A

Other Books in The Vintage Library
of Contemporary World Literature

The Burn

A NOVEL IN THREE BOOKS

(LATE SIXTIES—EARLY SEVENTIES)

Vassily Aksyonov

TRANSLATED FROM THE RUSSIAN

BY MICHAEL GLENNY

AVENTURA

The Vintage Library of Contemporary World Literature

VINTAGE BOOKS   A DIVISION OF RANDOM HOUSE   NEW YORK

Library of Congress Cataloging in Publication Data
Aksenov, Vasiliĭ Pavlovich, 1932–
The burn.
(Aventura: the Vintage library of contemporary
world literature)
Translation of: Ozhog.
I. Title.
PG3478.K70913 1985   891.73'44   85-40320
ISBN 0-394-74174-9 (pbk.)

CONTENTS

Book One
THE MEN'S CLUB

> . . . In truth, only a lout
> Can scoff at Russian life . . .
> —*Alexander Blok*

At last! The door! At the door of my apartment I sigh with relief. Now I can dive into something warm, into something of my own, into a pillow or a blanket, or I shall dive into the kitchen, where the vegetables are so beautifully arranged in piles, or perhaps I'll dive into a book . . . Strewn about on the floor are *The Adventures of Captain Blood, The Plays of T. S. Eliot*, and some professional journal, in other words . . . But perhaps I shall dive into a hot bath. I'll not answer the door, or pick up the phone. I'll sit in a bubble bath, lapped in simple uncomplicated soap bubbles, and forget all about the crazy nonsense in the outside world.

I crossed the threshold, groped blissfully in the twilight, and my household gods came floating toward me out of the darkness: the cowboy drawn on the bathroom door, my stuffed penguin, a key from the Vatican with its portrait of Pope John XXIII, the steering wheel of a car smashed up in my youth, the staff of Heracles, the bow of Artemis, you know the sort of thing – funny, jokey souvenirs (thanks to the kind thoughts of so many women) . . . my beloved *lares et penates*. Suddenly from the other end of the apartment a loud voice said very distinctly, "The home of the potato is South America!"

At that moment I was thrown into dire confusion and started to rush feverishly to and fro under the pressure of that terrible voice, which went on talking incomprehensibly. I broke out into a sticky sweat of fear until it dawned on me that somewhere the TV was still turned on. Obviously I had forgotten to switch it off yesterday, when I had been sitting in a blissful stupor in front of the flickering screen.

Realizing this, I rushed into the bedroom, jumped onto the bed, pulled off my shoes, wrapped myself in a blanket, switched on the bedside lamp, opened the magazine *Around the World*, and put it over my face. My heart was still beating, a muscle was still twitching in my neck, and behind my closed eyes the events of that day were still clamoring away like a party full of drunken louts.

Yet what had happened? In fact, nothing special. Come on, my friend, get the day sorted out. Get a hold of yourself. Start with the morning.

That morning I had trudged along the street to the metro, with nothing special happening behind me, except that something was making an awful creaking, rumbling, and clanking. Aware that this was nothing unusual, I didn't turn around, yet I was afraid. What if it *was* something out of the ordinary? Meanwhile, in the wind and bursts of rain a man with wildly tousled hair was approaching me. In one hand he held half a watermelon, which he was eating with a tablespoon as he walked along.

Astonished beyond measure at this sight, I realized that there was some connection between these two early-morning phenomena, and I turned around.

A boy of about ten was pulling along a rusty iron bedstead, on which were piles of tin basins, lengths of water pipe, faucets, scraps of wire, the bumper of a wheelchair, and something that looked like an old airplane propeller.

I quickly hurried on, stopped at the corner, and looked back again. The man with the watermelon was approaching the boy with the scrap metal. They drew level and stopped. The man dug his spoon deeper into the watermelon and offered it to the boy, who ate the contents of the spoon with relish and then said something angrily to the man, put his index finger to his temple, and turned it around, then started to maneuver his vehicle under the archway of a house. The man grinned guiltily with his shoulders and walked on unsteadily.

I wiped the sweat from my brow. Nothing terrible, nothing absurd, was happening; the world had not changed in the least during the past night. The boy was simply taking his quota of scrap metal to his local school, and the man, his dad, a pathetic alcoholic, in no way worse than me, was going from the watermelon stall to the Men's Club, the beer dive near the Pioneer Market. The only riddle was, where did he get the spoon? Had he really brought it with him from home? Surely he couldn't have shown such foresight?

All around me I was aware of the comfortable bustle of a Moscow street intersection, where people were selling pies, chocolate bars, apples, cigarettes, combs. I bought an apple, some meat pies, a chocolate bar, a pack of Stolichnaya cigarettes, and a comb, and combed my hair right there in front of a phone booth. How nice it all was! How full everything was of harmless fun!

As always, my neighbor Koreshok was standing by the metro entrance in a Napoleonic pose, a brutal man no more than one and a half meters tall but with a powerful, grim sort of sex appeal. His gigantic chest was thrust out, his hair combed sideways over his big ears, while blue silk pajamas flapped around his tiny legs.

I greeted Koreshok, but he did not even notice me. Just then several lab girls from the Film Institute were hurrying past, and Koreshok was watching them with a hot, sultry look, no doubt imagining himself and his penis let loose among this cheerful little bunch. In other words, everything was as it should be, and I started my calm descent into our subterranean marble palace.

It really is very pleasant to have one's own subterranean marble palace just around the corner. Even for us inhabitants of the Space Age, it is pleasant; but how delightful it must have been for the Muscovites of the 1930s. Such palaces, of course, greatly encouraged the Moscow populace because they significantly increased the amount of living space and imparted a secure and grandiose sense of patriotism.

The automatic change machines winked and flashed, but I headed for the last live cashier in our station. Nowadays, in the age of automation, this kindly tired woman, who has spent all her life in the marble palace, has less to do, and she even brings a book to work with her, which she glances at now and again with her radiant eye. I like changing my silver with her instead of in a machine: You can grumble about the weather, or make jokes about the female sex, and once, may I be rooted to the spot if I'm lying, I gave her a carnation.

I had already opened my mouth for some joke about what funny creatures women are when instead of my nice cashier I saw something quite different behind the glass. Staring at me was a huge unblinking creature of wax or clay, hair in solid curls, shoulders padded with solidified bags of fat, a being so immutable that the Creator seemed to have made it all of a piece as it was, without the preliminaries of gentle childhood and timid youth. A row of medal ribbons sat atop the new cashier's huge yet scarcely female bosom. Was one of them the Medal of Honor?

"But where's Nina Nikolayevna?" I asked perplexed.

Nothing, not a single curl, quivered; only the fingers made a slight movement, demanding money.

"But what's happened to Nina Nikolayevna?" I repeated my question, shoving a fifteen-kopek piece through the little window.

"She died," replied the newcomer without opening her lips, and threw me two five-kopek coins.

"Two?" I inquired.

"Two."

"Shouldn't there be three?"

"Yes, there should."

"But you're only giving me two?"

"Yes."

"I see. Sorry. Thank you."

Grabbing the coins and whistling a tune, I hurried to the turnstiles, as though nothing unusual had happened, as though everything was OK, whereas in fact everything wasn't OK; my heart was thumping, from terror, or from the strangeness, or from the frightening unfamiliarity of everything.

Brushing aside the disturbing recollections, I lay with the magazine *Around the World* over my face. Meanwhile, in another room of my apartment something improbable was afoot, some ghastly piece of telelife.

"Viktor Malayevich is a DOCTOR," said someone on the TV, with a heavy stress on the last word.

A pause. A slight cough.

". . . and he is also a PHILATELIST." This was said considerably more softly.

Another pause, the creak of chairs, and then in quite a normal, human voice: "Here you are, Viktor Malayevich."

A short, carefully modulated little cough from Viktor Malayevich. Clearly he is also a SMOKER.

"Here is a perforated stamp, red and black in color, without denomination of value . . ."

Why doesn't the damn tube burn out? I shall have to get up, expel the philatelists from my apartment, and make some tea, very strong tea. But I will not touch a drop of whiskey, even though an almost full bottle of White Horse is standing on the windowsill. Mashka brought it yesterday (or was it the day before yesterday? or three days ago?) from the foreign-currency store on the Bolshaya Dorogomilovskaya. What touching concern!

For all the six stops of his metro journey Aristarkh Apollinarievich Kunitser thought about the new cashier. No, she had not kept the third five-kopek piece out of greed, it seeks no profit, he was only showing me his implacability, he withheld my five kopeks, WITHHELD it without explaining the reason, it did not respond to my smile and would not have responded to tears either – their lordships don't like that.

Usually he began to cheer up as he approached his institute, where he was in charge of a huge top-secret laboratory. He would start thinking about his scientific work, about morality, about laser installations, about his male and female colleagues – who was having a "library day" today, who was having her period – about money, about moonlighting, and so on. Today, however, he could not get this morning's strange happenings out of his head: the scrap metal, the watermelon and the spoon, the clay bulldog sitting in Nina Nikolayevna's place, and his third five-kopek piece, which was now stuck in some unknown part of the subterranean kingdom.

The next surprise awaited Kunitser in the cloakroom of his own institute. A new attendant was looking at him with the frowning stare of a KGB officer. A grizzled crew cut, through which shone a blotchy, reddish-brown scalp; tufts of gray hair sticking out of the ears and eyebrows; an arrogant double chin; and eyes like small, hot black cherries, full of distaste, suspicion, and even – truly – contempt.

Kunitser gave a start. Those hot eyes, and not so much the eyes as the contempt in them, reminded him of something. What? The memory had already flown, having barely touched his brow like an owl's wing.

To hell with it! He threw the man his overcoat, took a numbered tag, and ran up the staircase, although he could not help looking back from behind a pillar.

The new attendant looked as solidly respectable as a retired general. He was now wearing glasses and studying page two of *Pravda*. He would have looked right in a professorial chair at the Academy of Social Sciences, at a desk in the Visa and Registration Office, or at worst, holding the reins of power in a house management office, but not in a cloakroom. Yes, he did look a bit out of place here, but he no longer, thank God, evoked any memories. OK, big deal! A new cloakroom attendant! He handed in his coat, got a tag, gave in his tag and got his coat back – that was the sum of his dealings with the man. Well, maybe he'd toss him twenty kopeks if he was feeling in a good mood.

. . . That lovely sunny day . . . snow crunching underfoot . . . an icicle, like a stalactite, hanging from the eaves . . .

... From the eaves of the schoolhouse, and across the street those four WHO DO NOT DRINK ...

Ah, nonsense! There was nothing special about the man, and the day had been absolutely ordinary. It was all just the tricks that a hangover plays on you – all these spasmodic recollections, the idiotic business of the five kopeks change. Must drink less! To hell with the damn poison! Weren't there enough pleasures in life? Women, for instance. Yachts, the cosmos, saxophones, lasers, thick books, clean paper, London, bronze, clay, granite ... Women, for instance.

That roaring sound – the program had switched to some huge, distant auditorium; *The Wisecrackers' Club*, a panel game, had started. Now the noise would go on at least until midnight. Odessa humor. He hadn't the strength to get up and turn it off. And there was no one else to ask. This was a fine state of affairs. The story of his life: There was no one to ask. He must get a remote-control gadget so that he could switch off the junk right from the bed. Yes, that was the solution – remote control!

Meanwhile, his hand of its own accord reached for the windowsill.

Oh, drosophila fly, mother of mutations!

At first, Kunitser did not even notice the girl who had slipped into his office. In the dusty twilight, among the folds of the heavy wine-red velvet drapes dating from the Stalin era, he caught a glimpse from the corner of his eye of a streak of luminescence; with half an eye he became aware of an outline, a little later a shape, still not entirely corporeal, semitransparent.

He stared and made out the details: her mini skirt, her soft knees, the small hands clutching a glass container to the region of her orifice of sin, the angular little shoulders that seemed ashamed of her small but beautiful breasts, and in the wine-red twilight, a face, half-childlike, that was also somehow ashamed of her breasts, her shoulders, and the meeting point of her legs.

Then he heard her voice, touched too with shame for her body, that small body created for sin and for sin alone.

"Good morning, Aristarkh Apollinarievich. I've been sent by Professor Martirosova from the Institute of Genetics. She made an arrangement with you. I have brought our drosophila."

He took in none of this because he was already walking toward her, quivering with overpowering desire, which she of course perceived at once and barely had enough time to put down her glass box on the floor. As he took her by the shoulders, she gave a brief sigh and helplessly threw back her head, offering her throat to his coarse, greedy mouth. Then she clasped him in her sweaty little hands and even helped with an obliging jump when he seated her on the windowsill.

Recovering from the first spasm of penetration, insertion, and consolidation, he noticed at his feet the glass container, in which were crawling innumerable tiny flies – and at once everything clicked into place.

Only yesterday he had been talking on the phone to Professor Martirosova, a lady of somewhat imposing proportions who was the champion tennis player of the whole research complex. The professor had asked him to shine his magic laser on a batch of her beloved drosophila flies, with which she was researching so successfully into mutation or some sort of fuckeration. At first, for form's sake, he had played hard to get and invented difficulties, pretending that he needed the laser himself (what for?), then he finally agreed: OK, send your little buzz bombs over here.

"Good," said the old witch. "I'll bring them over myself tomorrow." "You'll bring them yourself?" he asked in alarm. "Why not?" Martirosova's voice in the receiver became slightly husky and dropped noticeably in pitch, into the very depths of her athletic body. "But really, Professor, why should you go to so much trouble? I'll send one of my idle young assistants over to pick up your, er, verm – yes, your vermin." "You mean you don't want me to come?" "God forbid, Professor!" "That's not a nice way to treat a fellow scientist, you know." "I'm afraid I just act that way sometimes, Professor." "Very well then, I'll send a lab assistant over with them."

So this was Martirosova's lab assistant. She had brought the flies . . . this girl, who right now was moaning with her head thrown back, muttering something as her fingers reached for his face. This girl, this girl, this girl.

At that moment both of them began to writhe in the hot throes of orgasm, and when they came to their senses, they found that by some mysterious process of translocation, they were no longer on the windowsill but on the sofa.

He cleared his throat, went over to his desk, and sat down in the high-backed chair, stern and upright, for all the world like a college president. Suddenly, he caught her look of near-madness, and he dropped his head into his hands.

He was shattered by what had happened. From whence this sudden uncontrollable desire for another's flesh, the desire to stun, to madden, to shake this little creature, and then the feeling of pity, a nagging sense of guilt, of tenderness for this puny little girl, a desire to protect her from all harm?

The heartless brute managed to overcome his feelings of pity without much difficulty. Shuffling some papers on his desk, he asked in a neutral, businesslike voice, "Well now, have you brought me something from Martirosova?"

"Yes, some drosophila."

"These flies? How disgusting!"

"Oh, no, Aristarkh Apollinarievich. They're lovely. Under magnification they're truly beautiful." The flicker of a hopeful smile came into the girl's eyes. "We love our drosophila, you know. They're not really disgusting at all."

"I was only joking."

"I see." The hope and the smile were extinguished.

"Do you have a sense of humor?"

"People say I have."

"Excellent. Leave your vermin here and give my regards to the old witch."

He was already beginning to be irritated by her harrowed look, her unbuttoned blouse, the skirt bunched up around her waist, and her tear-filled eyes. She seemed aware of this and began hastily to button herself up. Then, with an obvious effort, she asked, "Aristarkh Apollinarievich, is it true that you—"

"Nonsense!" he shouted. "That's slander! Idiotic rumors! I'd like to get my hands on the bastards who spread that sort of gossip! The dirty rats are simply envious of my salary, that's all. If they only knew how I work my ass off to earn it! Never listen to anything people may say about me, no matter what trash they may invent. Rumors, rumors everywhere. Excuse me, I must be on edge. It's my nerves. Well, why are you just sitting there? There's such a thing as discipline, you know. Off you go!"

"I can't go . . . not without those things. Give them back to me and I'll go . . . No, I'm not going to cry, but I can't go without them."

"Without what, for God's sake?"

"You stuffed them into your pocket just now. They're in your pocket."

"Yes, you're right! Please forgive me. Here they are. I'll turn away. Is that OK? Your name's Inna, isn't it?"

When Kunitser turned around again, there was no one else in his office. The patch of sunlight had disappeared, and the folds of Stalinist velvet hung motionless. He picked up a powerful magnifying glass from his desk and peered at the flies in the little glass box. They were indeed beautiful: tiger-striped bodies, glittering little wings, tiny protruding eyes like chips of emerald.

The girl had vanished! There was no one there! She had appeared, had left the flies, and then had melted away into the velvet without a trace!

He rushed out of the room, flew down the stairs, and saw her in the huge empty hallway. Inna! he wanted to shout after her. Nina, Marina, or whatever your name is. Come back and never go away again. You're my salvation. But at that moment he noticed the new cloakroom attendant standing beside her. With the corners of his mouth turned down in a haughty, disagreeable expression, the attendant was talking to the girl as though lecturing her, scolding her. She hunched her shoulders, shivering, as she slipped into her coat. Suddenly, she ran off with a toss of her head, her heels clicking on the parquet, and disappeared altogether.

She wears Italian shoes at sixty rubles a pair, yet she only makes eighty rubles a month. The riddle of these little lab assistants. A monthly salary of eighty, but they can buy shoes at sixty. One of the great mysteries in Moscow.

"Seems to be in a hurry, doesn't she?" said Kunitser with an ingratiating cough, to the new attendant.

For some reason he felt a need to conceal from this man his impulsive pursuit, his strange unease, and to show instead that he was just a loyal, well-meaning halfwit, that he was not an intellectual but a regular guy, who could talk about girls, about ice hockey, about . . .

"Why are you not at your place of work, young man?" asked the cloakroom attendant, spitting out the words with the clear hint of a threat.

Kunitser was struck dumb. No one in the whole damn institute ever talked like THAT. He couldn't imagine even the chief or the head of the Security Section speaking in that tone of voice. Meanwhile, the attendant's burning little eyes were frisking Kunitser, rapidly feeling his entire face, searching his jacket, pants, shoes, flicking through his pockets and stopping at Kunitser's notebook that contained all his addresses, phone numbers, scraps of verse, and the formula that he had copied down in the toilet, the formula that had the outlines of a bird, the contours of a formula of genius.

"Do you have a match?" Aristarkh Apollinarievich asked, unnerved. Pleased with the humiliation he had induced, the attendant reached for his newspaper, saying, "The discipline here is obviously getting lax."

the bright deep snow
and sunlight in the corridors
an empty lesson a kick
hey Tolya von Steinbock
go on they're waiting for you there under the four statues
the only ones in Magadan WHO DO NOT DRINK
miner sailor milkmaid and Vanya the screw
black spot on the sunlit snow
a make of car called M
hurry Tolya
you can see the car's waiting and Sidorov
with his acne and his rotten teeth was always jumping
over the desks in the Chita style and yelling wildly
"When he scratches his balls that means trouble"
until he fell silent watching Von Steinbock
as he walked away down the long corridor.

A. A. Kunitser behaved most strangely. He walked up to the attendant and snatched the newspaper out of his hand. "I am not 'young man' to you but the director of Laboratory Number 4," he heard his own voice saying, vibrant with unfeigned indignation. "I am a doctor of sciences, a corresponding member of the Academy of Sciences, an honorary doctor of philosophy of Oxford University, deputy chairman of the district committee, a candidate member of the Party, a member of the Academic Council – and the discipline in this place is no business of yours!"

When he had finished barking out this litany, he noticed that the attendant was standing rigidly at attention, his eyes almost closed and his blotchy Adam's apple quivering.

"And how dare you read a newspaper during working hours!" roared the multiple title holder.

"What can I do, when all the rest have hanged themselves?" Breathing heavily, the attendant took out an enormous handkerchief, slightly frayed around the edges, and covered his mouth with it.

"You just watch those coats!" ordered Kunitser. "Your job is to carefully guard the staff's property. Got it?"

"Yes, sir!"

"And no rifling through the pockets! Understood?"

"Yes, sir!"

Should I ask him his name? thought Kunitser. I remember THE name, and the face. I'd recognize him. No, no, that's enough for one day, and it's a long time till evening. He's not the one. The one I'm looking for must be a general by now; he couldn't be a cloakroom attendant. Of course, this guy's one of them too, one of the Stalinist vermin. There are thousands of them still around . . . murderers, butchers, taking a well-earned rest.

Suddenly Kunitser was overcome with nausea, either from a lingering hangover or from disgust, and he reached the toilet and locked himself into a cubicle only just in time.

Oh, God, oh, God, is there no end to loneliness? Even then, in that spring, when the slush of the Nevsky Prospect was seeping through the worn-out soles of my shoes, in the twenty-fourth year of my life, when I wandered, a romantic masturbator, among the silent monuments of the Silver Age and read the appeals to join the ranks of the blood donors and thought of the donors of Budapest, even when I was penniless and abandoned on Aptekarsky Island on the night of the flood, I was not alone and could feel behind me the presence of mother Europe. She did not leave me, her flesh and blood; silent, great, nocturnal, she was there. Where are you now?

While the much-honored academician was throwing up, the secret formula soaked through from his notebook into his head, and from his head it was projected onto the tiles, where it now quivered, massive, broad-hipped, rather like a turkey or a phoenix. Kunitser leaped out of the toilet, dragging it by the tail. It groaned as he raced along the corridor to his laboratory. People coming toward him swerved out of his way. "Look out, guys, make way for the genius. That must be a new formula he's taking to his shit house!"

He burst into the laboratory. His team, stupefied from playing whist, rummy, battleship, and from reading the *Literary Gazette,* broke out into laughter. "Here's the chief again with a new bird!"

There was a hissing sound in the laboratory; it was hard to say whether it was the lasers working or someone frying sausages. Without a glance at his assistants, Kun began drawing his formula on the blackboard. He no longer felt ashamed of it, because its tail no longer looked like a wet broom but projected toward the northeast corner of the blackboard like a semierect phallus.

Half an hour later some kind soul handed him a bottle of beer. The formula, a steel bird now tamed, its feathers gently tinkling, was quivering on the blackboard, and looking slightly askance at the whole gang with one agate eye. With the beer gurgling inside him, Kun painted one of its toenails, stepped aside, and sat down on a box in the corner. The assistants began to discuss it. The telephone pealed in the laboratory – no doubt the Ministry of Defense had already gotten wind of the discovery. No one, however, picked up the receiver; let the ministry men come around themselves if they wanted to.

Kun heard the voice of his favorite student, the impudent Mala-medov, saying, "Hey, chief, how about drawing a finger stuck up its asshole?"

"If you do, I'll have your hand chopped off!" barked Kun, and immediately either fell asleep or lost consciousness; in other words, switched off.

When I came to my senses again, I was on the street. Past me trotted flocks of female lab assistants, typists, teaching assistants, the innocent victims of the capital. There was a smell of snow in the air, as though in a mountain pass. Above a street intersection, an illuminated adver-tisement for the Exhibition of Economic Achievements hissed with its superheated argon. A diplomatic Impala drove out of Sheremetievo Airport with an escort of mud-caked dump trucks. My pal Patrick Thunderjet, professor of Kremlinology (or criminology – what's the difference?) dozed on the back seat. I walked over to the metro.

In the metro. Humming. The shuffle of feet. Lies. Laughter. Barking. Laughing barking. Voice of a bookseller: "Latest news of machinations of international Zionism!" Naturally the first purchaser is a Jew. A Soviet Jew. A worker Jew. An intelligent, tired, worker Jew. An intelligent, tired, cunning worker Jew. An intelligent, tired, cunning, patriotically-minded worker Jew, an expert on space research, on the violin, on economics, a top-secret chess trainer of the indigenous population.

My observation of the Jew ceased: My view was cut off by two backsides, while I was pushed aside by a third. Like a fool I ride the metro while my car, a Zaporozhets, rots away by the roadside.

My next subterranean impression is of marinated water, or rather soda water colored by a cloud of syrup resembling the defensive excre-tions of a squid.

Damn the thing. Where the hell did it go? For a minute or longer

I searched my pockets for the five-kopek piece that had been there this morning. Surely the new cloakroom attendant can't have pinched it? So much for his looking like a general. Appearances are deceptive. One hears these words of wisdom all one's life, so by the age of forty one should have absorbed them. Obviously he pinched it. I'll raise the matter of this theft at tomorrow's Academic Council meeting and send a written complaint to the Party committee with a copy to the Central Committee of the Veterans' Trade Union. It's their job to sort it out. What do we PAY them for?

Just a minute. Suppose it's all a misunderstanding and I'm being unfair? I seem to remember eating something in the cafeteria today. Of course. I had a Russian salad for six kopeks and paid for it with the exact amount in copper, without getting any change – one big coin and a small one. I clearly remember the difficulty I had in forcing the five kopeks into the slot meant to take three-kopek pieces. What a good thing I remembered that; otherwise an innocent man might have gotten into serious trouble. In other words, I'd better stop playing the fool; that cloakroom attendant, in fact, doesn't remind me of anyone. He's just another slob; nothing special about him at all. So everything's OK. Today wasn't by any means a wasted day, and in some respects it produced some remarkable results.

Whistling boldly and cheerfully, a shatteringly successful man approached the long row of winking change machines.

That's civilization for you! In 1913, in tsarist Russia, there was not a single change machine. Nowadays, at this one station alone there are fourteen machines, and you can choose whichever one you like!

I looked carefully at the whole row of them and suddenly discovered that in fact there was no choice at all. Out of all those fourteen machines, ONE was not winking but was looking at me with a flat green eye; it was to that one that I must direct my steps, because it was Their Honor, a member of the underground bureau.

Obediently, forgetting everything, forgetting my family and the vast expanses of the universe, forgetting childhood and love, even forgetting and betraying Europe, my sleeping mother, I approached the machine and put into its maw – no, not a fifteen-kopek piece, I managed a bit of sleight of hand at the last moment (human nature is like that, and that's why we are unbeatable) – put into its maw a ten-kopek piece. It gave a contemptuous snarl; then came a low but rising hum, and I stood condemned to I knew not what and waited /and Our Father, Who art in Heaven, Hallowed be Thy name . . . From its iron womb, three five-kopek pieces fell into my palm.

"Three?" I inquired.

"Three," she replied.

"Shouldn't it be two?" I asked.

"Two," he growled.

"Are you giving me back the one I couldn't find this morning?" I asked.

It burst into laughter, immediately flung me through the turnstiles onto the platform and stuffed my mouth with a gag made of the *Moscow Evening News,* rammed someone's smelly old hat down over my ears, kicked my imitation-leather heels, sucked at the bottom of my pants, poured some loathsome pellets into my pockets: Off you go, cruise around the capital, great citizen.

The phone rang. It's Mashka, of course. Who else? What does she want from me? Maybe she really is a spy, as was whispered to me once in Geneva by the vice-president of the Society for Cultural Relations, whose own cover had been blown three times and who thus was no longer useful as a spy. I had set out to look for her in all the bars, and in true spy fashion she cunningly ran off with first one man, then another. Incidentally, if she really was a spy, in all the years of our liaison she never got anything out of me except what a woman usually extracts from a man – one secret only, the secret of life. No, Mashka is no spy; she is merely an unsuspecting tool of the cunning, long-term machinations of international imperiozionofellatiomaoism.

"Attention, please!" I said, speaking into the receiver through a blanket.

"Hi there," exclaimed Mademoiselle Marianne Coulagot. "Have you crawled under the blanket again? You can't imagine the shattering works by Kulich that I saw at Memozov's today! I think he'll soon be outdoing Fiox. Do you know him?"

"Attention, please," I said. "You are talking to Samson Apollinarievich Sabler's answering machine. Kindly record your message on the tape."

"More tricks!" said Mashka, laughing. "I suppose you've drunk the whole of my bottle? You'll never guess, kid, what a surprise I've got for you. Oh, I can't keep it to myself any longer, fool that I am. I'll bring it round to you this evening. It's all sparkly and warm. You will feed it, won't you? You see, its–"

"Attention, please," I interrupted her. "This is an answering machine–"

"A joke isn't funny the second time," she objected with unusual forcefulness. "Oh, yes! Here's something you can *really* howl about. Staggering news. Your friend Patrick Thunderjet has arrived!" I hung up and yanked the telephone cord out of its socket. For a few minutes I lay there, trying to make myself stop shivering, but in vain. Mashka's call had had its effect. It was quite clear what I had to do tonight.

Leaping out of bed, I took a healthy swig from the bottle; then, jumping out of my workaday pants as I went, I ran around the apartment, spat at the television screen, where some idiots were still competing in an exchange of carefully censored jokes, pulled my velvet Levi jeans out from the pile of dirty clothes, extracted my old alto sax from a heap of old shoes, and blew into it.

In whining tones the saxophone complained: "You've completely forgotten about me, you jerk."

"Can it!" I replied guiltily. "You're going out on a spree today!"

The instrument moaned tearfully, "Think you're so clever, don't you? Some genius you are! You're just shit! Threw your old pal into that stinking corner where your cat pisses! My valves are all rusty from cat's piss. That's no way to act, you slob. Romain Rolland said, 'Where there is no greatness of character, there can be no great man.' "

"You've quoted that wrong, and anyway stop being impertinent," I growled. "Come on, let's get going!"

At this, it crowed joyfully like a rooster, bleated, and giggled like a teenager in anticipation of an evening's bacchanalia.

The drink pulsated through my bloodstream, my heart beat with a muffled thump, objects changed their usual form and lost their frightening, mysterious significance, came closer, and created the delicious feeling of anxiety that you get when you're young. The spirit of youth, an evening of expectations – those are the first gifts of alcohol.

Before me lay Moscow by night, silent and clean. The dry, well-worn asphalt of the streets and the glass of phone booths gleamed under the streetlamps. In a quiet corner near a bakery, under some limp leaves, a flag swayed gently, just barely flicking, straightened itself, and quivered steadily, confidently, and secretly, living its own personal nocturnal life and thinking that no one was watching it. Seized by a sudden surge of love, I gazed at the flag for a long time. Poor thing. In the daytime it shouts propaganda at the bakery customers, while at night, it turns out, it patiently, gallantly, waits for someone.

* * *

It was past eleven o'clock when Samson Apollinarievich Sabler reached
the Blue Bird. Jazz enthusiasts were crowding around the entrance.
The café was packed. A hideous moaning sound came through the
half-open windows – it was Silvester playing his baritone, which
drowned out all the other sounds and even smothered the applause.
Sabler stood for a while listening to the voice of his friend, watched
the fans fighting the vigilante patrol around the entrance.

Finally, Silvester came to the end of his solo. Above the tinkling of
a piano, shouts could be heard: "Why don't they open up, the bastards?
There's still standing room inside!"

"Come on, you guys, let's push!"

"They say Samson's coming."

"The hell he is! Right now Samson's in Nakhodka in the Far East,
waiting for a package from Japan."

"Don't talk crap! Samson's standing right here!"

Everyone turned around and stared at him with delight. They had
good reason to be thrilled by the silent figure in jeans and short leather
jacket with an instrument case under his arm, the mysterious, famous
Samson.

"Samson's come! Now things'll really start swinging!"

"Hey, you sons of bitches, open up!"

"Hi, Samson! When did you get back from Nakhodka?"

"Just got off the plane," he said. "My ears are still stuffed up."

He noticed the flickering eyes of a man who obviously wanted more
than anything else to seem to be his close friend, an insider, a swinger,
and held out his hand to him. "Hi there, old boy."

"Samson!" The man almost died with happiness. "Did you get your
package from Japan?"

"Sure did. Got this sax."

"From Sadao Watanabe?"

"That's right."

"But, Samson, that looks just like your old sax," blurted out
someone standing behind him.

"No, it's a new one," Samson countered. "It's new, but it's just like
the old one. Specially made. Elka took away my old one in Vilnius."

"I told you so!" yelled the "close friend." "I told you Elka took his
old one in Vilnius! I told you so and you wouldn't believe me!"

"That's right; she took it away." Samson nodded and pushed his
way into the café.

Maeterlinck's *Blue Bird*. Chekhov's *Seagull*. The Steel Bird flies –

Where the soldiers cannot march, Where no armored train can roll.
The Bird – the Formula – the Hope of the Forces of Peace all over
the World. The Heron, Thin-legged, Wet and Ungainly. Do you
remember? The Muffled Cry of the Heron, Wherein was Heard the
Rustle of the Rain-Soaked Glades of Europe . . . The Slow Flight
of the Heron into Europe, Over the Church Towers of Poland, Over
the Sudetenland, Over Bavaria, Over Geneva, To the Marshes of
the Camargue, Onward to Andalusia . . .

Through the smoke the quartet could be seen on the stage: Silvester,
Alik Friedman, Pruzhinkin, and Ryss. A little way apart stood Fatface
Buzdykin, who was not playing but reading a sheet of music. When
Samson waved, the boys saw him, broke off in the middle of what
they were playing, and played the first phrase of "Take the A Train"
in honor of the new arrival.

Lord, how Samson loved them all. All except that idiot Buzdykin,
and he even felt quite tolerant toward the fool, despite their long-
standing quarrel over Czechoslovakia.

In that August of Sixty-Hate they had all been in the Crimea when
they heard the news; they had been just about to open their mouths
to start a furious howl, but instead they suddenly shut up. They didn't
understand what was really happening, which was why they didn't
protest, but only opened their mouths for vodka or to put the
mouthpieces of their instruments between their teeth. They did nothing
but play and drink, play and drink, play and drink, until they were
nearly aging from their terrible music, from vodka, and from keeping
silent – when suddenly Buzdykin flew in from the World Capital of
Peace and Progress and began saying filthy things about the Czechs,
along the lines of "Look what they wanted. We're not allowed to have
it, but they think they can!" Buzdykin had a personal grudge against
the Czechs: a year previously, they had given him shit because of
his pederastic inclinations. Samson, however, had not taken this into
account, and had created a scene that ended in a fistfight.

THEN IT HAD RAINED

and it was in the rain, after the fight, that we rampaged through the
camp site, a wild, drunken, ragged horde. The rain lashed us, flayed
us without mercy, fell unendingly and savagely on Koktebel, perhaps
as vengeance, perhaps for the remission of sins. Occasionally I glanced

around, goggle-eyed, and through the streaming rain I saw our gang, looking like a band of medieval marauders. I don't know exactly who was there. I think there was Lyova Malakhitov; and Yuzik Tsipkin, a doctor from the Arctic Circle; and a little chick in shorts called Nina, or maybe Inna or Marina, a hydrologist or a biologist or something, whom we had picked up near the beer truck and dragged around with us all day until in the end she fell by the wayside. And there was Academician Fokusov with two Odessa whores; and Shurik, an existentialist photographer from Lvov; and someone else too, from the people who probably weren't there at all – maybe the sculptor Radik Khvastishchev, maybe Genka Malkolmov the surgeon, maybe Pantelei Pantelei the writer, maybe Samson Sabler the saxophonist, maybe Arik Kunitser the top-secret scientist. And maybe there were even some who really weren't there: that woman with red-gold hair, with a bright, instantaneous smile that flashed on and off, a woman I had never met but had been waiting for all my life, and I realized her name was Alisa. And a kid I remembered, Tolya von Steinbock, seems he was there too.

We walked in stinking mud up to our ankles through the village of Planerskoye, while swollen streams carried all the resort sewage past us to the sea. The wooden outhouses blown down by the hurricane, the turds and liquid shit all floated down the rapids toward our sea, which yesterday had been crystal clear. All on the second day after the invasion!

At the camp site the whole gang sat down in a puddle, full of garbage and weeds, and started drinking from a bucket the Algerian wine that Houari Boumedienne sends us in the same tankers from which he pumps fuel for his MIGs, while Ganzelka's thin voice kept on yelling from a half-smashed transistor radio: "Don't stay silent! Friends! Lyova, Genka, Kolya, don't you dare be silent!"

We were not silent but were howling the favorite song of our childhood in off-key voices:

> Our armor's strong, our tanks are fast,
> Our men are full of courage,
> Soviet tankmen are on parade,
> Sons of their great motherland.

Suddenly we noticed that a multitude of eyes were looking at us.

It was a long silent row of people standing in line for the shower. They were huddled under a canopy waiting their turn to stand under the campsite's two rusty nipples, yet all around them the merciless rain had already been cascading down for two days and nights.

Then one of us – it may have been Lyova, it may have been me, perhaps Yuzik or someone else – jumped up, hairy, a torn shirt clinging to his body, barefoot, and swollen with rain, and yelled, "Why the hell are you standing in line for water, you idiots, when it's pouring rain? What's the idea? Do you mean to say that you're not the crazy ones but we are? There's more of you, so you're normal, and if there's fewer of us, so we're nuts. Is that it? Hey you, Unanimous Approval, you damn cowards, look at this great free natural shower – and you don't have to stand in line! Come out here! That's an order from higher authority! Vote unanimously and come out here! Maybe you'll wash yourselves clean!"

Our girls were sure the agitator would be killed on the spot, but Unanimous Approval said nothing, staring at us with looks that were uncomprehending, slightly glum but mostly quite calm. In the vast open spaces all around. . . . It was driving past us in buses and airplanes, carrying oranges and sausages from Moscow in string bags, competing on sports grounds to prove the advantages of socialism, singing oratorios in huge choirs, blowing brass instruments, forging, forging, forging "something made of iron," and charging across Central Europe with rifles ready, while the Danube in its snakelike course fled from the path of Its tank tracks.

Right here, in front of us, It was huddled on a dry patch of asphalt, standing in line under a sheet of tin for some chlorinated water, while all around rain poured down from the universe without respite and an oppressive black sky, which had swallowed the peak of Kara-Dag, half of Holy Mountain, and the whole of Syuryukkaya with its Pushkin-like profile, promised a further week's deluge. Therefore it was necessary, and all of us, dirty pigs, were to blame for what had happened.

By now Samsik had almost forgotten his fight with Buzdykin. It was a long time ago, and it had all been covered over with a layer of sticky mud. Everything connected with Czechoslovakia was being forgotten, just as Berlin and Poznań, Warsaw, Budapest, and Novocherkassk were forgotten in their time.

The audience gave Samsik a small ovation. "The mysterious Samsik, straight off the plane after flying across Wrangel Island from Wellen, where Stan Getz sent him his own sax on an Oil Alaska snowcat – whether as a gift or on loan isn't clear – at all events, Sam will be blowing it today. Don't worry. Look, he's already pushing his way through to the bar to fill up his tank. So the joint's going to be jumping so hard this evening you won't forget it for a long time!"

In the Blue Bird they only serve dry wine, but for Samsik Rimma the barmaid found a bottle of Bulgarian brandy. Silvester came up to the bar, and Rimma put a glass of fruit juice in front of him.

"Can't you do it without that?" Silvester pointed reproachfully at the brandy.

"On the contrary," replied Samsik, "with this I *can* do it."

Silvester shook his head. Through him, jazz fans all over the world rebuked Sabler for his debauchery. Silvester corresponded regularly with Thelonious Monk, Willis Conover, Leonard Feather and other jazz luminaries. He gave them our news, and in exchange he got records, sheet music, the magazine *Downbeat,* and so on. Naturally, the appropriate state officials examined all this mail with their appropriate organs, but they did not hinder it. The mail always arrived on time; not one stagecoach had yet gone astray on the dangerous roads of Europe.

Silvester looked like a Western intellectual. He always took note of fashion, and always followed it. Right now he had long hair and moustaches down to his chin, but Samsik remembered when he had a fifties-style crew cut. When he blew into his crooked horn, he looked like Satan himself and nothing like Silvester the vegetarian. Silvester had excluded all forms of temptation from his life: he never looked at a steak, never touched brandy, and the only thing he did to chicks was to pay them compliments. Jazz was his whole life.

"Still, you've come, man," Silvester said to Samson affectionately. "And with your instrument, too. We weren't expecting you."

"It was a crazy day; that's why I came," said Samsik. "I was depressed by a lot of stupid memories."

Someone jogged Samsik's left elbow. He turned around. It was Zheka Buzdykin, the runt of a sow's litter.

"Give us a drop, Samsik," he begged in a pathetic voice.

"So that's how they suck up nowadays, is it?" asked Samsik. "You pinch a drop of my life's blood and after that everything's forgiven and forgotten, is that it?"

As he said this he lifted up the bottle and pretended to be considering whether to pour the man a drink or not. Buzdykin looked at the bottle and whined humbly, "Cut it out, Sam. You're a musician and I'm a musician, so where's the quarrel between us?"

"When they rubbed your face in the shit in Prague, it was because you deserved it, right?"

"Sure, I deserved it." Buzdykin's face was covered in sweat.

Samsik tipped the bottle toward Buzdykin's glass but poured nothing out. "OK, you little runt. Tell me a joke about a tank."

"About a tank?" Buzdykin groaned.

"If you tell me a story about a tank, I'll fill up your glass."

"Don't give it to him," said Rimma. "He'll drink it, and then he'll start pestering little boys. You'll end up in jail, Zheka. This isn't Prague, you know."

Buzdykin shut his eyes and started babbling. "Little Red Riding Hood was walking through the forest and she met a Tank. 'Good day, Little Red Riding Hood,' said the Tank. 'Good day,' replied Little Red Riding Hood, 'and who are you?' 'I'm the Gray Wolf,' said the tank, playing it for laughs. 'If you're a wolf,' said Little Red Riding Hood, laughing, 'why do you have a prick sticking out of your forehead?' "

He began to quiver gently with his eyes closed, and when he opened them, there in front of him was a glass of the brown Bulgarian liquid.

"I'll never forget this, Samsik," Buzdykin said suddenly in a very firm voice and carried the full glass off to the toilet.

"Don't worry about him, Rimma," Samsik said to the barmaid. "They won't arrest him."

"You don't say?" she said in horror. "You mean, he's one of them? Seriously, Silvester?"

Silvester nodded modestly.

Samsik picked up the bottle and set off with it to the stage. Whistling was heard in the auditorium. While they had been sitting at the bar, the kids in the Blue Bird audience had had time to play in Greenwich Village and were now eager for new sensations. Samson and Silvester together – hey, this should be really something.

Samsik, old Sam, looked at the audience. The girls were all in jeans and T-shirts. One hooker was wearing an old-fashioned long dress with a train that dragged over the floor, and so to create more of an effect she wasn't sitting down. Another one, snub-nosed, with narrow little eyes, was covered in gold – earrings, bracelets, necklace. How come she's so rich?

Some of the boys were sucking on pipes and affecting glum looks like morose intellectuals; others wore blazers with gleaming brass buttons and behaving accordingly – like playboys. There were also some flower children, though they were more restrained in appearance than their London counterparts and so more acceptable to the Moscow police. Two or three Komsomol leaders were in the audience, wearing what had become their uniform – neat suit, white shirt, tie – looking like clerks in some ministry of youth. From being a sworn enemy, the Komsomol had lately changed into being the indulgent patron of jazz.

For a minute or two Samsik surveyed the audience, winked to a few acquaintances, bowed to the girls, then signaled to the band – OK, let's go!

Pruzhinkin, as always, began with his favorite "Take Five;" the audience responded noisily. Samsik blew into his horn a couple of times and suddenly closed his eyes – clearly and distinctly, like a movie, he recalled his debut as a musician.

It was in November 1956, one evening at the School of Mines in Leningrad, playing in the band of Kostya Rogov, the first Leningrad jazzman.

The dance hall was full of guys and chicks standing shoulder to shoulder, a pathetic and eager bunch of kids, drunk with the damp breeze from Europe that suddenly had started blowing in our direction. There were the wretched, universally despised *stilyagi*, with their narrow, stovepipe pants, trying to look like boys from Broadway; they would clip the collars of their Lentorg Soviet shirts, glue pieces of rubber to the soles of track shoes, and cut each others' hair in a Canadian crew cut.

Kostya Rogov took off his jacket, revealing his famous khaki shirt with shoulder tabs and a mysterious insignia on his left breast pocket: SW-007.

"Today, boys, let's start with 'Sentimental Journey,' " he said.

"By the way, there are some characters here from the Petrograd district committee of the Komsomol," warned the cautious drummer, Rafik Taziddinov, nicknamed Tazik.

"Forget it!" Rogov rolled up his sleeves as though preparing to fight, not play the piano. "We'll have a bash at 'Sentimental Journey,' then 'Lady Be Good,' and afterward we'll tear into 'The Woodchoppers' Ball' and bring the house down! Sam, come with me!"

He dragged me by the hand to the footlights and shouted to the audience, "Quiet, kids! Let me introduce the new alto saxophonist to all the friends of our band. Samson Sabler! Don't worry if his pants are baggy. The guy's OK. You can just call him Sam!"

The audience roared. I stood there alone, gripping my saxophone.

Sweat was pouring from my armpits; my face had broken out in blotches, and my knees were shaking. I couldn't for the life of me play "Sentimental Journey;" I felt I would faint – and fart as well, for good measure. I had to disappear before it was too late and throw up in some quiet place. I simply couldn't keep standing there alone with so many girls looking at me.

I made a rapid half-movement as though fainting when a few meters away in the crowd I suddenly saw those long, fair locks, cut off straight where they fell to the pouting breasts, and the little eyes looking at me with an expression unlike any I had seen in our girls, the half-open mouth. It was her, the Witch, Marina Vlady. I felt a sudden surge of courage and, to my own surprise, started to play.

Oh, Marina Vlady, girl of '56, girl who awakened my courage! Oh, Marina, Marina, Marina, standing up in a boat drifting over a Scandinavian lake under the sky at sunset! Oh, Marina, the first little bird from the West who flew toward the first sniff of the thaw in our God-forsaken land! You only have to make a sign, doll, and I'll instantly turn into a daring man of action; I'll wipe away the snot and set off to the ends of the earth to meet you. Oh, Marina – fascination, youth, the forest, voices in dark hallways, rapid footsteps running along a colonnade, the waiting for a secret rendezvous with demons of moonlight spattering your breasts.

As I started playing, Kostya immediately joined in and after him, the whole band, and she jumped for joy and clapped her hands – everyone was crazy about "Sentimental Journey" in those days.

> Here in Russia there's no jazz,
> And kids just puke up kvass.

A drunken bunch of mining students – the hosts of the ball – were howling these words in a corner of the dance hall. It was obvious now that a scandalous scene was unavoidable.

In those days "bourgeois" dances were still forbidden to young people, and they were only allowed to dance beautiful, elegant "national" dances – patriotic écossaises, minuets, *pas de patineur*, waltzes, gavottes. God knows whose stinking head spawned the idea of these dances. Surely Stalin himself can't have dreamed it up? And then again, perhaps he did. No doubt Stalin himself bent his mind to it, God rot his guts.

Lately, alas, the putrid breezes of "the thaw" have slightly spoiled the icebound parquet of those Komsomol balls, and in the ensuing flood some bourgeois character with a saxophone has crept in, namely, the pimply Samsik, cropped like a convict, in absurdly tight pants, a grubby one-ruble bill in his pocket, a twenty-year-old half-Pierrot, half-hooligan, the handsome Samsik *in propria persona.*

The spirit of disobedience, the idea of freedom, dashed from wall to wall like a mindless lunatic, and everyone started to dance, the chandeliers started to sway, and the plush drapes were swept crookedly aside from the windows, like an old woman's skirts – the gatecrashers were pouring into the hall.

In those days we hardly knew bebop, had only just heard of Charlie Parker and Dizzy Gillespie, had barely begun to improvise, but we were really into swing.

I suddenly saw my Marina Vlady dancing with some dude in a long checked jacket. I remembered that this dude had a Pobeda car, and I literally shook with jealousy and resentment. Suddenly my sax howled so bitterly, so despairingly that several people in the hall shivered with fright. It was the first instance of my sax moaning of its own accord. Kostya Rogov told me later that when he heard that sound, his guts collapsed, all his organs fell into a chasm – all except one, which filled with blood and began to stand – and at that moment Kostya realized that a new jazz was born. Maybe it was not even jazz but the breath of some mighty spirit blowing across oceans into my horn.

The Song of the Petrograd Sax, Fall Model 1956

I am poor,
  poor,
    poor,
Tell everybody I haven't a cent!
I am poor,
  poor,
    poor,
Tell everybody I haven't any rights!
Tell everybody I was conceived on rags in a prison hospital
By two enemies of the people, a Trotskyite man and a Bukharinite
  woman in a shameful act,
And I'm still ashamed of it to this day!
Tell everybody I learned from childhood to cheat society,
Clinging like ivy and mold and mildew
To nursery, kindergarten, school, and later to the Komsomol
Without any rights!

I am poor,
> poor,
>> poor,

Let everyone know that
I am a virgin in shit-stained underpants!
I'm a virgin, a coward with a miserable little cock, but,
Good God, I'm no hermaphrodite!
I am a man! I'm a son of this great earth!
I was bought by Samsik in a flea market from a drunken blind man
For a thousand rubles, which he saved by being a blood donor and
> a petty thief.

But Good God, I'm twenty years old and I'll be forty soon!
I'm a donor too and my blood is transfused through medical tubes
Into the collapsed vessels of my earth!
Tell everybody I'll burst before I shut up!
I'll howl until I give all my glittering blood,
Although I'm poor,
> poor,
>> poor.

I was terrified myself. I was at the end of my tether and suddenly noticed, when the last air bubbles croaked out of my sax, that no one in the hall was dancing and everyone was looking at me: Marina Vlady, her check-coated dude, and all the drunken mining students. Everyone was silent, and from the back of the hall, spreading and filling the vacuum with its sound, menacing as the sound of tank tracks: "Stop this provocation!"

Then streaks and squares of sunlight, black blobs of memories, and a transparent stalactite flashed before my eyes. I swayed on my feet, but Kostya Rogov supported me by putting his arms around me and spat out at the audience a stream of words in our semicomprehensible slang: "Kiss my ass! Your Big Daddy has kicked the bucket, so we're going to play you some jazz! We're going to give you some jitter-bugging in a minor key, and our genius Samsik here can play what he likes. And as for you, clothears, piss on you!"

And we played. But was it just a question of jazz? We longed to be part of the life of the whole world, part of that same "freedom-loving mankind" in whose ranks our elder brothers had so recently been fighting. Everyone was sick to death of living in our stinking shack, alongside the rotting corpse of Big Daddy. Everyone – Party members, People's Artists, KGB men, record-breaking coal miners – everyone,

except the bats hanging upside down in dark corners. And so we
played.

*A Story of S. A. Sabler's Youthful Days, Recorded from a Telephone
Conversation by the Moscow Writer P. A. Pantelei*

That evening Samsik, the adenoidal genius with the out-of-date residence permit, was arrested and taken to the headquarters of a
Komsomol vigilante squad. A body search produced the following
articles: a comb full of dandruff, a copy of the Polish magazine *Po
Prostu* containing a short story by Marek Hlasko, two soggy meat
dumplings wrapped in a handkerchief, a packet of condoms yellowed
with age, a blood-donor's record card, and a letter from Marina Vlady
written from Paris.

In the eerie silence of the Komsomol headquarters, the letter was
read aloud.

To: Monsieur Samson Sabler
c/o Madame Frieda Hitchcockovna Reznik
14 Shchors Prospect
Leningrad

My dear!
You invite me to come with you to the virgin lands. Alas, it is a
little too late to accept your invitation. Don't think, though, that
the traditional devotion of Russian women has been forgotten in
Paris. I am ready to follow you to any other God-forsaken hole – to
Réunion, to Tananarive, even to Marseille. I'll soon send you some
clothes, and when you get the chance send me some canned food.
Kisses,
Yours, Marina

"Comments superfluous," said the chief vigilante with the repellent
smile that he always assumed when confronting the class enemy.
"Why have I been arrested?" Samsik asked.
"You've been arrested for this," said the chief, pointing at the
musician's property laid out in front of him.
"But none of this was visible when I was walking along the street,"
said Samsik, perplexed.
"You're very clever, Sabler! Very clever, aren't you?" the chief
shouted from a mouth distorted with anger and disgust, his head
twitching at every word. His hair kept flopping in two wings divided

by his part, but he wanted it to lie flat against his head and give him an inspired look.

The headquarters was filled with girls and boys from Nevsky Prospect; the chief was master here, the lord of the night. On his orders Komsomol vigilantes slashed the seditious tight pants, cut off long hair, yanked off "stylish" ties, photographed all these "antisocial elements" in order to pillory them. The chief did not spare his prisoners and cruelly exacted revenge on them for their ideological immaturity, but also for his own clumsiness, for the excessive greasiness of his skin, for his rejection by the female sex, for his poor results in the school for young workers.

"OK, Vityusha and Valera, teach Sabler to love his country!"

A long-armed patternmaker and a bouncy toolmaker grabbed Samsik firmly. The young musician squealed, defending his honor. The chief leaned back in a prerevolutionary armchair and closed his eyes, imagining with relish that he was conducting an "active" investigation of Sabler, an interrogation of the kind once described to him by his brother-in-law, who had served in the security forces.

"Playing the fool again, Kryushkin," grumbled the regular police sergeant attached to the vigilantes.

"You've forgotten about Budapest, Sergeant," said the chief vigilante without opening his eyes. "It was young snivelers like these who caused all the trouble there." He suddenly jumped up and yelled, his eyes still closed, straight into Samsik's face as he hung in the grip of the two thugs: "How did you get that letter from Marina Vlady, you skunk?"

"She sent it to me," croaked Samsik weakly.

"I suppose you lived with her?" said Kryushkin with a repulsive laugh. His eyes were closed.

There was dead silence in the headquarters. Everyone in the room, prisoners and Komsomol vigilantes, waited tensely for the reply.

"We loved each other," Samsik whispered, dropping his head on his chest.

"You loved a *foreigner*?" asked Kryushkin, blazing impassively from behind firmly closed eyelids.

Fear gripped Samsik. It was true – she was a foreign citizen! She was not just a slim shadow on the sunset surface of the lake, not just a narrow-eyed face on the beach. She was a foreigner! It was only in Kuprin's story that she was a Byelorussian witch, a Russian subject; in the film, although she was a wild creature of the forest, she was still a foreigner. Yes, he was found out now and had nothing more to lose.

"Uh-huh, I loved a foreigner," he whispered.

Eyes closed, Kryushkin made a few incomprehensible circular motions with his head. Samsik felt a sudden surge of courage. "Aaah!" he growled. "Lift up his eyelids! He's not Kryushkin, boys, he's Vii!"

Suddenly a roar of laughter shook the former dragoon's guardhouse built in the Empire style. Both the prisoners and the guards, and even the police sergeant, laughed; everyone, it seemed, knew about this gruesome character from Gogol's stories of Ukrainian folklore.

"Vityusha, Valera, please, stop hurting me," Samsik begged them, amid the general noise, and the patternmaker and toolmaker willingly relaxed their painful grip and let him go.

"Vii! Vii!" Everyone guffawed, and Kryushkin rushed around beneath the Empire-style ceiling, as though he really was the horrible demon from the land of cotton underpants.

"Are you Komsomol members or not? Are you Russians or not?" he howled. "He loved a foreign woman, do you hear?"

"Well, isn't a foreign girl still a woman?" crowed Samsik, cocky with success.

"A woman, of course she's a woman!" came the triumphant shouts from all around, and the girls from the Liteiny Prospect even broke into a dance, like female monkeys on a hotplate. Someone wrenched open a window, and the smell of the water from the Neva River, mixed with snow and all the aromas of a great city, flooded into the headquarters.

The telephone rang. The sergeant picked up the receiver, listened, pushed his cap forward onto his nose, and said to Kryushkin in a bored voice, "It's Rogov, the district procurator. It seems, Kryushkin, you've arrested a famous musician." He passed the receiver into Kryushkin's shaking hands, and Samsik heard the distant voice of Kostya's father. "Hello. What's going on there? Release this musician Samson Sabler at once."

"Yes, Comrade Rogov. Very good, Comrade Rogov. At once, Comrade Rogov."

Kryushkin replaced the receiver, closed his eyes again, and pushed Samsik's property away from him. "Comrade Sabler, please take your things and return to your place of residence."

"To Shchors Prospect?" Samsik inquired cheerfully as he stuffed his shameful relics into his pockets. "Or to Decembrists Avenue? Or perhaps I should sneak back to the Fourth Company, Comrade Kryushkin?"

Replying, Kryushkin sounded like the voice of a ventriloquist suffering from typhoid fever: "Better go to Shchors. You'll never make it to Decembrists, still less to Fourth Company. They'll catch you on Sadovaya, and that's in another district, with a different procurator. Get me?"

Samsik thanked him and offered the chief his entire personal wealth, consisting of a couple of dumplings in a handkerchief. "Help yourself."

Sobbing, Kryushkin ate a dumpling in one gulp, and took only a delicate bite out of the second. Samsik actually broke out in a cold sweat of pity for this kid, with his crooked teeth and his face peppered with a swarm of blackheads, which many people mistook for coal dust from a locomotive.

"Ah, Kryushkin, you poor kid," he whispered.

"I have a hunchbacked sister to look after, Comrade Sabler," said Kryushkin, lying fluently. Samsik imagined this gray little runt Kryushkin with a fat, willful hunchbacked girl on his hands. It was straight out of Dostoyevsky!

"Kryushkin" – he put his hand on Kryushkin's shoulder – "Kryushkin, old fellow, will you let these other kids go?"

He nodded toward the *stilyagi*, who were standing nearby in silence, shuffling their feet with embarrassment.

"Of course I will," said Kryushkin humbly. "I'll just read them a poem first: maybe they'll understand something. You can go, Comrade Sabler. I'll just read them the poem." He stepped into the middle of the room and, with his eyes still shut, began in a calm, earnest voice: "OK, boys and girls, listen to this poem. It's him. I recognize him in his saucerlike eyeglasses, big as life preservers . . ."

Feeling his upper lip growing damp with emotion, Samsik went out of the headquarters building, because he knew the poem by heart and did not want to get upset again.

Toward midnight, People's Commissar Kirov gives back the avenue named after him to its former owners – the Horse Guards; silence descends on Horse Guards Avenue, and all its mirrorlike windows reflect a mysterious sight. Are they gleaming breastplates? Are they shakos?

I crossed the street over the clean, resonant asphalt, rummaged in a garbage bin, found the butt of an Aurora, leaned back against the cast-iron railings, and started to smoke. Behind me, the iron hoplites

in crested helmets clutched their lances. Meanwhile, Kryushkin gesticulated like an actor in the Komsomol vigilante headquarters, and the
sergeant, the *stilyagi,* and the young workers stared at him
thoughtfully.

It's perfectly possible to act like a human being and treat others the
same way, I remember thinking about Kryushkin, and I remember
bursting into tears.

"Why are you always rummaging in garbage cans, Samsik?" I heard
a voice say, full of gentle mockery. "Here, have a smoke!"

Beside me, offering a full pack of Auroras, stood none other than
Marina Vlady herself, wearing a tightly belted French raincoat.

"How did you get here?" I asked haltingly.

"I've been waiting for you." She laughed, and walked off toward
Leo Tolstoy Square, clicking her incredibly thin, pointed heels. Amazingly, we were completely alone on Horse Guards Avenue. I was the
only one there to admire her walk, and the wind from Aptekarsky
Island stirred her straw-colored hair for my benefit alone.

"Aren't you with that red-haired guy? The red-haired one in the
checked suit? The guy with the Pobeda?" I asked, dragging my left
foot so that the shoe sole, which had come loose during that alarming
evening, should not flap around too much.

"That's what *he* thinks," she replied sadly. "But in fact I'm your
chick, Samsik, your girl."

"What's your name?" I asked, gasping; yes, gasping.

"Arina Belyakova."

"Where are you studying?"

"Right here, at the medical school."

O ye gods of Greece and Rome!

"And where do you live?"

"On Barmaleyev Street. Do you know it?"

O ye gods of St. Petersburg, Finland, and the Neva!

"You don't have to drag your foot like that, Samsik! I don't care if
your old shoes flap when you walk. I love you anyway. Put your arm
around my shoulders. Don't be afraid."

Meanwhile, as Samsik was clasping Arina Belyakova's broad and
slightly bony shoulder, the situation in the vigilante headquarters had
undergone a sharp change.

Fired by the poetry, Kryushkin was aiming his metallic voice straight
at his target – the Empire-style chandelier:

The liquid in our veins is blood, not water!
We're walking through the barking of repeaters!

With renewed energy the vigilantes were slashing the *stilyagi*'s pants, shaving their heads in convictlike strips and tonsures, and photographing all these "antisocial elements." Cursing softly in the corner, the sergeant was drinking tea and sucking a pastille.

And on Barmaleyev Street, there was strange activity around Arina Belyakova's house. The inhabitants had left their house, a granite stronghold with black marble columns, the former embassy of the Emir of Bukhara in St. Petersburg.

"Sabotage," explained the house manager, a man of the old school. "The imperialist spies just won't let us live in peace and get on with constructive work, comrades. Anyway, it's not serious; the repairmen will come along soon and fix it."

The tenants, however, complained that he had once again called up the wrong people. He shouldn't have called the "comrades" from the KGB but just the plain, regular old fire brigade.

The house, in fact, was not yet on fire, but its entire utilities network – the electric cables, the telephones, the cable radio, the gas, the sewage, the heating – was heated to the ultimate degree and shining through the walls in all the colors of the spectrum, outlining the beautiful crackling framework in the gloomy darkness of Barmaleyev Street. The house was ready for love.

"We're in luck," whispered Arina Belyakova. "The oldsters will be sitting out in the street on their suitcases till morning."

She slipped behind an advertising pillar, pulling Samsik with her, ran with him across the open space, dashed into the courtyard, and started climbing the back stairs.

Samsik ran after her – what else could he do? – ran like a frightened hare after the white mane flickering in the darkness like a fox's tail, a hare pursuing a fox, his heart thumping with fear.

He knew perfectly well where things were heading – to the moment of truth, to a scandal, to catastrophe, to exposure! This medical student would not stop at necking and kissing, the delicious trembling that was known in their circles as pressing and that was the utmost limit of Samsik's dreams. He could even kiss, our poor Samsik. He could give French kisses (One girl had said, "You're a great French kisser, Samsik!"). This meant that in a diabolical surge of lust he could push his tongue through the teeth of the current victim (there had been three of them) and tickle the inside of her mouth with his tongue. Beyond that his soul did not penetrate, and whenever his jazz-playing friends started talking about hard-ons and screwing, Samsik could only put on a cynical, knowing grin, while his soul was still wandering like a frightened goat on the edge of a terrible, impenetrable forest.

Sometimes at night, when he woke up on a camp bed under the table at Frieda Hitchcockovna's place or on a straw mattress beside the gas cooker of Fourth Company, Samsik would fondle his body and proudly confirm his virility, his ability to copulate with persons of the opposite sex, but the very word "copulate" suddenly filled him with an inexplicable sense of despair. The physical reality of the act struck him as monstrous, impossible, and his proud pennant drooped like a wet rag.

Now, almost in tears, he stopped in the middle of a dark room, through whose wallpaper and carpets gleamed the overheated cables, while under the window the radiator shone like a glowworm.

"Ah, we're alone," whispered the girl.

"Why are you just standing there?"

"Oh, unbutton me here . . ."

"Oh, Samsik, darling . . . I've caught you don't be afraid don't be afraid I'm not a hooker I hardly know how to do it either like you keep touching me here touch this thing can I touch you don't be afraid kid don't run away . . ."

She touched him with her long fingers, touched him long and patiently. She was naked, shining as though through a kind of spider's web; in the over-heated twilight of this freaked-out house, the nipples of her breasts glowed like the eyes of some woodland creature. He suddenly forgot the terrible word "copulation," forgot himself, Samsik Sabler, forgot Marina Vlady and Arina Belyakova and jazz and Stalin and Tolya von Steinbock, and having forgotten it all, he took this woman and plunged with her from a precipice into a dark tunnel that was bent and curled like a snail's shell.

Seen from outside, it all looked fairly ridiculous: meaningless thrusts, hoarse, broken cries and squeals, the slapping of wet skin. But then it all came together, it all started to work, and after a time that to our hero seemed interminable but was really very short, Samsik came to his senses and he was a ma-a-an.

She was still stretched out limply on one side of the bed, biting the pillow and muttering something as she tried to quell her aroused but unsatisfied flesh, and then she suddenly noticed he was already smoking a cigarette. She lost her temper – hell, what a lover! – but then remembered her mission and smiled at him affectionately – OK, smoke away, kid!

Her mission was very important, though it must have seemed somewhat ridiculous to a European girl. For the six months since the showing of the movie *The Witch* in the Soviet Union, she had been walking the wet, uneasy streets of this city, where she had once run away from the School for Noble Young Ladies, and would unexpectedly, always unexpectedly, accost the local Samsiks, the pathetic little offspring of the Stalinist era, lead them away to crumbling houses of the Silver Age, and teach them to love, like some unforgettable image of freedom.

He threw away his cigarette and crawled over to kiss her.
"That's enough, Samsik," she said gently. "Go home. I have an exam tomorrow in internal medicine, so I must get some sleep."
He got out of bed and walked around the room, reverently touching his beloved's possessions: the thick medical textbooks and atlases, her briefcase, her white coat, and her stethoscope, coiled on the desk like a little snake.
"You're the one and only love of my whole life," he suddenly said.
She burst out laughing. "Careful, Samsik. Don't touch the walls. You'll get an electric shock!"
The power cable, thick as a fist, pulsated with a green glow two centimeters away from his shoulder.
"To me, you're the water, you're the tall pine trees overhead, you're the eucalyptus trees and the sequoias, you're the stars shining through the branches!" cried the lovesick Samsik. He made a sudden movement and immediately got an electric shock. The current flooded through his entire skeleton, turning him into an anatomical chart. He could not move from the spot or utter a word but stood there crackling and glowing, while she laughed like a madwoman.
Her laughter was insulting, the laugh of a bitch – there was no other word for it. What a bitch, what a bitch you are, he thought, but he could not speak: The diabolical electric current was raging through his body.
Suddenly she jumped out of bed, ran toward him, and shut out all

the light from him, first with her broad face with its slightly coarse Russian skin and then with her eyes, which seemed like the night sky. "Samsik, you crazy kid, I'm not your one and only. You're going to have plenty more one and onlies: my friend Brigitte and Claudia Cardinale and Sophia Loren and that fat Anita and Monica the intellectual and Julia-keep-your-hands-off. You'll have affairs, little Samsik, only don't give up your sax, and tell all your friends never to give up their instruments! Now blow. The voltage is dropping."

It was true; the power cables were fading and cooling, and the blue light of dawn could be seen outside. Arina Belyakova put on a short bathrobe while Samsik hurriedly combed his hair.

"Leave by the window," said Arina Belyakova. "Can't you hear those footsteps in the corridor? I think the comrades have arrived."

Indeed, energetic footsteps could be heard in the hallway, a firm but unperemptory knock, an urgent male voice: "Open up, please! State Security! A criminal is hiding in this house! Kindly open the door!"

"How polite they are," said Arina Belyakova. "Just like when Dzerzhinsky was in charge."

"It's your redheaded friend in the checked suit playing a trick," Samsik grunted.

"Maybe," she said. "But suppose it really is the KGB?"

"But I'm not a criminal!" he shouted.

The knocking on the door grew louder.

"Where can I see you again?" asked Samsik, already on the windowsill.

"You know the student canteen near the Erisman Hospital? I eat there every day between two and three. Go on, kid, blow. See you around!"

Revaluation of values. Fourteen years after that night, described by Pantelei after hearing it from someone else over the phone, Samson Apollinarievich Sabler was improvising a new tune in the Blue Bird café. "Revaluation of Values" was the name of the tune.

They had already played several American pieces, then one of Silvester's compositions called "The Look of the Mist" and Pruzhinkin's crazy rumpus "The Eternal Triangle," and everyone – musicians and audience – seemed to be swinging, but everyone realized that the evening hadn't really begun yet.

During an intermission, the quintet came down from the stage. Someone served Silvester a dish of cauliflower. Pruzhinkin tried to pick up the girl in the long dress – with apparent success. Ryss was drinking glass after glass of Tsinandali, a Georgian white wine. Some physicists from Novosibirsk were paying, and the drummer was trying to get high as quickly as possible at their expense.

Samsik was sitting at a table with an Asian girl, a sweet kid called Klara. Her father was a cook in Samarkand, which was why she was rich: precious stones in her ears and on her fingers, gold on her bosom. She was caressing Samsik's sweat-soaked back and murmuring something in Uzbek, but he couldn't tear himself away from his saxophone as he quietly tried out his new tune, noticing out of the corner of his eye that the boys were listening to him intently.

Revaluation of values – undervalued values. I've revalued, he played softly. I've undervalued, he played softly. Something was growing inside him, something close to rapture and clairvoyance, but he didn't yet know what it was going to turn into – a prayer or a riot. Tenderness and anger were mixed together in his sax now, like the mixture of gasoline and air in the carburetor of a car.

"What are you playing?" the daughter of the thief of Samarkand suddenly asked him.

"Sam!" Silvester called out in a loud voice. The cauliflower had obviously stuck in his throat. "Have you dreamed up something?"

"Something cool, daddy-o?" Pruzhinkin was fidgeting in his chair.

Sabler shrugged his shoulders, and just then the sweaty, fleshy face of Buzdykin loomed up in front of him. "I knew it!" he roared so that the whole café could hear. "I knew this lousy genius was on to something! It's revaluation, isn't it, Samsik? You've revalued, isn't that right? You've undervalued, right? OK you bastard, let's have it. Play! Come on, Samsik. Let your hair down!"

Almost weeping from some disgusting thoughts of his own, he gave Samsik a repulsive wink, as though they were accomplices in some filthy deal.

This is incredible, thought Samsik, this stool pigeon, this faggot, this alcoholic, understands my music better than all my friends. He glanced around the café and shuddered. He had a feeling that at the far end of the room, peering out from behind the cloakroom counter were two familiar, burning eyes, hidden by folds of withered skin, and that the nauseating smell of frying seal fat was being wafted toward him by some unknown means across a time lag of many years and making his throat tighten.

"Would you like to hear it, stoolie?" he asked Buzdykin maliciously. "Are you going to tape it?"

"I'll try." Buzdykin wiped his sweaty hands on his ass. "Don't worry. I'll tape it and send it you-know-where."

Samsik vaulted onto the stage and played the opening bars of the tune in a challengingly harsh tone, right into the face of the old hangman who was standing behind the cloakroom counter, all the way to Kolyma. The eyes – two hot little cherries – disappeared, and with them the smell too. Samson's friends abandoned their food, drinks, and girls, and ran to back him up.

Revaluation of values

I've revalued
I undervalued
   sunrise and sunsets down city streets
   lemon-yellow, lilac-colored mists
   camels' muzzles
   flat squadrons of distant torpedo boats
   rolling with the wind over little Europe
   shaded lamps under cables
   with the screech of streetcars
   with the tapping of heels
   together with a baby
   like greasy Mamlakat, the champion milkmaid, in a font of zinc
   who grew up under the sun of Stalinism
   under the glare of searchlights
   and was called our youth
I've revalued
I undervalued
   the smell of libraries
   untidy heaps of books and Anatole France
   and the angel squeezing through gap between the last few letters
   back to the beginning of the alphabet
   groping his way so uncertainly
   and in that labyrinth
   thrilling the heart with a special smell
   all these thousands of copulations
   flying and buzzing with the greed of desires
   tenderest contacts
   the gathering of honey
   and filling up the baggage of knowledge
I've revalued

I undervalued
   dribbling and passing
   goal kicks and tackles from the side
   tackles from below and heading
   painful clinches
   the goalie's flight to stop a corner
   lighted cigarette pressed to the cheek
   as a powerful argument
   pressing an opponent against the wall in a learned argument
   the specter of a barricade
   and the lessons young men of my age
   gave to the tanks
   that drove into their city
   early one morning
   in their youth
   and in their memories forever
I've revalued
I undervalued
   the absolute alcohol of arctic Kolyma
   Veuve Clicquot and the moonshine from Ryazan
   the stars of brandyness
   the brassy prize medallions on liquor labels
   the torn remains of crayfish like limbs on Kulikovo's battlefield
   and beer in steins with helmets like the seven knights of fable
   the warming feel of friendship
   of alcoholic friendship
   shared hangovers the agonies of hell
   which if one's in a bunch of good old friends
   are easily survived
I've revalued
I undervalued
   that seething Sanhedrin beneath an azure dome and tall white pillars
      like sequoias
   cold not red sequoias
   you made appeal to the sequoia
   in Lenin's likeness
   try appealing to the sharks
   with sharklike mouths and chins receding
   the shocked dismay of all your friends
   when faced with this menagerie
   the roar of this menagerie

Tallyho, tallyho, chase them abroad
into asylums into the grave
but for us for us the caviar
delicious meats and fats and juices
if need be through a tube stuck up our asshole
if need be through our nostrils through our ears
or through our pores
so long as it keeps flowing
I've revalued
I undervalued
    the border towns – Ungeny, Brest-Litovsk, Galician Chop
    borshch Byelorussian-style
    Swiss food and Argentinian liquor
    Sinjuko district with its relentless din
    the Seto bar and you Chieko
    furry coat of the she-ape and her tricks
    good luck
    and the paroxysm of patriotism
    in the bar in the toilet in the station
    under slushy snow behind the tracks of trucks
    beneath the golden dome of Great Ivan's belltower
    those furtive christenings of the flag with vodka
    behind the bakery in that secluded corner
    the shadow and the eye slits of a prison watchtower . . .
    Stalinist pig with slitlike eyes
    stinking bastards may history shit
    on your bemedaled muzzles
    may history shit on your traditions on your meda-
    meda-meda-meda-medals-squelch-squelch-pfoo-grrr-hrrr-
        sonsofbitches
I've revalued
I undervalued
    my lamp nocturnal
    booze or abstinence
    the joy of covering clean white paper with letters
    that wriggle like worms
    hieroglyphs like beetles
    Cyrillic curls of Russian
    the latticework of Gothic script
    and a staircase in the night
    all those consolations of the night

mysterious walkers through the park at night
through terraces mosaic in the moonlight
the touch of hands
till Chanticleer crows
the touching of cheeks
the whispers the silence
mysterious in the night . . .

How full the night is of many sounds!

The unexpected ending – "How full the night is of many sounds" – knocked his legs from under him. Samsik fell on all fours, leaving a damp trail across the stage as he barely managed to crawl to the piano, where he hid behind Ryss's bottom and burst into tears of pride and happiness.

His partners thought he was crying from shame, and after his performance they tried by every possible means to cover up, camouflage, and improvise on his tune. They didn't like their friend to be caught with his pants down in public, and they deployed all their virtuosity to hide his ignominy. Finally, the whole combo came in together, howling and roaring; Pruzhinkin screamed to distract the audience's attention, and the piece came to an end. Samsik then crawled out from behind the piano and went back to his Uzbek girl. Everywhere people were staring at him in perplexity: No one had ever heard music like that. Buzdykin, grinning triumphantly, was explaining something to Alexander Plastinkin, a senior member of the Komsomol Central Committee.

No sooner had Sabler sat down than Plastinkin came over to him, "Hi, Samsik," he said. "This Buzdykin character has been giving me, quite honestly, a pretty weird interpretation of your piece. He seems to think it's about the children of Stalinism, something about copulation, swearing, barricades, latrines, a whole lot of junk like that."

"What d'you expect, Shura?" Samsik replied with a sad smile. "It's his job. Or rather a combination of jobs, if you know what I mean."

Plastinkin smiled gently; he knew quite well what sort of work Buzdykin combined with his regular job. "Well, Samsik, I'm interpreting your piece as a struggle against petty-bourgeois mentality," he said cautiously. "What do you say to that?"

"That's right – the struggle against petty-bourgeois mentality," Sabler confirmed. "A straight fight against the petty-bourgeois mentality."

Plastinkin sighed with relief, slapped Sabler on the shoulder, and went out. Samsik understood Plastinkin perfectly: He too had to submit an official report on this pseudojazz bacchanalia. The struggle against petty-bourgeois mentality sounded just fine.

"Aren't you ashamed of playing that stuff, Samsik?" Klara whispered to him, giving Samsik's thigh a gentle pinch.

I guess I should be ashamed of it, he thought, now that he had cooled off a bit. It was not jazz; it wasn't even music. The authorities were right after all: "Russian boys" shouldn't be allowed to get too deeply involved in anything. Whether it was jazz or literature, they were always liable to get carried away, to spit bile and cough up bits of their lungs, to turn jazz into nonjazz and politics into nonpolitics. No, the authorities were wise, and that was a fact.

"Do you know how to smoke cigars?" he asked Klara the Asian girl with brutal frankness.

She smiled at him equally frankly with her eyes and then humbly lowered them – she was after all a woman of the East, an obedient slave. She had a very protuberant, slightly cretinous little forehead, and two or three tiny pimples at the corners of her mouth.

"Let's go!"

ABCDE

Samson Apollinarievich Sabler came out of the café into the street, and before he had even had time to take a gulp of the Moscow night air he saw, standing across the street under a powerful streetlamp, a huge dirty Impala, in which were his mistress Masha and his Anglo-American friend Patrick Thunderjet.

"So they've found me, goddamn bourgeois," he thought.

"Darling! Darling!" squealed Masha and jumped out of the car. She was wearing her invariable jeans and a red shirt, knotted under her breasts, revealing a gorgeous midriff, while her great big eyes danced the hula. She was very beautiful, as she always was at night when she had gotten through a half-liter of vodka.

Then a pair of giraffe's legs shod in worn-out Hush Puppies appeared, followed by Patrick, who scratched the hair on the back of his neck and stared at Klara. In his eyes, the Tatar girl was apparently in rapid motion, because he kept making strenuous efforts to get her in focus, swaying from side to side and flailing his elbows. He must have thought he was pushing his way through a dense crowd, for he was also nodding to the left and right and saying, "Sorry." Finally, he hauled a flask out of his hip pocket, took a gulp, and found that the situation at once grew clearer. He put his arms around Samsik's shoulders. "Hi there, you son of a bitch! We heard you playing."

"I fell flat on my face today," said Samsik.

"No, old man, it wasn't as bad as that," said Thunderjet, hiccuping. "You were playing pretty well on the whole, almost like last summer in Marienbad."

"Did I play last summer in Marienbad?" asked Samsik.

"Yes, you played very well," said Thunderjet, nodding. "But you played well today too. Say, where did you hear my tune, old boy? I played it only a week ago in Monterey."

"Listen to him!" Masha exclaimed indignantly, and gave Patrick a fierce slap on the face. "It's *our* tune – mine and Samsik's!"

Pat staggered again. He kissed the hand that had struck him and gripped the Tatar girl by the shoulders, bending over her like a boa constrictor over a rabbit. "Well, here you are, Chiriko, here you are at last," he whispered, and the whisper – a foreigner's whisper – sneaked its way around the street, frightening all the police spies and counterspies.

Masha sat down on the sidewalk and cheerfully burst into tears, while Patrick picked up Klara in his arms and said straight to her lips, "I'm sure you won't mind, will you, Chiriko, if I throw you into the car?"

Everyone climbed into the Impala, and Patrick started making wild jabs at the accelerator, gunning the car like a madman and clumsily shifting gears. The car roared and shuddered, its whole organism suffering horribly under the strain of continual drunken driving.

"Where do you live, comrade?" Klara asked the driver, as she sat beside him looking like a baby or a lapdog.

In reply, Patrick leaned over and thrust his tongue between her lips. Masha meanwhile appeared to be sobbing on Samsik's chest, but in fact her fingers were exploring to make sure that everything was in place. The car drove straight toward one of the concrete pillars of the Hotel Minsk.

ABCDE

Aristarkh Apollinarievich Kunitser, cursing his own scientific talents, left the top-secret nighttime conference to which he had been summoned at a most inconvenient moment – namely, just before his final attack on the bottle of White Horse. Now, walking down the marble staircase of the building that housed the top-secret scientific committee, he grumbled quietly to himself as he recalled the details of the meeting, at which the discovery he had made that morning in the toilet had been discussed as though it did not belong to him alone but to the whole of progressive mankind as a function of its (mankind's) relentless struggle for peace. As he walked down, growling under his breath, he rummaged vaguely in his briefcase among the papers, every one numbered and registered by the Security Section. When he finally found the White Horse, in which there was still a little left, he stopped grumbling and cheered up; having almost forgotten the details of that utterly vile (in the words of Lenin, the Great Teacher) meeting, he passed through the checkpoint and emerged into a delightful, deserted Moscow side street.

Before he had time to take a drink from the bottle, he saw an enormous black diplomatic car, with a drunken female hand waving to him out of the window. Seated in the car were Kunitser's mistress, Masha Coulagot, and his old Anglo-American friend Patrick Thunderjet.

"Hell, they've found me, goddamn spies," muttered Kunitser.

"Darling, at last we've found you!" squealed Masha and jumped out of the car. She was wearing her invariable jeans and a red shirt knotted under her breasts. The smooth skin of Masha's gorgeous midriff gleamed from the gap between her shirt and her jeans, while her eyes danced the hula. She was very beautiful, as she always was at night when she had gotten through a half-liter of vodka.

Then a pair of giraffe's legs shod in worn-out Hush Puppies appeared, followed by Patrick, who scratched the hair on the back of his neck and stared at the almost empty bottle of White Horse gleaming in Kunitser's hand.

The bottle was obviously dancing in front of his eyes as he made strenuous efforts to get it in focus, swaying from side to side and flailing his elbows. He must have thought he was pushing his way through a dense crowd, for he was also nodding to the left and right and saying, "Sorry." Finally, he managed to put his lips around the neck of the bottle, the life-saving ball of amber liquid rolled inside him, and he immediately straightened up, cheered up, and addressed the bottle with his usual amazing vivacity, "How fascinating you are, madam!"

"Pat, can't you see?" said Masha indignantly. "That's your friend Arik standing in front of you!"

"I can see, I can see," Patrick answered with jovial courtesy, saluting the bottle. "How's life, old man?"

"OK, thanks," I replied. "I made an important scientific discovery today."

"What is it?" exclaimed Masha.

"I'm not telling you."

"Why not, darling?"

"Because it belongs to my country."

"Important scientific discoveries belong to all mankind," she declared haughtily, almost contemptuously.

"That's what you think!" Kunitser yelled, his mouth twisted, almost weeping with chagrin. "You damn rootless, raceless cosmopolitans, and especially you, you whore, you White Russian bitch!"

Masha sat down on the sidewalk and cheerfully burst into tears. Patrick meanwhile, paying no attention to her, was sweet-talking the bottle.

"I like you, baby! Why don't you come along with me? Come in my car, you sweet little clockwork girl!"

Everyone climbed into the Impala, and Patrick started making wild jabs at the accelerator, gunning the car like a madman and clumsily shifting gears. The car roared and shuddered, its whole organism suffering horribly under the strain of continual drunken driving. Patrick was exchanging sweet nothings with the bottle as though it were a Japanese prostitute in the Sinjuko quarter, laughing happily and occasionally sucking at it. Masha appeared to be sobbing on Aristarkh's chest, but in fact her fingers were exploring to make sure that everything was in place. Meanwhile the car drove straight toward one of the concrete pillars of the Hotel Minsk.

ABCDE

Gennady Apollinarievich Malkolmov left the operating room in high spirits. How well everything had gone today! How marvelous it had been! What brilliant technique he had demonstrated during the operation. What anastomoses! What sutures! What an attractive forty-year-old surgeon-superman he was, this tanned brute, this almost-a-full-professor, surrounded by legends throughout the institute – Gennady Malkolmov! What an impression he had made on the assistants, but chiefly on one female student, Tinatina Shevardina! What unconcealed rapture had shone in her eyes! And how perfectly everything had worked out after the operation! How nonchalantly, without any prompting, the senior surgical nurse had offered him a full measuring glass of rectified spirit, and how magnificently he had downed it with a chaser of cold Borzhomi mineral water! How marvelously he had pulled it off, how youthfully and dashingly, just as in his student days in the late fifties! How very convenient it had been when Kaverznev appeared, a student who was perpetually in debt, an organizer of mass cultural events, and a dealer in live goods! And how this young scoundrel had excited the almost-a-full-professor when he had winked at him and said that Tinatina Shevardina was waiting for him at the park gates and that he, Kaverznev, had arranged a party to which Malkolmov and Shevardina were invited, and the token of gratitude that he expected in return for this so-called party was a mere trifle – just a passing grade for him, Kaverznev, for his surgery rotation!

As Malkolmov strode boldly through the park, the branches of the trees creaking in the breeze over his head, he felt like a pushy, successful senior, anticipating the pleasures of the "party," his coming affair with Shevardina, the liquor, the deafening pop music, and only occasionally did he feel a slight, oppressive awareness of corruption, dirt, tackiness, and banality, but only faintly, and it disappeared again immediately.

He walked out of the park into a quiet, deserted Moscow side street. The students were already waiting for him, all in trendy clothes, lolling picturesquely against the nineteenth-century cast-iron railings, the lights of the night flickering over Tinatina Shevardina's long legs. Four widely spaced crystal eyes appeared at the end of the street and slowly crawled toward the group at the gates.

Hell, that's ruined everything, thought Malkolmov. They've tracked me down, damn cosmopolitans!

He was not mistaken. A huge black diplomatic four-berth eight-cylinder limousine was approaching the institute grounds, and a drunken female hand was waving to him from the window. It was a little surprise dreamed up by his long-since ex-mistress Masha Coulagot and his old Anglo-American, or rather his intercontinental, pal Patrick Thunderjet.

"Genochka, darling! Here we are! Here we are!" squealed Masha and jumped out of the car. She was wearing her invariable jeans and a red shirt, knotted under breasts that pointed in different directions. Masha's gorgeous belly, smooth and rounded as a Volkswagen's roof, gleamed from the gap between her jeans and her shirt, while her eyes danced the hula. She was very beautiful, as she always was at night after she had gotten through a half-liter of vodka.

Then a pair of giraffe's legs appeared, shod in worn-out Hush Puppies followed by Patrick Thunderjet, who scratched the hair on the back of his neck and stared at the group of students – more precisely at Tinatina Shevardina and her two girl friends.

"Odd to see so many delicious tomatoes. How much do they cost in this garrison?" It wasn't very difficult to see that the American surgeon was the drunkest man in the party. It was quite likely that he thought the three Moscow female students were a gaggle of Saigon whores. He kept making strenuous efforts to get them in focus, swaying from side to side and flailing his elbows. He must have thought he was pushing his way through a dense crowd, for he was also nodding to the left and right and saying, "Sorry." When he finally managed to reach the three girls, he seized hold of them and relaxed blissfully, looking as though he were listening to an organ fugue being played in a cathedral.

At that point Malkolmov suddenly noticed that Patrick was wearing his, Malkolmov's, best shirt.

"You see, darling, Pat flew in today from God knows where on a Japanese plane and everything in his suitcase was so dirty and smelly that I had to go over to your place for some clothes," twittered Masha.

"You might have chosen something a bit less expensive," Malkolmov grumbled.

"But he's your best friend!" exclaimed Masha.

"I'm not talking to my friend," roared Malkolmov. "I'm telling *you* it's time you stopped handing out my clothes to all your studs that happen to be passing through town! This isn't London. There's no store like Liberty's just around the corner! Clothes are hard to get!"

Masha sat down on the sidewalk and cheerfully burst into tears. Patrick, who meanwhile had been swigging rectified spirit from a bottle hidden in Kaverznev's sleeve, came back to life and turned his attention to the three girls.

"Hey, kid, want a thousand piastres? Do you? And you? What a lovely girl! That's what's great about being in the service. Join the U.S. Army and see the world! Long live aggression! Come on, Genka, let's go!"

Everyone climbed into the Impala, and Patrick started gunning the car like a madman and clumsily shifting gears. The car roared and shuddered, its whole organism suffering horribly under the strain of continual drunken driving. The girls were laughing wildly, just like real prostitutes, and the odious Kaverznev was already trying out Patrick's Seiko watch on his own wrist. As for Masha, she appeared to be sobbing on Malkolmov's chest, but in fact her fingers were exploring to make sure that everything was in place. Meanwhile the car drove straight toward one of the concrete pillars of the Hotel Minsk.

ABCDE

Radius Apollinarievich Khvastishchev spent a long time that evening, devoid of thought or feeling (not to mention inspiration), polishing the marble tail of his sculpture *Humility*, until a young moon finally glanced into his studio and summoned him to abandon his tedious stint and hurry out into the streets of the capital in search of sources of inspiration, most likely to be found in the restaurant of the All-Russian Theatrical Society.

I will walk in briskly and sullenly, and I'll sit down alone, so that no one can come sneaking up with glasses, tumblers, and bottles. I shall order no liquor, so as not to attract any whores; I shall simply sit there and reflect on something great – the frieze at Pergamum, for instance, or the forms of Henry Moore, but preferably Pergamum, and in particular that group in which the hounds of Artemis are savaging the giants. I shall merely order something to set my teeth going, a salad, a bottle of mineral water, and some coffee, and don't expect any trouble from me tonight, you scum.

So mused the sculptor on one night of his fourth decade on the threshold of his fifth, on the threshold of his studio under a young moon, and watched as the elderly Stikhin the plumber, in his flapping shirt, and the young hippie Chudakov, a janitor wearing a sheepskin coat, approached him up the humpbacked slope of the street. In thinking these thoughts, the sculptor was concealing from himself the fact that he would, in fact, have liked to make up the third in this company, that he was ready to help consume all those disgusting bottles of port and madeira that Stikhin kept stashed away in his pants, and was certainly ready to take the train from the Kiev Station out to the student dormitory at the commercial school in Ochakovo.

Meanwhile, four crystal eyes were crawling down from the top of the steep little street, and a few seconds later Radius Khvastishchev saw a drunken female hand waving to him from the car. For this he was *not* ready. Approaching from below was his native element – the rowdy, drunken Muscovite brotherhood of male company – while approaching from above was something alien – his cosmopolitan mistress Masha Coulagot and their friend Patrick Thunderjet, a versatile, talented member of the international set. Hell, they've found me, those decadent aesthetes, damn foreigners!

"Darling, we've found you!" squealed Masha, and jumped out of the car. She was wearing her invariable jeans and a red shirt, knotted under her jutting breasts. Masha never wore a bra, which naturally never failed to shock the Moscow public. Masha's gorgeous midriff, one of nature's most perfect forms, gleamed from the gap between her jeans and her shirt. She was very beautiful, as she always was at night when she had gotten through a half-liter of vodka. Then a pair of giraffe's legs shod in worn-out Hush Puppies appeared, followed by the rest of that globe-trotting bum Patrick Thunderjet.

Patrick scratched the hair on the back of his neck and nodded with his long nose.

"Don't you see, Pat, it's your old friend, our celebrated genius!" Masha shouted into his ear.

"I can see, I can see," mumbled Thunderjet and, with the kindest of smiles, lurched toward Stikhin the plumber.

He found the way difficult. It was obvious that the plumber was constantly floating out of his field of vision, because he kept making strenuous efforts to keep him in focus, swaying from side to side and flailing his elbows. He must have thought he was pushing his way through a dense crowd, for he kept bending to the left and right and saying, "Sorry." Finally he managed to reach Stikhin, and grasped this Russian man around the hips with a lustful squelch.

Khvastishchev turned to Masha and said coldly, "By the way, you might refrain from this stupid sarcasm. I really am quite well known in the artistic circles of cultured society."

"Darling!" Masha clasped her hands. "You're a genius!"

Khvastishchev swung around on his heels. "We sleep together, don't we, ma'am? That's OK by me. But for God's sake, can't we do without these sickening 'darlings'? As for these Western petty bourgeois, especially upstarts like this—"

Masha sat down on the sidewalk and cheerfully burst into tears. Patrick, meanwhile, like a demon of homosexuality, was caressing Stikhin's unattractive hips, trembling each time he felt the concealed bottles.

"You and I, dad, were allies in World War II," he said affectionately to the plumber, and immediately, turning to the janitor, "and you and

I, kid, were allies in the Flower Power movement. Let's stick together, friends."

"Hey, this guy's OK," said Chudakov. "Got any dollars?"

"Why don't we have a get-together of all our friends who are in Moscow?" Patrick suggested. "Let's go to the Brazilian Embassy. Brazil's the country of the twenty-first century!"

"Sure, let's go," Chudakov agreed, "provided they don't chase us out."

Stikhin too said his piece: "If you want to make an exhibition of yourself, OK, go ahead. If you want to get a bloody nose, we won't stop you. You don't understand the Russians. You've got to realize that at bottom they're good-hearted."

With these words he hauled out of his pants three seventy-five-centiliter bottles of Madeira Rosé produced by the Ramensky Wine and Liquor Factory.

Everyone then climbed into the Impala, and Patrick started making wild jabs at the accelerator, gunning the car like a madman, and clumsily shifting gears. The car roared and shuddered, its whole organism suffering horribly under the strain of continual drunken driving. Patrick, Stikhin, and Chudakov were roaring out the song "I'm Standing at the Station." Masha appeared to be sobbing on Khvastishchev's chest, but in fact her fingers were exploring to make sure that everything was in place. They cruised around the streets and alleyways of Moscow for a long time, until they headed toward one of the concrete pillars of the Hotel Minsk.

ABCDE

A reception was in progress at the Brazilian Embassy, at which one of the guests was the Moscow writer Pantelei Apollinarievich Pantelei. Incidentally, it may not have been the Brazilian Embassy, and it could be that Pantelei had not even been invited but had seen the lights and movement of a party through the windows and had simply gate-crashed, fooling the police and the KGB with his authoritative, foreign appearance. At all events, he was in there.

He stood behind a curly fairy-tale pillar in the main hall of the embassy. The huge gala reception in honor of that country's national day was in full swing. Ambassadors, counselors, military attachés, Soviet civilian and military bureaucrats, the clergy, Soviet official writers and "dissidents," scientists and artists, cosmonauts, sportsmen, and ladies, ladies, and more ladies – fat ones, thin ones, pretty ones, witches, bitches, gold diggers, vampires, sweethearts, and wives – were slowly circulating under the astonished gaze of the mortally terrified Pantelei.

This was not, of course, the first time that Pantelei had been to one of these gatherings. In the past decade he had attended dozens, perhaps hundreds, of diplomatic receptions; he had never avoided them or pulled a snobbish face – "Oh, parties bore me" – and Pantelei the progressive Soviet writer had never found these receptions boring. He always ate his fill of delicious food and got half-drunk on sophisticated drinks, and sometimes he also managed to pick up a woman.

Today, however, he suddenly looked around and could recognize no one. He could not make out whether these were human beings milling around him or objects of some other kind; nor could he even understand the word "objects," and the concept of "around" seemed to him more like some kind of dim chaos. The horror of nonrecognition drew him to the fake-baroque pillar, which for some reason he found familiar. Staring at the pillar's curlicues encrusted with semiprecious stones from the Urals, he realized in utter despair that he could not tear himself away from this pillar, and that if he did, he would fall down and roll howling across the floor.

Suddenly he felt a touch on his shoulder and through empty space came the word "Hello." An electric current shocked him from the back of his neck to his heels. He turned around, saw Alisa, and recognized her.

That woman. That woman with her quick sly, glances, her mouth – now bitter, now impertinent – her wild mane of reddish-gold hair – he would have recognized her among a dozen other Moscow beauties.

"What on earth's the matter with you, Pantelei?" she said and immediately turned her eyes toward the crowd, on which she fixed her darting, mysterious, searching gaze. "May I stand here with you for a while?" she asked, without waiting for an answer to her solicitous question. "My husband respects you very much."

From the far end of the hall the tanned face of her husband, a famous tractor designer, was turned toward them with hopeless longing. Alisa's current lover, a long beanpole of a man, was sidling along the wall, smiling, with a glass in his hand.

Suddenly Pantelei, without realizing what he was doing but in a surge of wild joy, seized the lady by her delicate shoulder and turned her around to face him. His terror rolled away through the endless suite

of rooms and into the mirrors, into empty space, and the cacophony in
his ears was stilled.

"*Mon amour,*" Pantelei said to Alisa. "God has sent you to me.
You are my salvation."

Strangely, she did not try to pull away but looked attentively at him
and his fingers could feel her warm, yielding skin through the gold-
embroidered material.

Meanwhile her lover approached, wearing a long-tailed English
cutaway coat and a canary-yellow tie; he had the lazy, ironic eyes of
a debauchee beneath the Socratic dome of a man who was far from
stupid.

"Greetings," he droned in a nasal voice. "Just look at all these
people – and all for a few lines in a newspaper. Pantelei, old fellow,
why are you holding that woman by the shoulder when you hardly
know her? Let her go."

"Do you want a kick in the balls?" Pantelei said to him.

"Oh, well, if that's the way you feel . . ." The lover spread his
hands. "Tomorrow's paper will say, 'The reception took place in an
atmosphere of cold hostility.' "

Jokes apparently played a large part in the practice of their love.
Alisa was about to laugh, but the joke fell flat, and the beautiful
woman's face froze in silent, submissive expectation of her fate.

Sensing that something was wrong, her husband, the tractor
designer, barged through the crowd of diplomats like one of his creations pushing its way through the forests of Byelorussia.

"*Mon amour!*" Pantelei repeated loudly. It seemed appropriate,
under the circumstances, to address the object of his attentions in
French. "You are my destiny. Only now do I realize that it's you I
have been seeing for years in my dreams."

Faces of all shades of color turned toward him, and the thought
occurred to Pantelei that the gathering was sufficiently representative
for a declaration of love.

"Ladies and comrades!" he said with a charming smile, turning the
silent Alisa around by her shoulder as though showing her off to the
whole room. "Your attention please. Here is an interesting phenomenon of human psychology. I have seen this woman in dreams for
many years, although in my waking life I have only recently and
fleetingly made her acquaintance. If you can believe it, I even had the
impression in my dreams that I was stroking her thigh, this very thigh
that is now in front of me, and I cannot possibly be mistaken, although
I have never slept with this thigh."

He let go of Alisa's shoulder and reverentially stroked her thigh with the palm of his hand, and it was true: The path followed by his hand seemed familiar, immeasurably sweet, and the only possible path.

"That is all I wanted to say. Please forgive me." He bowed to Alisa and with unsteady but rapid steps made for the exit.

Proceeding down the corridor without further adventures, the crowd parting before him as though he were a president, Pantelei suddenly stumbled across a table behind which stood three handsome bartenders, presiding over a snow-white tablecloth on which paraded a company far more glittering than that which filled the halls of the embassy: there stood Gordon's Gin and Cinzano Dry and Queen Anne and Armagnac and Mumm and Campari and Rémy Martin and Ballantine's and Smirnoff and Benedictine surrounded by a guard of Schweppes and Coca-Cola.

Pantelei stopped at this table and glanced around. It suddenly seemed to him that he had hypnotized the crowd with his announcement about Alisa's thigh. Perhaps he had, even if only in part, because Pantelei was able, unhindered, to fill up a large cardboard box with magnificent drinks and to leave the embassy of the unidentified country without hindrance.

Only when he was outside, in the deserted silence of the street, did he hear the sounds of pursuit. He hid under the archway of a house, and his pursuers ran past him as though in medieval Paris. He was seized by a feeling of triumph. Now to go home and write all this down. But I mustn't forget anything: myself, Alisa, the liquor. And I mustn't forget that the pursuers galloped past as if we were in medieval Paris! He jumped out from under the archway and, sneaking through the back streets, quickly covered his tracks. How good to be living in the deserted hours of the night!

Pantelei unpacked his box and placed all his trophies out on the sidewalk, all those bottles of various sizes and shapes and brands. He had no doubt that someone would soon appear and carry him away somewhere out of that wonderful Moscow side street, where cool and harmless secrets leap like cats from roof to roof. Indeed, he did not have to sit there for long.

Four crystal eyes appeared in the dark womb, and into the light of the streetlamps drove a huge Impala, from which a drunken woman's hand was waving to Pantelei.

The mistress of Pantelei A. Pantelei, a Swiss citizen, Mademoiselle Marianne Coulagot—

. . . cool and harmless secrets leap like cats from roof to roof . . .
Mustn't forget that!

–and Pantelei's old friend, the third deputy of the sixth vice-president
of the International PEN Club, were driving together through innocent
nighttime Moscow.

Innocent Moscow!

Pantelei sat down on the sidewalk alongside his trophies, pretending
to be a street vendor. Let these ideological saboteurs see what an
assortment of goods the Moscow street traders are selling!

"Pantik, Pantik, here you are at last! Now we've hooked you!"
squealed Masha and jumped out of the car.

She was wearing her invariable jeans and a red shirt, knotted under
her freely bouncing breasts, which hid an ideological charge of unusual
explosive power. Br-r-r! Masha's gorgeous midriff, the epicenter of
the ideological struggle between Asia and Europe, gleamed from the
gap between her shirt and her jeans. She was very beautiful, as she
always was on nights when she had gotten through a half-liter of vodka.

Then a pair of giraffe's legs shod in worn-out Hush Puppies
appeared, followed by the rest of the so-called vice-president, who was
more like the drink-sodden center forward of a basketball team. He
scratched the hair on the back of his neck, suddenly saw my collection
laid out on the sidewalk, and leaped a pace backward with a wild
shriek.

"No, I don't want to. Not the UN again? Not UNESCO again?
Can't we at least go a month without that? Pantik, help me! Masha,
hold my nose!"

At that we all three embraced and sang a song from our distant
spring:

> Never, never shall we see in our dreams
> The misty West, the faithless, lying West . . .

So, off we went! Where to? Away! Away from London, from Paris,
from Moscow, nearer to our spring, to our drunken, disgraceful, irrevo-
cable springtime. Patrick made wild jabs at the accelerator, gunning
the car like a madman, and clumsily shifting gears. The car roared and
shuddered, its whole organism suffering horribly under the strain of
continual drunken driving. Then we sang a splendid American song
about those bastards who write on the walls of paradise and who are
therefore condemned to roll their own shit into little balls. So let them
roll! And the people who read their words of wisdom can eat those

little balls! We drove, sang and sobbed on each others' chests. Meanwhile, as she sobbed, Masha's fingers were exploring to make sure that
everything was in place. We drove, sang, and sobbed until the car
drove straight toward one of the concrete pillars of the Hotel Minsk.

The Surgeon-Pediatrician-Rheumatologist-Cardiologist-
Phthisiologist Gennady Apollinarievich Malkolmov Tells
the Story of His Youth to an Unknown Person at an
Unknown Time on an Unknown Telephone Line

We three – Masha, Patrick, and I – first met in August 1961 – in a
UN hospital in the jungles of Katanga. I had come there as the most
experienced Soviet specialist in African tuberculosis, Patrick as an
American osteopath, and Masha, or Marianne Coulagot, as she was
then called, was a Christian Sister of Mercy.

We were not exactly overburdened with work: Our chief source of
patients was a small tribe of hunting pygmies from the western coast.
Somehow the pygmies had heard about our hospital and the UN
food rations, whereupon they abandoned their settlements, walked
hundreds of miles through the jungle, and came to us wanting to be
cured. What fun it was! We hospitalized them all – the adult hunters,
the children, the pygmy girls, and the old women.

We also hospitalized the goddess of the tribe, a strange fair-skinned
creature with a distended stomach and a bottom that wobbled like two
down cushions – a silent creature lying on a ritual couch with her legs
spread wide open and held up on straps. It was curious to watch the
observance of the cult of Metamungwu (for such was the goddess's
name). The entire tribe stood around her – the women in one group,
the men in another. They all sang. The men, in order of seniority,
would approach the goddess to perform the ritual sex act, while the
women would caress the goddess on her forehead and stuff pieces of
food into her mouth, which she would quickly chew and swallow.

Metamungwu shocked the imagination of all the male personnel of
the hospital, whereas our women, with the exception of Masha, could
see nothing special in her.

In the evenings, when we all gathered on the veranda overlooking
the lake, I often advised Patrick to take part in the ritual, and he,
staring hard at Masha, promised to do so. Indeed, he soon began
strolling up and down the yard in front of the garage where the
goddess's couch was positioned and tried to talk to her, tell her jokes,
read her excerpts from the newspapers and the poetry of Ezra Pound,

until one day – everyone gasped in amazement – he taught her to smoke. After that, in the intervals between ritual copulation and eating, Metamungwu did nothing but puff cigarettes.

The pygmies were seized with holy terror and apparently decided to eliminate Mr. Thunderjet. Only sheer luck, I believe, saved the seducer on that occasion. One day he thought of pushing the mouth of a bottle into the mouth of the goddess, who, having taken a hearty gulp of Black & White whiskey, suddenly sat up for the first time in long decades and sang, in impeccable Spanish, an epithalamion in Patrick's honor, which sounded roughly as follows:

> Patrick Thunderjet
> Chiquito with the long nose
> And the angelic smile
> Patrick Thunderjet
> O prince
> O roses of the night
> O Patrick Thunderjet!

Observing this spectacle and hearing the epithalamion, the pygmies fell flat on their faces, expecting the end of the world. The director of the hospital, Professor Abbas, summoned Patrick and forbade him to pursue his friendship with the enigmatic creature.

How Masha laughed at that, how she laughed! Masha . . . Masha . . . Mademoiselle Coulagot . . . Strange as it is to recall it now, she and I too had our moments of "whispers and tender sighs" in the African bush. Who was this woman then, now a foreigner in Moscow and a drunken slut? In those days she was a Russian Frenchwoman, a third-generation émigré as pure and joyous as the dawn of Christianity.

"My grandfather was an officer," she prattled. "First a cavalryman, then an aviator. He fought a lot, *très bien,* and then retreated with the rest of the troops."

"With which troops?" I inquired with interest.

"With our troops – the Russians. He retreated to Europe."

"You're mistaken, my child," I said, kissing her in various places. "The *Russian* troops never retreated to any place. The Whites and the Entente scum retreated, but the Russians, that's to say the Reds, stayed put."

"But you've got it all wrong, dear!" Her eyes widened. "The entire *Russian* army retreated, but the Reds were nothing but Chinese, Latvians, and Jews."

"And the sailors and the Chekists," she added after a moment's thought.

"Clever guy, your grandfather," I said.

"Yes, he wasn't stupid," she agreed.

Oh, how she used to come in – ah, how well I remember how she came into our morning medical staff conference in her linen pants and blue denim shirt – a she-devil scattering cigarette ash and saying in her little birdlike voice, "*Ça va?*" and all the doctors (a Russian, a Yankee, an Italian, a Finn, a Pole, and the medical director, the Pakistani Abbas) answered her with their national smiles, "*Ça va!*" and well-being reigned in the jungles of Katanga under the UN flag.

Meanwhile the lovesick Patrick Thunderjet was suffering badly. One day he came to me in a state of distress and said that he couldn't sleep for one great thought. What was the thought? It was this: On the one hand, Miss Coulagot, as a Russian by blood, belonged to me, but on the other hand, she was after all a citizen of a Western nation, that is, of the Free World, and this might lead one to draw the opposite conclusion.

"Patrick, you're an intelligent man," I said, trying to reason with him, "and you must realize that the world is in a state of very unstable equilibrium. The power of the Warsaw Pact countries is so vast that you can't even imagine it."

"Is that so?" he said in amazement.

"I swear it! What's more, Pat, don't forget that we are now under the blue flag of the UN, the hope of all mankind."

He went off into the night and for a long time he made the twigs crunch in the forest around the hospital, scaring troops of monkeys and solitary hyenas.

One day I read Masha a poem by Gumilyov about an elegant giraffe from Lake Chad. She was astonished: "You're a Soviet Russian yet you read the poems of a 'White' Russian poet?" Ah, Masha, Masha . . . Another time, when she was listening to some of my tapes of Bulat Okudzhava singing his own songs, she suddenly burst into tears. What is it? Where does it come from? Whose is this voice flying here from the Soviet desert? She suddenly realized that she knew nothing about the homeland of the man who was her lover here in Africa.

Our erotic nights followed one after another, and we usually fell asleep exhausted and happy, like champions after winning several races. But one day I was suddenly overwhelmed by memories of the past, of the young Von Steinbock, of volcanic hills in the moonlight, of a green star over the Magadan Disinfection Center. I forgot about

Masha and began to pray. Suddenly she said with a sigh, "Why do they trust you?"

In fact, I never did quite understand why THEY trusted me. But then, why shouldn't THEY trust me? I'm very efficient at X-raying pygmies and collapsing ruined lungs; I even prescribed injections of streptomycin and vitamin B for the goddess Metamungwu, thereby, of course, helping to increase the prestige of my great country and to disperse the fetid miasma of anti-Soviet propaganda exuded by the tribes of Malawi. Why shouldn't THEY trust me?

Masha and I were so absorbed in each other that we did not even notice that war had broken out around us. Something did seem to be burning on the horizon. The staff acted nervously, twiddling the knobs on their transistors, from which announcers broadcast in French, English, and Swahili, but we simply gazed at each other and smiled. Masha, I believe, was seriously thinking of marrying me.

One day she and I were taking a romantic trip on the lake in a two-man canoe when a jet plane with strange recognition markings flew low over the water. With lightning speed a long line of splashes streaked past the canoe and faded in the distance; a minute later, a bloodstreaked bubble formed in the water and a crocodile broke surface, its belly ripped open by bullets.

"Boy, I'd like to shit on that bastard for fucking around like that!" I shouted, genuinely furious.

"Horrors! 'Shit!' 'Bastard!' 'Fucking!' What on earth does that mean? *Qu'est que c'est?*" Masha frowned comically. Her émigré ear could not always stomach some of the current expletives in our "great, mighty, free, and truthful" mother tongue.

Meanwhile the jet was coming back, spitting fire, the blood in the water increased, and on shore the isolation ward and a baobab tree in the hospital yard caught fire.

The night that followed was, objectively speaking, utterly terrifying. The fighting was getting close to our blessedly peaceful lake. Now and then the slopes of the mountains would be lit up by flashes, and the jungle echoed to the rattle of nearby machine-gun fire.

The entire staff gathered in the library. The Catholics (who were in the majority), headed by Father Claude, knelt down in front of a portable altar, the Muslims prostrated themselves on their prayer mats, the Buddhists sat with their eyes closed, Thunderjet and Lanz, the Uruguayan mechanic, together drained bottle after bottle of Black & White, while I read aloud to Masha from a Soviet textbook on

Darwinism. You ought to know, baby, what sort of education your future husband has had.

I carried this textbook with me wherever I went. It contained an illustration depicting the awful world of prehistoric animals – an extremely unpleasant sight for today's lord of the earth. Underwater, for instance, there swam a predatory, fast-moving marine lizard. The air was filled with sharp-clawed, fang-toothed pterodactyls with wings of leather membranes, while on shore a mad plesiosaurus was standing bowlegged under a gigantic horsetail fern. It was shocking to see that horde of absurd creatures, all obsessed by one idea – to eat someone else before being eaten themselves. The most interesting character in the picture, however, was one unfortunate dinosaur that had been deprived of its head. Everything else was there – the colossal, muscular, fleshy body, the long tail, the pillarlike neck. All was there except for one little detail – the head, the weight of which, as we know, is equal to one seven-thousandth of the weight of the whole body. Several months ago, someone had bitten off his head; he had not even had time to notice who it was, and now the wretched creature was paddling around unhappily in the shallow water, discouraged by the fact that he had nothing to eat with, not to mention that he couldn't even see any food, because his mouth and eyes are, after all, in his head.

AUTHOR'S NOTE. At this point we interrupt Gennady Apollinarievich's mumblings on the telephone to describe a curious chain of events.

In the last wet decade but one, while lying once on a decrepit folding camp bed behind a tiled stove, Samsik Sabler suddenly thought he was a poet and wrote something like the following lines on his shirt cuff:

> I curse, I hiccup, and I howl!
> I want to hide myself and spend my life
> Curled up and waiting, like some slimy reptile
> Among the pine needles and woodland ferns,
> Among the ancient giant sequoias
> That have survived the fires of earth,
> So that I'll never have to meet you,
> Never launch the boats into the rushing streams.

Who is "you?" What boats? What streams? The poet frowned gloomily. At a modest estimate, the poem would be worth two hundred old rubles if it only contained a single grain of common sense, to say nothing of ringing rhymes, original subject matter, self-discipline, and militancy, those essential qualities of Soviet poetry.

Later, when he was already famous, the sculptor Radius Khvastish-chev withdrew as a contender for the State Prize, in favor of the secretary of the Moscow Artists' Union; his reward was to be given a studio that was a converted vegetable store. While equipping these premises with plinths and armatures, the sculptor discovered, alongside an unexploded fragmentation bomb, a barrel of prewar vintage pickling brine containing the lower jaw of an animal somewhat smaller than a man. No doubt it was the jawbone of a dinosaur, he thought, glancing thoughtfully at the block of bluish marble that he had recently received from Yugoslavia as a token of gratitude for his statuette *The Youth of Marshal Tito*.

Pantik Pantelei and Arik Kunitser never met each other, which was not surprising, but once they both had courted the same lady, who was just on the point of leaving for a diplomatic post in the United States. While seeing her off, Arik had spent half a day wandering around among the cranes on the dockside, not daring to approach the white liner, where the lady was already enjoying a foretaste of being an American and where he had gazed at the jibs of these cranes, those long, long jibs and their slow movements. Pantik meanwhile, in an attempt to stifle his longing for the lady diplomat and his evil thoughts about her husband, went to the Zoological Museum and began studying life on earth from its origins to the present day.

Thus was established an undoubted, though very tenuous chain of circumstances: the textbook on Darwinism, the juvenile poem, the bones in the barrel of brine, the young lady diplomat, the dockside cranes, and the ticket of admission to the Zoological Museum.

"But why are you so obsessed with that stupid dinosaur?" Masha would sometimes ask me.

"Read this, you silly girl!" The Darwinist in me flared up at once. "Read this. 'It has now been definitely proved that a headless dinosaur could remain alive in the prehistoric environment for no less than a year and could even retain its reproductive functions.' " Well? How about that, eh?"

"Yes," my foolish Genevan would unwillingly concur. "It must have some significance."

* * *

The next morning a shattered unit of the UN armed forces – a bunch of unfortunate Indians in rattling blue helmets – beat a hasty retreat past the hospital. They left us their wounded and said they had been pursued all night by some awful people, several terrifying characters who appeared to have nothing else to do but show violence to the troops of the blue flag.

Dissolving a whole bottle of Alka-Seltzer tablets in soda, Masha managed to restore our chief surgeon, Patrick Thunderjet, to a divine state, and the whole hospital set to work.

In our ultramodern operating room, using three operating tables at once, without even thinking of danger, we operated on the wretched Indians who had been wounded by a gang of scoundrels. Under the influence of the ether-oxygen anesthetic, the Indians sang their religious hymns in plaintive voices. Masha, wrapped in her surgical gown, handed out clamps and sutures, while Patrick sawed off the leg of an Indian sergeant and cursed the romantic land of Scotland for having produced so many brands of whiskey.

Absorbed in our humanitarian task, we did not at first notice the armored car, towing a recoilless gun, which was slowly driving around the hospital yard outside the glass wall of the operating room. It was a marauding, open-topped armored car, manned by five villainous creatures – four white men and one black. They were lolling around in supermanlike poses, staring with sardonic smiles at the hospital and at the pygmies who were crowded around the dais of the goddess Metamungwu. Her legs spread out wide, as was her custom, the goddess was smoking and not paying the slightest attention to the new arrivals, although the tribe was clearly alarmed.

"To arms!" shouted our radiologist, a Japanese called Noma. "The mercenaries!"

"Gentlemen, please remain at your posts," said Professor Abbas. "We cannot abandon our wounded. Continue operating, gentlemen! We are protected by the Red Cross."

"And by the Lion and Crescent, the Hippocratic Serpent and Chalice, the Hammer and Sickle, the Vatican, Mecca, and the Kremlin." Patrick Thunderjet burst into uncontrollable laughter, exploding with all the bad-tempered spleen of a man with a hangover.

We went on operating, but meanwhile three of the men jumped over the side of the armored car and slowly moved toward the hospital. Two of them were dressed in camouflage suits, and one athletic figure was in jeans and a bulletproof vest, worn over his bare torso, for all the world like some Hollywood hero. All three of them had Stanley submachine guns dangling in front of their chests, while their hips were girded by massive belts stuffed with cartridges and grenades.

They were talking and laughing, but since we could hear no sounds through the glass walls of the operating room, they approached us gesticulating in a mute show full of evil portent. They came relentlessly closer, as though in a dream.

We all have "persecution" dreams, in which someone is approaching us with some vague but terrible purpose, getting nearer, nearer, nearer. And we still wait to see what will happen, while that someone comes nearer, nearer, nearer.

It was not a dream, however, and soon the trio disappeared from the screen; they had entered the building. We could no longer see them, but the sound of their footsteps could be heard coming – nearer and nearer – from the corridor.

"Alcohol!" The loud young voice must have belonged to the athletic figure in jeans. "Hey, you guys, I've found a stack of liquor here."

That was what I heard him say, but I had no idea of what language it was spoken in.

Scalpels and forceps froze in midair, the doctors exchanged glances, and Noma the Japanese whispered with a smile, "Let them drink it!"

At that moment Masha looked down the corridor and shouted, "That's methylated spirits! You mustn't drink it!"

"Oho! What a peach!" The three guffawed in unison, and a second later they were standing in the doorway of the operating room.

We went on working, pretending that we couldn't see the intruders, who were talking loudly as they stared around at the unfamiliar surroundings. I still could not make out the language they were speaking, but I understood them perfectly.

"Hey, Jan, look at all these cocksuckers!"

"Jesus Christ, all this hacking and hewing – it's enough to make you piss in your pants!"

"Shit, look at that – sterilization!"

"That's a long word, Philip. You're a clever guy. Watch out, they castrate people here for being clever!"

"Oh, I'm so afra-aid!"

"Jan and I'll screw that nice-looking chick, and these guys'll nip your balls off!"

At this, all three roared with horrible laughter, which they kept up for a long time, slapping each other on the buttocks, wiping away tears, even hiccuping. They seemed to have forgotten about us, until suddenly Alois Stakel, a male nurse, could stand the tension no longer and broke off their laughter by saying in his high-pitched voice, "*Guten Tag,* gentlemen!"

In reply to this greeting, the blond-haired athlete, who looked much worse at close quarters than from a distance, lifted up an imaginary skirt and made a curtsy. Another one of the mercenaries, a wiry-looking character of about forty, with a face as thin and sharp as a tomahawk, moved his right foot back and swept off an imaginary hat with a flourish that would have done credit to one of Dumas's musketeers. The third man, however, did not bother to strike a pose. Glowering, he stuck his thumbs into his belt and asked in French, "Who's in charge here?"

This massive, pockmarked creature, with tufts of gray hair protruding from the folds of his skin and out of his ears, with gray eyebrows, a flabby pouch under a chin as round as a kneecap, might have almost passed for an old man had it not been for the look in his eyes: mindless as the probe of a mine detector but at the same time ferocious as a lynx, a look that burned with untamable lynxlike fire.

This third man reminded me agonizingly of someone. Something very far away whirled in my head: snow, squares of sunlight, small Doric columns, a sheet of plywood, a flapping sheet of plywood, the taste of roasted sunflower seeds, amazement – where had they come from, these roasted sunflower seeds, at that time and place? – all that flashed like lightning through my head. And the next thought that followed was a riddle: Was all this an incident in the life of Tolya von Steinbock? Given a little more time, I would have recognized this villain, had not fear for Masha suddenly banished all these memories from my mind.

Meanwhile the senior mercenary was saying to our chief in a grim, businesslike tone, "This is what I have to say to you, monsieur. We won't touch your infirmary, but" – pointing to the operating tables and the gurneys lined up along the walls – "we're going to take these wrecks with us. We get paid extra money for dead bodies and prisoners. That's the name of the game. We've worked all night, smashing up a whole regiment of blue-hats, and we don't intend to miss out on our bonus pay. Got it?"

"No, gentlemen, we will not hand over the wounded," objected Professor Abbas. "They need treatment."

"They won't give them up," said the blond athlete, bursting into bitter tears. "We can say goodbye to our money, boys."

"Don't cry, Jan. We'll ask them nicely," said the "tomahawk" consolingly, stroking his bottom as though he were a woman. "We'll ask them nicely: Do us a favor, guys, and hand over these wrecks!"

"Go fuck yourself!" Patrick Thunderjet suddenly roared and thrust out his long, bony nose like a pistol. "Get out of here, you jerks. This is an operating room, not a cathouse!"

"Be quiet, Patrick!" his chief cut him off. "I apologize, gentlemen. My colleague is under a strain. But I must insist that you allow us to finish our work."

Grinning, the senior mercenary looked around at his comrades. "You see what bastards they are? These intellectuals can't bring themselves to talk decently to ordinary people."

He said this in an offended, almost plaintive tone, but suddenly burst out screaming with such fury, such blind frenzy, that again I almost remembered who he was: "Kill them all, boys!"

Instantly all three ran to different corners of the operating room, crouched down, and thrust their submachine guns forward.

And I had almost remembered him, almost, almost . . . but I won't be remembering anything any more . . . One more moment, one more . . . and I will never be avenged, avenged, avenged. There, I've remembered, I've remembered, but now, it's all over!

"You ought to be ashamed of yourself, gentlemen!" From somewhere came the voice of Masha, followed by Masha herself, who swayed around the operating room with her extremely lascivious gait, which harmonized so marvelously with the huge two-horned nun's cowl that she wore on her head. That walk of hers always drove me crazy. A whore! It was a whore's walk, offering the goods to potential customers, everything emphasized, everything on view. She was wearing her hospital gown over her naked body. But of course she was, it was hot!

"That's not the way soldiers act!" She approached the fair-haired mercenary. "Soldiers respect surgeons!" She moved toward the "tomahawk." "Any soldier may end up on the operating table." She sidled up to the senior mercenary and smiled as she fondled the muzzle of his submachine gun.

"Hm," the "leader" grunted, and seemed to shiver all over in delicious expectation.

"Peachy is right. Peachy's very clever," said the "tomahawk" and the blond boy, moving closer to Masha.

"OK," said the "leader" with a lopsided grin. "You motherfuckers can keep on patching up these wrecks, and we'll have a nice talk with

Peachy here. *Allez, mademoiselle.*" He gave Masha a slight prod with the barrel of his gun. "*Allez, allez.*"

And she went out, followed by our three incredible visitors, simpering and smirking like creatures in a nightmare.

She walked out, without turning around, as though I were not there at all, Masha – our savior, Judith, the sacred prostitute! Why had God sent such a trial for me to endure? What was I to do?

But I had a weapon in my hand, a surgical scalpel! I dashed forward, followed by Patrick, then by Noma and all the others. We can beat them! Of course, we may lose someone, but it won't be me, for sure! Whoever heard of losing me?

But suppose no one backed me up? In that case, I would be swatted like a fly. All my heroism would go down the tubes, and to no purpose: They would have raped Masha and rubbed me out. More likely, they would have rubbed me out first.

Yes, they've already packed me into a zinc coffin and shipped me off by plane to Moscow. Among the officials of the International Red Cross receiving my body at Sheremetievo Airport were my inconsolable relatives – Samson Apollinarievich Sabler, Radius Apollinarievich Khvastishchev, Aristarkh Apollinarievich Kunitser, and Pantelei Apollinarievich Pantelei – and other comrades. Then all the aforementioned were cremated; for a while the memory of them was visible over Moscow in a few playful curls of smoke and then dissolved in the sky.

Oh, Lord, send me now a holy fury, an all-consuming fury. Call it what you like, even plain, ordinary courage, but send it! These three thugs are going to wrench my beloved's legs open and take turns thrusting their stinking pricks into action, after which they'll invite the other two from the armored car and then one of them will want to have another go at her, and no doubt that gorilla, their leader, has a dong that hangs down to his knees.

How long it takes for you to make up your mind, how long it takes for your divine imagination to function!

She will, of course, willy-nilly experience pleasure from this monstrous assault and she will groan with pleasure, just as she groaned with you – no, even louder, much louder. Perhaps she will scream and shout with unimaginable pleasure, perhaps this will be the great moment of her life, perhaps without being aware of it she has always been waiting for these five stallions, hung with weapons?

How ready she was to offer herself in exchange for our lives! What will our lives be worth after this barter? What will my life be worth, the life for which I was so shamefully afraid?

But suppose she wasn't saving us? Not us, not me, but them, the wounded! THE WOUNDED! That was the meaning of it all! After all, we are supposed to save the wounded before all else! It is the duty, the sacred Duty of a doctor! Masha is a Christian nursing sister; she is saving the wounded, and you, a doctor, are supposed to be thinking of the wounded and not of your life, or your honor, or your woman, but only of the wounded – those Indians, those children of God. You should save them. Put up with anything, suffer anything, but save those wounded!

Here is another occasion when your strength, your faith, your personality, are being tested. Now all of them, your shadows, and Tolya von Steinbock, and Sanya, and Doctor Martin, are looking at you from the frozen hills of '48, and you should think hard about them; but there's no time for thought.

Suddenly, from across the corridor where they had taken Masha, we suddenly heard the bark of a heavy-caliber machine gun, followed by the deafening crash of breaking glass. The whole transparent wall of the operating room shattered into fragments, and it was as if we were rid of our deafness.

The hospital yard was filled with deafening howling, clatter, and whistling, so loud that even the machine gun could hardly be heard against it. The black mercenary was lying alongside Metamungwu's platform. At least a dozen arrows were sticking out of his body, but he was still twitching. An arrow was also protruding from the machine gunner's shoulder, but he continued to rotate the turret, pouring bullets into the hospital building, in the windows of which fighting pygmies still popped up here and there.

In fact corpses of pygmies were lying everywhere around the sacred dais, beneath which sat our two mechanics, Olafsson and Velasquez, their heads clutched in their hands. But despite their appalling losses, the tribe had not given up the fight.

By instinctive agreement, Patrick and I rushed into the corridor. Far ahead, along the blinding white walls, two broad-shouldered figures in camouflage suits were running toward the exit. I kicked open a door at random and found that I had guessed correctly: Masha, completely naked, was standing motionless by one wall of the spacious office, while the blond Jan, his pants down, was crawling around on the floor feverishly picking up his weapons and equipment.

Catching sight of us, he rolled over onto his side, seized a grenade, and was just about to pull out the pin when Patrick leaped forward feet first and landed slap in the middle of Jan's face. This whining super-soldier did not give in straight away, but there were three of us and his pants were around his ankles; after a short while, Jan went limp, his tongue lolling and his eyes screwed up in pain. There was a pair of handcuffs in his knapsack, which Patrick, with a dexterity that astounded me, snapped over the man's wrists. As for me, I tied up his legs with the venetian-blind cord, acting efficiently and with unaccustomed skill. We rolled his body over to the wall, and only then did we remember Masha. She was sitting in the corner, her head on her knees, her shoulders shaking. We lifted her up.

"Oh boys, boys," she cried, laying her head trustingly first on my chest, then on Patrick's. What had they done to her? I was ashamed to ask and – this was strange – all my feelings of male prestige had vanished and I realized that at last I was only thinking of her and not of myself.

Suddenly the blond kid came to his senses and started whimpering, "Finish me off, you guys! Hey, bignose, shoot me in the belly! Life's over for Jan Strudelmacher! I've made such a fool of myself. I'm done for! I haven't seen a woman for four years!" Squinting with his bloodshot eyes, he looked at the vinyl wallpaper, on which there was a thick streak of his secretion. "I hadn't even touched the chick when I came all at once. Shoot me, bignose!"

Patrick and I exchanged glances. Jan Strudelmacher – remember him? How could one forget a name like that! We smiled at each other: So that was where they had sprung from, these three mercenaries – Jan, Theodore, and Philip.

Once the whole troop had been commanded by a Swedish captain. He had led them across a dank and slushy Europe, until one morning, just as dawn was breaking, he lined them all up on the top of a hill and pointed with his sword down into the valley below, where a neat little town lay, looking like a cake with frosting.

"Are you bored with digging trenches, you scum, you hell's brood?" the captain asked democratically, himself the scion of a princely house from the arctic north.

"Yes, Comrade Captain!" the detachment shouted raggedly in reply.

Rows of plum trees stretched down the hill, and the band of riffraff, with a murmuring roar, streamed down between the avenues of trees

toward its booty. A ray of the rising sun had lit up the cross on the
church tower, but the town was still deep in blue slumber. It had, as
yet, no notion of the horror that was rolling down toward it from the
top of the hill. His halberd over his shoulder, Jan Strudelmacher ran
faster than the rest – he was always in a hurry. But the captain moved
more slowly than all of them, his mouth twisted in contempt: dogs,
carrion crows, filthy louts. But what could one do when you needed
the town as a strategic point and no such troops were to be found
anywhere in Europe? He, of course, had no suspicion that at the end
of that day the drunken Strudelmacher would rip his guts out in the
cellars of the count's mansion.

Later, Theodore the sergeant-major, sitting in an armchair, thumped
the oak table and made an announcement: "His Excellency Prince
Spitzbergen has perished in a heroic duel with the traitor Count
Rozbarsky. I am taking command. Bring me that swine of a count,
incorrigible cosmopolitan that he is, and we'll teach him to love his
country!"

It was then that I recognized him again, with his burning eyes like
black cherries beneath a cobblestone of a forehead – those two little
eyes that blazed in anticipation of the interrogation and that were
reflected everywhere, in all the lancet windows, and back from the
windows on to the Voroshilov Marksman badge on his massive chest
and on the buckle of the cloak that he had confiscated from the count.

When the count, barely alive, had been dragged in, Theodore rose
to meet him like a real professional interrogator; the others watched
with interest as he softly approached, leaned forward sympathetically,
and took a deep breath. The count raised his painracked eyes.

"Well, Sanya, have they been beating you?"

"Yes, citizen investigator."

"But they didn't beat you like this, did they?" And he rammed his
elbow into the count's eye, to the great delight, of course, of all the
young soldiery. The count was dragged away again.

So *that*'s who he is. Don't fool around any longer but remember
everything from start to finish – his first name, patronymic, surname,
rank, and there is nowhere for the young Von Steinbock to find refuge
among the plywood banners of our country, among its garlands, wheat
sheaves, and cogwheels. Then you will see the square shoulders of a
boyar's melton overcoat, the awkward movement of his neck above
the narrow Persian-lamb collar, and the merry, flashing little black eye
of the condescending victor.

"Why are you howling, kid? If you'reagoodboy-the-statewilltakechargeofyou-reducationnooneco-mestoharm-inourhandsun-lesshes-ashit!"

The smoke of this unexpected memory was stinging my eyes, preventing me from remembering it all down to the smallest detail, all their real names, when the corner of the room collapsed and a battlefield was revealed to us through tongues of flame. The armored car was driving around the yard, calmly annihilating the medical staff and the pygmies, then setting fire to the hospital building and destroying it. Loud music was playing: As they went, the bastards were playing Frank Sinatra's hit song of the time, "Strangers in the Night," through their loudspeaker. Roaring with laughter, Philip was turning the machine-gun turret, while Teddy, a vague grin on his face, was spraying bursts of napalm from a portable flame thrower. A third man, the driver, was turning the steering wheel, now and again taking a swig from a bottle of methylated spirits. All three were singing their own song in time to Sinatra's tune:

> Stool pigeons in the night
> Never sleep or make a sound,
> Like owls, in silent flight,
> They're digging up the ground.

Well, the moment had come to say goodbye. So long, Mister Soviet Union! So long, Comrade United States! So long, boys, the flags of the UN!

Patrick pulled off a hobnailed boot from Strudelmacher's foot and strode to the edge of the abyss, while I took down a saxophone from the wall (in keeping with all the rules of drama, a saxophone was hanging on the wall of this empty doctor's office, ready to drop on someone's head) and strode after him to the edge of the abyss. Naturally, the armored car came to a halt right under the shattered outside wall of our room.

"Bye," we all said, this brief word implying that the parting would not be for long. Then Patrick and I leaped onto the armored car. With a mighty swing I brought the saxophone down on Theodore's head, while Patrick dispatched Philip on a tourist trip to the banks of the Styx with a blow of the boot.

"You guys want another drink?" As he asked this question, the driver, Greaseface, turned around to us and did not even have time to be astonished before he followed his comrades into other regions.

His foot, however, pressed down hard on the accelerator and his hands gripped the wheel convulsively. Like an enraged rhinoceros, the armored car smashed through the wall and began racing around the hospital rooms. With sounds of smashing and ripping, we roared and crashed our way through the wards, treatment rooms, storerooms, and offices of what only yesterday had been a magnificent building. Finally, we burst into the library, shelves full of books flew in all directions, and the volume of an encyclopedia for the letter D fell on top of me from a great height. The volume opened before it hit me, and I just had time to notice the splendid, bewhiskered features of Charlie Darwin, who had naturally never suspected that he would be making such a major contribution to the education of the "new man" in Russia.

I came to my senses in the beautiful, smoke-laden twilight. The ruins of the hospital were still smoldering. The black mercenary, pierced by a dozen arrows like St. Sebastian, was silently wandering around the dais of the goddess Metamungwu. As he stumbled over the corpses, he bowed politely, saying, "Sorry, madam." He was humming a tune and clicking his fingers, laughing quietly at some private thoughts. Finally, he leaned on the dais and asked a vulture that was sitting on the far corner, "Excuse me, are colored people served here?"

No doubt this was preshock euphoria, and he thought he was in some den of iniquity.

I could now see everything properly. I clearly saw the vulture with its bare, scraggy neck and the disgusting red pouch under its beak. The vulture made no reply to the bleeding black mercenary. Maybe the bird was wondering whether they served vultures here.

I saw a great many birds all around. Suddenly, a pink flock of flamingoes flew overhead. Where were they going? It wasn't hard to guess: They were flying to childhood, to the land of stamp collectors.

Then two retired state procurators – marabou storks – settled glumly on the ruins of the garbage incinerator.

Peggy the mother hen, who had miraculously survived the carnage, was leading her brood of little crocodiles for their evening swim in the lake.

"Hey, fella, have you woken up?" I heard a faint voice and saw that none other than Jan Strudelmacher had collapsed against the side of the armored car. "Wanna drink?" In his handcuffed hands he proffered a bottle of methylated spirits with a death's head on the label.

"How can you drink that stuff?" I asked. "It makes normal people go blind."

"We go blind too," Jan said, smiling meekly. "But if you piss in it, you can drink it. Of course, you go a bit blind, but not completely and not forever. Right now, for instance, I can see you."

"OK, let's have it." I took the bottle from him and swallowed a mouthful. The smell was disgusting, but it had no taste.

"Drink some more, Gennady, and don't bear me a grudge," said the young scoundrel Strudelmacher cordially.

"Do you mean that we're all on the same side now? Like hell we are!" I said, but I could not tear myself away from the evil-smelling bottle.

Just then someone stirred under my feet and croaked grumpily, "Look at him swilling it down! By the way, there are people down here, too."

It was Philip. I handed him the bottle, and he cheerfully gargled it down, instantly forgetting the offense.

Soon the others recovered consciousness: Teddy, Patrick, and Greaseface the driver.

"Now I'll go get you some more methylated," announced Jan Strudelmacher, whereupon he fell to the ground and rolled back to the hospital ruins with remarkable speed.

"I see that there are human beings among you hired jackals," I said. "But you, Theodore, I find totally repulsive."

"The feeling's mutual," he grunted, crawling clumsily over Patrick's foot.

"Careful, you swine," Thunderjet hissed between clenched teeth.

"You swine, you swine, you swi-i-ine," chanted Theodore, like a woman stall keeper in a peasant market.

Greaseface the driver stretched luxuriously. "Stop bickering, kids. I'm going to give you something hot!"

He switched on the record player. The yard echoed to the stirring march "Sixteen Nations," performed by the Beatles. At the sound of this music, the survivors of the pygmy tribe crawled out of a hole and formed a line. Waving their deadly weapons, they filed around the dais of their departed goddess. They seemed to be celebrating a victory of historic significance.

Then the crippled warriors of the UN forces appeared, not yet fully recovered from the effects of anesthesia. They paraded in ranks around the flagstaff, toward which came Professor Abbas, holding a copy of the newspaper *Russian News*. As always at the sight of such touching international collaboration, I burst into tears.

"Don't cry, Comrade Malkolmov," said Abbas encouragingly. "You'd do better to listen to this heartening news." He began to read from the newspaper in a resounding voice: " 'Progressive public opinion throughout the world angrily condemns the banditlike attack by imperialist hirelings on the United Nations hospital in Katanga. The workers and technical staff of the Moscow Sioux and Sons factory unanimously condemn the machinations of the Zionist agency, Donbass: the workers of Yuzovka, Gorlovka, and Lugansk at town meetings declare unanimously, Hands off the Metamungwu pygmies and other freedom-loving peoples of Africa!' As you see, Mr. Malkolmov, as ever, total unity prevails in your country."

"What else do you expect?" mumbled Theodore, the "senior" mercenary, with a curious hint of pride in his voice. "It's the only normal country."

After a moment's reflection, he began applauding with his iron-hard hands. At once Philip and Greaseface joined in the applause, followed by Jan Strudelmacher. This young man, with incredible persistence, crawled up to the armored car, pushing a hefty bottle of methylated spirits with his nose and applauding loudly, despite his handcuffs. Soon all the survivors in the yard were applauding for all they were worth, and the evening culminated in stormy, unceasing applause that grew into an ovation. The last to give way was the fiercest opponent of totalitarianism, Patrick Thunderjet. The hands of the freedom-loving basketball player flashed in frenetic applause.

"You see, Patrick, we all have something in common," Strudelmacher said pointedly.

"Cock in your pocket, flea on a lasso!" the American barked in reply, using Berkeley campus slang.

A strange couple now appeared in the yard – the goddess Metamungwu and the chief of the tribe, a little old man called Kutsachku. The goddess was swaying along on high heels, her generous hips were draped in a twenties Charleston skirt, and her hair was *à la* Greta Garbo. The chief was wearing a lemon-and-blue checked jacket and spats that were yellowed with age. There was something touching, thrilling, and romantic about this appalling couple, these ghosts from the Roaring Twenties, the age when hope still fluttered over the continent of Europe, like the New Economic Policy.

"Gentlemen, my husband and I have come to say goodbye," said

Metamungwu in thoroughly respectable English. "Thank you very much for everything!"

"Are you pulling out, Helen?" asked Patrick.

"Yes, Mr. Thunderjet. We're flying to Geneva. We're thinking of opening a hairdressing salon."

"We're fed up with working our asses off for these pygmies. We've done our share for the dissemination of civilization," said Chief Kutsachku in a nasal whine. "Now it's time to think of ourselves."

"Farewell, my Africa!" the ex-goddess exclaimed sentimentally, leaning her cheek against the ceremonial couch on which she had spent the best part of forty years. "I shall miss a lot of things, living in Geneva." She glanced around with an ambiguous look. "Don't forget, gentlemen!"

"Greaseface, put on something suitable for the occasion," ordered Theodore.

" 'New Gray Hat,' played by Kid Ory, album number 44 in the national record library," announced Greaseface in a very learned voice, exactly like some Leningrad know-it-all.

To the quavering sound of dixieland, the bottle of methylated spirits floated its way to my mouth. Then a volume of the encyclopedia swam into my field of vision. To test what remained of my strength I picked up the volume and slammed it down on the crown of the "senior" mercenary's head. The boys, of course, were greatly amused.

"Ah, if only I could move my limbs," growled Theodore. "I'd teach you parasites to laugh."

"Right now you can listen, you dirty Sparafucile," Patrick said to him. "While your limbs are out of action, you can acquire a little intelligence, decency, and humanity. Gennady, read aloud to us from page thirty-five, eighth line from the top. Quiet, boys! What will happen? I dread to think! Read, Gennady!"

With my left eye I saw Masha walking barefoot over the smoldering remains of the hospital. She stopped on the burnt-out porch, quite naked and with little blue sparks leaping all over her body like will-o'-the-wisps. With my right eye I could see the large print, as though under a magnifying glass, and began to read it: " 'Dugong: Marine mammal, also known as the sea cow. Now almost wholly exterminated by progressive mankind . . .' "

Masha came down from the porch and walked toward me. She came nearer and nearer, then suddenly disappeared.

"My left eye has gone blind," I said.

"It doesn't matter. Read with the right eye," said Jan Strudelmacher.

"You read OK for Patrick, now read for me. Page one hundred and fifteen, eighth line from the bottom."

It was true; I could still see perfectly with my right eye. " '. . . At the present time, the last specimens of the dugong family survive in freedom in the region of the Arctic Ocean, zero degree latitude, all degrees longitude . . .' " As I was reading this, the print suddenly vanished and I regained the sight of my left eye, which saw close beside me Masha's bright, juicy lips, her childlike nose, and her thin, motherly neck.

"That's amazing – my right eye has stopped working," I said to Masha.

"It's all right, my dear," she whispered. "To hell with your right eye! The chief thing is that your left eye is working, so we can see each other."

"But the dugong, Masha, the dugong!" I exclaimed, and burst into tears like a child. "Just imagine – it's lying there at the north pole, on the very tip itself, and is feeding all mankind with its milk, its last milk! Do you understand, Masha?"

"I understand, Gennady."

Suddenly my left eye was extinguished, my love vanished, and into my right eye crawled Comrade Cheptsov, major of the security service (the name suddenly flared in front of me: Cheptsov, Cheptsov), Comrade Cheptsov in a sober civilian suit.

"Now read for me," he said in a tone of official disdain.

God, how I wanted not to read for HIM!

"The *Brockhaus and Efron Encyclopedia* is forbidden, comrade investigator," I mumbled evasively.

"We know that as well as you do!" he barked. "Read the *Soviet Encyclopedia*! Read, fuck you! Read, you son of a whore! You read it for that shit Patrick, didn't you? You read it for Junior Lieutenant Jan Strudelmacher, didn't you? And you don't want to read it to me, you cocksucker? You will read it; I shall not let you off."

He hit me on the nose with the open book and used one of the "methods of active interrogation"; I think he squeezed my scrotum with pincers. Then, of course, I began reading with great willingness: " 'DUGONG: First developed and studied by the great leader of peoples Joseph Vissarionovich Stalin in his unrelenting struggle against Lev Davidovich Bronstein. It was the great architect of progressive humanity who first established that the dugong belongs to the working class, because it (the dugong – Ed.) is of peasant origin. His majesty the standard-bearer of world peace, the Generalissimo with the brain of a scholar, the body of a philosopher, in the garments of a simple centaur . . . ' "

Alongside me, Cheptsov was breathing heavily and occasionally squealing as he reached the threshold of orgasm and each time put off the moment of supreme pleasure.

Suddenly the print vanished, and with it, Cheptsov. At first I was glad that I had gone blind in my right eye. I hoped that the left eye would now start functioning and I could see Masha again, but the days passed and I was blind in both eyes.

The Lament of Mademoiselle Marianne Coulagot

Oh, where are you, my homeland – unhomeland, distant and sweet, stormy
and snowbound, stretching to the back of beyond . . . weep for it!
What are you talking about? About hangmen? Fingermen? Oh, Genochka!
Tell me about that distant unhomeland where I've never been but have
only heard its envoys, poets, and violinists in Paris
No, no – not hangmen!
they're such good sportsmen
surely they're not pigs!
those springtime, birch-tree boys of Russia, my boys who live
in vast spaces of my unhomeland far from the rest of the world . . .
Do you hear the bell? It's Easter! Christ is risen! He is risen indeed!
So tell me about the boys, God's own children, those mysterious, unknown boys married to sluts
On Fridays in Paris it smells of *potage printanière*
Hey, they say, they're all so learned, so erudite, it's staggering,
but then why are they slaves, why are they cowards?
Ah, pine trees, sharp-needled pine trees,
Tell me what I must do?
I might have been a Komsomol
In my homeland.
Ah, grandfather dear,
Officer of the Guards,
Why, oh why, my dear,
Did you become an enemy of the USSR?
Easter cake and bagels, pretzels and toffee apples, and grandma in the window, and onion domes – it is like that, isn't it? Isn't it?

But you say it's all tractors, noise, oil, and mud . . .
You say – split half a can three ways . . . *qu'est que c'est?*
You say – nice piece of ass and hooker with the clap . . .
qu'est que c'est? Tell me, Genochka! *Qu'est que c'est* "screw"?
. . . Vast, deserted, cold, lashed by blizzards, blizzards all
over the land . . .
Genochka, why are you silent?

Masha, the nursing sister, took Patrick and me from Africa to Geneva,
passing us off as two brothers who had lost their reason and speech
from being bitten by some supertoxic superorganism. She fed us daily
on Swiss cream and Swiss chocolate. Soon we were able to walk again
and went to work at the European Institute of Economic Research,
an agency of the Common Market, which had pitched its tents on the
borders of the Helvetic Confederation and the French Republic. It
took us a longer time to recover the power of speech, but we earned
stacks of money. Even before we had exchanged a word, we parted:
Masha was assigned to an epidemic in Kurdistan, Patrick flew to the
States to apply for the astronaut program, while I changed my foreign
currency into ruble scrip and returned to Moscow, rich, famous, meaningfully silent. At the time, they said of me that I was the most eligible
bachelor in Moscow.

Meanwhile, the black diplomatic Impala was still racing toward the
concrete pillar of the Hotel Minsk. A few microseconds before disaster,
the driver suddenly sneezed and turned the steering wheel a fraction
in one direction. The car leaped past the pillar straight onto Gorky
Street, crossed the median strip, dove into a pedestrian underpass,
roaring like a tractor, shot out on the other side, swung back again
onto Moscow's main highway, did a three hundred and sixty degree
turn in front of a flood of traffic, and calmly drove up to the Hotel
National. No one had been harmed except for Traffic Officer Shchel-
gun, who began to hiccup violently when interrogated after the event
in the district headquarters of the KGB.

REPORT BY AGENT SILICATE, SUPERNUMERARY EMPLOYEE OF THE CITY CULTURAL AGENCY, FROM THE FOREIGN-CURRENCY BAR OF THE HOTEL NATIONAL, MOSCOW

(NB. This report is interspersed with an interior monologue by Silicate)

Dear comrades! At 0098 hours on May 32, I, Agent Silicate (L. P. Fruitozov), was on duty in the foreign-currency bar of the Hotel National. Present in the room were Mr. Magnusson, a Swedish expert on the paper industry; the Senegalese prince Joseph Calibava and his servant Pierre Play (both students at the Patrice Lumumba University); three Finnish ice-hockey players from the Turku Packers' Trade Union team; and no one else. From the Agency, the following were also on duty: Captain Diomidov ("Pete the bartender"), Senior Lieutenant Krivozubova ("Nyura the waitress"), Lieutenant Bakhrushin ("Tsadkin – artist"), Staff Sergeant Gaginadze ("Eddie – blackmarket dealer"), and Lieutenants Somova, Lomova, and Filchenko ("the girls - Nina, Inna, and Tamara").

0104 hours. Suddenly the doors were flung open noisily and on the threshold appeared the well-known suspicious element – intellectual – creative person of no fixed occupation, my close friend (whose name I forget) nicknamed Academician, as he is known in the Men's Club bar, which is in the open air near the Pioneer Market in the Timiryazev District. With him were Klara Khakimova, a freshman student in the Philodendron Department, Moscow University; a certain Marianne Coulagot, Academician's mistress and citizen of the Helvetic Confederation; also an enormous foreigner named Pat, who from his clothes might pass for a Soviet citizen.

Academician rushed up to me and immediately told me three ambiguous political jokes: the "eyebrows" joke (No. 1794/0040), the "meat" joke (No. 8805/1147), and the "computer" joke (No. 9564/2086).

As he came in, I shuddered inwardly!
My idol, my love, you're the darling of Russia!
If I were a woman, I'd never come out from under you!
Pigs, bitches, stoolies – hands off him!
How come Security's been idle for so long?
Clear-eyed youth, heroic sentinel!
The hopes of our country and our hard-pressed people rest on you!
"Friends," said my soaring falcon of the steppes. "Get acquainted,"
     and pointed to me.

"Before you stands the not ungifted poet Fruitozov!"
The Asiatic bitch frowned: "Does Fruitozov earn foreign currency
     with his poems?"
"What d'you mean? I came here quite by chance.
Ferlinghetti gave a dollar grant to support
My talent; they have a special fund for that."
"Crap! We know what you are; everyone in the university knows it!"
"Dear Academician, don't believe this lousy bitch, don't believe her,
     Russian falcon!"
"By the way, have you heard the latest?" And there and then, rapidly
Lest someone interrupt him, he whispered
The jokes about "eyebrows," "meat', and "computer."
How broad was his smile, our Mikula Selyaninovich, as he
With his Russian good humor turned to the bar, our national
     masterpiece:
"Hi there, Pete! Hi, Nyura! Hi, girls!
Hello, Tsadkin! *Gagemardjos,* Eddie!
Salaam, prince! Long live the paper industry, Mr. Swede! Let's
not be suspicious, friends, otherwise the whole of Russia could go up
the wall with persecution mania! Nyura, gin and tonic all round –
on me! Petya, switch off the muzak, we're going to recite some
     poetry!
Fruit, recite something short!"
"Certainly, I always keep something short ready to hand:
     'Blueness blueness blueness
     Slanting rain
     Greensward greensward
     Ah, mother Russia, to what sorcerer did you yield your beauty –
     To a heathen Judean or to Lebedev, the cur?' "
"Who's Lebedev?" cried the ladies.
"He's a poet; his real name's not Lebedev, he's a hostile element."
"Not bad, Fruit, strong stuff – and you really let Lebedev have it."
Such was my falcon's opinions, and incidentally they didn't notice
     the "Judean,"
So it's a lie when they say he has Jewish blood.
Of course it's a lie! We won't let the kikes have him!
And then he began to recite. At first his voice flowed quietly, like
Water from melted snow under a crust of snow in March, then for a
     moment or two it burst out
Like a fountain, and then it rang out like a Novgorod

Church bell, and shattered the rotten walls of the foreign-currency
   bar, in which
Fruitozov ruined his talent and sold his soul.

0142 hours. Academician began to recite a ten-minute poem entitled
"Noxious Fumes". It was tape-recorded by Captain Diomidov. For my
part, I wish to point out that the poem "Noxious Fumes" is a thinly
veiled Aesopian allusion to the allegedly poisonous atmosphere in my
own country.

Supplementary information: During the poetry recital, Mr. Magnusson sat down beside Marianne Coulagot and asked if he could make
love to her. Coulagot named the sum of one thousand dollars ($1,000).
The Swede objected that this was too expensive. Can't be helped,
that's the price, Coulagot replied, whereupon Magnusson went back
to his table.

The foreigner called Pat tried several times to interrupt the recital,
swore in Californian slang, and said that he was bored with all this
Russian poetry and its perpetual "subfucking," while all the time he
was trying to grope Klara Khakimova, the female student. I think
Pat can be classified as an ideological saboteur and that citizeness
Khakimova is definitely under the thumb of the forces of reaction.

Tears blinded me.
Shut up, you insignificant foreigner, you tomato-faced Dutchman!
How can you ever understand our pain, our fumes, the smoky hut
   of our Russian souls?
Genius! Let me kneel before you!
No, no, let me!
Don't touch me!
Look, you industrialists, princes, hookers: the not ungifted poet
   Fruitozov is on his knees before a genius!

I would also like to point out that Academician paid with traveler's
checks of the Soviet Bank for Foreign Trade and with British pounds,
and that it is no secret where he got them from: from CIA funds via
the journal *FOG*.

Then the following incident occurred. Mr. Magnusson returned to
our table and said to Marianne Coulagot that he accepted her price.
She said nothing in reply, because she was watching Academician, who
was dancing the tango with Tamara (Junior Lieutenant Filchenko). He
was loudly proclaiming the allegedly divine origin of her beauty and

intelligence. She (Filchenko) had allegedly been sent to him as a reward for his spiritual sufferings of the last decade, she alone would lighten the rest of his days for him, for she was open to love like a burgeoning lotus bud.

Comrades, I respectfully wish to cast doubt on the usefulness of the contact between Filchenko and Academician. From my own observation, and in the opinion of a number of our comrades, Filchenko is distinguished by the instability of her character; she sets too much store by her outward appearance and may easily neglect her official duties for the sake of erotic pleasure.

> That damned pop-eyed doll is embracing my sun!
> Just wait – I'll make your life hell!
> Beloved Academician, shall I never, never touch your rod?!
> I will fall at his feet and tell him all I know about Tamara!
> And I will sob out all my love for him into his lap.

Subsequent events confirmed my suppositions. Khakimova danced in an abandoned fashion with the hippielike foreigner Pat, with Mr. Magnusson, and with the Finnish ice-hockey players, but answered Prince Calibava's invitation with a contemptuous refusal, an indication of her racial prejudice. The special service photographers took several pictures. Magnusson reminded Coulagot that he accepted her price. She again made no reply and ignored the ten hundred-dollar bills, whose serial numbers I was unable to note, because at that moment the prince's servant Pierre Play began to slap his master on the cheeks, and I know why, but that is our internal affair. Coulagot, meanwhile, paid the bill and began whispering a series of male first names: Samsik, Gena, Arik, Radik, Pantelei . . . What an abundance of men, what effrontery! Mr. Magnusson then took out of his hip pocket another dollar bill (his reserve?) and began to wave this impressive quantity of convertible currency, shouting, "A thousand and one dollars for one night! Long live the sexual revolution! Down with the paper industry! Mao is coming! Are you ready?"

"Why are you crying, Coulagot?"
"And why are you, Fruit?"
"We are both crying for the same thing."
"I guessed as much. Let's embrace and cry together."
"OK, let's embrace."
"Can you feel I'm not wearing a bra, Fruit?"

"I'm not wearing a bra either, Masha."

"Tell me, Fruit, when my breasts press against you, do you really not feel anything?"

"I feel erotic arousal, Coulagot."

"So you're ambidextrous? Bravo! Bravo!"

"Masha, you must understand that my love for Him contains an element

of patriotic feeling, and for me his rod is partially a symbol,

something like Bogdan Khmelnitsky's mace or the spire of St. Peter's and St. Paul's cathedral."

"Ah," said she, "I can't exaggerate so poetically, for me it's just his prick."

"Coulagot, please, let's get out of this embrace.

I'm just about to suffocate, and you have nothing but vulgarities on your mind."

"Clear off, lousy Fruit! You know nothing.

I could have had three children by him, dear Fruit—

Five-year-old Lenochka, three-year-old Misha, and Stepochka, one year old . . .

You in your 'blue division' could never even imagine any such thing!"

The night, dear comrades, culminated in one of citizeness Coulagot's usual disgraceful scenes, with the smashing of crockery and shouts of "damn country," "slaves," "I love you all," "we'll all die in the same trough of swill," and so on. After signing a Crédit Lyonnais traveler's check, Coulagot fell asleep in the embrace of the goalkeeper of the Turku Smoke Eaters hockey team and was carried off by him to a hotel at 0390 hours.

Earlier, at 0380 hours, Academician and his friend Pat left the bar with two of the girls, Khakimova and Filchenko. Agent Silicate was unable to follow them, because he was taken aside by Mr. Magnusson for a serious conversation, about which a supplementary report will be issued; kindly do not believe anything said by Potapchenko, the old man from toilet No. 17.

With profound respect,

Supernumerary Agent L. P. Fruitozov, poet

She was astoundingly pretty. Of course I knew what she was, but still, how pretty she was! She went ahead of me down the vile staircase of creaking, yellow marble with steps worn down like prerevolutionary

table knives. This staircase did not, apparently, lead down to the
cloakroom and thence to the nocturnal street, but into a stuffy laundry,
where sick old women are washed or where they wash the underwear
of besieged regiments, or wash corpses, or boil up soap from stray
dogs, or make rakes by sawing up shinbones. But then she stopped on
that staircase, waiting for me, turned around, and smiled; her sweet,
curved silhouette and smooth birdlike head with those big Ukrainian
eyes and the thin hand, which in making that movement she placed
on an elaborate vase in a niche, a niche with a vase and a figure of
Cupid! And suddenly the foul laundry vanished from my mind, a
feeling of excitement arose in my memory, and that entire moment,
with its gestures, light, and sound took my breath away, as if

> From the gray caryatids
> A thin leaf of willow
> Fell onto the damp flagstones
> Of autumnal hospitals

It was a cold and translucent fall day, with sunset fast approaching,
when I emerged from the withered foliage of elder trees into the ruined
palace and passed under an arch, on which could still be read the
legend PRO CONSILIO SUO VIRGINIAE. I was walking on paving stones,
between which protruded tufts of reddish-brown grass, while above
me whole bushes were sprouting on balconies whose concrete had
fallen away to reveal the bare reinforcement rods. I was in a place of
desolation, a deserted vale of tears, a place where life had been
destroyed at some time in the past. Strangely enough, however, the
dreariness of the ruins and even the frozen lumps of excrement, the
broken-off noses and sexual organs of ancient statues, did not call
forth contemptuous pity and did not offend the eye. This once rich
and noisy house had been living now for so many decades in humble
but proud decay, with a dignity that was invulnerable to barbarians
and explosives, and no doubt every year for all that time some four-
teen-year-old boy like myself had pushed his way through the withered
elders onto the paving stones, and his skin had prickled with gooseflesh
from excitement. Through the empty windows and the holes in the
roof he had seen the translucent autumnal sky, full of flying crimson
leaves, and he had realized that the house was showing him a vision
of his own future life, including this tall thin figure with her smooth
birdlike head, with her huge Ukrainian eyes turning toward him – and

only God knew what else was in store for him and of what else that ruined and overgrown house on the threshold of his youth would remind him.

"Where are we going?" asked Filchenko.

"To my studio," Khvastishchev replied automatically.

At this point she grinned, and in a flash that crooked grin destroyed all the enchantment and reminded Khvastishchev that he was beastly drunk, that he was a playboy, a lazy punk, and that he was with a barroom hooker, a stool pigeon: Tamara the rip-off artist.

"Do you want to sculpt me?" Again she gave a pathetic, vulgar leer, completely submissive but at the same time with a nasty secret-police undercurrent of meaning.

But from whence had that momentary image of the ruined palace come and surely there had been some genuine emotion in Tamara's soul when she turned around LIKE THAT and put her hand on the vase LIKE THAT?

"Shut up, Tamara. Don't ask so many questions," said Khvastishchev roughly, taking the girl by the elbow and leading her to the cloakroom, just like a stern husband with an errant wife.

A wild scene was in progress at the cloakroom of the foreign-currency bar. Two vast but agile bottoms, adorned with silver lace, were scurrying back and forth across the floor – in just the way, no doubt, nuclear generals shuffle around across Mercator's map of the world in underground headquarters at night. Thunderjet was standing beside a mirror, in a thoughtful pose reminiscent of the Prince of Denmark, holding Klara in his arms; the girl was either asleep or had fainted, and her slightly bandy legs in wrinkled stockings were dangling helplessly, looking like a couple of long, week-old sausages.

"What are they looking for?" asked Khvastishchev, looking at the two scrabbling male cloakroom attendants in blue braid-trimmed uniforms.

"Gold," said Pat indifferently.

The old men's fingers were grabbing at round gold medallions and stuffing them into their pockets.

"It's Klara's necklace," said Tamara. "The stupid little fool dropped it and the chain broke."

"It's all gone through the floor – to the mice!" said one of the cloakroom attendants, giggling. "The parquet is full of cracks, because, to tell the truth, this hotel hasn't had any major repairs for two hundred years."

"Get up! The Day of Judgment is at hand!" rasped Khvastishchev, and gently kicked the second general's bottom.

A moment later there arose before him an impressive figure with a majestic goiter, sparse crew-cut hair, and two eyes like little black, sweet, overripe cherries. Another moment, and Khvastishchev recognized him and shuddered. "Put on this lady's coat," he said, struggling to control his tremor and pointing at Tamara.

"Well, well," said the cloakroom attendant in a self-confident, patronizing tone, in which there was even a hint of a boss doing a favor for a subordinate. "Am I not addressing the distinguished Comrade Radius Apollinarievich Khvastishchev?"

"How do you know?" Khvastishchev was perplexed, as perplexed as that pathetic Magadan schoolboy had once been at the sight of an ugly black car, its windows obscured by drawn blinds.

"I read this in the newspaper yesterday and I guessed at once that it was you." With a meaningful little smile, the attendant unbuttoned the flap of his tunic and pulled out a newspaper clipping, headlined in heavy type: RESPONSIBILITY TO THE PEOPLE. "It's your statement, Radius Apollinarievich: 'The very first duty of every artist,' you say, 'is to work for the people, to create sublime and beautiful images of our contemporaries.' " "Golden words, comrade sculptor!"

He spread out Tamara's fur coat before her on the plastic-topped counter, while he continued looking at Khvastishchev, who was leaning against the wall, trembling with humiliation and bottomless depression.

Beside the mirror, Patrick Thunderjet was declaiming Allen Ginsberg's poem *Howl* into Klara's ear.

"To work for the people, to create sublime and beautiful . . ." The voice of the terrible old man was still ringing in Khvastishchev's ears, or rather it was not the voice of this old man in a lackey's uniform but of the old man whom he recognized and whom he now remembered almost completely.

"You lout, you filthy lout," he muttered. "I'll show you."

Tamara brought her lips close to him.

"Radik, don't tangle with him. He's some kind of colonel; we're all under his thumb here."

"What's his name?" Khvastishchev asked boldly, squeezing Tamara's shoulder. Now everything would be cleared up. Now everything would be made absolutely clear.

"Shevtsov, I think," she said. "Yes, Shevtsov."

. . . The hideous mass of the black, oil-spattered train rumbled past me, five centimeters away from my huddled body . . .

"And you, young people, I think, didn't have any coats, did you?" asked the second cloakroom attendant, giggling. "These are not your coats, gentlemen," he said in English, his folksy, peasant voice burring the unfamiliar sounds.

"And that one is probably a general," whispered Tamara, "but he's harmless."

"We came here in the spring," Patrick calmly explained to the attendant. "We're springtime birds, daddy-o."

Khvastishchev plucked up courage and looked his old man straight in the eyes. The old man met his gaze unblinkingly; here, in this den of iniquity, he obviously felt absolutely self-confident.

I should spit in his ear, thought Khvastishchev. Grab it with two fingers and pull that tough old ear, that mini toilet bowl toward me and spit straight into that bush of gray hairs, into that deep pit, where a membrane, unusually sensitive for someone his age, was quivering behind layers of accumulated ear wax.

"I suppose you moonlight at this job?" said Khvastishchev.

"No, I moonlight at the other place," the attendant explained kindly.

"What? Isn't one salary enough?"

"No, it's not."

"So you get a pension plus two salaries?" said Khvastishchev, grinning stupidly. The cloakroom attendant frowned.

"You'd do better to total up your own income, Radius Apollinarievich."

"May I look at the back of your neck?" asked Khvastishchev.

Tamara clutched at his sleeve in fright.

"Come on, let's go! Don't mess with him!"

"Why not?" said the attendant, turning briskly to his left. "There you are. There's the back of my neck for you."

Khvastishchev pulled out a notepad and a felt pen and made a sketch of the detested neck.

"A magnificent nape," he said, thinking aloud.

"Like a prick with ears," said Patrick in English.

"Would you repeat that, please? I didn't quite catch it," said the second cloakroom attendant, straining to overhear them.

"I should like to sculpt you," said Khvastishchev. "You're my contemporary, so why shouldn't I make a sublime and beautiful image of you? Would you like to pose for me in my studio?"

"With medals or just with medal ribbons?" Shevtsov inquired sullenly.

"But of course with all your medals!" exclaimed Khvastishchev. "What fronts did you fight on?"

"I was a fighter on the invisible front, Radius Apollinarievich."

The second attendant coughed tactfully.

"Ah, hmm, does the invitation include me, too, old chap?"

Three foreign-sounding consonants and the sickeningly false "old chap" – the cunning old fox of a general was working hard at his camouflage.

"Of course, of course," Khvastishchev said, nodding. "You're welcome to come. We'll make a sublime and beautiful image out of you too."

The first cloakroom attendant was still standing with his back to the sculptor, and as he heard the last remark, two diagonal folds of skin came together, forming a letter X lying on its side.

"OK, see you soon!" said Khvastishchev, already savoring the thought of the meeting and of an evening of happy reminiscences. "Now let me thank you for giving this dear lady her coat."

Ha, ha! Khvastishchev's ten-ruble bill was met by two embarrassed looks and simply flapped uselessly in the air.

"This isn't a shish kebab stand, Radius Apollinarievich," said the first cloakroom attendant sternly.

"That money's no good here, old chap," explained the second attendant, kindly but with a steely glint in his eyes. "Only freely convertible currency, my friend."

"Pat, look in your pockets," said Khvastishchev to his friend. "Maybe you've got some kind of foreign currency we can give these monsters."

"Impossible – I'm holding a baby in my arms," said Patrick, "so I can't even blow my nose. Search for yourself."

The two cloakroom attendants tensed themselves and strained like pointers scenting game as they looked at Khvastishchev.

"OK, search his pockets!" The sculptor waved his hand, and they instantly pounced on Patrick, one diving for his left-hand pants pocket, the other for the right.

"An Indonesian rupiah!" muttered one of them. "That'll do. A Mongolian tugrik! OK – in a pinch. Convertible ruble scrip! We can use that. Traveler's checks! We can change 'em."

"Spanish pesetas!" whispered the other. "Fine. Ah, a lovely little greenback! A mark, a franc, a franc, a mark."

"Why do you want foreign currency, colonel?" Khvastishchev asked.

"For my daughter," he croaked. "To buy felt pens for my daughter. She's very talented."

"Crap! He's lying!" whined his companion. "He's always babbling about his daughter. His daughter – hell! He's saving it up to buy a car."

"Huh!" grunted Shevtsov, with a roar that was familiar from the distant days of youth and that came flying in from that cold country, where not only convertible currency but even ordinary money did not circulate. "Huh, you son of a bitch!" Skillfully he twisted his colleague's arm behind his back, forced him into a corner, and began applying some of his professional know-how. "And what are *you* saving up for? What are *you* saving for?"

Khvastishchev and Thunderjet watched this scene for some time. Shevtsov grunted with exertion, while his other half squealed unceasingly, like a piglet, but, as it seemed to the drunken guests, not without a certain pleasure.

"Not bad," Patrick grinned approvingly. "I've seen that treatment somewhere before, and it was being applied by an orangutan like this one, only I can't remember where it was."

"I can't remember either," muttered Khvastishchev. "I know him perfectly well, and I've seen him somewhere at very close quarters. Perhaps it was in some other life. Do you think I'm kidding, Pat? Do you think I'm scared of him? Watch me. I'll call him by the first name that comes into my head; I've forgotten his real name. So long, Oleg Vladlenovich!"

"So long," barked Shevtsov, without interrupting his esoteric activity.

"Good luck!" exclaimed his colleague excitedly from the very summit of the threshold of pain.

Khvastishchev and Thunderjet walked out of the hotel. From the entrance they watched a thick, whirling ground blizzard creeping in a broad front across Manège Square, heard it whistling, heard the overhead trolleybus wires humming. Above the cold, dark, sleepy city, above the grim turrets of the Historical Museum, above the whole of this failed Byzantium, they saw, surrounded by frosty rings, a blurred yellow blob – our last, last, oh, Lord, yes, our very, very last refuge.

Leaning her head on Khvastishchev's shoulder, Tamara, his dear little lieutenant, wept into his ear. "Oh, Radik dear, and Comrade Patrick, oh, how ashamed I feel."

"Why are you crying, Tamara?"

"Oh, I feel so ashamed of those two old men. They disgrace our

whole organization, those Stalinist degenerates! Comrades, please
don't think we're all like that. Many of the younger ones are even
very progressive. I swear, I'll make a complaint to the bureau . . .
bureau . . ."

"Don't cry, Tamara! Do you want to be carried, like Klara?"

"Bu-ur-eau-eau . . ." she mumbled as she fell asleep on his shoulder;
exhausted by secret service work, her eyelashes closed, and her Ukrainian eyes plunged into a Gogolesque night.

She was light as he picked her up in his arms.

Khvastishchev and Thunderjet slowly walked through a deserted
Moscow with girls in their arms. The ground blizzard whipped around
their legs, their heads were powdered with snow, the frost pinched
their noses, but their stomachs were warmed by female bodies and felt
good.

"Oh, if only the earth would swallow me up right here!"

"What are you moaning about?"

"But I called him by his name and patronymic, and he answered!
What did I call him, do you remember?"

"Don't try and kid me, old man!"

"I swear I've forgotten it – it's gone clean out of my head. I swear
by the memory of Tolya von Steinbock – do you remember, I told you
about him? I swear by the memory of the golden-haired Alisa – did I
tell you about her or not?"

"You're holding another woman in your arms at the moment."

"Oh, yes, sorry. Listen, I can't rest until I find out where I've seen
that old fart before."

"You bore me. And I'm bored by this frost, the eternal ally of the
working people. You need to drink three times more than you do. I'm
ridiculously sober! Do you have anything to drink at your pad?"

"Maybe half a bottle. I'm not sure."

"I don't know a single Russian who has any liquor stored at home.
You drink it all at once, you pigs!"

"Well, if there isn't any, we'll send Ivan. There he goes! Ivan! Ivan!"

A yellow patrol car with a winking violet light on the roof loomed
out of the snowy murkiness, and the cheerful, gangsterlike face of
Police Sergeant Ivan Migayev appeared in the window.

"Hi, sculptor! Taking some chicks home?" he inquired.

"Ivan, be a pal, take some money out of my pocket and go get us
some vodka!"

Sergeant Vanya didn't have to be asked twice but roared off past
the traffic lights and through the snow flurries to the Kazan Station.

A MIDSUMMER NIGHT'S DREAM AFTER FOUR BOTTLES
OF EXTRA, BROUGHT BY SERGEANT IVAN MIGAYEV
FROM THE KAZAN STATION TO THE STUDIO OF THE
SCULPTOR RADIUS APOLLINARIEVICH
KHVASTISHCHEV

That night I arrived on assignment at the district center. The settlement was apparently called Syromyaga.

Dozens of windows gleamed in the district soviet building, a goat was browsing on poplar fluff, the wheels of a Gaz truck were spinning around on the spot, getting nowhere.

The hospital was situated on a hill; the palm leaves swayed in the ocean breeze, now bristling up, now streaming out like a girl's hair.

Youth on the Air – the evening program, with the profile of the girl everyone knows.

Down below, the atoll lay curved in a strange serpentine shape, a narrow circle of dry land under the sun, apparently uninhabited, but shadows, followed by plumes of spray, were darting through the lines of breakers; surfers were scudding over the waves.

I pushed open the door and found myself inside a building, where someone was moving around, laughing and explaining, game playing with unnatural animation, and trying to muffle a cough with his sleeve.

"I beg you to see for yourself – everything is prepared, laid out on shelves in sterile packs. All the instruments needed for amputation, laparotomy, curettes for illegal curettage, forceps, scissors, planes, axes, a complete selection of tablets to last for four years, an ample supply of alcohol – help yourself! – and as for the nurse-housekeeper, she'll last you for fifty years."

I looked. A huge fetus was standing in a bowl, smiling meekly and affirming, "Don't worry, doctor, there's enough of everything here for you and your grandchildren for a couple of historical epochs."

"If you like I can take you in my car."

Having thus prepared his escape and conferred on himself the epithet "cunning," he went out into the corridor giggling and twirling his moustache, wearing eyeglasses, a hat, rain boots, a cloak, and a scarf, and carrying an umbrella.

Without moving from the spot, a dozen pairs of eyes rushed toward him, silently imploring him to save their owners from suffering, pain, and shame, from the pangs that accompany the early stages of dread diseases.

"Well now, let's see . . ."

"Just lift up your blouse, roll down your stocking, and bare your leg. Hm, yes, a most unusual case. Does it hurt here? No? What about here? Yes?"

Of course, the patients must be treated according to all the rules of medical science, but first we must make a tour of the island, go to the village store, to the office, like the famous governor Sancho Panza.

Quick! Jump into the zippy little Zaporozhets and drive off over the potholes and through the slush to Vorovskaya! Into a café, then make a phone call, scrounge some money, race down Sretenka, curse the foggy weather in Gnezdikovskoye, up Herzen Street to Sadovaya, loaf around Arbat, drink a beer, catch up on the gossip around the apartment house: Who's shacking up with whom, how much so-and-so paid to whom and why . . .

He went out and saw what looked like a synagogue. Coming out of the movie theater into the merciless pulsating heat of the sun, into the land of burdocks, and into the jungle of elder trees, he saw a very ancient building covered in dull, repetitious ornamentation, the creation of some unknown slave whose life, no doubt, bore no resemblance to the life of Frank Joshua, yachtsman.

The Assyrians, the Babylonians, the inhabitants of Urartu, were carrying something into their mosque, carrying something into the synagogue or church; in a word, they were carrying a heavy object into dense gloom.

They mustn't get me, he thought, trying to escape adroitly by slipping through the line of halberdiers, waggling his bottom and hoping thereby to distract the attention of the sullen guards. A loyal citizen apparently going casually about his lawful business, mincing his way past the halberds as he carried a folder containing the text of a lecture, lecture notes, a plastic sausage, and a badminton racket, through the endless ranks – quick, quick, quicker – smiling, nodding understandingly to the moustaches, the halberds, and the guards' stomachs.

And with a cry of horror he flung himself toward the fence, toward his damp burrow, where a glowworm flickered and where he tore at the horse sorrel with his teeth, seeking salvation in the buttercups until the ferns of childhood closed to form a shelter over him and he began to snore.

Pause. Aspirin

I was dropped as though by parachute into the silence of Spring Forest. Up in the sky, My World was still flying. It was quite large, changing the geometry of all its limbs, drawing three vapor trails behind it at the appropriate altitude.

Then, evidently discovering the loss, it began to dart hither and thither, to fidget and twitch. Its siren began to wail; offended, it shot up into the ionosphere, where it hung like a UFO, emitting rays.

Spring Wood was a thronging mass – tall, spreading, mossy, thick, thin, spotted, pink, green – ah, green! – curly and translucent, adorned with dewdrops and birds . . . and I was upset, almost depressed by the abundance of beautiful strangers.

But the Wood was gracious. Having spattered my face with a few drops, it said lazily, "Don't be annoyed, you godless scriptwriter, saboteur of bridges and steamers! Everything is flowering here, and in the fizzing of springtime even you are not so ugly."

Once I foolishly wrote that bare trees are more true and honest than those that wear a cap of green. Spring Wood had no doubt not forgotten this piece of impertinence, but thoughts of revenge, I could see, were quite alien to it. It said to me, "Buck up, alcoholic! Wander around, breathe, find out, remember! About the cedar and the oak, about pines and birches, about buds and pods, which you heard about in childhood, when you got an A in fifth grade for stamens and pistils, you little ragamuffin."

There's a positive ion on that branch. Its nose twitching, it is watching a negatively charged ion, prancing frivolously about and holding up the folds of its dress, like that mountain girl – oh, God, that mountain girl running downhill, her dress, her striped stockings, and her jacket flashing through the mysterious forest near Zakopane, in the Slavo-European empyrean.

He ran after her like a werewolf, bounding here and there, grunting and groaning, inexorably passing her from above and lying in wait for her below, behind a bush.

Then she fell into his grasp. Opening his slobbering mouth, he felt the bliss that a tick feels when it sinks its teeth into soft flesh, and covered her with his shoulder. With his shoulder as huge as a Caucasian cloak, with his hairy, slimy, wet shoulder, with his hideous shoulder he covered her and consoled her.

Later, when they met at parties, gently sipping dry martinis, chatting about theatrical tricks, carefully avoiding politics but hitting the martinis harder, they looked cautiously into each other's eyes, and everything that had happened at Zakopane was there.

Then, unable any longer to keep secret the answer to the riddle, they laughed quietly together, which caused a storm of anxiety in their corner of the room; thereupon John Carpenter, exchanging winks with Petya Plotnikov, invited his guests to the table, where dinner was served for a thousand nice people.

Have you ever seen decorated plates crunch their way noisily through a salad *à la parisienne*? I'm afraid so! Have you ever seen a lobster in aspic chewing spaghetti? Have you ever seen yesterday's meatballs, with a slightly musty taste, modestly laying claim to a portion of deviled chicken and chewing a lamprey, while the lamprey elegantly stuffs its belly with game pâté, which in turn gobbles kohlrabi, while that kohlrabi flings itself upon a turkey that is eating them all, the greedy swine.

With a nod, Smith spoke to Kuznetsov, and Rybakov with a slight bow said something to – of course – Fisher, while Taylor handed something with a smile to Portnyagin, and Plotnikov, quite unembarrassed, whispered to Carpenter* the phrase that was on all our tongues and racing around inside our heads. "Good health!" – that was the phrase, and a gentle wave of laughter flowed over the silverware.

Like little harness bells, like bells in a great monastery, the lamps were reflected in crystal towers, knives flashed, the battle had begun.

There, through the crystal, could be seen the comrade with whom one wet summer we admired a luxurious tapestry as we chewed eels, gulped beer, and listened ecstatically to the howl of modern jazz.

The tapestry had come by air from Toronto to our landlord, the unknown Saar, who, having fished from his little boat for fifty years, had never imagined that somewhere people were weaving such tapestries depicting shepherdesses that looked like cats, noblemen prancing around in the woods, sunset over a pond with swans, the swans' rounded flanks reminding us of the noblemen's bottoms.

"Art, however, moves in the most curious way; take, for instance, 'the word,' take 'cinematographer,' let's take 'sculpture,' let's cast an eye on the experimental theater. Contemporary art is moving in the most peculiar way toward disintegration."

So with a regal smile Lady Macbeth sprinkled kerosene over the conversation, and my comrade and I got up at once, our hair tousled, our moustaches twitching, and giggling as we scratched our hairy napes and stubbly cheeks.

---

*The Russian names Kuznetsov, Rybakov, Portnyagin, and Plotnikov are in meaning the equivalents, respectively, of Smith, Fisher, Taylor, and Carpenter.

"So long, guys. Thanks for the drink and the food, thanks for the fish and the culture, but we've both received a summons, so it's time for us to go."

"What summons, for God's sake? Forgive the indelicate question, but what summons?"

"To the john," we laughed. "The call of nature!"

"Two towels, a spoon, a knife, a mug . . . That'll be a ruble apiece. For the taxi."

We at once raced along the Bolshoi, stopping off at buffets and snack bars, leaving astern several beer bars and the humming Chvanovsky Restaurant. The Bolshoi Prospect unexpectedly curled around behind Tolstoy Square – yes, unexpectedly, always unexpectedly. On Karpovka, marble men stared ahead in mysterious thought, marmoreally perplexed, while copper porches, chilly and secretive, were alive and awaiting a visit from Blok's Unknown Woman, a visit from Blok himself. And there, as you turn onto the Moika from Zhelyabov Street, behind the Leningrad Chamber of Commerce, one sensed the expectation of a visit from a Jewish St. Petersburg girl and an acute presentiment of love.

Oh, seashore, seashore, waves, whirlpools, a shuttlecock frozen under pressure of the wind, openwork and lacy whorls *à la* Severyanin. Oh Baltic, oh Nida, oh Terioki . . . Your Long-footed Highness . . . footsteps of a Jewish girl on the beach . . .

> It was on the blue seashore
> At Terioki, perhaps on the Orinoco.

Now we arrived and saw garlands of chickens over the entrance into a building of the constructivist period, garlands of chickens plucked and entwined by their necks in a passionate appeal to man, their friend: Welcome!

We responded without delay and at once found ourselves inside that house, stinking and in semidarkness, among the shaking plywood of the corridors and the figures of irresponsible people flitting past.

"Here, I think, we must part," we said to each other with a portentous air.

"This way, friends!" A pedicurist waved to us with a towel like a wing.

"No, we're not coming to see you," and to the sound of falling sheet-metal, we went our separate ways, each of us humming about something personally important, gracious, and fundamental.

I pushed open a door, and immediately there rose up before me a creature, fiery-eyed, urgently impressive, a bumpy – yes, a bumpy – and rock-strewn chin, two pairs of cheeks, and a narrow orifice whence came forth in circles the ingratiatingly arrogant voice of a preacher, filling the premises with a superb rumbling sound.

The devilishly good aroma of a cigar, the devilish creaking of leather – good-quality boots, armchairs, and harness – a devilishly delicious Texas sandwich, devilish coffee, brandy, and whiskey, a devilish gleam in the cozy semigloom, devilish opportunities for growth, a devilish risk, devilish dreams.

"He, ho, hoo, ha, the human family is essentially nothing more than a fungoid spawn, a thin layer of mold, from which individuals emerge ephemerally onto the surface, and if they don't find their way into a soup, they die out of their own accord."

"Excuse me, but there are giants among us! Tolstoy and Goethe, wise men, poets, scientists who launch huge, roaring spaceships into the cosmos!"

"He, ho, hoo, ha, scientists and poets? They're just another variety, the inedible sort, a little taller but also smellier. Your mushroom spawn, brother, is unreliable stuff. The only reliable things are putrefaction and decay!"

"How can one live if one believes in such ideas?"

"It's impossible," he proclaimed.

"But what is this soup? You have just said that only a few persons have a chance, unlike their fellow creatures, of landing in some strange kind of soup."

He shuddered, rolling his eyes, lifting up his ring-covered extremities.

"If you like, we can now talk about this matter in a special way."

Smiles and nods and *double entendres,* winks, initiation into the secret, three turns, a whistle, a clap, a squat, and a dance on one knee.

"Ha, ha, ha! Lovely! Well done! Another turn on one knee! Do that pirouette again!"

I went out cautiously, pressing my hand to my mouth, and ran away.

There rushed toward me, but without moving from the spot, a dozen pairs of eyes, silently imploring me to save their owners from suffering, from pain and shame, from the pangs that accompany the early stages of dread diseases.

"Come on now, old lady, with your terrible hump, uncover your back! Don't be afraid, dear, don't cry. It won't hurt – I'm a doctor and clinician!"

The clinician saw an enormous abscess, which had swelled up like a transparent planet: Arteries, branching out in all directions like a map of the Amazon, throbbed violently, while on the edge, in lymph nodes swollen like sausages, an explosion was building up, and a scream was about to burst out of the old woman's feeble throat.

What was I to do?

Perhaps for an hour, perhaps for a minute, perhaps even for several days, Radius Khvastishchev had been sitting on the tail of his dinosaur *Humility* and looking at the back of its ugly neck. The tail – if this particular formation could be called a tail – had a rounded cavity that was an extremely comfortable place in which to sit or even to recline. More than once Khvastishchev had thanked heaven for guiding his chisel in the right direction and so providing this unexpected bonus, this broad, curving indentation in the marble, in which it was so pleasant to sit or recline, or sometimes – just imagine! – indulge in fun and games *à deux*.

Humility, which had already devoured Khvastishchev's car, his mortgage deposit, his record collection, and his ex-wife's jewelery, was an enormous monster, and for its convenience the early and greatly loved works of this once-famous sculptor were pushed into corners or crammed into storerooms.

A comfortable, delightful, beautiful cavity, Khvastishchev now thought, as he returned from a journey to the land of dreams. At least it provides some slight use for this hideous beast, he thought further as he stared with hatred at the horrible nostril of his unfinished work, from which protruded an ideally shaped human leg.

You marble whore; you've utterly ruined me, you bitch. They'll never let me go to Yugoslavia now. Everyone at the Moscow Society of Artists knows about you now, and elsewhere too.

The greenish-lilac twilight of a summer night flowed through the symbolic holes of *Humility,* through the "transverse spiritual artery" in its belly, which not even its creator understood or knew what it symbolized.

Anyway, why was this revolting, obscene, greedy heap of junk called *Humility*? You have torn away the mask and revealed *yourself* in this lump of marble, Radius Apollinarievich. You're still deceiving yourself, still convincing yourself that you love it, still making yourself feel pity for it, imagining a humble, stupid, but pure – ah, spiritually pure

– body of a dinosaur. But now look how it has turned out. The chisel won't let you lie!

But how can one get rid of the tendency to tell lies, get rid of the whole of this Judeo-Slavic complex? What prayer guided Henry Moore to his simple, pure forms? Why call a marble shape *Humility*? Why not just give it a number? You're still thinking you can influence the minds and emotions of your fellow citizens, contribute to their spiritual evolution, revolution, pollution, and God knows what else. They don't give a shit for your "appeals" to them.

The one thing that can astonish them is the dimensions. If, for instance, you managed to raise up above the city a *Humility* that was higher than a skyscraper, or, by contrast, to chisel it out of a grain of rice and tattoo on it the first ten pages of Lenin's philosophical study *Materialism and Empiriocriticism*, why then . . .

You must immediately file down and smooth away all those political, religious, and sexual symbols, smear that damn "transverse spiritual artery" with plaster of Paris, or, best of all, push the whole lump onto the firms of Vučetič or Tomsky; they will be able to find some use for it. Then at least you can buy some tickets to a vacation resort, so that for a month you won't have to worry about how you're going to feed yourself.

Behind Khvastishchev, the staircase creaked slowly and heavily. No doubt it was the utterly untalented and useless "King Herod" coming down from his upstairs garret. It was the same "King Herod" whose hips Khvastishchev had, many years ago, entwined with a garland of phalluses. Some symbol that was! It had reared itself up in front of a piece of female carrion from the SMOG group, but she wouldn't have it and gave him the brush-off. It was probably Herod going out for a beer.

But it turned out that it wasn't Herod. It was Patrick Thunderjet, the reptile!

"Oh bastards, bastards," Patrick began to moan from the staircase. "Russian bastards. Don't you have a refrigerator with some Löwenbräu beer in it?"

"There's usually a jar of pickling brine over there in the corner," Khvastishchev suggested.

"What's the time?"

"I've no idea."

"Where are the girls?"

"Ask me something easier."

With a groan, Patrick sauntered past the right flank of *Humility*.

Now and again he would grab at the marble and lower his head. Khvastishchev was afraid of climbing out of his cavity, because he knew that if he did so, his head would start to spin even faster. Girls? Did the American say "girls?" To be honest, Khvastishchev was mildly astonished by the long, lanky Patrick Thunderjet's appearance in his studio, and he remembered absolutely nothing about any girls. He racked his brains, and something floated to the surface: the Impala . . . Masha . . . certain scenes in the foreign-currency bar. But who were these girls? How infuriating! Which girls?

Patrick disappeared behind a bend in *Humility,* then reappeared on the other side, sat down on a chair, knocking some crockery onto the floor, groped around, and suddenly squealed with delight, "Hey! Eureka! Say, Radik, there's a whole pile of cigarette butts here! And a glass full of some liquid! I hope no one has puked into it. Shall I leave some for you?"

"Leave me half of it."

Patrick took a gulp, lit a cigarette, and suddenly roared with laughter, sounding like a young centaur from the islands of the Aegean Sea. "Ho, ho, ho, ho, ho! Do you remember that crappy dive called Middle Earth in that little cellar near Covent Garden market?"

He immediately burst cheerfully into a scatty song, as he had done in that happy, hopeful year of 196–:

It's Saturday, the latter day, the happy hippies' holiday!
A mile of dealers' stalls along the Portobello Road,
The flea market where you will find
organ-grinders, con men, shrimps, and female tramps,
limping fliers, flying lamps,
advocates and avocados,
cabbages and kings,
samurai swords and Samaritans' words,
nuts and bolts, miniskirts and maxishirts,
Scottish pipers and Guyanese snipers,
Spanish capes, magnetic tapes, Indian apes,
Arab hagglers, Chinese jugglers;
And tricorne hats
From Hymie Batz,
Shaggy dogs and cans of fogs,
Emus and cockatoos . . .
I stroll past the stalls
Admiring the balls.

I'm a champion stripper:
"Jackie the Ripper" –
Clumps of polyps up my nose,
Junk stashed in my pantyhose;
In spite of my fame
I've forgotten my name.
Here it smells of LSD –
But they won't bust *me*!

Against the greenish-lilac background, the wild profile of Patrick Thunderjet swayed in front of Khvastishchev, but he had the impression that he could still see Patrick's erstwhile dreamy, childlike smile.

"You know, Patrick, I simply can't believe that you and I will never go back to Portobello Road, that we won't push our way through that flea market again as we did that fall. I couldn't go on living if I thought that could never happen again."

Patrick stopped dancing. "Right now, old man, there's a stink floating all over Europe," he croaked.

"Surely there's not a stink in our London too?"

"It stinks everywhere!"

"You're right," Khvastishchev agreed after a moment's thought. "It stinks everywhere. The sixties are over and the seventies haven't begun yet. And will they ever begin, I wonder? Prague, Chicago . . ."

"The computers, though, give an encouraging forecast," said Thunderjet as he climbed into *Humility*'s cavity and lay down head-to-tail alongside Khvastishchev. "You and I, Radik, still have time to remember the days of our youth."

"Go fuck yourself, Pat," said Khvastishchev. "We'd do better to try and remember what happened last night, or rather this morning, and think of a way of getting rid of our hangovers."

"Look what I've found on the table." Thunderjet handed Khvastishchev a small sheet of paper, on which the following was written in large, schoolgirlish letters:

Radius Apollinarievich, and you, Patrick Thunderjet!
    Long may you live and enjoy life!
    May you learn the secrets of the human heart!
    When you meet good people, trust them!
    And try and avoid the bad ones!
Thanks for giving us a good time. We're leaving for Zagorsk, where there is hope that we may be able to enter a convent. For the

time being our address is: Workers' Dormitory, Soft Toy Factory, Zagorsk, Moscow Oblast. Please don't write to us.

Forever yours,
Toma and Klara

Toma and Klara . . . so that's what the girls were called! One of them, no doubt, was a member of the district committee, a member of the Komsomol, a weight lifter, and a gold digger; the other was a weepy, gypsylike little hooker, a waitress, a salesgirl. How on earth did we pick them up and what did we do with them? Why Zagorsk? And why the Soft Toy Factory?

As he strained to remember, a faint recollection began to form in Khvastishchev's brain, but as soon as it reached the very edge of his mind it slithered away into total confusion, into dim chaos, where there were no guiding landmarks, into another dimension – and that was terrifying. He realized that this was just his hangover playing tricks on him, but that didn't make it any easier to bear.

"Do you remember anything, Pat? How long were we drinking? What were we doing?"

"The only thing I remember," said Thunderjet, "is our conversation about the moon."

"Did we talk about the moon?" Khvastishchev asked cautiously.

"Don't you remember? You and I had a long and detailed discussion about the question of contact between the American and Soviet lunar stations. I remember we agreed that it was stupid to work on the same planet and not communicate with each other. In Antarctica we've been exchanging information for a hundred years, yet on the moon we're still keeping each other in the dark about 'secrets' that aren't secrets at all. I won't fly there next time if that stupid problem hasn't been resolved. We're not savages, so why do we each scratch around in the moondust on our own? There haven't been any secrets there for a long time. I'm sure that contact is possible even with the Dungflung base!" The American was getting very heated, waving his arms and banging his fists on the marble; his eyes flashed, as though they were actually discussing real problems.

Khvastishchev realized that his Yankee friend had gone even farther than he had last night, except that he had perhaps gone in a different direction.

"Are you talking about the Chinese, Pat?" he asked warily.

"And why not? They're just as good a scientists as we are. They risk their lives too, and they choke just the way we do when they swallow their space sausage or moon water. As a matter of principle, we should link up all our tunnels and make an international city on the moon. We must raise this matter immediately at the UN. Even if there's no peace on earth, then at least let reason triumph on the Spittoon!"

"What spittoon?" Khvastishchev inquired even more warily.

"You amaze me!" exclaimed the Yankee. "Weren't you the first one to say that seen from halfway the moon looked like a spittoon? Don't you remember how we laughed about it right up to the landing?"

"You mean you've landed on the moon, Pat?" asked Khvastishchev in a very quiet voice.

"This is incredible!" yelled Patrick in an absolutely firm voice, reminiscent of his earlier, healthy, young days, beaches and water skiing, muscular pleasures and wind in the hair. "Are you implying that I stayed in orbit while Planichka and Khartak landed? Have you gone off your head, Radik? After Khartak landed, both you and I were on the Spittoon no less than ten times, and we lived there for stretches of three months and longer."

He laid his cold hand on Khvastishchev's forehead and froze in this attitude for some time, apparently transformed into an excrescence on the body of *Humility*. Poor Pat! Now he would have to sit on the tail of the marble dinosaur until the sculptor knocked him off with a mallet. But perhaps the sculptor himself had long since become attached to it? That would be unpleasant – one could neither piss nor take anything to cure one's hangover.

Khvastishchev, caution itself, flung his legs over and slid out of the cavity. "Well, Pat?" he inquired. "Can you get up?"

Thunderjet jumped out of the cavity as lightly as a puppet. A weight fell from Khvastishchev's heart.

"Well, have you remembered about the moon?" Laughing benignly, Thunderjet patted his friend on the shoulder.

"Are there still bases there?" asked Khvastishchev.

"Of course there are. Four. Ours, yours, and two Chinese."

"Ah, now I remember."

"That's better," Patrick said with a sigh. "I was beginning to get worried about you."

He walked toward the door leading out of the studio, while behind his back Khvastishchev made the sign of the cross over him.

Moscow was completely deserted. Under a green sky its asphalt gleamed dully; suspended over the intersections, traffic lights winked; leaves swirled along the boulevards. It could have been night, it could have been morning, it could have been evening, it could have been before a nuclear attack, it could have been after.

They were walking along the boulevard, leaves swirling above them. As always, that swirl was driving them crazy and they were close to happiness. They wanted the boulevard not to come to an end too soon, they wanted it to take them to old Danzig, to the Ile de la Cité, or to Vienna.

"Hell . . . Hell . . . The leaves are being whipped by the wind," Patrick muttered. "You know, when I was a kid and the leaves were being whirled around overhead, I used to have a vision of the *Mayflower* hoisting its sails and returning home, back to old Europe."

Khvastishchev did not reply; he felt a sudden chill, and his legs unexpectedly refused to function. Thunderjet looked around and saw his friend standing in the middle of the avenue, staring at the foliage.

"What's the matter, Radik?"

"Pat, look! A clock! Can't you see? There's a clock hanging among the leaves!"

"Sure I can see it. It's half past three. That means that morning is on its way."

"Or maybe evening?" Khvastishchev was seized by a spasm, and before his friend's eyes, he suddenly began to tremble like a leaf.

"Steady!" barked Thunderjet. "At half past three on a summer afternoon it is completely light. It's broad daylight, not evening."

"Are you sure, Pat? Are you sure it's summer now?"

"Just look around, you blockhead! Can't you see the leaves are green? And the heat! Of course it's summer!"

"Is it really, Pat? Is it? But I'm shivering all over! Can't you see?"

"What you need, Radik, is a kick in the teeth. I guess that would stop your quaking!"

Suddenly Horror appeared among the foliage. Then it swung up into the sky, onto the pink-tinged upper stories of the houses, but the chief Horror, of course, was concealed in the words "half past three," and they thrashed from side to side in Khvastishchev's throat, like a sparrow in its death agony. The only human phenomenon in a world of spreading horror was Patrick's pair of eyes, but the shadow of the sun had started to fall on them too.

"Is it, Pat? Is it really? It's morning, you say? It's the north, you say? Or is it the south?" Khvastishchev was perishing, though he was still grasping at straws, as though still trying to deceive the incomprehensible, unbelieving Horror, but he could not keep it up and broke down, bursting into tears. "But what if this clock were to stop?"

Then he saw his friend's fist flying toward his face; he fell on his back and unexpectedly did not die but began to dream, in color and on wide screen, the

DREAM OF SHORTAGES

That evening in the theater on the balcony of night *The Barber of Seville* was being performed, but they DIDN'T PERFORM IT ALL!

I crawled up the green blinds in order to inscribe my love in the complaint book, my love for Rossini.

Dear Rossini, young Italian, your country, your nocturnal lights, your fountains, girls, and flutes, were given to me INCOMPLETE by deception!

I was clearly deceived, starting with the overture, which was missing the clarinet part; Rossini is missing in Russia and any survey would confirm this!

Dearest Herzen, don't waken Russia! Don't strive in vain, you love child! Let her be awakened by an Italian, a crazy tramp in torn lace!

I climbed up the shutters to the upper balcony, passing the windows, through which, floor by floor, there flowed Austria, verdant Oslo, France in her splendor, square and solid Berlin.

Down below strolled Vanya, the kindly cop on the beat, clasping under his arm a fur-bound complaint book, massive as a Goethe tome, as he whistled the passwords to his squad of stool pigeons.

The bold band of stool pigeons shook their ears like spaniels, leaped around like wirehaired fox terriers, spattered mud around like bulldogs.

On the balcony, amid the thunder of the theater, amid the clouds above the roofs of Russia, whiter than white and gentler than gentle, Rosina wove her fishnet stocking of intrigues.

Was she waiting for me? What was she lacking? Rumor has it that in Italy the demand for communism has increased. Their Piedmont is saturated with Marxism, though not too much.

As I climbed farther upward, the COMPLAINT BOOK boomed away beneath my feet, like some vast all-Russian overture. Down there, the battle of the age had already been in progress for fourteen centuries.

Everyone was short of something. The townspeople were making gunpowder and casting cannons. The princes were furious. The peas-

ants were trying to write in the complaint book with pitchforks. The
proletariat was digging up cobblestones.

It seemed to the Russians that they were short of lumber, that they
had been fooled over electricity, that the state was playing fast and
loose with their civil rights, that the Jews were bringing in materialism.

In actual fact, what our shaggy male dogs lacked was a blazing
symphony in a major key, an Italian woman in lace, quivering with
passion. What the Italians lacked was a good thick prick, a rough
tongue, a sturdy Tatar pole for stirring their tea or chocolate.

The complaint book hung above me like the Italian sky, full of vast
stars, and it was warmed by the heat of Vesuvius.

I had lost confidence in space. I was a cockroach clambering up the
shutters, along the cornices of the opera house, upward, downward. I
was following Rosina, and she, like a ship in the sea, was gliding over
brocade whirlpools, losing her tears in twists and folds of brocade.

Damn brutes. Can't you see the umbrella, the wineglass? Don't tilt
it, God damn you, don't tilt it!

When he came to his senses, Pantelei A. Pantelei found himself
sprawled out on a lawn. Beside him sat Patrick Thunderjet, the calming
weight of his hand resting on Pantelei's forehead.

"I haven't taken my eyes off the hands of the clock, old man," said
Patrick. "I'm ready to swear that the clock is still going. Right now
it's twenty minutes to four."

"A nice time," said Pantelei, sliding out from under his friend's
hand. "Nice day. An excellent century. A splendid age."

"Forgive me for socking you just now. Sorry, but I had to do it."

"Not only do I forgive you but I thank you, although I don't quite
understand why you did it."

"I know how it can happen, you see. I myself was once frightened
to death by seeing streams and stones."

"There are excellent streams in the Crimea! There are marvelous
stones in the Crimea! You and I must fly to the Crimea, Patrick
Thunderjet!"

"I haven't a cent, and you haven't a kopek. Someone has emptied
our pockets, my dear Pantelei."

"Let's go and empty someone else's pockets, Thunderjet! Have you
forgotten how we fought under the banner of Prince Spitzbergen? Get
up, American! Let's start our journey to wonderland!"

* * *

The line for Italian felt boots was winding its way in somnolent torpor around GUM, the state department store on Red Square, when it was approached from the direction of the Kremlin by two *déclassé* creatures wearing brand-name jeans, one of them tall, rangy, and barefoot. A pair of scarcely worn suede shoes, tied by their laces, was slung over his shoulder.

"Hey, man, won't you sell those shoes?" a citizeness of the city of Kherson inquired languidly.

She thought she was still asleep. For three days and nights she had been sleeping in the line for Italian felt boots, which apparently did not exist; now, against the background of the Kremlin's turrets and battlements, she suddenly saw a tall, thin alcoholic with a pair of suede shoes over his shoulder, looking like a prince!

"Glad to, ma'am," said the prince, galvanized into life. "How much are you offering for them?"

The citizeness smiled dreamily. "I'll give you five rubles, young man, a brand-new five-ruble bill."

Still not sufficiently awake to believe her own good luck, the citizeness took the suede beauties, and the lanky Yankee jumped for joy as he clutched the five-ruble bill. "Yippee!" he whooped. "We've made it!"

The news of the fantastic, unbelievable sale of a pair of brand-name suede shoes for a five-ruble bill spread through GUM like the spark along a safety fuse.

And then came the explosion. Forgetting the Italian felt boots, the line disintegrated, turned into a mob, and surrounded the two extraterrestrial visitors with footwear to sell. One of the visitors was admittedly already barefoot, but the other was wearing a beautiful pair of high-quality corduroy slippers. The mob waved its arms, shouting, as though at some spontaneous meeting in the days of the First Russian Revolution.

SELL YOUR SLIPPERS, FRIEND!

Such was the motive of this popular outburst. A full-blooded citizen of the Caucasus sprayed garlic-flavored saliva in the visitors' faces as he yelled, "I'll give you fifty!"

"These goddamn Georgians buy up everything!" came the shouts from all around.

"They haven't earned their filthy money!"

"Crooks!"

The visitor pulled off the slippers along with his socks, raised the whole lot above his head, and shouted, "I've been offered fifty rubles! Can anyone do better than fifty?"

"Seventy-five, dear, seventy-five," came the singsong voice of a woman vineyard keeper from Khorezm, stretching out her thin, harem-bred hands. "Here, my son, here."

"A hundred!" barked the Caucasian, thrust a hundred-ruble bill at the visitor, and snatched the slippers out of his hands.

"The slippers are yours! You can take the socks as a bonus! Hands off my pants! Comrades, comrades! Our pants are not for sale! Don't pull the jeans off my comrade!"

Dozens of nimble hands were fingering the visitors' denim pants, tugging at the zippers of their flies. "Sell them! Sell them! Sell us your Levi's, brother!"

Clutching their pants, the visitors fled. The mob followed them into the middle of Red Square, but stopped there. This marked the beginning of the zone of influence emanating from the sacred buildings of the Kremlin, and to enter this zone with thoughts of commerce on one's mind would have been sacrilege. Even the children in the mob knew the difference between GUM on one side of the square and the Kremlin on the other. Thanks to this awareness, the visitors were able to fade into the mysterious shadows; padding over the cobblestones with bare feet, they strolled toward the river, which was glowing pink under the dawn sky.

The line then calmly reformed itself and once more encircled the masterpiece of commercial architecture. The thought of Italian felt boots again took possession of the Muscovites and their comrades from out of town.

Later, three enormous trucks drove into the back entrance of GUM on Bumazhny Street, and from their great bellies emerged countless shoeboxes labeled in English "Made in Czechoslovakia, Dr. Indra and people."

"Something's being delivered." The rumor began to excite the crowd.

It turned out that the incoming goods were velvet slippers, at four rubles twenty a pair. Later still, all became clear: They were originally consigned to the Beryozka foreign-currency stores for tourists, but had then been downgraded and released for sale to the domestic consumer for rubles!

AT FIRST WE HAD NO WISH TO STEAL

The night pharmacist, who strangely enough had not yet lost all compassion for suffering humanity, gave us ten little bottles of tincture of valerian, a hefty bottle of Pantocrin – extract of deer antlers – and four small tubes of Bulgarian toothpaste.

We were in luck. Then came another stroke of good luck: In a cold, gloomy tunnel under an archway of the former Government House we discovered a long row of soda-dispensing machines. The miracle, of course, was not in finding them, since nowadays such machines are not hard to find. Our miracle, our stroke of good luck, lay in something else: There, in the rusty maw of one of the machines, stood a glass – intact.

We were about to settle down and spread out our supply of medication then and there, when suddenly a policeman leaped out of a doorway and ran down the tunnel toward us, loudly blowing his whistle. He was wearing a prewar uniform, with collar-tab badges instead of epaulettes, a white helmet, and cotton gloves. Who was he guarding in this puke-spattered building? Perhaps he wasn't even a policeman but the ghost of a policeman.

Anyway, we bolted and showed this guardian of the law a clean pair of heels. Cowardice, you say? Shameful behavior? No, gentlemen, there was nothing shameful in what we did. It makes no difference whether you are in Moscow, Tirana, or Cairo – running away from the police is not cowardice but plain common sense.

And that was how we stole the glass.

How delightful it was on the embankment by the water, or rather beside the oil slicks as they curled into spirals, pulling all kinds of floating junk behind them. There on the granite slopes we settled down. First we drank the valerian, then we opened the bottle of Pantocrin, with the spreading antlers of a reindeer on its label.

"What a shame we can't invite Tolya von Steinbock to join us here, and that we can't transport ourselves even for a moment to the Crimea, the Magadan heating conduit where ex-cons gulped Pantocrin and immediately tested its effect with some horizontal acrobatics on the bottom row of bunks.

"By the way, Pantocrin gives you such a hard-on that you can hang a bucket on your cock," said the First to the Second Person.

"What's the point?" said the Second Person angrily. "To satisfy all those hysterical women? You can count me out!"

The Second Person squeezed a tube of Pomorin toothpaste into the glass, scooped some oil out of the river, and then topped the glass with some of the aromatic solution, the aphrodisiac of Magadan. "Drink that! I guarantee you a month of sexual inactivity."

The First Person drank the sticky white liquid; before taking his first sip, the Second Person managed to clean his teeth.

Having consumed all their supplies, they stretched out blissfully under the planking of a landing stage used by the river buses. After a while the boards above them began to creak under the footsteps of a sailor, who was greeting the coming dawn with a muffled flow of obscene abuse.

The dome of the bell tower of Ivan the Great was already gleaming in the sun; above it the Orthodox cross was shining brightly and reflecting the rays of the sun. Soon the onion domes of the Cathedral of the Assumption and the Rizopolozheniye Church were also burning with sunlight. A breeze blew along the river, fanning our swollen faces and swirling upward, causing a slight tremor of the ruby-red stars surmounting each Kremlin turret, then flicked at the crimson flag flying above the green dome of Sverdlov Hall. Under the planks of the landing stage, the First Person suddenly felt his breath taken away by a surge of patriotism.

This had happened to him before. When returning home, for instance, from Japan via Poland after a three-month voyage in foreign seas you suddenly saw the crosses of the Kremlin merging in unnatural but somehow unbreakable union with the symbols of atheism, and you were seized by a spasm of patriotism, for you were looking at the lips and nipples of your Motherland, which still, despite a dreary coating of propagandist stucco, gave off the smell of milk.

"Do you love your flag?" the First Person asked the Second.

"I have no flag," muttered the Second Person.

"The flag of your country. I mean – the stars and stripes."

"That puke-covered bed sheet?"

"Well, I love my flag. I can't help it. I love them all: the tsarist tricolor, the St. Andrew's ensign, and the present red one."

PANTELEI APOLLINARIEVICH PANTELEI DESCRIBES, IN THE THIRD PERSON, THE OCCASION ON WHICH HIS YOUTH CAME TO AN END

It seemed as though it was only yesterday that beneath the dome of Sverdlov Hall the luckless head of Pantelei was drenched, as though by myriads of putrefactive bacteria, in the people's anger, represented by the anger of the Boss. Yet in fact eight years have passed since then, and that Boss, now an impotent old man, no longer represents anyone but himself.

The inside of that dome was lined with azure-blue tiles, but at the time it seemed to Pantelei that he was standing alone in a mountainous, icebound country under a dazzling sky that was totally indifferent to his fate.

The day in fact was March 8, Women's Day, the day of the country's menstrual cycle, and the low, pot-bellied clouds were dumping snowy sleet onto the Kremlin. Inside, although the white marble walls made it also seem snowy, it was hardly lonely: the hall buzzed with hundreds of voices, like a menagerie before feeding time.

"Pantelei, give an answer!"

"Pantelei to the rostrum!"

Should he go or not? Smiling vacantly, Pantelei had just finished combing his hair and was now sitting in his seat, twisting the comb in his fingers. Should he go, comrades? Around him were only the backs, heads, and necks of the liberals, until recently Pantelei's patrons, friends, and sycophants. Events had suddenly started to move fast; no one had expected this to happen, and therefore before the start of the session, "left-wingers" had sat down with "left-wingers," and the "right-wingers" had taken their usual positions. Now, instead of intelligent, keen-eyed, ironical faces, the unfortunate Pantelei was surrounded by nothing but the backs of their necks. Even the people sitting behind him had somehow managed to turn the backs of their necks toward him, although they were flapping their hands to the front in the interminable applause that was their salvation.

"Hey, you, come here!" the Boss said hoarsely into the microphone as he stood up on his raised platform, and the roar of the audience ceased instantly. "Come on, I can see you!" The finger, known to all the world from its mining adventures, pointed at the corner of the hall opposite from where Pantelei was sitting. "I see you, I see you. Don't try and hide! Everyone else was applauding except you! You with the glasses and the red sweater, I'm talking to you! Come up to the rostrum!"

The distinguishing marks of a wicked beatnik, "pidarast and apstractionist," were well known to the Boss from descriptions provided by his officials. The wicked beatnik always wore a sweater and glasses, had a little beard, loved noisy "jast music," and laughed at Stalinists. The Boss himself detested Stalin too and was gradually knocking the stuffing out of the dead monster, but Stalin was one thing and Stalinists were quite another: The wicked beatnik might not even stop at our culture, might undermine the very foundations of our culture with his venomous sarcasm. In general, give them an inch and they'll take a mile! They must be given a kick in the teeth before it was too late, they must be rooted out; there was already a whiff of smoke in the air that had an uncomfortably Hungarian smell to it. So his officials told him, and almost all of them had a university education and their class instincts never let them down.

The audience howled with triumph as it gazed at this classic beatnik, summoned forth by the commanding finger. There he is, the pernicious Pantelei, the schismatic who has been preventing our Polish comrades from building communism, whose mischievous prattling tongue babbles dangerous nonsense about the "thaw" and about the "heirs of Stalin." There he is, the very image of the enemy – remember him: red sweater and little beard, wire-framed glasses, and thin hair sticking wetly to his forehead.

Meanwhile Pantelei, his petrified bottom pressed firmly into his seat, held his breath. They had called on Silvester instead of him.

Silvester walked down the carpeted aisle to the rostrum, looking awkward and confused. He gesticulated and muttered, "What is all this to do with me, comrades? I've never given any interviews, comrades! I'm not Pantelei, comrades."

"Are you getting back at us because of your father?" The amplified voice of the Boss boomed out over the meeting.

This was another little gem of information provided by the clever officials: The wicked beatnik, of course, had a grudge against his country because his parents had died in the purges, and although no one denied that this was the fault of the cult of personality, still the apple never falls far from the apple tree, you know . . .

"Yes, my father was killed during the purges, but you yourself posthumously rehabilitated him," mumbled Silvester as he clambered up to the rostrum. Some of what he was saying reached the microphone and floated out over the auditorium like the incoherent groaning of a tenor saxophone.

Meanwhile the High Priest crawled under the legs of the members of the presidium to the Boss's posterior and whispered, "He's the wrong one, your excellency. There's been a slight mistake. That's not Pantelei, your excellency!"

"Go back to your place!" the Boss immediately barked at Silvester, who had already reached the rostrum, and then sat down, mopping the head that Hollywood had made famous, regretting the vain expenditure of ill will and therefore getting even angrier.

"Comrade Pantelei has the floor," announced the High Priest in a normal, businesslike tone of voice; he was a creature bearing an amazing resemblance to an anteater, with masticatory and olfactory appendages protruding from his plump body.

The glacier under Pantelei's feet started to slide rapidly downhill. This glacier had formed underneath him at the very start of the session, when a certain militant virago, exploiting the privilege afforded to her by Women's Day, had denounced Pantelei's international activities to the whole auditorium, in particular the interview he had given to the magazine *Panorama* in the city of Bydgoszcz in the province of Poznań. Now the glacier was rushing away from under his feet and carrying Pantelei with it straight to the rostrum.

Two thousand of the country's most prominent people stared at the obnoxious Pantelei with a certain disappointment. What? This ordinary-looking thirty-year-old whippersnapper in the usual gray suit and normal tie? Was this the dangerous subversive, the perfidious word spinner who had unlocked the hearts of Soviet youth with the skeleton key of decadence, the leader of the beatnik horde, who had caused clouds to gather over the Socialist Motherland? Perhaps this was simply camouflage, comrades? Of course it was mere camouflage, and Pantelei the Apostate obviously had a cross in his pants pocket, and under his shirt there hung pornographic pictures and the songs of Okudzhava, so that what we were seeing was nothing but a most cunning piece of camouflage, comrades. This sort of enemy was even more dangerous. With Silvester, at least, everything was on view. But Pantelei was trying to disguise himself!

Incidentally, the luckless Pantelei was indeed wearing a Catholic cross around his neck, left over from the days of Tolya von Steinbock. It was then, on the eve of their separation, that his mother and Martin, prisoners within a seven-kilometer radius of Magadan, had handed the youth this little devotional object adorned with a tiny silver figure of the crucified Christ. Subsequently, all five inheritors of the pathetic legacy kept the little cross, carefully guarding it from prying eyes, ashamed – yes, ashamed – of its archaic symbolism. Quite recently, in the casual, easygoing resort of Koktebel, young supermen had begun wearing crosses. Pantelei realized that his secret, shameful talisman had turned into a snobbish adornment meant to shock the "squares," and he wore it openly on his chest. It was then, most probably, that some anonymous informer had sent in a report about the cross to the appropriate authorities.

Now, as Pantelei walked toward the rostrum without a thought in his head, his arms and legs devoid of feeling, he had completely lost any sense of himself in that blue, icy space; but his brain, that unsleeping sentry of the feeble human organism, registered all the sounds and faces, all the remarks, about his tattoo and about the cross. Later, much later, perhaps in a dream, perhaps in a spell of drunken delirium, Pantelei remembered what it was that he had most feared in that august assembly: to be ordered to strip naked!

The rostrum towered above the auditorium, but even higher above it was the vast table of the presidium, from behind which fifteen faces stared at the approaching Pantelei. Were they stern? No! Were they threatening? No! Were they mocking, contemptuous, censorious, benevolent??? No, no, no, no!!! There were not even any traces of emotion on those faces. A face like these, any one of the fifteen, might loom up in front of you at night on a highway like a blinding headlight and drive past you without so much as blinking. In other words, they were absolutely ordinary faces, and only one face at the table was suffused with a bluish-red flush – the face of the Boss.

Once having mounted the rostrum, Pantelei did not present a very edifying spectacle. He felt the rostrum swaying beneath him like the crow's nest on a foremast, and with no land in sight on the horizon. His brain, however, was not sleeping; on the contrary, it was frantically dodging around inside its own labyrinth, seeking a loophole for escape. Suddenly Pantelei thought he heard the creak of a door, saw the flash of a narrow streak of light, and he began to move his tongue in front of the sweaty membrane of the microphone. He spoke as though pushing foul-smelling meat into a meat grinder, from which it oozed out in pale strings of dubious sausage meat.

"Dear comrades dear Nikita Kornponevich from this exalted rostrum I wish criticism directed against me justified criticism of the people makes one think about responsibility to the people to you madam I beg pardon slip of the tongue truly beautiful images of contemporaries and greatness of our everyday life despite attempts of imperialist agents dear comrades like my great teacher Mayakovsky who in the words of the unforgettable Joseph Vissarionovich was and remains I am not a communist but–"

The Boss's mighty bellow cut in as Pantelei paused for breath: "And are you proud of that, Pantelei? Are you proud that you aren't a communist? You heard him – he's not a communist! But I'm a communist and I'm proud of it, because I'm a son of my class and I will never renounce my father!" (Stormy, prolonged applause, shouts of "Long live Nikita Kornponevich!" "Glory to the leading class!" "Shame on Pantelei!" "Shame on Salazar, the hangman of Portugal!") "They've gone too far, you see. They write God knows what! They paint nothing but assholes! They make movies about shit in cesspools! Switch on the radio – nothing but noisy jast music! Go to a birthday party – nothing to drink, nothing to eat, just gossip and backbiting! We won't let you start a seditious Petöfi-style Writers' Club here! This isn't Hungary, you know! You'll get a rap over the knuckles, Mr. Pantelei! We'll take away your passport, and send you packing, with a kick in your ass, to the people who are feeding you! To Bonn!" (Stormy demonstrations of approval from the audience, cries of "Send Pantelei abroad!" "Send them all abroad!" "Crazy schizos, send them abroad – to Siberia!")

Pantelei (on the verge of fainting, in a frozen whisper): "Nikita Kornponevich, please allow me to sing a song!"

"I picked up a book the other day," the Boss went on quietly, gathering his strength for a new outburst. "It made me want to throw up, comrades. The oats didn't go to the horse, comrades." (Laughter, applause.) "No landscapes, comrades, no proper plot, not a single worker in the story, even at the district committee level. Neither fish, flesh, fowl, nor good red herring, comrades, but fortunately one swallow doesn't make a summer!" (Prolonged laughter, turning to tears.) "There was a time when for a book like that we'd have skinned the author alive! And his wife! And his children!" The Boss's voice had reached the very top of its register; suddenly, muffled by a cunning little smile, it dropped right down: "I refer, of course, comrades, to the great critic Vissarion Belinsky, and not to something else." (Stormy applause turning into the stamping of feet, voice with an Armenian accent: "That's enough democracy, it's time to use the rope!" Good-natured laughter: "Ah, these hot-blooded Transcaucasians!") "So there you have it, Mr. Pantelei! History is merciless to mongrels and renegades of all sorts, and especially to one – and we all know *who* that is!"

Pantelei (from the depths of unconsciousness): "Please let me sing, dear comrades!"

Shouts from the hall: "Don't let him sing!" "You can sing on the gallows – abroad!" "We know those songs of yours!"

The Boss raised his two cast-iron miner's fists. On his nylon sleeves glittered a pair of diamond cufflinks, a present from the people of Cambodia.

"We'll grind all the provocateurs and warmongers, all the Colorado potato beetles and maggots of the foreign press into the dust! Sing, Pantelei!"

The unfortunate revisionist was taken aback by this unexpected favor. He gripped the rostrum with both hands, took a deep breath, and was about to bellow "The Song of Stormy Youth" or "The March of the Communist Labor Brigades," when suddenly his mouth opened of its own accord and in a honeyed baritone started singing the totally irrelevant "Song of the Varangian Guest" from *Sadko*.

Nothing could have been more shameful. Pantelei lost consciousness, but even while unconscious he stubbornly went on singing, " . . . great is their god Odin, grim is the sea . . ."

The Boss listened, his face covered with his hand. The audience fell silent, gloating in malicious expectation. Senior Sergeant Gribochuyev, on duty in the cloakroom, had already prepared a sarcastic one-liner for Pantelei's benefit: "You're singing with someone else's voice, meester!" The aria came to an end.

"You don't sing too badly," the Boss muttered gloomily.

Pantelei came to his senses with a shudder, looked around, and saw the Boss's little cranberry eye gleaming through his fingers. It seemed to him that the Boss was winking at him, as though inviting him to have a drink.

"You don't sing badly, Pantelei. You are at least able to assimilate the legacy of the classics. You're better at singing than scribbling."

The Boss stood up, looked around the auditorium, saw among all the vaguely blinking intellectuals the tense faces of the "killers" poised to pounce, and thought maliciously, "The dogs are waiting. Once they were waiting like that to have *my* blood, when old Cockroach Whiskers made me dance the hopak. Well, you can go on waiting; you're not going to get your meat ration today."

He began to cough and clear his throat, and that coughing and throatclearing, which during the Cuban missile crisis of last fall had kept the whole civilized world in a state of hideous, sweaty fear, now kept this audience of "left-wingers" and "right-wingers," agitprop bosses, KGB men, and Soviet journalists in suspense.

Only Pantelei alone seemed not to be expecting anything. With both hands he gripped the sides of his rostrum, the ship of state, and sailed, sailed, sailed over the waves of history, but whither, "we may not know."

"You may sing with us, Pantelei, and develop your talent," the Boss

finally grunted. "If you sing with *them,* though, you'll ruin your talent
and we'll grind you into the dust. Who do you want to sing with?"

"With my people, with the Party, with you, Nikita Kornponevich!"
sang Pantelei, now in the gentlest lyric tenor, but, as the "right-
wingers" noticed, without sincere feeling and even with a certain
undertone of crafty slyness.

To everyone's surprise, the Boss smiled. "Very well, we'll trust you,
Comrade (COMRADE!) Pantelei. Practice, smooth the rough edges, work
at it. There's my hand on it!"

A powerful charge of live, revolutionary current surged through the
pores of Pantelei's sweaty palm. Excited shouts from the liberals
greeted this handshake, which was their salvation too, but Sergeant
Beriya Yagodovich Gribochuyev of the cloakroom guard was so
annoyed that he pinched his own left testicle: The setup hadn't worked;
old Kornponevich had failed to take the bait!

March 8 slurped underfoot like thin gruel; thin, gray, puffy, bluish-
drunken faces were lashed by an icy rain. Hordes of Muscovites
churned up the slush on Gorky [Bitter] Street in search of sweetness.
The sweet life on Bitter Street: Not many of the seekers can have been
disturbed by the crude paradox enshrined in those words.

Suddenly, among the stream of dirty cars on Manège Square there
flashed into view a bright patch of color, like a blob of yesterday's
Russian salad: a gypsy woman with a sack clutched to her bosom,
looking as though she had emerged from the capital's central garbage
dump.

A crowd of good-lifers, turning the corner at the Hotel National,
were running along the sidewalk and pointing at the gypsy woman:
"Stop thief!" "She stole a baby!"

No one, however, dared to jump over the pedestrian barrier and
chase the gypsy through the stream of traffic. The splashes from the
wheels would have dirtied their party clothes.

Pressed by the crowd against the huge plate-glass windows of the
National, three men who had just been let out of the Kremlin watched
the incident in silence: Silvester, Pantelei, and Nikodim, the leaders of
the nonexistent but already shattered army of the beatnik-revisionists.

The cars braked, skidded, piled up in heaps; the crowd roared and
called for the police. Without hurrying, the police gathered their forces
at the scene of action, but the big-breasted, big-bottomed gypsy woman
still ran, with a crazy gleam in her eyes, and escaped with her sack,

which the crowd claimed to be a stolen baby. Thus did she celebrate Women's Day.

The sun had softened the asphalt of Sophiiskaya Embankment, and it now showed the tire tracks of the Jaguars and Bentleys which were fanning out from the gates of the British Embassy. The asphalt was sinking beneath the heels of diplomats, like putrefying skin under a doctor's fingers. Two barefoot men, both well past their prime, were also imprinting the marks of their feet on the asphalt.

The two men were strolling arm in arm along the Moscow River, engaged in grave and earnest conversation, for all the world like professors from Moscow University or the academicians Ilyichov and Lysenko. A little van marked "Laundry Delivery," standing about two hundred meters away, was recording their words on magnetic tape.

"You think it's all our propaganda, but it's true – people are having their ears cut off. And toxic insecticides and electrodes on the genitals – that's true too. I was in Vietnam. I specially went into the very center of the inferno. I played the violin to those wretched brutes and drank with them. I actually counted severed ears with them. They were celebrating like madmen. I hate, I just hate what they call their motherland, that whore with sour milk in her tits. She has nothing in common with my childhood, with the things I remember with nostalgia."

"Well, as for *our* beautiful country, it has no need to brandish such horrors as severed ears. Castration, trepanation, clumsy sutures, dirt, suppuration, pus – those are our problems, and quite enough too. And yet, 'I love my country but with a strange love,' 'better the devil you know,' 'oh, my Russia, my bride,' and so on. I love it, don't you see?"

"All you Russians have this barbaric, profoundly provincial feeling about your country. You're always pretending to be some sort of shield for Europe, always droning on about the same old messianic idea. It's all nonsense! There's no such thing as the 'mysterious Slav soul,' just as there's nothing left of the 'great American dream' in today's world either. There are just two monstrous octopuses, two gigantic bags of half-dead protoplasm, which can only react to external stimuli in two ways: by contraction or by absorption. And it finds absorption, of course, much more pleasant than contraction."

"Ah, that's really scathing, that's brilliant! But all joking aside, this protoplasm of yours consists of human beings, of individual personalities, and each one of them has an intellect, a soul, a longing for God."

"Personality? Listen, you miscarried offspring of Stalinism, the only person who can claim to have a personality is the guy who manages to escape. Once you merge with a political or an antipolitical system, you become a producer or a consumer, a guardian or a destroyer; you're immediately slotted into some category."

"Do you think that by living within society each and every one of us is automatically bankrupt?"

"I'm afraid so! A few years back the only people I took seriously were those scatty flower children, but now even they have degenerated into revolutionaries; in other words, they've become an organized gang."

"But how is this fugitive individual personality to live? What can he or she believe in?"

"More than anything else in this world I would like to be a humble Christian and to believe in the crystal vault of heaven and in the limpid River Oceanus and in the turtle or the three elephants that are supposed to support the world, in the celestial Paradise Garden, in the snow-white feathers of the angels, but above all, to believe in Him, in His sufferings for our sake, and that He will come again."

"But don't you believe?"

Patrick did not reply, but turned away from me, and I suddenly had a clear recollection of an evening at the Third Medical Complex, the black roofs of the huts, the green sky, and the thin crescent moon over Wolf's Hill and Tolya von Steinbock walking alongside the political deportee Sanya Gurchenko, the crunch of snow under their feet, and their quiet conversation about the Paradise Garden.

It was hard for Von Steinbock to believe in it, but what is preventing you from believing, Patrick Thunderjet? Why these affected tirades? What is stopping you from believing in Christ? Perhaps as a child you didn't sit in a Methodist church but in a classroom listening to lectures on Marxism-Leninism? Perhaps you didn't read the Bible, but Chapter Four of Stalin's *Short Course* on Marxism and its "solely correct and truly scientific view of the world?"

I was on the point of losing my temper with Patrick, but then it occurred to me that, as usual, I was being unfair. As always, I cannot understand Westerners. A Russian will probably never be able to get under the skin of a Westerner. This tall American and I have been friends for years now, yet we can never fully understand each other. After all, a Westerner too needs something that he doesn't believe in, or perhaps my present faith is also nothing but an act of unbelief? Despair and anguish rasped over my skin like sandpaper.

Suddenly, behind us, a car engine could be heard gently purring; it gave a faint snort and stopped. We turned around and saw a gray-haired playboy, seated in an illustrated-magazine pose behind the wheel of a Mustang convertible. He was looking silently at Patrick with narrowed eyes. The unnatural, day-glo coloring of his face, the smooth skin, the flowered shirt, bright tie, and pale-pink flannel suit, the manly jaw, the car with automatic drive glittering with techno-logical goodies – it was the ideal image of a champion of the West in the Bolshevik camp, immaculate and not a hair out of place. The only thing that I didn't like about him were his eyes, that narrow-eyed stare, eyes that were so familiar they might have come from a Kolyma prison camp.

Patrick turned around, leaned on the parapet, and began looking into the oily waters of the fair Moscow River. He stuck out his ass; his sweater slid up and revealed a long, thin fir tree of hair running from his buttocks up his backbone. The result was absurd: The hard, persistent, piercing, carefully practiced look of the gray superman was now fastened upon Patrick's unattractive buttocks and was thus wasted.

"Thunderjet," the handsome man finally said, in the voice of Willis Conover. "The car that you took from the embassy car pool yesterday has been impounded by the Moscow City traffic police."

Patrick cast an imaginary fishing line and, with a carefree air, began humming "Go, Johnny, Go." The handsome man gave an outraged squeal, this time in quite a different voice: "Mr. Thunderjet! You have forgotten the purpose of your visit to this country! You missed a cocktail party at the level of deputy minister of education! How can you walk around town in that state? Who is that suspicious-looking character with you? You're a disgrace to the bald eagle!"

Patrick drooped guiltily.

"Sir, right now he's chasing a different sort of bald – or rather blond – head," I said to the handsome man.

"Ah, you understand English." The handsome man was embar-rassed. "Excuse me, I didn't mean to offend you. Are you a European?"

"Oh, yes! I am a son of this ragged-edged continent," I replied, with an obscure sense of pride.

"Please get into the car, gentlemen. This isn't California, you know. Look, do you see that van marked 'Laundry' by the bridge? Get me? And you were talking so seriously!"

Patrick suddenly swung around and hailed a passing taxi, "Hey there, chief! Can you drop me off at the Pioneer Market?"

When we were in the taxi, I asked Patrick, "Who's the good-looker?"
"From the embassy. Stool pigeon number one."

THE MEN'S CLUB

"One day, o Heaven, in the near future or past, there will grow out
of the slag concrete, there will arise from the scrap metal tall houses
like crystal tumblers with bubbles inside them, and nobody will eat
any living flesh because life will be like champagne!"

Thus did Pyotr Pavlovich Odudovsky attempt to console himself,
subduing his terrible attack of the morning shakes. As usual, he was
with his dog, Mura, standing in line, half-dead, for the Men's Club.
Mura was on her leash, running around her master's quivering legs,
and she was in a very bad mood. A cold, dirty wind was making her
fur stand on end and blowing all sorts of marketplace filth into her
eyes. Old and small, the mother of four litters, Mura knew all her
master's consolations by heart; she did not for a second believe in these
houses like crystal tumblers, and the invariable morning discussion of
the racial problem in the Men's Club irritated her beyond words.

"Be patient, Mura dear, it'll be opening any minute now," Pyotr
Pavlovich whispered imploringly; the little dog sympathized with her
master's spinning head and air pockets, and she put up with the situation, only now and again growling at the revolting, puke-covered shoes
of the alcoholics.

"Say, Alik, have you grown a moustache?" asked Kim, a loader
from the vegetable store. "Trying to turn into a Georgian?"

Alik Neyarky, in the recent past a leading ice-hockey player, folded
his bare arms, which looked like a boa constrictor in the process of
digesting several rabbits, and only grinned in reply.

"So, you think Georgians aren't human?" Sukhovertov, a nervous
male nurse, said to Kim in a squeaky, womanish voice. "I'm asking
you, Kim, you motherfucker, you filthy chauvinist – aren't Georgians
human?"

"Don't push your luck, Sukhovertov, don't push your luck, you dirty
little Mordovian swamp rat." Kim bared his teeth at Sukhovertov and,
turning away, began watching meat being chopped up behind the glass
walls of the market's meat section.

There, standing around the tiled semicircular chopping block, well
educated youths in brand-name eyeglasses, wearing tight imported
T-shirts, were slashing away with cleavers and scientifically hacking

carcasses into pieces. It was a sight that always consoled Kim whenever he felt unable to put up with all the closet half-castes and kikes any longer.

"It's all a pile of shit, comrades," said the internationalist Sukhovertov to no one in particular, grinding his teeth, and to calm himself he began staring into a corner of the fence around the store where there was a heap of old junk: a rusty winch, a carpenter's bench, a headboard, old rags, egg boxes, and milk cartons. In the morning, he felt calmed by the sight of scrap metal and salvage. He secretly imagined that this was his last reserve, that at the critical moment he would set fire to it all, warming himself a little at the blaze, and would use the metal to fashion something like a machine gun to mow down the social chauvinists, that is, the Chinese.

"Kim's right, he's right!" said a new arrival loudly; this was Ishanin, a grizzled Moscow hooligan left over from the thirties. "The entire countryside has flooded into Moscow without residence permits and has bought up all the bread. They're carrying off pretzels by the ton from the Kazan Station, the motherfuckers, goddamn sons of bitches. And we fight for Russia and bust our asses for the Soviets! Am I right, Kim?"

He pressed his fat, flabby stomach up against the loader, farting great whiffs of "Chinese mushrooms," that nauseating drink that in years past adorned every windowsill of the suburb of Petrovskaya.

"One of these days, Ishanin, you'll get fucked in the ass because of your Russia." Kim angrily pushed the old hooligan away from him. "You wouldn't believe it, comrades, but every evening he's carrying on under people's windows, always yelling, Russia, Russia. Yesterday I couldn't stand it any longer, and I poured a kettleful of boiling water all over him. Next time, Ishanin, I'm going to bust you in the kisser!"

Ishanin grunted and staggered back, but he seemed not to understand Kim's entirely reasonable remarks. Wiping his mouth with his cap, he turned to Odudovsky: "Could you possibly let me have thirtyseven kopeks, citizen? I've just come from the isolation hospital. They sent me there for some infectious thing – I'm very contagious."

Pyotr Pavlovich at once produced the required sum, although he knew quite well that Ishanin had been leaving the isolation hospital every day for twenty-five years.

Ishanin put the handful of coins into the bottomless pockets of his pants, wiped his nose and mouth once more on his cap, then suddenly flung himself with a howl at an unknown, tall, lanky man wearing a blue T-shirt. Ishanin's head was his most powerful weapon; his "headers" into the solar plexus always thrilled the veteran habitués of the Pioneer Market, and now the rising generation appreciated them too. The stranger, however, who knew nothing about the past, stared calmly with his alien Latvian eyes at the pointed head, with its tufts of gray hair, that was flying toward him.

"Hup!" Alik Neyarky suddenly let out a deafening grunt and stopped the dangerous charge at the last moment. Say what you like, our "knights of the ice" are well trained! Ishanin waved his legs and howled insanely in the iron arm lock of the ice-hockey star.

"You parasites, you prison-camp whores. Why, with your sort, I'd put it in your mouth. Fuck me in the mouth, I used to drive Marshal Tolbukhin's jeep. If there's a Russian among you, he'll believe me!" howled Ishanin.

A gust of autumn wind suddenly descended on the Men's Club, dousing the huddled men with a burst of cold raindrops and whipping up the wet leaves, cigarette butts, and scraps of paper on the asphalt into a little whirlwind. We all froze in weird poses: Kim, Sukhovertov, Patrick and I, Pyotr Pavlovich, two black students, Fima the butcher, and Alik Neyarky with Ishanin in his arms. And a moment later there arose from the heap of scrap metal Taisia Ryzhikova, a former crane driver, now a chronic alcoholic, who yelled in a horrible voice, "Our poor little white-winged seagull! Our own Valentina the space woman! They've married her off to a hick of a Chuvash!"

Everyone turned toward her. At once forgetting the bitter fate of the birdwoman from Yaroslavl, she minced coquettishly toward the Men's Club with her pigeon-toed walk, in her baggy flannel pants, wriggling her shoulders, from which hung a man's jacket without lapels.

On the counter of the beer joint stood a bowl of salt: FOR REGULAR CUSTOMERS! and Taisia dipped her finger into this bowl.

"I always feel like sucking something salty in the morning," she explained with a vague smile, and lowered her eyes, stiffened, and instantly and utterly, apparently forever, merged with the group of males.

By nine o'clock in the morning, about thirty or forty men had gathered around the bar. The racial problem was discussed with increasing bitterness.

"I did my army time in Moldavia, and I can tell you, those Moldavians are just like gypsies!"

"Where I come from, the potatoes are the size of goat turds, but the Latvians, the sons of bitches – why, their potatoes are the size of lumps of cow shit!"

"They cover them with shit! They shit straight on 'em! Those potatoes grow on Latvian shit!"

"The Koreans eat dogs, you know, and they think it's perfectly normal!"

"It's not the Russian Jews who do the fighting in Israel, but the ones who've always been there."

"We Russians get fucked in the ass by anyone who feels like it!"

"Now the Uzbeks, boys, *they* live well!"

"You're always talking crap about India – India this, India that! I could walk unarmed right through India and I'd strangle them all with my bare hands!"

"Any foreigner can spit in a Russian's eye and get away with it!"

"I was in the Komi Territory, OK? Well, the usual situation – the Karelian lies on the warm stove with a woman, while poor old Ivan the Russian slaves away in the forest!"

"We feed the whole world, the fuckers! We feed the Czechs, we feed the Mongols, we even feed those black-assed Arabs!"

"Extra brand of vodka costs four rubles twelve here, but in Syria our vodka costs fifty kopeks a liter, and nobody drinks it."

"What the fuck do they use it for, then?"

"They clean their guns with it!"

"Ah, the bastards! The sons of bitches!"

Suddenly the shutters in front of the bar were raised with a loud creak, and everyone saw behind the glass of the bar the familiar, glum face of Sophia Stepanovna. "Get in line, you soaks," she said in place of a greeting.

How on earth did our beloved Sophia Stepanovna slip into the bar unnoticed? thought Odudovsky. Surely she doesn't spend the night there? Perhaps she only pretends not to like us in the Men's Club. Maybe she couldn't live without us. I wonder if she sees it as her vocation – to bring us back to life, to cure us when we get the shakes, to lessen our male anguish? But of course, behind that grim exterior she has a heart of gold, of course she has.

Pyotr Pavlovich peered closely. Sophia Stepanovna was washing beer mugs. Her fat fingers, like fetuses pickled in alcohol, moved slowly; her dark though typically Russian features expressed no emotion except permanent, mild ill temper, but Pyotr Pavlovich could see her tender soul behind this exterior and was probably fonder of her than of his own wife, who at that moment was undoubtedly lying on her back with her legs wide open underneath some goatish nogoodnik.

Suddenly Sophia Stepanovna's face raised itself up from the mugs and for an instant something gleamed very brightly in her bloodshot left eye, in the way that a tin can or a sliver of glass sometimes flashes when caught by a ray of sunlight on some wretched city garbage dump.

The sore topic of the racial question long since forgotten in their longing for beer and their eyes all fixed on Sophia Stepanovna, the men all shuddered at this sudden spark of sunlight.

Meanwhile the optical phenomena continued: a golden, sickle-shaped smile broke through, a string of little pearls of sweat shone dully along her upper lip, and this entire rich visual feast was directed, as the men finally guessed, at Yefim the butcher.

"Come into the booth, Yefim," said Sophia Stepanovna with amazing feminine tenderness. "You can wash the mugs."

The Men's Club sighed in amazement: No one in the whole history of the Pioneer Market had ever been accorded such an honor. Pulling in his stomach, proudly swinging his shoulders, and slightly wiggling his little ass, Yefim the young anatomist made his way into the "booth." Instantly, female laughter came tinkling from the semidarkness, water began to pour at twice the speed, there was the clink of small change, and first one beer mug was shattered to fragments, then another, then a third.

"*Mazel tov*, Sophie, *mazel tov!*" roared Yefim. With his right hand he was washing mugs, while his left was caressing the immense ass of Sophia Stepanovna, and singing at the same time, "Come back to Mysore, where the waves break gently on the shore." I ask you, what more could a woman want?

My God, could Sophia Stepanovna Pishchalina, with her looks, ever dream of such a cheerful young man? Of course, good-looking men had made passes at her before, but they had all been given the instant brush-off because their advances were motivated by beer. Stupid prostitutes were prone to overestimate their malodorous charms and underestimate the proud and somber character of the Nymph of the Stream. And this young upstart from the meat trade is washing mugs with her and singing about Mysore, joking with her, spinning yarns about his time in the army, stroking her behind, and for some reason Sophia Stepanovna felt that he wasn't doing it for the beer, that he had the hots for her, old as she was. Even though Yefim, of course, drank beer and drank a lot of it – he never deprived himself of this – so OK, drink, Yefim, drink, if it does you good.

"Beer hits the spot," shouted the volunteer dishwasher. "Ain't that so, Sophy? Right, you guys?"

A tear was trembling on the end of Odudovsky's nose. Good luck to you, Yefim! And to you, Sophia Stepanovna! Kim stood there, baring his teeth in a half-wolfish grin: These goddamn butchers had got their paws on the beer now; next thing, they would be humping it away by the bucketful for the kikes to put in their refrigerators.

But at last the mugs were washed. Down into the city's sewers poured the sad, pale spirochetes, Koch's bacilli tormented by anti-biotics, the tough little devils of staphylococci born in the cavities of rotten teeth.

Here comes the beer! Down goes that first, insatiable gulp of half a mugful, whirlpools of beer around carious cliffs, blobs of froth in folds of the mucous membrane, bubbles on harsh stubble, a delicious shiver throughout the body, and, finally, the warm flush of euphoria, the sign of relief – life's worth living again!

Pyotr Pavlovich grasped two mugs with the fingers of his left hand and two more with his right hand. In his mouth he held the leash of his dog Mura and thus moved toward the wall of the market, to the little stone ledge where he usually settled down with his beer. Mura understood the seriousness of the moment and trotted close alongside, her little body aquiver, as though she too could feel the weight of four full mugs of beer. Putting down three mugs on the stone, Odudovsky made contact with the fourth, a contact of head-spinning intimacy, which is undoubtedly more sensual than all your sexual antics, madam.

The other gentlemen of the Men's Club grunted, groaned, and moaned. Each one took his first mug in solitude, like taking a woman. Then began the socializing. Once again the racial question began to pulsate, but at once the glands of internationalism supervened, and the secretion of brotherly love suppressed the outpourings of the spleen, the supposed seat of chauvinism.

"When I was in the army in East Germany, in our outfit there was an Armenian, a Tadjik, a Mari, and a Jew, who was the army champion in the triple jump. Dodik was his name, short for David. They were all good soldiers."

"And why not? They're all Soviet people, aren't they?"

"People are the same everywhere, ask even a 'negative.' Look, there are a couple of smokies, and they're drinking beer like the rest of us. Watch, I'll ask them. Hey, you guys. Excuse me, but what country are you from?"

"Can't you see? They're Africans."

"Thickhead! There are Africans and there are Africans. Where are you from, boys?"

"From Togo, monsieur. We're from Togo."

"Thanks. So they're Togolese. Glad to meet you."

"Hindi-russi-bhai-bhai!"

"Shut up, Ishanin, you asshole!"

"Have some dried roach, Togolese, Let's get acquainted. My name's Kim."

The black youths, with their doelike eyes, hunched up against the cold, cutting wind and glanced fearfully around the crowd of men, who were as unlike Africans as they were unlike Europeans. The Togolese were already used to the fact that in this strange, vast, badly lit city, people called them "negatives" or "smokies," and that empty taxis raced past them without stopping as though on the way to a fire, and that if Moscow girls talked to them at all they would start giggling nervously and looking around, as though afraid that a black spermatozoon might penetrate their white wombs right in front of all these other honest folk. So the Togolese were now pleasantly surprised by the attention shown to them by this yellow-faced gentleman in the blue bathrobe, Mr. Kim, that is, Kommunist International Movement, the initial letters of which formed the name of this outwardly unpleasant but inwardly nice forty-year-old gentleman. And in order to do something nice for him, they accepted some of his disgusting dried fish and smiled as they gulped it down.

Kim was very proud of his acquaintance with Ufwa and Bwali, the two Togolese. He glanced triumphantly at Sukhovertov – put that in your pipe and smoke it, you shitbag. A new spark of brotherly love had suddenly been struck in this hard-hearted old chauvinist.

We were all amazed and touched by the way in which Kim Koshulin, renowned for his hatred of other peoples, had suddenly struck up such a firm friendship with these blacks. At last, after a forty-year delay, his name, lovingly chosen by his parents in a flush of internationalist enthusiasm in the 1930s, had begun to correspond to reality. We were almost about to start arguing whether Kim would make an offer to the Togolese to split the cost of a bottle of vodka three ways, when Kim, having extracted a ruble and thirty-eight kopeks from each of his new friends, was already grubbing around in search of an empty can. Less than five minutes had passed before the newly formed trio had already downed a glass each of Yerofeyich – beer spiked with vodka.

Having drunk their Yerofeyich, the black students wanted to go, but the charming Mr. Kim clasped them around the waist and rolled his eyes in a cunning leer. "No, I'm not letting you go, Ufwal, or you, Boris! Drinking's OK, but we want to rap a bit, too. 'Cause we're all people, aren't we? Or aren't we? We're not monkeys who just look like people, are we? You and I are not crocodiles. Am I right or wrong? How'd you like me to show you a medium? By the way, he's Alexander Neyarky, once a famous hockey forward. He's a real medium – he can open a beer bottle with his foot. Alik, meet the comrades from the Congo! Togo, did you say? OK, you're right; the main thing is that they're people, that we should all act like human beings. Comrades, which of you has a bottle of beer?"

"Talk sense, Kim!" said the unusually animated Odudovsky, making a sweeping, theatrical gesture. "Who wants bottles of beer here? We're swimming in a sea of beer! It's a beer-drinker's nirvana!"

"Out of the way, asshole, with your bathtub!" shouted Kim, with an echo of yesterday's nightmare. "I need to show my friends here a trick. Alik, could you open a bottle of lemonade?"

Neyarky shrugged his square shoulders. "Just this once, OK."

A bottle of Sayana tonic water was placed on the asphalt in front of Alik, and almost without looking, with an amazing, lightning kick, he removed its metal cap. The bottle made not the slightest movement.

"And the bottle is intact!" screamed Kim. "The bottle is completely intact, comrades!"

He grasped Ufwa by the chest and sprayed his face with a fountain of his sickening yellow saliva. "The bottle's whole. Did you see that, you cunts? Could either of you do a thing like that? I expect you ate the German ambassador, and you have to get kikes from Tel Aviv to open bottles for you, don't you? You black-assed bastards, I'd beat the lot of you into pulp! Cocksuckers!"

Gray with fright, Ufwa tried to save his well-cut Parisian jacket. All those present realized that the idyll was over – Kim was off again! Sukhovertov, his chief opponent in the racial question, pulled Koshulin away from the Togolese, dragged him around the corner of the repair workshop, and sat him down on a pile of boxes.

"Now take it easy, Kim old man," mumbled Sukhovertov. "Say, Kim, what d'you think, will Spartak beat Shakhtyor?"

Sukhovertov could not bear to watch Kim disgrace himself: They were the same age and had spent their lives together, ever since the first postwar soccer championship, when that lousy team Zenith had won the doubleheader.

Kim let himself be hauled away, his fingers gripping the back of his neck, spitting and vomiting a stream of obscene, meaningless abuse.

The Togolese were just about to escape, when another, quite charming, Russian gentleman opened his arms wide to embrace them. It was strange that these black students had never even suspected that right alongside their dormitory was the meeting place of a club devoted to the protection of the developing countries.

Spread out on Pyotr Pavlovich's copy of *Socialist Industry* was a beautiful Ukrainian tomato cut up into large pieces, and several delicious little cucumbers, looking like newly hatched baby crocodiles, surrounding a little mound of Poltava sausage, while two miniature bottles of vodka weighted down the edges of this militant mouthpiece of Soviet industry.

"Help yourselves, mesdames and messieurs!" announced Odudovsky. "I am entirely at your disposal! Alik, would you care to join our little repast?"

"Wait a while, fellows," said the forward in English, winking to the two blacks. "I'm just going to conclude a little deal, and then I'll be right with you."

Clearly, not all the members of the Men's Club spent the mornings in a state of intoxicated prostration. Alik, for instance, had a business meeting with a mechanic from the cooperative service station, the mighty Uncle Tima. You give me a piston in exchange for a set of bearings, you give me a brake disk in exchange for an oil gasket, and so on, the normal business of the automobile racket.

So began the day for the Men's Club in the Pioneer Market. Some of its members felt themselves warmed by the summer sun, some seemed to be lashed by autumnal rain. Some luxuriated, as it were, in a pine bath, while some still seemed up to their necks in snow. Ishanin spent his time wallowing in perpetual slushy mud. Right now, longing to warm himself, he had clasped Taisia Ryzhikova to his body and was trying to button up his overcoat behind her back.

"Hey, Taska, shall I give you a hot rod today? Hows about a hot rod?" he said in a nasal whine.

Taisia smiled vaguely with the upturned whites of her eyes.

In the club I was known as Academician and regarded as one of the boys. I first met Alik Neyarky in the local funny farm after my first dose of Antabuse. Ishanin I once caught trying to rob my apartment; having smashed the locks, he had suddenly been fascinated by the fourth episode of a TV serial called *Adjutant to His Excellency,* and after a few sips of my whiskey he was dozing in front of the tube. Kim, Sukhovertov, and I used to "play the trumpet" together, that is, we would split a bottle of vodka three ways and drink it straight from the bottle in practically every unguarded hallway on our block. Pyotr

Pavlovich Odudovsky and I were once brought together by a common interest in the Hammapada, an enthusiasm for yoga and for India in general; we would call each other up at least ten times a day, and his wife even acquired her own key to my front door.

Often at night I would hear the soft padding of her bare feet in the corridor, then in my sleep I would see, right over my nose, her large naked breast with its pointed nipple, and feel the pricking of her long fingernails on reconnaissance around my perineum. I would have enjoyed these friendly visits if only Madame Odudovskaya had not been in the habit of wailing, at the most energetic moments, in a peculiar voice: "I'm taking off! I'm ta-a-aking o-o-ff!"

I tried to console myself with the thought that it was pretty hard to guess exactly from which apartment in our sixteen-story giant the wild creature was shouting at this particular moment. From the boulevard I had previously heard that cry more than once, but every time I had thought it was just a very well-done radio play.

Patrick Thunderjet greatly loved the Men's Club; he immediately felt at home there. "What a great bunch of guys they are," he would say, looking around at the blue of faces, the colors ranging from earthy to the purplish-blue of alcoholic blotches, adorned with hair-sprouting birthmarks, carbuncles, gold-capped teeth, lackluster eyes, and livid moles. "You can see at once that there's not a square among them! I'd move them all to California."

Following the example of Pyotr Pavlovich, we bought some food at the market and sat down cross-legged under the glass wall of the supermarket to enjoy our aristocratic breakfast. We spiked the beer with pepper vodka and orange liqueur. Between drinks we ate pieces of a strange, soapy, deep-water fish and Roquefort cheese, that putrid, shit-tasting dropout from the otherwise wholesome but dull family of Soviet cheeses, and little "hunter" sausages, stuffed with the revolting lard used by the Consumers' Union, and semiprocessed kidneys made from Indian poultry, and strawberry mousse made of Rumanian oil.

"Hey, Academician!" Alik Neyarky shouted to me from a distance. "I see you're taking the day off!"

"Friend of mine arrived today." I pointed to Patrick Thunderjet with a radish. "An American professor!"

Alik obviously wanted very much to join us, but the Togolese, finally drunk, were dancing a ritual dance around him, and the most that he could do was to clasp his hands over his head. In reply, Patrick blew him a kiss.

"Who's the hit man?" he inquired with enthusiasm.

"You guys barefoot?" Alik shouted to us, adding in English, "New fashion, isn't it?" He banged Ufwa's and Bwali's heads together and began to push his way toward us.

Behind the enormous glass wall that rose up behind us, the supermarket was already open. Now and then an almost miragelike picture appeared: some circus artiste or ballerina would come in, wearing jeans and a blue denim jacket, would pick up some prepackaged goods and depart, furiously wiggling her ass – it might just be Little Europe. But then the picture would at once be ruined by the appearance of an old woman with the downtrodden look of someone who had spent her life standing in line or some bowlegged Uzbek with medals on his velvet robe, and the mirage dissolved.

Suddenly the store manageress appeared and stopped on the other side of the glass wall in front of us. We observed her perfectly finished image. The large and spongy body was barely crammed into her starched white coat, nylons, and shaped, tight-fitting boots; on her head arose a towering edifice of hair. Even that terrifying apparition that haunted our childhood in the natural history textbook *The Hairy Man Adrian Yevtikheyev* could not have provided enough hair for this artifact. For the rest – a double chin like Marie Antoinette's; a button nose in the style of a prewar film star; the stern gaze of Madame Kalashnikova, head of the cultural department; and only in the very depths of her eyes, which were like the twin lakes Elton and Baskunchak, there shone the constant, agonizing desire to stand with her legs apart.

This creature also reminded me of someone from the past, I thought, just like the cashier in the metro, the cloakroom attendant at the institute, the cloakroom attendant in the bar, just like Theodore the mercenary in Katanga. They all recalled memories of something connected with layers of sunlit snow and a black spot on the snow, with a certain region of shame and a certain personality, the little tsar of that region. An informer? A security officer? A captain of the secret service? It must have been the alcohol playing tricks on me, the result of chronic neurosis.

The lips of the manageress moved. She was scolding us for something, pointing out that we had broken some regulation, and was threatening to stop our activity, but we could not hear what she was saying through the glass. The only thing that penetrated was the scent of a perfume called Lights of Moscow.

Just for luck, Patrick waved his hand between his legs. Although I was monstrously drunk, my Soviet reflexes were still working, and as

I envisaged a fifteen-day spell of unfreedom, I suggested to my friend that we should get the hell out of there. Patrick Thunderjet, however, seemed to know the female heart better than I did. He again waved his big hand at the manageress, and the lady suddenly gave a little sigh, seemed to shudder, and this time threatened us with only simulated sternness, then wrote something on a piece of paper and pressed it to the window for us to read: COMRADES SURELY YOU HAVE A HOME WHERE YOU CAN EAT YOUR FOOD, HAVEN'T YOU?

Without collusion we both instantly burst out sobbing so pathetically that the manageress, with all her peasant woman's nature, flung herself toward us, toward these two dirty, unhappy males (Wash them, wash them – BOTH! – Give them food and drink and put them to bed – BOTH OF THEM! – Tuck them in from both sides – BOTH SIDES!), pressed herself to the glass, and suddenly saw our bare feet! Horror transformed her animated features into a mask of popular anger. She recovered herself and carried her property away into the labyrinths of the world's most progressive system of retail trade. I at least knew *this* field better than Patrick did.

"If you don't have anywhere to sleep, boys, come to my place on Begovaya," we heard from behind us, and saw over our shoulders – I on my left, Patrick on his right – a large, bluish face whose eyelids were stuck tightly together.

"You see, boys, I'm a conductor on the Russia Indivisible Express. I don't get any sleep for ten days waiting for all the dirty tricks the Chinese may think up, and the next ten days I relax with whores. I don't mind the work, though, and you're welcome to come to my place on Begovaya. Only I warn you, the place is in a bit of a mess."

The conductor hiccuped and snorted, and a man in a straw hat, on the brim of which lay a thin border of last year's snow, announced in a loud voice, "Why should these boys drag themselves all the way to Begovaya? Just across the tracks I have a cottage in a forest reserve. I'll throw my wife out before I leave these two guys in the lurch!"

The Men's Club came to life and roared, "Who ever heard of leaving friends in the lurch! Better shoot them both! If they've got nowhere to sleep, let's go out to the Collective Farmers' Club at Dmitrov. Come on, Academician, stop farting around. Bring your Latvian along; there's an empty bed every night in our dormitory. We'll find room for you there!"

Suddenly we were surrounded; everyone pressed against us, sniveling and coughing. We were grunting under the pressure of either fraternal or homosexual sympathy, when suddenly from the windows of the nearby dental clinic there poured out an evil pall of black smoke, which spoiled everyone's mood.

The clinic had caught fire all at once, and now, before the eyes of everyone in the Pioneer Market, it was burning away sedately, without panic, without any signs of alarm, except for the occasional glimpse through the smoke of faces contorted with toothache.

Our manageress, meanwhile, had shown great efficiency: She was hurrying toward us with three vigilantes. As she ran, her right arm made a paddling motion, and she irritably flipped aside her left breast, which the rapid movement had caused to balloon out like a spinnaker. Her face was suddenly stamped with something Roman and imperial; she was now clearly acting in the name of the whole country, and her anger was positively godlike.

What a pity. This means the end of the trip, I thought. But just to be on the safe side, I yelled like a hooligan, "Patrick, blow the joint!"

The vigilante squad sliced into the beer-drinking community.

"Run! Run!" shouted Sophia Stepanovna in the lovely high-pitched voice of a teenage girl.

Wet hands grabbed at the manageress, but she charged forward like an experienced rugby player.

Patrick and I hurled ourselves under the vaulted glass roof of the market, rushed around among the carcasses in the meat section, crawled past rows of vegetable stalls, squashing strawberries, choking on pickles. The private sector of trade was on our side. A hail of potatoes and macerated apples flew toward our pursuers, but they broke through the market defenses and caught us. At the last moment, of course, the fire from the clinic spread to the glass walls of the market, which burst magnificently into flames. At once the fire engines drove up, emitting squads of helmeted firemen who reeled out endless hoses – the trap had closed.

The loudspeakers announced in thunderous tones, "The Mitropa train is arriving on Track 1! Passengers are requested to leave the cars and to register *nach Auschwitz, nach Auschwitz, nach Auschwitz!*"

Beneath the glass vaults, hissing a heroic symphony and emitting steam, a locomotive rolled in, swathed in Indonesian garlands with portraits of Vyacheslav Moiseyevich Bulganin and the ears attached to him. The locomotive headed straight for us, crunching melons as it came.

"Come on, let's go!" shouted Patrick and roared with laughter.

The steam, the noise, the stench of the Kursk Magnetic Anomaly, filled the glass cube, which of course soon exploded.

A DOUBLE: GAY COUPLET AND ACROBAT

The smell of old, stagnant urine brought me to my senses. I was sitting on a toilet, my head and shoulder leaning against a badly plastered wall, on which, not far from my eyes, was drawn a peculiar hairy object and a strange little pistol aimed at it.

"He's alive! He's come to!" announced the cheerful gangsterlike voice of Alik Neyarky from nearby.

In my fright I thought I was lying on the wall as though it were the floor and the toilet was somehow stuck to my behind. Then in a muddled way, spatial orientation began to come back to me. Lavatory graffiti, unknown faces of close friends, countless little cardboard tickets on the floor, pages of a race program – finally it sank into my consciousness that I was sitting on a john in the men's room of the city racetrack.

At one time this men's room had been fitted out with little enclosed cubicles with doors that locked. After losing your shirt, you could hang yourself in one of these closed cubicles without much trouble. People used to say that once, in the early fifties, a famous racetrack gambler called Mandarin, having scooped a quarter of the pari-mutuel pool on a "blind" bet, went to empty the superfluous brandy from his male organ, carelessly pulled open the door of the second cubicle, and saw hanging inside it his friend the transpolar flier Yaro-Golovansky. Then, so the story goes, Mandarin burst into bitter tears and traced the outline of his buddy on the wall with red pencil, not forgetting, drunk though he was, to add the contour of the airman's legendary pipe. Maybe the racetrack habitués are lying, but the outline, complete with pipe, has remained to this day on the wall of the second cubicle and can be seen showing through seven layers of enamel paint.

The new age of humanism has also left its mark on the men's room at the racetrack: The cubicle walls have been sawn off almost down to navel height, making it practically impossible to hang oneself.

From the blur of unknown friendly faces, a familiar one suddenly swam into focus – the racetrack regular Marcello, his inseparable cigarette holder between his teeth, his inseparable Ronson, and a "Campaign for Nuclear Disarmament" badge in his buttonhole. The sight of Marcello delighted me. I watched with pleasure as his supposedly imperturbable features played tricks with the supposedly tragic wrinkles around his supposedly Gothic nose and the Jacobin furrow on his brow.

"What did I do at the market, Marcello?" I asked him. "Be a pal and tell me. Let me have it straight. Don't leave a criminal in torment."

"Don't play the fool, Academician," said Marcello in his grating, monotonous voice. "You'd do better to give me a tip for the next race."

He handed me the race program, and I was overjoyed: Obviously I had done nothing very bad at the market, otherwise Marcello would hardly have offered his race program to a known criminal.

I looked at the form, spattered with little crosses, zeroes, and zigzags in Marcello's cryptic cuneiform, and I actually laughed with amazement – I immediately saw in it my sign, my lucky combination, an obvious winner.

"A double on Gay Couplet and Acrobat."

"Don't talk crap," grated Marcello. "Gay Couplet has had a hernia hanging down to his knees since last spring, and they use Acrobat to haul drums of oil down on the collective farm at Ramenskoye."

"A double on Gay Couplet and Acrobat," I repeated, thinking that if these two old nags didn't win, I'd better find a men's room with cubicles that locked.

"Place a ruble bet for me, Marcello. I'll pay you back later," I begged him.

Without altering his expression, the gambler nodded and started to go, but then turned around and stared at me intently; clearly I had sown the seeds of doubt in his brilliantined head.

The men's room suddenly emptied: everyone was hurrying to the betting windows. I got up from the john and walked over to a mirror.

> . . . Me, me, me . . . what a hideous word!
> Can that thing there be me?
> Did my mother really love a thing like that?

Staring at me from the mirror was an exceptionally pale creature with sunken cheeks and bags under the eyes. He might equally well have passed for twenty-eight or forty-eight. He was sallow, oh, how sallow, while those hollow cheeks, the long hair, the loathsome pallor, and the lips quivering on the brink of hysteria gave him both a certain viciousness and an oddly youthful look. The sternocleidomastoid muscle in his neck and the dark, thin sweater on his bony shoulders even added something of a sporting touch.

Looking at me was an obviously unreliable, socially alien, morbidly sexual, and suspicious type of person, whose sufferings were not worth a bent penny. I began to stare at him intently and suddenly realized that he was on the point of crying out, that he was barely restraining himself from breaking into a horrible, revolting kind of howl. I stared even harder into his alien gaze, and then I ran away, covering my face with my hands.

I lost my footing and slipped on the disgusting black slime that covered the tiled floor. From behind me, from the depths of the toilets, I could already hear an approaching howl, when I suddenly saw beneath me two bare, swollen, unbelievably dirty feet. They brought me back to my senses, because they were mine, undoubtedly mine. They were my very own unfortunate feet.

What on earth was I to DO with such feet? I couldn't even go out of the men's room on feet like that!

Suddenly the doors were flung open and in poured a noisy wave of roaring, grunting, laughter, and swearing. Shouting at the top of their lungs, the men angrily threw down wads of betting slips onto the floor, then ripped open their fly buttons and pulled out their tools.

"Hey, don't you piss in my pocket!"

From odd remarks I picked up that Gay Couplet had won the last race. Strangely enough, this news greatly encouraged me, and I stopped thinking of all my other horrors. I pushed my way through the gamblers and without fear – on the contrary, with great good humor – I glanced into the mirror, where a very close stranger was lurking in the crowd. Then I saw in the mirror that Marcello was approaching him, or rather me.

"There you are." He handed me a little blue betting slip for my double on Gay Couplet and Acrobat. "You've started off well; I've crashed. You owe me a ruble. By the way, it seems that no one except you has bet on that gelding. You know, I often bet against the stable too, but I have reliable information that the stable isn't betting today. There was a Party meeting yesterday, and one of the drivers denounced another, and there was an almighty row. Today everything is on the level – Marshal Budyonny is in the grandstand, the police band is playing, and only the favorites are supposed to win today. If that Acrobat of yours wins, I'll eat my glasses." He said all this in a monotone, standing in a fixed pose with a streak of smoke coming from his cigarette holder, while I shuffled from foot to foot, giggling stupidly.

"OK, Academician, let's go up to the grandstand."

"But I don't have any shoes. You see . . . it's kind of embarrassing . . ."

"Don't talk crap. You've got to be there to watch Acrobat drop out of the running at the second turn."

All was gaiety in the grandstand. Jostling in the crowd were drunken movie actors, traumatized athletes, tight-lipped kings of the black market, poverty-stricken writers, a few nice women – all more or less familiar faces from my trips around the bars. Before I had had time to look them over, I suddenly felt a quiver of excitement that foretold an imminent meeting, and in the next moment I saw the beautiful, reddish-blond Alisa.

"Hi there!" she said. "So it's you!"

She narrowed her eyes and looked as if she was expecting me to take some decisive step. What, here? Right here, in the racetrack grandstand, with everyone watching? I was overcome with confusion.

"What's so special about it?" I growled. "So it's me."

"That's what I said, so it's you," she retorted cheerfully and immediately lost all interest in me.

Her attention was taken up with her current lover, a habitué of Moscow café society, either an operetta singer or an officer in the international branch of the KGB.

Jealousy exploded inside me and lit up all the colors of the world around me. I saw the green oval of the grass racetrack and the flickering blobs of the jockeys' multicolored silks, the gleaming backbones and rumps of the horses, the windows of Moscow flashing in the sunlight, the clouds like curly-haired cupids, the trumpets of the police band, the white summer tunic of the legendary, bewhiskered cavalry marshal, the First Cavalry Army, and the First Five-Year Plan, and the First World War, and every other First you can think of.

"Hey, you, don't lose your temper!" said Alisa from behind the back of her escort. "You'd better meet my husband. He's a famous designer of tractors."

Looking at me was a middle-aged man, bursting with health and strength, looking like the astronaut David Scott. Now there's a real man, I thought, a real hero who completely outclasses all her other studs, all that cheap Moscow riffraff. Yes, I found myself liking the bemedaled Fokusov, my fellow runner in the stakes for Alisa's love.

"Glad to meet you, if we haven't met already," I said, giving him the chance not to remember about the disorderly goings on in Koktebel.

"Delighted," he replied, taking the chance with restrained gratitude.

"I believe you and I played tennis once," I lied, in order to do him another favor.

"When?" he asked in surprise.

"Right after a dress rehearsal at the Taganka and before dinner at the Uzbekistan." Tennis, the Taganka Theater, *lagman* soup at the Uzbekistan Restaurant – all the pastimes of the Moscow playboy; I admit I forgot to include the Finnish sauna. Out of the corner of my eye I noticed the international KGB man stroking Alisa's ass.

"Sorry, I don't remember," said Fokusov, embarrassed.

"I saw one of your offspring," I said. "A delicious creature."

Alisa's fingers, I noticed, were slithering over the hips of the good-looking piece of trash.

"Thank you," Fokusov beamed. "I miss them all the time, you know. If it weren't for my wife –"

"I understand, I understand."

I noticed that Alisa's mouth was half open and her eyes half closed, and the singer and/or KGB man was grinning very slightly; obviously that gentle stroking aroused many memories for him.

"Maybe I ought to chuck it all," said Fokusov lightly, showing me that he was capable of making fun of himself.

"You don't drink, I hope?" I inquired.

"Perhaps I should drink," he whispered. Gloom unexpectedly broke through all his protective layers, and he looked me straight in the eyes as though begging me not to reveal a secret.

Suddenly a plump, dark little woman, Silly Zoika, bobbed up in front of us. "Super news, comrades! Afanasy has gotten a new apartment and everyone's invited!"

"Yes, it's open house, open house!" slobbered her fiancé, a completely talentless songwriter called Afanasy Seven-For-Eight. "Please come. But there's nothing to eat yet in the house, gentlemen, so buy something – salmon, caviar, smoked eel – in the foreign-currency store, and come as you are. It's open house for stars of the arts and sciences. You come, and you . . . It will be a kingdom of poetry, music, party games, mild flirtation. We can surely keep within the limits of good taste, can't we, comrades?"

He wriggled his way around the dirty grandstand, treading on everyone's toes, looking into their eyes, and when he appeared between me and Fokusov, he began to tremble and quiver like a spawning perch. He had been drunk, of course, for at least three days, and he was emanating a sort of desperate nausea, that same sludge from which, I thought, I had just managed to drag myself out into the sane world, into a world of grass and horses, of the tanned sportsman who designed tractors, of his red-haired whore of a wife with her charming ruses, into a world lit up by the youthful glare of jealousy.

I jabbed my hand under Afanasy's ribs and rudely pushed him away from me.

"Academician is up to his usual tricks," said Afanasy with a twisted smile.

At that moment a bell rang and the horses were off.

"Apollo! Apollo!" "Botanist! Botanist!" "Spring Horizon!" roared the crowd.

I realized that I had not had time to notice the breed of my favorite, my lame cart horse from the Ramenskoye Machine-Tractor Station. Nevertheless I yelled the cherished name, "Acrobat! Acrobat!"

Several faces from the lower seats turned around as I shouted.

"The guy's crazy! He's rooting for Acrobat!"

Next moment the hospitable but vengeful Afanasy punched me hard from behind in the right kidney. I doubled up in pain.

The bastard, he's smashed my kidney! I dig him in the ribs and he goes for my kidney! Violence has triumphed, Count Tolstoy! Are you stroking my hair, madam? Do you want to soothe my pain by stroking me, madam? I'm waiting for you, distant wind of childhood. No, not you, madam? I see you're wearing a skirt of cowboy material. May I blow my nose? Are you married to a cowboy? I'm a cowboy! Take my gun, madam, and avenge the Ringo Kid.

While I fantasized thus, squatting on my haunches and grinding my teeth from the pain, Afanasy was sobbing on my shoulder, and the grandstand was roaring as though a TU-104 were accelerating along the runway to take off. The pain had stopped, and I straightened up at the very moment when the sweat-soaked, dappled Acrobat, its neck stretched out, was crossing the finish line. The other horses, heavy favorites, were limping along in a straggling bunch about fifty meters behind.

I never did discover what happened to that mare or to the rest of the horses, and at that moment I didn't care. The punch landed by the revolting Afanasy had flung Cinderella out of her first ball back into the kitchen. Everything sane, sportsmanlike, and amorous faded into the background and froze there in a frame, like a little picture to which no one is paying any attention. I was roaring with laughter like a madman, stuffing Marcello's Japanese glasses down his throat; laughing like a maniac as I saw the figure of my winnings hoisted on the pari-mutuel board − 2,680 rubles 97 kopeks. I laughed like a crazy fool, clasping my best friend and future co-author, Afanasy; laughed like a madman as I made an indecent proposition to Silly Zoika, his fiancée; laughed like a madman when she agreed to it; laughed like a madman as I gulped the brandy brought to me from the bar as part of the spoils of victory; laughed like a madman as I made for the pay-out window, surrounded by a mob of excited admirers; laughed like a madman as I took the money; laughed like a madman as I stuffed it down my shirtfront and pulled my belt tight lest I lose a single kopek.

"That's so as not to lose a single kopek," I explained to my admirers, laughing like a madman.

"With a win like that, it's customary to give something to the cashier," said Marcello, trying to maintain his fastidious expression.

"I won't give her a kopek!" I said, again bursting into laughter like a madman. "I prefer to send it to her later by mail. Give me your address, madam!"

I looked at the cashier in the window and shrieked with delight: It was my favorite cashier from the metro, Nina Nikolayevna. She looked at me with a gentle autumnal smile and recognized me – she recognized me, the darling.

"Good morning, Sergei Vladimirovich," she said in her sweet voice, and although she had called me by the wrong name, it was me she meant.

"Why aren't you in the metro, Nina my dear?" I exclaimed.

"The work's more interesting here," she explained with embarrassment. "It's more creative."

"I see, I see," I said hurriedly, nodding. "So you're alive, you're not dead, it was a lie."

My hand went to my shirtfront, but then stopped for some reason.

"Do you need money, Vera Nikolayevna?"

"It's up to you, Sergei Vladimirovich."

"I guess I'll send it to you by mail, anyway. Please give me your address."

"My address is always 'General Delivery, Central Post Office.' Don't send me any money if you don't want to, but simply write to me when you are discharged from the hospital."

"But I'm not planning to go to the hospital, Vera Nikolayevna!"

"That's good. I'm very glad to hear it." Smiling gently, she bent over her papers and started to add up some figures.

"Everything is the will of God," she said in a barely audible voice, and I suddenly realized with dazzling clarity that she was not referring to blind fate but to a living and intelligent God.

What had happened to me? To what depths had I sunk? Had I been drinking long? How long had I been standing with my bare feet on the floor and a wad of sticky money down my shirtfront?

The window's little oval shutter closed, and the rubbery tits of Silly Zoika crashed into my shoulders at full speed from behind.

"It seems someone else bet on the same double as you did!" she squealed. "Otherwise you'd have won more than five grand."

I knew of course that my unknown friend was somewhere here, and I was not very surprised when triumphant cries again reverberated from the ceiling of the pay-out hall. A pair of blackened feet, size forty-six, floated into the hall, borne along above the heads of the crowd. My unknown friend, the second winner, turned out to be Professor Patrick Thunderjet, doctor *gonorris causa* of Oxford and Prague. What joy – we had found each other again!

"It's lucky to be barefoot today," people all around were saying. "A couple of nuts have escaped from the funny farm."

Patrick had won exactly the same amount as I had – 2,680 rubles 97 kopeks – and, following my example, he had stuffed the whole bundle down his shirtfront. We burst into tears of happiness and embraced, pressing our money against each other.

Out on the street, Patrick wanted to know where to find the nearest police station. "I want to ask for political asylum in Moscow," he explained. "I like this neck of the woods."

At that moment there descended upon him the darling of the capital, Alik Neyarky, his cunning glance swiveling in every direction.

"Vood you laik a chick? I've found you a vuman, Pat, who'll make your head spin. She can do it any way you like, oll kainds ov lav, I promise you!"

"I don't feel like women at the moment. I am about to *act*! I'm going to make myself famous on television, so full speed ahead to the Ostankino TV tower! The confessions of an old American stool pigeon! For years I reported to the FBI on my friends Edward Albee, John Updike, Art Buchwald, and Bob Hope in order to get permission to travel to the world of socialism. Where is the police?"

"Here's the police," said Alik Neyarky, showing the ID card of a senior lieutenant of the Ministry of Internal Affairs.

The American began swinging himself around a lamppost. "Ah, Russia, my Russia, beloved homeland!" he shouted. "Bridges, we must build bridges! We must build them, and then we can burn our bridges and our boats!"

Meanwhile Silly Zoika and Afanasy Seven-For-Eight were still rushing around the racetrack collecting guests. When they seemed to have scooped up about a hundred people or so, they all set off in taxis and in official cars moonlighting as taxis somewhere in the direction of Izmailovo, or Chertanovo, or Khoroshovo, or it may have been Cherkizovo. Oh, those beautiful little villages that once belonged to the boyar Kuchka, what obscenities have been committed on your wooded slopes since the days when packs of hounds hunted here and Princess Ulita, that most ancient of Russian nymphomaniacs, held her orgies!

The party chartered an army amphibious truck. Inside, in the darkness, defended by good solid Urals armor, it was swarming with people looking for a glass. Naturally there were no glasses to be found, so we drank out of the bottle. There I switched off from reality and flew off into circumlunar regions, where I orbited without dreams and without memories.

I was awakened by the gleam of black, blue, and white tiles. Kneeling in front of me was Silly Zoika, with a bare midriff and fragments of a bra clinging to her voluptuous globes. Water was cascading everywhere, little rainbows shining in the spray around the faucets. Her eyes glistening, Silly Zoika was busy performing on my whistle, now acting the flutist, now the clarinetist, then inserting it into secret places, looking like the cat that has swallowed the canary. When the concert came to its inevitable end, she heaved a sigh of regret and her twin balloons seemed to deflate. Subsiding onto the rug, she shook her curly locks and uttered some incomprehensible gobbling sounds.

Patrick came in and sat down on the edge of the bathtub.

"M-m-m-mm," purred Silly Zoika and crawled over to his feet. Her eyes began to glisten again. "Mmm-mmm, another redcap to eat. Mmm."

Afanasy put his head through the door. "Academician, you're needed urgently!"

I went out of the bathroom, and he gripped me hard by the elbow. "Not bad, this apartment, is it?" He looked me in the eyes. "It's so convenient to have the bathroom and the john separate: You can wash while the other guy craps, and nobody's embarrassed. Wait until we get married in the fall, then we'll furnish the place; for the moment we don't have anything except three polar-bear skins, a present from a fan of my songs in the Arctic Circle. My lyrics are selling like hot cakes these days, old man. Your days are over; now it's the turn of us little guys. You must come and eat pies in the fall! Zoika's a genius at baking pies. See here, Academician, you're very arrogant and I'm doing my best to be friends with you when I could easily hand you over to the KGB, instead of which I'm making you an offer of co-authorship. How about us collaborating on an operetta but under my name? By the way, Academician, they're looking for you. You jumped! Ha, ha, ha, the Academician's frightened! Don't worry, it's only your wife, or rather the mother of your children, as she calls herself. Also, someone called Marianne called up for you – who's she? – and both the American Embassy and Intourist are looking for that American professor who's cleaning his teeth in the bathroom. And that's not all, Academician. Excuse the question, but you're not by any chance a Jew, are you? You seem to have rather curly hair. Let's have a look. Ah, no, you're not Jewish; that's good Russian flax on your head. Oh, yes, two nuns called up from Zagorsk; they are very anxious that you shouldn't go looking for them. I've given my address to practically everyone; sooner or later they'll all turn up here. Come on, Academician, let's go and join the guests. They're all listening to music.''

Afanasy's guests saw themselves as the intellectual elite. The music, of course, was something old. For Afanasy, music apparently stopped in the eighteenth century. I had heard this said by more than one Moscow snob. OK, let them say that, as long as they listen to European church music. There's always a chance that this long-lived music may change something for the better in this pigsty; at least it isn't harmed by being the object of a modish cult in Moscow.

Now that music is rocking, gently rocking your boat, and you float off in several directions at once, in all your ages at once; in your past you no longer see tedious slanders but only wistful charm, and you float through the hideous present into a calm future, and even this hideous present, drunken and shameful, is colored by the ancient charm of Europe.

The record ended and Alik Neyarky, with a brief sigh, arose from the bear skin.

"Iskyooz me. I must go to the bathroom for a moment and clean my teeth."

Afanasy crawled over another bear skin toward me and whispered with his slobbering maw, "What's the matter, Academician, feeling sad? Want something to eat? What a dog's life this is – you can't get so much as a piece of bread in Moscow after ten o'clock, can you? In the West, I expect, you only have to clap your hands and a hot-dog stand will roll up, isn't that so? What country are you planning to go to right now?"

"To Assland," I said. "Then I'm going to New Ballsland – the capital is Shit City. Ever hear of it?"

Trustingly, Afanasy laid his head on my knees. In the semidarkness his face took on almost classical proportions. "Persecution mania, that's what is destroying our intelligentsia," he said affably. "We can't close ranks and function as a team. Let me ask you a straight question: When is this whole bordello going to collapse?"

"There are enough whores in it to last out my time."

"I, on the other hand, hope it'll all go up in flames in a year or two. Your prognosis is not so optimistic, is it? I suppose you give it no less than five years, am I right? Listen, Academician, is it true that in the Pioneer Market today one of our people overturned some stalls and shouted slogans?"

"It's true," I said, and stopped a quarter-bottle of vodka with my foot as it rolled past us. "It's true, but not quite. It wasn't in the Pioneer Market but in the Byelorussian Station, and the poor guy wasn't shouting slogans but he was shouting 'Help' because he had fallen under the dining car of the Mitropa express."

"Oh, details, details!" exclaimed Afanasy, but I pressed the empty quarter-bottle against his Adam's apple, at which he obediently fell silent.

A new record started playing. Pergolesi. The guests were slithering over the bear skins to watch a rare sight – a stool pigeon being strangled in his own apartment.

The slightly moth-eaten maxiskirt of one of the ladies slid up and revealed the delicious, bulbous behind of our barmaid Sophia Stepanovna. Alongside the badly stuffed and slightly smelly head of the polar bear lay the head of a movie critic wearing green eyeglasses and smiling the wolfish smile of Kim the vegetable loader. Surely the whole of our popular Men's Club wasn't here in the role of the intellectual elite? Could it be that among the guests was . . . Yes, he was! The head of the polar bear was staring at me with a terrible, contemptuous look, in exactly the way that Captain Cheptsov used to look at Tolya von Steinbock. Captain Cheptsov! Do you remember, Alisa? Alisa, save me, I've remembered his name! Run, Alisa, he's getting close, just behind this mound. Throw away your snowshoes – the snow won't swallow you up!

Alisa Fokusova was standing alone against a background of a greenish, frost-covered window, silent and calm, as though she really had found safety in a hut of the Third Medical Complex. She was alone, and I only had to make the slightest effort in order to have her before her husband and her current lover appeared. Well, make that small effort, get up, push aside all these ugly faces. But then the husband and the lover entered the frosty square and the whole trio turned away – they were listening to the music of Pergolesi!

The bathroom door creaked and another trio emerged – Neyarky, Thunderjet, and Silly Zoika, who was chewing an enormous mouthful of ginseng.

"Squeeze him harder, my friend," Alik said to me, meaning my pressure on Afanasy's throat. "If you can't manage by yourself, we'll come and help you."

"He's still got to sing," I objected. "Sing, Seven-For-Eight, sing your favorite song!"

Afanasy cleared his throat and began singing like a distant, threatening choir:

> Oh, airplane, into the distance winging,
> Keep me safe in your heart, I beg;
> Beneath the airplane's wing is singing
> A piece of an airplane's leg.

"Now you're both in excellent shape," said Neyarky as he pinned badges of his sports club on our chests. "Have a good flight, boys! Keep your eyes peeled, though – syphilis stalks the streets in the south, you know!"

We walked down a badly lit glass corridor, while outside its walls the massive tails of huge aircraft loomed out of the smoky mist. In the nocturnal gloom, the lean torsos of Tupolevs and the ponderous bellies of Antonovs seemed so unsuitable in shape that they might have been quite unable to fly but simply have been meant to stand there as part of the scenery depicting an "airport at night," because our age cannot do without mass hallucinations.

"That Alik is a fool," grumbled Patrick. "He stuck the pin of his idiotic badge right into me."

"Me too," I said. "But it doesn't hurt at all."

"It doesn't hurt me either, but it's unpleasant. The sort of joke that Jan Strudelmacher would have played. I swear, I'll pay him back for it when we make camp under the walls of Danzig."

I shot a quick glance at Thunderjet, but he seemed to be expecting this glance and nodded to me with a very serious expression.

"Do you think that Alik was in our detachment back in those days?"

In the sunset haze I saw before me the helmets of a body of soldiers marching in step and their shoulders festooned with junk looted from the city of Magdeburg; I also saw our prince, floating along on horseback at the head of the column, but I could not recall a Jan Strudelmacher.

"I don't remember Jan. The centuries have blurred my memory."

"Yet you tramped along behind him for the best part of two years, until the Swedish cuirassiers hacked him to pieces in the battle of Kielce."

At that, there arose before me the vision of a broad back and blued steel shoulder plates, a sack of half-strangled turkeys, and the sable boa that had belonged to the duchess of Blois, a rusty crossbow, a Tatar sword and a tarred pigtail hanging over a leather collar.

"Now I remember! He had once been in the crew of a pirate ship and wore a pigtail that smelled of whale oil!"

"That's it." Patrick nodded with satisfaction. "And that is none other than your Alik Neyarky."

The boarding of the night plane took place calmly and peacefully. The passengers mounted the gangway yawning and talking almost in whispers; the lights in the passenger cabin were dimmed, and the stewardesses too were yawning.

Even so, there was one good lady in the back of the plane who started to make a fuss. "It's an insult to the rest of us! Look at them, getting into a plane with bare feet! Call out the vigilantes! You men, don't you see them?"

The voice of this woman was very familiar to me, while Patrick strained all his attention in the direction from which the voice was coming, and his unshaven cheeks began quivering.

"It's her, it's her. She's the leader of the National Unity Party of Bechuanaland! I'm scared, Joe! How did she get on this plane? Where are we flying to, Joe?"

"Relax, relax. I'm not Joe, and she's not the leader of anything, just the manageress of a Soviet store. Sit down, old man, we're taking off in a moment and they'll bring you a glass of hot milk."

I clasped my friend around the shoulders and sat him down in a seat. To distract his attention I asked him to tell me how he had paid back Jan Strudelmacher for his stupid practical joke.

Suddenly Patrick burst into roars of uncontrollable laughter, and his face was streaked with dirty tears.

"By bad luck, this jackal and I were once on the same basketball team. We came to San Diego for the playoff games, and they put us

up in a motel on the beach. The heat was unbelievable, even for those
parts, and that brute Jan spent all the time snoozing on his bed. One
day I took the boys into his room and shoved a live lobster up his
pants. Just imagine, he was used to saying "Good morning" to his
ever-stiff totem pole, but this time a monster with claws crawls out of
his pants! You're not laughing, Joe? Do you think it's disgusting? I
agree. But what can you do with these louts? Pigs, bastards – all they're
looking for is a scapegoat. In our outfit in Danang there was a young
medic, a quiet kid; so every evening without fail someone would piss
on his cot. Can you believe it, Joe, after that filthy trick with the
lobster the guys on the team actually began to respect me. That's
human nature for you! A wolf wouldn't dream of mocking his buddy.
Do you remember, we talked about it when we were in the spaceship?
I used to think that at least in space human nature would change for
the better, if only because of being weightless, but one day I saw Rusk
shove a piece of soap into Suarez's life-support system, and then he
rolled around with laughter as he watched his comrade twitching and
jerking. Then I realized that nothing would change, even if we were
to colonize Jupiter. All my life I've been pursued by cruel, stupid
practical jokes! I can't go on, Joe! I can't stand it any longer! I wouldn't
be surprised if even you were to stick a nail up my ass, or if the
stewardess gave me a glass of dissolved lime instead of milk. What is
it, Joe? Satanism? The victory of evil over good, the triumph of the
forces of darkness? Surely not. I guess even the devil must be ashamed
at the mean little tricks human beings play on one another!"

The breathless, gurgling sound of English being spoken from the
rear seats had begun to attract the other passengers' attention, and
they were turning around to look at us. At any moment we were likely
to find ourselves in a police station instead of the Crimea. I put my
hands over Patrick's eyes and mouth. "Go to sleep, old man."

He still went on growling, "Fuck . . . fuck . . . go fuck yourself . . .
fuck myself . . . fucking world . . ." but less and less loudly.

Finally a sign lit up – something about smoking or fastening seatbelts,
or about fastening unsmoked cigarette butts, or about smoking unfastened seatbelts, or something. The stewardess came down the aisle
laughing as she said, "Which of you is barefoot, comrades? There's a
lady who's upset about it."

The cabin door was still open, through which could be seen the
dark-blue, silvery night, and silence floated in, when suddenly . . .
Suddenly came cries of people in pursuit, a drunken man's shout of
resistance, and there clattered up the gangway and burst into the cabin

none other than Alik Neyarky himself in a flood of tears. His normally imperturbable, centurionlike features now looked like the face of old Auntie Paraskeva when the dough starts slithering away out of her hands. Such metamorphoses, incidentally, are not unknown in ice hockey. The defenseman Ragulin, for instance, when his team loses, begins to look like Grizodubova, the woman pilot of the 1930s.

Alik hurled himself bodily at us, kissed us and said, sobbing, "Boys! I got as far as the Udarnik movie theater and I suddenly thought, maybe I'd pricked you with the pins of my badges! I thought I remembered our Pat frowning a bit when I gave him a supporter's badge. I almost threw myself off the Kamenny Bridge, boys! Did I hurt you, friends? Let me take out those fucking pins! Don't be afraid. I once took a course in first aid. There we are! Is that better? Spit in my face, Arik! Spit! I've brought you a half-liter of vodka, you guys, dear boys, doves of peace and spring! That hooker Zoika, after she sucked us off, know what she said to me? She said, 'Turn them in to the KGB; you'll be promoted and we can get married.' 'Why you whore,' I said. 'You'd rather say goodbye to your virginity than Alik Neyarky drop his pals in it for the sake of another shitty star on his shoulder! I'll kill you! I'll kill you and myself and this airplane and Aeroflot and SAS and KLM . . . ' "

These terrible threats seemed at odds with the hockey forward's frightened expression. He was obviously trembling at the approach of the stewardess. I pushed him into his seat and walked toward the stewardess myself. "*Przepraszam, pany*, it's our scuba diver – he was left behind from our expedition because his sister was having a baby, but we can't wait. We're filming, and all the costs are in foreign currency!"

A wad of ten-ruble bills, pulled out of my shirtfront, clinched the argument. The stewardess nodded in silence, watching in horror as Alik, gesturing to Patrick, with a finger on the side of his nose, produced and stuffed into the American's mouth pieces of white fish, olives, pickles, salad, and blobs of mayonnaise. It was quite obvious that he had pinched it all from someone else's table at a restaurant.

"Don't be afraid," I whispered. "That man is building up the other one's faith in the human race."

Somehow or other the plane took off with all three of us on board. My companions immediately fell asleep and started snoring like two auxiliary jet engines, while I looked out of the window for a while, until the plane had entered its favored region – the space above the endless, dusty wilderness, where dreams wander.

A Midsummer Flight's Dream

That night on the Nevsky by the soda machine
    we capered around
    the machine belched
    in exchange for coppers the beer streamed out
    the kvass streamed
    and lemon urine
    streamed out too.
The machine grumbled at its sordid lot:
    "I hand out drinks to prowling drunks and hookers
    I pander to their passions
    in the guise of a cheap and sticky yucky soda machine
    though at my birth I was meant to be
    a living, breathing, supple leopard."
We laughed as we thought of terrible things
    we laughed as we thought of black black things
    yet the night was traditionally bright
    and we laughed as we gulped our lemonade
What common interests though
    what community of minds
    what unity of gesture could there be
    as the yellow traffic lights among the Admiralty foliage
    winked at us?
Our city was empty
    but for an excited crowd of Lenin statues –
    bald sacred heads and metal pants
    big tie
    decent vest
    and such very clean shoes –
    striding along, repeating that order reigned in the city
    that the city was sleeping only sleeping
    exhausted by the strange mysteries of the polar night
There goes a dandy – a parrot on his shoulder
    the ambassador of Democratic Guinea
    and a Greek from Petersburg Judea
    member of the Bavarian Academy
    dancer poet fiddler harpist
    Alice the Vixen
    the good Mr. Toby who was in the retreat to Dunkirk
    without a residence permit

and with a flea on a leash
We laughed all the way down the long long street
   to the Moscow Station
   and Klodt's four horses laughed along with us
   their mouths of bronze soundlessly opened
   and lumps of horse shit fell into the Fontanka
   making silent ripples in the water
For all its marble features
   this city was blind quite blind
   yet still there was something it could see –
   perhaps the silence –
   it shuddered in secret alarm
   looked through the gap between the drapes
   and with its marble features saw Hollow City
   on the threshold of enemy occupation
Ah so our city is occupied
   admit it
   yes we are expecting the enemy any minute
   yes I sadly admit it but
   from now on
   our life isn't worth a kopek
Let us be absolutely honest
   at any moment citizen you can be
   bumped off in the street
   and your wife
   can be raped in any doorway
But where are they?
They haven't shown up yet
But who are they?
Why do you have to ask such absurd and fruitless questions
   which only proclaim the banality of your mind?
All very well for you to make jokes like some aging
   satyr in rancid pants
   no one is chasing you –
   but where can I hide myself?
Father of many children am I
   with the looks of a handsome bitch
   my numerous wives in alleyways
   and a suitcase stuffed with money
Horrors
   here comes the occupying force

hear the creak of wheels
hear the sound of voices around the corner
They will drive cautiously along Brodsky
   turn into Naiman
   blaze along Rhine
   rush along Stakelberg to Auerbach
   and only pull up when they reach Pekurovskaya
It's time to sneak away
   there is a certain pharmacy
   inside is a bookstore and some folding cots
   steel shutters
   supplies of food
   and Coffin-Nail brand cigarettes
   no need to
   shun that brand
   smoke half a pack
   and you will gently float away toward Nirvana
   where the green dragon blooms like the lilies like the tender aloe
   where a hundred cobras wriggle in the swamp
   and amid them gleaming like a butterfly
   there swims a pinko Soviet Tarzan
But where is that pharmacy
   where is the butcher's shop
   where is our haven our refuge
   illumined by intellect and beauty
   where is the quiet house of prayer
   and where, pray, do they send the ashes
   of brave bewhiskered artists?
As we walked along the Nevsky
   an invisible tidal wave rolling at our heels
   devouring all traces
   sweeping away the bronze the marble and the gilt
   cleaning up the gobs of spittle
   swallowing up young people
   consuming urns, it cleansed the Hollow City
   devastated the wilderness, swallowing all that remained
   of long-past pleasures
Please come here
   it's quiet here and thoroughly respectable reliable and tasteful
   we're all friends here
   a solid Swiss defense

a mound of medicines like an altar
Bulat Okudzhava is sitting here
looking like some Buddha
sitting like a fakir in eyeglasses
over his chemicals
stirring the reagents with a glass rod
shuffling powders with a guileless smile
When Bulat oh, when did you master the science
in which even Gay-Lussac admitted failure?
IT WASN'T AN EASY MATTER, COMRADES!
Hardly had we settled down and taken off our overalls
hung our footcloths on the drier
opened a can of fish
poured some of the hard stuff into a glass
unwound the tight wrapping from a slab of bacon
when a broadcast was heard coming from the pipes
from a fig plant from the cans and from the ceilings
Please rise
a voice said to us
Please don't be cowards in this terrible hour
I beg all those wishing for certain destruction
I beg all lovers of senseless bravado
a huge leopard has appeared upon the Nevsky
he has a crooked fang
is desperately erudite
longing for encounters, he's ready to give battle in argument
on all the problems of matter and of spirit
on crusts on bits of this and that
he's coming nearer and his fang is burning
WELL COMRADES THE MOMENT OF TRUTH OF WHICH
INORGANIC CHEMISTRY WARNED US MORE THAN ONCE HAS COME
WE MUST ARISE COMRADES AND WHISTLING
CHAPTERS FROM THE HISTORY OF MANKIND PROCEED TO THE NEVSKY
LET'S GO COMRADES
DON'T BRING ANY FOOD OR UNDERWEAR

The aircraft was still floating over a wilderness of cotton, but gaps were already starting to appear in that wilderness. Down below were occasional glints of nocturnal lake or the bend of a river, like the flashes across a bedroom mirror made by the flickering beam of headlights.

Arms around each other's shoulders, Patrick and Alik were asleep.

The latter was holding an unfinished half-liter bottle of vodka gripped tightly between his knees. With some difficulty I extracted the bottle from his clutches, took a healthy swig, and leaned back in my seat. Behind me, two passengers were not only drinking but eating as well, accompanied by sounds of gurgling, lip smacking, and crunching. A very familiar voice was telling an intimate story: "Unfortunately, Petyusha, I was insufficiently informed about the degree of intimacy between Alla Alexeyevna and Yaroslavsky. She opened the chest of drawers in front of me and there I saw, Petyusha, ten bottles of brandy – the best brandy – and God knows how many bottles of dry white wine. 'There you are,' said Alla Alexeyevna, 'a present from the Georgian comrades after I had cooked their books for the quarterly balance.' You know me, Petyusha. I can keep myself in control and never lose my head, but Alla Alexeyevna herself is a person of some experience. In other words, she had me. Hardly had we consummated our intimacy when in came Yaroslavsky. I knew him from wartime days, when we both served in the rear echelon of the First Byelorussian Army Group; he was a solid Party man, a good worker in the real Stalinist mold, and I always respected him.

" 'Well, well,' he said. 'I see you haven't been wasting your time here but have been doing some work on the moral foundations of Soviet society.' "

"Imagine my embarrassment, Petyusha, when Alla Alexeyevna, with the merest flicker of a smile, began setting the table and serving suckling pig in aspic, bear steak with cranberries, salmon with horse-radish sauce, and braised goose.

"Yaroslavsky invited me to the table: 'Come, friends and comrades in arms, as they say. Dinner is served.' "

"We sat down to the meal. He tossed back a glass, I drank half a glass, then another glassful for him and half a glass for me. He smoked a Kent while I ate. In other words, Petyusha, Yaroslavsky had soon switched off from the real world around him, and then Alla Alexeyevna had me again."

The smooth, confident tone of the narrator was very familiar. I looked through the gap between the seats and saw two men, who were swigging with relish from a traveling hip flask and devouring food from a leather briefcase. Young Petyusha, the listener, was completely expressionless, and the object of Alla Alexeyevna's passion was a well-preserved man past sixty with the small protruding features of an anteater and three strands of reddish hair that boldly cut across his huge head.

"Excuse me," I said. "While fighting against insomnia, I couldn't help overhearing your instructive story."

"That's all right," he said. "My relations with Yaroslavsky are no secret to anyone."

"Excuse me. I believe you used to work in ideology, didn't you?"

He exchanged glances with Petyusha, and the two men laughed condescendingly, like people keeping a secret that is unknown to common folk.

"That was all in the past," he said. "Right now I'm in a different field."

"I remember your theoretical articles and your brilliant lectures. Don't you remember me?"

He looked intently at me, but only frowned. "There were so many of you."

He didn't remember me! It was amazing! But he had, as they say, "worked with me!" I was the chief object of his concern, his agonizing suspicions! The target of all his skills!

OK, so he might not remember Kunitser or Malkolmov, he might not remember poor old Sabler, he might just perhaps remember Khvastishchev, but surely he could not have forgotten his

MEETINGS WITH PANTELEI APOLLINARIEVICH PANTELEI

In times past this man was a High Priest, and more than once during the periods when the struggle for ideological purity was intensified, he summoned the unfortunate Pantelei to his presence.

Pantelei would make the by now familiar journey to the imposing modern building, where he would stop and inspect the large thermometer near the main entrance, trying to understand the mysterious oscillations of the mercury, which were clearly unconnected with the temperature of the terrestrial atmosphere. Despite the familiarity, he felt a churning sensation in the pit of his stomach. Before making his visits to that large building, Pantelei always tried to evacuate his stomach in the proper manner, but even so his guts usually rumbled; bubbles of anxiety coursed through his system and burst out at the most inappropriate moments.

In the hallway the officer would open his passport, checking the physical personage against the photographic representation (although Pantelei himself had long ceased to recognize himself in his passport photo), found his name on a list, and saluted, showing only by a barely noticeable smile that he knew more about Pantelei than the data given in his passport.

Pantelei found himself in a well-appointed but functional corridor, and the awareness that he, a biologically normal Pantelei, had thus without particular difficulty penetrated into the holy of holies, filled him with a delicious sense of participation and spiritual comfort. With some effort he reminded himself of the falsity of this emotion, of the fact that this thermometer, this officer, this slow-moving elevator, these mirrors and soft carpets, all these objects proclaiming soundness, solidity, and functional comfort, were no protection to him, Pantelei, but were simply transporting him to the place appointed for his regular brainwashing.

He dressed for this procedure with the utmost respectability, but even so, he always added at least one daring item to his attire – it might be his Oxford tie, his synthetic sealskin shoes, or his dark glasses, and sometimes he even pinned (to the lining of his jacket!) a Californian button with the inscription "Fuck Censorship."

Without for a moment forgetting the unenviable fate of the artist in a well organized society, but also reminding himself of his spiritual freedom, Pantelei entered the staff canteen and picked up a sausage. By taking the sausage, he once more stressed his creative independence, which must, as Lenin said, be treated with care, almost as though it were a raw egg, and smirked as he asked the serving girl the fantastically pointless question, "Are the sausages fresh today?"

Then, watched by the girl with cautious suspicion, he began to eat the sausage. He always ate with intellectual contempt but with physiological pleasure. The sausages in this canteen differed from ordinary sausages in the city stores as much as grapes, for instance, differ from elderberries.

"I hope I won't be poisoned," he joked gloomily with the girl, and set off at a slow, dignified pace toward the offices of the High Priest, where he again felt a sense of false security mingled with sticky-palmed anxiety.

And so the procedure would begin.

Pantelei enters the office. Deep in historical reflection, the High Priest is slowly turning around on a revolving piano stool. He pays not the slightest attention to Pantelei. Through the window can be seen the churches of old Moscow, the turrets of the museum, the spire of a skyscraper. It should all be rebuilt . . . and with the aid of theory, goddammit, we will rebuild it all.

"Ah, Comrade Pantelei." The High Priest yawns. "Excuse me, I've had hardly any sleep lately – these endless meetings on the arrangements for Lenin's centenary." Here the HP pauses, stares hard at Pantelei with an obscene grin, and repeats, "for Lenin's centenary." His features harden and his look is transformed into a steely frown. "*Vladimir Ilyich* Lenin," he says, stressing the great man's first name and patronymic with the hint of a vague threat, as though there were some other Lenin – Yurii Vasilievich Lenin, perhaps.

Pantelei shivers and sits down on a hard chair on HP's right.

"Well now, Comrade Pantelei, would you care for a cup of our Marxist tea?" says the High Priest insinuatingly, as though with each word he is hammering in pegs for a network of trip wires with which to trap Pantelei.

"Thank you. I won't say no," says the visitor, discreetly coughing into his fist.

"Excellent!" Delighted, the host executes a rapid circle on his own axis. He has caught him, caught the crypto-counterrevolutionary! Perceived his revisionist antiacceptance of the Party beverage!

Glasses of extremely strong tea appear, together with the regulation slices of lemon and a plate of cookies. With a hospitable gesture, the High Priest invites Pantelei, implying: Relax, enjoy yourself, have a cookie! Cigarettes are offered, and not just any old brand but Kazbek! Ah, the good old days, which for no good reason we have since defamed, those fighting times at the height of the Purge in 1937. Ah, those days have all vanished, along with the smoke rings from Stalin's favorite pipe! The High Priest surreptitiously helps himself to a Kent out of the drawer.

Well now, well now let's see, let's see. Everything is set up, the visitor's sensibilities have been dulled, and with every mouthful he plunges deeper into the labyrinth of traps. Now comes the moment for the unexpected blow.

"So what's going on, Pantelei? Seems you've been seducing women and girls, and" – the Priest opens the thick folder and glances into it as though to check his facts – "little boys?"

Got him! The dubious artist is pinned like a butterfly on the needle of his piercing, proletarian glance! But, but what's this? He is still resisting.

"All that about girls and boys is slander," Pantelei mutters, "but it happens occasionally with women."

"So you have been screwing women!" the Priest exclaims with delight. "A fuck or two now and then, eh? We know, we know." He riffles through the folder, giggling, as though looking for something and then pretending to hide it (photos of stool pigeons?) from Pantelei; suddenly he raises his grim, granite, inexorable glance from the papers, stares long and hard at Pantelei, then stretches out his arm and takes his visitor by the hand. "What's that?"

From the days of Tolya von Steinbock, Pantelei's hand still bears the mark of the Magadan "Crimea," a little blue anchor, around which are entwined like a royal cipher the initials "L.G."

"Oh, well, you know . . . the sins of one's youth," stammers Pantelei, desperately aware of how all this will be interpreted: revisionist, beatnik, pederast, criminal . . .

His gloomy thoughts are unexpectedly interrupted by a friendly slap and a giggle. The Priest winks mysteriously, unknots his tie, unbuttons his shirt, and suddenly with a lopsided grin, shows Pantelei his chest, on which a mighty tattooed eagle, carrying a naked female body in its claws, can clearly be seen through the silvery chest hair.

Then a real pantomime begins. To please the High Priest, Pantelei rolls up his sleeve and displays a tattooed dagger entwined with a snake on his forearm; with a romantic gleam in his eyes, the HP leaps out of his pants and exhibits the gnomic inscription THEY ARE TIRED on his surprisingly well-shaped legs. This friendly gesture by authority demands a response: Pantelei takes off his jacket, opens his shirt, and reveals a bottle, a deck of cards, and a whore's face above his breastbone and the legend "These are our downfall."

In joyful inspiration the Priest is by now walking across the carpet without his pants, to exhibit the most intimate spectacle of all, the three letters "FGB," tattooed on a certain little pendant of wrinkled skin.

"In the presence of ladies this expands into the inscription 'Fraternal Greetings to the girls of the Black Sea coast from the sailors of the Soviet Black Sea Fleet.' Such is the power of healthy – I stress *healthy* – instincts."

The striptease is over. Striving to calm his rapid breathing, the HP dresses himself by the window, looking out at the comings and goings of sleek black limousines, at the ideologically meaningless swarms of crows among the branches of trees along the boulevard.

"You will go to Pisa, Pantelei," he says hoarsely, "and there you can mount an exhibit. It can be as unofficial and avant-garde as you like. Then fly to Aachen, and there you can sing some subversive songs to your guitar, just to fool people. Afterward, Pantelyusha, you must go and see that shitbag Picasso. Your chief task is to persuade the great artist that his policy of distorting reality has reached a crisis: He must either give up his petty bourgeois abstractionism or hand over his Party membership card!"

"Supposing he won't hand it over?" asks Pantelei. "It's not our card, after all."

"If he won't hand it over, then to hell with him, but we must try! There is such a word as 'must,' Pantelyusha! Look at me. I have to sit here coping with you bunch of pricks, yet all the time I'm just longing to get back to scholarly work, to the archives, to the sources. Ah, how I long to . . ."

Can it be that no one will ever stand up and expose this "bottomless pit of humiliation," all this mockery, all these farcical pseudobattles and phony cordiality for what they are? Am I really so gutless that I can't at least blow my snot into his ugly, hypocritical mug? When will I stop playing hide-and-seek with myself and admit, finally, that I have recognized that cloakroom attendant, that he's the one, the Stalinist bastard, the very same Magadan death dealer?

I recognized him, but he didn't recognize me. They never do recognize us. There were so many of us, after all! In Germany they are still indicting Nazis and bringing them to justice, but our stinking hell hounds are getting pensions and even long-service medals. OK, let them have their medals, but they must, oh, Lord, they must at least be made aware of our contempt for them!

"See here, Fyodorich, stop yakking, gather up all these bones, and go dump them in the toilet. We're coming in to land," said the blank-faced Petyusha in a languid voice; he turned away from the dreadful HP to look out of the window, where the southern dawn was already lightening half the sky.

So that was it! The senior of this pair was the young, chinless, fair-haired, and slightly puffy-faced new-style "Petyusha," and in relation to him the so-called High Priest was nothing but a lackey, a clownish nonentity! So on which of them could I avenge myself, to which one should I show my contempt?

"Fyodorich" threw me a surreptitious glance, trying to guess whether I had worked out that he was the subordinate. Realizing that I had, he lowered his blushing head, giggled weakly, and began collecting all the chicken bones, skin, sturgeon gristle, and bits of string (Petyusha added to the pile by spitting out a half-chewed mouthful); having gathered it all together, he heaved himself to his feet, groaning slightly, and waddled off to the toilet.

Out of the window, Petyusha could see flickering lights amid the cherry-colored haze, and as he stretched, he said with an enigmatic smile, "A big, beautiful city!"

From the tone of his voice alone I immediately discerned he was a product of the Komsomol, raised in its grassroots organizations and reflecting its enthusiasm for Finnish saunas and international gatherings of progressive youth.

"They say that a colossal percentage of the men here are impotent," he said, pointing out of the window to the ground below. "In that case any kid –"

He said it – "kid!" He's one of us! The generation of Aksyonov's *Ticket to the Stars*!

"– any kid who can get it up is worth his weight in gold here."

He gave me a conspiratorial wink, meaning: We're not going to waste our stay here; we're going to have the time of our lives, aren't we?!

"Why is that so?" I asked. Involuntarily, I too felt a surge of delight under the influence of his enthusiasm: gold, silver, even to be worth one's weight in bronze in this situation was not bad at all!

"The city's surrounded by nuclear plants. The radioactive fallout creates a radiation level twice as high as normal. The women –"

"I guess the women must be gnashing their teeth in frustration!" I exclaimed.

"Just step outside your hotel," he said, grinning, "and they'll wear you out to a frazzle. That's the Urals for you."

An arrogant note could be heard in the word "Urals."

"You mean the Crimea, don't you?"

"No, I said the Urals."

"But we're flying to the Crimea!"

"You've obviously been overdoing it, kid."

"But look out there – that's obviously a Crimean sky!"

"The sky? I can see you're in a bad way, kid. You should have stayed at home."

"But why are you so convinced that this is the Urals?"

"I've been sent to the Urals on official business!"

I closed my eyes with shame and anguish. Nonentities, misfits, degenerates that we are, we're always going to the wrong place, flying to the wrong destination, slithering into the slough of despond – it serves us right!

Petyusha's condescending and far from sympathetic laughter was still ringing in my ears when the stewardess announced over the plane's loudspeakers, "Your attention, please. In half an hour our aircraft will be landing at Simferopol Airport in the Crimea!"

Still unable to believe that I had triumphed, I glanced at Petyusha. He looked as if he were the victim of a con trick on an international scale. Fyodorich consoled him by whispering, "When we land, we'll make a complaint to headquarters on the closed-circuit phone," as though their precious official phone link could turn Simferopol into Sverdlovsk.

I was delighted. You see, Petyusha, you're wrong! You were flying, like Heracles, to the land of the impotent, but instead, you found yourself in the land of shish kebab and garlic, where the men's pants split under the strain and the women are tired of love and where your modest endowment makes you good for nothing but kindling wood. So you see, Petyusha, now and then even you fall flat on your face, you sonofabitch, inheritor of generations of greatness, even though you may be able to boss a High Priest around. So you see, Petyusha, now and then an unpleasant surprise is lying in wait for you and your kind, you Komsomol volunteers striving onward to break proud new records, your handsome shoulders straightened as you face the sun and wind. Now and then Providence flicks a fingernail against the concrete forehead, loud laughter resounds from the heavens, and the peoples rejoice!

Chaos reigned in the aircraft. All the passengers, it appeared, had taken the wrong plane. Some had been intending to fly to Chelyabinsk, some to Ust-Ilim, some to Dzhezkazgan, but none of them, except the three alcoholics – two barefoot and one shod – had been bound for the Crimea.

SLEEPLESSNESS, HOMER, SWELLING SAILS

"Sleeplessness, Homer, swelling sails, I have read the list of ships until halfway . . . Sleeplessness, Homer, swelling sails, I have read the list of ships until halfway . . ."

"How does it go on from there?" asked Patrick.

"I can't remember."

"What are the rhymes? Sails–whales, I suppose," Alik suggested. "Halfway–pathway?"

"No, no, boys, you're wrong. I'll remember later. Just give me time and I'll remember the whole thing *and* the name of the author."

It was a fresh, windy day and we were sitting on the seashore at Yalta, on the granite steps against which green waves broke that looked like furious, slab-sided whales with crests of foam. There were no sails on the sea; they were all flying across the sky. Ragged and tattered, they flew to Hellas and at once came storming back here to us, whirling in circles, casting shadows on the bay, on the mountains, on the amphitheater of the town, whence they sailed back to their ancient homeland, for they had been born there.

> Tum-ti-tum-ti-tum were it not for Helen,
> What then were Troy alone to you, o Achaeans?
> What then were Troy alone to you, o Achaeans?
> What then were Troy . . .

Foam hissed around our feet, like myriads of white snakes curling into rings. Alik Neyarky looked at the horizon, where a flotilla of fishing boats was bobbing on the waves as they ran into harbor before an approaching storm. "How nice and fresh the sea air is," he drawled in a patronizing tone.

The little port of Yalta was full of fishing boats. They bobbed against the harbor walls, their rusty ironwork creaking, while behind them towered two gigantic liners, the *Ivan Franko* and the American *Constitution*. Even these two giants were rocking slightly, and the sounds of vague, indistinguishable music came from both of them, merging with the voice of the wind, the shrieking of the seagulls, the crash of the surf, the buzz of the crowd idling along the seafront, the music from several restaurants, the creak of rusting ships' metalwork, and was transformed into the quite distinctive music of a winter's day in Yalta.

But where is the broken bottle, required to complete the landscape? Ah, there it is; beyond the iron railings, in the shallow water by the breakwater, gleams a broken bottle, and in it – forgive me, classics! – there floats a cigarette butt. And so the picture was completed.

Now about the smells. What did it all smell of? What did our sense of smell smell? What did our sniffers sniff? What is a picture without smells? No writer worth his salt forgets about smells, unless his adenoids have grown so big that they're blocking his nostrils.

In the words of Neyarky, it smelled of *chebureki* in plum sauce, also of Uzbek shish kebab, of wine, girls, vodka, *chekushki*, and fresh dumplings. Of the last there could be no doubt, since an official event was in progress on the seafront: "The Festival of the Ukrainian Dumpling!"

In the words of Pat the American it smelled of sweat – of female sweat, male sweat, dogs' sweat, ships' sweat, the sweat of palm trees, and the sweat of our own sweat.

Finally, in the words of a poet hitherto unmentioned, it smelled of Turkey and Crimean Tatary, of Yaila, Marseille, Split, and the whole Mediterranean basin; it smelled, in fact, of the cradle of mankind.

In front of us on the granite steps stood three bottles of chilled rapture called champagne made at the Novy Svet – New World – factory and two bottles of Camus brandy at fifty rubles apiece.

The purchase of these noble beverages had already thrown the bar of the Hotel Oreanda into utter confusion. Shura the barmaid had never heard of Camus – neither the brandy nor the Nobel prizewinner. As far as she was concerned, there was only something called Kamus, the god of the bar, of whose purchase by three weird figures she felt bound immediately to notify the Proper Authorities. Who knows what these people are; they may have come from over the water and changed clothes at the offices of an Israeli spy ring, headed by some Goldstein or other, and disguised themselves as Soviet people, though forgetting to put on any shoes. Besides that, they pulled their money out of their shirtfronts, which was not exactly typical of decent Soviet citizens.

There and then in the presence of the purchasers, Shura the barmaid, a sinewy, muscular freak of the female gender, picked up the telephone receiver. "San Vanych," she said to the Proper Authorities, "there are three interesting-looking young men here who are buying Kamus, and –"

Alas, the vigilant lady was unable to finish her report. With an iron hand, the hockey forward gripped her painfully by the left breast, sat her down on a chair – sit there, you Mongolian toad – and snatched the receiver away from her. "Sanya! Hi, this is Alik Sandwich. Greetings from the capital! Who's your piece of ass? Will there be enough meat for three? OK! See you!"

Realizing who they were and thrilled by the amazing metamorphosis of her beloved "organs," the KGB, the barmaid closed her eyes with an understanding look – all is now clear, comrades – and placed a free portion of delicious Intourist goodies into a cellophane bag for us.

Now that bag lay in front of us, like a big, heavy jellyfish, and we abandoned ourselves to *la dolce vita* as we dipped into it. Life was once more quite tolerable.

"This is the life, you guys!" said Alik, laughing, and began to make gurgling, bubbling noises as he stuck two bottles at once – brandy and champagne – into his mouth.

"Ah, if only one could suppress the pangs of conscience," said Patrick, with a sigh.

"Go ahead and suppress them! Squash them like lice!" said the forward with a happy smile as he surfaced from the alcoholic depths.

"If only there wasn't this burning feeling, here inside," Pat said again with a sigh. "Sometimes I feel like going into an empty church and lying down naked on the stone floor."

"And my labors are calling me, friends," I said contritely. "A treatise on cooking salt. Lasers. The phoenix. Lymph – the liquid soul of mankind. That disgusting prehistoric pig *Humility*. My sax is getting sad again lying in the closet and the cat's pissing on it. I'm ashamed of myself, boys."

"Aw, forget it!" Alik stretched deliciously and scratched his back. "You know, an alky once gave me some golden advice. You only get one life, he said, so you have to live it so that at the end you don't feel sore or offended at the thought of so many wasted years. And that guy, a spartan character, could sink a couple of liters of vodka, fuck eight women, and next morning run ten kilometers cross-country!"

"But could he lie down naked on a stone floor and repent all his sins?" asked Patrick.

"I doubt it," said Alik.

"Did he seek redemption in hard but inspiring labor?" I asked.

"I doubt it." Alik spat into the sea.

"You see, Alik," said Patrick and I in unison, "your alky was a superman!"

Neyarky clasped us both around the shoulders and brought our heads close to his own strongly molded features. "Oh, you bastards! Oh, you hypocrites! Do you think I haven't recognized you? Why, as soon as you turned up at the Pioneer Market, you sons of bitches, I knew who you were! Have you forgotten, Malkolm, how you and I ransacked the house of the master of the bakers' guild in Württemberg? And you, Pat Pickleears, surely you remember that splendid night we spent in the mill at Graz? And how all three of us, for a hundred talers or so, turned the house of the duchess of Blois upside down? Maybe you remember, honorable Sir Samson, how the innkeeper of Brno squealed and how that crazy vivandière, Horse's Ass, roared with laughter when the soldiers gave her five gold pieces for every fuck? Stop playing at being little intellectuals. I know what drinkers you are, goddammit!

There's a lovely little town here waiting for us boys! Come on – let's slit open its belly and wrap its guts around our swords!"

I laughed as I listened to all this cheerful raving from Jan Strudelmacher – I mean Alik Neyarky. At that moment I took on quite a different role, leaning back with my elbows on the granite and stretching my legs toward the sea. A blob of yellowish foam dropped on to my feet. I grew younger and younger every minute. Away went fifteen years! I am drunk again, I am young again, I am happy and in love. I can feel every muscle, and a young, unknown world is calling to me from beneath the arches of its ancient colonnades, under the balconies and into the drainpipes, calling to me, THE MYSTERIOUS BEING OF THE NIGHT.

THE STOOL PIGEONS WHISPERED ALL NIGHT LONG
WRITING THEIR REPORTS ABOUT ME, WHILE I
MYSTERIOUS BEING OF THE NIGHT
WANDERED ALONE ON THE HIGHWAY

Somewhere in that crowd along the seafront a girl is coming toward us, looking like Biche Senielle, a white girl in cowboy costume, and she of course is dreaming of meeting me, the mysterious being of the night.

I had long been familiar with that state of being, that buoyant, godlike "Don Juanism," the distinctive quality of the "mysterious being of the night." It would come upon me at times, and not so infrequently, at a certain stage of being drunk, and although I have long been aware of its consequences, of the pain that is the price to be paid for bliss, I always welcomed it. The "mysterious being of the night" was, indeed, the invariable aim of all my travels. Funniest of all was the fact that I always met girls at such times and they at once realized who I was, that I was the "mysterious being of the night," and they always stayed with me without any further persuasion.

Meanwhile Alik Neyarky was keeping up his monologue. "Do you think I'm not drawn back to the skating rink? I am! Practically every evening Coach Tarasov calls up and begs me to come to a training session. But as far as I'm concerned, all those ice-hockey colonels can stick it up their ass, because I'm a free soldier of fortune with bull's blood in my veins and I know you can never expect any favors from Mother Nature, so our job is to grab them from her."

The crowd was alarmed by the boom of his resonant voice, which floated along the seafront almost as far as the Yalta lighthouse.

"Still, it would be nice to buy some shoes," said Patrick Thunderjet, scratching the back of his neck. "Many of the citizens seem to be staring at us rather strangely. I sense aggression in their looks."

"That doesn't worry me," I said. "I am the mysterious being of the night. I want to dot all the i's at once. Please do not judge me by the common yardstick. I am a creature of a special breed, I am the mysterious being of the night."

Patrick stared at me intently and whistled softly. "It's starting!"

My foreign friend had already encountered the "mysterious being of the night" and knew what it meant.

Some years back, a semiliterate young professor came to the University of Sussex under the Anglo-Soviet cultural exchange program. There he was suddenly transformed into the "mysterious being of the night." The students came to hear him lecture, but there was no professor. Only on the weekend was the "mysterious being" found, wearing nothing but swimming trunks, on the deserted November beach at nearby Brighton.

Alik blinked several times after my announcement, trying to make sense of it, then he got the message. "Wanna piece of ass, Genok? No problem! Go, boys, go!"

How disgusting! How vulgar! What are the police doing? What are they paid for? Grown men walking around barefoot! It's gotten so you can't tell who are ours and who are foreigners! Personally, I'd machine-gun the lot of them! Don't waste time talking – they should be made to do a job of work! Look, comrades, they've gone into that courtyard. God knows what dirty tricks they're up to! Come along, comrades, send in Alexander to deal with them – he's a champion weight lifter! Go on, Alexander, we're right behind you!

> Without you the world is empty how can I
> live through the next few hours
> look oh look a new ten-ruble bill
> is floating over the town
> a nice new pink new ten-ruble bill
> is floating overhead
> oh where have you vanished to
> tenderness

What's the matter with you, Alexander? Our gorgeous Alex! Your stomach's hurt? They punched me in the stomach. I was going to seize them by the scruff of the neck in my steellike hands, but they didn't say a word and hit me so hard that something down there has snapped. Doesn't matter; if it's left a mark you can be the star witness in court. What are they doing in there, Alexander? Relieving themselves. Can't you be a bit more precise? They were pissing, Comrade Retired Guards Major-General. You mean they were urinating and telling anti-Soviet jokes? I feel bad, Comrade Retired Guards Major-General. Ah, Alexander, Alexander, I wouldn't take you with me on patrol. Comrades, I shall now personally go and bring these parasites to their senses!

> Morning, morning starts at dawn
> greetings, greetings, incomprehensible country
> look girls, there's another ten rubles flying through the air
> Catch it! Catch it!
> oh, it's flown away into neutral waters
> the students have their own planet
> their candy and their newspaper
> and there are the virgin lands

What's the matter, Comrade Retired Guards Major-General? Colic? Help, the general's got colic! What colic, you stupid son of a bitch? I'm the victim of a provocation! Without a word of warning one of the parasites kicked me in a tender spot, another stuck this ten-ruble bill behind my tie – hey, hey, don't touch the material evidence! – while the third made the sign of the cross over me and kissed me. Me, a Marxist since 1937! He blessed me like a priest and kissed me with the lips of that Judas, Trotsky! These are enemies, comrades! Keep up the pursuit, while Alexander and I take a rest here. Do you have your dominoes with you, Alex?

A total revaluation of values was taking place in the shoe store on the seafront, in other words, stocktaking. The salesgirls, wearing men's rubber overshoes on their bare feet, were rushing around between pyramids of cardboard boxes, squealing whenever they fell into the inquisitive hands of the auditor, trembling like the women of Pompeii as they were buried under avalanches of surplus sneakers. The manager, a Jew suffering from eczema and who only the day before yesterday had publicly sworn his hatred of Israel, wheezed as he followed the auditor on his hunt, putting on a display of sensuality, lust, and masturbation as he whispered to his female staff, "Dear girls, please put up with it for the sake of the firm."

The auditor was proving to be energetic and insatiable. His feet were already adorned with an incredible pair of Italian shoes that looked like two Ferrari racing cars, the heels of a pair of imported moccasins were sticking out of his pockets, a pair of Swedish felt boots hung around his neck, but that was far from being enough for him. Having left the remains of a gigantic, unfinished veal escalope and several broken plates in the manager's office, the auditor was now hooting with pleasure as he grabbed at the salesgirls, groped with sensitive hands for a breast, a buttock, or a fold of fat on a female belly. Laughing with an excess of vitality, the auditor charged head-down at the cardboard barricades, scattering shoelaces, brushes, and shoe polish as he shouted, "What a job! I wouldn't wish it on my worst enemy!"

Suddenly the fun stopped – the presence of strangers was observed. Three life-size male dummies were standing inside the display window, one of whom was calmly trying on a pair of the firm's boots, while the other two were unambiguously wriggling their bare toes.

"Lobkover, something's wrong in your store," the auditor said reproachfully to the manager, releasing the Armenian girl Mura from his embrace.

The manager flung himself at the invading dummies and requested them to remove themselves immediately because the store was closed for inventory; otherwise they were liable to find themselves in jail.

"Two pairs of white sneakers at any price," the dummies begged hoarsely but politely.

The auditor, coughing as though a piece of sealing wax were stuck in his throat, was already edging toward the telephone.

"A – you are hindering the work of the finance authorities. B – you are being rude. C – a ten-ruble bill is sticking out of your fly. I shall call the police!"

Then something strange occurred. Nothing like it had ever happened to the auditor in all his auditing career: He was subjected to a display of violence as instantaneous and uncompromising as in a dream. What a moment before had been an all-powerful auditor now found himself on the floor beneath the steel-hard buttocks of his attacker. He groaned.

"Don't you like it? Doesn't it suit you?" asked his attacker kindly.

"Don't get upset, old boy. Here, take this as compensation for your suffering," said the second attacker as he thrust the very same ten-ruble bill under the auditor's nose.

"Love my love," the auditor heard the third man whisper in a gust of stinking, rancid breath. "You are an erotic man, and consequently you know the taste of freedom. There you are, my friend. There's a little gladiolus for you."

A disgusting gladiolus, looking rather like the curved, spiral horn of a mountain goat, approached the auditor's face, and he gratefully lost consciousness.

In the second half of the day to the sounds of a little song called The
    Talisman
but you must know you must know captain
the town has found another pink bill floating in the air
it was floating capriciously and despondently
as though before opening the door of the cage its owner
had fired a red-hot bullet into his high marble forehead
hundreds of eyes followed its flight
but nobody lost his personal dignity

Also moving with great dignity, there came along the seafront a girl called Natalya, – wasp-waisted, apple-breasted, forget-me-not-eyed, pouting-mouthed, maxi-dressed. From a distance, one could not detect the trembling of her outraged body; the little heels clicked confidently and the curls floated behind her in the Black Sea breeze, just as they do in a good movie. Yet Natalya was wallowing, drowning in an abyss of outrage and deadly insult, clutching at her last hope – the cynical noontide of youth, rubbed and worn until it shines.

What a squalid business – to be the victim of the oldest and cheapest con trick in the book, already reported hundreds of times in the world's press and even hinted at in the Soviet press. Invitation to act in a movie in Yalta, quarrel with parents, the flight, met at the airport with flowers, a studio car, an intoxicating evening in a picturesque little seaside town. Ah, Nathalie, any minute now you'll be introduced, any minute now someone mysterious will come in, someone from the twilight of *la nuit américaine,* someone in jeans, a grubby shirt, and dark glasses like Cybulski, a world-famous director . . . A huge juicy chicken Kiev cutlet and vodka, glass after glass . . . Ah, they should have given the girl an orange sherbet . . . Puffy, livid cheeks, a cheap jacket, a one-ruble tie, bad breath, another glass, and then some strange room, a lamp swinging from the ceiling overhead, and our little apples are being clutched by a strange pair of hands and squeezed, squeezed. What d'you think they are – tennis balls? And suddenly a piercing stab of fear for her beloved, expensive maxidress, legs forced painfully apart, and then the disgusting release, the tearful opening up. Do what you want to me and stick that thing in me that you're waving about and the more the better, only don't make me smell your stinking breath.

Next morning came a drab woman with an expense sheet who paid her ticket and gave her a miserly per diem and a ticket back home. I don't know anything about a screen test, dear, it's not my department. Then alongside our poor little wounded bird's head the phone rings and a hung-over forty-year-old voice inquires whether "pussycat" had woken up yet. Would she like her "daddy" to drive her up to the Uchansu Waterfall in an hour or so and hit the shish kebabs, which are famous for getting people better acquainted? Screen test? Don't know anything about screen tests, that's not my parish. What was that? Hey . . .

Life wasn't worth living anymore! She, the beautiful star of the Textile Institute, almost a professional model, daughter of a deputy minister, tennis player, dressed like a Westerner, had been – what do they call it? – SCREWED by some dirty old man. And he wasn't a director at all, just some unknown punk, but skillful – she had to admit it – skillful. Drunk as she was, she remembered his technique and couldn't help shivering all over. Ugh, how disgusting!

OK, no good crying over spilt milk. Big deal. So I threw one away for nothing, or as the hookers say, "One more, one less, what's the difference?" I'm not exactly a virgin, after all! My cherry was lost long ago, behind the lockers in the changing rooms at the Dynamo tennis club. So it's time to stop playing hard to get. I'll go back to Moscow and give it to anyone who wants it – to Tolya and Zhora and Grisha and Arkady, and to those two Togolese boys, but first of all I'll give it to my neighbor, Igor Valentinovich, who's as blue-jowled and fat as that monster last night. And I don't need any "mysterious beings of the night" either. I'm through with all that soft-lights-and-table-for-two crap. Sports, study, and healthy, energetic sex.

Before Natalya had even finished coming to her firm decision, she saw a "mysterious being of the night." Prancing along with a drunkard's urgent gait, white sneakers flashing, he came toward Natalya holding in his outstretched hands two bowls of steaming bouillon. When he caught sight of the girl, his face lit up with an enigmatic, mocking smile.

"Name?" he asked.

"Natalya," whispered our luckless film star, terrified.

"Ideology?"

"Marxist-Leninist."

She smiled, and everything that had happened yesterday vanished into oblivion; before her there was only today, only the joy of youth, like a tightening of the throat, like sunburn on a bright frosty day, like a happy meeting with a madman, with this "mysterious being of the night."

"Here, drink this!" He offered her a cup of bouillon and swallowed another in one gulp.

"Once more I'm drunk, once more I'm young, once more I'm happy and in bouillon," he declaimed, waving the empty cup around.

"With me?" Natalya giggled through the bouillon.

"With you, my gazelle! I'm in bouillon with you!"

He seized her by the hand and led her along the seafront toward a little square, where there lay a sad little stone lion, above which looked down on it a little stone eagle with only one wing.

As they ran, Natalya threw back her head, laughing as her hair flew out behind her, and the madman beamed and proudly looked her over as though she were a trophy of war or his own invention.

"A revolutionary of the 1870s perfect down to the last detail!"

Before the girl had realized what was happening, she was lifted up and placed on a nineteenth-century cast-iron pedestal, and for a moment her long dress billowed out, like the skirts of a nineteenth-century girl.

"Distribute the proclamations! Throw a bundle of proclamations into the crowd! Liberty! Equality! Fraternity!"

"Where am I to get these proclamations?" Natalya spread her hands. Between fifty and a hundred and fifty vacationers and inhabitants of the resort watched this scene with sullen curiosity, while from the far side of the square the proceedings were also observed dispassionately by fifteen large, bald individuals, disposed in a semicircle around a bronze statue, which, as usual, was staring at some point in the distance as though it had nothing to do with what was going on.

The "mysterious being" put his hand under his sweater.

"There you are. Take them. They're as good as proclamations, aren't they?"

A wad of ten-ruble bills quivered in Natalya's hand.

"Throw them!"

The bills flew into the crowd, like the money that cascaded onto the theater audience in Bulgakov's novel *The Master and Margarita*.

"We were born to make fairy tales into reality!" shouted the girl, at which she jumped down onto the pavement, and in a flurry of laughter, tears, and gentle kisses was led away into a dark doorway. There the madman kissed Natalya on her eyes, her mouth, her breasts, all her bodily organs, and then knelt down and kissed both her shoes.

"Go on, do it," whispered the girl, and after a moment's hesitation she thrust her fingers into his disheveled and far from clean hair.

THE REGIONAL FINALS OF THE CHILDREN'S GAME "SUMMER LIGHTNING"

were in progress several kilometers inland from the sea on the gray sun-baked hills, which incidentally greatly resembled the Golan Heights.

Armored personnel carriers, their worn-out engines roaring, loose mufflers booming, rickety tracks clanking, spitting out hot oil and screaming with frenzied children's voices, advanced to capture the crest of a hill and stopped. Young machine gunners leaped out onto ground that was scored by the explosions of seven-pound rockets. Flushed by weeks of uninterrupted fighting, the children's faces shone with fierce soldierly joy – victory! The detachment was the first to storm the ridge, and so could look forward to rewards from the military authorities of the region. And – who knows! – maybe at the national level too! Smoke and fire, powder and steel, fruit salad and dumplings!

A jeep drove up, carrying the detachment commander, retired Major-General Chuvikov, and the representative of the Komsomol regional committee, Yury Mayal.

"Well done, boys!" shouted the general to his troops. "Any casualties?"

"Seryozha La Fontaine has been throwing up, Comrade Retired Guards Major-General!" reported Olezhek Ananasiev, Chuvikov's best soldier.

"Send La Fontaine to the rear!" barked the general, his eyes under their winged brows smiling paternally. "There they'll teach him to love his country."

The boys burst into cheerful laughter. They had grown very fond of army humor and were used to making fun of La Fontaine, who stuttered. He was the son of a poor woman who sold soda pop in Alushta.

What eagles! The general nodded proudly to Mayal, referring to his little soldiers. No, all was not lost. We'll raise the new generation without any of Khrushchev's damned ideas about coexist– He couldn't pronounce the disgusting word without a half-liter of vodka inside him. Goddammit, they've raised a bunch of little snivelers who can only sing "Oh, my mama!" Why, in our day we sang a song that went:

> We defend the cause,
> The cause of mighty Lenin.
> We, the security boys,
> Will bash the enemy's heads in!

Another ten years' work on these kids, and maybe there'll be someone to beat the pants off the Chinese and put the fear of God into the Czechs and the Romanians.

"Vitaly Yegorich," said Yury Mayal imploringly, who after yesterday's performance was looking in no better shape than La Fontaine. "Give us a drink, Vitaly Yegorich."

"There you are, Komsomol, have a slug of that!"

Chuvikov handed the young man a hip flask of the most disgusting Georgian moonshine brandy, spat, and climbed out of his jeep.

Sick to his stomach, the Komsomol leader couldn't hold his drink down and left further military instruction to the veterans; he longed for only one thing – a Finnish sauna and some Danish beer.

The general walked up to the edge of the cliff and looked down on the frivolous town of Yalta.

Essentially, it would be possible to blow up, disembowel, and simply destroy this little town with one company of soldiers, provided, of course, that they were equipped with modern weapons. Three tactical missiles at different points for the first shock of surprise, then a burst of fire along the seafront with an automatic recoilless gun to increase the panic. After that, roll downhill in a column, spitting fire and shell, and split up in the town center: first platoon – to the telephone exchange; second platoon – to the port; third platoon – to lay mines under City Hall. Take no prisoners! Just like that. One, two, three, and it's in the bag! Speed is the essence of modern warfare! Unfortunately not everyone realized this yet!

Chuvikov had lived many years in Yalta, where he ran a big sanatorium, but this was the first time, strangely enough, that he had looked at the town from a truly military, and therefore the only correct, point of view.

This preceptor of the rising generation would no doubt have long

remained lost in these warlike reflections had he not suddenly noticed
an incredible optical illusion in the sky. There, up above, looking like
the hated doves of peace, were floating, now falling, now rising – good
God! – seven brand new pale-pink ten-ruble bills.

Before the general had had time to rub his eyes and dispel this
hallucination, he heard a sonic intrusion from below – the thoroughly
civilian whine of a car engine. An ancient taxi climbed up to the hilltop
of military glory, stopped, and sank down on its springs, whereupon
all four doors opened and a most obnoxious rabble climbed out into
the midst of the gunpowder smoke of Exercise Summer Lightning: a
strapping great hooker with an ass the size of a tank, a twitching little
sailor in a cream-colored shirt, a skinny, soot-colored bitch in a most
indecent minidress of synthetic brocade, and a long, lanky hippie in
white sneakers.

The last was clutching to his chest an armful of unimaginable goodies
– Yugoslav brandy, gin, whiskey, and slivovitz – while his other hand
held a fork impaling a juicy sausage, which he was slowly eating nibble
by nibble.

The party paid no attention either to the grim array of military hard-
ware, to the young patriots with their submachine guns, or to the
striking personality of the major-general. Sticking her zoological ass
into the air, the fat hooker knelt down to serve out the picnic, singing
"Tbiliso" and giggling as though ants were swarming in the rolls of
flesh around her waist. The black whore lay down on the rocks in a
reflective pose, looking exactly like an illustration to Pushkin's narrative poem *The Fountain of Bakhchisarai*. Her brocade dress had slid
up almost to her navel and revealed something pink and dirty but
desirable.

"Tomka," called out the black girl in a low voice, "which one of
them do you want to screw?"

"What about you, Lucy?"

"I don't care."

"I like the look of the Lithuanian, if you have no objection."

Clearly this orgy could not be tolerated for a second longer. The
general cupped his hands to form a megaphone and roared, "Leave
the maneuver zone immediately!"

At this, the picnickers turned around and for the first time noticed
all the military activity ten paces away from them. Their amazement
was so great that they stared at Chuvikov's contingent as though its
members were creatures from another planet. Needless to say, the
young warriors, in their turn, were staring with considerable interest

at this display of uninhibited behavior so alien to their ideals of patriotic asceticism. Suddenly, the tall, lanky hippie threw aside his sausage, flung his arms wide, and shrieked joyously in English, "Children!"

Raising a large box of assorted chocolates above his head and beating it as though it were a tambourine, he pranced toward the troop with the movements of an Indian nautch dancer.

"Come to supper, jingle bells, want a chocolate little elves?" sang this nogoodnik.

It is terrible to relate how quickly general, total, and uncontrolled disarmament took place. Submachine guns, mortars, and bazookas flew into the gray, withered feather grass, while the gangling and obviously non-Russian hippie leaped head-high with excitement and croaked something in the language of his potential enemies.

At first, the major-general was utterly perplexed. The whole scene struck him as a bad dream, a mirage; but then he pulled himself together and let out a howl. Running up to the edge of the cliff top, he waved an empty revolver at the picnic party: "I'll shoot you!"

"That's right, General." The taxi driver, seated on the trunk of his car, spat on the ground. "These parasites should all be put up against a wall. Otherwise we'll never stamp out syphilis."

The parasites, however, were not in the least frightened by the pistol. The two women jumped up on the rocks and started howling: "You've no right. Where's the law that says you can do this?" The sailor, eyes shining impudently, made inviting gestures, alternately tapping his Adam's apple and a bottle of liquor.

"Driver, turn around and get out of here!" Totally in the grip of his nightmare, Chuvikov aimed his gun at the women.

"Me?" The driver spat again. "I do what my passengers tell me. Got to stick to the rules."

"Run them down and crush them!" Chuvikov then yelled, rushing over to the armored troop carrier. "Crush them, Stepanych. They're Israeli agents!"

Stepanych, who in addition to being the sanatorium chauffeur was also a master sergeant in the army reserve and decorated with the Order of Glory, climbed out of the machine.

"Crush 'em yourself, Chuvikov! For the past week this heap of scrap has been more of a pain in the ass than my mother-in-law, and anyway I don't want to go to prison. There's the starter, there's the accelerator – crush 'em yourself if you want to."

With a savage roar, the huge machine started turning in circles on the spot, raising a cloud of dust. As he glared through the vision slits,

Chuvikov saw first the sea, then a piece of bare mountainside, then the sky crisscrossed with vapor trails – hey, you pilots, burn a skull and crossbones and a star on the top of my head – and then he suddenly saw his former army, his kids, the coming generation, his hope, the future liberators of Europe! The children were dancing around that tall idiot in white sneakers, who was bending down and no longer giving them chocolates but

FLOWERS!!!

An enemy, an inveterate enemy, ripe as a boil about to burst, flourishing like a gladiolus, a cunning internal enemy sent in from outside! *He's* the one who should be crushed first of all!

The armored car ceased its terrible but aimless circling, stopped, and suddenly headed toward the idyllic community of the friends of botany and freedom. Things might have ended nastily if the hippie in white sneakers hadn't jumped, with astonishing professionalism, into the armored vehicle and thrust a bunch of mountain poppies into the general's mouth.

General Vitaly Yegorovich Chuvikov regained consciousness to find himself in a far from unpleasant position. His head was resting on something soft (which later turned out to be Tamara's thighs), his belt was unfastened, allowing him to breathe freely for the first time in the whole warlike week, while he could see someone's hand holding a glass of amber-colored liquid near his mouth.

Of course, that damn hallucination was still floating in the sky – seven pink ten-ruble bills – and a cherry-red maelstrom caused by the opium-poppies was still swirling around inside his head, but the drink was good and invigorating, and his mind, as it should have done, soon grew clear.

"Would you like some more, Comrade Guards Major-General?"

"Of course." Chuvikov coughed sternly and was at once given another glassful, together with a half-chewed sausage bearing traces of lipstick.

Chuvikov then sat up, fully recovered, and saw around him the springtime of mankind, born in labor and struggle: the stars of Borzhomi mineral water and champagne bubbles, the fascinating mouths of ladies caught in the act of skillfully skinning blood sausages, and a guitar, and Mayal the Komsomol leader spread out over a granite rock like a rare fossil butterfly with a broken wing.

Beside him sat a youngish, intelligent-looking professor, who was looking at the general, having carefully and with human feeling tucked the strands of his long hair behind his ears, just like a nurse. Chuvikov said to him reproachfully, "You keep on pouring me out this veeski, but what's veeski to a Russian? No more than root beer! Incidentally, I much prefer our home-brewed proletarian moonshine."

With a long finger, the professor offered him a shiny, snotty marinated mushroom. "Vitaly Yegorovich, you are a human being and so am I. Right now I would like to spit in your face, you son of a bitch, you son of a goddamn whore, yet I'm not spitting at you but offering you a snack."

"Your first name, patronymic, surname, place of work?" inquired the general as he accepted the mushroom.

"Patrick Henry Thunderjet, professor at Oxford University, king of the May festival at Prague University, and deserter from the United States Army."

"Delighted to meeet you." Chuvikov simultaneously inclined nose and mushroom. "My name is Vitaly Yegorovich Chuvikov, Russian anarchist."

Through the enormous windows of the Café Oreanda, ships could be seen sailing over the sunset sea. Ah, what a romantic spot! You reach it from the seafront by climbing up a very steep stairway, you sit down at the window with an inscrutable, alienated look, you look out at the sea and the ships, you flick a Ronson and take a drag of your Winston. Now some smartass will say there is no sense in all these affected mannerisms. Wrong! Firstly, you are bound, in the end, to get disgustingly drunk here; secondly, you will go to bed with some bluestocking; thirdly, when you wake up the next morning you will remember how you walked into that café, how you smoked with a pensive look, you'll remember what you did afterward, and you'll think, What a shit I am, and a man always derives some benefit from such thoughts.

Alik Neyarky was sitting at a table surrounded by a whole group of people. They might have been doctors, circus artistes, or maybe the local crooks – it didn't matter who they were. What mattered was that these fans would produce a bottle of brandy, and no sooner had he taken a drink than a chick would get interested and start to play with the zipper of the hockey forward's fly under the table.

Swilling brandy, picking at a chicken, prodding the caviar with a finger, and now and again encouraging the inquisitive chick with his irresistible crooked smile, Alik held the floor and answered all the questions put to him by the sports fans.

One of them, for instance, asked him, "Will Firsov's forward line last for another season?"

To which he replied, "Chasing the puck is one thing, and defending one's country is another! There used to be a time when our coach, Anatoly Vladimirovich, would start turning on the psychological pressure and the guys on the team just farted at him. You sons of bitches, how come you let yourself be crushed against the barriers by those anemic Swedes? You're Russians, dammit! The whole might of our country is standing behind you! Peace! Labor! Freedom!"

Suddenly the hockey forward ground his teeth and swung his elbows. Glasses, scraps of food, and drops of liquor flew in all directions, and the snow-white sweater of his neighbor, a young black-marketeer and mountaineer, was splashed with brandy.

"You're overdoing it, madam, you're overdoing it a little," Alik spat out from the corner of his mouth. Then suddenly he banged his fist on the table, dropped his head onto his arms, and said in a muffled voice, trying to suppress his hiccups, "I shall continue. I shall continue to answer the television viewers" questions. At the present time my plans include going on a strictly secret flight to the moon within the program of the World Peace Council. Quiet! The task before us, comrades, is not an easy one, but we will be able to cope with it, provided that the Ice Hockey Federation supports us, of which we have little doubt. Quiet, you people!"

The forward's fist began to dance over the table, smashing the crockery, and came to a halt in a plate of fish in aspic. The fans exchanged frightened glances. Without raising his head, Alik went on in a muffled but grim voice: "All over the world people like you keep quiet when the real men are talking! OK, so it's decided – we leave as soon as we get the order from the Party Central Committee! With me are two old friends of mine from the Pioneer Market, fighters for the dignity of the individual. Stop giggling! OK, Tatyana, stop trying to jerk me off. I don't want it right now. Cool it. The moon is ours! The three of us will land on it, and progressive mankind can go suck itself off! Where are my two pals, the future heroes of the Fatherland? Answer me, where are they? Maybe you've handed them over to the police, you bastards? Perhaps you've opened a case against them? Well see here, you cretins, I work for State Security too! I'll book you all for running gambling joints!"

Alik growled and started noisily grinding his powerful teeth. The girl beside him, who had almost reached something like a feeling of blood relationship, shouted in businesslike tones, "A double coffee and an aspirin for Neyarky!"

The growling, however, stopped without the aid of aspirin. Neyarky drew himself up to his full and very considerable height and, in the sight of everyone in the Oreanda, leaned in anguish with both hands against the glass wall. "Where are you, my dear friends? Where are you, doves of peace and spring? Where are you, sages and poets?" he howled in a piteous voice, in the manner of Princess Yaroslavna's lament in *Prince Igor*. "Where is Neyarky's forward line? Oh, my uncompromising Academician! Oh, my flop-eared little Thunderjet, vere ar yoo? Sleeplessness and full sails, while we sail to the middle of the ocean we shall outstrip miracles as we drink from the neck of the bottle. Ah, the totalitarian system has destroyed these lads!"

The Oreanda's customers were shattered by this inspired improvisation, and one touring musician even started to accompany Neyarky on the flügelhorn.

As tears trickled down the centurion's hollow cheeks, his hand was already reaching for a little tubular-metal chair. A new explosion was building up. Suddenly a strong gust of wind flung open the door of the Oreanda, through which everyone could see the dark-green night sky and a single, neat little star twinkling in the distance. Then three pink ten-ruble bills, like messenger-doves, floated in through the door; after them, two people in black silk masks slipped into the café – a frivolous and indecent couple who, without the slightest doubt, had only just crawled out of bed. The new arrivals reached the middle of the room and hesitated. There were, of course, no free tables, and for some time they swayed, embracing, although not standing on one spot but moving as though to the rhythm of some antediluvian Argentine tango. Meanwhile, the ten-ruble bills were circling busily overhead, driven by the blades of a fan.

She was a creature of youthful grace, as witnessed by the delicate chin beneath the lower edge of the mask, the breasts like apples and the supple waist outlined by a maxidress in the romantic style.

"Who is that girl? Why don't I know her?" a young movie director in jeans and dark glasses called Kalitta asked his manager, the flabby, blue-jowled, hairy Kraisky, nicknamed Momma's Sweater. "We should be filming a girl like that, shot after shot after shot!"

"Suppose she turns out to have no nose?" said Momma's Sweater, giggling cautiously.

The man in the mask was middle-aged, unshaven, and poor, a fact proved by, if nothing else, his three-ruble white sneakers (although they were admittedly brand new), but there was also something mysterious about him, which was, of course, a touch of the "mysterious being of the night." This was evident from his clothes, which were freshly laundered, still wet, and gently steaming.

Oh, what a man, thought every woman in the café without exception. What a man, what a man!

Having finally stopped swaying, the couple went over to Neyarky's wrecked table and sat down on it amid the puddles and the fragments of glass. After sitting rigidly still for a few seconds, the masks suddenly drew close and kissed each other through their oral orifices.

They were watched in amazed silence (apart from Kalitta, who applauded gently), while Alik Neyarky slowly drew near, holding the chair by one metal leg in his outstretched hand. Everyone froze, expecting a nasty but interesting scene.

The hockey forward began from afar: "When I'm asked to name my favorite writer, I reply, Life! When I'm asked what I hate, I reply, War, hypocrisy, defeatism!"

He leaned one arm on the table, and with the other he waved his dreadful weapon.

"Correct, Comrade Neyarky!" said Shura the barmaid, suddenly coming to life. Ever since the morning she had been silent, shocked by the purchase of the bottle of Camus brandy. "This isn't a masked ball! Those people in masks need to be taught a lesson!"

Then the unexpected happened. Alik Neyarky threw away the chair and opened his arms wide: "Pantyukha! Genakha! Samsosha! Arka! Radik! I've found you! Where have you been, you old bastard? Where did you disappear to?"

The man in the mask embraced the hockey forward and started talking rapidly; his speech was like the headlong but wavering movement of a novice skier down a slalom course, when at any moment he may break his arms and legs: "In the Siberian snack bar, Jan! We lost each other in the snack bar. I went there to get a cup of bouillon and suddenly found myself in the gloom of mysterious night. Alone I traveled the length and breadth of that night, a mysterious being in the mysterious night, until I met this blue-blooded young creature. How are you, Jan? Kiss your little sister, old friend! She has laundered everything for me – pants, sweater, and even my underpants, how d'you like that, *Kamerad*? Have pity on her, Jan! I have been pitying her as hard as I can. Anyway, who wouldn't pity a blue-blooded young person who travels through a savage country without a body-guard?"

Alik did not have to be asked twice; he clasped the "young person" around her delicious buttocks and pressed himself against her, breathing hard.

"Relax, pussycat, this is just brotherly feeling."

"He must be saved, brother," whispered the graceful young creature in tones of sincere, exalted despair. "Brother, my beloved is a lost man. It may be that only I can save him."

"You're the one who's lost, kid! Academician and I are in perfectly good shape. Now let's sit down at a clean table and wait for our third friend, an American professor of sauerkraut. Hey, you people, give us a table, and make sure it's as clean as a hockey rink!"

A clean table was, of course, quickly produced, and they sat down in dignified silence. The girl cut a mask for Neyarky out of an Intourist napkin. The silent, masked trio totally cut themselves off from the life of this intellectuals' café, although they reminded everyone present of the proximity of frightening, infernal forces.

Soon, however, the rumbling of rusty tank tracks could be heard outside the windows of the Oreanda, and a strange procession drove out onto the seafront, crushing urns and statues in its path: three aging armored personnel carriers, full of children and flowers; a Volga taxi, crammed with a disorderly band of roaring drunks; and a four-wheel-drive GAZ, known as the Russian jeep, in which stood a veteran major-general waving to the public with a beaming look of victory on his grubby face, and a long, lanky hippie wearing a major-general's peaked cap.

The children were throwing handfuls of the heavily scented mountain flora out of the personnel carriers onto the scratched, scuffed asphalt and were singing a splendid song: "All men are brothers, so I'll embrace my Chinese friend, And tell him my greetings to Chairman Mao to send." Many people in the crowd were moved to tears – Exercise Summer Lightning was over!

"Uncle Pat! Uncle Pat!" shrieked the young warriors, turning to the hippie. "Teach us another song! You promised!"

They all loved the obliging Uncle Pat, who climbed up onto the folded hood of the jeep and with the active help of the general's cap struck up this song:

Now hearken to a story
My father used to tell,
Of the lips of Lady Gloria
And her little cap as well,
Her muslin cap, her lace-trimmed cap, her little cap as well!

"Her muslin cap, her lace-trimmed cap, her little cap as well!" sang
the children.

One night with Lady Gloria
The blacksmith's boy did spend,
And so you see my story
Will soon come to an end,
And the muslin cap, the rose-pink cap, was useful in the end!

"And the muslin cap, the rose-pink cap, was useful in the end!" roared
the children in chorus.

I sang of Lady Gloria
For praise I do not sigh;
For this same little story
Did Chaucer write, not I –
And good old Geoffrey Chaucer, he never told a lie!

"And good old Geoffrey Chaucer, he never told a lie!" the children
sang out joyfully.
"And good old Geoffrey Chaucer, he never told a lie!" the whole
seafront sang out joyfully: steel foundrymen and successful farmers,
policemen and soldiers, whores, fishermen, and foreign tourists,
whores, black marketeers, and vigilantes, tightrope walkers and movie-
makers, bureaucrats and junkies, pharmacists, speculators, and
whores.
A fierce universal enthusiasm, a fraternal sense of unity suddenly
gripped the seafront of the little resort town, and the mischievous
hippie known as Uncle Pat put both hands down his shirtfront and
flung out a whole sheaf of crisp new ten-ruble bills, pink as steamed
veal.

      drunkenness pink drunkenness was raging in our brains
      MEDITERRANEAN
      like the foam of the island of Crete

drunkenness twisted our steps around
the subtle corridors of Oreanda
down marble stairways we crashed
on tiled floors twirled pirouettes
burst into herds of dancers dancing the shake
into shithouses without end
and with hundreds of pissoirs
stretching along the motionless sea
like a rank of Roman legionnaires
like a mad speedboat
drunkenness swept us into
the horseshoe harbor of Split and on
to the polished cobblestones of Diocletian's palace
onward to visit the nymph Calypso amid
her ancient ever-desirable hills
onward to biblical valleys
to Romanesque cities 'neath rustling laurels
we plunged to the bottom of a well of cypresses
under a pure and dark-green sky
among statues of the luminaries
of Mediterranean civilization
we choked on what was perhaps
the very last night of our youth
choked on that night
choked on alcohol
on the hot pulse of the blood
on kisses

Out of a glorious feeling of vertigo that was like a flood of Russian salad, Major-General Chuvikov suddenly found himself on the restaurant stage. Instruments and music stands were strewn all around. Musicians were sprawled here and there in lifeless attitudes, and only Uncle Pat, with an expression of one about to faint, was stroking the cymbals with wire brushes in time to the hackneyed tune of "When the Saints Go Marching In."

The time has come for a direct hit, the general guessed, sitting down at the piano and singing, his fingers thumping the keys in the lower register:

> From Oryol to farthest Zamość
> Polish bones are rotting

And over all those buried bones
The feather grass is swaying . . .

"This is the operational plan, Patrick Henry. In three days we reach the Rhine – France will under no circumstances take more than two days! NATO? NATO is no obstacle. We'll simply blow it away like dust! The main problem will be to win the sympathy of the liberated peoples. Perhaps you can suggest something, Patrick Henry?"

"I want to go to the police," replied Professor Thunderjet in a faint voice.

"You want Polly's? You old goat. Tamara's ass isn't enough for him, he wants Polly's too! I approve of that!"

"The police, the Soviet police – I mean the militia," said Patrick Henry rather more clearly, removing a burning cigar from the mouth of the sleeping singer Viktor Buri and drawing in a lungful with a deep, grateful gulp.

"Attention, please. Everyone who's on their feet!" the general said into the microphone. "Our foreign friend is asking to be taken to the police station. We must help this progressive foreigner. Let's all go to the police, girls and boys!"

Those who were still on their feet (and there were not very many of them at the Oreanda) made approving noises. To the militia, to the militia, to the Soviet police! Why wait? We'll all go to the police station like law-abiding citizens. For once, no one's forcing us to go!

That evening the duty officer at the town police station, Lieutenant Yermakov, was engrossed in a work of Soviet literature, a novel called *The Sources* by a top-ranking writer – Vadim Mokeyevich Kozhemyakin. The novel, incidentally, bore the subtitle "Letters from the Frontline in the Ideological War." It's hero, a polygamous steelworker, an official of the N. Party district committee, and a television commentator on international affairs by the name of Mokey Vadimovich Kozhin, was right now in the very front line, namely in Paris on the Champs Elysées, where he was gazing contemptuously at the windows of the Citroën showroom. With all his skin, with all his hairy integument, with all his glands of internal and external secretion, but above all with his basic prick, Kozhin hated the false glitter of capitalism. What effrontery to flaunt everything, without regard for the fact that history has doomed it to extinction!

Lieutenant Yermakov knew in advance, without reading it, exactly what this book would be like. He also knew the author, V. M. Kozhemyakin – his books were always to be found in police stations, in the Bureau of Investigation, in the Party town committee – and he did not respect him. But somehow Yermakov enjoyed reading such books at night. You knew beforehand that the bad guys wouldn't win, that the plot would always develop along the correct lines, that the forces of progress would eventually triumph after a hard struggle – and this was very comforting during night duty in a town like Yalta.

The lieutenant had already served about ten years in Yalta, but he was still not used to the place. To him, this neurotic, tubercular, drunken town was like a dark, impenetrable night, a time of confusion and unrest, a continuation of the Civil War. If they were not picking up long-haired hippies with guitars, it would be some lady complaining that her little dog had been stolen, or someone would be fished out of the sea without proper papers.

Right now, even before Comrade Kozhin had had time to fire an answering salvo down the Champs Elysées, the police station became the scene of a happening more bizarre than anything you might see in a foreign film. The duty room was invaded by an incredible rabble of people, supporting one another, who were led by a well-known citizen of Yalta, director of the Nineteenth Party Congress Sanatorium, retired Major-General Chuvikov. The general was wearing his uniform tunic, but on his head was a woman's bathing cap adorned with nylon frills. Among the invaders were other familiar figures: Mayal, the town Komsomol organizer, wearing a jacket and pants, and two women registered at the Venereal Clinic, namely Kukina and Pergoryants, the latter wearing the general's peaked cap. Along with these local inhabitants came several vacationers: two men in masks, one in black, the other in white; a young girl, also in a mask, who was laughing pointlessly and kissing all the men; and a dubious-looking character with hair far too long for his age, of clearly foreign origin even though he had a Komsomol badge pinned directly onto the skin of his bare chest. Later the party was joined by a sailor of the merchant marine, who at once proceeded to disgrace his uniform by lying down on the floor.

At that moment, the only staff available to Yermakov was Sergeant Chebotaiko, and therefore, after appraising his visitors, he asked in a fairly polite and unprovocative tone, "What's the matter, citizens?"

The foreign element with the Komsomol badge in his skin stepped forward and announced clearly, "I am a professor of Oxford University, a consultant of NASA, and a UNESCO expert, but I want to make a break with my criminal past and I request the Soviet authorities to grant me political asylum."

"I see." Yermakov nodded and pointed to a chair. "Please sit down and write out a formal request to that effect."

He went into the next room and ordered Chebotaiko to summon all the patrolmen over the walkie-talkie, also to alert the nighttime vigilante squad.

When he returned to the duty room, a waltz was in progress. All the nocturnal visitors were silently and tenderly waltzing with each other, except for the defecting hippie, who was waltzing alone, waving his application form, and singing quietly to himself, "Shy and timid, I'm floating through my first waltz."

On his desk the lieutenant found two chocolate candies, a bright though slightly crumpled

ROSE!!!

together with a tinfoil dish containing a whole fish in aspic, and a cut-glass tumbler full of green chartreuse. The lieutenant strictly ignored the tumbler – no consumption of liquor allowed while on duty – but he ate the chocolates and the fish with no little pleasure. Putting aside *The Sources* and picking up the rose, the lieutenant sat at his desk and watched the dance.

There was something sad, something autumnal, about the dancers, something very hard to define but definitely unlike the characters in *The Sources,* either the good guys or the bad guys. Even the fat-assed Tamara Kukina, as she danced, had the air of a half-wilting chrysanthemum. Imperceptibly, the lieutenant too began to be moved by the lyrical melody of the waltz. Stop – he shook himself – there must be some people in society to fight for law and order and to prevent the population from sliding downhill to the level of a madhouse. Although he said this to himself, a treacherous, melancholy feeling of pity for these dotty alcoholics, together with gratitude for the delicious food, crept all the way up from bottom to top through his lymphatic vessels.

There is no knowing what conclusions Yermakov might have come to under the influence of the waltz had not at that moment the night patrols and a squad of select vigilantes entered the police station. It can only be said with certainty that Lieutenant Yermakov did not take part in the arrest of the visitors, the twisting of arms and legs, the pursuit of those who tried to escape, the thrusting head first into a motorcycle sidecar, the kicking, and everything else that accompanied and followed such actions.

PLEASE DO NOT COMPARE THIS DEWLAP WITH THE POUCH UNDER A PELICAN'S BILL, in which the stupid bird stores its wretched but essential supply of fish for food. This dewlap, spotted and flabby, is intended for collecting our Komsomol badges!

OH, HOW OUR BELOVED IMPORTUNATE GHOST HAS AGED after his spring in Magadan! How his skin and his mucous membranes have aged, but how strong his arms still are and how our underdeveloped little joints crack when we hoist a bundle on to our back!

ARE WE IN BULGARIA ALREADY? GUTEN TAG, BULGARIAN COMRADES! We were standing huddled in a miserable bunch in the hallway, when the Bulgarian variants of the KGB hustled us up against the wall. Put them up against the wall! Photograph them one by one! They're not going anywhere now! You're not abroad now! This is Bulgaria!

DO YOU KNOW A PIANO PIECE CALLED "MEMORIES OF YOUTH"? The pink grass that evening was, as always, motionless, and you strove so hard to summon up to the surface at least one little soap bubble of memory. Meanwhile, memory was sitting not far away under the statue of Artemis the huntress, in the form of a shy old woman, at whose feet lay a little dachshund and a newborn lion cub. From all sides the vast nocturnal city closed in upon us with its flat glass surfaces and dizzy canyons, which, as always on such evenings, teemed with prerevolutionary life.

MY FOREHEAD IS TWO FINGERS WIDE BUT THOUGHT LIES HIDDEN BEHIND IT, a most predatory, prematurely born thought stares out through my eyes, grows out through my skin like a regiment of energetic riflemen, while my ears, radar antennas, scan the deserted heavens!

Woken by the sound of falling water, I was brought to my senses by the acrid smell of urine. When I turned my head, I realized that I had been awakened by the sound of a cascade of acrid-smelling urine.

My head lay on the floor and, consequently, the rest of me was lying on the floor too. Near my head was a zinc-plated bathtub, into which were pouring two streams of liquid, one yellow and the other white.

The sources of these streams were two penises, bending over me like two medieval soldiers.

Turning in another direction, I also saw my wrinkled friend, shyly propping himself up on the hard bedding of his own hip. I then examined the hip that belonged to me – it had a blue bruise – my hairy shin, and inexpressive foot, beyond which was an iron cot; on it lay a naked man, his arms crossed on his chest as he laughed at the ceiling.

As the man's flank approached like a slow-moving barge, under the eighth rib could be seen a major excision and alongside it the flap of a skin transplant looking like a yellowing pod of a southern acacia.

Everything was like something else: penises like soldiers, a skin transplant like a seed pod. Certain objects recalled others. The lamp in the ceiling had a look of the Vigilant Eye of Fate.

The splashing sound of urine stopped; talking and growling in muffled voices, the two penises moved away with a shuffling of bare feet. I raised myself on one elbow and looked at the tub, though trying not to see my own face in it. In the tub was a reflection of the window, framed behind an iron grille, and hanging on that iron grille was a mournful naked figure with slack, drooping flanks. Then I realized what this place was – A SOBERING-UP STATION!

The man on the barred window shouted, "You haven't the right! I'm a member of a communist labor brigade! I have already saved a hundred thousand rubles-worth of fuel! My name is on the Board of Honor! Let me go, let me go, you murderous swine!"

It was a day of sun and crisp frost when Tolya von Steinbock dragged his knapsack full of food into the town headquarters of the security forces. From early childhood the boy had mistrusted bright cold weather like this. The still air, the motionless snowdrifts, the thermometer stuck firmly below zero – all these signs gave him a sense of impending disaster and of shame at his misfortune compared with the mass of citizens who had no such troubles.

The Magadan Security Forces were fond of their comfort and were quartered in a house adorned with four little Doric columns. The building was like a landowner's mansion, and had he felt so inclined, the young Von Steinbock could have imagined that he had come there to be hired as a tutor.

He did not, however, feel so inclined. He only wanted them to accept this abnormally large parcel of foodstuffs destined for a prisoner. Apart from that he was also hoping that there might be a repetition of that one happy occasion, when his mother had been driven from interrogation back to prison not in a paddy wagon but in a car, and he had been able to catch sight of her pale and unnaturally animated face.

On the porch, leaning against a column, stood a large, well-fed, powerfully built young man. A waist-length sheepskin jacket was thrown over his rounded shoulders; at his side hung a pistol in a holster. He was grinning with utter pleasure at his life, with the total perfection of his person – a knight of the revolution! – while to add to that pleasure he was chewing roasted sunflower seeds with an excess of leisurely gusto. How, you may ask, does one get roasted sunflower seeds on the edge of permafrost terrain in Eastern Siberia?

"Well, kid, is your momma inside?" he said in a kindly tone to Von Steinbock. "Brought something for momma to nosh, have you? Good! Go on inside! Don't stand around like you didn't belong!"

Tolya slipped into a dark corridor, feeling an aching sense of gratitude to the kindly giant.

That kindly giant, as it happened, "an enigmatic Russian soul with an innate potential reserve of goodness," was a soldier in the commandant's squad – in other words, the firing squad.

Ah, Tolya von Steinbock, timid creature full of obscure impulses, did you imagine, as you stood beneath the gilded fretwork frame of the security forces' wall newspaper *On Guard* that you would one day be related to the pimply saxophonist Samsik Sabler, that you would sleep in a marble hollow on the tail of your own dinosaur, that you would become renowned in Black Africa as the inventor of the microscope, that you would achieve fame as the author of books and scientific formulas and as a mysterious being of the night, a successor to Don Juan, yet always remaining the same Tolya von Steinbock, even lying on the concrete floor of a sobering-up station in a pool of poisonous drunkards' piss?

"Hey, you guys, give us a smoke! Hi there. Chuck us a Prima! I'm dying for a smoke! Are you people or dogs?"

By now three naked men were standing at the window, clasping the bars and yelling through the little open ventilation window. I crawled over to them on all fours, stood up, hauled myself up on the grille, and took my place between the lumpy buttocks.

Outside was a dark, empty street, the asphalt gleaming under the lamplight, the tops of the cypress trees barely moving, and not a living soul in sight.

"There's no one there," I muttered. "Who are you calling to?"

"No one there?" shouted a thin, flushed youth aggressively, his bushy side-whiskers somehow making his nakedness even more shameful. "Don't you count that guy over there?" He jabbed his finger toward an empty space. "Look, he's just coming from a fuck, and he's smoking a BT, selfish bastard! Just wait, you slob, you'll land in the sobering-up station too, and no bastard'll give you anything to smoke!"

"Just you wait," yelled the two others, "you won't get a damn thing!"

"Just wait!" I howled too. "You selfish shit!"

"Who's got a guarantee?!" the guy with the side-whiskers asked with even greater fury and immediately answered himself. "No one is guaranteed to get out of the sobering-up dump, because the police have gone completely ape. There's not even anyone very drunk here. You, kid, you were lying by the slop pail, and you were just asleep, weren't you?"

"That's right, I was just sleeping," I readily confirmed. "I was asleep and dreaming."

"What did I tell you?" he yelled, shaking the bars. "The real drunks are all shacked up with women and nobody touches them. And the fucking police don't even try to dry them out! Those fucking SS thugs just spend their time persecuting defenseless kids!"

"Look, there are three more walking along over there!" shouted my neighbor on the right, a bald, bloated, pink albino. "And they're all smoking! Hey midshipman, chuck me a butt end; be a pal!"

I looked at the empty street, at the blank slope of asphalt, and at the lamppost, and I remembered nothing, nothing, nothing that had ever happened in my life.

Even so, I did remember the "golden fifties," the swing craze, the solos for muted saxophone – boop-boop-boop-a-doop – and the crowd of girls at the back of the hall and the empty expanse of waxed parquet a minute before the start of the ball. Remember?

One dull, overcast summer morning Mr. Greenwood crawled out of bed and saw that the doors to the balcony were open, the chandelier overhead had not been switched off since the night before, the cigarette butts had not been thrown out, and not even all the vodka had been drunk. He went out onto the balcony and saw below him the empty park and a red-billed starling sitting on the shoulder of a plaster-of-Paris boy with a broken penis. Then his glance fastened on the cypress tree that faced him here every morning. The cypress was an ideal shape – a sort of three-story candle. Greenwood stared for a long time at the cypress without a thought in his head, and suddenly he felt that there was a woman in front of him. A woman? He was racked with an irrepressible desire to possess this smooth, green woman, but a second later he was overtaken by providential fear.

One day Herbert Penthouse, Jr., smoking his pipe, was walking to the Architects' House for a brandy, when below the belt and under his overcoat there appeared something that was round and about the size of a coconut. Herbert gasped with horror, and thoughts of how to remove this foreign body came suddenly galloping at him from afar, like a squadron of Budyonny's cavalry. He clutched at THAT PLACE, expecting to find something hard-lumpy-horrible-alien, but his fingers found nothing but tweed, and under the tweed he felt Penthouse, Jr.'s own damp little excrescence. He should carry a drink in a flat bottle and make sure that it was never empty. This was what real men of his age, pilots and writers, always did.

People of both sexes hurried purposefully past Tolya von Steinbock with folders under their arms. They exchanged greetings and laughs, as people do in ordinary offices, yet from behind one of the doors came the constant sound of a human voice wailing, although admittedly not loudly.

No one paid any attention to the lad with the knapsack, or perhaps they did not even see him in the dark corner under the wall newspaper. No one paid any attention to the moaning behind the door either, just as no one stopped to listen to the clicking of a typewriter behind another door.

Tolya was overcome by a feeling that he was having one of those frequently recurrent bad dreams, in which you realize that you are in a dangerous place, that you must get out at once because at any moment something terrible is going to happen but for some reason you cannot get away.

From the cheerful voices of the office workers he guessed that it was time for lunch; sure enough, the doors started to slam more and more frequently, and soon the corridor was deserted. Then the wailing grew louder, as though the wailer had decided that during the lunch break he would wail to his heart's content. Floorboards creaked at the end of the corridor, and Cheptsov appeared, yawning. This time he was in military uniform, but over his tunic he wore a sleeveless padded jerkin which hid his epaulettes. He stretched pleasurably as he walked, and gave a funny sort of snort, just as though he were shaking himself free from a pleasant but silly dream. He opened THAT door and let out the sound of wailing.

"Coming to lunch, Boris?" he asked into the open door.

Right in front of him Tolya saw a sun-filled room with net curtains on the windows and a portrait of Beriya above a desk. In the middle of the room, with his back to the door, his feet planted wide, stood a man wearing the same kind of padded jerkin as Cheptsov. Beyond him could be seen another man, sitting on a chair. The first man did something with his hands to the other man, at which the latter let out a wail.

"God, what melodrama!" said Cheptsov as he went into the room and lit a cigarette.

Since the door remained open, Tolya could see very well everything that was going on in the room.

"He's worn me to a frazzle, the fucking little fascist!" said the investigator called Boris in a weary voice, walking over to the wash-basin in the corner.

Cheptsov stuck a cigarette between Boris's teeth and lit a match.

The prisoner raised his head, and Tolya almost shrieked – it was Sanya Gurchenko, the bold Ringo Kid himself, the jaunty, cheerful Jewish deportee, the "paladin of Jesus Christ" who had bummed his way around Europe. It was impossible to see exactly what the skilled hands of the investigator Boris had done to him, because there were no marks on his ghastly-looking face, but he stopped wailing as soon as Boris went over to the washbasin.

"I think maybe you're overdoing it a bit, Boris," said Cheptsov softly.

"Well, I have nerves too, you know!" said his friend indignantly, as he went over to the desk and started putting some papers into a folder.

Cheptsov took a chair and sat down close to the prisoner. "Have they been beating you, Sanya?" he asked quietly, staring intently into the young man's face.

Gurchenko opened his eyes, blue eyes, which had forgotten God and looked as distant and lifeless as the whole of the northeast of the Eurasian landmass, cut off from both Russia and Europe.

"Yes they have, Citizen Captain," he whispered.

"Well, well," said Cheptsov as though encouraging him, as though summoning him back to life, and, amazingly enough, this summons was immediately heard by the tormented man. An insane flicker of hope, like the flash of a fish's tail, came into his eyes, and with a weak smile he licked his lips, giving a barely perceptible nod as a sign of gratitude for the sympathy, of which, it seems, the human soul stands in need, even in such a tiny dose as this.

"And did they hit you like this?" asked Cheptsov as he jabbed his elbow into Sanya's right eye. Gurchenko fell over sideways, the chair toppling with him. His eyeball was instantaneously suffused with blood.

"No, Citizen Captain. Before you did they didn't hit me like that."

As for the Yalta sobering-up station, there the wall newspaper was entitled *On Guard for Health*. The brass lettering of that title had once long ago been cut out by a celebrated client, the sculptor Radius Apollinarievich Khvastishchev. The specialist in applied physics, Doctor Aristarkh Apollinarievich Kunitser, had made the wall newspaper's artistic frame with a fretsaw, adorning it with bunches of grapes that resembled a scrotum of titanic proportions. The writer Pantelei Apollinarievich Pantelei had written a leading article for the newspaper; entitled "A Review of the Century in the Light of Its Fiftieth Anniversary," it began with the words "For more than a quarter of a century . . ." The famous physician Gennady Apollinarievich Malkolmov had daubed the whole thing with glue, while the saxophonist Samson Apollinarievich Sabler had drawn in one of the bottom corners a postmark with little wings, adding in a shaky hand, "Send letters."

"Who had headgear?" Captain Cheptsov suddenly asked right above my ear.

"I had a cap with earflaps, Comrade Duty Officer," said someone.

"And I had a sailor's cap."

"A fedora."

"A peaked cap."

"A beret."

"A skullcap."

"A sombrero."

"And I, Comrade Duty Officer, would like to have my hair back, please!"

The whole length of the little dark corridor was now filled with shivering, naked, sobbing, groaning men. I too was naked, I too was shivering and sobbing.

The male nurse, an old man with long arms, wearing a white coat spattered with blood, vomit, and iodine, stared across the barrier at these naked creatures with eternal, inexhaustible contempt. Looking at him, I remembered that only yesterday he had twisted my arms behind my back and pressed the point of his chin into the back of my neck. I recalled seeing the whole scene in the mirror – myself hunched over, my sexual organ dangling, and the old man pressed up against me from behind, with his blotchy dewlap, his gray crew-cut hair, and his two bestial, beady little eyes.

I apparently shouted, as people usually shout on such occasions, "Sadist! Fascist!" but at the same time I was trying to think who he reminded me of. Was it that captain in Magadan, whose name I simply could not retrieve from the depths of my memory, or was it the cloakroom attendant from Moscow? Or perhaps it was Sergeant-Major Theodorus, the mercenary?

Apart from these thoughts, through my drunken haze there suddenly came a stab of hatred, a familiar hatred, like that distant hatred of my youth, a hatred that called to mind a white stone parade ground, in one corner of which a lilac bush was shaking furiously in a gust of wind. Ah, I would have had no pity for this filthy rat, this Stalinist cannibal!

Lord save me and have mercy on me! Oh, Lord, forgive me and spare me! You must know, oh, Lord, that I don't have the strength to show pity for a man like this! DON'T ABANDON ME, OH, LORD!

"Which of you jokers is making funny remarks about his hair? I'm asking you, who is it?"

With an abrasive look in his eyes, the male nurse walked down the whole line of naked men until, of course, someone gave way and squealed, "It was Vasya, Vasya Valikovsky, it was Vasya trying to be funny. Why don't you own up, Vasya? Don't you have the guts? Want the rest of us to take the rap for what you said?"

The informer pushed Vasya Valikovsky forward, a well-known half-crazy alcoholic who used to haunt the town's public library.

"This won't be our last meeting, will it, Valikovsky?" said the nurse, rapping out each syllable very clearly. "You and I will meet again, and then we'll have some fun."

He began to distribute to their owners the various hats, into which, according to a good old Russian tradition, the staff of sobering-up stations throw all their patients' valuables when they undress them: eyeglasses, cufflinks, combs, hairpins, beads, amulets, knitting needles, hearing aids, slide rules, lorgnettes, nailfiles – all those dear, intimate private possessions (with the exception of weapons and poisons, which are confiscated).

Suddenly Valikovsky stretched out his thin, flabby neck, covered in withered cutaneous excrescences, raised his unevenly balding head, and shouted in a high-pitched voice, almost singing out on one quavering note, "You're a sadist! I shall complain to the Ministry of Health!"

All at once it flared up. A hurricane of disobedience gripped us, the naked, dirty, unshaven alcoholics, tormented by morning-after depression, disgraceful creatures racked with dizzy spells, palpitations, and nausea, a whirlwind of divine discontent and mutiny, like an injection of combustible fuel.

"Sadist, that's what he is, a sadist! Vasya's right, comrades!"

"Damn sadist, get out of this medical institution!"

"Down with the sadist!"

"He's sucked our blood, the filthy sadist!"

"I've been sobered up in Murmansk and in Tallinn, and nowhere else but here have I met such a sadist!"

"It's time you retired, you sadist!"

"What a son of a bitch! He tramples all over you in his boots! He squeezes your brains out, the sadist!"

"Who gave this sadist the right to do this?"

"We ought to write to Kosygin!"

"We ought to write to U Thant!"

"Write to Sakharov!"

"Why bother to write? Wait for him around the corner and then beat him to a pulp!"

"Sadist!"

"Ugh, you sadist!"

"No, no, friends! No violence! Passive resistance, but no violence!"

"Kneel down on the floor, you guys! We'll express our protest against this sadist's outrageous humiliations with our bare assholes!"

In all the years that I have lived in my country, nowhere, never – not in school, not at work, not on the streets, not in the metro, not in a stadium – have I been a witness, still less a participant, in a similar mass outburst of disobedience, such an upsurge of human dignity and anger. I had always thought that such occurrences were utterly out of the question, impossible in our country, yet suddenly in a dark corridor

that stank of vomit and nightmares, I took part in an act of insubordin-
ation, a desperate attempt to fling ourselves against the barbed wire
of the state's punitive machine.

Heads were held high, and no one was ashamed of anyone else
anymore. We all despised the worldwide power of sadism, we all
demanded to be treated with respect, we demanded the expulsion of
our tormentor. Everyone suddenly had a fleeting vision of the distant
silvery light of "free mankind," where we wouldn't be continually
oppressed and where we ourselves wouldn't misbehave. We were all
gripped with excitement, courage poured into us – do what you like,
only let it all show for once!

Above the noise of our rebellion there rang out the young voice of
the favorite habitué of the Yalta sobering-up station and the town
public library, Vasya Valikovsky. "Comrades, let's raise our voices in
protest against this bloodsucker of mankind disguised as a Soviet male
nurse! Comrades, patients, and convalescents, I am not mistaken when
I say that he belongs to that race of arthropods that was so brilliantly
and sarcastically pilloried by Academician Engels! Comrades, I am not
asking for this amphibian parasite to be punished but that he should
be morally condemned in the name of spiritual freedom! Comrades,
listen to the murmuring of the forests that have not yet been uprooted,
to the eternal call of the wilderness, to the whisper of the caressing
streams of the blue world of the night! Listen! Look!"

This is how the great miracle of the world will begin, I thought, this
is how the spiritual revolution will be set ablaze, the revolution
predicted by Count Tolstoy.

"I would keep my mouth shut if I were you, my friend," my neighbor
advised me in a very calm voice. "Shut up, or they'll stick you in the
funny farm. And you won't get out of there."

He sat down beside me, and I saw the terrible surgical wound in his
side and the skin transplant, looking like a dried-up banana. This good
man's large fist was gripping a quarter-liter bottle of pepper vodka.

"Three slugs," he croaked. "You can have three slugs of this stuff,
and no cheating!"

Gulp by gulp, Life, Humor, and Romance poured into me. "Thank
you, indestructible humanity!" I said as I stood up. "Truly, only the
higher primates are capable of such cunning – to have pepper vodka
as the hair of the dog without leaving the sobering-up station."

Slopping through the stinking puddles in their bare feet, the drunkards filed down the corridor to the duty room. In the doorway someone

gave Vasya Valikovsky a gentle rabbit punch to stop him from raising his voice again.

THE FRIENDS MEET AGAIN

Once again our paths crossed in the courtroom of a people's court, in which all the patients from the police sobering-up station met next morning. Neyarky and Thunderjet were sitting on a bench in the back row, looking full of fastidious dignity and solid wisdom, as though they were not the accused but the judges. They must have spent the night in other cells – sorry, wards – of the municipal humanitarium, because I hadn't seen them there. Strange to say, I had not thought of them once; it had not occurred to me to wonder at what bend in life's road, in what abyss, we might be fated to meet again. As it turned out, our meeting took place not a thousand miles away but in the people's court, the stern guardian of sober proletarian rule.

"Do you remember the poems?" asked Thunderjet through clenched teeth, as I pushed my way along the row and sat down beside him, trying not to look out of the window that was smeared with shit-colored paint. I immediately recited "Sleeplessness, Homer . . . ," the whole poem in full, and even remembered the name of the author – Osip Mandelstam.

"Look, there's the judge," said Patrick. "Do you recognize her, guys? It's a Celtic goddess that has been dug up and is now in the British Museum."

"Nothing of the sort," I objected. "She works as a ticket clerk at our metro station."

"Stop fantasizing," Alik interrupted us. "That person facing us is the president of the Greco-Roman Wrestling Federation – I forget the name."

The judge (he, she, or it) was sitting behind a table with a sour expression, and he (she, or it) was sniffing, as though we smelt of something indecent, while we in turn thought that it was she (he, or it) who was smelling of sewage.

"Where is the jury?" asked Patrick.

"There they are," said Alik, pointing.

Five policemen were sitting along the wall, and they too were turning up their noses, as though they were superior beings and we were the lowest of the low.

The door opened, and a new group of about thirty more of yesterday's revelers were pushed into the courtroom. Behind them, through the open doorway could be seen a street with a paddy wagon in the foreground. Along both sides of the street there flowed, in different directions, streams of people of both sexes, who had no doubt already passed through the sobering-up station and the courtroom and were now hurrying to work at some sort of forced labor. A little flock of under-age female alcoholic Lolitas, wearing school-uniform pinafores, crossed the street with peals of laughter. Two old women were waiting at a gateway for a third one, in order to send her out for a "jar" of moonshine. Among the crowd there occasionally could be seen the faces of male nurses, heavy, dull-kindly-inexorable, keeping a keen eye, mixed with a gleam of secret envy, on the crowd of their temporarily discharged patients. In the background was the sea, sobered and put to shame, which the tug *Roarer,* as black as a hangover, was punishing for yesterday's events.

"Come on, Abakumov, let's have your protégés," said the judge, yawning painfully and rustling the papers proferred by the fat-assed Sergeant Abakumov.

"Chkalov, Airplane Airplanovich," announced the judge in a dying voice, and one of the accused immediately jumped to his feet, a large robust man in blue Aeroflot uniform.

"Surname, first name, patronymic, year of birth," said the judge, glancing at the small round mirror concealed in the palm of her hand.

"Chkalov, Airplane Airplanovich, born in the nineteen thirtieth year after the great turning point," replied the aviator with cheerful willingness. "Like my great aviator namesake I belong to the skies. . . ."

"Place of work?"

"Commander of the Helicopter Detachment, Freight Transportation and Delivery Department of Tyumen, Siberia," reported the accused, not without pride.

"Abakumov, read the charge." On her nose the judge had found a festering blackhead, which she seized between two fingers as though it were an insect.

Abakumov gave his "evidence."

"Chkalov, A. A., being physically and mentally in a state of legal irresponsibility, ordered beer and music in the reception ward of the Second Five-Year Plan Sanatorium. Removing his outer clothing without instructions from the doctors, he then bombarded the medical personnel with various cakes and pastries that he had brought with him."

"What has made you behave like this, Airplane Airplanovich?" asked the judge, loosening the blackhead.

"Eight years without leave, Citizen Judge. The pressure just built up –" the helicopter pilot began in a muffled voice, choking with emotion.

The judge tugged cautiously at the blackhead. "What you did was ba-a-a-d, Chkalov. Supposing e-e-e-everyone behaved like that?"

"Things would be bad. There would be disorder," agreed the aviator, his head dropping and his shoulders shaking violently.

With a final movement, deft and elegant as a bullfighter's last thrust, the judge wrenched out the blackhead with its curly, suppurating little tail. A voluptuous smile flickered. The blackhead disappeared into a folder.

"Ten days!" it pronounced.

A sigh of amazement ran through the courtroom. The judge had cut it down by a third; the proper sentence for the helicopter pilot was fifteen days. And all because of a blackhead! The policemen exchanged glances – the Siberian aviator had been lucky.

The rest of the judicial proceedings were rushed through at record speed.

"Kolumbekov, Gamal Kamaletdinovich, born 1940, deckhand on a fishing trawler, having reduced himself to a state of intoxication, drank water from a drinking fountain without using a glass –"

"Fifteen days!"

"Dobzhenko, Eduard Yevlampievich, born 1950, makeup artist in a film studio, murdered the pet dog of Zilber, Agnia Solomonovna, with a pen knife. Comrade Zilber has been a member of the Party since 1905 –"

"Fifteen days!"

"Sidoruk, Erasmus Rotterdamovich –"

"Fifteen days!"

"Dkhodzuashvili, Avtandil Tarielovich –"

"Fifteen days!"

"Davinci, Leopold Leonardovich –"

"Fifteen days!"

"Makhnovich, Spartak, has forgotten his patronymic –"

"Fifteen days!"

Having thus flicked aside all of Sergeant Abakumov's protégés, the judge snorted irritably and demanded water, soap, and toothpaste. One of the brand-new convicts held a bowl for her while she performed her morning toilet, cleaned out her ears, blew through her nostrils,

and painted her lips with a Lights of Moscow lipstick. An egg sandwich
was then produced from a greasy sheet of newspaper. A snort of
disgust, then a weary pronouncement in a bass voice: "Damn woman.
Can't even make a decent sandwich. Never get married, boys!"

The courtroom broke out into sycophantic laughter, and the three
of us, three paladins of Europe, also laughed sycophantically – we'll
never get married, Citizen Judge!

"Well, Ryumin, now let's have your bunch. But look lively; we've
enough work to last us all day, and this evening I'm lecturing at the
University of Culture, dammit!"

The scruffy little Sergeant Ryumin pushed a folder toward the judge
and whispered to her heatedly, glancing at us as he did so. "A special
case," we could overhear him saying. "The KGB may be interested –
all the accused have university degrees and are half-Jewish."

"Come on, Ryumin, come on," the judge said, frowning irritably.
"Why put the cart before the horse? Proceed!"

Ryumin moved away with a huffy expression, placed a pair of Robespierre glasses on his nose, and began reading the charges with many
a meaningful stress on random and inappropriate words. "Messerschmitov, Wolf Apollinarievich, born 1932, doctor of nuclear-missile
sciences –"

I was already standing at attention – my patronymic had been read
out and therefore the charge concerned me.

"–while in a state of intoxication sold military secrets on board the
cruise ship *Constitution*. On being arrested, he vomited into the water
of the port of Yalta, kissed and punched members of the People's
Vigilantes, insulting them by calling them 'gendarmes' –"

"Fifteen days," said the judge with a yawn and turned over a page
of the almanac *Valiant Deeds*. "Try and keep it short, Ryumin. Brevity
is the sister of talent. Next."

"Brilliant-Gryunov, Alexander Makedonovich, professor of Germanic philology at the University of Syktyvkarsk –"

Alik Neyarky jumped up, with an embarrassed sideways glance in
our direction, implying that it wasn't his fault they had made him a
professor without his knowledge.

"–harassed passersby by stuffing salad into their mouths, which he
had obtained in a restaurant and pulled out of his pocket, sang songs
by Galich and Vysotsky, the words of which –"

"Fifteen days," the judge pronounced thoughtfully. Its fingers were
once more engaged in an avid search among the folds of its face.

"But I haven't finished yet, Comrade Major of Justice," squeaked

Sergeant Ryumin in an indignant falsetto. "I have not yet stated the crime with which Brilliant-Gryunov is charged."

"What-what-what?" the judge even forgot about the allure of blackheads and thrust her whole physiognomy forward. "Still mumbling that old junk? Isn't capital punishment enough for you? Watch out, or your amateur melodramatics will land you in trouble. Sit down, Brilliant-Gryunov, and don't worry. There's no going back to the past!"

"Thank you," sobbed Alik Neyarky, deeply moved, as he dropped all of his one hundred kilograms of hockey-playing muscle onto the bench.

The Robespierre glasses slipped to the back of his neck, and the sergeant instantly withered and grew wrinkled like a baked apple, giving a faint and inane giggle as though he were not a sergeant at all but one of God's dandelions.

"Patrick Percy Villington," he announced, moving on to the next case. "Captain of an atomic submarine, consultant to NATO, NASA, the CIA, and the FBI . . .'"

His tone was so meek that it sounded as if he was saying, Pyotr Sergeyevich Vilkin, kept in homeopathic pumpkin . . .

"Well?" growled the judge. The excessively zealous Ryumin was obviously getting on her nerves. "What then?"

"That's all, Comrade Major."

"Why was he arrested?"

"Er, he . . . he was just arrested." Ryumin was totally confused and wriggling with embarrassment. "Perhaps I was wrong to arrest him, Comrade Major. I admit my mistake and am prepared to apologize."

"Read the charge!" barked the judge.

"Arrested for pestering passersby with flowers and paper currency," babbled Ryumin.

"You did right to arrest him, Ryumin! Well done!"

The judge burst into laughter at the sight of the sergeant's face beaming with pleasure at the power that he exercised over this creature.

"And he undressed, Comrade Major!" squealed Ryumin joyfully, emboldened by this sign of approval.

"Did he reveal his sexual organs?"

"Yes sir! Or rather, not quite. But he was moving in that direction."

"I protest!" Pat suddenly yelled, jabbing the air with his bony, yellow finger. "I gave up exhibitionism ten years ago! I swear I see no point in it, sir!"

"Did you see that, Ryumin?" the judge said, shaking her head. "He is calling a representative of the law 'sir!' What is that called here?"

"It's called provocative behavior!" The sergeant's eyes started to turn white and pop out of their sockets.

"Well, Ryumin, what sentence do you suggest for him?" the judge asked, frowning.

"The death sentence!" Ryumin began quivering as though about to have an orgasm, but noticing the judge's mocking smile he subsided, cringing. "Ten years and five years' internal exile? Five years suspended? Or maybe we ought to let comrade Vilkin go for lack of evidence?"

"Wrong, Ryumin," boomed the judge in a patronizing tone. "Fifteen days is the correct sentence for this citizen, and fifteen days he shall have. Fifteen days for Villington!"

Humiliated and insulted, Sergeant Ryumin turned away to the wall and sobbed openly. No doubt at that moment he had lost all hope of returning to the glittering heights of punitive power from that beetroot-colored room in which each morning this modest seaside town dealt out its dreary punishments.

Meanwhile for us the magic tragic minutes had begun of the

FIRST MINUTES OF SERVITUDE

"Long live hard labor!" exclaimed Patrick, as we were led away to have our heads shaved. "Forced labor, gentlemen, is the pinnacle of human existence! You don't have to be a philosopher to realize that hunger is the highest form of satiety, and slavery is freedom taken to the point of ecstasy! Oh, the breadth, oh, the boundlessness of the enslaved springtime of the world – you intoxicate me! You will say, gentlemen, that I am quoting Pasternak, that I want to join the great tribe of *slaves*, that I am trying to fade into the background, and that with customary Norman perversity what I really long for is freedom? Nonsense! I will shortly attempt to prove to you that I am a worthy member of a chain gang, that I am prepared to munch with my scurvy-ridden jaws the meager but inevitable bread of servitude to the end of my days, to bear the blows of my good masters patiently and even gratefully, to sleep from taps to reveille, to evacuate the contents of my bowels strictly according to schedule, and I am prepared to call as witnesses all the convicts of the Nile, the Mississippi, and Kolyma!"

This flow of refined Óxford gobbledygook did not even cease when a barber, half-dead with a hangover, clipped the hair on our heads down to zero.

The door of the subterranean kingdom creaked, and a police voice blew like a cold draft over the freshly-cropped crowns, still rather shy in their fresh nakedness: "Vilkin, get your buckets and go fetch the chow!"

Patrick seized two buckets and strolled off down the corridor with a bold smile. The orderlies from two other work teams were already crowding around the hand-out window, but our professor proved bolder than they. Less than five minutes had passed before he was galloping back with one bucket of steaming soup and half a bucket of rancid buckwheat groats.

"Okay, boys, grab your spoons! Don't despair! Life's good! Russia's all around us! Come on, let's go!"

"So are you the boss of our team, Patrick?"

"Just call me Pete. Cheer up, boys, there's a great workday ahead of us – unloading meat, loading fish, scouring barrels, and amateur dramatic rehearsals! So don't stand there shivering, you fucking pricks, you sons of whores, you trichomonad cocksuckers!"

"He's got what it takes, this Estonian. Sure has!"

"He'll keep us on our toes, this guy!"

"Arbeit macht frei, Genossen!"

The sun's crooked smile lit up the southern coast of the Crimea from Sevastopol to Novy Svet, but over the mountains above Yaila there hung clouds of radioactive lead, which had already swallowed up the whole of Europe. Everything of mine was there, all that was dear to me – everyone and everything – was stranded in those clouds, and I could no longer remember anyone.

A single car came out of the clouds down the rusty cable of the funicular toward our last seashore, and for a moment I had the impression that in it, huddled close together, were two souls dear to me – Alisa the Vixen and Dog Toby from the Land of Fools, but the car did not come down as far as us and, turning around in the transparent mist, it disappeared into the darkness without coming back again.

The sun was reflected in the chilly puddles on the last shore and on the heads of us sinners, the prisoners of officialdom, shaved bare by the blunt razor of a police barber, but it did not warm them. Ah, no, there was no warmth in the bright sun. It only made us feel prickly and uncomfortable and even vile, but there was nowhere to run away

to: nothing was left of the warmth of the sun, and clouds were moving
in from the north.

Oh, God, oh, my God! Citizen guard, may I leave the ranks for a
minute. Do you want to piss, Messerschmitov? No, I have to go back
to the recent past, to that hot Yugoslavian night when he, my double,
so bold and mysterious, climbed up a drainpipe to the second floor of
the *Excelsior*, leaving stains from his alcoholic breath on the fresh,
romantic, moonlit wall.

"Pani Greta, don't chase me away. It's me, that Russian poet; yes,
yes, the crazy one. Don't talk like that but give me a cigarette instead.
Ouch! I've scraped my hands bare on that damn pipe and you don't
even care. Oh, you do care? Then care for me with your breasts, care
for me with all your belly, care for me, care for me with your lips,
Pani Greta, and let the Security Police pinpoint all our organs. But let
me pull it out all the same; after all, we are artists and foreigners, why
should we be afraid of the international secret police. We are the
offspring of poor desecrated Europe. You're a girl, I'm a boy, so let's
have a roll head over heels, with delicious squeals, on your damn
bed!"

"But it's not my bed, *Kamerad*!"

"Of course, to a certain degree it's not your bed – it belongs to the
people's state. But you, *la paloma*, are paying for this stall with foreign
currency and therefore you can allow yourself in your clinging, transparent draperies to have pity on a Russian laureate. Care for him with
your long legs, take him to yourself, warm him – to hell with your
television primness – care for him, care for him untiringly. Take him
in your hands and keep on doing it, now turn over and thrust your
nose into the pillow and care for your new friend with nothing but
your rear end, and now, and now, smear yourself all over his body,
cling to him for a long time, forever, and if you want to go away, he
will let you go for one minute just so that you don't get pregnant."

"Well, now, tell me about your life. What kind of education did you
have? What have you read?"

"I was educated at the College of St. Augustine on the outskirts of
Lausanne, then I went to –"

A knock on the door interrupted the European girl's revelations.
From the corridor came the rancid, nicotine-ridden sound of Dr. Chris-
tina Becker, her preceptress and senior Party comrade, clearing her
throat.

"Go away, go away Russian! *Zum Teufel* immediately! Go to the deffil, you bastard!"

"Wait, you little fool! Shut up or you'll blow everything! Just shut up and that old she-goat of yours will fade away and then I can quietly fade away too."

But *pani* lost her head and rushed all over the room between the patches of moonlight and neon light, picking up the clothes of the progressive militant – jeans, T-shirt, shoes – and throwing them out the window. Ah, the sight of her as she dashed back and forth, tall and slim, with her jutting Negroid nipples, and how she muttered in horror, "Go away, go away."

"You're as frightened of Genosse Becker as if she wasn't your comrade but your lawful spouse."

The little *pani* burst into noiseless tears, and the knocking grew louder. Then my double jumped off the balcony into a flower bed, and as he began fumbling for his clothes among the flowers, he suddenly began to tremble, inflamed by the happiness of that night.

An Adriatic night, he naked amid the flowers. From above came the sound of a hoarse, peevish voice and the creaking of parquet under a Party boot; then out of the darkness fluttered the long thin arm of his partner in sin, and there fell at his feet, like a love letter, his abandoned under-pants. The Adriatic night was coming to an end. The sun had already lit up the top stories of the new hotel on the island. Ahead lay another day of his young, victorious maturity, of self-assured escapades by the spoiled child of Europe, the "representative of the new wave." Vulgar, dirty sensualist, trying to be a young man again! Get lost, you piss-artist!

One after another the trucks rolled up and with dull thuds unloaded frozen carcasses twenty meters or so from the gaping black maw leading into the meat section of the Seaview Restaurant. The helots picked up a carcass apiece and hurried toward the black hole, where they slithered down the greasy wooden ramp toward the gigantic, ever-rumbling meat grinder in the yellow factorylike depths.

Pick up that lump of meat, you son of a bitch, you crab louse, and move your feet! When did that lump, which bears no resemblance to meat, become what it is – just a lump? They say that this mutton was brought to the surface from the underground strategic reserves, laid down thirty years ago by the farsighted Marshal Timoshenko.

The customers of the Seaview, free people it would seem, did not complain about the meat. They simply smacked their lips, the shits, imagining themselves lords of the earth, not suspecting that the iron cots were ready for them, too, in the sobering-up station, and that the soup made from the guts of deepwater fish was already being boiled in readiness for them.

All around, the absolutely normal, respectable life of a resort town was in full swing. Miners were strolling around the park in their expensive suits, treating themselves to meat patties and dry wine, enjoying to the full their right to leisure, throwing rubber quoits, hitting the targets in the shooting gallery, pinching the broad bottoms of haughty girls. A writer with a philosophical look was feeding the seabirds. A violinist was standing under a cypress tree in a traditional pose, sawing away at some sentimental tune. There was dancing on the deck of a steamer sailing off the headland. Tennis players could be seen through the gaps in a hedge as they flickered back and forth. A lame girl with a thick book was sitting on a bench, staring fixedly at the tennis court, perhaps even without envying the way the players leaped about. Someone was sauntering along an avenue, yawning, dying of boredom, and scattering orange peels. Someone else flew urgently past in insatiable thirst for pleasure. An old woman sat totally unoccupied, totally thoughtless, without pose or pretention, while a large, purebred tomcat warmed her left leg. In other words, everything around was alive, everything in that seaside park was pulsating in various rhythms; but all of it, strange to relate, lived and pulsated under the patronage of an enormous severed head, sawn out of thick plywood by an unknown artist and painted an unnatural color. The head was in profile and seemed to be straining forward in some direction; alas, this urge was not supported by any movement of its body because it had none, but stopped at the sternocleidomastoid muscle, which had been neatly sawn through in the middle of the neck by a power saw. The aim and function of this head in a seaside park was defined by the inscription that curled itself around the head and affirmed that this cosmically dead head was yet more alive than all the living.

TO WORK, COMRADES!

said Sergeant Ryumin, when he had lined us up in front of a public toilet that was stuck to the cliffside like some mysterious hermit's cell.

Somehow none of the passersby noticed our little file of shaved-headed, bleary-eyed men, although we were standing in full view of everybody in front of the public toilet, which was scheduled to be restored after many years of undeserved oblivion. A remarkable structure, built without the use of slave labor by rip-off artists in the dawn of the post-Stalin era, it might have been mistaken, as already mentioned, either for a hermitage built in the romantic style, a movie set, or, at the most, a stylized beer bar. In fact, it looked like anything but a public lavatory. The facade was generously wreathed in stucco garlands of southern flora, and the entrances were adorned with fake bronze lamps in the late Empire style. In other words, if according to some prophetic forecasts of our glittering future we may expect to have solid-gold public toilets, then this one too was by no means cheap.

So there we stood, in front of this toilet, with crowbars and shovels at the ready, like a company of mercenaries before an attack, while our leader, an executioner who had himself once stood in front of a firing squad, kept striking flint against steel in an attempt to light his stinking pipe. His puny little body was hunched up inside his breastplate, and brief flashes of a secret, jackallike smile occasionally lit up his upper lip.

"To work, comrades!" he repeated in a subdued voice. "Let us begin and end our work without noise and fuss, as we say in Valhalla."

After this speech he shrieked, "Vilkin, start chipping!" and Patrick Thunderjet struck the door with his crowbar.

At once a piece of brown incrustation flaked off and we saw. . . I don't know what the others saw, but what flared up before my eyes was a sudden scene of horror.

Feeling as though I had been jabbed in the solar plexus with a stick and lashed behind the knees with an iron rod, I fell, bent into three, gasping for air, moaning at the horrific sight before my eyes and seeing further horrors all around me – in the wild, insensate tops of the cypress trees, in the monstrous sea, and in the sky of a blue so dark it was almost black, and in the whole unrecognizable world.

Horror crushed me from all sides ever more strongly, as though I were plunging into the depths of the ocean; it was already seeping through my skin, my arms becoming impossibly heavy as the horror simultaneously crawled up my backbone like lead.

"Give him some vodka!" shouted Alik. "Ryumin, you son of a bitch, go get some vodka!"

"I'll give you vodka! I'll fix you, right here and now!" Ryumin fumbled at his holster, into which he had long since put a flask in place of his automatic. "I shall book you, *Professor* Brilliant-Gryunov, you filthy kike, under Article 143 for mutiny at your place of work!"

Huddled together, the slaves of the resort could only stare in silence at the horror-stricken and bitterly sobbing Wolf Apollinarievich Messerschmitov, whom no one could help.

The professor of Germanic philology, however, was not content to play the coward. Lifting Ryumin into the air with his two enormous hands, he said, "As for you, motherfucker, I shall eat you alive and won't even spit out the buttons!" and flung him against the wall.

After that, he and Pete Vilkin the plumber picked up the twitching body of their friend and carried him at a run to the open terrace of a cocktail lounge, known as the

SOUTHERN SALUTE

"Hi there, big boys," said Veronika the barmaid with a smile. "How come you all three look like Yul Brynner?"

"Can't you see, you dumb broad?" Alik barked at her. "Why are you standing around like it was none of your business?"

Big tears rolled down Patrick's face as he slapped his suffering friend's cheeks. Although the victim's head was lolling from side to side, suddenly Veronika, a woman of great experience, caught sight of his eyes and shuddered. The experienced woman could not recognize herself in those protruding, bloodshot eyes. Standing right beside her, as it happened, was her special pride, her own invention – a cocktail called Fireball – and she at once offered it to the suffering man. The two friends clasped his head and pressed on his lower jaw with their fingers. As the thick liquid, yellow with blobs of green, poured down the unfortunate man's throat, he immediately closed his eyes and, after the first convulsive gulp, suddenly took the glass quite calmly and leaned forward with his elbows on the bar.

"That's a Fireball, isn't it, Veronika?" I asked the barmaid. I had long had a soft spot for this woman with the frank looks of a whore, a vulgar southern variety of the golden-haired Muscovite Alisa, the wife of the tractor designer.

"You've guessed it, friend; it's a Fireball," replied Veronika in a hoarse voice and put a lighter to a cigarette with a shaking hand. She hungrily drew in a lungful of smoke.

"I often think, Veronika, about the recipe for that drink. At first sight it's a disgusting-looking liquid, a mixture of liquor and snot, but there is something in it which gives the muck a thrilling taste of excitement. Tell us the secret, Veronika! How does a bubble of magic fantasy get into this filth? I expect you put something of your own into it, don't you, Veronika, you old hooker?"

Veronika answered these familiar jibes with a forced laugh and glanced cautiously around. I too glanced around. All around me was the warm, dense, luxuriant evening in which certain outlines were floating. Pressing against me on both sides were a couple of shaved-headed criminals, who had obviously just been released from a penal colony. At any other time I might perhaps have been frightened by criminals, but right now the embolism of excitement was starting to course through my bloodstream, and I laughed as I seized them both by the nape of the neck and banged their foreheads together.

Instead of stabbing me with their terrible knives, the two crooks burst out laughing and kissed me on both cheeks. I at once realized that I was one of them, one of these criminals, and that I had either been amnestied or was on the run.

"Veronika," one or all of us said to the barmaid, "we shall be shot tonight, so set 'em up, mix those cocktails, shake that shaker, turn on the music. Suck our cocks if you like, don't be shy! There you are, Veronika; there's something on account, paid with our precious medieval medallions, and since the drinking has started in earnest, Veronika, bottoms up – and no heeltaps!"

"They're looking for you, boys," said our lady friend in a low voice. "They've picked up your trail."

Sure enough, down the central avenue of the park, scattering the terrified public, a trio was approaching the terrace of the Southern Salute: the writer Tikhonov, chairman of the Committee for the Defense of Peace; Vice-President Spiro Agnew; and the coach of Neyarky's ice-hockey team, Colonel Tarasov. The three of them together, although individually so different, reminded me of my favorite cloakroom attendant.

"*Guten Morgen!*" said Spiro Agnew, raising his beaver hat. "We've tracked you down, boys!" With a sly look he wagged a threatening finger. "We've come straight from the Party town committee. It's all fixed; you can come back now."

"But we like it here," we objected. "We've no place to go back to."

"You must return to your place of residence and as fast as possible," said Tikhonov sullenly. "You ought to be ashamed of yourselves!" He banged on the ground with a copy of Tolstoy's staff. "You, Pantelei, were scheduled to go on a trip around the hot spots of the planet and you have to disgrace yourself here in white slippers! And you, Thunderjet, are not a very good advertisement for the American military, are you? I shall not even mention Neyarky. This comrade has put his personal interests before his social obligations! It's unheard of!"

"You're mistaken, gentlemen," we mumbled vaguely. "We're not who you think we are. We're just out of prison. We're all sick with active syphilis. We're relaxing, having a bite to eat –"

"Atten-*tion*!" roared Tarasov in a deafening voice. "Tomorrow, you pox-ridden bunch, I'm going to put you all behind the puck naked! Then we'll see how you move! Meanwhile we'll start with the injections!"

I ran wildly through the undergrowth of box, laurel, beech, and elder. I kept on running and running like a wild horse, like a wild herd, and was beginning to get accustomed to this mad flight and to the bleeding scratches on my skin, to the fierce subtropical thorns, when I suddenly saw horror again. I jumped through a dog-rose bush into a little glade where an old woman with a cat was sitting peacefully under a lamp. Oh, there was nothing more terrifying in all the world than that old woman and her cat, sitting on a horrible bench under an unimaginable streetlamp!

After that, the body of Messerschmitov, fugitive from an antialcoholic punitive labor brigade, was given over to the tender mercies of the medical personnel, who came running up, wearing epaulettes and steel helmets.

A Dream When Unconscious

That night we arrived arm in arm with a Zaporozhets car
at a private view in the Gothic quarter of old Moscow
at a marble tavern
The editor in a Peruvian overcoat
irritating the capital with his sporting waist
arranged the disposition of the chairs
not forgetting an armchair for himself
And then with a crafty smile there entered
Comrade Zerchaninov in charge of sensations
your attention please he said hospitably
a splendid trick has been prepared for you
Allons enfants to the foothills of the Pamirs
at a depth of five hundred bestial inches

lives a shaman rabbi bishop lama
an experienced Mongolian sheep breeder
From morning to night he interprets Marx
cuts out shapes with a fretsaw
and with meditation or rather masturbation
he fills his modest leisure time
You only have to travel five thousand kilometers
up steep mountainsides down avalanche slopes
through a dark country perilous as China
and you will reach it
Just then with peals of laughter
there galloped down the yellow corridors
a little herd of shorthand typists
skirts hitched up hair disheveled
rouge smeared all over their cheeks
Go man go, squealed the girls from the VD clinic
that's it old man what a violin
what a bow excellent string
Members of the editorial board please turn left
room seven fourth brigade
hut six ninth avenue
section eight for whites
zone D
The manager of the shop smirking disgracefully
and wiping his hands with a towel
nodded to the left
this way boys
I've just come from there myself
in all my life I've never experienced such pleasures
spiritual pleasures I mean
of course not carnal
pure joy for the mind and the soul
As we moved toward them out of the fissures
the people came tumbling with their rations and with scarce goods
with fresh foreign-currency scrip on their shoulders
Outside the windows were glimpses of meadows
where herds of scrip leaped and gamboled
and grazed in the oasis actively devouring
the life-giving chlorophyll of foreign currency
All around our pallid faces peered through the glass
a hundred million stupid consumers

the aquarium sweated with desire
but a wind of anger brightened the glass
Let us sweep away national frontiers
the international purchaser has rights
and the simple Buryat is no worse
than the shaggy Jew
and I dare say much better
Meanwhile the scrip was spawning
no one had ever seen such whores
who promised so many new
subcutaneous pleasures for the mind
As we went forward the powerful Zaporozhets
cleared the way with its bumpers
its cooling fan whistling
angrily waving its windshield wipers
Stop chirped the birds
stop the sirens sang to us
what good to you is philosophy boys
whined with his tail the three-headed dog Cerberus
For there is love so sang to us Calypso
There are sails so sang the Argonauts
There is the motherland sang Yevtushenko
There is martini sang Ernest Hemingway
No friends the truth is dearer to us
what's more the door we long for is so near
to walk along Piccadilly for a few bars
to turn onto the Nevsky through the Arc de Triomphe
swim across the wall and jump over the Spree
then to the Nikitsky Gate through Rockefeller Center
then
Is the oracle receiving visitors?
Yes, of course! What is the question to be?
About the problems of the creative artist.
How much is your subscription?
Not a lot and not a little
a forty-year-old hack with a small car
in a shabby little jacket from Liberty's
Please go through that door, but remember that the length of the
    audience
is strictly regulated

therefore if you feel a desire
to punish . . .
"Excuse me, miss?"
"That's right. If you want to punish the teacher, then
go to work without delay."
I expected to see an Olympian figure
with Sartre's ugly mug and Tolstoy's beard
in Socratic chiton crowned with bay leaves
with an owl on his shoulder and the herbivorous
serpent of wisdom on his Grecian shoulder
In front of me there sat a squalid fascist
Katuk the SS man – Yezhov – Lin Piao
in a sagging uniform
with pseudo female
despondent features.
Does the whole truth lie in revenge on evildoing?
in the attempt to torture
in punishment through pain
in the partial mortification of a scoundrel
of a molester of a sadist or a hangman?
"Go to work, please," he said, nodding. "There on the wall
are pincers, thumbscrews, needles . . ."

"What must I do?" said the flabbergasted visitor in a hoarse voice.

"Punish me. Cause me unheard-of, inhuman pain. Punish me for all
the crimes committed against humanity and God – in other words,
torture me."

With his hairless eyelids he tried to conceal the sparkle that flashed
in the depths of his pupils as he took down from the wall a massive
pair of pincers and handed them to the visitor.

"And what if I just kill you, you monster?" shrieked the visitor.

"That is no punishment," he said with a grin. "You'd do better to
squeeze my scrotum with these pincers. How I shall scream! Your soul
will start to feel better at once."

Suddenly from the glowing coals in the stove came a squeaky little
voice, which might have been a woman's or a child's: "Papa! Papa!
Papa französisch!"

"What's that?" The avenger lowered the pincers. "Who's that?"

"God knows." The prophet shrugged his shoulders wearily.
"Someone who is suffering, a daughter, perhaps, or a wife."

"Who is she shouting at?"

"At me, who else? There's no one else here. For years now she has been shouting, shouting, shouting, begging, begging, begging. *Ich bin papa, papa,* he-he, *papa französisch . . .la guerre, la guerre . . .*"

Book Two
FIVE IN SOLITARY

Down to Gehenna or up to the Throne,
He travels the fastest who travels alone.
—*Rudyard Kipling*

Before embarking on the second book of this narrative, the author is obliged to state that he aspires to penetrate with extraordinary profundity into the problem that he has chosen.

But does any problem of such seriousness exist at all? Do the author's pretentions to profundity have any foundation?

Time and paper will show; but the author cannot renounce his aspirations, because it is characteristic of any serious Russian book to tackle serious problems.

In Europe there are frivolous democracies with mild climates, where an intellectual spends his life flitting from a dentist's drill to the wheel of a Citroën, from a computer to an espresso bar, from the conductor's podium to a woman's bed, and where literature is something almost as refined, witty, and useful as a silver dish of oysters laid out on brown seaweed and garnished with cracked ice.

Russia, with its six-month winter, its tsarism, Marxism, and Stalinism, is not like that. What we like is some heavy, masochistic problem, which we can prod with a tired, exhausted, not very clean but very honest finger. That is what we need, and it is not our fault.

Not our fault? Really? But who let the genie out of the bottle, who cut themselves off from the people, who groveled before the people, who grew fat on the backs of the people, who let the Tatars into the city, invited the Varangians to come and rule over them, licked the boots of Europe, isolated themselves from Europe, struggled madly against the government, submitted obediently to dim-witted dictators? We did all that – we, the Russian intelligentsia.

But are we to blame for it all? Should we not be seeking the prime cause of our present state of decay in the inclination of the earth's axis, in the explosions on the sun, in the deplorable weakness of our arm of the Gulf Stream?

Reflections of this sort, however, will not get the narrative moving forward. It is time to begin, having first said a prayer, and without any fancy tricks.

So I survived the treatment and recovered. I survived, the sleeves of the straitjacket having failed to break my spinal cord. My recovery was so complete that I was not even quite sure about the authenticity of the personalities and events of the Men's Club.

Now I am a sober, calm, thoughtful, hard-working citizen, with documents that are in perfect order, the owner-driver of a small car, a shareholder in a housing cooperative, an amateur sportsman, an exacting artist, a moderate oppositionist, a gambler, a jogger, a middle-grade celebrity, a semimiddle-aged semi-intellectual – in other words, a normal Muscovite, and scarcely anybody in this city knows that a so-called torpedo is sewn under my skin. Only rarely nowadays do I dream wild, rhythmic dreams; on the contrary, I am often visited by logically structured reminiscences that are like the flashbacks to be found in normal books.

NAVIGATION IN NAGAEVO BAY

was closed in November, when the bay froze over, and until that date the columns of prisoners marched around the clock day after day right through the town from the port to the disinfection center.

The center of Magadan, incidentally, looked thoroughly respectable, and indeed, by the standards of the time, quite splendid: there were five-story buildings at the intersection of Stalin Prospect and Kolyma Highway, buildings with grocery stores, a pharmacy, a movie theater built by Japanese prisoners of war, a school with large square windows, the large villa belonging to the boss of Dalstroy – the Far-Eastern Construction Corporation – General Nikishov, where he lived with his all-powerful wife (known as Junior Lieutenant Gridasova), and the monumental Palace of Culture with the four bronze figures on its pediment – a sailor, a milkmaid, a miner, and a Red Army soldier, known locally as the only ones who don't drink.

The dreary processions of convicts were not allowed to disfigure the splendid town center. They flowed into town through side streets and only emerged onto Stalin Prospect at the point where there were no more stone houses, only wooden ones, although these were relatively decent two story tenements used to house the free, nonconvict workers. Painted pink and greenish, they looked like lumps of sugar candy.

With curious and not always Russian eyes the convicts would stare at these little houses, at the tulle curtains and potted plants in the windows. Perhaps these peaceful little frame houses, located at the end of their long march, had the effect of giving the prisoners a surprise and even a little hope. No doubt they were even more cheered by the sight of the kindergarten, with its stools shaped like red mushrooms with white-spotted caps, with its slide built in the shape of an elephant, with its swings, crocodiles, and hares, all of which made such a peaceful picture beneath the benevolent gaze of an athletically built Standard-Bearer of Peace in All the World who adorned the facade.

After that the columns would trudge past the power plant; past the municipal bathhouse; past the rubble-strewn market, where a handful of Yakut traders sold "sea-beast fat," that is, seal blubber, and frozen blueberries; past a new group of huts housing internal exiles and ex-convicts, unpainted, not new-looking but crooked and dark, just like the fate of all prison-camp inmates.

Finally there arose the watchtowers of the disinfection station, and in the square in front of this institution every gang of prisoners had to wait, squatting on their haunches.

The column squatted and fell silent. The guards, with dogs and with rifles held at the ready, like shepherds amid a large flock of sheep, strolled around among the variegated headgear, among which could be seen here and there European fedoras, Polish round-brimmed square-crowned *konfederatki*, battered forage caps of other small, unknown armies, and even checked cloth caps.

In the predawn mist of the early morning, when Tolya walked from his suburb to school in the center, one after another these columns would come flowing toward him. Their characteristic sound was the shuffling of hundreds of shoe soles, the muffled, indistinguishable talk, the shouts of the guards, the growling of the dogs. In the dim bluish half-light, white blobs of faces floated past, while here and there in the column someone would cast a glow on the tip of his nose and his chin as he sucked on a handmade cigarette rolled in newspaper.

"No smoking there! Lengthen the pace!" a guard would bark, rattling the bolt of his rifle for greater intimidation.

On the way back from school, Tolya's route took him in the same direction as the prisoners: The hut in which he lived was located beyond the Disinfection Center, at the foot of a hill. In those daylight hours he could clearly see the prisoners' faces and he caught their stares as they looked at him.

During the first days after arriving from the "mainland," he understood nothing and pestered his mother, Martin, and Aunt Varya: Who are those people marching in columns? Are they bandits, enemies of the people, fascists? And why are there so many of them? The adults maintained an evasive silence to spare the tender soul of the young sportsman, though they could not lie: only yesterday they too had been marching in those columns. In time Tolya grew accustomed to the convicts and stopped noticing them, just as a pedestrian in the big city doesn't notice the traffic when he walks along the sidewalk.

Tolya's head was already full of the usual schoolboy matters, the preoccupations of early youth: his falling in love with a girl of the Magadan aristocracy, the colonel's daughter, Lyudmila Guly; his translations from Goethe made in her honor; also the image of the early Mayakovsky, which had captured his imagination.

. . . black top-hat and cape with upturned collar, challenging look, sensitive lips . . . "the futurist Vladimir Mayakovsky, electrovelograph by Samsonov, 1913, Kazan" . . .

> I shall shout at the sun with an insolent grin:
> It's fun to roll my r's on the mirror-smooth asphalt!

Tolya walked along the wooden sidewalks of Stalin Prospect with a springy step, light and free, a sportsman and a futurist, and at the same time an ordinary Soviet schoolboy; in no way was he the offspring of a perfidious family of serpents, an apple fallen not far from the apple tree.

Later he came to realize what revulsion the land of Dalstroy felt toward his family and what strange compassion the favorite of this land, the town of Magadan, would now and again show to him.

They wrote essays on themes of freedom: "Man Should Strive for Excellence in All Things" or "We Have Been Given Glittering Wings." The bronze quartet "who didn't drink" gazed in through the classroom window. Lyudmila Guly tossed her bangs like a pony and chewed the cap of her fountain pen. The heart of Tolya Bokov (secretly Von Steinbock) beat faster as he diligently applied himself. What a marvelous school! What happiness! Everywhere else separate schools for boys and girls had long since been introduced, yet here Tolya was sitting in warmth and comfort writing about glittering wings and very near him the divine Lyudmila Guly, daughter of a colonel in the Directorate of the Northeastern Corrective Labor Camps, was frowning with anguish at the specter of getting a D for her composition.

Oh, youth, youth, golden carnivals! The thumping jazz band of political prisoners, the famous homosexual tenor serving a fifteen-year sentence, Lyudmila Guly waltzing in a white dress with the look of a thoughtful pony. Ah, if only I could give her my "glittering wings" and take over responsibility for the awful garbage she has written on the subject "The Image of Pechorin, the Superfluous Man of His Time," ah, if only I could save her! How terrible it was – in the aristocratic families of Magadan they beat their children if they got a D! With the buckle end of an officer's leather belt on those divine and already fully mature buttocks! Kidnap her! Run off with her, away from such insults! For her sake become a thief, a highwayman, a gold prospector!

Tolya was very strangely dressed. His legs were encased in tight stovepipe pants, vintage 1914, that had belonged to his grandfather the pharmacist. Around his shoulders drooped a jacket, altered to Martin's order from a Hungarian officer's greatcoat in the workshops of the Quarantine Camp by the best tailor in the Romanian city of Jassy. The jacket was bulky, with patch pockets, a single vent in the back and drooping shoulders. Tolya had no inkling that he was, in fact, dressed in the very latest American style. He was ashamed of his outfit and envied the aristocrats of the class in their short jackets and baggy pants made of Shockworker-brand material.

One day Tolya was walking in the school corridor toward the cafeteria when he suddenly saw in the rays of sunlight ahead of him the slim little figure of Lyuda Guly. They were quite alone in the huge corridor and approaching each other.

Tolya saw her, saw her so clearly that he felt like disappearing through the floor; with eyes as sharp as a hare's he saw her affectionate and interested look, saw the adorable smile on the face of the young goddess. She came toward him, clicking her little hoofs and tossing her bangs, and he only had to open his stupid mouth and say something, anything (hi, Lyuda, how's about a movie – skating – basketball – the wall newspaper – semolina and milk – the Kuomintang rabble?) and no doubt Tolya would have entered upon an intoxicating, romantic episode of his youth – the friendship of a boy from the last hut in town with the daughter of the terrible colonel. After which would come the firing squad, Cavaradossi's aria, doves on red-tiled rooftops.

Lyudmila Guly walked past, but then stopped and half-turned around, expectantly, but he, the mere nobody, after a trembling moment, went dumbly on his way, barely able to drag one leg of his grandfather's pants after the other.

His grandfather Nathan von Steinbock, a graduate of the University of Zürich, had dreamed all his life of owning his own pharmacy. He was very able and industrious, and worked in several Moscow pharmacies: Rubanovsky's, Lev's, and Ferein's. At last, his grinding of powders, his weighing of pills on highly accurate scales with transparent celluloid pans, as well as the quiet good manners that he had learned in Europe, bore fruit. Out in the suburbs, on a weed-grown lot blackened by locomotive dust, arose Von Steinbock's Pharmacy, a real pharmacy with frosted-glass globes over the entrance, with a silver-plated National cash register, and a selection of dried herbs, chemicals, and medicines in little revolving drawers. Alas, even this triumph was dogged by the black humor of fate: The pharmacy opened in late 1916, only a few months before the Revolution.

In the spring of 1917 his grandfather came rushing into his apartment, his fur coat flapping open, waving a bundle of newspapers. "Rebecca! Kerensky's in the government! Just imagine – Kerensky! That means goodbye to the Pale of Settlement!" Only a few years later the grim, yellow-skinned official of the Moscow City Pharmacy Administration, citizen Steinbock, flung his eldest daughter, Tatyana, out of the house for "joining the usurpers," in other words, for joining the Komsomol. What happened was exactly what forty years later we sang about our mothers:

> Soon she will be leaving home,
> Soon there'll be a fight at home!
> A goddess of the Komsomol . . .
> Ah, brothers, that's a different story . . .

In 1937, after the arrest of Tatyana the communist, the "warriors of the Ministry of Internal Affairs' also came to arrest old Von Steinbock and his wife. Vigilant neighbors had informed the authorities that the apartment of these unreconstructed bourgeois was stuffed with hidden gold: Russian ten-ruble coins, napoleons, louis d'or, doubloons, and zecchini. Von Steinbock's little store of gold was enough to pay for the new fourteen-engine propaganda airplane *Erasmus of Rotterdam*!

"You filthy kike, you have raised a Trotskyite in your family!" the investigator shouted at the old pharmacist.

"I beg your pardon, but Trotskyism is one of the splinter groups of communism, isn't it? I repudiate communism in all its forms," the pharmacist objected.

"Gold! Where have you hidden the gold, you filthy son of a whore, you bitch's guts, you horse's ass?!" yelled Sergeant Theodorus into the face of the monk hanging from a meat hook.

"Look for it yourself, search . . ." The monk smiled weakly. He passed beyond the threshold of pain and drifted farther and farther away.

In the cellars of the Ministry of Internal Affairs, the so-called Black Lake, Nathan von Steinbock fell ill with galloping consumption. His clothes were handed back to old Rebecca, who had been released for lack of evidence.

And so it was that in due course the witnesses of these dramatic historical events (a pair of drainpipe trousers made by the English firm of Coruscus) bore the shy Tolya away from Lyudmila the colonel's daughter and into the john, where, with their feet propped up on the toilet bowls for effect, two of his classmates, Pop ["priest"] and Ryba ["fish"] – in other words, Popov and Rybnikov – were smoking.

"By the way, Lyuda Guly already . . . you know . . ." said Ryba, hitting his clenched fist with the palm of his right hand as though knocking in a peg.

"Sez who!" said Pop with a grin.

"I'm telling you! There was an officer traveling in their sleeping compartment from Moscow to Khabarovsk. While old man Guly was asleep, the officer fucked Lyuda all the way."

"Ryba! You shit!" Tolya yelled in fury and "overwhelmed his opponent with a hail of blows."

"Tolya! Bok! Stop it! What the hell's gotten into you?" The cowardly but muscular Pop grabbed Tolya's green jacket from behind. The attack was unexpected. The sleek and strong Ryba was left sitting, gasping, in the drainage gutter of the urinal immediately under the classic graffito "Fresh air, sunlight, onanism, make a healthy organism."

Tolya staggered out of the john.

". . . she longs, it seems, for carnal pleasures . . ."

He went into the cafeteria and spent a long time simply staring at his semolina and milk. The Fiji Islands . . .

". . . how could that officer 'fuck' such an angel?"

He went into the gymnasium, grabbed a basketball, and hurled it from the center almost straight into the basket.

The sinful Lyudmila appeared in the gymnasium doorway and stopped there, leaning against the doorpost. It was enough to make anyone burst into tears!

Being a fairly authoritative figure in school basketball, Tolya quickly organized a scratch game and began showing off his "class" – dribbling, feints, passing on the move – breaking off now and again to leap over the high jump in the "Western roll" style or to bounce off the trampoline (admittedly not very successfully, because he gave himself a nasty bruise on the base of the spine), but he achieved his aim: He attracted her attention and evoked a peal of laughter like tinkling sleighbells, which made him jump for joy. Sin, the fall from grace, the officer, the train compartment, were instantly forgotten – she came, the fallen angel came to watch me! And he flung himself back into the basketball mêlée – OK, now I'll score by doing an extended leap, like Alachachyan! He darted forward, flew up toward the backboard, and while still in the air, he saw the grinning Pop and Ryba waiting for him. Sparks flashed before his eyes – he had been "boxed"!

Blood was flowing from his upper lip when he picked himself up from the floor. The laughter in the gymnasium hadn't stopped. Far from it, the sleighbells were now pealing furiously and without restraint, even with a certain madness, and everyone around was laughing. What? Surely they and She were not laughing at someone with a cut face, laughing at him with his bloodstained mug?

"Tolya, your pants have split in the back," he heard Ryba's voice say. "Go to the locker room; we'll cover you."

Thirty-three years of this violent century had made themselves felt – the English stitching had parted, and the famous law of dialectics had come into effect: quantity had passed into qualitative change! The split in the seat of his pants now revealed a vile, protruding pouch of well-worn Soviet cotton underpants. Through the blood and the tears of despair, through the wreckage of his ruined chariot of love, there floated into his memory an old prewar aphorism: FOREIGN GOODS LOOK FINE, BUT THEY DON'T LAST!

* * *

Horses, tractors, convoys of trucks, and columns of prisoners moved past me in steady, monotonous succession.

Yet I longed not to be different from the others, longed to live in that Stalinist world and to deceive myself by writing essays on topics that presupposed I was living in freedom, by playing basketball, by getting into scraps with the sons of jailers, and by falling in love with their daughters. I longed not to have to regard myself as a pariah in that Stalinist world, to accept the slogans and the lies and the leader himself as primordial values, not to be afraid of filling out questionnaires and not to pay attention to the columns of forced laborers.

At sixteen I was already a perfect slave in a world of slaves, but I wanted to be an utterly average, ordinary slave like all the rest. To admit that I was an outcast in that world, a slave of a lower category, meant that I could acquire a little bit of freedom, even if it meant only sniffing the smell of freedom, the smell of alienation from that world, the smell of risk; it meant that my life would be a challenge. But the organism of a young athlete did not want that.

Sometimes I saw specters of freedom: It might be the wind from the ocean suddenly blowing in through the mouth of Nagaevo Bay, it might be a face in a crowd of prisoners that startled me with its fleeting look of untamed defiance, it might be an unfamiliar star suspended over the boundless expanse of imprisoning snow, or perhaps the words "remember, you said, Jack London, money, love, passion . . ."

It may be that in 1949 Magadan was, in a sense, the freest town in Russia: In it there lived the special deportees and the special contingent, which included those categorized as SHE (Socially Harmful Elements) and SDE (Socially Dangerous Elements), nationalists, Social Democrats, Social Revolutionaries, Catholics, Muslims, Buddhists . . . people who recognized themselves as the lowest of slaves and who, therefore, had challenged fate.

One day, muttering some verses composed in honour of his Lorelei, Tolya was wandering around a slum district of the town known as Shanghai. A blizzard was blowing and its howl was the only sound. Suddenly Tolya heard voices and laughter coming from below ground, and right at his feet he saw a strip of light. In front of him was a manhole leading into an underground conduit for steam-heating pipes. The square wooden cover of the manhole was raised, and it was from there that the sound of voices and laughter was floating out into the snowbound night.

Tolya bent down and saw an underground tunnel in which a whole colony of people were encrusted vertically and horizontally along the hot pipes, like underwater coral. Some were asleep, some were smoking, some were eating food out of cans; someone was drinking a thick, sticky black liquid out of the spout of a teapot. A gentleman wearing a tie was reading a book. Two women, undressed down to their bras, were cursing angrily but not despairingly. A little to the side, some people, grouped in starfish formation, were playing cards. An old woman was cooking something on a kerosene stove. A young man was combing lice out of his thick hair onto a sheet of newspaper, where he squashed them with his fingernail. A dog sitting beside him was also engaged, in its own way, in a battle against parasites. At the very lowest level a pair of knees could be seen, bent and spread wide; there, copulation was in progress. No one seemed upset by living underground; on the contrary, Tolya had the impression that all these people were blissfully content in their refuge.

Later he learned from Martin that this tunnel was called the Crimea, and that ex-convicts released from prison lived there while waiting for a steamer to take them back to the "mainland." There were several such underground heating conduits in the town, and indeed the people in them were not distressed or suffering in any way: After the camps, it was a thoroughly good place to live.

"And perhaps it's a good place before the camps too?" Tolya then asked Martin. The latter did not reply but only smiled.

Martin was still serving his third term of imprisonment under Article fifty-eight, Paragraphs seven and eleven, of the Criminal Code – "Group Activity of a Counterrevolutionary and Terrorist Nature." Tolya's mother had been imprisoned under the same article, but she had already completed her ten-year course of correction and was now a more or less free citizen, an ordinary (ordinary, Tolya!) housekeeper in a children's orphanage.

"Mama, what is Martin in for?" Tolya once asked at the beginning of his life in Kolyma.

It was the stupidest possible question to ask in Magadan. Even the State Security men never asked "What are you in for?" The normal question, short and to the point, was phrased differently: "Which article?"

"Which article are you in for?" "Fifty-eight? That's obvious; but which paragraphs?" "Espionage and ten." "Those are easy paragraphs. You're lucky." That was how people talked to each other.

Mama thought for a moment, then threw Tolya a quick sideways glance and was slightly embarrassed when the boy caught her rapid, furtive look. "You see, Tolya, Martin holds very firm beliefs. He is also too trusting and never hides his views."

"What's wrong with that?" Tolya asked in amazement.

"Oh, Tolya!" There was so much exasperation and pain in his mother's exclamation.

The boy said nothing, waiting for a sensible answer.

"Well, on top of that," his mother mumbled, "Martin, you see, is a German, a Volga German."

"Ah, now I see!" cried the boy and at once ceased his questioning. The answer turned out to be simple: He was born a German, so it was only right and proper that he should be in prison!

That particular period in Martin's life was one of pure bliss. For the past eighteen months he had been on parole. He could freely leave the prison-camp compound and move around the town unescorted, which he did from morning till night, treating officers' families by the fashionable method of homeopathic medicine. He would stride around town with a springy gait, thickset, in a black overcoat and hat with a little black doctor's bag, always ready to open his thin lips, to flash his big teeth and make anyone a gift of his smile.

He had the look of a real doctor, a good real doctor, and indeed he was a real doctor, what they call one of nature's doctors. He would stare keenly at passersby, analyzing their ailments, and was always ready to strike up a conversation either with the ladies of the Magadan aristocracy as they languidly strolled past in their furs or with quite ordinary folk. He loved talking to all and sundry about their illnesses, never interrupted people as they described their aches and pains, and always heard them out to the end. He beamed with pleasure whenever he met people he had cured, and he would walk around that dangerous town confidently but always on the lookout, always ready for anything – good news or bad news – but also prepared for humiliation. In just such a way, no doubt, the serf architect Voronikhin used to walk once among the buildings he had designed.

Martin was obliged, however, to sleep nights in the Quarantine Camp, which was four kilometers outside of town. If a patrol had caught him in town after curfew, he could easily have been given a fourth prison term.

And so, oblivious to the prisoners, sunk in grief, Tolya was walking one diamond-bright evening toward the black hill, at the foot of which was his home. On his way he saw a long column of female prisoners coming toward the Disinfection Center. In the opposite direction there came marching from the bathhouse a squad of Japanese prisoners flying a red flag and singing "Katyusha." Their unfamiliar looks, combined with the stereotyped sympathy toward the "unfortunate peoples of Asia" instilled into every Soviet person since childhood, helped the Japanese prisoners of war to fool the prison-camp authorities. Whenever five of them gathered together, they always hoisted a red flag and struck up the "Internationale" or "Katyusha." Ah, what class consciousness, said the the brass hats from the Ministry of Internal Affairs approvingly; the foreign proletariat knows instinctively who is their enemy and who is their friend. As a result, the Japanese were allowed to march around the town without an escort and with their mouths permanently open in song.

Suddenly, as the squad met the column of female prisoners, the singing stopped.

"Madam, russky madam" said the Japanese, giggling.

"Ah, I could do with one of those little yellow creatures right now," said a deep female voice with a sigh just beside him. The column was marching along the same wooden sidewalk as Tolya. Although he heard the sigh, Tolya did not, of course, turn his head; but out of the corner of his eye he nevertheless saw the huge, hideous, mass of marching women, dressed in motley rags, in quilted pants full of holes, with knapsacks on their shoulders and tea-kettles on their belts, some in hats fastened to their heads with seersucker towels, some even with traces of lipstick.

The bright slashes of these painted mouths among all the gray, dirty faces struck Tolya as grossly indecent. Trying to breathe through his mouth in order not to smell the stench given off by these women, he naturally also tried to suppress the horrible thought that only a year ago his mother and Aunt Varya had been marching in columns like these.

"A yellow one, a black one, I'd even take a striped one," groaned another female voice, followed by an unambiguous, gasping sigh. The women laughed and Tolya shuddered. The guard walking ahead of Tolya shuddered too.

"Cut out the talking!" he barked, with a hint of something like fear in his voice.

"Oh, what wouldn't I give for something between my legs right now!" came a desperate little voice from the back of the column.

"Hey, guard! Vanya! Let's go around the corner and you can have me dog-style!"

This produced an even louder burst of laughter; the guard only twitched his shoulder and said nothing.

Tolya was so embarrassed, he didn't know which way to look. What did that mean, "dog-style?" It sounded unspeakable. What was he to do? Should he run away?

"Wouldn't you like that young kid there, Sophie? Look at him, fresh as a daisy! I'll bet he's still a virgin, too, with a lovely sweet, pink little cock! Like an Eskimo!"

"Oh, momma, make me young again!"

Realizing that they were talking about him, Tolya broke out in a cold sweat. He blushed a telltale pink and heard a roaring sound in his ears.

"He's blushing. Look at him blushing, girls!"

"Come over here, kid. We'll teach you all you need to know!"

"Leave the boy alone, you old bag!"

"She's right. Why bother with a boy when you can use your fingers?"

Unable to restrain himself any longer and overcome by mindless fury, Tolya turned his head and saw the faces of a dozen or so old peasant women staring at him. I'll tell them what I think of them with so many four-letter words, he thought, and that'll show them what sort of kids live in Magadan!

Suddenly he saw in the column, so near that he could have reached out and touched her, a Girl, almost a child, of around his age or slightly older. A Real Girl, quite unlike Lyudmila Guly; he realized at once that it was His Girl.

She was mine, mine, mine, the one and only girl of my whole life!

She was wearing a thin black overcoat, a black scarf, and some hideous, filthy rags wrapped around her feet. Although she found it hard to keep up the pace, she was light, thin, airy, and delicate. She was the Girl from the Little Tavern with whom the Rough Sea Captain Fell in Love! Golden wisps of hair peeped out from under her nunlike scarf. The whites of her eyes were huge and pure, tinged very faintly with blue, as though the iris could not quite contain all that blueness, the color of the skies of Europe.

Oh, God, how timid she was – and how near! I could have stretched out my hand to her; she could have jumped over the ditch and walked alongside me on the raised wooden sidewalk.

Tolya and the girl gazed at each other, unable to tear their eyes away. The women in the column continued to roar with laughter, but he no longer heard them.

"Tell me, please, what is this place we have come to?" her voice suddenly rustled in a captivating mixture of Polish and Russian.

"This is Magadan, Alisa," I said. "It is the capital of the Kolyma Region. Right now they will work you over in the Disinfection Center, then they'll send you to the Quarantine Camp for two weeks. There the eight criminals who work as male nurses will rape you. You will get sick from the trauma, and when you recover, you'll be made to march to the women's camp at Elgen, which means 'dead' in the native language, and when they put you to work in a lumber camp, then you will get sick again – and this time for good. Are you Polish or English?"

"My father is Polish and my mother is English," she replied, shivering.

"Alas, neither your father nor your mother will ever learn what fate befell their daughter."

"But that can't be so!" she exclaimed in horror. "It's impossible," she said in English, adding fondly in Polish, "*Moj kochany!* Samsik, Gena, Arik, Radik, Pantelei, save me. That mustn't happen!"

"It won't happen!" I cried. "I'll save you!"

I stretched my hand out to her. She gripped it hard, jumped over the ditch, and I pulled her around the corner of the nearest prison-camp compound, behind a fence.

"Quiet, Alisa, just don't make a sound," I whispered as I took off her once-smart overcoat, now stinking of sweat and urine, then her jacket, quilted pants, and foot wrappings. "Now you are naked, Alisa, now you are nearly safe."

I pushed her down behind the front of my sweater and she snuggled up against my body with her soft, satiny warm skin, a skin that was full of electric charges; her hair tickled my chest, and her lips whispered right over my heart something unintelligible in all the thirty languages of Europe – and she was saved.

"Tell me, please, what is this place we have come to?" her voice suddenly rustled in a captivating mixture of Polish and Russian.

Oh, God, how timid she was – and how near! I could have stretched out my hand to her, she could have jumped over the ditch and walked alongside me on the raised wooden sidewalk.

Tolya turned away and could just hear her muffled, barely audible sobs. She realized that a Magadan Komsomol was not going to answer her. She went on mumbling, still looking at him, but no longer with any hope, already foreseeing the Quarantine Camp, the brutal male nurses, and the lumber camp.

"We've been a whole month getting here, those goats did terrible things to me, I can't take it much longer, where are they sending us, I'm only seventeen, I don't know anyone in this country, I feel terrible . . ." She muttered on like this, in a mixture of Polish, Russian, and Engl –

By then the column, and Tolya with it, had drawn level with the "free" public bathhouse. There, on a frozen snowdrift underneath a streetlamp, a couple of dozen men, who had clearly seen everything in their time, obvious denizens of the underworld, were standing with their arms akimbo like generals taking the salute at a parade.

"Hi there, you lovely lady gymnasts! Welcome to Magadan!" bawled one of them.

"Hey, I'll be damned, that's Seryoga the Wolf," squealed a voice like a circular saw.

Suddenly the marchers stopped and the guards began rushing about. Voices yelled from the snowdrift, "Back again, Nina? Did anyone of you girls meet Masha Seryogina at the transit camp? Hey, girls, did they ship you here on the *Felix*? Did you see Sima Pryskina? Girls, catch these cigarettes! Catch this candy, you fucking hookers!"

"Hey, girls, that's my guy there! Hi there, Chinky, you handsome bastard! Good to see you, cocksucker! Is Yura Lepekhin here yet? Anyone there from the silver mines? Throw us some soap, boys! I'm begging you, let's have some soap!"

Thus they screamed from the women's column, whose ranks had finally broken up in confusion.

"Tamara, there's a pair of woolen underpants in that bundle!"

From the snowdrift came flying bundles, parcels, packs of cigarettes, cakes of soap, bottles of cologne, cans of food, and loaves of bread. Tolya was pushed against a sagging fence, and he fell down in the snow, from where, shaken, he watched the incredible scene. Who were those fearless men and what made them do these desperate things against all regulations?

And the women were happy! They were clustered here at this God-forsaken spot on the edge of the world, under a thick dark-green sky, through which a new moon had just broken, and their eyes shone like the eyes of young women as they caught their unexpected presents and yelled out names that were, no doubt, quite random.

"Fimka! Zhora! Hassan, you bare-assed bastard! Hi, boys!"

The guards pushed their way through all this chaos with eyes white with fear, rattling their rifle bolts, shouting and swinging their rifle butts. Finally, the officer in command of the escort fired his pistol into the air.

Suddenly Tolya saw His Girl. She was lying on her side in the snow. Her hair had come completely loose from her scarf and covered her face in a golden cascade, while one sharp little elbow was stuck up in the air like a bugler holding his instrument. Tolya took a step toward her and noticed that she was drinking in convulsive gulps from the narrow screw-topped mouth of a bottle of Mermaid cologne.

"Alisa!" I called out to her.

She did not hear. Angrily, desperately she bit off the neck of the cologne bottle, which made her lip bleed but enabled her to drink more easily. Very quickly she emptied the bottle and collapsed facedown in the snow.

At that moment a young man in fur-lined boots and a quilted jacket, fastened tightly around his waist with an army belt, came sliding down the snowdrift straight toward her, toward the so-called Alisa. He knelt in front of the girl and put his hands on her shoulders. "Don't be afraid, Alisa," he said, and went on in the same attractive mishmash of Polish, Russian, and English. "Don't be afraid! Don't be afraid of syphilis, don't be afraid of the taiga! This is the end of the line. I have some influence in the Quarantine Camp! I'm in with all the crooks, so you don't have to be afraid of anything! And we'll go back home again one day and you will be singing 'Red Poppies on Monte Cassino!' "

Alisa smiled a senseless, happy smile. "Oh, Maciek, Maciek, do you still remember our father and mother? Don't forget Elzbieta, Maciek!"

Hungrily, frenziedly, he began caressing her hair and bloodstained mouth. Her head was uncovered, her curls frozen into little icicles hanging over her forehead, but through them her eyes, turned upward to the moon, gleamed brightly and boldly.

A guard ran up and swung his rifle butt at the youth. I saw it coming down toward the young daredevil's head, but inexplicably something stopped it from reaching its target. I then saw the young man leap backward toward the fence, kicking the guard's feet from under him as he did so. I saw the lieutenant in command of the escort fire at his back several times, again and again, but he missed – in some incomprehensible way he missed.

"Lift up the fence rails, kid," the daredevil ordered Tolya.

Tolya lifted up several of the rails, pulled aside a tangle of rusty barbed wire, and the guy immediately squeezed through the gap. Before following him, Tolya glanced around and saw that the girl was now standing in the laughing, jostling crowd of women, slim and straight as a poker and oblivious of everyone around her.

He crawled through the hole and dropped the planks back into place. Before him was a bluish-white wilderness of snow, across which that strange and bold young man was running, stumbling at every step. A guard dog, snarling with fury, was rapidly catching up with him. Tolya imagined himself in the young man's place, and the thought made him feel so weak from fear that he fell down in the snow. The youth, meanwhile, stopped, swung around, and flung himself at the dog, teeth bared. Clearly taken aback by this unexpected attack, the dog sat back on its hind legs. The young man gripped the animal by the throat, picked it up from the ground, and flung it aside; paying no further heed to the dog, he then strode over to Tolya.

"A man is stronger than a *Hund*," he said. "Even the biggest *Hund* is still smaller than a man."

He stretched out his hand to Tolya and helped him get up. Feeling for a path under the snow, they soon came to the empty Magadan market, where the rows of stalls could just be seen reflecting the moonlight, the ice between them yellow with urine.

As usual, the only person in the market was Perfisha, a crazy deaf-mute Yakut. All day long he would stand there selling frozen seal meat; he always stamped up and down on the same spot, never slept, never ate, and smiled a hopeful smile as thin as the crescent moon. Several frozen seals lay on the stall in front of him: three full-grown seals and one little seal pup, their kindly looking, whiskered muzzles pointing upward. No one ever bought a seal from Perfisha or even tried to haggle over the price, but he was obviously resigned to his fate and simply kept stamping his feet, smiling and quietly humming to himself.

The bold young man shook hands with Perfisha, pulled out a box of carpentry tools from under the stall, then with a quick glance and a smile at Tolya he drew a crackling hundred-ruble bill with its picture of the Kremlin from behind his shirtfront, placed it in front of Perfisha, and picked up one of the seals.

"What do you want a seal for?" asked Tolya.

"I want to buy it!" he answered with a sly grin.

Perfisha made negative-sounding noises, swept the hundred-ruble bill off the counter, and pulled the seal toward him. He tugged at it once, twice, and suddenly, baring his teeth, pulled out a knife and lunged at the young man. His response was to burst out laughing, drop the seal, and offer Perfisha a cigarette.

"You think he's selling this rotten old meat, don't you?" he asked Tolya mysteriously. "The fact is, he kind of worships these creatures,

works magic with them. This market is like a church for him, and the
seals are his gods, you might say. Get it?"

Smiling his blissful smile, Perfisha was once more stamping his feet
behind the counter, and Tolya suddenly understood that these were
not just random, pointless movements but a kind of ritual dance. The
frozen animals really did look like kindly idols, excavated from some
archaeological site.

"He'll never sell them to anyone," said the daredevil young man, a
strange note of pride in his voice. "He'd lay down his life for them! I
like Perfisha!"

He picked up his toolbox and strode off toward the exit, Tolya
following him. Soon they were back on the narrow path, this time
walking side by side, shoulder to shoulder, frequently slipping and
slithering off the path into the snow.

"You don't happen to know a place called the Third Medical
Complex, do you?" asked the young man.

"I live there," replied Tolya.

"Will you show me the way?"

"Of course."

"Then let's get acquainted," proposed the bold youth. "My name's
Sanya Gurchenko."

"Tolya Bokov."

"Glad to know you. Is Bokov your real name?"

This terrible question was asked in such a casual tone that Von
Steinbock unexpectedly admitted, "Not quite."

"And mine's not quite Gurchenko either," said Sanya with a smile.
They shook hands.

"And that girl, who you . . . who you . . . whom I . . ." mumbled
Tolya.

"That, brother, is quite another story," Gurchenko answered curtly,
and turning his face away from Tolya, he began whistling softly.

The snow crunched under their feet. Through back alleyways and
vacant lots they bypassed the Disinfection Center, in front of which
the female prisoners were now squatting on their haunches. Now and
again Tolya glanced at the sharply delineated features of his new-found
acquaintance, who had a challenging, sarcastic look to him that was
rare in Magadan.

"I'm a special deportee," said Gurchenko. "And who might you
be?"

"I'm just a schoolboy," said Tolya, finding himself unexpectedly
embarrassed. "I'm in the local high school, in the ninth grade."

"You mean you're a freebie?" Sanya stuck out his lower lip and frowned.

For the first time in his life Tolya suddenly realized that he didn't have to be ashamed of his parents, that on the contrary, this man would despise him if he turned out to be an ordinary "freebie."

"My mother did ten years. They let her out last year."

"So you're one of us!" Sanya gave a cheerful laugh. "Fifty-eight?"

Again Tolya felt a new sensation: The thing that he usually tried to hide, of which he was as ashamed as though it were some kind of suppurating pustule, that accursed "fifty-eight," was nothing shameful in Sanya Gurchenko's eyes; indeed, it wasn't even bad but was the most natural of human conditions and everything else was slightly suspect, something not quite normal.

"Yes, of course, fifty-eight," he replied casually.

Now Sanya slapped him confidingly on the shoulder, laughed, and looked into his face.

"*Parlez français?*"

"No." Tolya twitched his nose.

"Speak English?"

"So-so."

"*Sprechen sie Deutsch?*"

"*Verstehen wenig.* Do you really know three languages, Sanya?"

"Italiano, too. You see, Tolya, I have a talent for languages. When I was fifteen the Krauts took me with them when they retreated from Rostov, and after a month working on a farm near Baden, I could speak German like a native. Then I was picked up by a French unit, so I learned French, too. After that the Americans came, and without noticing it, I found myself speaking English. Ah, Tolya, it was fun in Europe in those days! My God! If only you'd been there!"

"Did you really travel all over Europe? Where did you go?" Thrilled and amazed, Tolya stared at his companion. He felt complete trust in him, indeed he already almost worshiped him.

"Ask me where I didn't go!" exclaimed Sanya. "Munich, Hamburg, Paris, Nice –" There he suddenly stopped, and Tolya at once understood why he had stopped.

"And how did you come to be here?" he asked cautiously.

"The commies fucking well bamboozled me like any sucker, fool that I was!" Sanya exclaimed, as cheerfully as before. "I had a pal called Domenico, an Italian, and we were in Rome, on our way to Argentina to make a fast buck. The Argentines happened to be recruiting construction workers in Rome for a big project in Córdoba, in Argen-

tina. One day we were walking along the Via del Corso, both wearing
American duds and smoking Chesterfields, girls swooning at the sight
of us, and suddenly I saw – I could fuck myself when I think of it! – a
huge poster with a picture of an old dame in a scarf stretching out her
hand toward me, and she was looking me in the eye, no matter which
way I turned. D'you see, Tolya? The commies bought me real cheap!'

"What are 'commies?' ' "

"The communists, of course. You see, Tolya, *lieber Freund*, the
words on the poster were in Russian: 'Son! Mother Russia is calling
you!' Believe it or not, I sat down right there beside that poster and
burst into tears, although I admit I was very drunk at the time. I cried
and cried and, can you believe it, I didn't think of my mother and
father but of a shitty old soccer ball I used to kick around on a garbage
heap, and the smell of that garbage, a bare poplar tree, an Armenian
guy on a bicycle, and a song called 'The Day Has Faded.' Do you
understand?"

"I understand you, Sanya," Tolya replied quietly.

"Anyway, to make a long story short, two weeks later, along with
fifty other Russian displaced persons from all over Europe, I was put
on a steamer in Naples – they made speeches and had a band playing
for us, the sons of bitches – and we all sailed to Odessa. Special prison
railroad cars with barred windows were already waiting for us when
we arrived. So, cursing and swearing, we rumbled all the way across
a sixth of the world's land surface straight to the port of Vanino in the
Far East, and from there we were shipped here on board the *Felix*,
like those women we saw today."

"It's fantastic!" exclaimed Tolya. "And you could have been living
a normal, peaceful life in Argentina!"

"I doubt it," said Sanya thoughtfully. "After that job in Córdoba
was over, Domenico and I were planning to go on to Australia."

To Tolya all these places like Paris, Argentina, and Naples were
farther away than the planets of the solar system. To all the young
inhabitants of this "One Sixth of the World," geography seemed a
completely abstract science, and none of them saw any serious purpose
in learning foreign languages. "We don't need the shores of Turkey,
and what is Africa to us," in the words of the patriotic song that they
used to hear sung on the radio. We're not interested in what's going
on out there beyond the barbed wire of the Soviet frontier: here are *We*
– Russians, the Soviet people; out there are *They* – ghosts, phantoms,
foreigners.

* * *

"Well, we sure seem to have gone in for citrus fruit in a big way this year!" said Colonel Guly after dinner as he complacently put aside his newspaper, feeling benevolent sympathy for Them, the workers of Europe who were groaning under the heel of the Marshall Plan, while the American occupiers doped them with Coca-Cola, deafened them with nerve-jangling "jast music," and raped their daughters.

"Come here, Lyudmila. Bring me your report card!"

"Oh, come on, dad, must I?"

His wife (from the sofa): "Georgii, are you at it again?"

"Bring it here, Lyudmila. I want to check out your progress on the political battlefront!"

As he watched his daughter going out of the room – ah, that delicious round little bottom! – he was aware, not without pleasure, that his blood was still a young man's blood and that right now it was pulsing hard into his chief extremity! Still without taking his eyes off his approaching daughter – nice little breasts, nice little tummy, everything where it should be! – the colonel was already unbuckling his officer's belt. The lazy little girl was bound to have a D somewhere in her schoolwork, whether it was for the image of Pechorin or that goddamn Darwinism, and this would be the pretext for some pleasurable moments: pushing her down on the bed, pulling up her skirt, and then a few paternal homilies expressed on her pink, rounded buttocks. "We don't need – one! The shores of Turkey – two! And what is Africa to us – three! We don't need it, don't need it, don't need it!"

The hill was now rising up in front of Tolya and Sanya like a gigantic black wall, as though it was that notorious Iron Curtain behind which the West lay concealed. The brilliant sickle of a crescent moon peeped over the top like a spying prison guard. At the foot of the hill, along a white road, stood a row of black wooden huts. At night, with their hideous defects hidden from view, they appeared perfectly sound, solid, and even cozy dwellings, their windows giving out a friendly glow, and it was immediately obvious that these were not prison-camp buildings but regular homes.

"Say, look at that moon, like a guard on a prison wall," said Sanya, laughing. "Any minute now it'll open fire on us!"

Tolya was very surprised that they had both had the same thought about the moon. "But, Sanya, suppose it's not a guard? Suppose it's a scout or a spy from the other side?"

"From what side?" Gurchenko threw Tolya a rapid glance. "From what other side?"

Suddenly a dark wave of fear overwhelmed Tolya. His legs turned weak with terror. "Oh, I didn't mean anything, just . . . a sort of poetic thought . . . like a metaphor. By the way, this is the Third Medical Complex. Which house do you want?"

"Number 6." Gurchenko took out a slip of paper, struck a match, and read, "Number 6, apartment 8."

The dark fear spread farther inside him, and his stomach heaved. It was his address. Who was this young man and what did he want with them? Was he from THERE? From that neat little landowner's mansion with the colonnaded porch, from THAT organization? Right now, no doubt, Martin was at home and he was probably . . . Of course, this Gurchenko was from *there*. That was why he was so bold and cheeky! And cunning, too – they had trained him to talk like that, as if he were just another prisoner. What was Tolya to do? How could he warn Martin?

"I've been asked to repair a window frame," said Sanya.

He shook his carpenter's tools and marched ahead as though he had forgotten about Tolya, whistling something sad that wasn't exactly a tune, formless but melancholy. Ashamed, Tolya threw aside his suspicions.

As they entered room 8, Martin was kneeling in front of a little portable altar and praying. Softly but quite audibly he was reciting in Latin, "*Pater noster, qui es in caelis: Sanctificetur nomen tuum!*"

He looked over his shoulder and smiled. "Ah, Sanya!"

Tolya watched as he stretched out his hand to Gurchenko, clearly not intending it to be shaken, with the back of the hand upward, and Gurchenko knelt down and kissed that muscular, heavily veined hand.

Martin made the sign of the cross over Gurchenko. Then they both knelt before the altar and completed the prayer together: "*Adveniat regnum tuum: Fiat voluntas tua, sicut in caelo, et in terra. Panem nostrum quotidianum da nobis hodie: Et demitte nobis debita nostra, sicut et nos dimittimus debitoribus nostris. Et ne nos inducas in tentationem. Sed libera nos a malo. Amen.*"

The little altar consisted of three parts, like a triple mirror. On the left side of the triptych was glued a postcard-size picture of *Descent from the Cross*, on the right side was a reproduction of Raphael's *Sistine Madonna*, while in the middle a crucifixion had been drawn directly on the plywood by a none-too-skillful hand.

Tolya stood in the doorway behind the two kneeling men and looked at Martin's bare, shaved head and Sanya's thick, unruly head of hair. He had long known that Martin was a believer, that he prayed, and that he possessed this folding altar, a tiny Bible, and rosary. All this was in such wildly unimaginable contradiction to Tolya's ideal of an athletic Komsomol youth, with his longing to be an average "healthy member of society," it was all so shameful, that Tolya tried somehow not to notice it and, of course, not to ask any questions.

Yet he liked Martin. He was always very bright and breezy, this Martin: He would step over the threshold, wipe the icicles away from his eyebrows, flash his great teeth in a smile, and say cheerfully, "The frost has gotten much fiercer, my children!"

From his visits to the prison officers" houses he would bring home delicious food, money, and odds and ends of clothing. Sometimes he played on the flute, sitting in front of the frost-bound window and drawing from his instrument a gentle, old-fashioned tune. Tolya became very attached to him, although he was desperately ashamed of this member of his new family, whom he had never dreamed of meeting here when he had flown from the "mainland" to join his mother. What an unexpected man he was – a German, a prisoner, a homeopathist, and a Catholic! The church and Catholicism were things that Tolya found old-fashioned and vicious, a kind of disease that gave off a bad smell. OK, so Tolya had made up his mind not to ask questions – he had already burnt his fingers from asking certain questions – OK, so he would leave Martin in peace. After all, he was already a pretty old man.

Yet now Tolya had seen this bold, smart young lad of almost his own age, who reminded him of the Ringo Kid in the film *Stagecoach*, kneeling in front of a Catholic altar while Martin blessed him with the sign of the cross and they whispered the Latin words of a prayer together! Surely Sanya wasn't a practicing Catholic too? And what about Martin? Perhaps he wasn't just a simple Catholic but a priest too, a padre? Where am I?

"Which is the broken window frame, Philip Yegorovich?" Sanya asked as he stood up.

Martin took a can of sprats and bottle of port wine out of a trunk. "I see you have already gotten acquainted with Tolya."

"And under pretty strange circumstances, too," muttered Tolya.

"What happened?" Martin looked up in some alarm.

"Oh, it was nothing special." Sanya made a dismissive gesture and winked conspiratorially at Tolya, meaning, Don't give me away. "Near the bathhouse someone threw a packet of tea into a column of women prisoners and the guards kicked up a fuss."

"I hope you didn't throw it, Sanya?"

"Really, Philip Yegorovich!"

"Be careful, my children." Martin took off his glasses, wiped them, and put them back on his nose. "Be very careful!"

"And who are you to talk?!" asked Tolya with a spitefulness that surprised even himself.

His spiteful tone was understood. Sanya stared at him very hard, noticing the Komsomol badge on his jacket, grinned without saying anything, and climbed up on the windowsill with his tools. Martin said nothing either, but glanced at his watch and sat down at the table, placing his hands, palms down, on the tablecloth. The wine and the sprats remained unopened. As for the model student of the Magadan High School, member of the Komsomol, star of the town's junior basketball team, he retired behind a screen to his own corner, sat down on his bed, and opened Academician Timofeyev's textbook on Russian literature.

He held the book in front of him, oblivious to the printed words, and reflected on the events of the last few days: about the shame of his torn pants and his split lip, about Colonel Guly's belt, about the bottle of Mermaid cologne, about the strangely public yet private temple of Perfisha the Yakut, about the altar, about the crucifixion. Who had crucified Him? Why was He the Son of God? How did He rise from the dead? Why did oppressed people turn to Him? Who am I and who can I turn to? Why did I come into this world and where will I go when I leave it? I have sensed the proximity of a terrifying threshold, across which there is the piercing fear of incomprehension, an agonizing awareness of my own littleness, insignificance, and uselessness in the incredible universe of suns and planets. The only way of banishing these thoughts was by a violent shake of the head.

The tapping of a hammer. The tinkle of breaking glass. Somewhere far away a flute gently played the melody of Beethoven's *Scottish Song*. Then there was silence. Tolya realized that there was no one else in the room and set about making preparations.

The electric cord was partly sufficient and was included in his plan. Tolya lengthened it by tying to it the belt of his mother's bathrobe and a towel; then he found a whole coil of clothesline behind the radiator. Hurrah! Now I can manage without any unreliable dodges! This excellent rope will easily bear my sixty-five kilograms! The next important step was to take the lamp off the hook in the ceiling.

Everything had to be done quickly, neatly, and efficiently before his mother or Aunt Varya came back.

Tolya switched off the light, climbed up on the table, cut the cord with a kitchen knife, and carefully lowered the heavy pink, fringed lampshade. Why spoil it? After they take the body down, they can use the lamp again.

Outside the window rose the steep, grim mass of Wolf's Hill, cutting out three quarters of the sky. The rest of the sky, however, was enough to flood the room with bright moonlight. All the objects in the room threw sharp, distinct shadows, and the shadow of the noose on the wall was absurdly clear. Was the moon really so bright tonight?

The shadow of a head slipped through the shadow of a noose made of a looped clothesline. The door creaked, and on the threshold appeared the figure of Martin. He stood there silently peering into the solemn, moonlit gloom of the room, and behind him, amid smoky yellow fumes, seethed the loathsome, bustling life of the corridor: Someone was hurrying past with a skillet, someone with a saucepan, someone with a bucket of dirty slops, another with a mop, while nearby stood Paulina, the woman from the next apartment. She was in an odd pose, half with her back to the open door, half sideways; at any rate, her intensely desirable breasts were thrust out forward and her shamefully desirable bottom jutted out behind her.

"I, a Young Pioneer of the Union of Soviet Socialist Republics, do solemnly swear in the presence of my comrades," Tolya muttered hastily, afraid that everything would be ruined and that in another moment it would be too late.

"Come with me, Tolya," said Martin quietly.

"Over the hill?" guessed the boy.

He remained standing with the noose around his neck and went with Martin along the creaking passage and down the staircase, then along a winding pathway toward the hill. They walked through the thick darkness under a glittering sky.

"What drew you to the noose?" Martin asked without turning around

"But surely you know?" cried Tolya, and sang out rejoicing, "Fifty-eight, paragraphs eight and fourteen KRTD,* and fifty-eight, paragraphs ten and eleven with loss of civil rights and without, and my pants split while she was watching and that girl bit off the neck of the bottle and Perfisha has his frozen gods and you are a homeopathist

*Russian initials for "Counter-Revolutionary Trotskyite Activity."

and a Catholic priest and I'm a Komsomol and I'm sixteen years
old!"

He burst out sobbing and walked to the edge of the table. The toes
of his shoes hung over the abyss.

"You mustn't do that," said Martin sternly.

"But why not?"

"It is a great sin. God commands you not to do it!"

"I don't believe in Him," said Tolya with a laugh. "What am I to
Him?"

"He needs every human being," said Martin with his previous
severity and fell into powdery blue snow up to his chest.

Tolya stood over him on the edge of the firm path, and also on the
edge of the dining table.

"You believe in Him although you don't know it," Martin went on,
making no attempt to clamber out of the snowy ditch and only rubbed
his bald head, deep in thought. "You know Tolya, that in this world"
– with a movement of his arm he embraced the glittering but starless
sky and the strangely altered, angular landscape, wild but obviously
not belonging to Kolyma – "in this world a great battle is in progress.
God is fighting against the one who is called the Devil, against the
Darkness, against Nothingness, against Emptiness. God needs
everyone for this struggle. God needs the actions of human beings."

"How do you know?"

"I don't know, I believe."

"Perhaps he needs me to step off this table?"

"No, no, He doesn't need that," muttered Martin, climbing out of
his snow-filled pit. "It is a sin, a sin, a sin."

"But perhaps I need it more than He doesn't need it?" shouted
Tolya spitefully.

"You don't think that!" Martin raised his hands in horror. "Admit
that you're simply playing at atheism out of bravado!"

Tolya made no reply and began rapidly clambering up the pathway
toward the gleaming silvery crest. This time it was Martin who followed
in his footsteps, breathing heavily.

He did not know whether it was for a long or a short time that he
teetered on the edge of the table. At all events, they reached the crest
of the hill and before them lay spread out an endless expanse of hilly
countryside, over which a shining heavenly body hung in absolute
tranquility.

"Why have we come here?" Tolya asked Martin.

"I don't know," the latter answered softly. "You must realize that I am no more than a human being, just as you are."

Without making the slightest movement, the shining body observed them intently.

"What shall we see here? The future life or the past?"

Laughing soundlessly, a detachment of marauders in motley uniforms strode past them, wearing breastplates and scraps of precious velvet, in a drunken mood of wolfish merriment, smeared in blood, mud, and wine.

Toward this detachment there came slowly through the dwarf stone pine another group of people, pale and dead tired, also spattered with blood – their own – with arms crossed on their chest, in dignity and peace.

Now something is going to happen, thought Tolya. Now the battle will break out, now I will learn at least one answer. Alas, both groups went their separate ways in silence and moved away into the boundless snows.

Nobody knows anything, and the cold on this plateau is piercing me to the bone. The shame and the cold were too much for a sixteen-year-old.

Tolya swayed nearer to the edge, the rope tightened beneath his Adam's apple, that lump of gristle that had only recently formed itself in his throat.

"And what about your mother?" Martin then cried very loudly, his voice carrying far in space.

The marauders and the men of righteousness turned around for a moment, and Tolya sat down in the snow and sniveled like a little child.

At once they turned back to the hut. Martin led Tolya by the hand, but Tolya still sniffed and sniveled in terrible but now childish, innocent misery. His pride had evaporated at the sound of that one word "mother."

Of course, the young Von Steinbock was still swaying on the edge of the table with his head in the noose and reciting his Pioneer oath "to serve the cause of Lenin and Stalin," but it was not, to tell the truth, meant very seriously.

The shaman Perfisha was hopping around in the corridor, and his idols, the seals, were dancing with him, their stone-hard frozen bodies banging and bumping as they pranced. Perfisha was singing Cavaradossi's aria but in his own peculiar way, accompanied by grunts and much slapping of his buttocks and thighs. All the neighbors, in fact, were dancing around together with all their utensils, and only Paulina, the woman from next door, continued to stand in the same provocative pose, declaring in a booming voice, like a radio announcer, "This year, as planned, we have sharply increased the citrus-fruit harvest! The country will soon be inundated with the products of our sun-drenched plantations!"

Tolya turned to Martin. "May I embrace her, Philip Yegorovich?"

"You may, Tolya, you may."

From behind, Tolya put his arms around Paulina and clasped her breasts, pressing his groin against her bottom. Unimaginable bliss pierced him through and through. The moment of shame drew near.

Somewhere far away a red silk Pioneer kerchief fluttered before the eyes of young Von Steinbock. Our older brothers are marching in ranks; each one is twenty years old. The standard-bearers are there on the flanks, flags streaming out, blood-red and bold! In steady lines the columns advance, and you too belong to that drum beat, to that great army! I'm a Pioneer, I'm the same as all the rest!

The woman Paulina wiggled her buttocks, and the blessed, despairing moment of shame was accomplished, spurting forth in irresistible bursts.

All wet, Tolya lay on his narrow bed, afraid to move: The creaking of springs, of course, might give away his secret to the people behind the screen.

Through the gaps in the screen he could see the brightly lit table, around which sat his strange family: his mother; her husband, the doctor-prisoner Martin; and her friend from prison known to Tolya as Auntie Varya. With them was a guest, Sanya Gurchenko, the carpenter-deportee. They were drinking port wine and eating sprats. Tolya's mother was cheerfully describing how the head of the personnel department of children's institutions, Madame Stupitsyna, had by chance heard her playing the piano and had suggested that she be promoted from housekeeper to music teacher, but the deputy head of the department, Madame Ikhanina, had objected forcefully that it would be ideologically incorrect to entrust the musical education of preschoolers to a former convict. But in reply to the two ladies' inquiries the telephone had barked that under the conditions of a severe shortage of qualified staff such questions should be decided on purely practical grounds, and therefore Tolya's mother would soon stop counting sheets and little pairs of soiled underpants and would move up to a new level of social responsibility, to play the noble instrument made by the Red October factory, which "stood, encased in wood, against the wall, giving forth entrancing sounds when touched by fingers."

Everyone laughed. Then Aunt Varya suddenly remembered that Martin was late for curfew. This meant trouble – he would be put in solitary and then sent to the mines!

Nonsense! Martin burst out laughing and explained that he had already bribed the guards at the Quarantine Camp so heavily that he did not even have to spend the night in the camp but only went there in order not to disturb the guards and because order was order, *die Ordnung!*

"I'll go with you, Philip Yegorovich," said Gurchenko as he stood up, remarking with pleasure, "Your window frame, comrades, is now in perfect shape. *C'est magnifique!*"

As they said goodbye, Sanya and Tolya's mother spoke to each other in French, and it was obvious that both of them derived great pleasure from talking in a foreign language.

When the men had left, his mother asked Aunt Varya in a low voice, "What do you think is the matter with Tolya?"

"In my opinion, he is in love," said Aunt Varya.

"Oh Lord!" said Tolya's mother with a sigh. "Now my son is in love. Oh, God, oh, God."

ONE DAY IN 197–

the former Guards officer Serafim Ignatievich Coulagot, as he came to the end of his evening stroll in London's Kensington Gardens, noticed an anonymous artificial satellite moving across the sky toward the setting sun.

Once, long ago, Serafim Ignatievich, a fearless, poetic youth of the Gumilyov type, had dreamed of flying over Königsberg in the bomber *Knight of Russia*, and therefore for the rest of his life any flying object attracted his glance, which although permanently outraged by the October Revolution, was as keen and inquisitive as ever.

"Children! Pay attention, you little devils!" the old man called out, and the children, born to his daughter Manyechka from a succession of unknown fathers, some of whom may even have been Bolsheviks, came running up to the officer's calloused feet.

"Perhaps it's a Russian bomb, is it, Grandpa?" suggested the oldest grandchild, laughing as he followed his grandfather's pointing finger.

ON THE SAME DAY

the sculptor Radius Apollinarievich Khvastishchev, in a smock spattered with clay, alabaster, yesterday's cake, India ink, lipstick, Prussian blue, and Bulgarian salad, was sitting on the tail of his marble offspring and tinkering with a blowtorch. While his hands were clumsily occupied in this mechanical work, his spirit in the meantime, having seized upon an idea, was soaring over the squares of Moscow in a creative search, seeking a suitable place for a hitherto unseen, gigantic sculptural group, the circular frieze *Moebius*, a model of eternity, the future path of mankind.

Yesterday's tempting proposal made by a Texas oil tycoon had this morning been curtly and rudely rejected by telephone. Khvastishchev's creations belonged to his Motherland, to Moscow, because the umbilical cord through which he drew the creative juices from his native soil had not yet run dry, dear tycoon!

ON THE SAME DAY

Samson Apollinarievich Sabler, with his usual vacant look, was strolling quietly around the Sivtsev Vrazhek District of Moscow, gently humming through his slightly swollen young man's nose, quietly grieving over the creative ideas that he had left scattered around in various bars, mildly hungering for the pound of sliced salami hidden under the saxophone in his instrument case, while calmly and resignedly contemplating the sunset of his career, his youth, and his dreams.

Suddenly, above a huge gray building that looked like some horrible parliament house, he saw in the blue haze an aerial eel. Emitting the opening bars of a minor-key but thoroughly erotic tune, the eel wriggled down straight into Samsik's hands. This eel turned out to be nothing more than a long paper printout of an electrocardiograph. Where had it flown from? Surely not out of the windows of the Central Committee's special clinic?

Staring at the mysterious jagged lines, Samsik went into a bar serving semiprepared food and sat down at a little toy table.

"Since when are you a doctor!" said the waitress serving out the semiprepared bouillon, apparently so offended by someone that she didn't even say the words but mouthed them with her young sausage-like lips.

Instantly Samsik cheered up, opened his instrument case, and quite without embarrassment began eating the sliced salami. Then he took out the sax and played the beginning of a new tune, passing it around on approval, as it were. Let it go the rounds of Moscow all day and some jackal of a plagiarist could gobble it up tomorrow morning somewhere on the Solyanka for all he cared.

"Since when are you a musician!" mouthed the waitress.

Ah, even if only for a moment he felt himself a teenager again, a spotty masturbator, a "melancholy vagabond, one of the moonlight wanderers," a European champion arisen out of this God-forsaken corner of the world.

ON THE SAME DAY

in his capacity as a consultant Gennady Apollinarievich Malkolmov arrived at the secret section of the UPVDOSIVADO and CHIS clinic.

The monumental granite structure with a plinth of black marble resembled the parliament building of some small totalitarian country inhabited by a bad and cruel people. There was, of course, no sign-board or inscription on this institution, but the long line of black limousines (their windows screened by blinds like the windows of a brothel) that stretched along the façade and the cast-iron railings announced eloquently to the general citizenry, Don't poke your nose in here if you value your life!

The high-ranking doctors of this exclusive clinic stared mistrustfully at the consultant's long, lank hair and bohemian moustache as he walked in their company down the endless corridors of this temple of healing. He was conducted into a spacious office and shown a brand-new cardiogram that had just rolled out of an ultramodern West German machine.

"Well, professor, what does my EKG look like?" asked a command-ing, condescending bass voice. Malkolmov saw through the spider's web of wires a blotchy pink, sappy, elderly body and above the body a pair of insistent little eyes, like two hot beads, and a contemptuous fold of willful, sardonic lips.

Holding the EKG, Malkolmov walked over to the window. Outside, down below in the narrow alleyway, there tottered the frail little figure of a musician with an instrument in a case. From above, Malkolmov mentally sent greetings to that familiar figure and then threw down to it the shiny imported cardiogram. The long EKG strip quickly took on the role of an aerial Muscovite eel. It immediately caught the attention of the musician and curled affectedly as it wriggled down into his hands. Malkolmov smiled sadly.

"So what about my EKG, Professor? Hurry up with your diagnosis, or I'll be late for a portrait sitting with the sculptor."

"Even the Kremlin wall might envy your EKG – it's so normal, comrade guards comrade," said Malkolmov, paying no attention to the warning gestures of the resident physicians or their horrified looks.

"That suits me," said the patient with a chortle.

Malkolmov looked into his eyes and at once noticed from the iris that the patient's organism had a catastrophic lack of Lymph-D, but said nothing; this was not what he had been summoned for, and in any case did such patients even need Lymph-D, an idealistic substance that had been unmasked at the last session of the presidium of the Academy of Medical Sciences?

ON THE SAME DAY

in a quadrangle on the campus of the University of Sussex a revolutionary assault was in preparation.

All night long the revolutionaries had been lighting campfires, dancing the hula, playing cards, smoking grass, working themselves up, discussing the problem of union with the working class – which for some reason seemed very undesirous of such a union – and, of course, fucking one another on all the steps of the vice-chancellor's staircase. They were waiting for the arrival of the mass media, for who makes a revolution nowadays without the television cameras?

The co-chairpersons of the revolutionary committee, Johnny Dior and Eurydice Cliquot, together with delegates from the sexual minorities, were working out a plan for the insurrection. As soon as the TV people had set up their lighting equipment, the storming of the library would begin. Simultaneously, effigies of the professors and senior lecturers would burst into flame, while portraits of the saints – Lenin, Mao, Stalin, Trotsky, Hitler, Che Guevara, and Yasir Arafat – would rise into the dawn sky. Then they would blow up the totem pole of bourgeois liberalism, a fifty-meter obelisk inscribed with the names of bourgeois scholars.

Now the first rays of a crimson, pastoral sun were illuminating the fluffy, tinsellike clouds over the county of Sussex. That mythical bird, the bittern, shrieked hysterically from a neighboring swamp. For the last time Eurydice passed her pimply young tongue over the offspring of the House of Dior, who was already exhausted before the revolution had even begun, looked up into the sky, and shrieked with amazement and fury.

On top of the university obelisk could be seen a folding cot, and sitting on it was Patrick Percy Thunderjet, professor in the Department of Slavic Studies.

The appearance of the indecently alcoholic professor at such an inaccessible height was as magical as it was scandalous. The revolutionaries were shocked. The telescopic lenses all began pointing upward, and enthusiasm for storming the empty library evaporated.

How this reactionary had managed to reach the top of this smooth column, and with a cot, a case of beer, and a thick book as well, was never explained. For several hours the aim of his ascent also remained unclear.

"I am trying to build a bridge between two decades," Thunderjet replied vaguely from the top of the pillar in reply to a telephone inquiry from the philosopher Sartre in Paris.

Finally, when the events of the day were in full swing, the professor got up and requested the attention of those below. "In the name of and under instructions from the youth of Simferopol and Yalta, I will now piss on your revolution," he said amid the silence and, having first apologized to the young ladies present, thereupon carried out his promise.

ON THE SAME DAY

the scientific, administrative, political, and security bosses of a top-secret institution were conferring in the holy of holies, on the topmost floor of a corner tower that looked like the top of a cream cake.

"I would think twice, comrades, before leaving him in charge of such a sensitive department as Laboratory Number 4," said the Party Committee. "The opinion has been expressed that he is not just a sick man but is exhibiting a certain definite tendency in his views."

"I would not describe it as a definite tendency," Security put in, quietly but firmly. "Observation has yielded contradictory data. During his last drinking binge, Kunitser more than once shouted curses at Sophia Vlasevna, as he calls my organization, but several times he also sobbed and demanded freedom for Angela Davis. He has not only condemned what they call the invasion of Czechoslovakia but the bombing of Vietnam, too. So the picture is not quite clear, comrades."

"Forget it, guys," Science smiled carelessly. "I talked to Kun in his own language and he swore to me that he would never touch another drop. Kun is profoundly shaken by what happened to him. He says that all this boozing conflicts with his personal, moral, and religious convictions."

"Religious?" Party Committee started up at the word.

"Well, you know, that's a manner of speaking. The chief thing is that he is a genius, and his formula has given us a powerful boost."

"Will he really not touch another drop?" inquired Administration gloomily. "You realize how important this is, don't you? can he at least keep it up until the experiment is finished?"

The intercom apparatus on the desk gave a low buzz, a red light flashed, and a secretary's voice announced meaningfully, "Aristarkh Apollinarievich has arrived."

"Kun, are you there? Come in, old man!" exclaimed Party Committee joyfully, and ran to open the door.

Kunitser came in looking pale, with sunken cheeks and unfocused eyes, settled himself on the edge of the desk, then said in a dull voice, "Our tin can has completed three orbits. Everything is normal."

"Where is it now, Kun?" asked the scientist softly.

Aristarkh Apollinarievich looked at his watch. "Right now it is over London, to be exact, over Kensington Gardens, and in five minutes it'll be over the Irish Sea."

"You haven't switched on the device, have you?" asked Security cautiously.

"Would you want me to switch it on over Kensington Gardens?" Kun turned even whiter, almost blue, and his cheek twitched.

"Oh, come now, Kun," said Security, smiling. "What do you take me for? After all, children might be walking there."

ON THE SAME DAY

almost at nightfall the golden-haired vixen Alisa, in a brand-new red Volkswagen, was driving through Moscow on urgent business. This little car, a masterpiece of Western mass-consumption technology, had been recently sent to her by mail by an old friend of Academician Fokusov, the progressive cosmopolitan Norman Guttiero Normans.

Fokusov and Normans, two progressive playboys, had a great deal in common: many years of the hard struggle for peace, meetings at various hot spots of the planet, conferences, dinners, cocktail parties. Recently they also had Alisa in common.

In his heart of hearts the Academician had been angered by the gift of a Volkswagen: The brief but stormy friendship between Alisa and Normans had been made known in their circle, and now, what d'you know – a Volkswagen! Was it just a sentimental greeting or – who knows? – the payment of a prearranged fee for services rendered? He did not, of course, show his indignation, but merely refused to pay the customs duty of two hundred percent. How it all ended, we have already seen – Alisa was driving around Moscow in her Volkswagen on urgent business.

She was a little excited, as she always was before the start of a new affair, but there was something special about her present excitement. Lately she had completely lost the ability to relax, and all her dashing adventures, phone calls, sudden disappearances, unexpected flights to the south, in fact all things that made up her life, were now tinged with a certain latent unease.

Recently in Yalta she was descending by cable car from the Gorka Restaurant at Darsan. She was drunk and cheerful. Traveling with her in the little two-seater car was the arrogant Galeotti, a movie cameraman. He had put his arm around her, whispered indecent suggestions in her ear, and she had laughed, all the while knowing that she would not be sleeping with him that day but with the man who was coming down in the next car, an imperturbable character with a pipe between his teeth, who to all appearances was not interested in "that sort of thing." Suddenly she forgot about both her companion and the imperturbable man; she was seized by a mysterious excitement, a strange feeling that at this very moment something unique that concerned herself alone had flown past her like an invisible bird and was just about to vanish forever.

Down below at that moment a winding little Yalta street had come into view, where a file of about fifteen men was shuffling along with spades over their shoulders, followed by a bored policeman.

Today, that same feeling of the passing of an irreplaceable moment arose in her several times as she drove across Moscow to meet her new stud. First, while held up by a red light at an intersection, she had heard the wild voice of a saxophone floating up from some cellar. Then, at the three-lane turning into Gorky Street, she had noticed something like a dark-colored snake writhing in the air above the streetlamps, disappearing in the blaze of light from the windows, then reappearing at rooftop height before being snatched by the wind to float up and away. It might have been a note of music or the fragment of a cardiogram or simply a Muscovite aerial eel, witness to our secrets.

He was waiting for her at the agreed place, a tall good-looking young man, naturally, wearing a blazer, naturally, carrying a flat attaché case. Why the hell do I have anything to do with this slob, she thought glumly as she opened the door for him. As she pulled away from the sidewalk, she glimpsed the yellow electric letters of the latest news flickering above the roof of the *Izvestiya* offices: ". . . in Leningrad the work of the European con . . ."

Everything flew away, fled, rolled past her. She felt the faint twinge of a moment's passing melancholy. Now they were driving through a succession of small dark streets. The young man, half-turned toward her, was smoking a Kent and smiling with a lopsided grin. Winking at him, she turned her head away and saw through a window a bare wall, shelves, a marble sculpture. Then it was all gone, left behind.

They were now driving into the pitch blackness of a blind alley, alongside a temporarily halted construction project. She stopped the car, turned off all the lights, and switched off the ignition. In the silence she heard the hiss of a zipper and stretched out her hand. It's a good thing, she thought, that's it's completely dark as I hold this hot, hard, pulsating little brute in my hand. It makes it easier to imagine that it's not this slob but someone else. Before bending down, she looked up at the sky, where it seemed to her that among the motionless stars one was moving, slowly passing from Sirius toward Andromeda.

ON THE SAME DAY

under a glass dome, beneath the translucent sky of that city to which Mandelstam dreamed of returning one day with his friends, where among the stained-glass windows of doorways, the ghosts of the Silver Age still wander at night, under the dome of the Intourist hotel an ordinary "working" dinner of the European Community of Writers was in progress at the expense of the Literary Fund.

From their corner, two full-time secretaries of the Writers' Union kept a fatherly eye on the chomping European writers and smiled hospitably, while carrying on a far from carefree, indeed an apprehensive, conversation: They were jointly responsible for this dinner, and if any disaster were to occur, both of them would be out of favor "up there." For that reason the secretaries were now obliged to confer, suppressing their mutual detestation and their rivalry for the biggest slice of the cake of fame.

"Who's that wandering about between the tables, the one with the long hair? Have those smartass local boys from Leningrad managed to gate-crash again? Who's checking on invitations at the door?"

"That's Pantelei, a member of our delegation."

"What? Pantelei's been included in our delegation? I must say I sometimes find it hard to understand –"

"Forget it! The guy came to his senses a long time ago, and he hasn't signed any more letters of protest."

"He may not be signing anything, but he's been saying plenty. He's an alcoholic and a cynic, if not a subversive."

"Where did you hear that?"

"From 'up there,' of course."

"I see, I see. By the way, look over there – Fengaud is sitting alone. Go and do your stuff with Fengaud, and I'll invite Pantelei to my own table."

Fengaud, a frail little intellectual so nervous that he responded to the slightest external stimulus with a quivering of internal sensors, was vouchsafed his first glimpse of the typical Soviet bureaucrat. The bureaucrat was walking toward him, playing with a gnarled boxwood walking stick in his huge, puffy hand. Horrified yet fascinated, Fengaud observed the approach of this man-mountain in its vast gray suit. Fengaud was amazed to see how precisely the advancing individual corresponded to the image of the Soviet bureaucrat that he had built up in his own imagination.

And yet today of all days the bureaucrat had wanted to be simply a writer, one of the boys among his fellow writers, all Europeans together, and he would have been extremely annoyed if he had known that the little Frenchman saw him as a typical Soviet bureaucrat. In fact, before the start of the congress, under the watchful eye of his European-educated wife, much had been done to eliminate from his outward appearance a great deal of the bureaucratic gristle, padding, and stuffing and to add to the image a certain simple writerlike chic, liberalism, and even playfulness – hence the boxwood cane with a carved head of Mephistopheles, hence the bow tie (like Alexei Tolstoy, who was, after all, a count), hence the mignonette in his buttonhole, hence the pipe with the bowl carved to look like a devil. God, the things one has to do to deceive the bourgeois; why, they had even restyled his pants by cutting out the comfortable bagginess around the crotch and thus squeezing his hernia.

The secretary could not know that in the sophisticated imagination of the gentleman from Montparnasse a Soviet bureaucrat looked exactly as he did, down to the smallest detail – complete with boxwood cane, mignonette, bow tie, pipe bowl carved into a devil's head, but above all with that very same blue jowl, that tiny little nose sunk between two buttocklike cheeks, and those two dishonest, piggy little eyes.

Long ago, before the Revolution, the secretary had been a corporal in the imperial Cadet Corps, although in his memoirs he wrote vaguely and inconsistently about his "Komsomol youth," and then about his service in the tsarist navy fighting against the foe, followed by hints of his aristocratic origins, which, of course, he had repudiated at the trumpet call of the October Revolution, an action that deserved – and won – compensatory rewards from the new regime.

When addressing audiences of foreign guests, whether devoted friends or fierce antagonists of the Soviet system, he often used foreign words. Sometimes with a crafty, conspiratorial little smile he would say "ladies and gentlemen" (tensely hoping that it would *not* come out as the proverbial "lady and hamilton"), and then he might even get his tongue around "attention please," in a cold sweat lest he say "tension peas."

As he came up to Fengaud, the secretary put one arm around the tender forty-year-old neck, the other behind the Frenchman's lean, sinewy bottom – an ambiguous gesture, to say the least – and boomed right over the angular avant-garde little head a string of sweet, deceptive words designed to attract the hearer irresistibly to the tenets of socialist realism. "Well, my dear scriptorius, let me wish you as we Russians say – *bon appétit*! Welcome!"

Behind his elbow the trained interpreter had already conveyed to the stunned Fengaud, "Good evening, Monsieur Fengaud! For years I have been following your researches into a biological monotype that is not culturally determined and is therefore free."

"Did you translate correctly?" asked the secretary. "Did you tell him 'welcome?' Not 'well, chum,' but meaning 'do come to the table' or 'dinner is served.' "

"All's well, Hal Sich," whispered the interpreter confidentially, implying that he was one hundred percent Russian too, even though he was obliged to earn his living by talking double Dutch.

Fengaud's nervous system quivered like an aspen in a hurricane. "Thank you, monsieur," he managed to say, as he disentangled himself from the fumes of cologne and brandy. An ancient Gallic gene in the depths of his organism summoned its Jewish brothers to battle. "I am truly shattered to learn that my modest labors are known to such a highly placed individual in such a distant country."

"What's that? What's he saying?" The secretary shook the interpreter. The sound of a foreign language, as usual, both irritated and amused him.

"All's well, Hal Sich," answered the interpreter nonchalantly with a smile. "He says it's cold outside but the warmth of Russian hospitality has melted our hearts."

"Bully for you! Well said!" The secretary slapped Fengaud on the shoulder. "Eat, eat, Monsieur Fengaud. Don't stand on ceremony; eat everything that's on the table, and if it's not enough, we'll order more. Well, bottoms up! To the beautiful land of France! *Pour belle France!* Ah, Paree, Paree."

Meanwhile the other secretary, in a thoroughly friendly, confidential spirit of one writer to another was dining with Pantelei, encouraging him with pats on the shoulder, a political joke or two, and a liberal line of talk. "You know, old man, I don't like these bullyboys of ours either. Thinking people should stick together. You, for example, why don't you drop in on my magazine?"

"Yes, I'll drop in sometime," mumbled Pantelei.

"I don't mean just drop in for a piss when you happen to be passing by on the boulevard. If you bring me something not too long, even if it's in your special style, I'll publish it. Do you have something like that?"

"Yes, I do," Pantelei smiled. "It's called 'The Rusty Funicular.' "

Suddenly the interpreter ran up, lathered in perspiration. How had he managed to work up such a sweat in only twenty paces?

"Andr Ukich, Fengaud has gone crazy, Hal Sich is as red as a beetroot. They were talking about the *nouveau roman*, but Hal Sich is completely out of his depth and I can't quite keep up either."

The secretary chuckled with satisfaction: This was the moment when it became obvious that nowadays you couldn't go far with nothing but bullyboys in charge of the Writers' Union.

"Come on, Pantelei, let's go and cope with this Frenchman!"

Hal Sich found intelligent conversation exhausting, whereas Andr Ukich clearly enjoyed it. Pantelei said nothing and smoked. He felt sorry for the drunken Fengaud and could imagine the agony he would suffer tomorrow, one little Frenchman alone in this vast bureaucratic country where you couldn't even get Alka-Seltzer. Fengaud was getting drunker by the minute, spouting ever greater nonsense about structuralism. Suddenly he went silent and stared at Pantelei as though he had only just noticed him.

"Excuse me, I've suddenly realized – you're Pantelei, aren't you? Forgive me. Somebody mentioned your name to me the day before yesterday. He asked me to send you his regards."

"Who?" asked the interpreter, without waiting for Pantelei's reaction. "Who asked you to send his regards to Pantelei?"

"It was some curé or other. I met him in La Coupole café. I don't remember his name. Some curé . . . Excuse me, do you happen to know a curé in Paris?"

"Do you know a curé, Pant?" asked the interpreter casually.

The idiot, the drunken fool, thought Pantelei. He couldn't have chosen a worse moment to send me greetings from Paris – and from a priest, too.

Hal Sich stared at Fengaud in glassy-eyed horror, Andr Ukich smiled a vague, ambiguous smile, the interpreter stared at Pantelei with frank, professional curiosity, while the Frenchman, the stupid prick, wiped his steamed-up glasses.

"Of course. I know more than one," Pantelei said to the interpreter. "I have pretty good connections with the Vatican. So you can pass that on, pussycat, to the proper quarters."

"IT HAPPENED IN ROME

one intolerably hot and sultry night in September, on the little square in front of the Trevi Fountain. Do you remember that fountain, old man?"

"Of course I do. Anita Ekberg and Marcello Mastroianni bathed in it in the film *La Dolce Vita*. As if I could forget it! As if I could forget Anita!"

"Yes, that's it – a great pile of baroque sculpture, poison-blue water, its cracked bottom covered with coins, and all around it the babble of Babel, the whir of movie cameras, the fumes of alcohol, nicotine, and perfume rising into the autumn night sky of the Eternal City. It was the same everywhere during that season: on the Piazza di Spagna, the Via del Corso, the Via Nazionale, and in Trastevere – crowds of overexcited tourists were surging everywhere. That year, Rome was truly the center of the world. Its ancient renown had merged with a new one, created by films about sin and novels written by homosexuals.

"All the sidewalk café tables were full, and in the bars people were standing shoulder to shoulder, swilling gin and tonic, iced Campari, and beer. Amid all this, as you may have guessed, old man, I wanted a drink too.''

"I can guess that. I wanted a drink then too.''

"Just imagine, I was completely alone in Rome. A Soviet citizen alone in Rome and with plenty of Italian lire in my pocket! It was a sensation, a triumph of the new era! Our delegation had flown back to Moscow that morning, and I had been allowed to go on from Rome to Belgrade to take part in a symposium. How about that, eh? The KGB man in charge of our party had spent two whole nights on the phone to Moscow to wangle me that permission, and he had succeeded. He was a most charming fellow, an old hand from the days of the Cheka who had taken part in the pacification of Turkestan.''

"Its funny you should say that, old man.''

"Why, old boy?''

"Because the same thing happened to me: Rome, hot and sultry weather, an old Chekist phoning Moscow. The only difference was that my nice old KGB man had been a specialist in the Baltic states, dealing with the Forest Brotherhood, those anti-Soviet guerrillas, and I wasn't going to Belgrade but to Ljubljana.''

"OK, perhaps you'd like to tell me the rest of your story?''

"No, why should I? Do go on. I was just surprised by the coincidence. You know, Rome, the hot weather, longing for a drink . . . And didn't you want a woman, too, old man?''

"Like crazy! I wanted one so much that I felt dizzy and trembled shamefully in every limb. Maybe you saw me that evening by the Trevi Fountain?''

"Unlikely. I was pacing up and down the Piazza di Spagna like a jackal. Go on with your story.''

"I suddenly saw that one place was free at a little table beside a drainpipe. The other seat at the table was occupied by a priest, who was leaning with one shoulder against the moldy wall. He was smoking and staring ahead at one spot as though dazzled by the countless rainbows created by the jets of the fountain, and he didn't immediately respond when I asked if I might sit at his table.''

"But *how* did you ask him, old man?''

"Don't be sarcastic. I asked him in Italian, '*Permesso?*' And he answered in English, 'Go ahead.' He took me for an American.''

"I bet that pleased you!''

"Of course it did. It's always nice for us when people don't recognize us as Russians. It's come to a pretty pass when we're ashamed of our

own nationality! In fact, I was so annoyed with myself that instead of
a gin and tonic, which was the fashionable drink that summer, I ordered
a triple vodka and tossed it off in one gulp – just to show that I was a
real one hundred percent Russian and could take my drink like a man!

"The priest didn't even notice this piece of bravado. He was lost in
thought. But I earned a gentle round of applause from a scraggy,
middle-aged Englishwoman who was sitting at the next table. In those
days in Rome, you remember, there was a special mood in the air at
night, a sense of a kind of brotherhood, as if we were all carefree,
footloose cosmopolitans – the free world, the decline of civilization,
flower power, and so on. She was so well groomed, clean, and fragrant,
that thin woman! Beside her sat her companion, such a liberal, self-
deprecating, and elegant Englishman! And I was such a sweaty,
clumsy, and scruffy Russian! The triple vodka quickly had its effect,
and with a charming smile I said to the lady in the dialect of Moscow's
Pioneer Market, 'How would you like me to give you a hot rod?'

" 'I beg your pardon?' she said with the most genuine kindliness and
attention, her clean features reaching out to me through the attractions
of Helena Rubinstein. Her companion, with a courteous inclination of
his head and a wrinkling of his brow, attempted to penetrate the
obscure world of this barbaric language.

" 'It's you who should pardon me, my dear Madame Whore,' I went
on ceremoniously. 'The fact is, in the words of the song, "I haven't
seen a woman for four long years," so I would be delighted to screw
you anywhere you like, even in a toilet if need be. Sincerely, yours
truly,' – I said in English – 'you'll be fucked while you're still asleep,
vous comprenez?'

" 'Excuse us, sir,' said the Tory intellectual as he scratched his
moustache with his fingernail and gave me a friendly smile. 'Neither
my wife nor I understand your language. Are you a Serb? Perhaps
you'd care to join us for a drink?'

"I found myself liking him, so out of shame I ceased lusting after
his skinny woman. For a second I considered accepting their invitation,
when suddenly my priestly neighbor leaned very slightly in my direction
and with a smile through the cigarette smoke said in perfect Russian
thieves" slang, 'Watch it, kid, or those dudes could land you in shits-
ville. Quite a few people in the West know Russian, and there are
even some of us, as you see, who dig the scene.'

"I tell you, old man, that I would have been less amazed if the statues
of the Trevi Fountain had come alive! I was absolutely dumbfounded!"

"And scared, too, I'll bet!"

"And how! A string of the most terrifying initials and names ran through my head – NTS,* CIA, KGB, the Holy Inquisition, trap. *agent provocateur.* . . . I thought some terrible force had planted one of their agents on me! Someone was after me!"

"But how could they have planted a man when it was *you* who sat at *his* table?"

"Exactly. But that thought only came to me afterward. For several minutes I sat there speechless and I could hear, as though through layers of cotton and from a great distance, the English couple get up, the cast-iron legs of their chairs scraping over the asphalt, the woman's voice saying, 'Do you know, I had the impression that that Serb was asking me to go to bed with him,' to which the man's voice replied, 'In that case you'd better give him our phone number.' Several minutes must have passed before I pulled myself together. All the while the priest said nothing and stirred his cup of coffee with a little spoon. Finally I was able to look him over very carefully.

"He was a little – perhaps a lot – over forty. Strongly marked features, a close haircut, graying slightly at the temples, a tanned face marred by several old scars – he looked more like a professional ice-hockey player than a priest. Under his black cassock, topped by a clerical collar, one could sense a lean, trained, athletic body. None of this was particularly surprising; nowadays there are plenty of sporting Jesuits. What was extraordinary was the fact that there was an elusive something in his looks that was definitely Soviet, something typical of Soviet people of his generation – specifically of *his* generation and not of ours."

"You're right. Each generation has some kind of invisible wrinkle that marks its features."

" 'Excuse me, I had the impression that you spoke to me in Russian,' I said cautiously to the priest.

" 'You were not mistaken.' He raised his eyes, and at once his face was transformed by humility, gentleness, and fatherly concern; he was clearly a Catholic priest and nothing else.

" 'But . . . as far as I can see . . . you are a Catholic priest.'

" 'Indeed,' he smiled. 'I am a member of the Order of the Knights Templars and I work in a Catholic library. By nationality I am Russian."

" 'It's fantastic! But you know all the very latest slang!'

*"NTS": Russian initials of "National Labor Union", an actively anti-Soviet emigfe political party.

"He laughed. 'I hope you'll forgive me. The situation was too tempting not to have a little joke and I couldn't resist it.'

" 'But you –' I began, and stopped myself.

" 'Yes, yes,' he said with a nod. 'You're not mistaken.'

" 'But how? And when?'

" 'Aha, that's a long story!'

"He raised his eyes heavenward and clasped his hands in the traditional Catholic gesture, but this time his gesture was ironic, and for a moment the priest's eyes glittered with such a spirit of audacity and recklessness that I even felt an inward stab of boyish excitement. He could have played a part in a cowboy movie, that priest.

" 'Shall we have a drink?' I suggested.

" 'Isn't it dangerous for you to drink with me?'

" 'Why should it be?' I said with feigned surprise, but he gently patted my arm.

" 'Don't think I don't know that circumstances vary for different people and that it's dangerous for some Soviet visitors to drink with a Catholic priest in the center of Rome and not dangerous for others. So I'm asking you, to which category do you belong?'

" 'I'm in no danger,' I said, 'but I belong to a third category: I'll stake my –'

" 'You'll stake your –' He smiled.

" ' –balls on it!' I exclaimed.

"And we both burst into laughter. We had a drink, and then another, after which we set off on a walk around the narrow streets of old Rome, reminiscent of the corridors of some noble but crumbling palace in which a permanent, insane carnival was in progress. In one of the little alleyways alongside the Palazzo Madama my new friend found his Fiat, and we began to cruise around the labyrinth of Rome. That night was a very special night in my life, a night like a beacon. After such a night you could go into the wastes of Siberia, you could even go to prison, but the glow of that night would continue to brighten your life for a long time. The empty eye sockets of the Colosseum, the scraggy cats that haunt the Forum, crayfish roasted on a spit in a real trattoria."

"Was that in Trastevere?"

"Yes, alcoholics, prostitutes, queers, roaming hordes of foreigners, crosses, domes, statues, arches, hippies lying around in heaps here and there. At the gates of the Vatican, my priest and I even managed to get involved in a fight."

"With some Americans?"

"Yes, with some American sailors. The priest and I were sitting on the steps of St. Peter's when a whole bunch of American sailors appeared, wearing their little white cook's hats. They had been brought in buses from Naples, on shore leave from ships of the Sixth Fleet. As usual, they were fooling around and behaving outrageously. This gang wanted to go into the Vatican and have a cup of coffee with Pope Paul VI.

"They were creating an uproar around the gates, harassing the Swiss Guards, and then – can you believe it? – my priest went up to the ringleader, a two-meter-tall hunk of muscle who was waving a bottle of chianti, and said to him in English, 'My son, get these oafs of yours away from here or your balls will be hanging from your ears,' and backed up his words with a hefty swing to the man's torso. Well, all hell broke loose! We were well and truly pulped."

"But at least the sailors went away and stopped making trouble."

"How do you know?"

"But exactly the same story happened to me! When you were telling it to me, I got goose pimples, because it all happened to me, except for a few minor details. Well, go on. What happened then?"

"Nothing much happened after that. We sat down on the steps of the cathedral again and went on with our conversation."

"On philosophical themes?"

"Yes, on philosophical themes."

"But what exactly were you talking about? About life? Or about death? About love? About retribution? About compassion? About man's duty to God? About God's debt to us? About the life of God? Or perhaps about His death?"

"Yes, old man, we talked about all that, but I was in a state of great elation and I can't exactly remember which way the conversation went. That wasn't really the point."

"No, that *was* the point, old boy. I was also pretty high, but I can still remember some of it."

"Perhaps you'd like to tell me? Try at least."

"I remember, we talked about something strange, about a

THIRD MODEL

" 'Tell me about God,' I asked him. 'Where does he live and what does he look like?'

" 'God lives beyond the crystal vault of heaven, at the very zenith,' he replied. 'That is where paradise is. The weather is always fine, everyone is nice to everyone else – it is the abode of the righteous. God is an old gray man with a big white beard and kind green eyes."

" 'That's very nice for the righteous,' I said, 'but what is there for us sinners except the skillets of hell? Let me ask you three questions: Do we need God? Does God need us? Does God exist?'

" 'How can I answer such questions? Do you think my garb gives me the right to give you the answers? It gives me no special rights; it only places me under an obligation."

" 'So it also places you under an obligation not to dodge questions like this. You must at least try to answer them."

" 'Very well, let me try. I think that throughout our lives, in all our searching, we are saying that we, both believers and so-called atheists, all need God. We always have before us two models for comparison: a thing or an idea as the first model, and then a thing or an idea for comparison with it. The second model may be better or worse than the first. But we only seek a third model; agonizingly, and so far without results, we try to create a third model and through it to see the face of God.'

" 'What's so clever about that? Won't the third model simply be even better or even worse than the second one?'

" 'Oh, no. Whether it's worse or better, it's still the same second model, only with expanded qualities. However, there does also exist in the world a third model for comparison; it is not better and not worse – it is completely different. Sometimes man comes close to it in his moments of creativity – in music, in poetry, in mathematics – but he only just comes close, he only senses its presence. You don't understand? It is impossible to understand. But do you feel it? The inexplicable – that is the third model. Take, for instance, those strange, biologically inexplicable attributes of human nature: compassion toward one's neighbor, charity, the urge for justice. These are the higher, inexplicable emotions. Others, such as cowardice, anger, even courage, are physiologically comprehensible feelings, and Freud has explained them all, including even the most complex combinations of them. The higher emotions, however, are inexplicable, fantastic, and it is with them that the precepts of Christianity are concerned. Christianity is like the breakthrough into space, that most courageous and far-reaching spurt toward the third model. Christianity, being itself fantastic, relies on fantastic emotions and proves the existence of the fantastic. When you come to think of it, biological life itself is a fantastic phenomenon, isn't it?'

" 'There are other religions too. They are also seeking what you call the "third model".' "

" 'I do not deny the sublimity of other religions, but Christianity, with its example of self-sacrifice, with its Sermon on the Mount, with its belief in resurrection, is the most fantastic, the most emotional, and the boldest of all religions. In addition, it is the most democratic one. It convinces even the simplest souls. It is Christianity that is in the forefront of man's great search.'

" 'Great, you say?'

" 'You, of course, don't regard it as great, do you?'

" 'More often than not, I don't. Especially when I have a hangover. When that happens, I think that all human history is just the heaving of an ant heap, that we are perpetually lying to ourselves, that we endlessly exaggerate our own significance in the universe and the importance of our ideas and actions, that we are utterly puny in this world, totally insignificant creatures on a worthless little planet.'

" 'We are as infinitesimally small as we are infinitely great.'

" 'Oh, lord, all these metaphorical expressions!'

" 'No, I am not talking in metaphors at all, I am simply talking of dimensions, of scale. Some scientists maintain that an elementary particle can contain within it a whole universe. How many universes, therefore, are there in our bodies, in our worthless little planet?'

" 'Phew, that's terrible to think about. Now we're dealing with something really frightening.'

" 'It's not frightening at all. Think about it more often and you'll see it's like the little chink of light in a *camera obscura*.'

" 'But in that case it must mean that an ant is equally as infinitely great as it is infinitesimally small! So what is the difference between men and ants?'

" 'Difference? There we go, stuck once again between our usual two models. Why do you need a difference? Don't you see that our concepts of dimension, our idea of scale, our notion of difference, don't exist in the real world?'

" 'I think I see what you're getting at. If we cannot debase ourselves by the thought of our own insignificance, of our nullity, then all our deeds and actions really are meaningful and important. Is that it?'

" 'That's correct, but that is only half of my idea. The other half is that if our concepts of scale are purely conditioned and we cannot imagine ourselves as "giants who stride from pole to pole, who change the course of rivers," then it means that it is not so much our *actions* that are important and meaningful – since no matter what we may do, such actions in themselves are neither small nor great – as the spiritual meaning of our actions; in other words, the quality that belongs in the realm of the fantastic, that is what is capable of breaking through toward the "third model," into the truly real world.'

" 'I see what you mean. You are saying that our actions, or rather the spiritual meaning of them, are interesting and important to God.'

" 'Exactly. It seems to me that the Almighty is more interested in that than in the revolutions of heavenly bodies and the movement of lumps of rock.'

" 'So God exists?'

" 'Of course! He lives beyond the crystal vault of heaven, in the paradise garden. His angels fight against the powers of evil, and sometimes they fly home on leave and lie down at His feet on the silky grass. He plays to them on the lute and gives them renewed strength to go on fighting. It is delightful there where He is. The climate is ideal, without all the cars and smog that we have in our Holy City of Rome.' "

AND IN THE GOLD OF SUNRISE,
THE MELTING AIMLESS PATH
THE AIMLESS RESTLESS SEEKER

"That, I think, is what that priest and I were talking about that night on the steps of St. Peter's Cathedral."

"Perhaps, old man, you and I both dreamed this?"

"Then there appeared over Rome fleecy, colored cirrus clouds – lilac, emerald, orange – and I recalled the line by Blok, '. . . and in the gold of sunrise, the melting aimless path, the aimless restless seeker,' and I quickly sobered up as the city did so too; I was seized by a fit of the early-morning shakes, irritation, heartburn, disquiet. Then he slapped me hard on the shoulder, handed me a little piece of cardboard, stood up, and walked over to his car. In my palm lay the visiting card of the Englishwoman from the café. I've completely forgotten her name."

"Mine was called Elizabeth Stevens, editor in chief. That was printed on her card, and then in felt pen was added her Rome address, 'Albergo Milano,' and the phone number."

"Yes, something of the sort. I caught up with the priest and asked him, 'Shall I go and see her?'

" 'Why not?' He smiled. 'She is a charming creature and very unhappy. Perhaps "that Serb" can make her happy?' He then drove me to the Albergo Milano, where we parted."

"And what did you do?"

"Naturally I went up to her room. We gave each other a great deal of pleasure. She was a delightful lady. When I left the hotel, I felt light, buoyant, young, hungry, thirsty, ready for labor and defense. I went straight to the station and took the train to Belgrade."

"To Ljubljana."

"*You* went to Ljubljana, but I went right on to Belgrade. I was expected at a symposium on the topic 'Ideas and Facts.' "

"You know, old man, it really is the most extraordinary coincidence. The symposium in Ljubljana was entitled 'The Factual Value of Ideas.' Tell me, old boy, when did this happen to you?"

"In 1965."

"And it happened to me in 1966. And what was the name of your nocturnal companion?"

"He was called Father Alexander."

AND IN THE GOLD OF SUNRISE,
THE MELTING AIMLESS PATH,
THE AIMLESS RESTLESS SEEKER

The reminiscences of the two friends were suddenly interrupted. The light in the studio went out, the shadows thickened, and the outlines of Khvastishchev's monstrous sculptures stood out more sharply against the white wall.

They did not immediately understand what had happened. Khvastishchev naturally thought that something strange had occurred to his precious organism. After the last "journey to the edge of the night," he occasionally had the feeling that at any moment he would be transported somewhere else, into another dimension; this made him catch his breath and sweat like a pig, as though something shameful was happening.

Khvastishchev's friend, the sculptor Igor Serebro, was also frightened when he noticed that the windows of the subbasement were darkened by the wheels of an enormous limousine. Surely it wasn't a Chaika? It looked like a Chaika!

Khvastishchev was no stranger to limousines. Mercedes and Cadillacs, Citroëns, and Jaguars, quite often used to turn around in the entrance of his alleyway, but they always parked on the other side. In exchange for a half-liter of vodka and a snack, the police sergeant Vanya put a blue circle with a diagonal red line – Park Here at Your Peril! – on Khvastishchev's side. Chaikas, however, were quite another matter. Vanya was in the habit of saying that "traffic signs don't apply to them," which, of course, was entirely just – it was their city, after all, and they were the bosses.

"Seems like a Chaika has stopped outside," said Igor Serebro in some perplexity. "Maybe it's from the Korean Embassy. Perhaps they want to commission you to make busts of Kim, Il, and Sung? Or perhaps Furtseva, the Minister of Culture, has come to see you?"

"Well, why not?" said Khvastishchev angrily. "I've had plenty of official personages here – Malraux and Simon de Noiry. So why shouldn't Katya Furtseva come too?" He scratched the back of his neck and suddenly burst into a laugh of nervous bravado. "Or perhaps the 'comrades' have come to get me?"

Igor objected vigorously, "They don't drive Chaikas, and in any case, why on earth should they bother about you, mister honorary graduate of the University of Dushanbe?"

The doors of the studio opened directly onto the street without a hallway. These doors were flung open, and in the bright square of sunlight Khvastishchev saw his faithful motorized centaur, Sergeant Vanya.

"Hi there, Radik," he said hoarsely. "Some devil has come to see you."

"So I see," said the sculptor with a nod. "What's his number?"

"The car belongs to the Executive Committee." Vanya gave the crooks" two-finger salute and hurried away.

Why is it that the Moscow police and chauffeurs call the people who drive in Chaikas devils? It can't be due to the influence of Dostoyevsky. Some connoisseurs of popular humor, such as the writer Pantelei, suggest that since the Russian word is *bes,* it is a Russification of the American word "boss." The bosses are coming, or the *besy* – the devils – are coming. What's the difference?

Khvastishchev was extremely irritated: The unexpected visitor had interruped his interesting and important reminiscences with a friend. He and Serebro seldom saw each other.

His old friend Igor was a spirited, impetuous scoundrel with an artistic temperament – sometimes effervescent and full of enthusiasm, sometimes irony itself, sometimes bold, sometimes cowardly – that made him totally unpredictable. He was the favorite of all Moscow. Everyone expected him to do something for them, but he was extremely elusive, never did what was expected of him, and always made other people dance to his tune. Never once had Khvastishchev been able to find Serebro at home, reach him by phone, or catch him anywhere. Yet Serebro, by contrast, always managed to call up Khvastishchev and always found him at home in his studio whenever he needed him.

And Igor often needed Khvastishchev. Sometimes Igor brought foreigners to see him as one of the practitioners of "Russian underground art," or Igor would bring some girl, whom he would dazzle and then undermine her will to resist. At other times it was Igor who invited Khvastishchev to a private viewing of his work, followed by all kinds of scurrilous escapades, and sometimes he dragged him into some public act, after which Khvastishchev was obliged to spend several years kneading clay for Tomsky or Vucceticc in order not to starve to death.

Occasionally Khvastishchev got angry: Why does this bastard make use of me just as he likes? Why does he treat me like a toy? Then he thought, Igor sees the whole world as a toy kingdom; he is so childlike that he even treats himself like a toy. He is openly absurd, but at least he is original, honest, and talented, and one day he will change; I like him and I expect great things of him. After all, he and I went into the attack side by side during our little *Sturm und Drang* period, we both got bloody noses for our pains, and we both licked our wounds in our lairs at the end of the sixties. At all events, we are friends.

Today Khvastishchev was very touched when Serebro appeared: He had turned up for no particular purpose except to chat, with a bottle of Johnnie Walker in his pocket. Annoyed to discover that his friend had given up drinking, he climbed up into his favorite hollow amid the primeval sexual symbols of *Humility,* and they both plunged into their strange, delightful reminiscences. And then the "devil" suddenly arrived.

In the square of sunlight formed as the door was flung open, there appeared a black shape that looked like a target used for rifle practice. The shape strode into the studio and turned out to be a portly old man in strange garb that was a sort of Kremlin uniform, namely, an expensive but badly made suit, white shirt, and tie.

"*Zdravstvuite,*" he said, somehow managing to pronounce every letter of that difficult Russian word of greeting. "Is this the home of Radius Apollinarievich Khvastishchev the sculptor?"

Khvastishchev's heart started to thump, his blood vessels began to pulsate, and vague negative emotions, like bubbles of marsh gas, bombarded the coating of tranquilizers around his nerve endings. The cold, thick, gelatinous blood of the Mesozoic Age, the horrors of the Thirty Years' War, lice, evacuation, standing in line to get into prison, standing in line for the medical checkup, bubbles in the veins . . . Pulling himself together, he jumped over the tail of *Humility,* pulled up his jeans, and boomed in a self-assured bass, "Good morning. I am the sculptor."

Hands met in a shake, and the visitor, without relaxing his grip, glanced around the studio with a look of graciously condescending mockery. "Very curious taste in furniture!"

Grizzled, slightly curly hair cut *en brosse.* A low but protuberant forehead. An elephantine upper lip. A nose like a dill pickle. A pelican's crop. Three rows of orders and medal ribbons of varying degrees of distinction on his left breast, which was as solid as Mount Khalkhin-Gol. His right breast was so spattered with small badges and emblems that it looked like an encampment of the Golden Horde. Though not good-looking, he carried himself with dignity.

"Are you a master of the art of realistic portraiture, Comrade Khvastishchev?"

"Excuse me, but with whom have I the honor and to what do I owe the pleasure?" asked Khvastishchev, having completely come to his senses, speaking with suitable calm and thinly veiled irony, in other words as a "dissident" artist should.

At that moment a door slammed on the mezzanine, and Klara squeaked, with her usual perfect timing, "Radik, some 'devil' has come to see you in a Chaika."

Rubbing their sleepy eyes, Klara and Tamara, the two failed nuns, appeared on the staircase, both of them, of course, without pants – one was wearing pantyhose, the other a pair of indecent lace panties.

"What . . . what . . . what does this mean?" The visitor's jaw dropped.

Khvastishchev explained in some embarrassment, "They are my pupils. My nieces and pupils. Tamara and Klara, members of the Komsomol."

The two little hookers, quite unfazed, came downstairs and greeted the visitor with a deep curtsy. Just then, the fine, well-built, fiery-eyed Igor Serebro, with a bottle in one hand and a smoked perch in the other, leaped from behind the obscene protuberances of the marble monster and spun around like a top.

"Introduce me too, maestro!"

"And this is my apprentice, who prepares the clay," said

Khvastishchev, clearing his throat. "He was put in my care by the police to be reformed and reeducated. Igor, a chair for our guest! Klara, coffee! Tamara, a smile, please! Fan dance? No, I absolutely forbid it! My dear comrade, I am all ears!"

The visitor sat down firmly and heavily on the chair and gave Khvastishchev a quizzical look. The sculptor's whole body was all question, almost entreaty.

"Well, Comrade Khvastishchev, I have made inquiries about your creative skills, and after weighing all the pros and cons, I have come to a positive conclusion."

"Hurrah!" whooped the girls. "That means they won't take away the studio! They won't throw us out! Devil, you're our savior."

Khvastishchev was actually rather touched by such a sincere expression of womanly love and did not even shout at the girls when Klara started to do a belly dance and Tamara tried to show their visitor the fan dance. Genuinely moved, he picked up his pan pipes and played a few bars of an old-fashioned minuet in his guest's ear. Meanwhile the "apprentice" danced around a mop like a Spanish gigolo. Choosing his moment, he whispered to Khvastishchev, "This is turning into a scandalous scene!"

"Oh, oh, oh," groaned the visitor. "Remove your nieces, Radius Apollinarievich! And please don't whistle in my ear. I can't hear with that ear, anyway. Concussion."

"The war?!" Serebro exclaimed triumphantly.

The visitor shook his head in negation.

"A construction site? A dam?"

With a fleeting smile, the visitor again shook his head.

"Surely not the Revolution?"

The visitor clutched his head in his hands. The girls were squealing as they pranced around him like a whole platoon of Egyptian soldiers on the banks of the Suez Canal.

"A paper weight?" Khvastishchev shouted into the concussed ear.

The visitor glanced downward with such a pained look that the sculptor immediately realized that he had hit the bull's-eye.

"Girls! Stop doing the fan dance! Bring us some coffee, you young hookers!"

For a few seconds the visitor sat in stony silence, then opened his mouth: "You invited me for a session of portrait sculpture and what do I find here? A horde of half-dressed people whistling into my ears! Now, see here –"

"I quite agree. It's disgraceful," said Serebro, and instantly disappeared behind the dinosaur's back.

"I invited you?" Khvastishchev asked quietly.

"Maybe I should go away?"

"When did I invite you? Was it long ago?"

"Perhaps you are unwell, Radius Apollinarievich?"

"Just a moment! Vait a minit, ser!" Khvastishchev slipped around behind *Humility* to recover his composure. On the way he grabbed the Tatar girl by the ass and whispered to her, "Find out his name!"

Out of sight of the visitor, he collapsed against the stone monster and closed his eyes.

"What's all this crap?" asked Igor. "Did you really invite him to pose for you?"

"I may have done," Khvastishchev mumbled. "You know, I was on a bender for a whole week, and I could have invited all sorts of people. But I don't remember this devil. I thought I never came into contact with devils, but who knows . . . He does remind me of someone, but I can't remember who it is. God knows. I suppose I must have invited him."

"Are you going to sculpt him?" Igor looked through the "transverse spiritual artery." "Klara is already sitting on his knees. She's started to work on him. In another minute she'll jerk the old man off."

"Klara!" Khvastishchev called out.

She ran over, prancing and cavorting. "His name's Lygher! Imagine, what a funny name: Lygher, Boris Yevdokimovich."

Khvastishchev made a face, as though from a sudden spasm of nausea. "Go upstairs with Tamara. I don't want to see either of you down here again!"

He was suddenly seized by a vague despondency and anguish, a fit of the shakes. The whole scene – the buffoonery, the half-naked girls, his ill-omened mood of that morning and the bubbles of phylogenesis – it had all served to undermine and shatter his already weak defenses, to send cold drafts whistling up his monk's habit. The relentless call of the gutter was pulling him back to the world of squalid Moscow bars, unmade beds, sour beer, and the madness of that false, deceptive freedom bestowed by alcohol. But no, I won't give in! I must sculpt something, Something Big, I must tell of my dream, I must serve God, Mother Europe, and Mother Volga! Peace in silence. Perform the mysterious, nocturnal service to my materials – stone, clay, metal . . . However, if I were to snatch that bottle out of my friend's hand right now and drink half of it in one gulp, I wouldn't have to wait for those sacred moments of inspiration – the world would change instantly, everything would glitter, a shiver of creative exultation would run through me from the top of my head to the soles of my feet!

"If you don't want to sculpt him, then I will," said Serebro. "An excellent specimen of the cloven-hoofed stage of evolution."

Igor was the creator of a famous series of busts that went by the laconic general title of *Fathers*. These were portraits of typical representatives of the Soviet aristocracy: a milkmaid, a metalworker, a Party official, a cotton grower, a general, a writer. There was nothing grotesque about them, nothing ironic, no hint of nose thumbing, nothing but ideal bronze, photographically exact portraits to which no one could possibly object. But when the collection was exhibited, people who knew Serebro, and there were quite a few of them around Moscow, laughed up their sleeves and exchanged winks. "What a collection! Serebro has really stuck the knife into them, now let them come and look at themselves." Meanwhile "they" came and looked, and liked what they saw. His controversial talent, "they" said, was developing in the right direction. This collection, incidentally, won Igor a State Prize, previously known as the Stalin Prize.

Khvastishchev looked through the "transverse spiritual artery." After the disappearance of the two awful "Komsomol" girls, Boris Yevdokimovich Lygher imagined himself to be alone. He yawned nervously and, glancing around, with a quick furtive movement straightened his false teeth, then calmly produced a comb from behind his medals and combed his sparse but quite real hair. The narrow aperture of the "transverse spiritual artery" gave the impression of bringing Lygher closer to Khvastishchev. The sculptor stared at the old man's face, at the pendulous bags of skin, the sclerotic crow's-feet, the still sparse patches of senile pigmentation, the tufts of gray hairs protruding from his ears and nostrils. Listening to his wheezy breath, he thought of how the air was already irritating the linings of his exhausted bronchial tubes. He was suddenly filled with a warm, almost painful feeling of sympathy for his visitor.

There is no point in looking for that monstrous Chekist in every elderly man. This is simply an old man. A piece of old human flesh, and flesh, in the philosopher Berdyaev's opinion, is not matter but is simply form, a vessel. Pity and affection are the emotions appropriate to the contemplation of human flesh, all that connecting tissue, veins, cartilage, bones, lymph – oh, lymph! – blood, horny formations, everything that so quickly ages and decays. This is your father, not a hangman. Sculpt him as your father. Sculpt the essence of the man that emerges from the cocoon of orders, medals, and badges. Make his eyes big and put blue stones into them! And down below sculpt huge medals with all the folds of their banners, with their swords, with all the teeth of their cog wheels, their sun rays, and inscriptions. Sculpt his weak human skin!

"Since I invited him, I shall have to do his portrait," Khvastishchev said to his friend.

"And quite right, too!" said Serebro encouragingly. "Temporary compromises are sometimes necessary."

So saying, his friend departed from the studio. Just like that, he upped and left without having asked for anything, without having offered anything. How about that, eh? Did this mean that old Serebro had simply dropped in to find out how his old pal Khvastishchev was getting on, to gossip and philosophize a bit? Perhaps age was, after all, beginning to tell on them, and along with patches of mold, spots before the eyes, and ringing in the ears, even their boorish generation was developing a taste for true friendship?

"We'll start work at once, Boris Yevdokimovich!"

With unusual jauntiness Khvastishchev leaped out from his refuge. "I shall have to fix up a sort of pedestal for you. The subject should always be raised up higher than the artist. Such is the immutable Marxist law, remarked upon by Lomonosov, long before Marx himself: 'Clothed in corruption, villainy shakes the earth . . .' Do you remember that passage? I'm glad I'm dealing with an intelligent man. To convey intellect in sculpture is not an easy matter. You can't just do it with one stroke of the trowel. You agree? I'm glad! What post do you hold? I understand, I shall be as silent as the grave . . . 'men whose names we do not know,' is that it? By the way, what are we going to call this sculpture of ours? Are you surprised that I'm already thinking of a title for it? The fact is I already feel that we are close to having a success on our hands. My liver, like a blacksmith's bellows, is pumping the mauve blood of inspiration into my brain. I shall exhibit your bust in the Manège Exhibition Hall as the culmination of an important stage in the search for the positive hero. Ah, that eternal quest! The quest with open visor, with a hammer under the kneecap, with a sickle under the balls! You search and search, and all the time those heroes are alongside you, driving past in Chaikas!"

Lygher had already seated himself on an improvised pedestal made up of three mattresses that had seen absolutely everything humans can do on mattresses, while the sculptor, without once closing his runaway mouth, was working successfully and with absolute concentration (his tongue, of course, wagged automatically), and the only moments when he shuddered were when the sitter tapped his cigarette case with the long cardboard mouthpiece of a Russian cigarette. Finally, the model managed to break through the flow of the artist's prattle.

"You and I, Radius Apollinarievich, should understand each other right from the start," said the sitter ponderously and even with a certain melancholy. "I know that my age, the Chaika, my decorations, and so on evoke certain associations in your mind. You would be wrong, however, to regard me as a dull conservative, one of yesterday's men. Do you think that we, the men at the helm, didn't suffer injustice and oppression during a certain period of the recent past? I'll tell you a short but instructive story about something that happened to me.

"It was in 1949 – No, I tell a lie, it was in the first quarter of 1950. I was expecting a promotion, a major promotion to a higher post and transfer from a northern unit of our system to one farther west. I was about your age at the time, full of energy and devoid of any evil forebodings. A phone call from the high-ups: Come and report! I went. I felt no doubts, no nagging little suspicions; the only thing that bothered me was that my belt squeaked a little. 'May I come in? Reporting on your orders.' 'Sit down. Sit down, you don't have to stand at attention! Sit down, Comrade LAGERSTEIN! Sit down in that armchair; your race likes a soft seat.'

"Can you imagine what a blow this was? By that sarcastic remark he was implying that I was a Jew! Not everyone, you'll agree, could stand such a shock. There had been occasions in that office when certain comrades had cracked under the strain: Some had had fits, some had vomited, or some even had a heart attack.

" 'Pardon me, Comrade General,' I said, 'I didn't quite understand what you were saying.'

" 'Indeed, Lagerstein,' said he, 'you never would be able to quite understand me, because you are not an internationalist. You have been concealing your racial origins, and in our state that is unforgivable.'

" 'Comrade General, you are looking at a man who is pure Russian on both sides of his family!'

" 'Now, now,' he said, 'don't get excited.' And he proceeded to taunt me with a gross imitation of a Jewish accent.

"Ah, Radius Apollinarievich, to this day I still tremble with indignation whenever I recall his sneering, teasing tone of voice. Tell me, now, you surely don't think I give cause to be mocked in that way, do I?"

"Yes, you do," said Khavastishchev without thinking.

"I knew it!" Lygher shrieked, as though he had just fired a shot, his eyes flashing as angrily as those of Shchors, the legendary hero of the Civil War.

An outburst of such force in this age of emotional inertia! To fix it in his memory, Khvastishchev then and there, using a felt pen on the linoleum floor, sketched the curl of his upper lip and the angry flourish of his eyebrows.

"I knew it, I knew it," Lygher whispered in tragic tones, his bronchial tubes whistling as he bent down from his pedestal, for all the world like Macbeth crouched over the corpse of one of his victims.

"Yes, there is something un-Russian about you, Boris Yevdokimovich," said Khvastishchev, still paying no attention to what he was saying.

The antique chair on the pedestal creaked under the pressure of the large body. At this, Khvastishchev lost his temper. "I'm joking. There's nothing Jewish about you – just the boorishness of a peasant from Pskov."

"All my life," said the visitor quietly from his wobbling chair, "all my life I have been persecuted for that slight curl in my hair, for the way I pronounce the letter r. For some reason, my name always makes everyone suspicious. Lygher, I tell everybody, should be stressed on the *first* syllable. Not Ly-*gher,* not La-*gher,* still less Lagerstein. And we're not from Pskov, Radius Apollinarievich, but from Tula. The *Ly*ghers have lived in Tula for a century and a half; they were specialists in making spigots for samovars."

"And where did they live before that?" Khvastishchev inquired with an ulterior motive. Suddenly the sitter began to giggle helplessly and looked at him with one eye between his thumb and index finger.

"The fact is, Radius Apollinarievich, that the Lyghers are descended from a French prisoner of war who had perfidiously invaded our country."

"You mean – not your country, but ours?" asked Khvastishchev.

"Why not ours? *He* invaded *our* country! This shameless frog eater invaded our country!"

"But if he hadn't invaded it, then you wouldn't have existed." Khvastishchev suggested forcefully. "In other words, before he invaded it, this country wasn't yours at all, Boris Yevdokimovich."

"If he hadn't invaded, I would have been a pure one hundred percent Russian," Lygher explained. "I wouldn't have had this curl in my hair and I would have pronounced a regular Russian r and everything would have been normal. I would have had a normal Russian name like Kartashov or Voronov."

"So he invaded, this curlyhead who burred his r's," Khvastishchev said to himself with a strange feeling of inspiration.

"Yes, he invaded and was already celebrating the French victory when he was given such a fright that he fled all the way to Tula."

Lygher's *Schadenfreude* toward his unfortunate ancestor was absolutely sincere. "He must have gone around Tula saying to everyone *'la guerre,'* meaning *'c'est la guerre'* – the war is to blame, forgive me, good people. Hence *Ly*-gher and the proletarian dynasty of that name, after which they were all pure Russians and even revolutionaries, Radius Apollinarievich. You know what it was like at a certain time. A tiny blot on your family history and a man could be deprived of everything – career, wife, children." He took his hand away from his face and sighed with relief. "You're the first person I've confessed this to. Purely for mutual confidence, for a sense of creative fellowship."

"And do they know about the curlyheaded Monsieur La Guerre *up top*?" asked Khvastishchev.

"I'm afraid they do," said his visitor. "I sometimes sense certain hints of it, although France is pursuing a realistic policy toward the Soviet Union. If it weren't for that wretched little Frenchman, Radius Apollinarievich, I wouldn't be riding around in a Chaika but in a better class of car."

Oho! Khvastishchev whistled to himself and thought, What a strange bird!

Suddenly he was distracted from his modeling clay as the words "strange bird" caused him to fly away to distant regions. For some reason he suddenly remembered how

THE YOUNG VON STEINBOCK

inspired by his acceptance into the Komsomol, thrilled by the spectacle of the ice breaking up in Nagaevo Bay, and also by Mayakovsky's early poems about city life and by his own essay on Gorky's *City of the Yellow Devil* (which had recently been read aloud in class as a model piece of work), had strode along Stalin Prospect in a state of euphoria, moving so fast that the boards of the wooden sidewalk did not even bend beneath his feet.

Hell, the world's not such a bad place after all, and the other kids in the class are all my friends. We're all Komsomol members together, and Ryba, the Komsomol organizer, is one of us, and now I'm no different from all the rest, and my pants are wide and made of wool, and my jacket has padded shoulders and a half-belt in the back, and they hardly ever ask me about my parents. Why, even in the district committee they didn't ask about them! Tell us, they said, about the successes of the Chinese People's Liberation Army, and they smiled and no one even mentioned my parents. The Komsomol doesn't bother about such things; for them, it's much more important for a guy to be a good sportsman, to get good grades in school, and to know the right answers in politics. Away with writing poetry, moping, and thinking unsuitable thoughts! All that will be left behind in the Third Medical Complex, and will evaporate as you get closer to the center, closer to that happy crossroads where Lyudmila Guly spends quiet Komsomol evenings relaxing with her little Komsomol girlfriends and the loud-speaker on top of its pole sings "Flower of the Fragrant Prairies."

One day, Lyudmila Guly, you and I will be given the job of editing the wall newspaper, he thought, as he pushed open the door of the school's history library. There, in the musty gloom of the Punic Wars, he saw his heroine with Ryba, the Komsomol organizer. With a lasci-vious grin on his lips, the Komsomol organizer was groping under the beautiful girl's blouse. Suddenly his face lit up – he had found what he was looking for! A moment later his expression grew serious again: The Komsomol organizer was absorbed in a session of heavy petting.

"Shall we make friends, Lyudka?" he hissed. "Shall we?"

For the moment she said nothing.

Ryba, smooth and greasy-haired, mouth puckered as though about to suck, a creature as drab and gray as a flannel rag, son of the prison-camp quartermaster, and an absolute little camp quartermaster yourself, you have kidnapped my love, my quivering Lyudmila, you're squeezing her left breast, sucking the juices out of my flower of the fragrant prairies. Beneath the portrait of Cromwell you are pushing your disgusting paw in between those two precious knees.

"Get out, Bokov!" Lyudmila suddenly barked angrily at Tolya. At that moment she thrust out her chin, and suddenly the swinish features of the whole Directorate of the Northeastern Corrective Labor Camps were clearly visible in the historical semi-darkness.

Squares, diamonds and trapezoids of sunlight patterned the floor of the school hallway. Raucous laughter came from the chemistry lab, where the seventh grade was fooling around with reagents. Through the geometrical patterns and the dusty sunbeams Tolya slouched his way to the classroom, which was hung with portraits of Fourier, Saint-Simon, and Radishchev. Today I'm the class monitor and the black-board hasn't been wiped clean, there's no chalk, I haven't brought any of the things that I'm supposed to bring to class, there'll be a row, my beloved has been raped, and I don't really belong in the Komsomol at all.

"What is the meaning of this?" asked the geometry teacher through clenched teeth, an anemic woman whose bangs were still curly from their semiannual perm. "Why have you brought these portraits of utopian socialists into my class? Very well, we will sort that out later. Give me the class roll and sit down. Abakumova, Abalkin, Blinchikov, Blum, Vilimonov . . ." As she read out the names on the class roll, the children answered "yes" or "present." When the geometry teacher reached the name "Guly," Tolya realized that his name had not been called out.

"Kirova, Kulinich, Lordkipanidze . . ." Without even looking at the sheet, clearly knowing all the names by heart, the nauseating, thin-lipped old maid droned on in a monotone.

Perhaps she's going to throw me out? I won't go! Just because I brought those pictures of pre-Marxist socialists by mistake. Big deal. They're not doing any harm. There's Beriya's picture hanging above the blackboard, and he's not doing anyone any harm, is he? So what's wrong with Saint-Simon? The next lesson is history, anyway.

"Opryachnikova, Ordzhania, Faizullin, Von Steinbock . . ."

Responses came from the pimply-faced Opryachnikova, the pimply-faced Ordzhania, the pimply-faced Faizullin, but not from the pimply-faced Von Steinbock. He was absent. Aristocratic names with a "Von" were not included in class registers. The name "Von Steinbock", with its overtones of both nobility and Jewishness, so out of place in the kingdom of the victorious proletariat, had long ago been suppressed by Tolya's father, Apollinary, an active revolutionary from the Putilov factory in St. Petersburg, who had renamed himself Bokov. "That will sound wonderful, Von-Stein-Bokov!" was the sarcastic comment of Tolya's grandfather, an incorrigible Constitutional Democrat, but later he accepted it – oh, well, the new name would maybe make life a lot easier for his grandchildren. Apollinary Bokov – ouch! Where is your rough red Russian shirt?

"Is Von Steinbock present?" the geometry teacher asked loudly, staring straight ahead and sticking her chin out like some great histor-ical personage, though not, of course, a utopian socialist.

For a few seconds the class exchanged perplexed glances, then a young mobster called Sidor giggled and the rest broke out into loud guffaws. The youthful mind finds everything funny – you have only to stick up your finger and the young will laugh at you, so the name Von Steinbock caused an absolute riot of hilarity.

"I am asking a question: Is a student by the name of Von Steinbock present in this class?" The pioneer of the Far North raised her voice even higher.

"There's no one of that name here, Eleodora Lukovna," gasped Vika Opryachnikova, the class group leader, through tears of laughter.

"Oh, yes, there is!" The geometry teacher slammed the class roll shut and screamed, "There is a pseudo-student here who is hiding his true face, who has fallen like an apple not far from the apple tree of his parentage in our Soviet cherry orchard, where the chips fly when we cut down such trees, and where the hammer is not answerable for what the saw does! With the cosine we are building gigantic hypotenuses, we are growing watermelons on compost in square greenhouses, under the guidance of our great leader we are changing the courses of rivers by planting protective windbreaks of trees, but the snake-headed Hydra of the enemies of the people, stinking of putrefaction, slithers its way into our great friendly family of nations!"

Her eyes white with hatred, the geometry teacher shrieked so horribly that the class was reduced to frightened silence. Suddenly, something utterly strange happened: Eleodora Lukovna clutched at her own breasts, her left hand grasping the left breast, her right hand the right, and began squeezing her defenseless mammary glands with an expression of despair totally incomprehensible to the roomful of ninth graders. Amazingly, not even this made them laugh.

"Stand up, Von Steinbock!" the geometry teacher suddenly said in an exhausted, flat, indeed somewhat guilty, voice.

Saint-Simon, Fourier, and Radishchev encouraged him: Stand up Von Steinbock, our wretched confrère, have a little courage even if you haven't any convictions! Beriya, on the other hand, advised him not to stand up. It's no business of mine, he seemed to be saying. Get on with teaching geometry, you stinking bitch, and keep your nose out of things that don't concern you.

Lyudmila Guly's mouth made an O, her eyebrows arched until they looked like the wings of a bird. Sidor opened a mouth full of rotten teeth in the frozen grimace of a big-time con man.

The door creaked, and the aroma of the Third Medical Complex – the smell of twice-cooked, adulterated, rancid seal blubber – wafted into the classroom, followed by an ugly face with a tubercular flush and wrapped in a bright flowered scarf. The face began to wink at Tolya with both eyes, beckoning him to follow her out into the hallway, but for a long time the boy either couldn't or wouldn't understand that this ugly mug had appeared for his own good, that everything today was "going his way."

"Tolya, I've come to fetch you. Come on, Tolya," the face called out to him, sobbing, and then Von Steinbock finally recognized it as belonging to the janitor from their hut, remembering that her little nose had been partly eaten away, either by lupus or by the ordinary Kolyma syphilis bug.

IN AN ALLEY THAT WAS BLUE AND HALF-BLINDED BY SUNLIGHT

the sculptor Radius Apollinarievich Khvastishchev stared after the disappearing Chaika and wondered why there was something about this "devil" that awakened such distinct memories, and whether those memories would return at the next sitting. Vanya rode up. Without getting off of the seat, he offered the sculptor a Lucky Strike.

"Some devil that was," he said with a guffaw. "He was just a damn chauffeur."

"A chauffeur?"

"Sure. I saw him get behind the wheel, and there was no one else in the car. He was no devil, Radik, just an ordinary shit shoveler from the Central Car Pool, or maybe from the Palace of Marriages."

"The sunset of an empire," said Khvastishchev to Vanya, who agreed, opened the throttle, and roared off to bring some law and order to Peace Prospect.

IN AN ALLEY THAT IS BLUE AND HALF-BLINDED BY SUNLIGHT

the fluff from the poplar trees is blowing in the air, so I guess summer has come.

What on earth is the matter with me? I don't love anyone, my appetite is good, I like cakes and chocolates, I can talk for hours about carburetors, Cardan shafts, bearings, and pistons, I don't answer letters, I read nothing but junk, and I listen to the Beacon radio station – and no human being can sink lower than that!

Now and again I think everything is falling apart and that is the only fundamental thought that enters my head. Human individuals are seeking contact, I think as I look out of the car windows at people meeting each other, full of hope, at the metro station, at all those scenes that only recently filled me with such excitement. The sun has started to set later, I think as I gaze at the evening horizon, which once used to call to mind the specter of my beloved Europe. Heyerdahl has proved that the ocean is being polluted, and instead of the blinding, roaring, far-flowing ocean, I see revolting black clots of oil with white suckers all over them.

Without thought, without feeling, without any clear aim, I go into a telephone booth, which smells like a public lavatory. In fact, I think to myself, there is nothing repulsive about the smell of urine, one only has to get used to it. I remember a story someone told once over dinner in the Actors' Restaurant, where some personage, obviously fond of coining aphorisms, was announcing sententiously, "A nation that pisses in phone booths is not ready for democracy." The discussion then went on around and around that newly minted aphorism like a wooden horse on a carousel. At that point, I think, the writer Pantelei Pantelei intervened and stated that he was obliged to disagree. He, Pantelei, apparently had seen often enough gentlemen at night in Munich and Oslo abusing telephone booths, yet the nation of Munich had made great progress in democracy, to say nothing of the nation of Oslo. "What's more," Pantelei seemed to have shouted, apparently touched to the quick by this aphorism, "since we're calling a spade a spade, when I was young I myself pissed more than once in phone booths on the Petrograd Side of Leningrad, yet I was and still am a genuine democrat and a liberal!" They say that a depressed silence fell on the table after that, and the discussion ground to a creaking halt.

To hell with them all, I thought, as, tormented by the heat, depression and the stink, I read the number written on the wall immediately above the telephone: 226–4156. The number had been written by three different means: the first three figures by ballpoint pen, the two next figures in lipstick, and the final two had been scratched by some sharp object. A hard, stubborn fingernail, no doubt, had finished the job. A most important human quality – stubbornness! 226 – two times the number of the famous twenty-six Baku commissars shot during the Civil War; 41 – my shoe size; 56 – the year of the "thaw," humidity,

Samsik's year. Now I could remember it, now I could call up the number from any phone booth – Baku, feet, saxophone!

On this day and not on any other, on the sunny side of the street, stacked with new cooperative apartment houses, in a wretched piss-soaked phone booth on the melted asphalt, alongside the Fiats, motionless and dazzling as they burn in the sun, under a fluffy June snowfall, I, the lyrical hero of this book, began to dial those numbers. Suddenly it seemed to me that the telephone had come alive and my finger was not going into a fingerhole on the dial but into quivering pulp. Aha, I thought, there they are again – the tricks that abstinence plays on you.

The quivering of the pulpy substance and the current along the wires, urgent and intermittent . . . My exhausted biocurrent running like mice through the monstrous labyrinth of the capital's telephone system. Where is it running to?

WHERE INDEED ARE WE GOING?

At the end of the street there appeared a familiar, flabby figure. As it emerged from a doorway, the four brass buttons on its jacket all gleamed at once.

Finally, my biocurrent reached its destination and like a calf butted its forehead against a membrane, began to push, to moo piteously, to implore. How touching and pitiful, what a resemblance to a spermatozoon, how like one of those solitary little globules with its tiny, twitching tail!

At the other end of the line, in some unknown part of town, down an endless corridor, came the sound of a large pair of heels, and the master of the house, reflected simultaneously in three mirrors – a huge one on the wall, a distant one in the bathroom, and a tiny hand mirror – like a spreading patch of efficient perplexity, shut out his apartment with a "hel-lo-oo" spoken in a rounded baritone; my biocurrent, however, worn out but cunning like all hunted vermin, had already leaped across the scarcely visible gap between voice and ear.

"Greetings," I said to the stranger.

"What can I do for you?" – a dry charge of electricity, Bengal lights flashing in a frosty night.

"Is your wife at home?" I asked at random, as though his wife should have been waiting for me on the shores of the Caspian holding a clean pair of moccasins, with the song "Sentimental Journey" on her lips – his *wife,* and not his daughter or his mother, not some whore, not section chief Sylvia Omarovna, but the wife of this electric stingray called Hello.

"Who wants her?"

The phrase rolled back and forth over the pebbles with a polite threat, like a demonstration of armored forces.

"The question is not who wants her but whether she's at home," I said.

"Ha, ha, ha!" he said. "Now you're talking almost without an accent."

"I never had an accent," I said.

"Excuse me, but are you calling from the Board?"

"No, from a phone booth."

"Interesting," said he.

"What's interesting?" I said.

"Interesting to know who wants my wife. Who are you?"

"An operator," I said.

Silence reigned, then the electric stingray crackled back with less assurance: "What do you have?"

"There are a few goodies on the horizon," I said. "Shoosy-poozies, pantsy-wantsies, French bread, leather goods. Of course, only for greenbacks, you understand."

"Did my wife give you this phone number?"

"Well, maybe it wasn't your wife, maybe it was your daughter or your mother or some whore, or maybe Sylvia Omarovna, your section chief." He burst out laughing.

"When are you going to stop playing your idiotic games, Kostik? It's pretty stupid, after all!"

"But it worked, didn't it?" I lisped cunningly. "You must admit it worked, old man."

"One of these days I'll pull your ears off." He laughed in a friendly voice. "Hang on a minute, she's just getting out of the bathtub."

"Oho, so there'll be something worth seeing," I said with a giggle, getting into the part of Kostik.

"Ah, you rat, Kostik. Alisa! Alisa! You're wanted on the phone!"

CO-OM-ING!

somewhere among the rocky cliffs, in the clefts, through the under-growth of wisteria and azaleas there rang out HER cheerful voice. Alisa!

I'm coming! She's always coming! I was choking with excitement in a currant-black cloud, in a thundercloud charged with electricity, in lilac-colored air in which the oxygen is replaced by helium, in which the helium-swollen gladiolus thirsts for the vulva, in which the moon-flowing magnolia, the wilting moon lily, thirst for the phallus. Alisa! I cry in the ruins of the palace, where centuries ago an explosion prepared everything for her arrival: gaps in the walls, views of the sea, and young trees between them. I'm coming! she answers from below, and like a little red tongue of fire she is flitting up narrow stairways cut out of the stone monolith like a spark running along a safety fuse, past the fallen columns and fragments of capitals, skipping lightly over the moss-grown blocks of stone, in which peeping out through the slime of the revolutionary age are ancient Roman torsos, breasts, necks, chins, fragments of former prisoners of the exploded nouveau riche. Not a century has passed since it happened, since the ill-omened Attila passed over us, Attila the farter, a puff of lilac smoke. How much we needed such young men . . . Is that by Bagritsky? The ruined castle on the vast slope, and there down below, the green bank of the White army, the last few kilometers to the sea. Run, run, my Alisa, come up from below and appear above the shore: Either I am an officer who has exchanged his ship's deck for love or I am an enlisted marauder, rolling head over heels in a torrent of mud. Or perhaps I'm a fugitive trade unionist, who is on the run for having smashed the tiles of the sobering-up station, or a pastry-cook prince, who has erected in your honor an ancient Byzantine monster on the hilltop. But now you're right down at the bottom, beneath me; right underneath me your flanks are spread wide open in love, all of you is underneath me, and above us is the tranquil sky. All of you is spread-eagled beneath me, your hair spread out, your groaning lips half-open, your misty lymph-suffused eyes swiveling, arms flung out, legs wide apart, and I am pounding into you, thrusting farther into you at each stroke, and now I am carrying you away, my poor weak one. Down the hillside, along the moonlit path, across the tennis courts and artillery batteries, I carry you, small and numbed, I give an almost bestial growl and nearly weep with tenderness as I bear you, and you hang on to me, whispering and wide open, now you are all mine, as I am yours. So on we go and will go forever, but stones are rolling somewhere and we fly into the bushes – madness! and head over heels, weeping ah, so many victims! we roll, roll, roll downward, but we already have a premonition that we will rise up again.

"Alisa!"

"Coming, coming! Hell, I'm all tangled up. Wait, will you? Can't you wait just a minute? Hi, Kostik! What do you want? Is this another one of your jokes? Because of you I'm standing here all wet! Get screwed, you shit!"

A click and the wild howl of a siren – run for your lives! Shattered, I come out of the phone booth into the blazing sunlight. Who was that woman? Surely she wasn't the same one I knew already, with whom I'd even talked, the wife of a famous tractor designer, the Alisa whom everyone knows and who is the talk of Moscow? In that case – what could have been simpler? – why not rap with her and make a date for a fuck? So why did I start getting such strange nudges of memory, memories from the incredibly distant past? So whence the sudden vision of a ruined castle, and even before that, yes, yes, the vision of a rusty funicular and something else? All the hallucinations of abstinence, nothing more.

FOUR BRASS BUTTONS

embossed with the emblem of the New York Rotary Club, a long drooping moustache, and smoky dark glasses. Toward him came a checked jacket made in London, a Lee shirt unbuttoned to the navel, all old and worn out with the exception of a dime-sized medallion around his neck, made of the metal that never ages – gold.

The writer Pantelei Apollinarievich Pantelei met by chance in the street his friend the rogue in the elegant blazer.

"Wait a minute for me, old man, I need you badly," said the "blazer" briskly and cheerfully.

"I'll wait," said Pantelei, concealing his amazement that someone still needed him. Leaning against a wall, he watched the "blazer" go into the phone booth, dial a number, and stroke his prominent bald patch, his lips twitching and smirking and his thick eyebrows jumping up and down as he talked, like a couple of whores signaling to a customer. Suddenly, for no apparent reason, Pantelei's whole languid and inert being was pierced by a wild, inhuman stab of jealousy. He instantly felt something new, some kind of vital acceleration, like Ella Fitzgerald's rhythm approach to "Mac the Knife." His friend leaped out of the booth, rubbing his hands vigorously together. "Sorry to keep you, old man. Just fixing a date for a fuck."

A minute later they were already at the other end of the world, tearing along at ninety kilometers into the gloom of the tunnel under

Mayakovsky Square. Half-blind, they flew into the molten tin of Insurrection Square and out again. The "blazer," resting his entire left arm on the steering wheel, raced his Mercedes at a furious pace around Moscow, never looking to either side and paying no attention to anyone except Pantelei. He was saying something with passionate insistence, pointing at Pantelei with his right hand, but instead of listening to him the writer was recalling his own days of living at this insane tempo.

He remembered once seeing a woman at the sanatorium. Standing at a wash-basin with a foolish, pensive look on her face, she was washing her breasts. Then without a second's reflection he leaped over the balcony, ran along the corridor, and unerringly flung open the door of her room. He even wrenched off the door handle, it seems. In those days he was a drunken hooligan of a poet, free from all laws and conventions, and everyone gave in to him without a struggle. *Und der Haifisch! Der hat Zähne! Und die hat er im Gesicht! Und Macheath der hat ein Messer! Doch das Messer sieht man nicht!*

"Guess what! John Lennon has agreed to play Raskolnikov! Cinerama, stereo sound – we've got the lot! Over to you, Pantelei! Do you agree?"

He finally realized what the "blazer" was saying to him, this well-known Moscow "fixer," who always seemed to smell of bull's sperm from a mile away. He suddenly wanted to play a really dirty trick on the "blazer," something painful and offensive, to bite off all his brass New York buttons, for instance, wrench the cover off his clutch housing, stuff all the garbage, ashes, and cigarette butts into some part of his anatomy, the self-satisfied son of a bitch!

Before another minute had passed, Pantelei felt ashamed of himself: Hell, if it's OK for me to wrench off door handles and burst into an unknown woman's room singing a song, why shouldn't he be allowed to "make a date for a fuck"? He removed a single hair from the navy-blue material.

"Sorry, I didn't hear what you said. I was daydreaming for a moment. Would you mind repeating your idea?"

As a penance, Pantelei had to listen all over again to the tedious creative project of this gilded offspring of the Party élite, and at the same time to be given a considerable chunk of his life's story.

Suddenly they were crawling along at a turtle's pace in the turtle soup of Zubovsky Boulevard over the skulls and potsherds of the great epoch that was still recorded by giant X's on the Telephone Exchange building, that epoch when there was none of today's traffic in Moscow, and the only vehicles on the Sadovoye Ring were whistling police cars and a few "daddy's Pobedas" driving along beneath the eternal neon-lit appeal to the Soviet public: "If you want to be intelligent, *Pravda* in every apartment."

Perhaps it was actually the "blazer's" daddy who had composed that verse, wishing to continue Mayakovsky's tradition of writing rhyming copy for the Moscow Trading Trust,* that verse whose crackling glow from the roof of the Generals' House used to illuminate our drunken youth. It was, after all, in the spirit of that appeal that daddy had composed the words of the Soviet national anthem, for which he had been decorated with a golden medallion the size of a half-ruble piece. Yes, much had changed since those days, and even the national anthem had become just an anonymous, wordless noise for a brass band. Much had changed, though not everything: that crackling, poisonous gas was still there at the intersection and daddy, too, was still with us, his position unshakable.

It turned out that in the fairly recent past the "blazer" had married the wife of the Luxembourg ambassador, or someone of that sort, and that in accordance with the appropriate Soviet law (there was, it seems, such a law) he had gone with her to Paris. For three months, old man! All legal and above board! The balding, hirsute Soviet husband was allowed to spend three months of every year with his extraterrestrial wife beyond the confines of the system.

There, in the foreign capital, our Red Guardsman encountered the ills of rotting capitalism. "You know what it's like, old man, the stench of decay, outbursts of rebellion. Anyway, it was in La Coupole, old man! Yes, it was there that I conceived the idea of a free and passionate adaptation of the novel by our fellow countryman Fyodor Mikhailovich Dostoyevsky. You see, in the West nowadays there are colossal opportunities for visual synthesis. Just imagine, five screens above a vast stage and on it the tiny figure of John Lennon with a guitar. Does the idea interest you?"

"Very much," said Pantelei, and swore to himself that he would today find out all about the "blazer's" date for a fuck. Who had he fixed it with? Who was this woman? For some reason Pantelei regarded it as an extremely important, highly personal matter; somehow he was simply maddened by the thought that the "blazer" would be screwing some woman today, as though he had stolen her from him, Pantelei.

"And in one corner of the stage there'll be a ten-meter-high piece

*One of the enterprises for which Mayakovsky wrote advertising slogans and jingles during Lenin's New Economic Policy in the 1920s.

of kinetic sculpture out of foil, Duralumin, and neon tubes. This, of course, is —"

"The old woman moneylender?" suggested Pantelei.

"What?" the "blazer" suddenly screamed with horror, as though he had just seen the kinetic monster right in front of him. His moustache stood on end; his fingers abandoned the steering wheel and pressed against his forehead.

As though in a silent nightmare, the automatic-drive Mercedes swerved leftward from the right-hand lane, presenting its left side to the mad stream of rushing traffic, then crossed the median strip, turned three hundred degrees, and came to a stop.

The sheer improbability of this terrible, instantaneous swing across the highway shattered Pantelei, but like any normal citizen, he immediately forgot about the danger and began imagining the even more terrifying action that the police would now take. Like all people of our time, he was more worried by the problem of punishment than of crime.

Three police inspectors started running toward them from different directions, shouting into their walkie-talkies as they ran. Another officer jumped out of his glass traffic-control booth. From the direction of Zubovsky Boulevard, a blue and yellow police Volga was already racing along the center lane reserved for official cars, while a police motorcycle was heading toward them from the Crimean Bridge.

The driver's head, meanwhile, was slumped forward on the steering wheel. He was grinding his teeth, coughing, and breathing in short gasps. Had he gone out of his mind? Pantelei shook him by the shoulder.

"A stroke of genius," croaked the "blazer" in a strangled voice and raised his head. His face was suffused with the fire glittering from his eyes. The joyous fire of inspiration. The madness of the creative artist.

"A stroke of genius!" he exclaimed, and leaned over to embrace Pantelei, breathing into his face with fumes of onion, pepper sauce, and half-digested pastrami. "The old moneylender as a ten-meter kinetic sculpture made of Duralumin! No, I was right. We need you and no one else! Your paradoxical brain, none other! I'm going to send a telegram to Von Steinbock today!"

Seeing that the Mercedes was not trying to get away, the police now approached at a walk. All the officers had the calm, even affable expression of sadists.

"Who? Who are you sending a telegram to?" Pantelei asked cautiously, unable to believe his ears, not trusting the reliability of the link between his organs of hearing and his deeply hidden organ of memory. Any interconnection between these organs often struck him as absolute nonsense.

"My friend Henri von Steinbock. Haven't you heard of him? He's a composer of genius and a producer who's ready to take risks. That's the kind of guy he is." The "blazer" stuck his right thumb up in the air, like an ancient Japanese drawing of a penis, while with his left hand he casually extended a little red booklet out of the window.

A strange ripple of live electricity suddenly passed through the forces of order: The booklet floated from hand to hand, melting bricks, opening pearls, dissipating thunderclouds, and spreading around it azure skies, comfort, warmth and joy.

"We weren't expecting this," said the captain from the glass booth as he returned the booklet. "An unexpected surprise, you might say. May I give you the compliments of the whole precinct? Do be a little more careful, please. Good luck. Captain Bushuyev reporting."

"What happened?" muttered Pantelei when all the police officers had gone.

"Nothing special. I'm an honorary member of the Moscow police force, you see. I once put on some lunatic play about the heroes in gray uniforms, well, you can imagine what happened – wild success, diplomas, decorations. Anyway, back to my idea. This Henri von Steinbock – rich, lives well, artistic temperament, and all that jazz – is going to finance the whole show. What a lineup: Von Steinbock, Salvador Dali, John Lennon, Pantelei Pantelei, and me! The whole of Europe will be pissing in its pants!"

"Not to mention Dostoyevsky," Pantelei added modestly.

"Of course, plus Fyodor Mikhailovich," the "blazer" agreed casually.

They left the car in a quiet alley and set off on foot. The alley was smiling, patriarchal, all aquiver with new young leaves and dappled with light. It was hard to imagine that the mad whirl of traffic on the Sadovoye Ring was nearby. A simple, kindly old woman was coming toward Pantelei and the "blazer;" she was pushing a baby carriage, from which the hazel-brown eyes of a tiny baby girl were looking at them with an intent and friendly stare.

They were walking on the pavement with their shades and moustaches, hung with all kinds of little chains, charms, rings, the little badges of their pseudofree caste, as the baby carriage rolled along the sidewalk and the tiny little girl, not showing the slightest fear, said, "Uncles," raised her little finger, and laughed. Yet there was so much about them that would probably have frightened another child.

The "blazer" was half a head taller than Pantelei and half a shoulder's width broader. Why the hell do they always latch on to me, thought Pantelei, these spoilt upper-crusters and ambassadors' brothers-in-law? What on earth do I have in common with these hereditary members of the boss class, with their little red books, their Mercedes, their obliging girlfriends, and all their Parises? I have my own Paris, the real one . . . every moment . . . *omnia mea mecum porto*, especially now that I've even stopped drinking vodka with them.

"Uncles," said the kind old woman to her baby. "Look, Vanya, two uncles."

The little girl turned out to be Vanya, a little boy.

"Listen, what would you do if suddenly some awful disaster were to happen?" Pantelei asked the "blazer." "Right here in this alley, at this instant? Some flood, or a gas attack, or a wild riot?"

He was extremely surprised at his own question, but the "blazer" not at all. After hemming and hawing a few moments in thought, he replied, "I would pick up this little Vanya here and try to get away. What would you do?"

"I'd do the same. Put the kid under my arm and blow," said Pantelei, excited.

"What else?" muttered the "blazer."

"Well, of course," said Pantelei, "you'd never manage to save the old woman if the street was full of poison gas."

"No, you couldn't save the old woman," the "blazer" agreed. "Gas spreads very quickly. No good even trying. You'd never be able to get her away."

"Exactly," Pantelei agreed with a nod. "You've got to save anyone you can, like that kid, for instance."

The "blazer" suddenly took a checked cap out of his pocket and put it on his balding head. The effect was very handsome and charming.

"Where are we going?" asked Pantelei.

"To some bar, of course! We've got to develop my idea!"

"Is he Russian, this pal of yours Von Steinbock?"

"He's a Russian Jew," the "blazer" replied simply. "But what a guy!"

He must be one of the "White" Von Steinbocks from Samara, thought Pantelei.

TWO VON STEINBOCKS ON A VERANDA:

Try and picture it – in the late spring of 1917 two men in vests, holding heavy newspapers on canes, just as if they were in a Swiss café; celluloid collars, narrow-striped English shirts, black silk backs to their vests pinched in at the waist with elastic, lean bottoms, luxuriant moustaches, and gray sideburns, innocent and transparent Jewish eyes.

Forgotten are the tinctures, solutions, all that *aqua destillata* and *unguentum quantum satis*; forgotten are the mademoiselles, the marquisettes, and the bells of Corneville.

"Listen, Yasha, our children won't have to bend their backs any longer! We're taking the European road! A democratic republic! Racial equality!"

"Ach, Nathan, we must get out!"

"Listen, Yasha, my daughters and your sons will no longer be the victims of that savage Asiatic xenophobia!"

"Ach, Nathan, I don't know what xenophobia is, but we must get out!"

"Listen, Yasha, you're not anti-Russian, are you?"

"Ach, Nathan, I'm a businessman. We've got to get out before it's too late."

"Yasha, I love this country! This spring has made me feel Russian. For the first time I realized that I'm not a 'lousy kike' but a citizen of the Russian Republic! I'm full of pride for my country. Look, despite outbursts by the insurgents, we are going to have free elections and the Constituent Assembly will speak its weighty word!"

"Ach, Nathan, you're a fool!"

"And you, Yasha, are an ignoramus, a small businessman, a shmuck from the shtetl with a limited horizon!"

The arguments degenerated into threatening swoops with newspapers flicking close to proud Ashkenazy noses, later even into the semblance of a brawl among the flower beds, among the pansies, gilly flower, and wallflowers. The long democratic summer was approaching the hollyhocks' flowering time and its own dusty extinction.

The summer expired amid the mounting fury of the awakened people. Occasionally two slender second lieutenants in white gloves would appear on the veranda, Yasha's sons, Solya and Nonya.

"There's proof for you, you hairy shmuck! Jews – officers in the Russian army! Have you ever seen the likes of it before? Boys, say something to your ignorant father!"

Smiling condescendingly, the two lieutenants quoted the speeches of their young prime minister.

"Meshuggene! You're all meshuggene! The goyim have filled your ears with shit! We must get out, meshuggene, get out, get out!"

"But how do we go, and where to?"

"Ah, now that's another matter . . ."

"We'll sail down to Baku by steamer, and from there we'll go to America. Listen to your stupid father, you poor boys! Leave them alone. They've nothing but women's assholes on their minds! So we sail down by steamer, do we? Yes, by steamer. To Baku? To Baku! And from there to America? Yes, to America. Baku's a big port. Steamers go from there to America. Boys, do you hear this mangy imbecile? Your father's a real hairy shmuck!"

"What's the matter, you young pigs? Why are you laughing, pigs?"

"You don't really mean it, do you, Pa? What nonsense! The Caspian Sea is a lake!"

"*Guter Gott!* What pigs have I begotten!"

"Pa, the Revolution didn't give us officers' epaulettes so that we could run away!"

The arguments continued, booming out over the Volga, and the weather got worse, the people's fury became ever more heated, and the sky above the republic began to look like the curtain of the tragicomic puppet theater that was about to go up at any moment.

"My girls don't feel they are Jewesses any longer!"

"We must get out and go! By train to Vladivostok, to the Pacific Ocean!"

"Another spring like this, gentlemen, and I shall renounce my noble 'von.' "

"Across the La Pérouse Strait and from there to the healthy city of San Francisco!"

The family was already packing up its "von", wrapping it in wadding, ready to be shipped to the narrow Gothic valleys of Europe, where it had been born in the Middle Ages, like the alchemists'' homunculus, out of nothing, out of the dense miasma of Jewry, out of corruption and cunning deceit.

What social injustice there had been in those far-off times! Some Jews were given the name Arsch ("asshole"), others were named Rappoport ("rag picker"), while the boldest and most unscrupulous of our forefathers showered copyists with silver in exchange for writing a "von" in front of their names, and no doubt they didn't stop at silver either – they gave the copyists home-distilled plum brandy to drink, and perhaps intimidated them, too.

So now let's send the despised "von" back to Europe, to that stuffy little old dump in Württemberg, to the Hohenzollerns; and the Steinbocks, citizens of free Russia, will applaud the Constituent Assembly along with all other free peoples!

"Ach, Nathan! You can take the ferry from Helsingfors to Stockholm, and from there you can go to Christiania in Norway. I know my geography now, and I won't try and sail on a lake instead of a sea!"

The argument was decided for them on a day of bad weather, of hurricane and slush, amid whirls of wet yellow leaves, a day of twilight and autumnal purple: Russia dropped back into her old rut.

Subsequently the Samara Von Steinbocks, who never did manage to send their despised "von" abroad, transformed themselves into dubious facsimiles of European Jews under the liberal multiparty government of the Republic of Simbirsk, and the brave young lieutenants Solya and Nonya served faithfully with gun in hand and never turned around when anyone shouted, "Hey, kike!"

The Kazan Steinbocks, on the other hand, who had abandoned their "von", lived through discomfort, hostility, and coldness, as though someone were wrenching out their whiskers while they were asleep. There was no occasion to applaud the Constituent Assembly; on the contrary, in exchange for starvation rations they were forced to serve the insurgents and, mutating prematurely into a certain likeness of the famous picture *Menshikov in Exile,* to wait gloomily beside a cold stove for the restoration of the legitimate government, to cram themselves into one room, to cook in the communal kitchen of what once had been their own apartment, to steep themselves in the mothball smell of privation and calamity.

The Samara branch of the family, by contrast, did sail down the Volga to Baku, where, their numbers considerably reduced by having to pass through a roaring epidemic of typhus, they nevertheless organized their final emigration from one sixth of the earth's land surface to the other five sixths. Their relatives who stayed behind in Russia never did learn how they lived in that overly large portion of the world, how they multiplied, and how they wore yellow stars, how they were incinerated in gas ovens, and how they made "big geld."

The stay-at-homes had their own troubles too, sir. First their daughters grew up and joined the Komsomol, then a cheerful young proletarian appeared on the doorstep, and having sneezed, introduced himself as an industrial apprentice from Petrograd with the pleasant-sounding name of Bokov.

"Hi there, Mom and Dad! My name's Apollinary Bokov, but you can call me Polya. I'm to be chairman of the city soviet in your town."

"*Qu'est que c'est?*" The old people's Württemberg noses twitched in unison.

So it began – *qu'est que c'est, qu'est que c'est,* what's that? And to this day, *qu'est que c'est?*

As we can see, Tolya had every right not to respond to that awful name with its telltale "von," which, in any case, had long since been sent back to the place it came from; his legal name was Anatoly Apollinarievich Bokov, and to hell with the whole bunch of you! All those old skeletons in the family closet have long ago crumbled to dust along with grandfather's vests, ties, and collars. In the logic of things, surely here on the very eastern rim of the vast Asian continent, among the icy waters and the permafrost, no one could know about that "von!" But, it appears, somebody did know. In that small town, no more than a dot on the map, there was an even smaller dot, so tiny as to be utterly insignificant, where they *did* know everything.

So now he was standing at the main entrance to the school, flights of steps curving away to the right and left, as though on show in an arena of shame. The hideous, noseless face of his guide said nothing, but only breathed heavily alongside him, making occasional odd, embarrassed grunting sounds. He asked no questions, because there was no point: Disaster had struck, and now there was no hiding from the shame.

Shame – clean, snowy, and sunlit – stretched out in front of him. The expanse of shame was crisscrossed with wooden, raised sidewalks, along which the Magadan public flowed in various directions. On the right and left extremities of shame were the two wings of his school, one in the shade, the other in the sun, and from which hung a massive, yellowish, translucent stalactite, one of the adornments of the landscape of shame. The backdrop to shame was the Palace of Culture. The sharp, cubist geometry of shadows decorated the background of shame, and the bronze statues of a frontier guard, a milkmaid, a miner, and a sailor – THE FOUR WHO DON'T DRINK – crowned its upper level. The people on the wooden sidewalks were moving hurriedly, striving to leave the scene of shame as quickly as possible, feeling that they were out of place here, because shame is static, precise, and beautiful, without a single puff of smoke, without a single whisp in the sky, without hope.

Tolya glanced around, seeking the center of shame, the essential black spot, and found it at once without having to search for long – on Stalin Prospect, between the school and the Palace of Culture, stood a black Emka car. He headed straight for the center, crossing the lower half of shame.

This, Tolya, marked the end of your vain attempts to break into the category of average people, to become an ordinary schoolboy and Komsomol member, a friend of the pretty little Lyudmila, and a local basketball star. You walked toward the black Emka, with its pink blinds, feeling amid the blinding snow that the whole class was watching you and your shameful companion, THE OFFICIAL WITNESS.

He had suddenly guessed that this syphilitic woman from the Medical Complex was an official witness, and, having still not fully perceived the further course of events, still afraid to pronounce mentally the word "ARREST" but with that word already lodged within him, he gripped the door handle of the Emka.

No, there was no courage in the soul of young Von Steinbock at that moment. All his mental images had evaporated at that moment. Gone were his romantic role models – the young Mayakovsky, Jack London's gold prospector, the European tramp, the fearless lover. Here the future person or persons that he might become no longer existed; all that remained was something trembling, bluish-pale, still half childish and ashamed, in soiled underpants that smelled of urine and sperm. That something opened the door of the Emka and was immediately gripped in the face by a man's two hot, greedy, and mocking eyes like ripe cherries.

The fold of a cheek on the lambskin collar of an expensive overcoat, the sickle of flesh at the back of the neck, the heavy hammer of the forehead, the little lambskin hat with a leather crown – all this was somehow lifeless, so solid and sound that it was unnatural. But the two eyes were full of life, the life streaming from them was positively scorching! Power, strength, scorn for all wretched creatures, for his unworthy victims, and, above all, pleasure, intoxication with power, and contempt.

"Ah, there he is, our young hero. Come on, sit down, sit down, our hole-in-the-pants hero." The voice of the man who had turned around to Tolya from the front seat sounded completely ordinary, almost kindly.

A faint hope twitched in the pit of Tolya's stomach. Suppose nothing particular was happening after all? It squirmed and vanished; no hope.

There were two people on the back seat: another lambskin collar with a face, a slack, indifferent, yellow face with sagging skin, and beside it, a lady. Indeed, Tolya's mother looked like a real lady from some prewar film – a dark-brown fox fur around her shoulders, a felt hat adorned with a silly little felt flower shaped like a propeller.

"Move over a bit, Steinbock," the yellow-faced man said to Tolya's mother in a colorless voice, and moved himself a little to one side.

His mother, to complete the nightmarish silliness and incongruity of her "free" outfit, also had a muff, a fur, prerevolutionary muff in which, looking like Anna Karenina, she was hiding the little hands that had grown calloused from wielding a logger's saw and pounding piano keys in a kindergarten.

"Tolya, try not to be upset. The most terrible thing has happened. I have been arrested again," she announced in a flat, expressionless voice.

She moved over and made room for her son on the back seat. The door slammed, and the soldier-driver pulled the blinds down more firmly.

"They came for me while I was at work," his mother continued in the same steady voice, only with a pause or two. "I asked to be allowed to fetch you from school in order to say goodbye, and these gentlemen were so kind –"

"Don't be such a creep, Steinbock!" barked the massive neck from the front seat, a flash of cherry shooting at us from under a frown. "What d'you mean, 'gentlemen?' "

They were driving along now, and soon, shimmering ahead of them with its welcoming dark-blue bulk was Wolf's Hill, beyond whose crest certain mysteries had occurred quite recently. Tolya noticed how the passersby turned at the sound of the car's engine, froze at the sight of the Emka, and then, petrified, disappeared as the car's pink blinds shut them out of sight. Unable to obey his mother's appeal, Tolya was miserable, shaking with sobs.

"I meant to say 'officers,' " his mother corrected herself.

"Well say it then." This time the neck did not move.

"In my day the words 'gentleman' and 'officer' were almost synonymous," said mother with animation, even smiling, at which she convulsively pulled her right hand out of her muff.

The yellow-faced man with sagging skin gave her a keen glance, but a little too late – his mother's hand had already grasped Tolya's and

was squeezing it hard: Don't cry, don't cry, don't humiliate yourself!
Tolya knew he was humiliating himself, knew that his mother found
it intolerable to hear her grown-up son crying. How shameful to cry
in that lambskin captivity! It wasn't him crying, not Tolya Bokov, not
young Von Steinbock. He would never cry, whether he were white or
red, he would never cry in front of these pigs! It was something else
in him that was crying, something small with wet, sticky fur, a little
living creature caught unawares, trembling, and there was no power
that could stop it.

The cheek was on the lambskin collar again, and the hat pushed
down over the eyebrows in a distinctly gangsterish style. The pupils
were suffused with a mobster's bloodshot menace. Subsequently Tolya
was to notice on more than one occasion the similarity between
hardened crooks and these so-called officers.

"We will try and explain to you the difference between those words,"
the neck announced slowly, and added with pleasure, "Steinbock."

Tolya's mother's grip weakened, and he suddenly realized that she
was afraid. Something like anger, hot and coiled, stirred inside him
and almost stopped the flow of his tears, but then the little damp and
furry creature twitched harder and he started crying even more.

Then they stopped at the Third Medical Complex. Several inhabitants and their children looked on in silence as the procession made its
way from the Emka to the hut: First a security officer in an expensive,
heavy overcoat; then a lady in a hat, fox fur, and muff, the kindergarten
music teacher, almost an ITR;* then the tall boy who had flown in
that fall from the "mainland"; then another officer; and last of all an
apathetic reenlisted sergeant.

The yellow-faced Major Paly was sitting at the table and writing the
official record of the search, while the thickset, well-fed Captain
Cheptsov, with an assumed air of fastidious boredom, walked around
the room, pulling out things at random from the bookshelf, out of the
drawer of the wobbly table, overturning the pillowcases embroidered
by Aunt Varya. The floorboards of the crumbling building creaked
dangerously under his feet. Paly smoked ceaselessly and kept raising
his eyebrows as though trying to pull up the skin because it was
slithering off his face. Cheptsov hemmed and hawed as he leafed

---

*Russian initials of an official phrase designating a particular category of prisoners who
were relatively privileged – "engineers and technicians".

through the books, put something aside for confiscation, and boomed to his colleague over his shoulder, "Dostoyevsky *The Possessed,* Alighieri *Divine Comedy,* six issues of the magazine *America* for 1946, two brass crosses . . ."

Suddenly, without a word, he offered Tolya's mother a pack of Belomor cigarettes, and to Tolya's amazement his mother took a cigarette, thanked him, and with absolute self-possession drew in a lungful of smoke.

Everything was quiet, routine, unfussy. At first his mother was tapping the heel of her boot on the floor, but then Paly asked her to stop tapping because the table was wobbly enough anyway and it was hard to write, and her heel ceased its aimless tapping.

Everything would have been quite routine but for Tolya's sobbing. What was happening to him and how many tears does a person have in him? He clenched his teeth, gulped, wiped his face with his hands and sleeve, brushed away the snot, and sobbed on and on. He tried to weep and sob politely, in order to disturb Major Paly as little as possible while the latter wrote out the official report, and for that reason Tolya moved away, to continue weeping and trembling at a slight distance from that round table, which not long ago Martin had brought to them, piece by piece, from the carpentry workshop at the Quarantine Camp.

His mother was sitting beside the major, one elbow leaning on the table, and saying quietly; "Tolya, listen to me carefully. Write to your aunts at once and tell them what has happened. Ask Varya to take some money out of her savings-bank account and buy you an airplane ticket to Leningrad, but don't go until the end of the semester, or you will lose this school year. You will be sent money to live on by you know who. Listen to me, please . . . and don't forget your scarf."

Suddenly the table tilted under the weight of Captain Cheptsov's hand. "Why do you have these crosses?" the captain asked Tolya's mother in a gentle, almost conciliatory tone.

"They . . . they are simply ornaments," she replied, and lowered her eyes.

Part of Tolya still acted as a disinterested observer, and he watched the scene intently as though from a distance or through the wrong end of a pair of binoculars. Thus he noticed the numerous bags of skin on Paly's face and listened to the abstracted way he smacked his lips. It was such a curious sound, as if the recording officer wanted to stress something by the smacking of his lips, but when you glanced at him in alarm, you realized that it was, in fact, a completely meaningless

sound, merely his way of removing the saliva from his mouth. The
same observer also detected something of the boxer in Captain
Cheptsov's stance, with his arms that hung slightly in front of his torso,
the movements of his neck and his sloping shoulders. That detached
observer, as though peering out from the depths of a tunnel, also
noticed his mother's embarrassment when she was asked about the
crosses, and realized that his mother was not just afraid. She was also
ashamed of her secret religious faith. But why, why was she ashamed?

"And what is this?" asked Cheptsov with a guffaw as he flung down
Martin's little folding altarpiece, looking like a child's stand-up book.

Tolya's mother broke out in red spots, and then her whole face
turned crimson.

"It's . . . they're . . . pictures by Leonardo and Raphael . . . just
reproductions."

She was ashamed because she was still a *Soviet* person, the detached
observer suddenly guessed. Soviet-indoctrinated, despite two years in
isolation for "political" offenses and eight years in the Kolyma camps,
she still thought like a Soviet person, just as I do too. That was the
reason for her beastly shame!

"I don't believe you, Stei-ein-bock." Cheptsov leaned slightly
forward over Tolya's mother, like a boxer. His tunic fitted tightly over
his back and showed up the solid fat around his sides.

Tolya was still crying, sniveling, and sniffing, but the detached
observer in him imagined the captain undressed: a huge figure of a
man, with resilient buttocks, a hairy, protruding stomach, a heavy,
pendulous penis like that of the dominant male of a herd of seals, a
wrinkled old killer.

The same detached observer noticed the change that occurred in
Tolya's mother a moment later. Something inside her seemed to click;
the "Soviet shame" was switched off and drained away from her facial
expression. The eyes narrowed, and she said in her previous defensive,
cunning voice with its extremely "intellectual" tone, "Come, come,
Captain! The old masters often used biblical subject matter to reflect
the life of ordinary people. Really, Captain!"

Once, Tolya had heard his mother say to Martin, "I was always
extremely kind and polite to them, as though they were officers of the
tsar's Horse Guards; it disarmed them."

Cheptsov sensed the change of tack, the sly female feint. Dis-
appointed, he growled, "Taking refuge in superstition, Steinbock?"

What more, one might have thought, did the captain want? The
criminal was in his hands, so just be glad of it and hang onto her! No,

Captain Cheptsov was an all-or-nothing man. He thirsted for total capitulation and none of your slippery Jewish dodges!

"Get on with the search, Cheptsov," the major put in drily at this point. "Have you found any correspondence?"

The captain threw a bundle of letters on the table, smirked at his cold, unemotional boss, and started to climb into his immensely heavy overcoat. He was suddenly overcome with boredom by this whole case, and his good mood was ruined: He had imagined the arrest of an inveterate Trotskyite as being somewhat different. That old fool Paly suppressed any sort of initiative; he could never get over having dealt with those Estonians. Someone should warn him.

Next, Cheptsov kicked the screen and barged into the corner occupied by the Komsomol member Bokov. He prodded textbooks, fastidiously pushed aside Jack London, yanked off the blanket, and began to show a sudden interest in Tolya's sheet, which looked like the map of an unknown archipelago. The traces of a conquistador's dreams. He looked over the screen at Tolya as though he had only just seen him, gave him a conspiratorial wink, and boomed at him in a voice that even betrayed a certain admiration, "Hey, you jerk off? Good for you!"

The captain's mood improved slightly. "Get ready, Steinbock!"

Again the dressing up as a slightly faded beauty: fur boa, muff, the hat with the propeller. From the end of the corridor came the scratchy music of a foxtrot – ah, the golden thirties, the dawn of fascism. One of the tenants was trying to pretend that nothing unusual was happening.

It was only now that Tolya at last grasped the full implications of the event: His mother was being taken away to an unknown place, for an unknown reason, and for an unknown length of time. Without wasting any words, but also without cruelty, brutality, or violence, they were removing his mother, whom he had only come to know in the last few months, who still made him feel embarrassed, who in the evenings recited to him from memory the poetry of Blok, Pasternak, Mayakovsky, Gumilyov, Akhmatova, and who used to recall, or perhaps invent, funny stories about his childhood that had occurred before the catastrophe of her first arrest. She had almost become his real mother. What reason had he to feel ashamed? Why had the Komsomol, the basketball team, Lyudka, and all the rest of it ever seemed more important than his mother?

"Mother!" screamed Tolya, and at once his senseless sobbing stopped.

"Allow me to help you on with your coat, madam." With two fingers Cheptsov mockingly held out Tolya's mother's twice-refaced overcoat with the quilted lining hanging out. But she did not give in, and with the bright, incongruously lipsticked mouth in her broad white face, she retorted with cold "high society" hatred, "Excuse me, Captain, but I am not an officer's wife."

She snatched the coat and put it on in a flash. Cheptsov laughed and strode out of the room, and Paly said apathetically but entirely politely, "Say goodbye to your son, Tatyana Nathanovna."

The experienced security officer allowed mother and son to touch for exactly as many seconds as was proper to the ritual of arrest. He then took the prisoner by the elbow and gave her a gentle push, like a good but emotionally uninvolved doctor. "Now that's enough, Tatyana Nathanovna, you've said goodbye."

The door closed.

"Mama!" howled Tolya, and in that cry there was no longer a trace of his earlier senseless weeping but a real, live emotion – despair. There was also, perhaps, a touch of hatred in it.

The door opened and Cheptsov, his fur hat leading, marched in – he had forgotten his briefcase.

"What are you yelling for, you whore's brat?" he said quietly, looking around for something, and walked softly over to Tolya.

Tolya restrained himself for a horrible few moments. Cheptsov was standing in front of him with a frozen smile, as though putting himself on show so that Tolya would remember this image of the all-powerful enemy for the rest of his life: low forehead, two arched eyebrows, eyes like hot little cherries, snub nose, and incipient double chin – the whole simple, strong, ponderous, and unambiguous. Another minute, hold out for just another minute! At any second he may go for you, this bull, and will start to maul you and push you around as though you were a woman! You won't be able to stop him! If only Tolya could hit him in the forehead with a sledgehammer! If only he could plunge a pitchfork into his double chin!

"Little slob! You're just a puddle of chocolate-colored shit!" Cheptsov laughed, straightened his hat, picked up the briefcase containing the confiscated articles, and went out.

"BUT WHAT PROSPECTS WE HAVE!

Don't you realize? Henri will finance the whole project and write the music. Julie Christie will play Sonya, Robert Hossein will be Svidrigailov . . .''

Pantelei was still unable to shake off the wave of memories that had suddenly come over him. Although the prospects were gradually beginning to sink into his consciousness, he still could not reply, could still only stare with lowered head at one spot in front of him, at the long narrow dish containing the snacks for which this actors' club was famous, the "assorted seafood:" a few halves of hard-boiled eggs holding little blobs of caviar, slices of red fish that looked like sandbanks on the shores of the Caspian Sea, sprats like mummies in sand, and all of it slightly withered, slightly blurred, not quite real, not up to the standard of foreign-currency bars, and, of course, a long way off from what was served in the Kremlin, but even so a tasty dish for the plebs of the artistic world.

"But what have we to do with all this?" he finally asked his enthusiastic friend, the semi-Luxembourg husband of a semidiplomatic semiwife.

"Don't you see? They can't do it without us!" said the latter in a.nazement. "You write the screenplay, I direct it!"

"But why should they want *us* of all people?" Pantelei continued to insist with dull incomprehension. "Why can't they use some Albedike and some Truffauñuel?"

"No, it can't be done without us," said the "blazer" firmly. "We are his fellow countrymen."

"Whose?"

"Dostoyevsky's!"

"Ah, I didn't quite see that right away. It makes sense. The authentic Russian touch, building bridges between East and West."

"So you agree, Pantelei?"

"Of course I agree. How could I fail to agree? I'm not such an idiot as to turn down an offer like that."

Using his napkin to pick up the sweating bottle of vodka, the "blazer" poured some of the colorless, harmless-looking liquid into two glasses. Pantelei watched this movement as though in a trance. It had been a long time since he had seen those strange, rhythmic dreams. For a month after his "drying-out" cure he had had the same vision every night: wine glasses and tumblers being filled up, the rattling of bottles, throats gulping down alcohol, little bubbles of gas, and nothing left of his past but the intoxicating midnight breeze.

"Don't give me any. I'm on the wagon," he said.

"Yes, I'm basically on the wagon too. I got fed up with our disgusting Russian drinking habits," said the "blazer." "We just don't know how to drink in a civilized manner, you know, yet there exists a genuine art of imbibing alcohol, which is completely unknown in this Tatary of ours."

He smiled a smile that radiated intelligence and charm. He does understand everything, after all, thought Pantelei, and he is laughing at himself. He's not dumb, this young man, not dumb at all. But what is it that happens to them all as soon as they start talking about their "art?" Where does their sense of humor disappear to? They get so deadly serious; they start to take off into stratosphere and make out as if they're talking to the great shades of the past.

"Yes, but seriously, I'm not drinking, not in the European style and not in Tatar style either."

"You should play tennis, old man," the "blazer" said sincerely to Pantelei, and immediately tossed back a glassful.

Agonized, Pantelei watched the movement of his Adam's apple, and after drumming his fingers on the table for a few moments, he said fussily, "But how come you and I have completely forgotten Leo Tolstoy? It'll look as if we're not treating the matter seriously – he was an author too, after all. Just think: Anna Karenina – Sophia Loren, Karenin – Carlo Ponti, Israeli ambassador to the United Nations –"

"Yes, yes!" The "blazer's" eyes began to sparkle like figures flashing on the quotation board of the Stock Exchange. "Go on!"

"Seryozha, of course, would be played by Ringo Starr, who is a twenty-eight-year-old hippie who has fought his way out of Tibet –"

"Yes, yes!" The figures chased each other in mad succession. "Keep going!"

"And of course Vronsky would be an American astronaut just back from the moon –"

"Pure genius!" he shrieked, knocking over everything around him on the table and pressing his fingers against his temples.

"Oh, my poor, poor Blazer Sergeyevich Mukhachov-Bagrationsky!"

"But what about the Russian contingent?" he whispered, "apart from you and me?"

"I have an idea, Sergeyevich. Look, why don't we bring in our Khvastishchev instead of Salvador Dali?"

"Radik? Another stroke of genius! He's an old pal of mine! Radik is a titanic figure, a colossus, a Russian and a cosmic genius!"

Suddenly he pushed his glass aside, sighed deeply, and for no apparent reason ran a comb through his hair.

"Sorry, old man, Radik won't do. He's an alcoholic, old man. He needs to be sent on a cure. You know how much I like him – he and I have a lot in common – but they'd never give him an exit visa. Apparently, not long ago in Yalta he assaulted a general and bit off all his buttons. He swallowed the general's buttons. And then, he has signed various subversive documents."

So that's how it is, thought Pantelei; at last you've started talking in your normal language, your old dad's language. A spasm of fury seized Pantelei's throat and he barked hoarsely, "And what about me, you son of a bitch? Why do you ask *me* to do this job? Don't you know anything about me? Or haven't you checked out my file yet, Mr. Honorary Policeman?"

To Pantelei's amazement, no angry scene ensued; what's more, the "blazer" appeared not to have heard his outburst. He suddenly froze with the fork in his mouth and stared at the far end of the bar, where a strange and most elegant movement had suddenly arisen between the carved wooden pillars flanking the entrance, where there now appeared several flashes of bright color, fresh brilliant colors that were not stale, not worn out, not bought in secondhand stores, not from Moscow. As they approached, they turned out on inspection to be three birds of paradise, ballerinas with smooth Russian hairdos.

The "blazer" had already forgotten his global projects and stood up with his arms open wide in an embrace.

"Here, come here, girls! Natasha, Sasha, Paulina! Vadim Nikolaye-vich, do sit down with us."

They were the prima ballerinas Kokoshkina, Mitroshkina, and Para-moshkina, nimble envoys of Soviet art who, according to a long-term strategic plan, were preparing the ground in Europe for the ultimate proletarian revolution.

Being in their homeland for the first time in a long while, the girls were still surprised at the Russian smells, the crumpled faces, the lack of decent clothes, the whole decor of our native pigsty with its permanent sense of being just about to erupt into a noisy brawl.

They had been brought to the bar by Vadim Serebryanikov, a friend of Pantelei's, or rather a former friend, a former leader of the "new wave," a former first violin in the orchestra of "new voices," a mighty chromosome of the fourth generation, founder of three or four active avant-garde studios (now, of course, forgotten), a former exponent of the "ideas of the sixties," now a totally sold-out official culture merchant, conductor of an academic choir with affiliates all over the country, a Party-approved star, and an inveterate alcoholic.

Not long ago people had argued about Serebryanikov: Had he sold out totally or not quite? Now there was no longer any argument: He had become untouchable, he had gone over to "them," into an orbit where they use a different set of rules from ours. Only on the days of his drinking bouts, which, it had to be admitted, were becoming less and less frequent, would Vadim Nikolayevich turn up in his old haunts to create mayhem with his old pals, torment himself with remorse in front of any riffraff; then he would disappear to an anonymous address and for three or four days he would MOAN, BARE HIS SOUL, BEG FOR SYMPATHY, crawl around the garbage dumps, and then suddenly – vanish. Where to? Where did he go? Some thought he went to a psychiatric hospital, others thought he went to prison, while still others, more simply, guessed that he had crawled away to nurse his hangover. And then, equally suddenly, he would reappear – and not just anywhere, but on the television screen. Clean, dapper, wearing most attractive glasses, with an intellectual's slight tremor in his voice, Vadim Nikolayevich would discuss on screen such matters as the inter-action between various national cultures within the Soviet Union, the dominant literary theme of the day, the crisis of his unfortunate Western colleagues. His drinking companions of yesterday would curse him for a bastard, a filthy sellout, scum, adding, "Look what he's become. We want none of him!"

Pantelei never swore at his former friend, neither inwardly nor aloud. He remembered not only the bars and seedy dives. Something else linked him to Vadim: the stage at the Polytechnic Institute, for instance, a forbidden play that they had both written and never did get performed, joint ideas of theirs that never came to anything either, dreams that they shared, which, although smothered in vomit, might still have been washed clean, as they sometimes proposed on the rare occasions when they met.

Now they were sitting together at the same table, and that table began to acquire more and more people clustering around it, like the growths on a piece of underwater coral. The three girls, the stars of Russia, could only turn their heads in dumb amazement, could only flutter their Dior eyelashes and open their foreign-currency mouths at the sight of ever more literary octopuses, hairy squids from the movies, theatrical cuttlefish attaching themselves to the coral. It all grew and grew. Arms waved in wild gesture. They were all friends – none of them were excluded – and they were all a bunch of louts. Independence had turned into arrogance; they were all trying to show their independence, above all by insulting the man at the head of the table, Vadim Nikolayevich.

Thus, for instance, a certain writer put his face into Vadim's soup and started to eat it with the lower half of his face, while the upper half continued to insult the owner of the soup by calling him a collaborationist. Another example: A well-known satirist used one hand to stroke the knees of Vadim's girlfriends and the other to draw an endless succession of caricatures, each one more disgraceful than the last, which he shoved in front of his host with a repulsive laugh. Finally, a third example, in accordance with the law of triads: A certain lousy poet, drunk at the mere proximity of the great man, at the chance of tickling him below the navel, sidled up to Vadim Nikolayevich, wearing a filthy tweed jacket, and flung onto the table a heavy, sealed wad of money, either his royalties for the film *The Cornerstone* or for the latest installment of the soap opera *Your Majesty,* or simply a subsidy from secret government funds.

Serebryanikov sat there drooping, as though crushed by a heavy weight, with a contemptuous, meaningful smile on his lips as he stared at an uneaten piece of salmon that was floating, curled up like a maggot, in someone's unfinished cup of coffee, into which it had fallen via the inscrutable ways of nature. He was afraid to raise his head, because then the whole room would start to turn around, and he was hardly able – or perhaps just able – to hear the insults of his friends and the gentle twittering of the ballerinas. He had already forgotten what had happened that morning – that burst of irrepressible excitement that he had felt in the piercing breeze that was blowing around the business center of Moscow – had forgotten that instinctive upsurge of memories about nothing, perhaps about his youth. One – and he ordered the car to stop! Two – and in a side-street the three ballerinas appeared, like an illustration to his memories about nothing, about his youth perhaps.

Talonov, his driver, at once carried out his instructions and did not remind his boss about the foreign delegation, the honorary degree ceremony, the anniversary concert, the talk with leading steelworkers about the way forward for Soviet art. In the end, the sexual organ decides everything, as Driver Talonov had always believed, and his intuition had never let him down. Go on, boss, have fun, while I amuse myself cruising around dear old Moscow!

Pantelei looked at his friend's thinning hair, the furrows plowed in it by years of exertion on the Party's behalf, at his puffy face in which almost nothing human remained, and he thought glumly, There's practically nothing human left in you, my friend, except the tendency to decay. There's almost nothing left in you at all, nothing of the young, madcap d'Artagnan, nothing crazy except your unstoppable slide into old age, my friend, our failed leader. How wrong we were in those days to think that your intrigues were our intrigues too, that your shrewdness was our shrewdness, your inflated talent was the same artistic talent that the rest of us had. How easily they bought you, body and soul, and how easily, too, they split us up, divided us, cut us off from each other, heated us in the furnace, and hammered us into different shapes.

"Pantelyusha!" the "blazer" suddenly shouted. "Tell us the plot of *The Three Sisters* in a few words."

At the name "Pantelyusha" Vadim's face expressed a certain alarm; his glance rose up from the floating scrap of salmon, slid along the faces of everyone present like a wet rag, but could discern nothing, and his eyes only grew blearier. Then Vadim's head fell onto the edge of the table, and he grunted, "If Pantelei shows up, tell him he's a bastard!"

The great man's finger stirred the cold coffee, and he fished out the object of his attention, a sliver of uneaten red fish, to show it to the whole table, as much as to say, Here's another wretched wordless creature, and it wants to live too! After that, Vadim Nikolayevich collapsed altogether, drooping as he rested in the nursing home of physical decay.

THE PLOT OF THE PLAY *THE THREE SISTERS* IS AS FOLLOWS

Nothing is achieved without hard work, and figure skating is no exception. From childhood the sisters had grown up in sports clubs under the solicitous eyes of the senior coaches – lithe men and ponderous, muscular women.

Why am I here? Who am I waiting for? Kokoshkina, Mitroshkina, and Paramoshkina? Why don't I slip out in the twinkling of an eye and leave the story unfinished?

Although the sisters belonged to a generation that could not imagine life without the Intervision system, their apartment was a masterpiece of the Old Russian style. Their mother, who had been the champion rifle shot of the Red Army, had collected samovars battered in the struggles for independence, while their father, a passionate ornithologist, spent his days in a charming exchange of whistles and tweets with his goldfinches, siskins, and thrushes, and every morning, his stomach rumbling, he would drink raw eggs. The family grew up together with the nation.

"Just imagine, girls! Tuzenbakh – Elvis Presley; Vershinin – Frank Sinatra; Solyony – Adamo! Everything we want! Coproduction financed by the Principality of Monaco! Polyphony! Polygamy! Three sisters are dancing, our kids are singing! To Moscow! To Moscow!" The "blazer's" hands moved under the table as though he were developing a film there.

In their preschool phase the sisters were interested in periodic bleeding from the womb, and for that reason were always covered in scratches: Their cat Sicilia did not wish to be the object of their curiosity.

"Do you like the poetry of Joseph Brodsky?" Kokoshkina asked her neighbor, the poet Fyodorov-Smirnov, during a pause.

The girl had asked this question out of a wish to raise herself a little out of the general rut of animal urges, to save herself, if only for a while, from being groped by sweaty paws, to show that she was not just a little dancing figurine, a sex object for men, but also a person with a mind of her own. Such instinctive adroitness is not rare among simple-minded creatures.

"Brodsky?" The poet flushed the color of tomato sauce. They were long-term rivals.

The girl went on, unaware of having made a *faux pas*. "Do you remember those lines of his? How do they go?

> Seven years ago he laid his hand on her eyelids
> Lest the snow make her frown, but the eyelids,
> Not believing his wish was to shield them,
> Fluttered like butterflies as he held them.

"Shit!" roared Fyodorov-Smirnov. "Brodsky thinks he's Lermontov! If he's Lermontov, who the hell am I supposed to be?!"

They studied in school, but didn't understand very much. For instance, what was the point of the Russian "matryoshka" doll, with its endless copies of itself in ever smaller sizes enclosed within it? Or what chance did an under-age virgin have of playing any role in the contemporary youth movement? Why were the women of the progressive socialist countries not launching a campaign for painless abortion?

The youngest sister, racked by her own "accursed" problems, turned up one day at the youth club attached to the Museum of Paleontology. What is the reproductive principle of the triton? How do duck-billed platypuses of different sex copulate? Can a male flamingo make love to a female heron? Her older sisters came running up in a panic – you've gone to the wrong museum, you little fool!

Their development progressed to maturity, and the sisters, attending the sessions of the Krasnopresnensky district committee of the Komsomol or the Party cell of the Pechora café, would call out to the migrating birds: To Moscow! To Moscow!

In Western countries, as the rebellion of the young spread wider, in Russia everything was basically calm, and only in Slavophile circles of the capital of all Slavs were rumors being circulated in whispers that the Jews of Scandinavia had invented rubber genitals.

"Oh, what a pity we don't have a tape recorder," said the "blazer" regretfully. "This is a ready-made scenario, or a libretto. Forgive me, Pantelyusha, but we will now drink to you. Let us drink, my friends to synthetic art, to libido, to success!"

Why am I here? I must get out at once, crawl up to my loft, bow to Our Lady the Consoler of the Afflicted, switch on the lamp over my table, put on a record of Chicago jazz, and lay a clean sheet of paper on my desk. How much longer can I go on being shaken up in this vile train? Surely I can jump out of it while it's moving even at the risk of my life? Who put us on this rattling train, with these rattling bottles and glasses and all this sticky food? Where did we board it? Where did we take our seats on its vomit-covered velvet seats? Where was that platform, spattered with gobs of spit? Where is our baggage being taken to: our childhood, our freedom, our creative work? Where is it locked up? Under what lead seals is it secured? We guess that our creaking monster is rumbling across the green hilly countryside, over translucent waters, while on the horizon there arise now the chains of mountain ranges, now the outlines of cities. We guess that we are crossing huge squares with crowds of people gripped by passion. We guess all this, but we see nothing, and all we do is pour ourselves drinks and eat and dully remasticate our stale ideas. We make friends and join groups because we are too frightened simply to get up from the table, wrench open the door, and ask with plain, straightforward anger, Where are you taking us?

"Do you have a pad, old man?"

"Why do you want to know, Fyodorov-Smirnov?"

"We must get these three little sisters off to some pad, but fast, while they're still in heat, or they'll start having hysterics. Take 'em and fuck 'em!"

The time had come to part. The youngest of the three sisters was carried away by a Tanzanian to a nature reserve on Lake Victoria, where he fucked her. The middle sister danced her way into the sinful clutches of a Greek secret agent, with whom she was sent on a Party mission to Zimbabwe, where she was handed over to a racist white planter who exploited her mercilessly, in other words fucked her. There's no denying, though, that the third sister struck gold: She became the legal wife of a real live Swiss and now resides handsomely in a respectable Swiss-German *Haus* that stands foursquare amid the chaos of Europe like a citadel of common sense and regular though thoroughly moderate copulation. Belonging as they do to the free world, all three graces destroy the sperm by the French method, and when they meet on their spring vacations in cafés to drink chocolate, they recall the meat pies and suckling pig of Moscow, which to this day they still regard as the symbol of all that is new and progressive. To Moscow! To Moscow!

"What horrible things you say!" Sasha Mitroshkina suddenly burst out fervently, her little nose quivering with bravery.

Pantelei broke out in a cold sweat of shame.

"You're right, Ninelle, the ending is a bit flat."

"It's not flat. It's disgusting, boring, lousy," Mitroshkina said, almost in tears. "Aren't you ashamed to sneer at Russia and Europe like that? Once you were my favorite writer, you were my inner world, but now I see you're nothing but a louse! Look at that stinking goat Fyodorov-Smirnov sitting beside you, trying to fix up a 'pad.' Well he may be repulsive, but at least he's easy enough to understand, whereas there is nothing human left in you, my dear!"

She began sobbing and leaned her little head on her pink hand. Her delicate hair, without a single speck of dandruff, lay alongside a revolting plate of salad.

"He doesn't drink, so no wonder he's so degraded," the satirist boomed contemptuously.

"Out of the mouths of babes and sucklings shall the truth come forth!" Comrade Vadim Nikolayevich Serebryanikov suddenly said in a very loud, very sober and scathing voice. He had raised his head and was now looking Pantelei straight in the eye with a cold, sober stare.

"The girl's right, Pantelei. The fire of cynicism burns the cynic himself first of all!"

"Ah, you shit!" Pantelei instantly forgot about the three sisters and about the vodka that was splashing all over the table like a whore in a bath-tub. Everything in him hardened and rang with hatred. "Scum!" he said to his friend. "That's why they put such a value on you, you nonentity! They know that when they need you, you can pull yourself together and trot out some quotation and dig up a convenient way of saying that black's white. That's why they even forgive you your attacks of senile decay!"

Serebryanikov carefully pocketed his now slightly thinner wad of money, and then stood up. "Come outside!"

"Hey, boys, let's not have a fight," begged the "blazer." "We're all Europeans, after all."

Fyodorov-Smirnov gave a sneering laugh, and Pantelei decided that, once he had dealt with Vadim, he would come back and beat up this filthy anti-Semitic jackal, after which he would take the ballerinas away to his loft and screw all three of them, and he wouldn't write anything today, tomorrow, or ever again. I'm thinking like a drunkard, he thought to himself, even though I haven't touched a drop for weeks. Now I'll come back after this fight and I'll drink!

THE TOILET WAS CLEAN

except for the imprint of a sweaty billiard player's hand on the towel.

Vadim Serebryanikov and Pantelei Pantelei stood pissing in silence, side by side as though they were good friends. Both moved, shook themselves, and zipped themselves up almost simultaneously, then turned and smiled guiltily at each other.

"Look, let's forget it," said Vadim. "You know I've never yet dropped any of our pals in the shit."

"I know," said Pantelei.

"In fact, quite the opposite: Whenever any of the kids are in real trouble I help them, I pull them out of it."

"I know," said Pantelei.

"But you're the only one who never comes to see me."

"Well, I still manage to scrape by one way or another."

"Your name is still your salvation, Pantelyusha."

"Yes, I guess it is."

"D'you want me to tell you a secret? They don't like you UP THERE."

"But why, Grayhead? Why don't they like me?"

"You shoot your mouth off too much, Pant. You stick your neck out. You always used to talk a lot before, but then everyone was gabbing away. The difference is that since '68 they've all stopped blabbing, except you. You still keep on spouting the same stuff as before."

"In that case, I must be saying the right things."

"You're behind the times. Nowadays it's a bad thing to gab and shoot the shit, and they don't like people who do. Perhaps you think they don't hear you? They hear you all right! Those boys have bugged every wall, they're everywhere. Incidentally, there are some decent, regular guys among them, but above all, they don't like chatterboxes. They get needled by chatterers who are out of step with the times."

"I hope I never get in step with *your* times."

"Now, now, you don't really mean that, do you?" Vadim glanced over his shoulder to where there was nobody.

"Listen, surely you and I can have a serious talk in the john," said Pantelei, almost imploringly. "You're not running any risks *here*, are you?"

Serebryanikov gave a frank and cheerful burst of laughter. His old laughter. The favorite laugh of a favorite actor, the rosy-cheeked movie hero who played riggers, steel erectors, fishermen, and carpenters, the famous Serebryanikov laugh in which only those who knew him well could catch the very faint tinkle of the psychopath.

"It's just these places, ha, ha, ha, that are specially bugged because people think they're absolutely safe, ha, ha, ha!"

Reflections were distorted in the black wall tiles: An arm would hang separately from a body, a head would slither apart into two unequal halves. Once again Pantelei was seized by a crazy feeling of alienation from his real surroundings and he almost shouted, "You've all gone clean out of your minds, you saps, you cowards! Sleep with a woman and a week later they tell you she's a plant, a stool pigeon, a lieutenant in the KGB. Talk to someone about Dostoyevsky and you're done for – it turns out the other guy's a paid informer. Sit down to a meal and they make warning noises and nod at the walls. Go for a piss – keep your mouth shut! It's pure Orwell. And if that's the case, then it's time to get out of here! If that's so, it's impossible to live here any longer. We've got to get out!"

"But where to?"

A forearm cut in half raised itself and lay on an empty square of tile, while in the neighboring tile above it a pair of lips and the tip of a nose swam into view.

Footsteps were heard behind them, and out of the black tiled space the friends were approached by the lower half of a torso and an almost sideways view of hips and belly. The upper part of the torso was completely cut off and moved independently, with the head, like an owl, sitting on its left shoulder. Amid this dark disjointed mass there shone a gleam from the medal worn by winners of the State Prize. The prizewinning urine flowed calmly and simply alongside Pantelei.

"We must get out!" Pantelei announced to the medal. "Through the historic homeland with a Jewish visa, to Labrador if necessary, even unto the deepest, icebound asshole of the world! Get out, and let THEM have everything of ours that we leave behind: Tolstoyevsky, and the middle section of the Moika Canal, and the bronze stallions that we once tamed with such zeal, and even our girls, all the girls of the fifties, sixties, and seventies – let THEM devour everything that belongs to us! Get out, escape! Go, Russians, go!"

At the end of this passionate and audacious appeal Pantelei suddenly realized that no one was listening to him. Serebryanikov and the anonymous prizewinner were calmly discussing the prospects for the sale of a batch of Mercedes in Moscow BY SUBSCRIPTION LIST and for internal currency – ordinary rubles. The whole business was to be handled by Zamyslov, and one must take care not to miss the opportunity.

"OK, Pantik, don't get steamed up," Vadim said finally, patting him on the shoulder. "All that's just good clean fun. Let's go."

They came out of the men's room and sat down in the semidarkness under the staircase on a couple of torn leather armchairs, which, according to legend, had been the favorite resting place of those two pillars of socialist realism, James Aldridge and Boris Polevoi. It was in these very armchairs, so the story went, that Colonel Polevoi had once had a heart-to-heart with James Aldridge.

"Instead of spouting all that crap, Pantelyusha, you'd do much better to write something for my outfit," said Serebryanikov. "Write me an outline, and I guarantee you an advance and a contract."

Swinging his superbly made English shoe, the tips of which were only slightly spattered with vomit, Serebryanikov began describing which category of contract he would sign and how much of an advance he would offer, but Pantelei wasn't listening. He was looking at the blunt-toed English shoe, and he felt it was a good, kind, amusing friend of his youth. How great it would be to work together with this shoe and not to think vile thoughts! To turn up every morning – just like having a steady job! – in the empty auditorium, to sit side by side at the director's desk, drink coffee, smoke, talk about real things: where it seemed a bit overwritten, where it struck a false note, where it needed tightening up a bit, and where, on the other hand, they could let it go over the top.

Ye gods of Olympus, he and I could put on a real knockout of a show, slick but not tacky, funny enough to raise belly laughs, and as bitter as fate. He is a touch over forty and I'm getting on for forty; we're both still in the prime of life, but we have a lot of experience behind us. It's all there in our memories, on paper, on the stage, on the screen; it's all at our fingertips. We can give Aristophanes something to worry about, we can rampage like a crazy mob through the taverns of old London, we can weigh Aeschylus and Euripides in the balance, build a hellish tower higher than the Ostankino television tower, invent hell, invent a whole island of funny and good-natured nonsense with mountains and palm trees – in other words, paradise – hang an Unidentified Flying Object from the flies of the theater, we can turn a girl into a heron and, of course, vice versa!

"Well, do you have an idea for an outline?" asked Vadim.

"I have an idea about a heron," Pantelei replied cautiously. "A heron. A big, stupid bird."

Serebryanikov's face at once took on a meditative look, and Pantelei stared hard at him.

What was the maestro thinking about? If he's wondering whether the idea would get past the censor or not, then I'll smash his face in with my elbow and abandon him in this armchair that Polevoi used to fart into when he was a young man. But if he's thinking about the muffled nocturnal cries of the marsh bird, about its slow nocturnal flights from Lithuania to Poland, about its insatiable passion in the remotest parts of damp, sleeping Europe, if he's thinking of the heron as the symbol of our youth, our girl . . . ah, then I will clean his shoes with my tie!

"Is the heron a girl?" Serebryanikov's eyes suddenly came to life, his features sharpened. "Almost a little girl. She's ashamed of her legs – her knees stick out so. A modern paraphrase of *The Seagull*. Am I right? A silly, stupidly shy, deliciously attractive nymph of the marshes. Have I guessed it? At night our hero hears her muffled cries, the beat of her wings. He thinks of an image of Europe. The gorgeousness and the wetness of life. Is that it?"

Pantelei started to unknot his tie. He almost burst into tears. My old pal Vadyukha – he had no trouble in understanding me. It required only a single word, a single gesture for him to grasp what I was thinking. And why shouldn't he grasp it? He and I, after all, are a single whole, two halves of one "ego," one half the signer of letters of protest, the other half director of an academic choir. But to hell with all that: We were both able to draw the same image of the heron from the depths of our soul.

Happy and young again, the two emerged from under the staircase and with an independent air, even with a certain disdain, like representatives of a still extant "fourth generation," they walked past the billiard room, where the fifth – the "blazer" – generation was pushing the representatives of the third – the "frontline" – generation out of the seats in which they had long been comfortably ensconced. Then they passed by the abominable brandy bar, where Vadim slowed down a little and glanced slyly at Pantelei, as he used to do in the old days when they slowed down at the sight of any liquor bottle. Pantelei, however, gave him a prod. They successfully rolled on past the bar and reached the large main staircase that led up to a famous bust.

"Gorky, Vladislav Makarovich," said Vadim, and honored the bust with a deep bow.

They then passed through the main hall, beneath the feet of a striking portrait.

"Mayakovsky, Yury Yakovlevich," Pantelei explained to Vadim, as though the latter were a foreigner and he a hospitable *sovieticus*.

After that they stomped along a dark passage, at the end of which a small figure in cast iron stood on a cylindrical telephone stand.

"Simonov, Lev Lukich," Vadim nodded to the figure with a certain familiarity, opened a door, and they found themselves on a balcony above the barroom.

At a first glance into the alcoholic kingdom it was evident that the evening was moving toward its crisis point, in other words, toward a hysterical explosion of scandalous behavior and punch-ups. The coral, which they had recently left, now looked like an octopus. Its tentacles were pulling in more and more denizens of the deep and extracting five- and three-ruble bills from them.

Pantelei glanced uneasily at Vadim and was appalled at what he saw – his friend the creative artist had vanished: Vadim Nikolayevich was gazing downward with the eyes of an alcoholic sleepwalker.

ALL IS FORGOTTEN

Vadim, remember the heron! A sand spit in Lithuania, a deserted little bay, a boardinghouse with rusty water pipes.

ALL IS FORGOTTEN

"Let's go see what's going on! Let's go have a drink! C'mon, let's go!"

Vadim, we're not taking one step downstairs until we recall how our hero came back from Africa to that boardinghouse and nobody there wanted to listen to him. Don't you remember how excitedly he spoke to them all – to his wife, to his son, to his mistress, to his uncle – but no one would listen to him? Remember how he plunged into the silence outside, where the only thing to be heard was the cry of the heron!

ALL IS FORGOTTEN

"Pantelyukha, you slob, bring me a bottle! I can't face it without a bottle! Look, that mirror's crushing me, crushing me, crushing me!"

"Vadyukha, you son of a bitch, surely you haven't forgotten how one night the heron appeared at a bus stop, and how the rain trickled down from her raincoat onto her wet knees. If you start drinking, you cocksucker, you'll forget how many acts there are in our play, you'll forget the prologue and the epilogue, you'll forget all the days of our youth!"

"Oh, fuck your heron and our youth, too. Can't you see I'm falling? Either take me downstairs or fetch me a bottle or strangle me right here on the spot."

"I'd rather strangle you!"

Suddenly Pantelei fell silent. From above he saw an elegant party appear at the back of the hall under the tall, pointed stained-glass window: It was the tractor designer with his wife and their companions.

They sat apart, as though separate from the rest of the room, as though totally unconnected with the mounting uproar, as though nothing around held the slightest interest for them, almost as though they were foreigners.

Meanwhile Alisa, my Alisa, was talking to someone with restrained, beautiful gestures as if aware that she was inaudible, like a movie actress playing a foreign woman, a sort of magic woman, the dream of the white race. It was as if she were sitting in front of a camera largely concerned about her gestures and articulation, keeping in mind a still unrecorded soundtrack, for which someone – could it be Pantelei? – would write a phenomenal new script instead of the nonsense she was talking now.

There she was, carefully and reflectively pushing back a long golden lock of hair and putting it in place behind her ear. Eyelids lowered, a second's silence as she listened to someone else's lines, then the flying up again, blue fire in the eyes, white fire in the mouth, the momentary spark as a fiery little tongue darted in and out again, a vivid flash of sensuality.

ALL IS FORGOTTEN

Baku-foot-saxophone! What nonsense! I shall carry her off today and never give her back. I'll smash anyone's teeth in. Knock any wall down. Baku-foot-saxophone! What nonsense is that?

"Let me take you downstairs, Vadyukha!"

"Save me, friend, don't strangle me," croaked Serebryanikov. "I'll give you an advance, I'll give you a contract. Please save me first, give me a drink, and then you can strangle me, Comrade Colonel. After all, we're on the same side here."

Pantelei dragged Serebryanikov downstairs into the barroom, and there, under the carved oak staircase, he seated the People's Artist at the grand piano.

"Linka," he called out to a waitress, "bring Vadim a glass of brandy. Look after him, and when your shift's over, take him home with you, OK? And call me in the morning."

"OK," the kind, reliable, earth-mother agreed readily, and even, perhaps, with delight.

There was yet another magnet of this uninhabited island – Linka's vast derrière, the sight of which brought a sense of calm to the soul of every "cultural worker:" Let the Russian soul go crazy; all's well, it seemed to say, because the rear is secure!

In the shadow under the staircase Pantelei hesitated for another second: I shall now step forward and the earth will heave beneath me and into the foul, stinking magma will vanish all my good intentions, all my hard work, my play, my novel, the loft, the lamp, the icon.

OH, COULD I BUT STRETCH OUT MY HAND TO MY BELOVED

and carry her away from here in a rattling old Zaporozhets and set off with her to Lithuania, where you don't understand what anyone is saying and they pretend not to understand you. To travel together, sitting side by side in comfortable old clothes, to drive at a steady speed along the Minsk Highway and toward evening turn off into a country byroad, to tumble together on a thick old blanket, to touch her lips, hold her face in one's hand, unbutton her sweater and touch her nipples, grasp her fimly by the shoulders, take a hard grip on her crotch and torment her with tenderness, torment her with tenderness for as long as the heavens allow us, and afterward with eyes forever united to watch the confused nocturnal pattern of the stars, with ears forever conjoined to listen to the music of the night, to talk quietly to her about writing, about death, about the classics, about God, and then go to sleep like that and in the morning jump up, make jokes, horse around, and then drive on, with only one main objective in view – the next night's stop.

So we traveled from year to year, so we travel from year to year, so we will travel from year to year, and she gave birth, and she gives birth and she will give birth under bushes, in roadside ditches, in haystacks. I assisted, assist, will assist her labor, will massage her distended and blue-veined belly, catch her wild shrieks with my mouth, warm the over-stretched lips of her vagina with my hand, cut the umbilical cord, swaddle the babies and place them beside her flanks so exhausted by vagabond love. Then we left, leave, will leave our children to be raised in the towns and villages of Eastern Europe lest they disturb our journeys, and when we have reached, reach, will reach the end of our road, we shall gather all our children together and have watched, watch, will watch their jolly games by the fireside, beside the swimming pool, on the terrace of our beautiful house, because with the years we have acquired, are acquiring, will acquire wealth, age, and retirement.

Pantelei came to his senses when he reached the middle of the room. Countless old friends, holding glasses in their hands, were converging on him from all directions: "I like you, old man, but you don't like me. Do you like me too? Then why don't you say so? If you have words in you, you ought to say them; after all, there aren't so many of us left, old man. We're all numbered in the Big Ledger in the sky."

Slipping out of his friends' garlicky embraces, Pantelei saw that he was being watched by THAT party, and Alisa, holding her hair with her left hand, was laughing and saying something to her companions while the tractor designer was nodding with an impenetrable fastidious look and turning away.

She stood up and started walking in a northwesterly direction. Of course, of course, that was how she walked, walks, will walk in her inimitable manner: a charming and simple gliding movement with sudden aggressive bursts of speed and shameless cutting of corners, and then once more the stately minuet. Behind him, Pantelei could hear comments being passed on her progress: "Look, it's Alisa Foku-sova . . . How old d'you think she is? . . . even so, she looks pretty good . . . No bra, bare feet . . ."

Her northwesterly course changed abruptly to its opposite, a southeasterly course, followed by a few steps eastward, a turn, another turn, and then, with her mane flying like a battle flag, Alisa headed westward. Pantelei finally guessed that she was threading her way past the tables . . . to him! Was it possible? Her husband was here, after all, and she had already agreed to meet the "blazer" today for a blow job, and in any case there were all these people here.

"How does she grab you?" asked the anti-Semitic poet Fyodorov-Smirnov, sidling up with a glass in his hand and chewing something with his red, carrotlike lips. "Nice piece of ass? I screwed her!"

Fyodorov-Smirnov is the commonest Russian surname. It's not Ivanov or Petrov or Sidorov. The three brothers Ivan, Petr, and Sidor are the triple spirit of Russian anarchism: A twitch of the shoulder, a wave of the arm, and since the booze is flowing freely, slice up the last pickle and let's go the whole hog! That's all past history. The present-day Russian is Fyodorov-Smirnov. Whenever he meets me and smiles at me in that way of his, I shudder all over in anticipation of the feel of his hand, damp as a wet dog. His lips are like carrots and his sweaty look is horrible; he gives the impression of having overeaten yet still being hungry. Fyodorov-Smirnov, I want to say to him, you and I are not enemies and we're not friends, still less are we fellow countrymen. I am Pantelei, blood brother to Ivan, Petr, and Sidor but not to you, Fyodorov-Smirnov!

Alisa found her way out of the labyrinth of tables and was now heading straight for Pantelei. Unfastened jeans, a stained hippie-style T-shirt, all the colors of her clothes, her face, and her body were now playing together in harmony, like mid-tempo rock'n'roll.

"Look at that slick chick, but I had her like a hooker," Fyodorov-Smirnov murmured into Pantelei's ear.

He was just about to sneak away, but Pantelei held him by the arm:
Wait, wait, Fyodorov-Smirnov; the moment that will be the peak of
the evening is approaching, and you and I are going to be at the center
of events.

"We were just having an argument," Alisa said cheerfully. "Is it
yours, that story about the gas stove that's going around Moscow?"

With fleeting astonishment she glanced at Fyodorov-Smirnov, who
was quivering slightly in Pantelei's grip.

"Alisa, and you, Fyodorov-Smirnov," said Pantelei, "don't you have
anything to say to each other?"

"What?" Alisa was quite amazed. "To him? How do you do,
monsieur?" Then a loud whisper into Pantelei's ear: "Who on earth
is he?"

Fyodorov-Smirnov sucked vodka through his teeth, and his carrotlike lips tried to assume an expression of sophisticated cynicism.
"Chuck it, Alisa. Don't you recognize, he-he, your old friends? Don't
you remember? By the way, there's a pad just around the corner from
here. Shall we push off together? Just for an hour or so, a quickie and
then back again. What d'you say?"

There then occurred a short, or rather an indefinite break in time,
but Alisa did not even have time to raise her eyebrows before another
avalanche of seconds poured out and Pantelei fastened his fingers
around Fyodorov-Smirnov's throat.

Not even the philosopher Plato could have decided who was right
and who was wrong in this business. What made Pantelei seize the
damp throat of his unpleasant colleague? Brute instinct or a mysterious
yet honorable burst of anger? What made Fyodorov-Smirnov slander
the charming lady? Anti-Semitism, envy of Pantelei, or the fact that
he was hopelessly in love with an unattainable dream? What made
such a charming lady lie down under this stinking creature? Some
human emotion, such as despair, or just an itching fanny, like a bitch
in heat? The answers to all this are known in the place where all is
known, but not here, not where we are, not in our order of things.

WHAT HAPPENED TO PANTELEI

My coarse shirt split into shreds along every one of its rotten seams,
and shivering in these rags, I put all my heart and soul into strangling
him until I forgot about him. Then I roared off with her in a taxi down
Sadovoye and kissed her laughing mouth, and on we raced, and I

kissed her until I forgot. Then I made love to her in a high-speed elevator, in its surging rises and head-spinning falls and at the stops between floors, where I put her down on her knees in front of me and lifted her up by her arms and pressed her against the wall, then turned her around with her back to me and took her on the floor of the elevator, then sat her on my knees and made love to her endlessly until I forgot.

It was not these events, however, that became the climax of the evening in the writers' club. What happened was something more amusing than the usual brawl between two writers and the customary sequel of carrying off the charming lady and making love to her in an express elevator. The rest of the company, incidentally, did not even notice when Pantelei seized Fyodorov-Smirnov by the throat:

IT WAS DISTRACTED BY THE APPEARANCE OF A EUROPEAN WOMAN

In the doorway there appeared a suede-clad deity, a veritable angel of suede. When she was at home in Europe she never wore suede, except for hunting, but having lived a long time in Moscow and spending her time in a permanent state of irritation, she never took off her suede.

She had discovered that suede is the symbol of material success in our capital city. It gave her particular pleasure to shock the Moscow riffraff by an abundance of expensive suede: a long suede skirt with a slit up the front right to the crotch, suede shorts, high-heeled suede boots, suede jackets, little suede capes bunched up behind her back, a suede umbrella, a suede shopping bag with which she would occasionally appear at the Central Market.

The objective was achieved: The Moscow market traders would swoon with rapture; all this suede luxury did not even arouse the base emotion of envy but only delight. Our European woman, who had started out simply meaning to shock people, gradually acquired a taste for it, for she noticed that she only had to appear on the New Arbat in her suede for people to start awarding her points as though she were a figure-skating star – 5.8, 5.9, 6.0! What the lady failed to notice was that she had turned from a sophisticated European into an ordinary Moscow prick teaser.

So now there she was, shouting from the doorway like any shrew, "Pig, traitor, where is my Mercedes with its suede roof?"

Standing in the door, she had noticed her Russian husband in the company of several charming ballerinas, drunk, disheveled, painfully obvious as the man for whom she had paid the high price of her diplomatic immunity.

A Russian husband, you see, is like the Russian ruble – five, six, nine to one! You, *mein Lieber*, handsome as you are with your muscular, hairy thighs, are a filthy jackal. You devour everything I have, you send me out to the Georgian black marketeers to get Danish beer, you bolt your food and spit, and you only take me when you've had a few drinks, no doubt imagining to yourself that you're having a ballerina. You only love me when there's brandy inside you, only because of my Mercedes, because of Paris, where you, you Russian bear, *Schwein*, pig, discuss your artistic plans with prostitutes and homosexuals.

How shameful it all was from the very beginning, from the very first night! She had thought that all Russian men were sort of naive peasant shepherds and wanted to show him a nice, sophisticated, European trick or two, but he, the monster, debauched her – just like that! – with his massive cannon. And in the morning he had thrown up, and then immediately driven off in her Mercedes without even waiting for the documents!

"Give me the keys, you pig! And gather up all your hookers. What a bunch! The rate of exchange for them is six to one too, and my dear Adolf still adores me and will take me back any day, and he'll throw his dirty little Uzbek girl out of the embassy at once! Just you wait! I'll tell Adolf everything, and he'll pass it on to the proper official in the Ministry of Culture!"

At this point the intellectual, artistic "blazer" yelled his reply in a bull-like roar, "Keep your hair on, you crab louse! Adolf will never cause me any trouble!"

"*Warum, warum!*" screamed the European woman.

"Because he's in our pay!" he said, roaring with laughter.

I COULD TOLERATE ALL THIS NO LONGER

I was walking slowly along a wet nocturnal sidewalk. Across the street, along which cars were passing in an endless stream, I saw a solid row of yellow houses, their facades brightly lit by argon lamps. There was not a soul in or around them; a suffocating airlessness seized me in front of these houses, and I saw only the simulacrum of a soul under an archway, where a chain of glistening puddles stretched out into the

distance, until it was crossed by an alleyway, at the end of which a
tree could be dimly made out, a black tree with branches outlined like
a cluster of bronchi, like the faint simulacrum of a soul.

To lean my cheek against the tree. To stand a few minutes in silence.
To keep at least a few remnants of human dignity. A bronchial tree,
an arterial cluster. The heart of Russia.

There, in the heart of Russia, from the porch of a village store, if I
had been a Russian writer, spread out beneath my gaze would have
been a pleasant valley crossed by a quietly flowing river, meditative
bronchial black poplar trees, the long necks of age-old well cranes,
and were I a Russian doctor, I would have felt the steady pulse and
the even breathing of my motherland, and before me would have
stretched the wide open spaces of purity untouched by corruption.

GENNADY APOLLINARIEVICH MALKOLMOV

crossed the nocturnal street. One of the cars slowed down questioningly, another banged into its rear bumper with uncaring effrontery.
Malkolmov walked under the damp, warm, and dark archway, through
which could be seen the alleyway leading to the ponds and to the tall,
handsome, or, as they say in Moscow, Central-Committee-type houses.

Along the alley toward the ponds moved the two impudent cars,
while a third, cautious, car came crawling toward them. Another car,
the hum of its engine barely audible, nosed out of a gateway. Seven
or eight cars were asleep alongside the enormous, grim building of the
Sound Archive.

By night and by day the building that houses the Sound Archive
maintains a menacing silence and induces a feeling of momentary
terror in passersby. No one could ever say exactly what caused that
terror. There doesn't seem to be anything very special about the Sound
Archive; it is just a very ordinary, gloomy-looking building, of which
there are hundreds in Moscow. Well, of course, it is the place where
in dull, dusty silence they store state secrets in the form of a variety
of sounds – shots, lovers' groans, festive march music. What's so special
about that? No, say what you like, everyone who passes it is seized by
a momentary shiver of fright. Perhaps something nasty happened here
in the past: did Beriya hold his orgies here, or did Stalin's illegitimate
son idle his life away here, watched over by a company of the Guards?
Nobody can say for certain what it is.

Standing in front of the hostile building, Malkolmov fought hard against fear and overcame it. Proud of his moral willpower, Malkolmov struggled with fear twice more, then walked past the intimidating pile with complete indifference. Shamed, the Sound Archive House pulled down a strip of black marble low on its forehead and from its medieval windows of the late thirties it gloomily watched him go past.

Yet another car swung around the corner. It skidded in a puddle, smacked against a projecting granite ledge of the archive, and drove off toward Sadovoye Ring, swerving drunkenly. Silence returned to the scene.

"Oh, Lord!" whispered Malkolmov. "My God!"

Right in front of him, a large male body lay spread-eagled in a puddle. The brass buttons of his blazer glinted in the moonlight. Malkolmov came closer and saw thick tufts of chest hair sticking out from a hopelessly torn, not to say lacerated, shirt.

Malkolmov thought with some relief that this man was not, of course, someone of his circle. People of his circle did not lie unconscious in puddles at that hour. They were sitting in the quiet of their little apartments listening to Bach's B-minor Mass, they were toiling humbly and studiously at some imperishable opus, perhaps working on the globally vital problem of Lymph-D, smoking quietly and drinking strong tea, gently dreaming of salvation in the heart of Russia. Yes, this was obviously not someone of his circle.

"All the same, I would save her," said the man in the puddle in a loud voice.

"Who?" asked Malkolmov.

"Why, the old woman, of course," he said irritably, as though reminding Malkolmov of a recently interrupted conversation. "Surely you remember that little problem? You put it to me yourself." Here he clasped his hands under the back of his neck as if he were lying on a sofa and not in a puddle. "If a cloud of poison gas came floating down the street and it was a question of which of them to save, the little boy or that withered old hag, in other words if one had to make the choice, I would carry them both to safety, the little boy and the old woman. Do you see? That would be my choice. You can't leave an old woman to certain death, even if we die in the attempt to save her. That's my decision, d'you see?"

He sat up, scooped some water out of the puddle, and wiped his face.

"I see I've made a mistake," he croaked. "You're clearly not Pantelei. You're someone else. Who are you, nocturnal wanderer?"

"I am a humble Russian physician," said Malkolmov, and bowed.

"And I'm a humble puddle dweller. I wonder whether a Russian physician can give a person an injection that will cure all his troubles?"

"Not every Russian physician, but you happen to have found one who can."

As they walked to the secret clinic of the UPVDOSIVADO and the CHIS, the pond dweller gave Malkolmov a mournful account of his life: "I am the nonexistent son of somewhat undistinguished parents. This evening has turned out to be unexpectedly catastrophic for me. My best works have been torn up, soiled, vilified. Nothing like this ever happened to my parents. It happened to my grandparents, but never to my parents. Shall we say a prayer?"

In front of them, at the back of a garden surrounded by a fence, shone a bright Orthodox cross atop a small, recently restored church, which comfortably housed two organizations: a museum of clay toys and a society for the blind. It was clear that these organizations lived peaceably side by side and accommodated themselves to each other, and the church had of course gained by this arrangement – it positively gleamed with its white walls, green designs, and gold stars on the little blue onion domes. Furthermore, it was maintained by the state as a monument of Russian architecture, and this too helped it to prolong its three-hundred-year life with dignity.

Malkolmov and his companion, the nocturnal sufferer, knelt down and prayed.

"You cross yourself in a strange way," said the sufferer. "When you make the sign of the cross, it looks odd and kind of wrong."

"It's the Catholic sign of the cross," Malkolmov explained. "Unlike the Orthodox custom of pinching three fingers together, it is made with the open palm and from the left shoulder to the right. That's how I'm used to doing it."

"You mean you've been crossing yourself for a long time?" A certain note of jealousy could be heard in the stranger's voice.

"I didn't mean to say anything about myself. I was just going to remark that God is one and the same for both the Orthodox and the Catholics."

"Jesus Christ Superstar," said the unknown sufferer respectfully, in English. "Incidentally, he's coming back into fashion again."

For a moment Malkolmov was slightly annoyed at his companion, as though offended on Christ's behalf, but then he thought better of it – what a fool I am to be annoyed at a puddle dweller!

"Get up, you silly fool! We've done enough praying. Let's go see about this shot."

*   *   *

The secret hundred-gram hypodermic injected a mixture of top-secret vitamins into the nocturnal patient's veins. As he left the treatment room, Malkolmov looked back. The patient had been reanimated with astonishing speed by secret nutrients. As he lay on the couch, large, cheerful, and impudent, he was stroking the ass of Nurse Marina, a captain in the Medical Service. No, thought Malkolmov, that man will always manage to survive in this country, since even when he falls into a dirty puddle he manages to be picked out of it, not by some mere general practitioner or the usual emergency service, but by a luminary of medical science, a genius, a consultant attached to UPVDOSIVADO and CHIS!

Malkolmov himself, however, was not so lucky that night: He simply wanted to get out of the clinic into the fresh air, and he lost his way. He wandered down the endless, styrofoam-lined corridors of this temple of healing, where he met not a single soul and could find not the slightest hint of an exit. Well, he finally said to himself, let's not waste the time and let's indulge in some thought. So now he was walking around the labyrinth and thinking about the lymphatic system. For years now, segment by segment, he had been studying and describing the lymphatic paths and ganglia of man and other primates. What quantities of lymph he had filtered, centrifuged, transplanted, replaced, substituted, transferred! The mysterious Lymph-D – that was the aim of his unceasing quest.

Years ago, in the late fifties, an argument started about a far from wholly rational topic in some intellectual slum of one of the world's capitals. In those days, intellectuals everywhere were constantly imagining that they had uncovered something phony, some form of deception. Among other things, they thought they had discovered something phony in natural physiology. It's all false, false. So their countertheory ran as follows: When you cut your finger, the appropriate liquid flows from it, a mixture of erythrocytes, leucocytes, and all the rest of the junk. Now if you lacerate your soul, something like "invisible tears" flow from it, and surely isn't this Lymph-D? So they started to argue. Some shouted that even if some substance like your so-called Lymph-D did exist in man, Genka, it would never be possible to isolate it or even identify it! Malkolmov went crazy, shouting, Philistines, freaks, you don't understand anything! And do *you* understand anything, oh great man? I? Even though I don't understand, I sense, I sometimes feel, the proximity of a mystery; sometimes under the microscope I see what look like strange question marks posed by fate. He's drunk, you guys! He's as drunk as a skunk! Then one of the girls, hair the color of wheat, high and jutting breasts – the sex symbol of those days – suggested that he seek advice in neighboring, related areas in which the creative younger generation was engaged. Unexpectedly, Malkolmov approved of this suggestion. The girl, whose face afterward he never could remember, began phoning around to other intellectual slums, to the haunts of the "new wave" of youth, to some sculptor, to a jazz musician, to a writer, a physicist . . .

Everywhere they went, they drank, argued, and picked up girls. No one, of course, doubted the existence of Lymph-D, but they were all convinced that it was not a matter for medical science. Doctors, they said, should stick to curing archbishops' colds, but when it came to discovering the secrets of nature, that was a job for them, the poets and philosophers, and more particularly for the physicists. Malkolmov then lost his temper, called them all idiots, and left their company, though not forgetting to grab the girl, to whom he bitterly made love for the rest of the night.

Next morning, having forgotten the girl, he began to study the lymphatic system, hoping one day to stumble across the secret doorway in that boundless lactolymphatic labyrinth. He studied it, too, on his days of secret inspiration, when nausea at everyday life, at his professional success, and at everything else surged up in his throat. The nausea would pass, insight would come in its stead, to be again succeeded by nausea of another kind.

Then the bottle made its appearance on the table. Malkolmov climbed into his student jeans, cruised around Moscow, woke up occasionally in other cities, sometimes in the south, sometimes in Siberia, gave stormy expression to his feelings, that is to say spouted all kinds of nonsense in various fluttering avenues of plane trees, and then it seemed to him that he was close to the longed-for doorway, just a little bit more – and then . . . when he had sobered up again, he couldn't remember what that "little bit more" was.

"A little bit more," that seductive siren-whore, beckoned him on from bottle to bottle, from disappointment to disappointment, but never let him get his hands on her. When you're drunk, it's as if you were floating down a mountain stream: The current is strong, but your goal seems near, even though the way to it is endless. Sober, you're always going uphill, the way is shorter, harder, more certain, but your goal is infinitely distant.

Around a corner of the corridor a flickering light was dawning. Having not yet had time to plunge into scientific speculation, Malkolmov quickened his pace, hoping that around the corner he would find an exit to the street. He turned the corner, but instead of a door he saw before him a television screen showing a picture without sound. The peak viewing hours of Moscow's television now being over, in this dark hallway of a secret clinic an ideological commentator, a general, was giving his nightly talk on current events. The sound was not switched on, so the general only moved his lips. Whenever he lowered his eyes toward his invisible piece of paper, his chin sank into numerous folds of flabby skin, and we saw before us the thoroughly familiar figure of a tedious, glum bureaucrat. What was this bureaucrat saying to us?. The usual clichés: " . . . based on the decisions . . . to raise boundlessly loyal . . . selfless exertions for the good of . . . expresses unanimous approval . . ." Whenever he raised his head for a moment, looking out of the folds of skin was the little pointed muzzle of a young polecat.

And does the mysterious, cosmic Lymph-D also flow within that little polecat? That morning a musician, an aging youth with a saxophone in a case, had plodded on his way beneath the windows of that same clinic. He had caught the EKG printout that was thrown to him and, grinning, went into a store selling semiprepared foods, from whence there suddenly issued the delightful laughter of his crazy young saxophone. That night a character with brass buttons had lain in a dirty puddle and discussed the ethics of saving a little boy and an old woman. Indeed that old woman, God's forget-me-not, had appeared more than once in the course of the day, pushing a baby carriage containing a rosy-cheeked little boy. Now a polecatlike bureaucrat is flashing his missile-sharp teeth at mankind from the television screen. And in all of them flows my long-sought Lymph-D.

You're obviously not going to find your way out of this place, so sit down in this soft, secret armchair and watch that face. In front of you is a remarkable face. In front of you is

THE EVOLUTION OF A TYPE DISCOVERED BY ZOSHCHENKO

Zoshchenko and Bulgakov discovered this type in the twenties. By now the boor who harassed the dwellers in the overcrowded, shared apartments of those days has completed his development, has achieved the dream of his nights of nightmare – general's stars; he has equipped himself with the lenses of common sense and joined the legion of television personalities. In a previous stage of development he was called Zhdanov. Passing through the bloody sweat-room of the thirties, Zoshchenko's bathhouse attendant and Bulgakov's dog-turned-man known as Sharik became Zhdanov, Stalin's "cultural policeman." The Columbuses who had discovered the type were declared monsters. The stolid, respectable, normal Zhdanov hated his discoverer and labeled him a monster, a social throwback, a piece of garbage left over from the burnt-out Silver Age of Russian literature.

There, in essence, is the chief conflict of our time, ideally abbreviated to the scheme ZOSHCHENKO V. ZHDANOV.

Do you remember how at school, back in the days of Tolya von Steinbock, we had to bone up on all the historic decrees and speeches of Sharik-Zhdanov, in which, with his decaying teeth, he chewed his discoverer, Zoshchenko, into small pieces, and with him the Nightingale of Tsarskoye Selo, the poetess Anna Akhmatova? Even in our heart of hearts we never doubted Sharik's bathhouse attendant's pronouncements, and particularly the chief, fundamental, one: "Soviet society is no place for you." And even when a little whiff of rebellion began to ruffle the surface, when we were already giggling over Zoshchenko's banned story about a monkey and were copying Ahkmatova's poems in letters to our girl friends, in our heart of hearts, in the very deepest recesses of our soul, we were still convinced that Zhdanov's world was normal and that Zoshchenko's world was abnormal, decadent, and shameful. In the days of our youth, Sharik's bathhouse world swelled up from the ingurgitation of much blood and assumed the features of grim, unshakable greatness. It was our patron, our benefactor, and our controller, the only real and normal world, and the remote concept of Zoshch_nko, whichever way one looked at it, was in the end nothing but a tiny, suppurating little pimple.

Several years had to pass before we could see, as though with our own eyes, a lonely little figure sitting sadly but calmly on a bench on a St. Petersburg boulevard. There was calm in the neat but worn suit, calm in the left leg, strangely twisted around the equally calm right leg, calm in the hand lifting a calm cigarette to the lips, calm in the glance following the backs of friends hurrying past and failing to recognize him. Anti-bathhouse attendant, anti-Sharik, anti-Zhdanov, their hated discoverer had recognized them with his sole defensive weapon – Awareness. It took several years to comprehend the true force of that weapon.

Then we admitted that it was this world, the world of calm little loners, the world of the poets, that was the true world, and that the other one, huge and as juicy as a swollen blister, was false, ephemeral, and already reeking of decay.

Are you sure, however, that Calm has come to you too, that Awareness has dawned upon you too? You can find such crushing metaphors to describe the pig-polecat on the TV, but are you sure that you don't really want to switch on the sound now, reject all your subversive little thoughts, and sink into the soporific jumble of that ideological speech and revel in the comforts of loyalty, the bliss of conformism?

"See here, thinking aloud on topics like that under the vaulted ceilings of UPVDOSIVADO and CHIS, that's going a bit too far!"

Malkolmov turned his head. At the far end of the hall, reclining in a similar armchair, was his old friend, the famous surgeon Zilberantsev. He was puffing at a cigar and laughing.

"Zilber! What the hell are you doing here?"

"Hi there, Malkolm, you damn fool! I came here much earlier and switched off the sound. Just wanted to sit in peace for a while. I sat down and watched that big shot, and suddenly you showed up! It was fantastic!"

"What's fantastic about it?"

"The fact that I was just thinking about you, Malkolm. About you and about him." Zilberantsev pointed his cigar at the screen, where the pig-polecat was at that moment waving a pointer at a map of the Sinai Peninsula.

Malkolmov and Zilberantsev were the same age. They were once classmates and had also played on the same basketball team. For a long time their lives had run in close parallel: love affairs, drunken binges, rapid progress in medicine, Ph.D. dissertations, UNESCO scholarships, jobs overseas . . . so much so that back in those days it would never have occurred to them that one day they would branch out and take quite different paths. Each regarded himself as a genius and had never envied the other. Furthermore, they also understood each other. Zilberantsev was probably the only person who understood certain so-called nonsensical ideas of Malkolmov's and took them seriously.

Recently, however, their careers had begun to diverge. It happened little by little, imperceptibly: Zilberantsev joined the staff of UPVDO-SIVADO and CHIS, while Malkolmov refused to become a member of the permanent staff and remained an independent consultant; one had signed a letter in defense of Sinyavsky and Daniel, while on that day the other one happened to be leaving town; one was no doubt jetting around on the international conference circuit, lecturing on the achievements of Soviet science, while the other was just earning the means to keep himself in brandy by moonlighting in emergency rooms. Not long ago something absurd had happened. At a meeting of a scientific association they had started to ridicule Malkolmov's Lymph-D as being an idealistic-metaphysical-surrealistic substance, and Zilberantsev had kept quiet, though later, after the session, he had encouraged his friend with a demonstrative pat on the shoulder.

"Yes, I was thinking about you and about him, when suddenly you appear and start philosophizing aloud, and on that very subject," said Zilberantsev.

"On that very subject? Were you thinking about the same thing?" Malkolmov asked in astonishment.

"About the same thing, only differently. I was thinking about Lymph-D. It flows in everyone: in you, in me, and in that general – but in what concentrations?"

"So you were also thinking about yourself?" Malkolmov couldn't resist saying.

"Yes, about myself. I am I. You are you. The general is the general. But we don't all have the same moral level, or an equal moral potential. Perhaps it is this metaphysical soup of yours that determines the moral potential?" Malkolmov held his breath, while Zilberantsev sat calmly puffing on his Upmann cigar.

"Do you mean that seriously?" Malkolmov asked quietly.

"Never been more serious."

"And you know?"

"I know you have a whole flask containing at least five hundred cc's, no less."

"And do you know who the donor was?"

"Yes, you yourself."

"How can you know all this?"

Zilberantsev stood up and switched on the sound: "The Arab peoples know very well who their true friend is . . . the peoples of the world will place a reliable barrier in the way . . . the entire Soviet people salutes and approves the peace-loving policies . . ." A march started to play, banners were carried into the hall, young Komsomol members wearing white sword belts raised high their bared blades. Under the cover of all this noise Zilberantsev said into Malkolmov's ear, "An anonymous informer's report about you and your ideas came into the Security Section and I was called in for a consultation. I told them it was all junk and that although you were a good physician you were an incorrigible fantasist. Now let's get out of here. We can go on talking out on the street."

The exit turned out to be quite near. Zilberantsev simply opened a door and they found themselves on a deserted nocturnal sidewalk, under rustling lime trees, in a relaxed, sleepy city ready for friendly revelations.

"Just imagine what prospects could open up if your discovery were to be put into circulation!" said Zilberantsev with all the warmth of his youthful past. "I know you'll reply that it's your property and that you don't want to share it with all these pigs. I know you've been collecting the contents of that flask for over fifteen years, donating it at your most private moments. You see, Malkolm, I remember all our conversations and even our drunken babbling; my brain is made like that – don't think I'm a stool pigeon. But that little supply of Lymph-D already opens up the field for a colossal experiment if we were to get the state to sponsor it, and I will see to that. You and I could become world-famous – you the Mozart and I the Salieri – but I won't poison you because I love you, because without you I am a nonentity. But you, Genasha old fellow, will be a nonentity without me because, forgive me, you're an alcoholic and without me you could crack up. To this day you're haunted by the ghost of that sadistic officer you once told me about, that time in Pyatigorsk when we bought an iron cot from the night watchman and slept on it outside the Party town committee. You keep thinking you see that man's ugly mug in every old cloakroom attendant. You have kids scattered all over the world – in Africa, in Paris, God knows where else. You're an unstable type. You don't fit in. But who cares about the fame. What the fuck would we do with it anyway? The fact is that in the final analysis you and I need to justify our existence, and that Lymph-D of yours is liquid soul or something like that. And suppose on this basis we could find a universal panacea for all the troubles of mankind? Just think of the prospects – to be able to raise the moral level to its optimum point on the scale! To be able to test everyone for their Lymph-D level, just as we can now test them for hemoglobin! Create a nation with a high and constant level of moral strength and you make it unbeatable! Then to confront the rest of mankind, and not with missiles but with the most advanced scientific discovery: Lymph-D! A new era! Maybe nothing would come of it, maybe it's all garbage, but we must at least try it, you and I! I know what's holding you back, what's bugging you, but just take a careful look at today's specimen of the human race, that character who was reading us a speech from the TV screen. He's nothing like that recurrent memory of yours, and the eyes of that respectable, steady, reliable bureaucrat are nothing like those hot, beady little eyes of that sadist you told me about that day we once flew to Chelyabinsk instead of Sochi when we were drunk. Whom are you seeking? Just think: Even though you haven't been avenged for his humiliation of you when you were a boy, you are an active and important member of society and you will become a world-famous genius. And what about him? A pathetic old man living on a pension, who can do nothing but write letters complaining there are too many Jews on the editorial board of *The Week*. Just think of the absurdity of the situation if you were to meet! You must have seen those old men sitting around on suburban park benches in raincoats listening to transistor radios. To hell with all that nonsense! Tell me, do you agree to start the project?"

"No," said Malkolmov firmly. "I do not agree."

CHEPTSOV DID NOT FEEL HIMSELF AN OLD MAN AT ALL

and indeed he wasn't old; he had been able to retire early because, owing to the nature of his work, certain years had counted as two years, some even as three. Cheptsov had earned his pension in often tough and rugged conditions, and the reward for his fidelity to the cause of Lenin and Stalin was the miserable sum of one hundred and seventy rubles per month. There you sit, madam, counting those ten-ruble bills, and not even looking at me through your little window, yet if you were to take a look at the far from fruitless years of my past, you could see things that would make the polish peel off your nails from shock, and you wouldn't flick through those seventeen pink ten-ruble bills quite so carelessly.

Count away, count away, little madam. A ten-ruble bill for the early thirties. In our canvas-topped boots we joined the security forces in answer to the summons of the Komsomol and were immediately flung into the hottest sector. Another ten rubles for those years of feverish activity. The three-man tribunals worked almost right around the clock in those days, and the executioners never slept at all. We played chess, read novels, danced with each other in the commandant's office – anything, so as not to fall asleep. Later, of course, we got used to the routine and we slept the magnificent, dreamless sleep of youth, and that, of course, was thanks to the high level of ideological training. When you realize that you're not dealing with human beings but are exterminating mad dogs, you can sleep soundly without dreaming. Still, madam, you can pull another ten-ruble bill out of your shitty peace-loving budget in memory of those sleepless nights of the past.

The war, the "blocking battalions" to stop any troops who felt like retreating, SMERSH the counterespionage network, the forests of Lithuania – no, I've no reason to feel ashamed. Count away, madam, and we won't upset your nerves. You can sit there quietly behind your teller's counter in the bank like a good, modest socialist toiler, manicure and all, yet you might have become a whore in an American bordello, one of those that would have been set up all over our sacred soil if it hadn't been for the advance into Korea in '50! That old bitch, that old gray-haired whore Sergei Sergeyevich Smirnov and his "No one is forgotten, nothing has been forgotten – you'll see!" The traitors, the Vlassovites and kikes are let off scot free, but there's nothing but an embarrassed silence when it comes to the country's *real* heroes!

You're all bastards, corn weevils! They sob into their handkerchiefs, you see, about the "regrettable mistakes" made by a great man; they're ashamed of their own past, you see; they sashay around in foreign ties; they hug foreign presidents . . . peace on earth . . . détente . . . coex . . . coex . . . cocksuckers!

If they'd kept faith with the old ways, there'd be no need for any damned "coex" in the world! The year 1962 was planned to be the one in which capitalism collapsed worldwide! "Into battle to the death for everlasting peace." Millions sang it at the top of their lungs! Stalin used to be visited every month by his clever Oriental friend, and he himself flew to Peking more than once in total secrecy. Nowadays they can't do anything in secret. It all seeps out into the open; they're just too fond of having their pictures taken, the slobs! Everything's been given away by that degenerate corn planter Khrushchev and the idiots that came after him.

Open a paper, what do you see? Nothing but "talks on a mutually acceptable basis"! The shame of it, the ineradicable shame! A hundred and seventy lousy rubles a month – what a reward! If only it could be three hundred, or even two hundred and fifty! If only I got half-pay on retirement, or say a free ticket to Foros, even the right to use their polyclinic, like that nonentity Lygher! Traitors to the workers" cause, revisionists . . . Oh, forget it!

That favorite last phrase of his interior monologues, that threatening "Oh, forget it," Cheptsov spoke aloud as he came out of the bank. He said it so passionately and emphatically that two young passersby, two young lads lounging along the sidewalk in their blatant, impudent

"I-don't-give-a-fuck" attitude, even turned their heads to look. They even fixed their impudent, vacant, goggle-eyed stares on the somber figure, but then immediately forgot him, their long, hateful locks of hair waving in the breeze.

Cheptsov directed his ponderous body toward the park. His black waterproof cape hung below his knees, and his velour hat was firmly rammed down to his ears. This figure exuded gloom and ill fortune, yet Khachaturian's charming music to *The Widow of Valencia* could be heard coming from it – there was a transistor radio in his pocket tuned in to the Beacon station. Cheptsov moved at a slow measured pace, although no one would have thought of him as an old man.

Now and again he felt brief twinges of old age, but they were always followed by a powerful surge of assertive masculinity, and then he would quickly forget the twinges. He could always walk much faster and more vigorously when he had some goal in mind. Angrily thrusting aside the intimations of incipient old age, Cheptsov nevertheless adopted a steady, unhurried gait, as though camouflaging himself as an old man . Unconsciously he sometimes used to try on the mask of old age – just in case, as it were – for somewhere within the innermost depths of his soul he occasionally felt that old age was his last defense, his ultimate excuse. Thus, on his daily walks in Timiryazev Park, he often surprised some passersby: From behind he looked like an old man, whereas from the front he was a vigorous man in the prime of life.

"I never imagined, comrade, that you were an admirer of light instrumental music," an old woman said to him with all the inappropriate gush of a teenage Komsomol member; a familiar sight in this oasis of ozone, this elderly woman still had a completely smooth face with full lips and a thoroughly feminine bustline, but her legs were swollen, elephantine. Out of habit, Cheptsov mumbled something indistinct in reply and walked on. The old woman's playful tone infuriated him. Surely this decrepit old trade-union whore didn't see him as a possible match?

The park of the Timiryazev Agricultural Academy, apart from its interest as a landscaped botanical garden, is also of interest as the place where pensioners come to do their "courting." Here, amid the beds of experimental flora, Cupid has made a nest for assignations between the senior citizenry, where widowers or widows can find themselves a mate on the basis of shared cultural interests or to improve their housing situation or simply out of the promptings of the heart. There even used to be a sort of club here, where once a week an eighty-year-old veteran of Budyonny's cavalry army would bring along his accordion, and the old women would dance in couples, as though showing themselves off to the old men sitting around and clapping in time to the music. On the paths of Timiryazev Park intellectual pensioners would exchange books or subscription tickets to concerts, and they too would pair off.

This idyll, and the shameful frivolity of the Timiryazev oldsters, infuriated Cheptsov, particularly when now and then a human ruin whose prime had been in the early thirties would cast sly glances in his direction. Cheptsov would have given up these walks long ago, but years of excessive smoking, combined with his current job, which required him to work in a place that was full of smoke and stench, plus the unpleasant smells at home – all this had had its effect, and his body craved oxygen.

Sometimes Cheptsov allowed himself to play little practical jokes: He would frighten the old folk. His game was to approach a group of domino players and stand behind them. He would simply stand behind the backs of the giggling, wheezing, cackling old men and clasp his big, powerful hands in front of him. Inevitably his steady stare would make one of the domino players cringe, turn around, shiver with fear, and nudge his neighbors. They had recognized him! They knew! The older generation remembered that stare only too well and knew what it meant. Once recognized, Cheptsov would remain standing by the domino players for a few more minutes, wondering with which article of the Criminal Code to charge this or that old man, and then, still silent, he would walk away with a feeling of satisfaction and head for the ponds, where he usually enjoyed another and equally strong form of emotional pleasure.

There, near the ponds, was the start of a long path with rustling treetops, at the end of which gleamed the convex windowpanes of a small but historically important palace. As he looked past the tall, regular trees toward the palace, Cheptsov experienced an intense feeling of hatred. The feeling was, one might say, unfocused. It was not the palace that he hated; it had long since become national property, a citadel of progressive science. Nor did Cheptsov hate the path either; the rising generation, which in every sense of the word was relieving his own generation, strolled along that path. No, of course he didn't hate the palace or the path as such. What Cheptsov probably hated was the palace being at the end of the path. It was precisely the fact that the path was crowned by the palace that evoked in him a powerful feeling of masculine hatred.

His cheeks still quivering with detestation, he walked on to a dark and damp corner of the park, took two walnuts out of his pocket, and tapped them against each other. At the sound of his tapping, a little creature, a squirrel, ran down from a pine tree straight into his hands. He fed the little rodent with tidbits, tickled its frail little flanks, and sometimes even touched his lips to the comic little tufts that sprouted from its ears.

Then he would walk along past some cast-iron railings, where he sometimes thought about his soul. He knew, of course, that no such thing as a soul existed in nature, yet he imagined his own soul as a large, dark, dry sack full of innumerable pockets, recesses, and partitions. More often than not, however, he did not think about his soul, but after feeding the squirrel, he would walk the street and take a streetcar all the way home. As he did today. . .

While still in the elevator, he could hear the tapping of a typewriter in the back room of his apartment. Nina was at home and was once again hard at work "moonlighting," as she shamefacedly called the job of typing out the dissertations of various careerist kikes. Well, so what. The girl would only have to put up with this for another year or two. It was her own fault – her tastes were too expensive! Yesterday she had spent forty rubles on some French perfume. Half her monthly salary! A quarter of the pension he received for years of faithful service! And all for just a little medicine bottle, which those lousy Frenchmen didn't even fill up to the top – either that or the shopgirls in Moscow poured some of it out before selling it. The scent, of course, would send anyone out of their mind!

Opening the door with his key, he stopped, as always, before crossing the threshold, expecting to hear a shriek from Paulina Ignatievna. One might think it would have been possible to get used to it after all these years, but he never had gotten used to it and every time he waited for that cry with a little cold shiver up and down his spine.

"*La guerre*! *La guerre*! Papa! Papa! Papa *französisch*!"

There it was, that tinny, birdlike, stupid, mocking shriek, followed by a sob that would then break off and . . . silence.

Then he entered, and without looking behind the screen, he merely said in that direction, "Yes, yes. Wait a moment. Coming."

He went through into the kitchen and took out of his black briefcase a carton of milk, a container of yogurt, and some rolls; from the kitchen he could see Nina's thin back, mane of blond hair, and shoulders quivering from her rapid typing.

"Is that you, Dad?" Nina shouted without turning around. "But I thought today you . . ."

As usual she didn't finish the sentence and went back to her tap-tapping.

Obviously she had thought he was on duty in the institute today, but he had come to an arrangement with Philippich and was going to take his place on the night shift in the bar.

"Dad, do me a favor, will you?" she asked plaintively.

"Do you want a cup of tea?"

"Yes, and make it good and strong!"

He put the kettle on the gas, changed into a pair of soft slippers, and took off his tunic and hung it up in the closet; there, for a second, he clutched Nina's already worn corduroy jeans (she had banged away at the keys for a whole week to buy these American rags!), fleetingly sniffed the crotch of the jeans (forty rubles, perfume, enemy, spring), shut the closet, went in to Paulina Ignatievna, extracted the bedpan from underneath her, glanced at its contents (good stool today, no traces of blood or mucus), carried the bedpan into the bathroom, emptied it, and washed it out with bleach, then replaced the bedpan under Paulina Ignatievna and wiped her face with a damp towel.

He liked Paulina Ignatievna today; her eyes were blue today. Whenever she got angry, her eyes turned green, and when she stopped wanting to live, her eyes went white. Today they were blue, which meant that this evening pleased her – the steady clatter of her daughter's typewriter, the shuffling of her husband's slippers. She liked it when everyone was at home, and maybe at such times she forgot what had happened to her. It was indeed high time to forget – twenty years have passed, Paulina Ignatievna!

Cheptsov returned to the kitchen and set about making the tea. They told you the truth back then, Paulina Ignatievna, but you took it so hard that you fell apart on the spot . . . Papa *französisch*! In those days, maybe, there were real grounds for your collapse, but by today's standards, well . . . if only you knew, Paulina Ignatievna. Nowadays you can't spit on Gorky Street without hitting a Frenchman, and those other ones, who are the cause of all the latest trouble, can emigrate to Palestine without hindrance in order to strengthen a hostile state, which is another minus point to enter against the people who are responsible for it.

He poured out Nina's tea into a huge earthenware cup decorated with roosters (to the girl, this cup was a symbol of home and paternal benevolence in her hours of relaxation in the evening), put a few slices of lemon in the saucer, scooped up a handful of candy, even poured some honey into a little bowl, and carried it all into his daughter's room.

Over Nina's shoulder he read the sentence she was just typing: ". . . fight against the violation of civil rights and for the release of . . ." He put down the cup and the bowl in front of Nina and stacked the candy beside it in a heap. He took a little extra gulp of air: "Drink up, kid."

If only he could allow himself, just once, to put his hands on her shoulders and gently squeeze them. When you stood behind her and looked down, you could see that there was something goatlike about her small jutting breasts. A little she-goat.

She had once had a phase of enthusiasm for mime, and had practiced it at home in a mauve leotard to that sickening anti-Soviet music. Twisting and gyrating in front of a mirror, she had suddenly caught sight of him watching her. It was silly of him to have been so careless as to look at her like that. She shuddered, realizing at once that his look was not the look of a father but of a man, an ordinary man who desired her; shuddering, she bent herself into a clumsy pose, with her arms and legs all tangled up, like a wounded goat.

Nothing of the sort ever happened again. Cheptsov tried to look at Nina in the same way that he looked at other people – imperturbably, sullenly, with an expression of glum boredom. This cost him no little effort, especially whenever she came home at night from God knows where, from her disgusting mime studio, for instance, which was full of fucking long-haired alcoholics, junkies, the scum of society, all sorts of so-called "scientists" in quotation marks and writers, Katya Furtseva's fancy men – ah, forget it. Those tall young studs, with straight shoulders and quivering, greedy thighs . . . From her languid look, her sunken cheeks, the tongue furtively licking her lips, he always recognized unerringly – "she's been fucked today" – and it cost him a great deal to restrain himself from jumping on her and throwing everything to the winds!

She, the little girl whose underwear he had washed ever since Paulina Ignatievna had suffered her appalling trauma, she, whom he had raised and taught to the best of his limited ability, whose every sigh he understood only too well, although he talked to her very little, she was being spreadeagled, squeezed, sucked, and fucked by some shit called Aristarkh Kunitser, who smelled like a subversive from a mile off!

She took a candy, sipped the tea, and banged out the end of the sentence: " . . . heroes of the Democratic Movement – General Grigorenki, Vladimir Bukovsky, Natalya Gorbanevskaya, Andrei Amalrik, and hundreds of others!"

He read all this and instantly, from behind her back, ripped the sheet of paper out of the machine. She jumped up with a shriek and ran into a corner of the room. Seeing her father with the crumpled sheet in his hand, she held her breath – it was so unexpected that she clearly expected something awful to happen.

"So *that*'s what you're doing," he whispered, staring at the paper. It was a subversive proclamation, and the paper was cheap, thin, underground paper, on which nearly ten copies could be typed at once.

"Hey, dad, hand it over!" She stretched out her hand. She knew the power she had over him. "It's mean to peek over people's shoulders!"

She even laughed her husky little laugh. Never before had she laughed at HIM like THAT. She was laughing like a woman, instinctively wishing to subjugate him. It was that laughter and that female arrogance that finally detonated within him a kind of infernal machine, a little brown storehouse full of bombs – and a brown fountain exploded into the air.

He lunged forward and knocked her off her feet with two terrible blows across the face. Then, kneeling on the floor, he turned her over on her stomach and pulled up her skirt. With his right hand he pulled the belt out of his pants, folded it in two, and started to lash her across the whorish little lace panties stretched over her bottom. Then he rolled her over onto her back and started slapping her on the cheeks again with the palm of his hand, after which he tore open her blouse, gripped her little nanny goat's breasts and pressed his mouth to hers. With an instantaneous, unconscious movement he ripped off her panties, and then, without the slightest haste, even with a certain solemnity, he pulled out his hot, rockhard, evil-smelling penis. He was actually surprised at its dimensions, either because he had not seen it in the firing position for such a long time or because it had never looked quite like this before. Then he entered her, settled himself in a comfortable position, and set to work.

She groaned and bit her lips as she turned away to avoid his kisses. All the time that he was pumping away, her eyes were closed, but suddenly she began to groan loudly and sensually, her eyes opened for a moment, and he saw in them a bottomless, intoxicated smile. He rammed her to the end, to the very core, and this had never happened to him before with any woman. Proud of having scaled such heights, he kept up the work on the limp, pathetic, and still more desirable body and brought her to another orgasm, until she moaned again, and once again he looked into the bottomless eyes of the opposite sex. Then he himself uttered a kind of growl and squeezed something out of himself, slackened, and finally released her from beneath his hairy stomach.

"*La guerre! La guerre!* Papa *französisch!*" came the cry from beyond the forests of Mozhaisk on the field of the battle of Borodino.

He realized that Paulina Ignatievna had heard everything, had guessed what was going on, and now no longer wanted to go on living. He squinted sideways at Nina. She was staring at him hard and intently with an unfathomable expression.

"Don't worry, Nina, I'm not your father at all," he said gently and placed his hand on her pubic mound. "I'm not your natural father. I'm no blood relation to you. Just another man. Now I must tell you about our secret."

AND HE TOLD HER THE SECRET

"You are the daughter of Colonel Boris Yevdokimovich Lygher, and your mother Paulina Ignatievna was his lawful spouse. Ah, Nina, your mother was simply the most gorgeous lady in Magadan and deservedly enjoyed great authority in our circle! She played music, sang operetta arias, had a superb knowledge of classical literature, and with all that she was a true member of the Party. In our little world everyone knew that if Paulina Ignatievna invited you to one of her five o'clock teas, you would leave it spiritually enriched. You were only about three when I started coming to your house. The company of your mother raised me to a new level.

"It was a difficult time, the early part of 1953. We were preparing for a new purge to rid Dalstroy of hostile elements. Evidence was pouring in from the Center. Under those conditions, I always gained great moral support from Paulina Ignatievna.

"One day I visited Paulina Ignatievna at a moment when your father, my immediate superior, was absent. I could not resist the outward attractions of Paulina Ignatievna. I became physically intimate with her.

"But I did not hide behind a *fait accompli.* With a clean Party conscience and an officer's sense of honor, I asked Paulina Ignatievna to leave Colonel Lygher and unite her life with mine. The proposal was rejected, but our meetings continued.

"Paulina Ignatievna was a remarkable woman. I shall never cease to be amazed by her! She combined our meetings with giving me French lessons. She taught the subject in the Magadan High School, where she was not only secretary of the Party committee but active in social and political work, helping the students, even the children of former convicts. She was a guiding spirit in both cultural activities and political instruction. Excuse me, I'm going to smoke."

As he took out a pack of cigarettes, he glanced fleetingly at Nina. In the past, at the mere sight of a cigarette, she would shout, "Daddy, don't you dare!" with pretended fury, on grounds of the harmful effects of nicotine. Now, however, she did not give so much as a twitch of an eyebrow. Lying naked on her side, her head propped on one hand, she was listening in silence with an inscrutable expression as he told her the "secret." Seeing the cigarette in his mouth, she tapped her lips with two fingers as a sign that she too wanted a smoke. No doubt she had made the same gesture to all her other studs – "give me one too." He lit a cigarette for her and actually felt a slight tremor at the new sensation. Now he wasn't her father, she wasn't his daughter, they were lovers! Surely this was happiness?

"Well?" said Nina, her unfathomable stare still fixed on him.

He nodded to show his willingness to go on with the story right away. He filled his lungs with smoke and tried to think back to twenty years ago, to that spring in Magadan when the mists used to creep along the streets, above them a faint blue haze. He tried to recall as clearly as possible Paulina as she had been in those days, and suddenly an odd thought came to him: And were all the officers of the State Security Administration so attracted to this woman because her political and social activities somehow gave a touch of reason and humanity to their filthy, criminal work?

Yes, he had actually thought those words – "filthy, criminal!" Furious with himself, he wondered just how such dreadful words came into his mind. Of course, they came involuntarily, from the same source as all subversive thoughts, from the same dirty, rotten corners! We were not criminals! We were doing our duty as shining knights of the Revolution and we had nothing to be ashamed of! No need to point to that little Pole, Dzerzhinsky, who had started it all, either; even without him the security forces would have produced any number of heroes to serve the cause of the dictatorship of the proletariat! Ah, forget it!

"I'm now coming to the main part of the story," he continued. "The general called me in and handed me some documents containing evidence about your father, Boris Yevdokimovich Lygher. The documents had just arrived from Moscow, ordering us to clarify certain biographical details about Colonel Lygher, because he had been found to have foreign origins – French, to be exact. Among the documents was a handwritten, unsigned report stating that Colonel Lygher had close connections with the 'rootless cosmopolitans,' a phrase of the time that meant Jews, and a terrible accusation in those last weeks of Stalin's life.

" 'Did you write that report?' the general asked me. 'We know all about you, Cheptsov, we know all about you and Madame Lygher, but in this particular instance we don't condemn you. Do the necessary with these papers and send Lygher to me.'

"I rushed from headquarters straight to Paulina Ignatievna. No, I had not denounced Boris Yevdokimovich. I admit I didn't like him. I wanted to have such a marvelous comrade as Paulina Ignatievna all to myself. I realized only too well that the inevitable arrest of Colonel Lygher was bound to affect his wife as well.

"I ran into the house. There before me was Paulina Ignatievna. She was busy with the kid, that's to say with you, Nina, teaching you about art – she was showing you Repin's picture *The Zaporozhian Cossacks Writing a Letter to the Sultan of Turkey* and telling you the story of how this masterpiece came to be painted. It was an unforgettable moment – a ray of sunshine falling on Paulina Ignatievna's blue crêpe-de-chine dress.

" 'Paulina Ignatievna, you must immediately sue for divorce! Your husband is a traitor!'

"Those were stern times, Nina. Many people thought that we officials of the security forces were devoid of human feelings. Not so! Perhaps I was a little too brusque, but only out of a desire to save Paulina Ignatievna. I was ready to submit an immediate application for a transfer to another sector or to the 'mainland,' to leave and take you both with me. Paulina didn't understand.

" 'How dare you! Blackmailer! Get out!'

" 'Paulina, your husband's name isn't Lygher at all. It's Lagher – *la guerre*. He's been concealing his real nationality. He's a Frenchman, if not a Jew! I needn't tell *you* that *"la guerre'* means "war" in French!'

" '*La guerre! La guerre!*' she suddenly screamed wildly. 'Papa! Papa *französisch*!' And she fell backward onto the parquet."

Cheptsov stopped for a moment and cleared his throat. Now he had told his "daughter" everything, or almost everything. No, he wouldn't tell her about the laugh that Paulina Ignatievna gave. He couldn't describe such a terrible laugh in words. He had never heard anything like it, even at interrogations.

"And that was the start of her illness. Your father came home in the evening, and we had it all out. He was shattered by his interview with the general and agreed to give you and the paralyzed Paulina Ignatievna to me. He packed his things and left the next morning. He was not arrested, only removed from his job. It was the spring of 1953, and already there was a whiff of Khrushchev's rotten liberalism in the air."

Cheptsov was getting increasingly agitated and nervous. He lit another cigarette and paced up and down the room, his whole one hundred kilograms crushing the parquet floor at every step. Suddenly he recalled how the floor of that dilapidated hut on the outskirts of Magadan had buckled under his weight when they had arrested that dyed-in-the-wool Trotskyite woman back in '49. Raphael's *Sistine Madonna,* brass Catholic crosses, books by reactionary writers . . . He could remember no other details of that arrest.

"Put your pants on!" he suddenly heard a hostile voice say.

"What?" he gave a start, aware of his nakedness.

"Put your pants on. You look disgusting," said Nina, his little girl.

As he grabbed his pants he saw in the mirror a repulsive old man in a green officers' shirt, from which protruded a gray hairy stomach and beneath it a dark, wrinkled penis in a fluffy gray bush. An old man with a little broken nose, a huge dewlap, and hands trembling with obsequious desire to please this little girl. For the first time he saw himself as an old man and was appalled. His dream of happiness had burst like a soap bubble.

"Bloodsucker, toad. You're inhuman!" Gutsalov the guerrilla from the Caucasus had shouted at him during an interrogation. "I swear that everything about you is monstrous, inhuman!" That scum, who had raised his hand against everything that was sacred – against the Motherland, against Stalin – had the gall to claim humane treatment! Anyway, he had been treated entirely according to regulations, so he should have been cursing the regulations!

He tightened his belt to haul in his paunch, tidied himself up in front of the mirror, frowned, and tried to banish the specter of a wretched old man. You can't frighten us, we won't give way! Don't try and scare us with your pathetic God! He doesn't exist, that's for sure.

From this moment on we're going to start a new life, Retired Comrade Lieutenant-Colonel. There's enough money, both rubles and foreign currency, that's the main thing. I'll hire a nurse for Paulina

Ignatievna, take Nina to the Beryozka foreign-currency store and buy her whatever she wants, and we'll go off to the south for three months. And as for my miserable partner at the cloakroom in the foreign-currency bar, that shit Lygher who humiliates himself before any Swede for a krona, I'll never tell her about him. She'll never know about that nonentity, who'll do anything for money. Two cloakroom jobs aren't enough for him; he even moonlights by driving a Chaika for the Palace of Marriages. He'll do anything for money, that little "frog eater from Bordeaux." I'll be both father and husband to the girl.

He turned around. She was now sitting in the corner, curled up in a ball, and still staring at him with that unfathomable look. No doubt she had been watching him with that look while he was putting on his pants in front of the mirror. That calm, inscrutable stare. He had been just about to tell her all about his exciting plans, when suddenly a strange signal from a car horn came from the street through the open window, a sound like the neighing of a horse. Nina jumped up as if a spring had been released inside her, clutched her blouse to her chest, and ran over to the window.

Cheptsov also went to the window and saw below a brand-new, gleaming Zhiguli car. No wonder the slang name for these little cars was kike wagon – from it emerged Aristarkh Kunitser, a real sharp dresser in his gray suit and broad-knotted tie, looking like some spruce young Englishman, just as though he had never worn a straitjacket, as though he wasn't an alcoholic but a genuinely clever, talented scientist of national stature.

Then began a scene which Cheptsov experienced as an absurd dream. Movements, sounds, insinuations, smells – all added up to a sense of something incomprehensible and sinister.

It was a fine warm evening, and down below Kunitser took off his dark glasses. From above, from below, from all sides came the sounds of music-hall songs, mostly foreign, as Kunitser waved to Nina and turned toward the front door of their apartment house. The windows of the houses across the park glowed red with the reflection of the setting sun, and suddenly Cheptsov guessed a terrible truth – Nina and Kunitser were having an affair! The treetops were rustling in the park as Nina shot past him like a bullet, emerged from the bathroom moments later in jeans and a tight T-shirt, thrust a comb into her tangled hair, and bit her lips. A breeze blew into the apartment, carrying with it the aroma of the blessed south and of his forgotten youth, and from it, his youth, a picture floated up before his mind's eye: a longed-for vision of boyhood, the wife of the chairman of the provincial executive committee driving past him in her rumbling Packard. Then Kunitser appeared in the apartment, was immediately seized by Nina and dragged toward the door, lest he hear the shameful cry *"La guerre, la guerre."* Even so, the shout rang out, and Cheptsov thought he heard in it a note of triumph. For the first time he detected a shade of emotion in that senseless cry. The sound made Kunitser jump and he stopped in the doorway. Slowly, like a slow-motion film, he turned around and saw Cheptsov in a corner of the hallway, still not fully dressed, with an open fly and dangling arms. Some strong emotion flashed across the face of the pseudoscientist and froze into a repulsive grimace.

"You?" he said slowly. "Is your name Cheptsov?"

"You are not mistaken, Aristarkh Apollinarievich," said Cheptsov quietly but distinctly and gestured invitingly toward the kitchen. "What's the hurry? Have some tea. Homemade jam. Strawberry. Picked them myself. Nina made the jam."

I'll lull his vigilance with jam and old-world manners, and then I'll strike unexpectedly! So Nina can see which of us is the real man!

Kunitser suddenly took a tottering step toward him. His face was now shining with a brassy gleam. He seemed to be trembling. Obviously crazy.

"Tea and jam? Thank you. I'll never turn down an offer like that!"

"La guerre! La guerre! Papa *französisch!"* Paulina Ignatievna was obviously on the side of the potential enemy.

Kunitser gripped his head in his hands and began to press his temples.

"Did you hear that, *'la guerre?'* Where have I heard that before? Did you hear it? Was I hearing things? Papa *französisch?"* He stared around like a hunted beast.

Nina, who was hanging onto his shoulder and trying to pull him toward the door, whispered hotly, "We'll be late! Come on, Aristarkh, let's go."

She looked over Kunitser's shoulder at Cheptsov, and her face was twisted with loathing and repulsion. Go away, you spider, she seemed to be saying, you vampire, you inhuman monster!

Kunitser looked at her with amazement, as though seeing her for the first time. He turned and looked at Cheptsov, then again at Nina and once more at Cheptsov. He seemed drawn more strongly to Cheptsov than to Nina, but he allowed himself to be pulled out of the door.

The lock clicked. The elevator went down.

"*La guerre! La guerre!*"

Breathing hard, his eyes dull, Cheptsov flung aside the screen, swung his outstretched arm, and slapped Paulina Ignatievna's detested face with all his strength.

For the first time in twenty years the colonel's wife broke off her cry unfinished. She stared at Cheptsov with her clear eyes. He had the impression that she was about to say something. Perturbed, he began pacing around the apartment. This cramped and stuffy apartment, it was worse than a coffin! All its smells, all the slime, the carbolic acid, the packets of Hungarian goulash soup, the panties, the sweat, the French perfume, that stinking French woman's filth – all was suffocating him, pressing in on his temples. All his life! Expiation . . .

Expiation? The long mirror fell over sideways, papers flew in all directions, the typewriter slid noiselessly to the floor. He slipped on the spot where Nina had been lying, and the slimy feel of the varnished floor there brought on a new surge of passion. That's how you'll die, you lousy little bitch! She's gone out with that scum, that kike, that degenerate, as though nothing had happened, as though this wasn't a historic day in our family life! I'll kill you, I'll fuck you to death, I'll split you up the middle!

When he came to his senses, he caught sight of his right arm, lying on the floor like a log of wood. The hand was clutching a sheet of paper. Was the arm paralyzed? A pity. It had been a good arm. It had done a lot to bring clarity into the class struggle for the greater glory of the Fatherland.

Suddenly the hand raised itself of its own accord and brought the crumpled piece of paper close to his face. His other hand released itself from under his body in order to smooth out the piece of paper.

"Fight against the violation of civil rights and for the release of the heroes of the Democratic Movement – General Grigorenko, Vladimir Bukovsky, Natalya Gorbanevskaya, Andrei Amalrik, and hundreds of others!"

So everything was now clear. In the emotional turmoil Nina had forgotten her little "job," and obviously that counterrevolutionary in the Zhiguli had come with the intention of collecting it. He could heave a deep sigh of relief. How simple it all was now! He must do his duty. All was now clear and straightforward: duty, honor, struggle! You'll all go to prison. Soviet science would manage quite well without Kunitser; no one was indispensable. Nina would have to taste prison slops too. When duty calls, a patriot must be prepared to sacrifice even his daughter. Like Pavlik Morozov, who informed on his parents! No, you kikes, we won't let you gnaw at the bastions of socialism with your miserable little teeth!

He got up from the floor, picked up the fallen mirror, combed his hair, and put on his tunic. Anguish and gloom had not yet given way to the primitive emotion of gut patriotism. An old man with a quivering jaw looked at him out of the mirror.

Kunitser will be arrested immediately. Seven years in a strict-regime prison camp plus three years' internal exile! Nina, of course, won't get more than a year, being an unsuspecting accomplice, and anyway things aren't what they used to be in the old days . . . . Had he, Lieutenant-Colonel Cheptsov, actually said that: ". . . things aren't what they used to be in the old days"? Ah, if only the old days were back again!

A few minutes later he was all set to do his duty: shaved, buttoned up, all the subversive documentation, the sheets of paper and carbon paper placed in an old but still robust portfolio that was stamped in gold on its watered-silk cover: "Participant in the Regional Party Conference 1952." Something, however, was still missing. What was it? Ah, yes – vodka.

He opened the kitchen closet, unsealed a bottle of Extra, poured himself a shot, and – down it went! Then he ate a pinch of Hungarian goulash soup powder. A second glass – bottoms up! He tipped some more soup powder into his cupped palm and stuffed it into his gaping mouth. Good! He poured the remainder into the glass, which disappeared in one gulp. He sucked his thumb. He had been going to take his raincoat. To hell with it! He had intended to wear his fedora. Forget it! Instead he picked up his old service cap and jammed it on his head. Either the cap had shrunk or his head had expanded. So what! *Sehrrr gut! Trrès biennn!* A plastic daisy as a parting gift for Paulina Ignatievna. Not talking, eh, you bitch? Let me give you a kiss! Sleep away, baby, in the dark of your dreamless night! Adieu, madam! *La guerre!*

The old women sitting in the warm evening air on the bench beside the front door were amazed to see an unfamiliar man in semimilitary garb leave the house with a red portfolio under his arm and stride off boldly toward the streetcar stop. His back, bottom, flanks, the back of his neck, were unrecognizable.

AN ACCIDENT SITUATION

arose when Aristarkh Kunitser, without looking to either side, shot out of a side street onto the highway. With much squealing of brakes, both streams of traffic came to a halt, the drivers burst out into cascades of foul language, and the blue Zhiguli, as if nothing had happened, made a left turn and drove off. Amid the general uproar, the driver of an official car, one Talonov, said thoughtfully as he watched the Zhiguli disappear with a woman's head resting on its driver's shoulder, "If the Moscow girls don't stop playing with their boyfriends' sexual organs while they're driving, the accident rate is going to increase."

Vadim Nikolayevich Serebryanikov, who was sprawled on the back seat, laughed in his sleep.

Nina looked at the profile of her beloved Aristarkh. He had apparently not even noticed the danger at the intersection. He was biting his lips, deep in thought, this man with the beloved profile. Ah, how happy Nina was at that moment – now putting her head on her lover's shoulder, now staring into his eyes . . . She had even forgotten that an hour ago she had been raped by her putative father. Suddenly the beloved one himself reminded her of it. "That man . . . that Cheptsov . . . what is he? Some relation of yours?"

Nina felt a moment of confusion. What should she say? If only Aristarkh had come for her yesterday and not today. Anyway, now wasn't the time to tell him about all those strange secrets. Better to lie, better to pretend that today was yesterday.

"My father."

Aristarkh suddenly made a sharp right turn out of the center lane and, under the very nose of an enormous concrete-mixer truck, shot under the archway of a building and stopped there.

"He was a hangman, your father. He tortured my mother. You weren't even born when he was an executioner. He tortured people under interrogation. I saw him hit a bound man in the eye with his elbow."

"You . . . saw . . . Cheptsov hit a man in the eye?" she asked, hardly breathing.

"Yes. A bound man," Aristarkh emphasized cruelly. "With his elbow. In the eye. You are the daughter of a torturer and a judicial murderer."

"No!" she screamed. "No! No!"

Aristarkh leaned his head on the steering wheel and closed his eyes.

A WINDOW COVERED IN FROST FLOWERS

Frosty pine trees, overlapping one another. Pine branches. A few little stars. The lifeless fiesta of a frost-bound window, and only at the top, near the ventilation pane, was a live disk, the oily trace of the moon.

"Hi, Tolya. Where's your mother?"

Martin came in from the frosty outdoors, rubbing his hands cheerfully. He took off his coat, rubbed his hands again, patted Tolya on the shoulder, and sat down on their hard, ugly sofa. His mind was obviously still on his work, still wrapped up in his worries, his prescriptions, complaints, and symptoms, and that was why he didn't notice that Tolya was smoking.

Tolya was smoking a Kazbek cigarette and drinking sweet port from a large dark bottle. He had found the cigarettes and the wine in a kitchen drawer a few hours after his mother's arrest. Now he was sitting at the table, dully smoking his first cigarette and drinking wine for the first time in his life. He felt no sensations except a slight dryness in the mouth. With the indifference of a forty-year-old misanthrope, he drew in and blew out the smoke, sipped the wine. He stared dully at Martin.

Martin was sitting on the sofa, straight-backed and smiling. He has amazingly white and even teeth, thought Tolya, I wish I had teeth like that. Just like American teeth. Americans are famous for having superb teeth. The Ringo Kid had teeth exactly like those.

"So what, then? Mother not back yet?"

"Mother's gone," said Tolya calmly. "She's been arrested."

Martin did not exclaim or jump to his feet, but simply covered his face with his hands and wept bitterly.

Tolya watched Martin as though from a distance, as though looking at a movie screen from the auditorium. He watched him with dim-witted surprise – the sight of a broad-shouldered man with a sturdy bald head weeping like a child was astonishing.

"Poor woman, poor woman," Martin kept repeating in a barely audible voice, tears running down between his fingers and dripping from the knotted veins on the backs of his hands.

Suddenly Tolya had a flash of insight – he saw everything sharply and in its true light, and perceived the difference between his own tears and Martin's. Several hours ago, it was not he who had been crying but a little wet animal inside him, that little "tolik" who wanted to be just a regular Komsomol and student; he had wept from fear at the terrible changes about to take place in his life. When Martin cried, the man himself was crying, crying for Tolya's mother.

Tolya threw away his cigarette and pushed the wine aside. He stood up and walked over to Martin. "Don't cry, Philip Yegorovich," he said in a strange, hoarse bass voice. "I've already cried enough for the two of us."

Martin heard him and remembered Tolya's existence. While he was crying, with his face covered, he had of course forgotten about Tolya, thinking only of the boy's mother. Perhaps he had remembered some moments when they had made love, the sad and shameful love-making between the male and female zones of the prison camp – what can be sadder and more shameful than the love of two convicts? Perhaps he had also remembered some moments of happiness – for where is the love that brings no happiness? He lowered his hands and wiped his face with his sleeve.

"Tolya, my dear, don't be afraid," he said in his usual voice. "Forgive me, Tolya, but I am going to pray. For your mother and for you."

"They took away your altar," said Tolya.

Martin knelt down in front of the empty corner, folded his hands together, brought them to his chest, and lowered his head to them. In front of him was only an empty corner, but to one side stood a rickety bookcase on which were little busts of Tolya's mother's favorite writers – Pushkin, Blok, Mayakovsky, Goethe. These busts had been carved in bone by a skilled "light-duty" prisoner from the Quarantine Camp. He had made them to Martin's order in gratitude for the latter's help in getting him a cushy job in the sick bay, where it was, of course, somewhat warmer than in the uranium mines. These busts always wobbled slightly, because the whole hut trembled a little and with it the rickety little bookcase.

"Philip Yegorovich, teach me to pray," Tolya asked, kneeling down beside his stepfather.

"He prays who believes," said Martin quietly.

"What about someone who wants to believe?"

"He who wants to believe already believes."

"So teach me to pray," Tolya whispered, tearing off his Komsomol badge from his jacket and throwing it away.

"Repeat after me," said Martin, staring fixedly into the empty corner. "*Pater noster* . . ."

"*Pater noster*," said Tolya.

"*Pater noster, qui es in caelis: Sanctificetur nomen* TUUM . . ."

"Pater noster, qui es in caelis: Sanctificetur nomen TUUM . . ."
Then they sat at the table in silence for a long time and did not
touch either the wine or the cigarettes. When his stepfather was about
to go, Tolya asked him, "Philip Yegorovich, you're not really a doctor,
are you? You're a priest, aren't you?"
"No, Tolya, I am a doctor. I graduated from the University of
Kharkov. But in the camps I helped my fellow Catholics to celebrate
the rites of our religion. I had to say the mass for the dead, marry
people, and even baptize newborn babies – everything happens in the
camps. You might say that I'm almost a priest. I'm a camp priest,
Tolya."

THE THIRD MAN FOR A THREESOME

was being sought by Alik Neyarky and Pyotr Pavlovich Odudovsky
behind the Children's World department store. Why did they need
him? Why bother with a third man to split a bottle of vodka? Surely
it wasn't too hard to finish a bottle off between the two of them? Such,
however, is the Russian tradition that has grown up over the years.
The custom is to split the first bottle three ways, to choose the grimiest
possible entrance hallway, spread out a few snacks on a radiator, and
have a little heart-to-heart chat – to swap experiences, as it were. An
ingrained, genetically implanted nostalgia for the warm, cozy beer bars
that the poet Yesenin was so fond of or for those long-vanished cab-
drivers' taverns, is alive to this day in the Muscovite soul. You might
think that nowadays, in the 1970s, all the preconditions exist for
consuming liquor at home – television sets and modern sanitation –
but the old spirit of the Moscow taverns still survives and it draws
certain restless citizens out to the crossroads, to doorways, to garbage
cans, to "threesomes." They did not, of course, have to search for long.
"There's a suitable comrade over there."
The "suitable comrade" was standing by the big plate-glass window
of Children's World, facing Dzerzhinsky Square and looking at the
imposing curved frontage of the building housing the headquarters of
the KGB (once the head office of the Salamander Insurance
Company). He was wearing a threadbare military tunic, a faded service
cap, and a pair of brown pants that were considerably too short for
him. The comrade's broad bottom was thrust out in the direction of
the Hotel Berlin with a certain air of challenge. In his whole attitude,
in the careless way he was leaning against the window, the "suitable

comrade" seemed to be hurling a challenge to fate and to implacable Cronus himself. A red portfolio protruded from under his arm, like the stump of a once-mighty wing.

"Definitely an interesting man."

The two friends approached Cheptsov. Without beating around the bush, Alik showed him the neck of a vodka bottle sticking out from under his shirtfront.

"Excuse me, sir, would you care to take part?"

"I don't drink," came the gloomy reply. Two small black eyes looked out from under shaggy brows with a glare that was positively scorching.

"Where have I seen that ugly mug before?" frowned Neyarky.

"Ha, ha, ha! Allow me to doubt you," said Odudovsky cheerfully, and with comic horror waved his hand in front of his nose as though trying to dispel the "suitable comrade's" liquor-laden breath.

Odudovsky was in an excellent early-evening mood. He had already polished off half a bottle of red wine on Stoleshnikov Street, a ten-ruble bill was rustling in his pocket, and he was thoroughly adapted to a bachelor's existence – ah, there's more to life than what lies between your thighs, madam!

The "suitable comrade" did not respond to humor but merely emitted a strange, short sound that was half grunt, half groan.

"We get the message!" With an iron grip, Alik took him by the arm. "Go, go, Budyonny's cavalry!"

From the other side, Odudovsky seized hold of the red portfolio, and the newly created trio set off down Pushechnaya, moving away from Children's World and consequently away from KGB headquarters, those two mighty institutions of Russia's capital city.

Odudovsky had organized everything to perfection: the hallway, the glass, and the radiator. A dim light from a soot-stained window fell on the mosaic-tiled floor, on which were still preserved the old-fashioned letters of the maker's name: "Kronhaus and Company: Moscow – Berlin – St. Petersburg."

"I think I've seen you before, comrade," Neyarky said to Cheptsov. "Our paths have already crossed somewhere."

"I've known you for some time, puck chaser," said Cheptsov, with a hint of the professional in his voice.

"You mean you've seen him on TV?" exclaimed Odudovsky. "You see, Alik, you're as popular as ever!"

"No, in the restaurant of the Hotel National," said Cheptsov, "being rude, chasing girls, and usually burping. All three shifts know you very well, Mr. Master of Sport."

FIVE IN SOLITARY

"Kiryanich!" Alik embraced Cheptsov. "Hey, Lev, he's the check-room guy from the foreign-currency bar at the National. He's a real pal, one of us for fuck's sake!"

Two weeks before, Alik had been dropped again from the team for slack play and loss of speed. The fact was that Alik had gotten bored with hockey and started to take an interest in Moscow life again, not, unfortunately, in the productive labor of its factories but in various forms of masculine entertainment. He was an incorrigible male, was this popular sportsman, a roaring boy who never wasted time in regrets: In weight and physical strength he was the equal, and more, of Gordie Howe, although the defense lines in Soviet hockey are generally on the weak side.

"My daughter is a criminal," Cheptsov muttered to his new companions.

"Nowadays, generalissimo, there's more to crime than stealing horses!" rasped Alik.

"My daughter is guilty of crimes against the state," Cheptsov explained.

"That is a fairly broad category," said Odudovsky with a subtle smile, as he lifted a sprat out of the can with two fingers and shook the oil from it.

Alik could not believe his eyes: The grim cloakroom attendant from the National suddenly burst into tears.

"My daughter . . . my little girl . . . raised her . . . washed her panties . . . put a lot of money and effort . . . pretty and clever . . . crimes against the state . . . just look at this, comrades!"

The white tapes, somewhat out of place against the red watered silk, flew open to reveal the subversive proclamation "Fight against the violation of civil rights and for the release of the heroes of the Democratic Movement . . ."

"Freedom," said Neyarky, savoring the word. "Freedom is a sweet-tasting word. Everyone needs freedom, like they need air."

"Freedom is the recognition of necessity!" Odudovsky chimed in proudly. "You must admit, comrades, that the classics knew how to put things into words!"

"Sure thing," Alik agreed.

"But freedom for the right class!" Cheptsov suddenly howled in fury, stamping his feet. "Just read that and see *who* the heroes are! Not Angela Davis, not Mikis fucking Theodorakis, but Russians – degenerate, subversive Russians!"

"Easy now, generalissimo, take a look at this," Neyarky said at this point, showing him another bottle of vodka peeping out from under his jacket. "Relax, we'll survive."

Once again twilight descended on Cheptsov. What was he doing? Why was he drinking vodka and baring his soul to this déclassé riffraff? Why didn't he go to the man in charge of foreign-currency bars, Major Golubkov, and hand over the portfolio tied with its white tapes? Why had his step faltered on Pushechnaya near that store window full of dolls, cribs, and teddy bears? Why had he hung around there for half an hour, eyeing the passing women, and why did he actually try not to look at the secret KGB building?

The silly, weak old man outside Children's World was thinking how to save his daughter, or rather not his daughter but his mistress. I shall save Nina my mistress and keep it a secret from her. I shall say that I found the leaflets at my daytime job at the institute and that they fell out of Aristarkh Kunitser's raincoat. Good idea. Now I must go, go . . . go. Why aren't you going?

The wild, drunken sunset behind his back wouldn't let him go. Only the hated Aristarkh would suffer – so go and make your report! The sunset would not let him go. It enveloped him from all sides, and its yellow reflections shone everywhere. Why don't I go? Is it because I don't want to add to an already long list of crimes? Crimes?! You old fool, you've already fallen under the influence of their subversive propaganda. Do you call your faithful, uncompromising service to the state a *crime*? I don't want any more arrests and interrogations, I don't want any more of it! I'm old, I'm an honest man, I'm a keen amateur gardener, I used to be an honest veterinarian! Behind him the sun suddenly sank below the noisy backdrop of Moscow and he realized that now the twilight would not let him go. After that the night would bar his way and he probably wouldn't live to see the morning.

"You want to inform on your daughter, do you? That's not a very nice thing for anyone to do," said Alik Neyarky in a moralizing tone, breathing sprat-flavored olive oil into Cheptsov's face. "I did a spell in the security forces too, Kiryanich, but I never once informed on anyone."

Cheptsov drank the rest of the fiery vodka and started to talk rapidly, jerkily, his words interrupted by sobs. "I have a daughter, dear comrades . . . lovely creature. She has little breasts like a nanny goat's, dear comrades. There's a little hollow in the back of her neck where her skin is as tender and smooth as it is on her belly – not a hair, not a pimple . . . I tell you guys, a daughter like that can send you out of your mind . . . Such huge eyes, you've never seen anything like them

. . . but she cuts her hair short, the little fool, although it's naturally soft and fluffy – it could look like the waves on the Volga like it says in the song . . . She's so gentle and slender, her shoulder blades stick out from her back, and down here, you know, her little ribs even show through . . . And my daughter's lips are red with a fine film of moisture over them, and when she lies on her side, it makes a line like that . . . Look, that sort of line . . . It's enough to send you out of your mind . . ."

"What a remarkable portrait of a daughter!" said Odudovsky, frightened.

"It's quite obvious," said Alik. "In the village of Odintsovo, where my wife, Tamara, lives, there's a retired colonel who also fucks his daughter. It happens, Kiryanich, it happens; you're not the only one."

"And it happened in the olden days, too," Odudovsky added approvingly. "You only have to think of the Borgia family."

Cheptsov knelt down, took aim, and with all his force rammed his head against the radiator. Then he did it again.

IN THE YELLOW TWILIGHT OF A CUL-DE-SAC

Kunitser was sitting, or rather sprawling, stretched out as far as the seat of his Zhiguli would allow. Nina's head, her fluffy hair cut short, lay on his knees, sobbing and sighing. The windows of a canteen kitchen faced the street, from where in the yellow twilight came the grinding sound of a huge potato-peeling machine. Kunitser looked at Nina's head.

This is not my love, this is only a part of my love. A little creature who came to me one day holding a little glass box . . . Where is my love? Where did I lose her? Sometimes I have a moment of clear vision, a gap in the clouds, and in it a faint memory. I want to hold on to that moment, but it flies away. Where is my love?

My pimply little prince, my Tolya von Steinbock, you once caught sight of an exhausted girl convict with golden hair, lying on her side in the snow and trying to bite off the neck of a bottle of cologne. Her name was Alisa.

Everything is floating past me, as though all the doors and windows of the room where I'm standing have been opened at once and a malevolent draft is blowing away sheets of paper, envelopes, stamps. All gone, as though that meeting were not written in the book of my fate.

THE JOURNEY WILL BE DANGEROUS

was the title of the film that Tolya von Steinbock was seeing for the seventh time.

It was, in fact, that classic Western *Stagecoach,* with John Wayne playing the lead, but the audience in the Gornyak Movie Theater of Magadan, including of course Von Steinbock, knew neither the film's real title nor the names of the actors. It was one of the "pirated" films: The title and credits were excised, a new title invented, and an introductory text added, explaining that spectators would be seeing an episode from the struggle of freedom-loving Indian tribes against the white colonizers. It didn't matter that the audience's sympathies were inevitably enlisted against the freedom-loving Indian tribes, who peppered the little stagecoach with arrows, and that they applauded the white colonizer, the Ringo Kid, when he jumped from the roof of the coach onto the back of a horse and then at a gallop brought down two Apache warriors with his Winchester. What was important was that the outward forms of propaganda were observed, and the spectator, willy-nilly, was supposed to have been given yet another dose of serum labeled "struggle for national liberation."

For the seventh time Tolya von Steinbock had come to see how the Ringo Kid walked across the screen, how he sauntered around with his long legs in those amazing cowboy pants with metal rivets, how he wiped the dust from his face, how he caught in the air the Winchester thrown to him by the sheriff, how he showed his white teeth in a slow cautious smile, how he kissed a woman . . . Tolya thought he could easily see the film seventy times.

A hero of incredible valor and boldness, who wouldn't think twice about giving his life for freedom! The Ringo Kid inspired Tolya with self-assurance; he imagined seeing his tall figure on the streets of Magadan, and naturally, as he came out of the theater, he felt a little like the Ringo Kid himself.

Among the quilted jackets, sheepskin jerkins, and overcoats of the crowd shuffling out of the theater he suddenly noted a plush coat of artificial fur. The springy legs of the Ringo Kid suddenly went limp – it was Lyudmila Guly! She turned in profile. Yes, that was her nose, her lovely forehead, her lips! She had noticed him! Didn't she blush? She swung her heavy braid of hair from her back around to her chest. That challenging laugh!

"Hey, kids, Von Steinbock thinks he's the Ringo Kid!"

Three of his classmates – Pop, Ryba, and Sidor – came up to the scarlet-faced Von Steinbock, while the taunting beauty stood at a distance with a girl friend and giggled in mockery. Shame, a feeling of delicious languor, a vague guess: She *is* interested in me after all! He almost crapped in his pants with excitement.

"Why aren't you coming to school, Bokov?" asked Ryba.

"Say, Tolya," said Pop, "you know there's an algebra test tomorrow, don't you?"

"Hi, Bok. How come you missed training? Freewheeling, eh?" Sidor gave Tolya a friendly nudge, spat to one side, and winked.

Tolya could see from their eyes that they all knew about his mother's arrest and were now, strange as it might seem, showing him their approval.

"I'm going to come to training," he said with a desperate attempt to summon the image of the Ringo Kid to his aid, hunching his shoulders, thrusting his hands into his pockets, and walking away with a nonchalant air. "And I don't give a shit about the test."

The stroll past his "comforters" went off brilliantly – he looked cocky, cool, and independent. It certainly made an impression on Lyuda. She actually opened her mouth!

"Von Steinbock!" he heard her say behind him in a mocking yet also very slightly disconcerted voice. It was an attempt to reassert her superiority, implying, Don't forget who we are, and who *you* are – a "von" and a Steinbock to boot!

He stopped in a doorway to turn up his coat collar and light a cigarette. He had carried it off perfectly! Out of the corner of his eye he had noticed Lyudmila's face light up in a flash of admiration. Yes, she was obviously not indifferent to him, and he loved her even more, even though he now knew that she was a bitch.

A savage wind was whipping along the Kolyma Highway, past the long row of solid stone houses, real city houses in which the families of the officers of the Ministry of Internal Affairs lived. At times this place could give the illusion of being a big city.

At this point the Ringo Kid image faded away. Instead, in his long overcoat that flapped in the wind, Tolya von Steinbock imagined himself as a big-city youth at the turn of the century, a companion of the young Mayakovsky, a futurist poet:

> All at once I daubed a sketch of tedious life,
> By splashing on the color from a glass of tea!
> And on a plate of galantine my knife
> Described the slanting cheekbones of the sea!

He was so thrilled that he came out in goose pimples.

Alas, the city came to an end around the next corner, where it gave way to a jumble of huts, fences, and prison-camp watchtowers; there, Tolya remembered, three times higher than the solid yellow pine fencing, was "Vaskov's House," the Magadan prison, where his mother was locked up and where he had to take her a food parcel tomorrow.

Depression and misgiving at the thought of tomorrow's prison visit gave him a pain in the stomach. Tolya leaned against the railings surrounding the brightly lit window of a grocery store. A beautiful pile of cans of lard, the last faint smile of Lend-Lease. A crowd of people seethed inside the store. Just suppose he, the Ringo Kid, could walk into that store now in his reefer jacket with two rows of steel buttons, a cartridge belt slung around his hips, and a warning smile – take it easy, you guys, don't push! – on his lips. Everyone in there would simply freeze, all those officers and officers' wives, stupid and fat and squat. And just suppose he were to stride up to the gates of "Vaskov's House," where the prisoners' relatives were all standing in line to hand in their food parcels, looking anxiously into the face of every guard. He wouldn't wait in line! He would put a bundle of dynamite under the gates and blow them open to burst in and set all the prisoners free! Word of honor, the Ringo Kid would have dealt single-handed with all the guards in the Magadan jailhouse, that bunch of bandy-legged, clumsy, stupid "screws" with blobs of frozen snot under their noses. With great pleasure he imagined the encounter between the Ringo Kid and Captain Cheptsov of the Ministry of State Security! Hell, a dozen or so Ringo Kids would have ripped the guts out of the whole Magadan gendarmerie and all those armed guards, the whole Directorate of the Northeastern Corrective Labor Camps, all the Special Camps, the Penal Units, and the Prison Labor Administration, and liberated everyone!

This whirlwind of fantasy was interrupted by a kindly female voice. "Aren't you Tolya Bokov? Hello!"

Tolya gave a start, looked around, and saw a pretty young officer's wife lit up by the light from the store window. She was wearing a sable fur coat and a fluffy Orenburg scarf. Her round face, with its lively coloring and sparkling eyes, would have been quite beautiful had it not been for her chin, which was large enough to give her a rather too provincial look. This was the first time that Tolya had met this young lady of the local elite, who taught French at his school. Recognizing her, he was struck dumb with embarrassment because he couldn't remember her name and patronymic; he had never encountered her in school, because he took English instead of French.

"I'm Paulina Ignatievna," the lady prompted him in a cheerful, friendly voice, and suddenly put the boy's arm in hers. "I'd like you to be my escort for a little while, young man."

They set off along the sidewalk, she leaning on his arm. Von Steinbock was taking a lady by the arm for the first time in his life!

"I'm so glad I met you, Tolya. I was just going to send for you. You see, I'm the secretary of the school's Party committee."

She kept her face constantly turned toward Tolya, looking at him most attentively as though studying his character.

"Poor boy," she suddenly said in such a kind voice that Tolya, to his shame, all but burst into tears. "You participate in all sorts of school activities, you play volleyball," she said, slightly more officially but still with warmth and sympathy.

"Basketball," Tolya corrected her.

"And you don't lack ability; I have made inquiries. You enjoy a certain authority among your classmates. You've been accepted into the Komsomol."

If only she knew that I had thrown away my badge! thought Tolya.

"Tolya, why have you stopped coming to school? I have read your essays. They're sincerely patriotic. You're a good Soviet boy, Tolya! There is a principle in our country: The son is not answerable for his father."

As she spoke that phrase, the lady made a curious gesture, using one hand or perhaps two to trace shapes in the air that might have been ovals or squares with rounded corners.

"But surely it's also true, isn't it, that the apple never falls far from the apple tree?" asked Tolya. "When I was in the third grade a teacher told me that."

"Oh, Tolya!" the lady exclaimed heatedly. "She was a bad teacher! She hadn't studied the works of Comrade Stalin properly!"

She did not have far to go, and soon they stopped in front of a five-story building in the center of town. It looked welcoming and festive inside the brightly lit windows, through one of which came the words of a sweet, squeaky little song sung by Zoya Rozhdestvenskaya:

> Give me the sun and the moon,
> Love me alone!

"You mustn't become embittered and cut yourself off from the group," said the lady as she firmly shook Tolya by the hand. Her fur coat was slightly open, and from its depths came forth the aromas of a sweet, overpowering perfume and a large warm bosom.

Von Steinbock shuddered slightly from an unexpectedly sharp upsurge of sexual desire. This did not pass unnoticed. The lady gave a barely perceptible smile. "All will be well," she said with quite unusual warmth. "I have discussed things and made inquiries. My husband . . ."

Talk of the devil . . . Tolya did not have time to hear the end of her hopeful remarks, because at that moment a black Emka with blinds on the windows rolled up to the building, exactly like that car of shame in which his mother had been brought to fetch him when she was arrested. Perhaps it was the same one? Out of it came three solidly built officers, who leaped over the mound of frozen, shoveled snow along the sidewalk, laden with bottles of brandy and champagne. The first one, with colonel's epaulettes, shouted cheerfully, "Paulina, how are things on the food front? The whole regiment's here!"

The officers drew Paulina Ignatievna toward the porch with much laughter, loud shouting, and even a certain element of humor as they each played the role of being her page. There was a slight scrimmage in the doorway, Paulina Ignatievna turned around, and Tolya heard her say to her husband, "That poor boy . . ."

All three officers looked at Tolya and one of them bent down to Paulina Ignatievna's ear, his teeth and the whites of his eyes gleaming. It was Cheptsov. Tolya guessed at once what was being said to the glittering lady, and his guess was confirmed.

"Oh, for heaven's sake, Cheptsov!" The lady waved her glove at him. "Go on, go inside!"

The officers squeezed through the door and she waved goodbye to Tolya with the same glove, managing to convey a slight but detectable hint of flirtatiousness. "Be sure to come and see me in school. Tomorrow. Don't forget. I'll be expecting you."

The door closed.

"Damn State Security bitch," Tolya whispered, quivering with anger.

High society! Aristocratic manners! Expert on the works of Stalin! And he had almost given in to her, had weakened, had suddenly been hotly aware of what prospects might be opening up for him: plush curtains, cream-colored night-lights. I don't need your sympathy, you Gulys, Cheptsovs, and Lyghers! I am a wolf, a wolf's cub. It's true – the apple *doesn't* fall far from the apple tree, and the son *is* answerable for his father!

The Lyghers . . . Yes, yes, he remembered now. She was the wife of Colonel Lygher; Philip Yegorovich had once spoken of her in tones of respect. But then he spoke of all his patients with respect, as though sickness and physical complaints in themselves gave people the right to be respected. He wondered what that bitch had complained of.

But perhaps sickness really does confer the right to respect? Perhaps that is how a believing Christian should behave – forgive everyone, never seek vengeance? OK, so be it; but does a Christian have the right to feel contempt?

What is contempt? Is it a superior emotion? Is it spiritual or biological? Did Jesus feel contempt for his executioners? Did he really feel only love for them? "Father forgive them, for they know not what they do." We can never fully attain Jesus' perfection, but then from the standpoint of our ordinary, everyday logic, doesn't contempt mean revenge? Isn't there violence in contempt?

Suddenly, as often happens in Magadan, it started to snow hard, so hard that all the lights were blotted out. Tolya was now walking head down against the snowfall. He did not particularly notice the change in the weather – his head was too full of the avenging Ringo Kid and the all-forgiving Christ.

After Martin had read him the Gospel according to St. Matthew, Tolya often imagined to himself the scene of Christ's crucifixion. They were driving a huge rusty nail through His hand, so that He could no longer take His hand away from the crosspiece. Now they were driving one through His other hand – how easily a nail goes through human flesh! – and now He could never loosen Himself from that curious structure. Just to be on the safe side they were tying his feet to the upright – it's more secure that way. Totally helpless, totally in the executioners'' power. Who invented crucifixion? Whose brain first conceived the idea? No wild beast could have thought of it. Wild beasts only kill their enemies, but never gloat over their slow death. The urge to gloat over the destruction of a victim is a purely human characteristic. Yet there are also other purely human qualities – compassion, for instance. Cruel mockery and compassion – both coexist in man, but not in animals.

The sun overhead. Wounds crawling with flies. No way of getting loose from the cross. Golgotha, a hillock of clay crackling in the heat of the sun. Somewhere nearby is the city garbage dump. He is always painted with a cloth around His loins, but almost certainly there was no loincloth and the guards mocked His nakedness. "They know not what they do." Was that all? Was there no contempt? Is contempt a human quality? The cross is a crude representation of a man flying. What is this strange creature – man?

At the crossroads there came such a violent flurry of snow that Tolya was actually spun around by its force. The streetlamp above him swung wildly. In its uncertain, flickering beams Tolya could just make out a group of citizens, hunched up as they slowly made their way down the middle of the street. How strange they looked, that party of both sexes in a blizzard, amid the hutted, barbed-wire desolation of Magadan! Felt fedoras, fox-fur boas, trench coats with patch pockets, high-heeled shoes. Behind the group trudged a squat, burly "man with a gun." A newcomer would have been amazed at this encounter in a blizzard, but Tolya was not in the least surprised; he had often met such people. They were convict actors being escorted to do a show in the Palace of Culture.

Tolya slogged his way back to the Third Medical Complex, back to their room, where in the absence of any women it was smelling more and more of the "abomination of desolation." Aunt Varya had also been arrested. Rumors were going around that all those who had served out their sentences under Article 58 of the Criminal Code were being rearrested. They would not be charged with any new offenses; Martin knew this for certain from his patients. Instead, they would simply be arrested again on the same charges that had been made against them in 1937 and for which they had already served their ten years. On what grounds? Decision of the appropriate authorities, that was the only answer.

Tolya had already thrown the jurisdiction of all "appropriate" and "supreme" authorities into the trash can, along with his Komsomol badge, on that night not long ago. All supreme authority, that is, with the exception of the Highest of All. Stalin, among whose many honorifics was the appellation "Best Friend of All Soviet Athletes," still held a certain place in his heart.

Sanya Gurchenko used to say, "He's the biggest swine of all. He should be hanged by his balls."

Martin had declared with calm conviction, "Hitler and Stalin are two incarnations of the Antichrist."

In Tolya's mind, the great leader was somehow split in two. There was the generalissimo in full-dress uniform, the standard-bearer of peace in his big epaulettes, enough medals to make a coat of chain mail, sculpted in bronze, granite, and plaster of Paris – this Stalin was, perhaps, the "biggest swine of all" and the "incarnation of the Antichrist." The other was a kindly uncle with a pipe, with eyes screwed up in a look of cunning, "with the head of a scholar in the garb of a simple soldier," this Stalin, of course, knew nothing about the evil deeds ascribed to him. He wanted to do good for people, he lowered prices every year, he was to be seen bent over a map of the massive system of windbreaks against erosion, formed by planting long rows of trees at carefully selected locations: "We shall conquer nature!" he would say in his Georgian accent. The generals were deceiving him about the true state of affairs in the country! If only he would come to Kolyma and see for himself! But he would never come to Kolyma.

And I'm never going back to school, never going into a classroom with its portrait of Marshal Beriya. I'll never accept the charity of any of the Magadan colonels' wives. I'll become a hobo, an electrician, a miner, a fisherman. After all, there are plenty of wide open spaces in the Soviet Union where there isn't any barbed wire! Later, perhaps, I'll acquire an education: Perhaps I'll become a doctor, or a math professor, or a sculptor, or a musician. Or maybe I won't get an education at all and just become a nobody. One thing is clear, though – I will be a free man and I will always write poetry. I'll write poems and I won't show them to anyone. I'll just carry them around with me in a pillowcase, like Velemir Khlebnikov, the futurist poet. One day Lyudka, who will marry Ryba and become a colonel's wife, will meet an exhausted tramp in a leather jacket, and then she will shudder and think bitterly, What a little fool I was!

Preoccupied with these inner debates and struggles, Tolya von Steinbock was passing through the shady quarter of Magadan known as Shanghai when he was suddenly faced with a column of steam spiraling up into the air and noticed a dim light streaming out around his feet. Stepping aside, he realized that he had almost tripped over the cover of an underground steam-heating conduit, that same "Crimea" whose discovery had so surprised him once before. This time he could see nothing but steam as he peered through the crack between the manhole cover and the ground, although bursts of laughter could be heard issuing from that maelstrom of steam. He was just about to walk away when the cover suddenly creaked, an arm appeared, and a very familiar voice shouted, "So long, you subterranean devils!"

A second later, Sanya Gurchenko, cheerful, nimble, and strong, arose in front of Tolya. "Who's this I see? Where've you been, Tolya?"

"At the movies. I went to see the Ringo Kid."

"Aha!" Sanya exclaimed. "He's a great guy, the Ringo Kid! I could do with a couple of dozen of his sort here. We'd soon shake this place up!"

Tolya was amazed at the parallel with his own thoughts. "You're like him yourself, Sanya. You're the Ringo Kid of Magadan."

"You flatter me." Gurchenko put his arm around Tolya's shoulders. "I'm not as good a shot as he is. Still, I'm not bad with a machine gun. It's great fun, you know, when machine guns start to chatter! Once three of us wiped out a whole *Sonderkommando* of the SS. And d'you know why? Because we were having more fun than they and we could use our automatic weapons better than they!" He looked into Tolya's face. "Say, how are you making out? Have the bastards given you permission to see your mother?"

"No."

"Ah, the bastards, the filthy pigs, the sons of whores, the stinking crab lice," Gurchenko swore pleasurably, adding, "Shit!"

"Listen, *Kamerad*," he said. "D'you have any chow at home?"

"Martin brings it. There's quite enough." Tolya lit a cigarette and glanced sideways at Gurchenko. "Sanya, what were you doing . . . down there in the 'Crimea?' "

"A pal of mine lives there," Gurchenko said with a grin. "I go there because it's like going to a club. And it's much more interesting than your shitty Palace of Culture. It's a pity, though, that the women are doing their washing down there today and you can't breathe because of the steam."

"Sanya, I suppose you couldn't take me down there, could you?"

"Sure, let's go now if you like," said Gurchenko, but suddenly checked himself and added with embarrassment, "Still, Tolya, it's not a good idea for kids under sixteen to go there . . ."

"But I'm way past seventeen!"

Gurchenko still hesitated, thinking it over. As he took a drag of his cigarette, the red glow lit up his eyes, which were examining Von Steinbock with ironic approval.

"*Gut!*" he said finally. "Let's drop down the hole. Only stick close to me at all times."

He raised the cover and lowered himself into the steaming abyss. Tolya followed him. They found themselves on a strongly built wooden staircase, rather like a ship's companionway. Ten steps down. Not a glimmer to be seen. After the frosty cold above, they were enveloped in damp heat. The stairs came to an end, and Tolya could see that they were standing on a large, thick pipe. The pipe was so hot that it burned him even through the thick soles of his American shoes, yet two figures were sitting on it in nothing but their underwear.

His eyes were by now a little accustomed to the gloom, and Tolya noticed that one of the figures looked like a real prerevolutionary professor, a type very familiar from books: a little Menshevik-style pointed beard and steel-rimmed pince-nez. The "professor" was scratching his chest underneath a prison shirt of coarse cotton and at the same time reading a thick, handsome-looking book with evident pleasure. How on earth could he read the print in all that steam?

"So you came back, Alexander Georgievich? Welcome again," the Professor said to Sanya in a kindly voice. "Pantagruel and I had just decided to move up higher and breathe some fresh air."

The man called Pantagruel was sitting a little distance away and could just be vaguely distinguished as a round, pinkish shape dressed in a sleeveless navy undershirt.

"Hey, Panta, still counting lice?" Sanya shouted to him.

"Uh-huh," Pantagruel replied. "I've squashed sixteen today, and Nikolai Selyodkin's only gotten seven."

"Have you put them somewhere so that your figure can be checked out?" Gurchenko asked with businesslike professionalism.

"Sure. We've put them on a loaf of white bread. Nikolai Selyodkin complains that his lice grip on tighter and that's why they're harder to catch, but I tell him it makes no difference – an insect is an insect."

"Excuse me, young man, but have you come to take up residence here?" the "professor" asked Tolya.

"He's a visitor," Sanya explained. "Friend of mine. What are you reading, Doctor?"

"Apuleius. Our great leader Lenin would have said, 'An enormously entertaining little booklet!' "

Sanya and Tolya walked down the steep slope until they came to a brick wall. They moved sideways to where there was an opening, beyond which Tolya could see what looked like a spacious cave. Steam-heating pipes snaked along the walls of the cave, and in the gaps and recesses around them he could just make out swarms of people. There were no fewer than five tiers, and at the farthest end, where a jet of steam was spurting from a pipe, a squealing bunch of sweating women was busy doing laundry.

Suddenly, through the general hum of voices, right under Tolya's feet, two male voices cut the air, one a hoarse bass and the other a cracked falsetto.

"You filthy pig, you counterrevolutionary, fuck off before I stick you one between the ribs so you won't see the sun again in a month of Sundays!" screamed the falsetto, gasping for breath in the humid air. "Fuck off, you lousy political, or give me back my packet of tea!"

"Firstly, don't you dare call me a counterrevolutionary, you ugly little crook!" replied the bass with a hoarse laugh. "And don't think you can scare the shit out of me. I've seen plenty of your sort. I swung a shovel digging the Volkhov Canal, I helped build up the country's industry, while you are just an abscess in the body of society!"

"Cocksucker, lump of horseshit, I'll slit you wide open with this file!" said the falsetto in a choked voice.

They started brawling. Sanya jumped into the steam, and Tolya, without a moment's thought, followed him.

In an alcove, built out of planks and cardboard, two men were rolling around, locked in a struggle, gasping and grunting. Sanya lunged forward, and with a practiced motion – no doubt a trick learned at unarmed combat in the army – he knocked a sharpened file out of one of the protagonists' hands. The two enemies let go of each other and looked at Gurchenko, breathing hard: a flabby man with curly black hair and a skinny, ash-blond youth who might have been the mascot of a soccer team.

"Now, now, boys!" Sanya shook his head, then shouted to someone down below, "Eagle Owl, a couple of guys on the fifth have been breaking the rules!"

"Just think for a moment, Sanya," boomed the man with the curly black hair. "Fancy him accusing me of such absurd things! There was a time when I had three thousand louts like young Spike here under my command!"

"Call me a lout if you like, but you took it!" whined the blond boy. "I don't care if I never get out of this place alive, Comrade Gurchenko, but Top Brass pinched my two packets of second-grade Georgian tea!"

"There they are. Your packets are lying over there in the corner," said Top Brass contemptuously but with a tremor in his voice. "You kicked them over there with your own dirty feet."

Spike dove into the corner and at once reemerged with two packets of tea. His features now shone with such radiant happiness that he might have found Aladdin's magic lamp instead of tea.

"There they are, my lovely little packets! Say, Top Brass, you don't really mind me trying to sharpen my file on you, do you? Come on, let's go! Let's brew some *chifir!* Hey, Sanya, quit standing around there like you didn't belong! Squat down!"

"Sit down, Sanya, and you too, comrade." Top Brass moved over to make room on his bunk and, lowering his voice, added, "I despise criminal prisoners. I always beat up crooks when I get the chance. That's my principle: Bash them. Wherever I was, they were scared of me – at Khatanga, in Seimchan, in transit. Me, steal his tea? I who was once –" He broke off in a fit of coughing.

Sanya and Tolya crawled into the alcove. Spike was already at work pumping up the Primus stove to boil the tea – two whole packets in an old tin can that had once held stewed pork. This was the first time that Tolya had seen *chifir* made, the famous narcotic drink that his classmates used to talk about with bated breath in the men's room.

Chifir intrigued schoolboys even more than hard liquor or cigarettes. It was said to induce such hallucinations that you imagined yourself God knows where – in Paris or the Himalayas, if not in the very lushest regions of paradise itself.

"How do all these people get here, Sanya?" asked Tolya. "It's a mystery to me. Surely the bosses at the top know about these heating tunnels, don't they?"

"Of course they know, but they turn a blind eye to them. Where else are people to go? When a con finishes his sentence, the sea may be frozen up for another five months before ships can sail again to take him back home. There's no room in hostels or dormitories. What am I to do, sir? Freeze to death in a ditch? OK, OK, you know where you can go – shove off and find a place in the 'Crimea'! Apart from the 'Crimea' there are at least six more of these tunnels, most of them named after warm places in the south. There's 'Odessa,' 'Alupka,' 'Baku,' and three more without names. Everyone in the Kolyma camps knows about these hotels. And there are lots of them who just won't budge once they get in here. Wild horses couldn't drag them away. They live here for a few years and completely forget about the 'mainland.' No ex-con can ever be sure that he can get fixed up on the 'mainland' as comfortably as he can here – it's warm and you'll never starve. Even children are born here, Tolya. When the steam clears a little, you'll be able to see children and animals down below."

From far down the tunnel came the sound of a sweet voice, coming closer as it sang an aria from some operetta,

> . . . there's a little bit of devil in everyone,
> But the power of women's charms
> Melts your heart when in her arms . . .

On the other side of the tunnel Tolya could see a creature wearing an army tunic, the front bulging with a large bust, and with a large bulbous ass in a pair of quilted pants. There was a glimpse of a white face and bright red lips.

"Shit! Piss off, Valka!" Gurchenko spat.

"Gurchenko, Gurchenko, you're a horrid boy," said the creature coquettishly, and laid a huge manicured paw on Sanya's knee.

Sanya pushed the paw away with disgust and gave the singer a kick in the ass. The creature faded away in a burst of hysterical laughter.

"That's Valka Pshonka," Sanya explained. "Queer. Sticks a couple of enema bulbs inside the tunic and a pillow up his pants."

"What for?" Tolya asked in amazement. "What's the point, Sanya? And what's 'queer?' "

"Well, queer . . ." Sanya grinned. "Well, they don't want women . . ." He stopped, embarrassed, and glanced sideways at Tolya. "OK, kid, you don't need to know everything at once. I don't suppose you know much about women either, do you? My only advice to you is, keep away from those guys. They play on their team, we play on ours. And women, Tolya, are the better half of freedom-loving mankind."

Meanwhile the better half had finished doing the laundry, the cloud of steam was thinning out, and visibility in the "Crimea" had improved. Tolya could see the women attacking Valka Pshonka when he (or she) tried to wash his revolting bra in their washtubs. They battered him with rolling pins, tore his tunic, and yanked out the enema bulbs: "Now we'll pull off your prick, then you *will* be a woman!" The transvestite's sobbing features were occasionally visible with makeup smeared over his face and forehead.

Into the crowd waded the president, or "godfather," of the "Crimea," nicknamed Eagle Owl. He looked like the eighteenth-century rebel Emelyan Pugachov – black hair in a mop cut, a short beard, broad shoulders in a tight cream-colored pajama top fastened with loops of plaited braid. Eagle Owl mercilessly thrashed the women, but with the flat of his hand and without hurting them much. The women squealed and shook their fists at the "godfather," though not daring to hit him – he wielded great authority.

Finally, the hubbub in the tunnel died down, and Tolya actually saw some children. On the lowest level, a little boy was pedaling back and forth on a tricycle. Eagle Owl climbed wearily up a ladder, and when he reached their "alcove," he said quietly to Spike, who was busy with the Primus stove, "If you sharpen another file, you shithead, we'll chuck you out of here."

The "godfather's" slightly bleary eyes fixed their gaze on Tolya and turned to Gurchenko with a questioning look.

"This is Tolya von Steinbock," said Sanya. "His mother was arrested the other day. You know Tanya, don't you? Martin's wife."

Eagle Owl stared at Tolya for several seconds in silence and then winked at him with both eyes at once. "Want some chow, Von?"

"Thanks, I'm not hungry," Tolya muttered.

"Come down below, Sanya," Eagle Owl then said, apparently losing all interest in Tolya. "Lenka tells me Engineer is coming."

"No! Seriously?" Gurchenko seemed delighted by this news. "That's great!" He jumped up and banged his head on the bunk above, but did not even notice it.

A second later Sanya and Eagle Owl had climbed down and disappeared behind rows of wash strung up to dry. Tolya stayed in the "alcove" with Spike and Top Brass. The latter was reading in the local newspaper, the *Pacific Star,* an article about the progress in retaining snow for irrigation purposes in the Amur region, and with a serious expression was underlining various passages in red pencil, including whole paragraphs of speeches made by Party leaders.

"By the way," he suddenly announced to no one in particular, "before the tragic mistake made by the security forces when they arrested me, I occupied a very senior post in my hometown, and now I intend to start all over again from zero. It's never too late if you know the system and the style of leadership. It may be behind a counter, it may be in a small workshop – the great thing is to make a start."

"Bullshit! You, Top Brass, behind a counter! Like hell!" said Spike in a querulous voice, weeping either from fraternal emotion or from the gas given off by the Primus stove. "You and I are going to shove off to Georgia and buy you a Party membership card on the black market in Telavi. My pals tell me that in Georgia they can fix you up with a Party card for cash. I'm on the level, Top Brass! Don't be offended! On the Telavi black market you can buy any piece of paper you need to start a new life."

"Ready!" Spike suddenly shouted with excitement and took the canful of bubbling *chifir* off the Primus. "OK, Von, since you're the guest you can try it first. Go on, help yourself."

Tolya stared at the can in holy terror. Boundless prospects, like the dream visions he experienced when he had diphtheria, opened up before him. What vast spaces! What a labyrinth of mirrors! There, in the corridors of infinity, stood Von, the hardened *chifir*-drinker and

longtime inhabitant of the "Crimea," legs planted wide and fists clenched behind his back.

"What are you waiting for, Von? Drink up!"

The corrupt little eye of a senior apparatchik peeped out from behind
the newspaper as Top Brass exchanged winks with Spike.

The *chifir* was simultaneously hot, viscous, sweet, and bitter.
Suddenly Tolya felt a spasm in his throat and his head began to spin.
Spike caught the can.

Then the mirror-lined diphtheria wards parted and I found myself
in a delightfully comfortable and warm place, a fabulous cave. Mischievous, mysteriously fascinating sorcery was taking place all around. My
faithful friends were struggling comically, like two clumsy bear cubs,
over the can full of the magic drink. While they were fighting, I
took another sip. Everything was wonderful, and down below joyous
mysteries were awaiting me. Smoothly and rhythmically, like an ante-
lope in an animated film, I descended from the fifth level and laid my
weightless, curly, golden head upon the plump legs of a sleeping
goddess, perhaps Aphrodite herself. As my head lay on these legs I
observed the approach of another goddess, this time Artemis, who
was, as is proper for a huntress, somewhat muscular and scrawny. But
gorgeous! Who can deny the attraction of Artemis, huntress of the
forest? She urges on her hounds – sic 'em, Panther, go Puffball! – and
pulls me by the hands into her hunter's cabin of fir branches.

"Hey, kiddo, you high on *chifir*?"

Useless question. One of Artemis's black locks falls over her blue
eye. My name's Lenka. Nonsense! How moist you are, o lips of
Artemis! What greedy, delicious lips! A breeze rustles. A curtain?
Nonsense! A puff of Mediterranean wind. Don't be afraid, you little
fool, no one can see us. Where are you hiding it? Nonsense! The
youths of Hellas are afraid of nothing! Take it if you need it, it's all I
have, Artemis! Silly boy, that's all I need. Nonsense, Artemis! Forgive
me, but you're talking nonsense. Where is your quiver, your arrows,
where are the magic hounds Panther and Puffball, the terror of giants?
What, Artemis, are you mounting astride me? Do you covet the laurels
of the Amazons? You're a brave rider, Artemis, but that crooked grin
doesn't suit you. Lenka's my name, Lenka. What are you muttering
about, you little fool? Show it to me, let me stroke it, the dear little
thing.

Three people crawled into Artemis's hideaway – Emelyan Pugachov,
the Ringo Kid, and the Enemy of the People. There was no mistaking

the last: a dark gray suit with neatly pressed lapels, tie, vest, an English spy's moustache, and cold eyes, a typical enemy of the people.

"I spotted you, Enemy of the People! But don't worry, I'm by origin an enemy of the people myself. I love my Russian people and its enemies. The apple doesn't fall far from the apple tree. In the period of reconstruction, cadres are all-important. Come in and don't be embarrassed, Emelyan, and you, Ringo, and you, my dear Enemy of the People. Welcome to the grotto of Artemis. Sincerely yours, Anatoly von Steinbock, esquire."

Gurchenko, Eagle Owl, and Engineer transferred their gaze from Lenka-Paprika to the boy Von Steinbock, who was lolling on a ragged blanket in a corner of Lenka's pad, the fly of his pants still open.

"I warn you, Lenka, you will come to a sticky end if you carry on like this," said Eagle Owl with ill-concealed exasperation.

Paprika bared her teeth in a crooked smile.

"What did I do? It was Spike who gave him the *chifir*."

"What were you doing with him?"

"What I was doing doesn't matter. I'm clean. I had a negative test yesterday – I'm not one of your syphilitics."

"I'll bite your nose off," the mighty Eagle Owl threatened her, but in a tired voice that held no ill will.

Lenka's bandit charms had no effect on Sanya. He simply gave her a resounding slap on the face and asked, "You deserved that, didn't you?"

Lenka-Paprika took no offense at the slap in the face, and only smiled over her bony shoulder at Sanya with her eyes. She straightened the pillow under Tolya's head as he lay there mumbling beatifically, and lit a hand-rolled cigarette, another not entirely harmless habit.

"Now, listen, children of the underground . . ."

With an unpleasant smirk on his face, Engineer glanced around at those present. Tolya was not altogether wrong in calling him Enemy of the People. He was genuinely at odds with the Soviet people, and throughout his conscious life he had fought actively and efficiently against that people, that is to say against the "bosses" beloved of the people and against the system of unanimity so loved by the people. Among the Kolyma prison population there actually were people, incredible as it might seem, who had taken part in real conspiracies and oppositional groups and not in the fictitious ones invented by State Security. These extremely rare individuals managed, as a rule, to adapt to prison life far better than members of the countless army of "innocent sufferers."

"Now listen, children of the underground," Engineer began in a repellent voice. "You must play out your operatic dramas without me. I have only fifteen minutes to spare. I doubt if the cause will be greatly served if a police raid nabs the deputy chief engineer of the port of Nagaevo in a heating tunnel, along with the crooks and prostitutes. Let's get straight to business. We have established that when the ship has finished unloading, the crew of the *Felix* starts hitting the bottle and the security on board gets noticeably weaker. The problem is as follows: Do we take the ship from the pier, or do we sneak on board and take her over once she's at sea? By the way, are you sure that boy's asleep?"

"The kid's sound asleep." Lenka stroked Tolya's hair.

I may or may not have been asleep, but I saw something, maybe in my sleep, maybe while awake. I was riding on something. For some reason I was lying at the bottom of a glass wall behind which a bunch of strange and terrible people were hatching a daring plot to hijack the steamship *Felix Dzerzhinsky* and escape to America.

As I looked around in anguish at my Motherland, I saw a sun-baked asphalt yard and a white wall, past which was walking a red-haired woman in a long, vividly colored Russian peasant's dress. I was standing in the shade of an acacia and could sense the nearby waves slapping wearily against the concrete seafront. The sea was tired from its ceaseless raids on the shore; the cypresses were tired of photosynthesis and could barely move their exhausted tops. I had never been here before, but I knew this was my own, tired country. Everything around me was weary, and only this woman was fully alive and active as she walked briskly over the burning-hot asphalt, carelessly tossing her auburn hair as she went, kicking little stones out of her sandals, wrinkling her nose, and smiling boldly, challengingly, and aggressively at someone invisible; it might have been to me and she might have been Alisa . . .

One day I will dream of her hip lying under my hand.

It should be explained that the convict ship bearing the proud name of Felix Dzerzhinsky, founder of the Soviet secret police, had previously been a Dutch cable-laying vessel and had peacefully laid cables across the Atlantic until our brothers in class, the German Nazis, seized her as a prize. Then either Churchill or Truman – or it may have been Marshal Badoglio for all I know – handed her over as part of the spoils of war to our whiskered cockroach in exchange for a herd of Don Cossack horses. Since the cockroach's chief concern was how to cope with prisoners, the Dutch cable layer became a prison-transport named after a renegade Pole.

Whether in my sleep or on a chessboard, or on sandy slopes of the pine forests of childhood, so softly lit up by the light of a gentle dawn, or perhaps amid the damp ferns and molehills in front of me, there was revealed the plan of the conspirators, the enemies of our country, the enemies of the people and of the Directorate of the Northeastern Corrective Labor Camps.

They have weapons. They are going to put them to use. Instead of landing in their favorite port of Vanino, the peaceful, unsuspecting prison guards are going to find themselves in Yokohama or San Francisco, and there, instead of their dear, obedient convicts, they will be met by the aggressive local military intoxicated with Coca-Cola, poisonous chewing gum, and ear-splitting jazz music.

I won't go. I have very many bonds with my native country. More than you think, Captain Cheptsov. Yes, my country, embodied by two old women, one from Ryazan, the other from Vyatka, standing on a porch on a July night of 1937 and wailing at the top of their voices as they watched a girl, a Komsomol and a member of the security forces, bundle me into an Emka – me, the five-year-old offspring of enemies of my country, in other words, my parents. Of course, of course, Captain, the Emka with blinds on its windows is my country too!

The Motherland scraped its bare branches against the windows of the state orphanage for children of enemies of the people. Oh, how gray, how damp is the sky of my native country!

She conducts physicals in the medical room of the local military commandant's office. Stand up with your back to me! Bend down! Strain! My Motherland doesn't like it when a lump appears out of the back passageway. Like any whore, she prefers young soldiers without hemorrhoids.

Sooner or later, on a mysterious night I shall lie down in bed with my Motherland and run my hand over the curve of her hip and put my hand on her breasts, and she will touch my stomach with hers, she will whisper that she loves me and ask me to love her in return.

The Motherland and I will celebrate my twentieth birthday, my thirtieth . . . She will call me at night to her corrupt and beautiful nighttime cities, to the capital she herself has defiled; she will whistle in my ears tunes of nostalgia for other countries. A drunken cosmic sky, a history full of gallows and drumbeats, my Jewish Russia, my cardboard, my plywood and red calico socialism, so dear and so nauseating.

My Motherland had decided to hijack a piece of her own floating territory, the Dutch cable layer, the convict-carrying ship *Felix*. The heirs of my country, runaways, deserters, free men, *chifir* drinkers, descendants of Pugachov, Russian cowboys, had hatched this audacious plot!

My Motherland is not audacious. She may be cruel, but she is meek. She breathes through her mouth because she has adenoids and nostrils blocked by Stalinism, and her forehead, beautiful as the dome of the Monastery of the Trinity, is covered in pimples. My Motherland is going to engage in a life-and-death struggle on the ship's deck. My Motherland wants to run away from herself to America.

I don't want to run away! I toss from side to side, from the past into the future. Don't carry me away, don't carry me away to America!

Tolya awoke when a ray of morning sunlight touched his face. The ray came from above, from the manhole; dust was now floating peacefully in it as though the setting were a country house. Along with the sunlight, a peaceful morning conversation also penetrated Tolya's consciousness.

"They say that Stalin has decided to sell Kolyma to Averell Harriman," said the nearby voice of Pantagruel.

"With the people or without them?" another asked with lively interest, no doubt the voice of his perpetual rival, Nikolai Selyodkin.

"With the people, of course. So keep on squashing your lice, Nikolai. In America they disinfect lousy people with electricity."

"The Declaration of the Rights of Man is inscribed on the banners of Jefferson and Lincoln!" said the Professor solemnly but not too seriously.

"The rights of man, but not of convicts!" put in Lenka-Paprika. "In America even prostitutes are treated as human beings, and men who jerk off are used for manure."

The authoritative bass voice of Top Brass intervened. "Stalin and H. G. Wells came to an agreement: Kolyma will be handed over without the people. The ground must be cleared for private enterprise, because Soviet people are not adapted to capitalism."

Tolya found himself lying on a torn, ragged blanket. On the same blanket, Sanya Gurchenko slept the marvelous undisturbed sleep of youth. Beside him was Lenka. She was smoking, with one hand holding a cigarette to her mouth and the other stroking Sanya's curls. Sanya's head was lying on her stomach.

At the feet of this couple sprawled the disheveled Engineer, curled up in an uncomfortable position. Not a trace remained of his English elegance: His tie was unknotted, his jacket was stained with white slime, his pants were bunched up, showing a pair of elastic garters and a rolled-down silk sock. Alongside his bare, unpleasantly white leg lay a small hypodermic syringe and several broken ampules.

Eagle Owl was sitting, leaning against the wall. With his hands clasped around his knees and breathing regularly, he was asleep with open eyes. Although his eyes were open, the pupils had rolled up and disappeared beneath his eye sockets, giving Eagle Owl's head the look of an ancient sculpture.

Meanwhile, on the other side of the blinds, the inhabitants of the heating tunnel were peacefully eating breakfast and discussing the political prospects of Kolyma.

Tolya suddenly had a feeling that there was nothing at all under the blanket on which he was lying – nothing but a vast expanse of air. There was no earth, only an abyss. To convince himself of the solidity of existence he had to bang it with his heel.

It looked as if Engineer was dangerously ill, apparently with a heart attack. The shots had not done him much good, as could be seen from his blue lips covered in dried spittle and the blue tinge of his nostrils. Sanya must be woken up and made to help.

"Look, Lenka, Engineer looks real bad."

"You awake, kid?" Without moving, Lenka looked at him and gave a throaty laugh. "How's your little dingdong? Doesn't hurt, does it?"

"Thanks, I'm OK, Lenka."

"And I thank you, comrade student, for getting my name right. Yesterday you kept calling me Artemis, as though I was an Armenian."

"But, Lenka, look at Engineer – he's in a bad way."

"Not to worry," She waved her cigarette. "The guy was shooting up just a bit more than he should have. He'll sleep it off. You cold, kid? Snuggle up closer to us."

Suddenly the curtain was wrenched aside and Tolya saw Martin's face in front of him, with a look of near-fury – his thin lips pressed together, his eyes burning beneath the brim of his hard hat. Tolya had never even imagined that Martin could look like this.

"You!" Martin shouted, raising a large fist. "You!" The fist unclenched, and his hand hung down in despair. "You will drive me to the grave, Anatoly! And you help to kill your mother too!"

When he was excited, he spoke Russian very badly, as though he had just come off the farm in his native Crimea, as though he had not spent eighteen years in the melting pot of Soviet, and therefore Russian, prison camps.

"I haven't done anything. I just came here by chance . . ." mumbled Tolya, jumping up, pulling on his pants, fighting against headache and nausea, looking for his cap and mittens.

Martin squatted down and made a careful examination of the broken ampules. Then he took Engineer's pulse and looked sternly at Lenka.

"Nothing happened, Philip Yegorych." In a tearful voice she began making excuses like a naughty little girl. "The guys were shooting up, but the kid was already asleep by then. He only drank tea, just tea . . ."

Gurchenko opened his eyes and immediately, catching sight of Martin, shook himself and sat up.

"You must come and see me, Sanya," Martin said to him firmly in German. "This can't go on. It's a sin, a grave sin."

"*Ich verstehe.*" Sanya hung his head. "*Jawohl,* Philip Yegorych."

Eagle Owl and Engineer did not wake up. Tolya and Martin clambered out of Lenka's "den" and began to climb up to the surface.

Tolya was dazzled by the sunlight on the glittering expanse of white. Fresh snow covered the roofs and hilltops, everything around was white and blue, and the only two blobs of different color on the whole panorama were the red flag above the Dalstroy headquarters building and the yellowish-brown smoke coming from the chimney of the town's centralized heating plant.

"It's easy to paint pictures like this," Tolya said with a giggle. He still could not rid himself of the feeling that last night he had been somewhere on the edge of the future, and this strange morning mood of humor was, so to speak, a voice from the future.

"What? What did you say?" Martin turned toward him, and froze in a half-turned attitude on the path between the banks of shoveled snow.

"I was saying that no doubt God found it quite easy to paint a picture like this – blue sky, white snow, a red flag, and yellowish-brown smoke."

"What were Engineer, Eagle Owl, and Sanya talking about yesterday?" asked Martin in a low voice.

"I don't remember. I was asleep. Or maybe I wasn't asleep. Perhaps I was making a journey. I was far away."

"Were they talking about a steamer? About the *Felix Dzerzhinsky*?"

"Yes!" Tolya recalled it all with excitement. "They were planning to hijack the steamer and escape to America! They were such bold, desperate people! I simply –"

"Look behind you, Tolya," said Martin quietly.

Tolya immediately realized that something terrible had happened. He very much wanted not to look around, but he couldn't help it. Don't look around, keep on walking, enjoying the blue of the sky. If you look around, another gaping hole will be torn in your life, in your shining blue sky, a terrible gap will open up in God's simple, sunlit picture. To keep walking along the path without looking around, though, meant being a traitor. There's nothing you can do, but even so, if you look around, at least you won't be a traitor. Tolya slowly turned around.

Over the bumpy wheel tracks in the snow, not yet driven over since last night's snowfall, a canvas-covered army truck was crawling along slowly. It stopped at the place from which they had just emerged, the manhole cover into the heating tunnel. A couple of dozen soldiers wearing sheepskin jerkins and armed with submachine guns jumped out of the truck into the snow. Without haste, they surrounded the manhole cover. A black Emka, skidding, its engine racing, drove up to the scene and disgorged the leading actors. One of them was wearing a familiar bulky overcoat with a lambskin collar and a lambskin hat with leather top: the back of his bull-like neck was shaved, and he held a pistol in his fist. He raised the wooden cover and gestured to the soldiers with his pistol: "Get down there!" The soldiers climbed down the hole slowly, like badly functioning robots. All the men taking part in the raid looked clumsy, sluggish, and slightly ridiculous, but the guns in their hands were handy, purposeful, and modern. No doubt the man who designed them had a feel for guns.

"Someone must have informed on them," said Martin. "They're done for. Sanya's done for. Now let's go and don't turn around anymore."

They walked for a long time along the path through the snow. Martin was expecting to hear shots and the sounds of a struggle, but it was quiet except for a few vague shouts, something like "ands . . . ind . . . ack!"

At last they reached the civilized part of town, with its frozen, raised wooden sidewalks that creaked underfoot. Across the street shone broad and clear, like the whole phony facade of Kolyma socialism, the big windows of the Magadan High School, the favorite creation of General Nikishov.

"Now go and *take* that algebra test," said Martin. "Go on, Tolya, my boy. You must take that test. Go and solve those problems."

Tolya turned toward the school. What a hole gaped before him!

What a jagged patch torn out of God's picture! How could he face that torn patch and go on living?

Martin made the sign of the cross over him. "Your mother will soon be let out of prison. She has been sentenced to permanent exile in Magadan. I asked them; they promised. And they've kept their promise. Permanent exile – at least it's tolerable . . ."

I LOVE RACING AROUND MOSCOW AT NIGHT

thought Malkolmov. When you sit alongside the driver in a minibus you sometimes have the feeling that you're not driving but flying, floating, or gliding, depending on the speed. The nocturnal city rolls away beneath you – the well-worn asphalt pavement, the "stop" lines, dotted and solid, the directional arrows, and the zebra-type pedestrian crossings. The specially equipped Volkswagen, complete with siren and revolving violet-colored beacon on the roof, never waits for the green light. It eases out of the line of vehicles, slowly approaches the intersection, and then, having switched on the siren, surges forward. No police officer ever stops the van marked RESUSCITATION in big red letters.

The Boulevard Ring from Solyanka to Trubnaya Square is like a roller coaster. A steep climb up to Yauza Boulevard, across Pokrovka and Kirovskaya, a slight drop followed by a little rise up to Sretenka Street, and then a steep drop down to Trubnaya Square. How charming and strange it all is here! What's strange about it? you will say. What is strange is that the line of those roofs thrills me even now, at the age of forty, almost as much as it did when I wasn't yet sixteen: those little *art nouveau* turrets and peeling frescoes in the turn-of-the-century World of Art style; that projecting corner of a constructivist building; those three tall plate-glass windows and behind them a huge glass chandelier, which suffered so much at the loss of its first owners; that remnant of a monastery wall and the little People's Will house built up against it; that tall, un-Russian spire of an Orthodox church; a florist's shop; a secondhand store, a well-known fence for stolen goods; a public lavatory; a police station; the headquarters of the Red Cross.

On yesterday's program of the West German Russian-language radio station, Heinrich Böll made a wonderful remark about Solzhenitsyn: "a sense of divine bitterness . . ."

I feel a sense of earthly but piercing bitterness whenever I drive from Solyanka to Trubnaya Square. It's odd, but that feeling is very similar to the youthful fascination that I felt at sixteen. But was it fascination? And is it bitterness that I feel now?

At Trubnaya Square the bright lights and complex system of exit ramps brought him back to the matter in hand. At this point, Malkolmov put out his cigarette and wondered whether he was committing a professional misdemeanor. He had answered this emergency call on his own initiative, without being ordered out by the dispatcher.

Ten minutes ago he had been called to the telephone and a very familiar, drunken voice had barked into his ear, "Listen, old man, are you my friend or a three-ruble whore? Get over here to the Kuznetsky Bridge and save a dying man. Come at once, or I'll throw up! A hero of the First Cavalry Army has collapsed in my arms. All citizens are equal, but some are more equal than others. Medicine in the service of progress! I can't hang on much longer!"

Malkolmov had then raced from the doctors' on-call room straight out into the yard, where three imported Volkswagen first-aid vans were parked. His reflex action on getting a phone call of this kind was to get going, and fast. Remembering similar nighttime calls that he himself had made, he realized at once that the caller was some drunken, distraught, quivering friend, a member of the Order of Men, an organization persecuted in the Soviet Union. The incident might, in fact, call for nothing more than a Valium, but he always flung himself into action and raced off at full tilt without stopping to consider.

"There's no left turn here, Gennady Apollinarievich," warned the driver.

"Doesn't matter. Turn left anyway and switch on the siren," Malkolmov ordered.

On the corner of Neglinnaya and Cherkassky a yellow traffic light was blinking and a solitary streetlamp swung from a pole carrying the trolleybus overhead wires. Two people were standing in front of the Musica store, which looked like a nineteenth-century governor's palace in some small colonial country. They were holding a third man by his arms and legs, his bottom dangling down almost to the level of the sidewalk and his head flung back as though his neck were no longer supported by any trace of a backbone. The first man was easily recognizable as Alik Neyarky, the famous hockey player, while the second could with difficulty be discerned as Pyotr Pavlovich Odudovsky, the invalid intellectual; the third person was a corpse.

Malkolmov leaped out of the Volkswagen, followed by the rest of the team. The rear door of the ambulance was opened. The bright interior light was switched on. The corpse-person – weighing at least one hundred kilograms! – was carried inside, where everything was made ready: hypodermics, tubing, the heart-lung machine, all the necessary drugs, intubator, an oxygen mask. The doors were slammed shut, and they drove off.

Half of the man's head and his entire face were covered in clotted blood, while fresh blood was still oozing from some deep wounds behind his ears.

"Igor, tourniquet! Tamara, swab!" Malkolmov ordered.

As the ambulance drove smoothly through the nocturnal space, the process of resuscitation was able to continue undisturbed – such is the excellence of West German springs and shock absorbers! Malkolmov slowly injected adrenaline and watched the blood-pressure gauge. At last the needle twitched and began to crawl upward. The prostrate body emitted a hoarse grunt; a bubble of blood formed on the lips and burst. It was only then that Malkolmov noticed through the fuzz of gray hair a tattoo just below the right nipple: a hammer and sickle and the words "Kola Peninsula 1939." He stared into the face of the reviving man.

With gentle, rapid movements Tamara cleaned the face, revealing the bony ridge above bushy eyebrows, a vertical gully between nose and upper lip, a small broken nose, a harsh, sneering upper lip, and a huge, mottled goitrous double chin.

HAVE THEY BEEN BEATING YOU, SANYA?

"Yes, they have, Citizen Captain."

"And did they hit you like this?"

. . . Gurchenko was tied to the chair and therefore fell over sideways, the chair toppling with him. His eyeball was instantaneously suffused with blood.

"No, Citizen Captain. Before you did they didn't hit me like that."

Malkolmov opened the sliding window into the driver's cab. "You here, Alik? Keeping your friend company?"

"That's right, old man." Three days' worth of alcoholic breath wafted through the little window. "Say, you wouldn't happen to have seventy grams of pure alcohol, would you?"

"Alik, who is this guy and what happened to him?"

"He's Kiryanich, the cloakroom attendant from the foreign-currency bar at the National. Get it? A big cheese. We were splitting a bottle three ways, and he began hitting his head against the radiator and singing 'The Song of the Varyag.' He's a shady character, old fellow. Shadows of our forgotten ancestors. Come on, don't be mean, give us some of that alcohol!"

Tamara produced an identity card from the patient's tunic and read, " 'Cheptsov, S. K., Lieutenant-Colonel, retired . . . ' The rest is all smudged and illegible, Gennady Apollinarievich."

So there's no doubt. It's him! Tolya von Steinbock, avenger from Magadan, where are you now?

TAKING REFUGE IN SUPERSTITION, STEINBOCK?

. . . imagine him undressed – huge, with resilient buttocks, a hairy protruding stomach, a heavy pendulous penis, like that of the dominant male of a herd of seals, a wrinkled old killer . . .

"What are you yelling for, you whore's brat?"

. . . Stop crying, Tolya, remember the image of your enemy – low forehead, eyes like hot little cherries . . .

"Little slob! You're just a puddle of chocolate-colored shit!"

. . . Weakness, the fear of helplessness . . . you're in the hands of the *apparat,* in the huge, inhuman, subterranean grip of the state!

Now he is in your hands, in your long fingers. Your two hands are saving the life of a sadist; they are resus-cit-ating a criminal.

Your hands are the hands of an intellectual, but they are an exact copy of the hands of your father Apollinary, a St. Petersburg proletarian, a revolutionary, and subsequently a Party bureaucrat, and later still an unrepentant political prisoner. Your hands are incapable of exacting revenge. They are used to operating on patients and palpating women; they have no feel for weapons and they even dislike clenching themselves into fists.

OK, don't take revenge. Instead, just pull the needle out of his vein and leave the rest to nature. It wasn't you who banged his stinking head against a radiator. He did it himself! So let him kill himself! You haven't the right to save him!

The ambulance stopped and immediately stretcher bearers ran up. The service worked smoothly and well, because time on call at night in the emergency room was paid at double rates.

AS GURCHENKO LAY ON THE FLOOR

of the interrogation room, looking past the officers' legs he suddenly saw Tolya standing in the corridor under the wall newspaper. He immediately stopped groaning with pain, although only the Almighty knows how much he wanted to howl and shriek at that moment.

He was silent even when Captain Cheptsov kicked him in the kidneys and groin, and when Cheptsov put his boot on Sanya's face and stood on it, jokingly balancing on one foot.

"Stepan, Stepan," said Boris, the investigator, in a somewhat uneasy tone of voice. "Don't go beyond the regulation methods!"

"I'd squash them all and to hell with the regulations!" said Cheptsov, jumping on Sanya's face. "All their children, all their relations and friends! You know, I can't bear to look at all these bastards!"

Smiling gently and puffing pleasurably on a cigarette, Boris the investigator walked around Captain Cheptsov, who was quivering with class feeling, and suddenly noticed Tolya von Steinbock in his long black overcoat, standing frozen with horror beneath the wall newspaper *On Guard* in a square of sunlight.

KUN HAS ARRIVED

said Professor Argentov, glancing out the window and catching sight of Aristarkh Kunitser's car, a blue smudge down below in the courtyard.

Two Russian lads, Ivan and Pyotr, Russian intellectuals of the new type, came over to the window. These young men were greatly appreciated in Moscow's "dissident" circles; they were valued for various reasons, not least because they were one hundred percent Russians – they were *so* Russian, in fact, that even the feature writers of the *Literary Gazette* would have found it hard to direct even a hint of anti-Semitism at them.

"Why have you invited him? Do you respect him?" Ivan and Pyotr asked Argentov. "They say he's a playboy and an alcoholic."

"Kun is my closest friend!" Argentov objected hotly. "You boys were still crazy about ice hockey when Kun and I raised the question of the legitimacy of the single-party system at the Integral Club in Novosibirsk."

"Kun!" he shouted down below. "Hey, Kunitsa!"

The front doors of the Zhiguli opened, and Professor Kunitser and a thin girl in jeans got out of the car.

"Why are they together?" said Ivan, puzzled. "That's the girl who does our typing. I gave her the appeal from *Europa civiltà* to copy."

"Strange," said Pyotr. "What can they have in common?"

"Bed, perhaps?" replied Argentov with a laugh, putting a hand on each of the young men's shoulders. "My fellow revolutionaries, I must inform you that despite the struggle we are all engaged in, here and there some people keep fucking."

They came up in the elevator. Nina was crying. She had turned away from him, huddling into a corner and trembling. Above her head and her tousled hair shone our guiding star, the sacramental three-letter inscription that appears in any Russian elevator on the day after it goes into service.

Kunitser was standing in another corner of the elevator, looking at the weeping girl. She's not my love. Where is my love, where did she slip out of my grasp? I embrace Nina . . . but you're only something like my love, slightly, only just like my love, my beloved! It's not because of you that I'm rebelling against the institute, against "progressive science," it's because of your stepfather, my dear little bitch. I shall never, ever again do anything for Soviet society, because *they* are still in charge, they – the stepfathers, the cloakroom men, the Stalinist sadists – and not us! They can complete the experiment without me! Let them search for me! No doubt they've already unleashed their Doberman pinschers all over town looking for the formula's creator. They can manage without me! NO ONE IS INDISPENSABLE, as Stalin used to say. And if they can't manage, then to hell with them and to hell with my formula, to hell with scientific research. I've finished with all that forever!

"So he raped you, did he?"

Kunitser suddenly noticed a mirror in the elevator and saw himself in it – pale, with a lopsided smile and untidily mussed-up hair.

"He raped you!" he repeated emphatically. "Don't be afraid of words! Your so-called father raped you!"

"No, no he didn't." She turned and faced him, eyes lowered, nose and lips puffy from crying. She seemed to want to bury her face in his chest, but couldn't make up her mind to do it. "No, Arik, he didn't rape me, it wasn't like that. I was raped, I know that. He simply took me as though fate had destined me for him. It was an unimaginable moment, just as though . . . as though . . ."

Kunitser was seized by a fit of shuddering, and he took a step toward her as if to help her. At last she clasped him and pressed her face to his chest.

"What is your name, what is your name?" he murmured. "I saw you once when I was young. You were Polish, you were an English girl, you were in a convoy of women prisoners. You and I will go away to the ocean, to a mountainside, where the forest thins out and where the moon goes down to take a rest."

"Yes, I know," she muttered, as though sunk in oblivion. "You walk and walk through the forest, when suddenly you reach the edge of the woods and there sits the moon. And they also say that the moon gives no warmth."

"Nonsense!" he exclaimed. "The moon gives plenty of warmth! I say that as a mathematician! I know it all already! I heard that cry of 'la guerre, la guerre' long ago! I even imagined long ago that maybe you are" – he looked hopefully into her eyes – "Alisa?"

She drew away and wiped her face. "I'm Nina, not Alisa. What are you going to do with him?"

NOW THREE PAIRS OF EYES WERE LOOKING AT TOLYA VON STEINBOCK

or rather five eyes, because the sixth, put out of action by Captain Cheptsov, no longer counted.

"And what does this mean? Who is this?!" Investigator Boris barked a moment later. He barked the words fiercely, but still gave Cheptsov a cautious sidelong glance, wondering what they should do. Extraneous witnesses are not exactly desirable when an interrogation goes beyond the limits set by the regulations.

"Take it easy," said von Steinbock with a smile. "Stay where you are, guys!"

He took off his overcoat and came into the interrogation room. The officers both were frightened. They found themselves without arms.

At the next moment Tolya was throwing a chair at Cheptsov and hitting another officer in the stomach.

It was done! After a while Tolya and Sanya were out the door and rushing down the road in an MGB car.

"Look!" Sanya said to Tolya with his husky voice. "They are trying to catch us!"

*"Never mind!" Tolya laughed. "Look here! My favorite candy! Dynamite!"**

---

*The text in italics appeared in English in the original Russian-language text.

Cheptsov said nothing to his colleague, but strode out into the corridor, gripped Von Steinbock by the shoulders, turned him around, and kicked him so hard in the behind that Tolya slid right down to the end of the corridor, past the doors behind which could be heard the clink of crockery and the cheerful voices of the staff at their lunch. Cheptsov flung the knapsack full of food after Tolya. Something in it smashed – no doubt a bottle of milk.

Cheptsov laughed and laughed and laughed.

The door opened onto a frosty day, a frosty day, a frosty day.

The guard on the steps of the patriarchal mansion was being ingratiating to Colonel Lygher's wife.

"Poor boy, poor boy, poor boy," she smiled with red lips.

"ARE YOU GOING TO KILL HIM?"

Nina whispered, barely audibly.

"Was she conceived, I wonder, on that frosty day, on that frosty day, amid that frost?"

"I am a Christian," said Kunitser.

"You can't be!" cried Nina, as though in fear.

"Why not?"

"Well . . . for one thing, you're partly Jewish . . . and then, and then . . . it's absurd: A 'Christian' – it's somehow passé, out of date."

Kunitser wrenched his necktie loose as he started to choke with fury. "You little idiot! It's your shitty Marxism that's already out of date. Christianity has only just been born! A mere two thousand years ago! Only two thousand years! To God, two thousand years is nothing, and the Devil still has time to die twenty more times!"

"How naïve you are," whispered Nina. "My poor, poor, poor boy."

That's the limit! She has picked up the baton from her mother! Obviously all that big-deal compassion is in their blood.

"And then . . . and then . . ." the girl whispered so quietly that she could hardly be heard, "a Christian couldn't do what you've been doing with me . . ."

Suddenly an electric charge ran through Aristarkh. This child was accusing him, standing in a dirty elevator under a graffito that said "prick." He stretched out his arms to her. "My dear, forgive me. Now, I do believe. You must be right."

The astonished features of Argentov appeared on the other side of the grille of the elevator door. "See here, Kun, necking in an elevator at your age! You're incorrigible!"

They went in. Argentov's junk-strewn and labyrinthine apartment was full of people. Kunitser knew hardly any of his old pal's friends. And there had been a time when he had spent most of his life here.

IT HAD BEEN A FRATERNITY

Right here, on this wall, they had once calculated out the ethical formula of socialism. In those days, in the late fifties, the apartment had also been full of people, but everyone knew each other; they were friends, brothers:

> Oh, our youthful sentiments,
> Oh, those furious arguments,
> Oh, those all-night meetings!

The son of a bitch, now famous and respectable, in those days had seemed like a strange giraffe, trotting confidently through the streets of Moscow. He used to shake off the snow and right there in the doorway would start booming away about Cuba, about Fidel, about the Staircase, the Apple, and the Rough Sea.

The Moscow Ant had sung here too. The whole apartment fell respectfully silent, and even the drunkards corked their bottles whenever he put one foot on a stool, rested his guitar on his knee, and gazed up at the dark ceiling with his watery, vacant eyes. He, the Ant, had changed as well, and no longer came here.

The drunken cosmopolitan, Patrick Thunderjet, would burst in loaded with bottles bought for hard currency. A crowd of red-cheeked, snow-covered Georgians would enter, led by Our Girl, the adopted daughter of hunchbacked Tiflis. Overflowing with vitality, poetry and wine, Our Girl would immediately forget her Georgians and give herself to any others who were temporarily deprived of their share of the good things of life, to the whole of orphaned mankind. A bunch of Lithuanian supermen would arrive and seat themselves solidly around a table, not understanding much of what was going on around them but unreservedly prepared to join the brotherhood of the new Moscow intelligentsia. Tape recordings, new books, pictures by crazy abstract artists, political jokes, guitars, icons, manuscripts written on tissue paper, jokes, jokes, and more jokes. They were all poor and unknown, but later they suddenly became rich and famous.

Trivial, useless things suddenly acquired a special, nonmonetary value. More and more foreign languages were heard here; ever more smartly dressed women started coming, and as they touched threadbare carpets, sagging couches, and soot-blackened samovars, turned them into superprecious objects. The den became enveloped in a chemical aura of fame – "the haunt of Moscow's intellectual elite."

Toward morning we would leave for other houses. There seemed to be plenty of houses open to us in Moscow; we felt there were a great many of us and that all of Moscow was already ours.

A ground wind was blowing through Moscow as we sang in the streets, saddened by the early morning hour:

> Once there was a soldier boy
> Armed with gun and saber,
> But he was just a childish toy
> A soldier made of paper.

And we too, the paper soldiers of our generation, will perish for nothing, for peanuts – so we sang, saddened by the early morning hour, but in our heart of hearts we believed in the strength of Okudzhava's "paper soldiers." "And our intentions will be pure on Insurrection Square at half past five," we declaimed, and the words seemed a guarantee of our victory.

In the damp winter of 1966, Moscow put two such lads from one of *our* houses on trial. Then four more. Then more, singly, in pairs, in whole batches.

They demoted *our* professors, fired *our* theater directors, closed *our* cafés. The question that we raised as to the legitimacy of the single-party system was decided, and in a sense that even forbade asking the question. The epoch of Lenin's centennial began. The Neanderthal features of that old *Pravda* hawk Yurii Zhukov dominated the television screens. Shuffling a stack of censored books by erotic Parisian writers, he spoke of the crisis of bourgeois culture.

It was then that Argentov's home experienced its culminating moment: Here, behind the Chinese screen by the fireplace, littered with empty bottles, to the strains of the song "Lenochka Potapova" was composed the first collective letter to the defender of all true communists, Louis Aragon.

That day also marked the collapse of Argentov's house, and the carefree Moscow of the "men of the sixties" burnt up with a bright blue flame. The disintegration began.

True, letters continued to be written, and in ever greater quantities – to the Writers' Union, to the Academy of Sciences, to the Presidium of the Supreme Soviet, to the Party Central Committee, to the United Nations . . . The Letter of the Twelve, the Letter of the Sixty-Four, the Letter of the Twenty-Seven . . . In defense of Ginzburg and Galanskov, in support of Sakharov, to congratulate Solzhenitsyn . . . All the letters were written from Marxist positions, in defense of "Leninist standards" and against the "alarming symptoms of a rebirth of Stalinism."

The regime maintained a sullen silence, without responding to those damned intellectuals, but simply did its job sluggishly, obtusely, "uncompromisingly": tightened screws, hamstrung tendons, castrated. In that unwillingness to clarify attitudes "by means of mutual correspondence" lay the destruction of the "sixties," of the Soviet "new wave," of the socialist renaissance.

But we're on your side, we're Soviet people too. We are only showing concern, expressing our involvement in public affairs, but they don't even answer us! All they do is put the screws on us, hamstring us, castrate us, squeeze our windpipes. How could the elitist liberals know that the Regime saw in their effusions a certain danger to their sacred pork-barrel system?

The "Moscow houses" darkened and emptied, the guitars fell silent. More and more Argentov's house began to smell of bilious vomit, bleach, and the male menopause.

The wheel of history, with a flat tire, rolled on its rim into the Centennial Era. There was a lot of natural gas in the country – "eternal fires" were lighting up all over the place; the plastics industry fashioned grim missiles for the rising generation; gilded belts were tightened on bellies stuffed with potato fat.

One day, during a night of falling stars, in the early hours of a morning the color of dill pickles, with surly, dumb astonishment, Unanimous Approval occupied a fraternal socialist country to ensure that it was no longer fraternal but safely under its skin.

Then for the first time in Argentov's house the fur began to fly. Some shouted that it was time to go out into the streets and join the Five demonstrating on Red Square! Others wept: "But those are our boys on those tanks, our boys who applauded us, who read our books!" Still others, with cold-blooded pedantry – so comforting! – held forth about the "bag of protoplasm that only reacts to pain stimuli." There were even those who condemned Dubček for "adventurism" and blamed all the Czechs: "What did they expect? Did they really think they could have what we can't have?"

Until suddenly one of them, who was sitting on the windowsill – "highly intelligent, a celebrity" – simply tipped over, fell into the street, and disappeared. He had said nothing to anyone, left nothing behind, had sat silently throughout the whole argument, only now and again rubbing his pale face, and suddenly he fell out the window – perhaps he had just suddenly decided to do it, perhaps he had felt dizzy, perhaps Argentov's house spun around at that moment, lost its gravitational pull, and simply nudged the man out onto the asphalt below.

He lay down there on his side as though drunk, with a dark stain spreading ever wider beneath him. It was as if the asphalt were melting.

Then it started: noise, shouting, people running. Siren screaming, an ambulance drove up. The doctor, Genka Malkolmov, well known as "one of us," tore through the crowd.

When everything had quietened down, only two men were left – Argentov and Kunitser, two old friends and fellow scientists. They went into the kitchen to eat borshch, and at this point a family emerged timidly from the depths of the apartment – a wife and children, a mother-in-law, an invalid uncle – the family about which everyone, including Argentov himself, had forgotten during that "swinging decade," the decade that had just come to an end to the howl of an ambulance siren. It turned out that Argentov's apartment was not just "one of the refuges of Moscow's intellectual elite" but also an ordinary home with all the necessary attributes, including a family. In those days quite a number of families were reborn in Moscow.

Kunitser had never managed to establish or create a strong family. Lamenting the lost sixties, he had wandered among the remnants of the decade and tried to avoid the house of his old friend. For some reason he was even slightly ashamed to remember the house. Was it because on that evening he had been one of those who had joined in the call to "go out into the streets?" He preferred not to remember certain details, and instead he lamented the vanished years even more bitterly and unrestrainedly than people lament their misspent youth.

Lately, though, Argentov's name had again started to pop up here and there. People were saying that his family had once more retreated to the nether regions of the apartment. It was rumored that the house had become a sort of "headquarters of free thought," that everything was much more serious now – no guitars, no alcohol . . .

And indeed Kunitser and Nina saw nothing on the table but some weak tea and a plate of bagels. No less than fifteen people were drinking tea to the sound of soft music. It was unlikely that anyone was listening to the music; it simply made it more difficult for the KGB eavesdroppers to function, as was later explained to Kunitser.

Everyone in the room glanced at the new arrivals, and then quietly resumed their low-toned conversations. Kunitser looked from face to face, but found no one he knew, then looked at the walls, which reminded him of other days, and at the ceiling, which still bore the marks of a pair of size forty-five shoes walking toward the fan, a frivolous but delightful practical joke played by the "men of the sixties."

"Friends, this is Aristarkh Kunitser, my old friend. Yes, *the* Kunitser," Argentov introduced him. "And with him is Nina, his young friend."

Kunitser shook hands with all those present, or bowed. He didn't know what Argentov meant by "*the* Kunitser." Was he referring to *the* Kunitser who had been sentenced to fifteen days" forced labor after a night in the Yalta sobering-up station? Did he mean *the* Kunitser who, barefoot and swollen, had sold cedar cones on the streets of Simferopol? Or *the* Kunitser who had lain in the alcoholic ward with an Antabuse drip rammed into his buttock?

"Scientist with a worldwide reputation," he heard a woman's voice whisper behind his back.

Ah, so he was *that* Kunitser!

He liked Argentov's new friends. There was no bohemian atmosphere. The people were serious, clear-eyed, very plainly dressed, polite, and restrained – real intellectuals. Now these were the right sort of people to associate with, and not with a bunch of drunks, gamblers, and lovers of Caucasian cooking. Alas, you're a stranger in the company of real intellectuals and at home only in the stinking dens of Moscow's lunatic fringe. How good it would be to join these new people, to be reborn, to clear one's mind, to shake up one's intellectual baggage. The thought so attracted him that he even forgot about his encounter with Cheptsov and about Nina's confessions. No doubt Argent had purposely invited him today in order to draw him into their company. Now there was a friend for you, a real friend!

Suddenly Kunitser caught sight of an old acquaintance, a member of the erstwhile "fraternity." In the past, if this man had worn a jacket, it had invariably been the last word in chic, probably something ultra-English dating from the Great War era, adorned with some strange emblem, such as a badge or a little bell. Now he was wearing just the plainest and most ordinary of jackets.

"Hi there, old man," Kunitser whispered to him.

"Hi, Aristarkh," was the equally unpretentious response, accompanied by a move to make room for him on the sofa.

The master of the house came up, threw an open American magazine onto Kunitser's knees, and pointed to a particular place on the page, which was outlined by a windowlike shape in red felt pen. Above the window was a picture of the appetizing rear end of a girl clad in woolen pantyhose. To the left of it stood the imposing shape of a bottle of Cutty Sark whiskey, to the right was a caricature of Nixon with puffedout cheeks, and below, some comic strips. The text in the window read: "Continued from page sixteen . . . Old Soviet leadership supposes nothing will change in this country, but . . . (see page forty-one)."

"How did we come to be here? How do you know these people? Why have you brought me here?" Nina whispered in his ear.

She was very upset. A young man with a round, ruddy, and very Russian face was staring hard at her from the opposite corner of the room.

"Mr. Kunitser, would you allow me to ask you a few questions?" someone asked him from behind.

One of the very plainly dressed men standing by the wall behind the sofa offered his visiting card. He was the correspondent of the magazine that had been marked with the "window."

"Naturally, your incognito will be strictly observed."

A subdued, tactful hum of talk flowed in from all around the room. Finally, Argentov disturbed the scene by announcing in a loud, cheerful voice, "We are here, Kun, to hear a paper read by Yakov Shalashnikov. Go on, Yakov. Kun will, of course, pick up the drift of your thoughts at once."

In his worn leather jacket Yakov Shalashnikov might have looked like a taxi driver had he not been so obviously nearsighted. He brought a magnifying glass on a long wooden handle up to his right eye and began reading aloud.

It was an essay on the development of totalitarian thinking in Russia. According to Shalashnikov, Russia had not yet completed the process of Europeanization begun by Peter the Great. Shalashnikov contended that the present-day enthusiasts for the purity of ideology and for a relentless struggle against all forms of dissidence, the inventors of all those typical propaganda clichés, such as "feelings of legitimate pride," "a huge surge in the workers'' zeal," and "examples of genuine patri-

otism," were none other than the heirs of those pre-Petrine government clerks, the sweaty and louse-ridden forefathers of Russia's eternal
bureaucracy, who obstructed Peter's reforms and hindered the barbers.

The speaker drew parallels between the Old Muscovite legislation
and the articles published by present-day ideologists. In the sixties, of
course, these parallels would have evoked a storm of excited applause,
and people would have laughed until they cried. Now the audience
listened seriously and showed no emotion. One of the young men
periodically collected the pages that had already been read and carried
them into the next room. The twin spools of a small tape recorder
revolved on a table in front of the speaker.

In the middle of the paper's delivery the front door slammed and a
tall, middle-aged man carrying a heavy briefcase passed rapidly through
the room without stopping to greet anyone. Kunitser noticed that the
arrival of this man produced something like a wave of relief in the
room, and two charming but somewhat desiccated ladies actually
exchanged smiling glances.

From his seat deep among the broken springs of Argentov's sofa –
ah, what memories! – Kunitser could see the new arrival go into the
adjoining room, throw his briefcase into a corner, take off his jacket,
hang it on a coat hanger, slit open the serge lining with a razor blade,
and extract from it a sheet of thin but opaque paper. It might not have
been paper but some kind of cloth specially prepared for transportation
inside the lining of an ordinary Soviet jacket.

Just then the man caught sight of Kunitser looking at him, but
showed no embarrassment; on the contrary, he gave a cheerful wink
and proudly waved the sheet that he had just extracted from his jacket.
Argentov moved over, quietly shut the door, and also winked to
Kunitser, as though the latter were *one of them*. The stranger's handsome, rather horsey features remained imprinted on his visual memory.
The word "COURIER" happened to come into Kunitser's mind, and the
random thought proved to be a correct guess. But, of course, he's a
courier, their courier.

The speaker continued in a dispassionate tone. "Wherein lies the
meaning, the aim, of the so-called visual propaganda that has
permeated Soviet society since the moment of its birth and that now
exceeds even the Stalin period in scale and volume? Do these endless
slogans – The Ideas of Lenin are Eternal; People and Party are One;
Our Aim is Communism – convince anyone? Do these thousands upon
thousands of plywood, plaster, marble, and cast-iron statues of Lenin
inspire anyone? No, they neither convince nor inspire, but they are

not supposed to convince or inspire. The statues of Lenin, the slogans, and growth charts perform the same function as the palisades and sentry boxes of old Russia: For every present-day Russian, they define the limits of his stagnant, provincial little world. Their message is, Not a step beyond the boundary! These things, which seem absurd and pointless to any enlightened socialist, are regarded as the only possible methods for use by the opponents of Peter the Great's Westernizing reforms – in other words, by Soviet communists. Naturally, a Russian Social Democrat is not simply a supporter of the Petrine reforms – the essence of Social Democracy is broader and more profound. But it is our view that even in our practical, everyday activities we should be aware of the origins of our present-day bureaucracy, its historiosophical and national meaning. Our struggle . . ."

So that's it! thought Kunitser. So that's what it's all about! Argentov has been organizing a Social Democratic movement. Not bad!

The master of the house beckoned to him from the kitchen door. Kunitser tiptoed across the room and went into the kitchen. Argentov closed the door after him.

"A Social Democratic discussion circle, am I right?" Kunitser asked.

"Not a discussion circle, but a party," Argentov corrected him gently.

He was now exhibiting an entirely new quality – gentleness. In the past decade the professor had been a real rock'n'roller in a leather jacket, noisy and abrasive. Now – gentleness. Was gentleness, perhaps, the style of the seventies? Or was he only putting it on for this evening for the benefit of Kunitser, the novice, in order not to scare him?

"A party, Kun, a real party. We have resurrected Russian Social Democracy. As a matter of principle we are working differently from all those legal groups and committees, like Sakharov's. Do you remember our disastrous 'meeting in memory of the victims of Stalinism?' Do you remember how the old Stalinist diehards sneered at us? That was the time when we should have gone underground. Now we are on a completely conspiratorial footing, but I've invited you because I trust you as I trust myself. I'm devilishly glad you've kicked the drinking habit. It's time to get to work, Kun!"

Argentov's kitchen was now as neat and tidy as though it had been licked clean. Neat square jars for granular foods stood in rows on the shelves, marked "Tea," "Buckwheat," "Coffee," "Millet," "Flour." The table was covered by a vinyl tablecloth decorated with pictures of antique automobiles.

Kunitser looked away. Suddenly, out of the blue, he had the sickening feeling of being in a little boat at the mercy of the elements: anxiety, isolation, despair – and the bow buries itself into a wave; excitement, hope – the boat shoots up onto a crest, a vast expanse all around you . . .

"Couldn't you manage without all this, Argentum, old man?" He pressed his hand to his eyes. "I mean couldn't you do it without a political party? What about science, Argentum old man, the infinitude of science? What do you have to say about science, Argentum old man, about music, about the beauty of nature, and in particular about Mount Elbrus? Are you sure, Argentum old man, that you can't manage without a party?"

Argentov sat down on the edge of the table and stroked his bald patch, smiling a charming smile. Even in his student days he had developed a splendid bald patch. It had never hindered him. He had a special quality, typical of strong characters: Every gesture and grimace that he made, every word and sound that he uttered, announced to those around him, Yes, it's me, this is what I am – before you stands the completed image of Nikodim Argentov!

Kunitser had never managed to achieve this completeness; he always felt that he was either overdoing it or failing somewhere, and as a young man he had at times quite simply suffered from a feeling of his own absurdity.

"No, Kun, it can't be done without a party. Do you remember how, when we were young, we calculated on that wall the necessity and inevitability of opposition? What a pity that formula wasn't preserved." His clean, straightforward, intelligent friend stared thoughtfully at the rooftops of Moscow bathed in the evening sun. "You see, somebody had to start. Why not us? We're not dreaming of a crown of thorns. But if someone has to start, if it's inevitable, then why shouldn't we be the ones to start? Everyone can't just go on endlessly saying 'Why me?' Whatever happens, someone has got to say 'Why not me?' After all, it's inevitable, we worked it out . . . then why shouldn't you and I say it?"

"It's logical!" Kunitser's boat shot up onto the crest of a wave. "That's something I can understand! I'll join your party, Argentum old man! I hope we won't limit ourselves to reading papers. Where can I start distributing leaflets?"

His remark about leaflets was said jokingly, in the heat of enthusiasm, but when he looked at his friend's face he broke off.

"For a start, Kun, you can distribute our program in your hush-hush lab. According to our information, the atmosphere there is absolutely ready for it."

The glittering, spray-tossed, wind-blown expanse seethed around Kunitser's boat. Here at last was a real cause! Enough of that fucking around in the canteen and the toilets! Proclamations, programs, action! And enough, quite enough, of sneering at the intelligentsia. No more of it!

"In essence our program is hardly any different from the program of historic Social Democracy, but . . ." Argentov slid off the table and rubbed his hands together hard and cheerfully. "Do you have a smoke?"

Kunitser took out a pack of Gitanes. Argentov's little eyes glittered sarcastically. "No, sorry, I don't smoke those."

"But you always used to love Gitanes!" exclaimed Kunitser in astonishment.

"I've been smoking our Prima for a long time now."

He opened the kitchen door a little and asked, "Verochka, give us a cigarette."

Suddenly he saw something shocking in the apartment, and he froze in the doorway with his mouth wide open. There, in the big room, something was happening. People were busily but somewhat chaotically moving the furniture. There was a muddled sound of footsteps and voices. Someone was asking questions, someone else was answering, but most noticeable of all was that most of the Social Democrats were strangely silent.

Verochka's foxy little face thrust itself into the kitchen. "Argentov, THEY have arrived."

"Who are 'they?' " he asked in a whisper.

"Them. The comrades."

Argentov pulled the door wide open. From behind him Kunitser could see THEM, three young men, two of them almost boys with fluffy sideburns, wearing neat little suits, and a third one of about thirty, with a university graduate's badge in the lapel of his jacket. Presumably the third young man was a product of law school and the first two, perhaps, were still studying by correspondence course.

Oddly enough, Kunitser felt no particular excitement, still less fear. He calmly compared THESE with THOSE, with the ghosts of his boyhood, remembering how Cheptsov had seethed with passion and how dispassionate these ones were.

The three young KGB specialists showed not a hint of sarcasm, mockery, or cruelty toward the arrested Social Democrats. They did their job calmly and efficiently as they collected books, papers, spools of tape, typewriters, and politely asked people to open their briefcases. All the material was carried out to the landing by two other, more plainly, dressed young men, their assistants.

"Do you have a search warrant?" Argentov asked in a firm, stern voice.

"Yes, yes, of course," replied the "graduate's badge" in a slightly vague but very polite tone, and produced the warrant as though it were a travel ticket.

With a challenging gesture, Argentov noisily placed a chair at the table, sat down, put his glasses on his nose, and began to study the warrant intently. He was showing his comrades by personal example how they should behave.

Everyone, as it happened, kept their dignity. Kunitser came out of the kitchen and watched them all carefully. The whole scene struck him as entirely dignified, indeed even normal: Nothing special, just a raid on a secret meeting of Social Democrats. Only Nina, huddled in a corner of the sofa, seemed to be on the verge of hysteria.

"And that, really, is all," said the "graduate's badge" after a while. "Kulkov, Miloserdov, and Grossman will have to come with us."

The "fluffy sideburns" produced a warrant for the arrest of the two young men, Pyotr and Ivan, and of Grossman the courier.

"And you, Mr. Nolan, are expected at the Press Department of the Ministry of Foreign Affairs," said the "badge," turning to the foreign journalist. "If you like, we can give you a lift there in our car. After all" – here he allowed himself to smile for the first time – "you did come here by trolleybus."

The "fluffy sideburns" gave Argentov a copy of the official record of the search to sign.

"And what will happen to the others?" Argentov asked sharply.

The "badge" tugged at the zipper on his portfolio.

"Nothing. You may continue your tea party or go home. We have no instructions concerning the rest of you."

"See here, I am the host!" Argentov almost shouted. He seemed to be reduced to a state of near-fury by so unexpectedly being left in freedom. "I am Argentov!"

"Nikodim Vasilievich, surely you don't think we don't know who you are?" said the "badge" quietly, and put on his soft fedora. "Goodbye, Nikodim Vasilievich. Goodbye . . . ahem . . . comrades." In the door he suddenly turned and faced Kunitser. "And good evening to you, Aristarkh Apollinarievich!"

"Up your asshole!" Kunitser surprisingly blurted out.

The only response to this pointless outburst was a wild shout of laughter from Argentov and Nina's muffled sobbing. The "graduate's badge" only kept staring at Kunitser and just gave a very slight frown.

The door closed behind the uninvited guests, the prisoners Kulkov, Miloserdov, and Grossman, and the foreigner Nolan. All the rest remained seated in absolute silence, while outside, the endless evening of a dusty Moscow summer slowly expired.

In the eastern windows the sky was turning a deep blue, and only on the spire of a skyscraper at the Red Gates could there still be seen shining the afterglow of the sunset. In the western windows a dusty gold was giving way to a kind of sea-green spotted with little glowing coals along the skyline of the New Arbat and Kutuzov Prospect.

Kunitser and Argentov tried not to look out of the windows. Having all their lives been keenly conscious of the passage of wasted time, they found in such sunsets a certain hope, a certain hint of the future, a certain music. Wait for the ships, wait for the ships, wait for the ships . . . Now, not for the first time, both of them felt that they had lived too long, as if beyond the limits of the sunset they saw no vision of either divine or mathematical significance.

Night was falling, falling, falling . . . The mirror reflected a neon s'gn: "Men's Shoes." In the dark room no one could make out the source of a phrase that rang out: "Oh, ye unthinking and tardy of heart to believe all that the prophets have foretold!"

A MULTITUDE OF DISEASES

was suddenly discovered to be plaguing Samsik, Samson Apollinarie-vich Sabler. Now and again in the past, white blobs had floated before his eyes, he had felt dizzy, an occasional stab in the heart, and his bronchial tubes had wheezed. Previously he had never regarded these phenomena as signs of sickness but had only complained to his pals that he felt lousy.

This morning, at rehearsal, however, Samsik had passed right out, and the other guys, frightened, had carried him off to the Institute of Emergency Treatment, where one of the doctors was a jazz fan and a "friend" of musicians. Their friend was not on duty, but thanks to his influence they were still given good service, and the talented organism of Samson Sabler, leader of The Giants combo, received a thorough examination.

The result was (a) extreme hypertension, (b) stenosis of the mitral valve, (c) duodenal ulcer, (d) polyarthritis, (e) bronchiectasis. In other words, he'd live.

"You, Samson Apollinarievich, have contributed a great deal toward the destruction of your own body," the charming, golden-haired lady doctor with round, steppe-dweller's features announced to Sabler.

"Tell me, please, couldn't you and I meet someplace?" asked Samsik as he buttoned up his shirt.

"Why not?" said the doctor, surprised. "I must warn you that emphysema is developing as a result of playing the saxophone. You even have the right to claim compensation on the basis of medical diagnosis of an occupational health hazard. I'll give you a certificate to that effect."

"Thank you very much," said Samsik. "I appreciate that. So at least I'm assured of a crust of bread. But tell me, please, couldn't you and I meet somewhere?"

"Of course," said the lady doctor firmly, and signed a prescription with her bold signature: "Dr. Belyakova, A. V."

Samsik jumped up from the couch like a young man. His vision was a bit hazy, there was a slight pain in his side, but his mood was terrific – he felt high. "In that case, come to the concert we're giving today at the Institute of Refrigeration Research! We're going to go right over the top!"

What did all these diseases matter to Samsik compared to the creative surge that he had been experiencing in the last few months? After his spell in the sobering-up station, after his sentence of hard labor in a municipal work gang, Samsik had been about to set out for the third bank of the Mississippi, but he had changed his mind. What, and give up the chance of ever playing his own stuff again, of ever setting people swinging again? Never again express the feelings of his rotting generation? Never revaluate all those values that were so deeply in hock?

For a long time he took refuge behind the screen around the bed of his common-law wife, Milka Koretko, where he lay sorrowing, at the end of his rope, tormenting himself with regret and shame for his lost years, terrified of the future and afraid that there might not even be a future for him.

There was a time (it seemed like yesterday) when Milka Koretko had been a solid fan, a musician's groupie, and people had actually fought over her (I can see it now – there she is, running through a snowstorm in a minidress, chased by Shura Skop of the Komsomol

Central Committee, and behind them, under a streetlamp, two guys are bashing each other to death, one in a red jacket, the other wearing yellow. It may have been yesterday, it may have been a hundred years ago). But now Milka had cooled it, had put on weight, and was working as a floor supervisor in an Intourist hotel.

For all those days that he lay behind Milka's screen, Samsik's past enveloped him like pea-soup fog, as though he were barely alive, the murk only occasionally enlivened by little brightly colored scenes.

"My boy, my poor old boy," Milka wept over him when she came home from work with a drink or two inside her.

He pretended to be asleep and summoned up a dream. He still remembered the time when he used to dream rhythmic dreams that were much more interesting than real life. Once he managed to conjure up something like this:

that night, in some deserted mountain village
'mid icicles and pine-branch stalactites
I saw the Moon . . . it shone
no, no, it didn't shine – but simply hung
above my head, just like a little fish
a pinkish little fish with fins,
a little tail, quite plain, and with a human eye.
the little fish was sewn on silk
with packthread, but beyond a doubt
it was the Moon and it amazed me
by such a transformation . . . so I called
some friends of mine to come and see
the rare phenomenon of this fishlet, alias Moon, the midnight
    luminary
my friends, though, didn't come; I don't know why they stayed away
    from my dream vision . . .
I was anxious lest the feathery clouds might cover it,
might screen the fish from sight without a trace . . .
and then my friends came up to me.
Well, where's the fish? the clouds had covered all
the boundless sky . . . so where's your Moon?
above us hung the clouds,
the fish had vanished but the Moon remained,
lying on a bed of cotton, like a brooch,
like a lump of artificial ice
milky-white suspended over Moscow . . .

over the mountain country or was it over Moscow?
most likely, over both . . .
so much, then, for your Moon! some moon!
a nameless friend just laughed
jumped up and pulled it from the cloud
and flung it to the ground and smashed it
into little fragments colored like the sea . . .
colors of July, pearl of December . . .
then was revealed a mirage in the cotton:
a deep dark hole within the moonlight . . .

This dream was repeated several times, and although Samsik knew
that its origin was quite elementary and came from a fish embroidered
on the screen, he nevertheless convinced himself that this dream had
a profound, mysterious, and beneficent meaning.

Suddenly something remarkable really did happen: dream and reality
merged. The hole in the cotton widened to incredible proportions, and
the dark-blue night sky was strewn with little fleecy clouds. The light
fell on an eighteenth-century cobbled street, along which clip-clopped
a horse harnessed to a carriage ornamented with rococo curlicues.
After a while the horse stopped beneath a row of white columns, gently
stamping the ground with its left hind hoof and waving its golden tail.

Samsik's nostrils caught the damp, slightly smoky smell of Europe
– oil shale mixed with pastry, cakes, leather, tobacco, and metal. Very
thick, dark silk! A dress darker than night, yet shining, too! The rustle
of the dress in the breeze, the rustle of an auburn mane! Someone
female ran down the steps, hiding nose and lips in black lace, eyes
glittering.

The modestly anonymous craftsmen of the past have bequeathed us
many a masterpiece in cast iron. Along one such masterwork of cast
iron the dress rustled and hissed and then, as though momentarily
inflated, like a dark-blue rose bursting into flower, disappeared inside
the carriage. It was her! Alisa? Marina?

Samsik then emerged from behind the screen, went to the place
where he had to go, calmly emptied his bladder, cleaned his teeth,
combed his hair – all very calmly! – picked up his saxophone, kissed
the sleeping Milka, and departed. On the staircase he remembered
something, returned, and left Milka's daughter, Katerina, a modest
present, made up of his personal possessions: a Parker pen, a Ronson
lighter, his polarized glasses, and a Holiday tortoise-shell comb. All
this might be of use to the growing child in the not too distant future.

Samsik's footsteps rang loudly across the nocturnal caves of Moscow. At the moment when he emerged from a tiled pedestrian underpass on Sadovoye, he saw Marina Vlady. Volodya Vysotsky was driving his wife home in his tiny Renault from the airport after her arrival on the night plane from Paris.

Volodya braked slightly, and seemed to wave to Samsik – they were slightly acquainted. His wife, however, said something with a stern look – she and Samsik were slightly unacquainted – and the couple, shifting gear, sped away over the hump of Sadovoye, only the car's rear lights glinting cheerfully.

Samsik then ran on, seized with artistic excitement. A creative idea lent wings to his heels. The sax under his arm clattered its valves like a little man, a frozen, bent, little prisoner starving for love.

The policeman in the sentry box alongside the American Embassy called up to warn the appropriate authorities of a citizen running through the night. The authorities then radioed to three patrol cars who were circulating in the vicinity of Insurrection Square. They, in turn, using their walkie-talkies, warned officers on the beat and motorcycle patrols about the "fugitive." Very soon the citizen was spotted. Not surprising – after all, a human being isn't exactly a needle!

There was Samsik dashing to and fro in front of an enormous gray wall in the light of six powerful headlights. The police perhaps thought this was the last death agony of a criminal, but Samsik was not in the least scared by the good old Soviet police – they had, thank God, seen him safely through more than forty years of his life.

So now a big thank you to the officers of the Moscow police! Without them, perhaps, the creative idea would never have been born, the circuit wouldn't have connected up, and the saxophone wouldn't have been blown up by a huge bronchiectasis.

Samsik's six shadows flickered back and forth over the wall, soon joined by the shadows of the approaching police officers. The sax wailed and the creative thought was born: *The Battle Between the Gods and the Giants*.

"Look, look, comrades!" cried Samsik, pointing at the wall. "Porphyrion wrestling with Heracles! Alcyoneus fighting the Goddess of the Night! The ether is the domain of Zeus! Time to stop? Just a minute, let me finish! I'll tell you about the thought that didn't want to lie and the tongue that told lies about the thought!"

There are not a few sensitive fair-minded men in the Moscow police. The officers lit cigarettes, allowed the saxophonist to have his say, and only then invited him to get into one of the patrol sidecars.

Pacified, Samsik jumped into the sidecar with the ease born of practice, and closed his eyes, whispering; "O Cronus, devourer of your own children. A revolt against whom? Against Cronus, of course! That is the essence. Don't you understand, sergeant? The essence of art is the revolt against Cronus!"

"I'm looking at you, comrade artist, and I'm puzzled. You seem like a kid somehow, and yet – how old are you?"

"And you, my glorious centaur?"

"I was born in '52."

"Theoretically you could be my son. By the way, what's your name?"

"Sergei Plotnikov."

"No, doesn't fit," said Samsik with relief. "Your name means 'carpenter' and I knew a girl called Jane Carpenter once, but that was considerably later."

The Pergamum frieze. The battle of the gods and giants. Some years ago Samsik had been in a drunken party that took him to some sculptor's studio. There Samsik had gotten himself all messed up with clay and covered in lime, had swallowed some filthy concoction and collapsed in a corner. From that corner, through the smoke and people's legs, he had caught sight of some photographs of a bas-relief stuck to plywood – broken torsos, heads with missing noses, bulging muscles, figures and faces mutilated by time yet still poised in grim determination, in other words, something from ancient Greece.

Samsik lay in the corner, his head resting on the knees of a bronze statue, while all over the studio the sculptor's guests raised a hideous din, neighing like war-horses, glasses clinking like the clashing of armor, in fact much as if the marble battle were still going on. Through the almost unbearable noise, Samsik could hear the drunken voice of the sculptor breaking off from a screech into a hoarse gasp.

He was shouting something about a Texan-Jewish cowboy, who was buying from him outright the whole idea of a modern Pergamum frieze, a *Moebius* model of eternity, buying his talent, all his blood and sperm. But the lousy capitalist could go suck an egg; the whole thing would stay here, where it was born, in Moscow, the Third Rome – after all, one day even the Bolsheviks would mature sufficiently to appreciate art, one day even the Soviet bureaucracy would be racked with guilt, and he, the modest genius, would meanwhile bide his time in poverty and obscurity.

The next morning, straight from the Men's Club, that's to say from the beer bar at the Pioneer Market, Samsik set off for the Lenin Library, took out an appallingly heavy volume of engravings, and extracted from it new knowledge about the battle between the gods and the giants. A musical idea was born in his still drunkenly grinning brain then, but by the evening of the same day he had already smothered it with hack work, fucking around, smoking hash, drinking, chewing the fat, and humping chicks.

So the years passed and Samsik clean forgot his idea, as he had forgotten other bursts of inspiration, when suddenly, while lying at death's door behind Milka's screen, he remembered it! That night, right from the police station, he called up his best friend Silvester to interest him in the idea. By morning, under the keen, friendly eye of Police Captain Yermakov (recently transferred to Moscow from the southern shore of the Crimea) the idea had gripped no less than ten musicians, and thus was born the jazz and rock group The Giants.

Silvester was happy and proud. Ah, you and I, old man, will do great things! We'll unite two generations, the forty-year-olds and the twenty-year-olds, jazz and rock! Twenty-year-old vocalists and forty-year-old instrumentalists, beat and improvisation! We shall rebel against Cronus and fill up the gaps in the Pergamum frieze!

Among other things, the idea included not only a uniting of generations but also a synthesis of several muses. Developing Samsik's idea, Silvester commissioned the writer Pantelei to compose a script for the concert. The sets would be designed by the sculptor Khvastishchev. Words, sounds, and graphics – what more could one want!

All that remained was to find a sponsor. The thoroughly battered generation of the forty-year-olds understood very well that without a sponsor they would be eaten up alive. Various possibilities were discussed. Contenders for the role of Maecenas included The All-Russian Association of the Blind, Academician Fokusov's outfit, the State Archive.

Meanwhile rehearsals had begun, for which they had found the ideal location – the boiler room of the Soviet Shareholder cooperative apartment house. Before three days had passed, of course, a bunch of Moscow's nogoodniks began gathering around the boiler room: children of dubious elements, pro-Western youth, hippies, black-market dealers, various know-it-alls, jazz fans, and, of course, amateur stool pigeons.

The hostile press often reports that in Moscow rumors propagate like fruit flies. And where, one might ask, do the rumors come from? It is to all appearances a sullen, tight-lipped city, equipped with the last word in word filters and jamming devices. But no sooner does, shall we say, Brezhnev shed a few tears over a little scarlet flower or

a tiny pearly cloud than a rumor immediately springs into life: A new
economic policy is being prepared or peace is about to break out in
the Middle East, or on the contrary, an old economic policy or an
intensification of the ideological struggle is on the way.

Even Samsik – heaven knows, no Brezhnev he! – caused rumors to
start emanating from the boiler room of the Soviet Shareholder: The
story was that a new, shattering form of jazz was in the making that
would rock both America and Poland back on their heels.

It's always like that in Russia. Even the most mediocre modernist
in the arts, an admirer of everything in the West, who damns everything
home-grown, is secretly convinced in his heart of hearts that the world's
greatest talent will emerge from Russia, and it only has to be nurtured
for it to burst forth and astonish the whole world no less than the first
atomic mushroom cloud or ballistic missile.

It wasn't long before Silvester was called up by Alexander Kuzmich
Skop, a highly placed official in the Moscow city committee of the
Komsomol, wanting to know the source of all this "unhealthy furor."

"But what furor?" Silvester was horrified. "What are you talking
about, Shura? We're absorbing the classical heritage of ancient
mythology. In fact, we're striking a covert blow at the Greek junta!
Now listen, Shura, you know something about music."

And right there Silvester boomed into the phone four whole bars
from the number "Cerberus the Three-Headed Dog." Skop calmed
down but insisted on sending a vigilante squad to the boiler room all
the same, in order to check it all out on the spot. Silvester did not
object. Being cunning, he realized that a nice little bust-up would do
them no harm but would, if anything, give the group a certain reputation for daring, like, for instance, the Taganka Theater.

Silvester did not divulge these diplomatic subtleties to his old friend
Samsik, who was wholly absorbed in the artistic side of the project.
Along with his boys – guitarists, drummers, sound technicians, and
soloists – he was reveling in the chance of playing in the boiler room
of the mighty and, of course, semicriminal housing cooperative. All
of Moscow's hippiedom had provided them with costumes for the
forthcoming concert, together with Lucky Strike cigarettes and cans of
Danish beer. It was somewhat warm in those infernal regions, but the
boys liked the heat. They stripped to the waist and imagined themselves
on the beach at Monterey or in the bazaars of Marrakesh. There was
a whiff of grass in the air.

One day a funny thing happened. By way of practice, Samsik was
improvising on a theme from the American group Chicago and leaning

with his bare back against a bend in a red-hot pipe. The theme was very close to his heart – "The Fateful Questions of Nineteen Sixty-Eight." Samsik was carried away – if one can say that of a man who was making his instrument give forth a series of hoarse, monotonous yelps, like the squeals of a dog being slaughtered, mixed with dark, confused clucking sounds.

Members of the younger generation, with whom Samsik, according to Silvester's plan, was meant to form a link, put down their guitars and looked at their leader with amazement. Thin, bathed in sweat, with a little brass cross sticking to his sweaty, hollow chest, Samsik Sabler was rhyming "Prague" with "Chicago."

Suddenly, something from far away came closer. He closed his eyes and blew something tender and sad, a simple memory of the days of his youth. He could see steam, clouds of steam, and through it people wearing prison underwear sitting on heating pipes, like clusters of some wild, tumorlike growth. In this new elegy that he was playing, there was not a single note of protest or rebellion, but on the contrary it expressed a gentle, disconsolate theme from his own personal fate.

The younger generation thumped indignantly on their drumheads, strings, and the keys of the electronic organ. No one was interested in the leader's personal fate. The leader fell away from the pipe and collapsed face down. His back was smoking, the skin peeling off in clumps – a second-degree burn. He'd really done it this time!

Somehow or other "The Pergamum Frieze" was made ready, and all the equipment was transferred from the boiler room to the air-conditioned climate of the lecture hall of the Institute of Refrigeration Research. Incredible are the turns of fate! In the infernal skillets of the Soviet Shareholder no one had imagined that they would ultimately find such a mighty, prestigious – and cool – sponsor!

The concert was set up for today. Samsik, suffering from a stitch in his side, ran up the staircase of the Institute of Emergency Treatment and imagined the

PHLEGRAEAN MARSHES

where the company was assembled that morning: Porphyrion and Ephialtes, Alcyoneus and Clytius, Nisiros, Polybotes and Enceladus, and Gratian, and Hippolytus, and Otho . . .

Samsik quickened his pace as he climbed the main staircase of the former St. Nicholas's Hospital, up the yellowing marble steps that were worn down to black in places, and landed in a low-ceilinged semidark hallway, resembling an ancient temple, at the end of which two bearded men were holding up a portico adorned with Roman numerals, with suspended above them the invariable slogan: "Put the ideas of the Twenty-fourth Congress into effect!"

. . . and Agrius and Thoas, and how many more, terrible ones, were
    there?
We rebelled in the mud and foul weather
Beneath a low-lying pack of endless clouds . . .
They flew like evil omens
Above our army. We seemed to ourselves
A band of footpads and cutthroats,
But youth, uncouth and furious,
Writhed in our arms and snakelike legs!

Samsik was wandering over the old tiled floor of the hallway when he saw in a dark corner three hospital cots, on which three alcoholics, beaten up in some nocturnal Moscow brawl, lay under nets like wild animals. He stared. Didn't those men have snakes instead of legs? Nonsense! Why such crassly obvious parallels? They were just ordinary, wretched human legs. There was a foot sticking out, encased in plaster. Why keep them under nets?

One was lying motionless and silent, and only his facial muscles regularly, every few seconds, contracted in a grimace and then relaxed again, as steadily as a winking lighthouse. The second was groaning hoarsely, his head thrown back on the pillow, while his large, pointed Adam's apple moved up and down. Only the third man spoke: "Seryozhka, switch on the headlights! Where are you going, you stupid fucker? It's already ten to seven! Switch on the headlights and let's go!"

Covered in black hematomas and cuts, one eye closed, he tried to raise his arms to grasp something, to snatch at something from his delirium, but every time his arms dropped helplessly. In his case too the net was pointless.

We were expecting attacks, thunderbolts, wild flashes of lightning and the other psychic effects that Zeus was so fond of, but all was quiet, endlessly silent, without even the sound of water splashing in the limitless Phlegraean marshes. This was our world – the vast swamp, gray water, gray grass – and there we were rebelling! As we stood and waited, we were beginning to think that nothing was going to happen, there would be no response, and therefore no rebellion, when suddenly in the far distance, where a moment ago no one was to be seen, there rose up a man as huge and tall as an oak, and it was a god. A short sob, like a gulp, came from our ranks.

Greetings, oh, punitive god, great and gilded! Invincible, smiling an enigmatic little smile, you stand there beneath the low gray sky, arms crossed on your chest. Heavily armed, you do not move from the spot. What is your name, god? Hephaestus? Apollo? Hermes? We have never seen a live god before, until our rebellion, and now we see you, oh, unknown god, sent to punish us. Why are you silent?

Several male nurses appeared; without ceremony, and with much grinding and squeaking, they turned the three cots around on the tiled floor and pushed them toward the inner rooms of the ïnstitute.

"Seryozhka! Seryozhka! You're wrong, you son of a bitch!" yelled one of the trio, in such a terrible voice that Samsik lost consciousness for a moment and thus, unconscious, reached the doorway, and only there, as he looked around him, did he realize that the nets were hung over the beds for a purpose: Seryozhka's friend was thrashing about like an Ussuri tiger.

Samsik threw all his weight against the heavy door. The cool air of early nighttime pulled him out of the despairing hospital atmosphere and brought him back to active life. From the steps of the institute he saw a vast crowd of cars crawling slowly toward a crossroads. As he made his way down, clutching the railings, he again tried to imagine the field of battle, this time in the terms given to him over the phone by the writer Pantelei.

"Right," he had said from some distant place, in a ringing, sober voice, like a real classicist. "Imagine the streets of the West before a revolution. The streets of the European capitals humming with revolution, a strongly spiced pizza, a pound of rotten eggs. Then – can you see it, boys? – a bottle apiece, a bottle of champagne. Mumm, and a rubber dumdum bullet for each in the back of the neck. Here are rubber revolutions, the street theater of capital cities at night, dense clots of nocturnal pollution, the braying of electronic donkeys. Now let us return to the bright Grecian world, surrounded by a total absence of civilization, that is, by darkness. There too things were not all that simple. Tantalus insulted the gods, and for that he was punished with what we nowadays might call a drying-out cure. Demeter, mourning for Persephone, ate Pelops's shoulder, and that was that. Niobe, daughter of Tantalus, also displayed *hubris* (old Cockroach Whiskers was right: 'The apple never falls far from the apple tree'), and for that Apollo and Artemis shot her children dead with arrows. In other words, the comrades boldly abandoned the principles of dull, abstract humanism, and in keeping with the given situation, they firmly took a tactical approach to the aphorism 'The son is not responsible for the deeds of the father.'

"As you see, boys, the frustration against Olympus had been building up for some time, and you must be aware of this when you play the theme of the Unknown God."

The sight of a solitary, silent god amid the swamps is enough to alarm any mortal, even one conceived and hatched out by Mother Gaea from a drop of Uranus's blood. Some of the giants even thought that their wild, absurd life was now justified when they saw one of the Olympian multitude.

Why were we born? Rebellion and death resulting from it are the meaning of our marshy existence. Why don't we keep on rebelling? Why do we tremble with veneration at the first god we see, a spy-god? Indeed, are we rebelling at all?

An ultramodern resuscitation ambulance, rear and top lights pulsating, drew up to the main entrance of the institute. Out of it leaped a man, unrecognizable in the darkness, who ran up the steps and, in a voice that was brisk and businesslike though slightly tinged with hysteria, shouted "Call up Zilberansky at once! Ask him to come! Please!" and disappeared.

The ambulance demonstrated its life-saving capabilities. It hummed, snorted, opened itself up. Out of it was expelled a wheeled stretcher, carrying a heavy, prone body. Then the ambulance drove away, the paramedics departed, and for a few seconds Samsik was left alone with the weighty body.

In the absolute silence that ensued he realized that this encounter lay outside the power of time. The massive body lay motionless, like a stone idol from the Scythian burial mounds. Hephaestus, the blacksmith god, quietly descended the steps and raised his lantern. From out of the darkness the dim light illuminated a coarse, strong-willed face with a protuberant brow and upper lip, an inadequate forehead, and a little nose. The face, which in life had been something of a caricature, bore in death the features of somewhat obtuse grandeur typical of the guardians of underground arsenals.

AFTER THE RELEASE OF TOLYA'S MOTHER

and of Aunt Varya, or rather after their transfer to the category of permanent exiles, the strange family in the Third Medical Complex rejoiced. Inveterate Trotskyites were only allowed to move within a seven-kilometer radius of their spiritual center, Vaskov's House, but even inside that radius there were so many possibilities for enjoying a "normal human life"! One could go to the stores and shop there, order medicines from the pharmacy, have clothes made at the tailor's, listen to the radio, and derive the greatest possible pleasure from all this.

One day, when the weather was fine, Tolya and his mother set off to the photographer's to have her picture taken as a memento. In the studio they saw Captain Cheptsov. He was posing for his photograph, sitting bolt upright and holding his hands on his knees in a pharaonic pose.

On another occasion Tolya ran into Cheptsov face to face in the town library. The captain was selecting some books to read, mostly classics – Turgenev, Nekrasov, Gorky.

The third time, in the summer on the shores of Talaya Bay, Tolya, his mother, and Aunt Varya were walking through thickets of dwarf stone pine when they suddenly came out onto a meadow, where Cheptsov, wearing a silk undershirt, was playing volleyball with several women.

In other words, within that small radius (seven kilometers) meetings with Captain Cheptsov occurred fairly often, and each time the captain gave neither Tolya nor his mother so much as a glance. Perhaps, indeed, he simply did not notice them at all. Or perhaps he had merely forgotten all about them.

But he had not forgotten them. Tolya realized this at the First of May parade in 1950. Together with two of his friends from the basket-ball team, Tolya was carrying an enormous portrait of Stalin the Standard-Bearer of Peace. Tolya was gripping the right-hand pole with his left hand, and thus seemed to fulfill the role of the right flanker as they passed the podium on which stood the Magadan big shots, a herd of pigs decked out in gold epaulettes. Below the stand was a bunch of more junior officers, and among them, of course, to Tolya's good fortune, there protruded Captain Cheptsov's huge, padded chest.

As their eyes met, Cheptsov showed that he had recognized him. In fact, of course, he had always recognized him, but had simply not regarded him as a human being. Now his glance moved from the Standard-Bearer to Tolya's glum face, and he smiled his fleshy, mocking smile.

On that occasion Von Steinbock almost stared him down – almost. To have responded fully to Cheptsov's look would have been impossible: That would have meant wrenching the pole out of the portrait of Stalin, flinging himself at Cheptsov, and hammering, hammering at that look and at the smile, in revenge for it all – for the sniveling and the sobs, for the way Cheptsov had handed mother her coat, for beating up the Ringo Kid, for booting Von Steinbock in the ass, and for the photographic studio, the library, the volleyball, and now for this First of May parade.

"We were born to turn fairy tales into reality, to overcome space, time, and distance. Reason has given us steel arms and wings, and instead of a heart, an internal combustion engine!" Who, in those days, could have looked from the Magadan square into the future and seen darkness in the forecourt of St. Nicholas's Hospital, Hephaestus holding his lantern over the body of Cheptsov in rigor mortis? We all imagine that life is nothing but a succession of moments, and we never think that the gods are at work.

Suddenly there came a burst of bright light. Orderlies ran up and pushed the stretcher away, while the hospital forecourt was invaded by Samsik's horde of hippies, The Giants, the younger generation.

"Sam!" yelled the twenty-year-old lead guitarist, Makkar, running ahead of the others, his long shaggy hair flying in all directions, wearing baggy, bell-bottomed brocade pants. "You're way off base, daddy-o!"

"You're off base, you've goofed, you're not cool!" shouted the kids, and Tar Baby, the nineteen-year-old drummer, actually shook their leader unceremoniously. "People are all arriving at the refrigerator, momma! They've already called up from the American Embassy! They'll skin you alive, Massa Sam! *Unkl Silver he's enkshus*, got it? He's having kittens! We can't start the show without you, daddy!"

At this, Samsik crowed with happiness like a rooster. He felt good among these young kids. He really wanted to bridge the generation gap, to link these cool cats, the offspring of Moscow's bohemian fringe, with those ghostly Leningraders of his youth, the Samsiks of '56 in thick-soled, Soviet-made copies of American baseball shoes (known as shit squashers) and tight, narrow pants. Like it or not, you Party-line apparatchiks, you Marxist pencil pushers, you can't eradicate that "insignificant proportion of our otherwise ideologically healthy generation," and you will never completely stifle the European spirit that has always been a part of Russia!

"You, childrenski, you socksuckers!" he addressed The Giants. "You, successors to the balding fifties and the rusting sixties, you are the corrosion of the seventies. I appeal to you, my friends! What is the meaning of rebellion, and *is* there any meaning to it?"

"Sounds to me like he's been hitting the bottle, guys!" said Makkar in amazement. "Have you, daddy? Or maybe you've been shooting up?"

Samsik raised his arms, inviting the whole mob to the Phlegraean marshes, to the peninsula of Pellene, which is

NOT SO VERY FAR FROM HERE.

First to come to his senses was Porphyrion, ringleader of the revolt, who wiped the blissful smile from his face with his hairy hands.

"Hey you, big boy!" he shouted to the solitary god. "Who are you? Name? What's your name? Even if you're Apollo, we'll make you eat shit! We'll have our revenge!"

"What for?" The motionless god asked the question silently, merely by a slight shimmer of his aura.

"For everything! We'll have our revenge!"

The giants choked on the bloody word. There was a smell of steaming entrails. Sink our teeth, our teeth, into the god's liver. Vengeance! Vengeance on Zeus for his greatness, for his wisdom, for his arrogance, for his endless offspring, for his throne, for the lightning, for our male members, which have never known love. Vengeance on them all for their nectar, their ambrosia, even though we don't give a damn for the stuff. Vengeance on them for being different, for their bright, sunny world of mythology in which they roam about so happily! Vengeance!

And at once the whole expanse of the marshes was filled with a glittering host. The spy-god was lost in the crowd of golden gods and goddesses, advancing on the giants in rustling garments and the faint clinking of swords, arrows, and armor. A window opened in the sky, and a mighty shaft of the sun's rays descended upon the swamp, as though to illuminate the field of battle for the future sculptor. The gods advanced in a steady, businesslike fashion, with no particular display of solemnity, clearly not intending to take long in dealing with this filthy scum, this froth, these mere bubbles of the earthly imagination.

> Bubbles! We have burst
> Over Europe,
> But while we float hither,
> Don't lose hope!
> A hurricane over your Gothic!
> Bubbles!
> Make ready the javelins!
> You have till dawn!

He knew, of course, that the whole of THEIR Moscow would come to the concert, all the "people," but when clusters of hippies, sitting on concrete slabs, began appearing a few blocks away from the Institute of Refrigeration Research, he began to feel slightly uneasy.

The Institute of Refrigeration Research was located in the back of a large complex of apartment houses amid a chaotic muddle of small factories, fences, and foundation pits of buildings that were dug during the last five-year-plan and never completed, abandoned bulldozers, cranes, generators, and a mass of newly dumped concrete blocks.

A taxi cautiously picked its way through this "Shanghai." The driver glanced at the figures of hippies flitting back and forth in the light of occasional headlights, and at one moment he actually stopped when a concrete pipe loomed up out of the darkness; on it were sitting the three Max-Rayevsky sisters, wearing broad-brimmed hats and their grandmothers' feather boas, with doll-like little faces painted to the point of utter indecency.

"Hey, look at the way they've done themselves up!" The taxi-driver roared with laughter. "What a bunch of scarecrows! Gypsies! Well, here goes!"

He released the clutch pedal so hard that the Volga leaped across a trench dug for heating pipes, splashed into a puddle, burst through some wire, and flopped onto an unexpected strip of asphalt, along which he drove up to the grass and metal of the research institute, all its floors ablaze with light, like a ghost of the Federal Republic of Germany.

A crowd was already standing here quite peacefully and without breaking down the doors. In general, it was dry, warm, peaceful, and sweet, in other words, a thoroughly pleasant London atmosphere. A few Zhigulis, two Volkswagens, and a four-berth Ford camper completed the illusion.

"Who invited the foreigners? Was it you, Makkar?" asked Samsik sternly. "Why, kids? Why make waves?"

"Why make waves?" This, one might say, was the slogan of Samsik's generation. OK, play; OK, have fun, but just make sure you don't make waves! Live it up, do your thing, be brave, only don't tread on the toes of the powers that be!

The children of the Khrushchev generation were not yet afraid of the powers that be. Not that they were particularly brave; they simply had not had much experience of the fury of the authorities when roused. Moscow's hippiedom had not yet acquired sufficient experience. The world seemed entirely natural and normal: We are hippies, the good guys, and they, the vigilantes, are the squares, the bad guys, who hassle us. Apart from these, there are the foreigners, the Yanks, the West Germans, the black marketeers . . . and, when you're high, casual sexual encounters as cool as bees gathering honey!

Last year they had planned to demonstrate against the war in Vietnam, the idea being to show our kids' solidarity with the *un*square people who were demonstrating in Trafalgar Square. They had gathered in front of the American Embassy with slogans in English: "Get out of Vietnam!" and "We demand troop withdrawal!" They made the V for Victory sign with their fingers. The general effect was cool, man, like at Berkeley, and it was also against imperialism and for peace. So why the hell did the police have to show up? Three paddy wagons full of friendly Soviet police, and the demonstration by progressive youth was liquidated. Did they fuck you up? Sure, they fucked us up. And why, did you ask? Why? Hell, for demonstrating against the Vietnam war. After all, they held meetings against it in all the factories. Aha, yes, it's OK to hold meetings in factories, but the police all over the world bash *us* up. There you are. So why make waves and upset the bosses? Who said anything about annoying the bosses? All that happened was that Tar Baby called up and said, "OK, guys, let's go to the embassy and make a bit of a ruckus." And we made a ruckus. So everything was normal, then? Everything normal, daddy. And what about democracy in the Soviet Union? What's the score on that, kiddo? I guess democracy's pretty fucked up here, daddy-o.

Silvester was already on the stage, setting up the equipment, shouting instructions to the sound technicians – the twin Veksler brothers – clicking his fingers, sometimes jumping up and down, sometimes freezing on the spot and muttering to himself. Catching sight of Samsik, he rushed up to him. "Thank God you're here! Let me give you a kiss. Are you going to play for us, Sam? Try the Alcyoneus theme. Let me give you a kiss! Now remember, Sam old man. Makkar will sing his words, and then you come in here and give us twelve bars of improvisation. Sam, you old yellow-eyes, let me give you a kiss! Do you remember Alcyoneus?"

"How could I forget it." Samsik picked up his saxophone and closed his eyes.

They were advancing on us like waves. Each one of them was as elusive as a wave and, like a wave, unforgettable. A horde of bright-visaged beings of such nobility! Oh, how hideous were our snakelike legs and how repulsive were our matted locks smeared with traces of nights spent in the swamps, our joints swollen with rheumatism and our muscles like moss-grown rocks!

"Oh, brothers!" said the young Alcyoneus. "In truth, never even in my dreams have I seen such a handsome god as that one with the dogs! Look, brothers, see the twin bulges on his chest! I cannot in truth imagine what they might be, but they send me out of my mind! See, giants, how boldly he carries before him those slightly quivering protuberances as though they were ordinary things!"

"You're not afraid of death, are you, Alcyoneus?" asked Porphyrion grimly.

"Of course not, Porphyrion, not at all! It's just that I've started to get an idea, that I understand why . . . why I was given that third little snake that dangles between my two snakelike legs. Look, Porphyrion, my little snake has raised its head. It too seems to like that god with those tender but firm bulges! Oh, Porphyrion . . ."

A sound flew across the swamp. Heracles loosed the bowstring and an arrow, tipped with poison from the Lernean Hydra, pierced the breast of the mighty but naïve Alcyoneus.

"Poor youth," said Porphyrion with a sigh. "He did not have time to meet even a single heifer belonging to the rich men of the West."

A rock hurled by Porphyrion, somersaulting through the air, flew toward the bright host. The battle had begun.

Samsik stopped playing and smiled his not too Hollywoodish smile at the boys. "Not bad, eh?"

The boys looked at him with satisfaction. "Pure fifties," said Makkar.

"What?" Samsik was worried. "Something wrong?"

"It was great, leader," the boys reassured him. "You really hit the spot. The golden fifties. You played sheer nostalgia."

"Interesting." Samsik wrinkled his nose. "I had no idea I was indulging in nostalgia. I was just playing and trying to make it as good as possible."

"By the way, comrades, there's a problem that interests me." With his mane of hair and luxuriant moustache, Tar Baby, covered in medallions, bracelets, and rings, made the remark in the uncharacteristic tone of a semi-intellectual technician. He was visibly excited. "Of course, as a musician, I'm not in the same class as Samson Apollinarievich, but there's this problem that interests me. OK, I'm playing in this drama, but I must admit that I'm not thinking about giants. In fact, comrades, I don't think about anything at all when I'm playing. I feel something very strong, and that's enough for me. Maybe we should just shit on all this literature? If I'm wrong, I hope the comrades will put me right."

"Tar Baby!" Silvester shrieked like a madman, flinging himself at the young musician and waving his arms. "You're right – and you're wrong! Come on, I'll explain it all to you. I'll open your eyes!"

All this enthusiasm, these hectic leaps and foaming lips, gripping people with sweaty hands in a fury of inspiration, all this was just like the old Silvester, and Samsik loved it. In general, he loved the atmosphere of rehearsals, when people shouted and blew off steam, and everyone was as relaxed as though he was at home – that was the *real* high. To be honest, Samsik never fully responded to the public when the show was on. He always remained what he was, a shy, awkward jerk from Barmaleyev Street. Rehearsals – now there he was in his element. There he really loved playing and looked for compliments. "Silvester, maybe I wasn't playing so good?" he asked his old friend, knowing perfectly well that he would praise him.

"You played like a genius, old yellow-tooth," said Silvester approvingly, and then clapped his hand to his forehead. "Oh, I completely forgot. There's been a rash of phone calls for you. Academician Fokusov sent his best and promised to come with his wife and friends . . . And who else? Oh, yes, Volodya Vysotsky. He's also coming to the concert, along with Marina Vlady."

At once Samsik's head began to swim. How idiotic that his body should react like this to good news – nausea, a jump in blood pressure . . . What was Marina Vlady anyway? Just a mirage, a puff of French smoke. After all, today I met Arina Belyakova, my first woman, and I didn't give myself away, so as not to embarrass her. Anyway, what is Marina Vlady now? A member of the Central Committee of the French Communist Party! It's obviously time to forget the old image. So what, let 'em come. I shall be delighted and I'll try not to fall flat on my face when "my friend from far away" comes to our concert.

"They're already in the hall," Misha Veksler whispered to him. "I was shattered! It's the first time I've seen Vysotsky in the flesh."

In the still almost empty hall Samsik caught sight of something pink or blue or lemon-yellow, and alongside it was Vysotsky.

"Hi there, Sabler!" Vysotsky shouted. "I hope we're not in the way?"

Samsik made a long, deep bow, holding his saxophone to one side in his outstretched hand. "I have toothache today. I'm not in form. I fainted this morning," he said in a plaintive voice from the stage, thinking at the same time; What am I saying, slob that I am? He continued, "The food's to blame, of course. The pilfering in canteens has gotten beyond all bounds. Sometimes you can't tell the difference between meatloaf and bread. Bachelor life. Heartburn and colic are the price of freedom."

"Shut up, old man," said Vysotsky calmly. "What's the matter with you?"

The brightly colored blur beside him laughed. That same distant laugh of a girl from the golden shores of the West! Take your glasses off, madam. You're not at a Central Committee meeting now! You're my guest, in the palace of jazz and freon refrigeration systems! Get up, Madame Comrade Vlady, and to hell with that shawl of yours that keeps changing color! You and I are the same color and we'll never betray it!

Do you remember, behind Tolstoy Square on the Petrograd Side of Leningrad, there used to be a little turn off from the Bolshoi Prospekt: the walls of two six-story houses, the marble figures of Venetians, stone, tiles, and bronze, a "memorial of the Silver Age?" Do you remember – dark, gloomy doorways with stained-glass windows, a row of pruned lime trees – just a step away from your medical school, remember? You were always hurrying to seminars, but I, a bold urban guerrilla, always intercepted you and turned you around, and we would walk down that little forgotten cul-de-sac off the end of the avenue, where there was no traffic, where one's footsteps always echoed, and where it was as deserted as though the Bolsheviks had won the Revolution and then gone away again, leaving the city without any of their capital investment, only the memory of them. You usually used to say, "OK, let's go to your place on Barmaleyev, and maybe . . ." Involuntarily your hand clenched into a fist. We would walk from there to Barmaleyev Street and we did that "maybe," but do you know, that wasn't what I was always dreaming of. I was always dreaming of meeting you again in an echoing silence amid huge marble houses and of us walking through the interiors, my gaze moving from your face to the smoke-blackened Venetian figures and back again from the Venetians to you. I'm not sure you perceived that street in the same way that I did. I'm not sure whether you even remember it now. Was it you with me in those days? Or was it plain, ordinary Arina Belyakova? Or was it the mythical Alisa, who melted into the Siberian tundra in 1949? I'm not sure about you.

All this passed through Samsik's memory when he was no longer talking to his distinguished guests but just sitting quietly behind a curtain in a corner of the stage, looking at the painted backdrop, which the boys had now set up. On the backdrop, among the other products of Radius Khvastishchev's fantasy there were photographs of the Pergamum frieze, in the form in which it is now preserved on Museum Island in East Berlin.

A headless Zeus is wrestling with three giants. He has no left arm, and all that remains of his right arm is the shoulder joint and the hand, grasping the tail of a bunch of spent thunderbolts. It was not the giants, of course, who caused the god to suffer this terrible loss. A deep crack has split the hip of one of the giants, lumps of marble have fallen away from Porphyrion's buttocks, he has lost an arm and the tip of his nose, but it is not the gods who had crippled him thus.

Moment by moment. Battle. Evil deeds. Gesture follows gesture: The thrust of a lance, the shooting of an arrow, stones flung from a sling – they all occur, they all emerge as though from the sea, only to fall

at once back into the sea, remaining only in the shaky memories of
eyewitnesses and in the imagination of artists, nowhere else. But
memory and imagination can be perpetuated in marble or recorded on
magnetic tape.

They were enemies in the Phlegraean marshes on the peninsula of
Pellene, yet they became allies in Pergamum. They raised a wave of
marble and thus withstood the pressure of time: horses rearing, teeth
bared, muscles flexed, hair flying, weapons . . . In the Pergamum
marble, both gods and giants fought together against Cronus.

Ladies and gentlemen, dear comrades, you see before you a field of
battle. As you see, this bas-relief has suffered serious damage over the
long centuries. Note here, for instance, the fragment of a waist, a tuft
of hair, the hilt of a sword . . . empty, doomed space. Any of the
spectators may mentally add his or her own person to the frieze.

According to the concept of Khvastishchev, the sculptor, who for
some reason has not turned up at the concert, the empty spaces of the
Pergamum frieze will be filled, during the course of the music-drama,
with the children of the twentieth century – Stalin, Hitler, Mamlakat,
Che Guevara, Brigitte Bardot, Salvador Allende, Cassius Clay, Haile
Selassie, Christiaan Barnard, Valentina Tereshkova, Khrushchev, Neil
Armstrong, Solzhenitsyn – together with fragments of outstanding
events of modern times, such as the battle on the Boulevard Gay-
Lussac or a meeting of the workers of the Ilyich factory protesting the
evil deeds of Tel Aviv.

And now, here they are, lined up on stage under the slogan "Put the
ideas of the Twenty-fourth Party Congress into effect!" and against
the background of the Pergamum frieze, the jazz group The Giants,
under the leadership of Sabler and Silvester, all in jeans of different
colors and bright shirts, with Makkar wearing brocade pants and a
little vest over his bare torso.

"This might as well be in the West," said Marina Vlady, thinking
this would be a good stick to beat the critics of Soviet socialism.
"Where's the boredom? Where is the barefaced propaganda? Where
is the oppression of creative youth?"

Samsik stared into the auditorium and almost choked with happiness.
This was his great moment! In front of him was a hall full of people
who were spiritually close to him and as remote from Captain Cheptsov
as it was possible to be! There was Marina Vlady, dreamgirl of his
youth, and there sat Doctor Arina Belyakova, his first love, to whom

he had today revealed nothing but his blood pressure, but who had undoubtedly recognized him, for otherwise she wouldn't have come to the concert.

Everything around me here tonight – the West, Moscow, jazz, young people – is dear to me, and none of it reminds me of you, Cheptsov! Around me are our friends, our instruments and our powerful amplifiers. We have brought our bodies and our generations together, we have linked them up with electricity, with the energy system of the whole free world, a world that includes our Soviet Motherland, too! So drop dead, you dumb, thick-skulled sons of bitches! Today we're going to play jazz!

ZILBERANSKY ARRIVED AT ST. NICHOLAS'S HOSPITAL

or rather at the Semashko Institute of Emergency Treatment only half an hour after being called. "What's the problem, Gennady?" he inquired from the doorway. Declining the white coat offered him by a nurse, he strode over to the operating table.

He had obviously come straight from some pleasurable occasion, either from a cocktail party or from his mistress. He exuded the complete playboy's bouquet: a touch of Rémy Martin brandy, a dash of Yardley's aftershave, and a whiff of Kent cigarettes. He also reeked of sperm and female erotic secretions.

Malkolmov nodded toward the table, where the body of Cheptsov lay motionless and stiffening. A jungle of tubes stretched from the body to a positive Manhattan of ultramodern life-saving machinery that surrounded the table.

Zilberansky cast a rapid glance at the machines. The needles on all the dials lay motionless, and the only sign that they were functioning correctly was the winking of the different colored indicator lights. Rolling up his tweed sleeve, Zilberansky pulled back Cheptsov's eyelids in the time-honored fashion and tested the pupils for reaction to light.

"Done for," he said. "This is no longer clinical death, Gennady. It's the real thing."

"We did everything," said Malkolmov emphatically. "It's all on record. There are witnesses. I did everything; my conscience is clear. It's all on record."

Zilberansky looked intently at Malkolmov, trying to catch his glance as it wandered over the equipment and the sheaf of clinical notes.

Then he turned to the nurses: "I would like you all to leave the room, please."

They left the two men alone with Cheptsov's corpse. Zilberansky offered Malkolmov a Kent. They lit their cigarettes.

"Who is this man?" asked Zilberansky.

"I can't understand how he slipped through our fingers," Malkolmov muttered. "He should be alive. I saved him. All systems were functioning properly, and we did everything according to the rules."

"Who is this man?" Zilberansky walked around the table and put his hands on his old friend's shoulders. "Answer me! Don't keep looking away from me! I've almost guessed who it is already. Don't be evasive, Genka! You've described that face to me so many times. Is it him? The one you can't get out of your memory? The *Chekist* from Magadan?"

"Sadist! Stalinist! Filthy pig!" The words burst forth from Malkolmov, his twisted, sweat-soaked features quivering. "Why couldn't I save him?"

"You wanted your revenge on him," said Zilberansky quietly.

"By slapping his face perhaps! By sarcasm or contempt!" Malkolmov went on, shouting. "But not by taking his life! I don't need his dreary little life! I had every reason for wanting to save him!"

"Any other doctor in your place would have saved him." Zilberansky's eyes glittered thoughtfully through the cigarette smoke.

Malkolmov dragged on his cigarette as though he were inhaling oxygen. "Any other doctor?" he said in between lungfuls of smoke. "This sort of thing can happen to any doctor. Don't you think? Hasn't it ever happened to you?"

"That's enough smoking, for Christ's sake!" shouted Zilberansky, flinging open the window, seizing Malkolmov, and shaking him. "Now relax! Sit down! Listen to me carefully. You are an old medieval obscurantist, an alchemist, and a charlatan, and I'm going to try and talk to you in your own language. That man's a corpse because for some reason the ligaments binding his soul to his body weakened and snapped. Something essential to his soul flowed out of him, and his soul departed, perhaps because it was afraid of your vengeance –"

"What is his soul like?" Malkolmov asked. "Like a vampire's?"

"Hardly," said Zilberansky reflectively. "More like a jellyfish's perhaps? Anyway, that's not important. If you want to save him, if it's really so essential to you, then, dear Apollinarievich, – just think about what you must do."

Malkolmov already understood what he meant. He put his head

under a faucet and, through the water streaming over his face, asked his friend, "Would you do it if you were in my place?"

"Never," came the firm answer. "I would stick firmly to the instructions; nothing more. I'm an atheist."

"You're only saying that because you've never been in this situation yourself."

"Maybe. But do you understand what I'm getting at?"

"Yes, I do."

What he had in mind, of course, was Malkolmov's Lymph-D, the substance that he had recently referred to as "liquid soul." The stuff was in a flask nearby, locked up in a safe in Malkolmov's laboratory, in the basement of the institute.

It's down there waiting for me, thought Malkolmov, waiting to burst into action, waiting for the moment of creative rebirth. And for all these years I have been waiting for it too, wherever I have been, in every cesspool, on every slope, and at every turn, and my Masha is waiting for it as she moves from one stranger's bed to another in unfamiliar towns, and my children are waiting for it, those children who have never seen their father yet and have never even heard of him. In fact, all enlightened mankind is waiting for it.

"Are you sure, Zilber?" asked Malkolmov, his wet teeth chattering.

Now it was the turn of his friend, the mighty, flourishing, self-confident Zilberansky, to be evasive. "See here. As far as I'm concerned, you can go to hell," he muttered. "Find some of your Catholic priests and get them to help you solve your problems. I'm not a padre."

"Very well then," said Malkolmov. "In that case I'll ask you another question: Are you sure that Lymph-D will help him?" He nodded toward the rigid body.

Zilberansky opened another window and stood quite still with his back to Malkolmov. After a minute he shrugged his shoulders.

Leaving the treatment room, his heels clattering on the resonant tiled floor of the long corridor, Malkolmov smiled at his team – "Don't hang around here, you guys! Go get some rest!" – and went downstairs into the hallway. There he met a colleague (the woman doctor who looked like Marina Vlady), borrowed three kopeks from her for the vending machine, and quenched his thirst with a pear-flavored soda. Then shuffling out of the hallway and down into the basement, he unlocked his little cell, sighed – phew, the dust! – and opened the safe, from whence he took a flask and returned by the same route, slapping the vending machine on the side as he went: Keep up the good work, old man!

Zilberansky was seated on the windowledge and smoking; against the background of a dusty Moscow night, his profile had something noble about it. He was thinking to himself: I expect you imagine, Gennady, that I'm advising you to use up your Lymph-D for unworthy, Salieri-like reasons.

Malkolmov was thinking: Have you gone off your head, Zilber? How could I guess that something like this would happen? Who else but you could I trust?

Zilberansky slipped down from the windowledge and helped Malkolmov set up the drip. Malkolmov was barely able to find a wiry, knotted vein under the rockhard skin in which to insert the needle. Somehow or other he got the needle in, opened the valve on the drip, walked away from the corpse, and found a chair near a glass-fronted cabinet full of instruments and materials.

When the first sigh escaped from Cheptsov's lips, and the needle indicating arterial pressure began moving upward, Malkolmov opened the glass cabinet and, having selected a round bottle, took out the glass stopper and began gulping down the colorless, transparent contents.

"What are you drinking?" asked Zilberansky.

"Alcohol," said Malkolmov, pausing for breath. "Pure, undiluted . . . Ah, that hits the spot!"

HAVING INSERTED THREE FINGERS INTO KLARA

Radius Apollinarievich Khvastishchev bent them into various shapes. With the other hand he was squeezing her breasts, first the left one and then the right one, and gently tweaking her nipples.

Radius Apollinarievich was lying on his back, with Klara at his head and Tamara at his feet. The latter was occupied with his male member, purring and groaning softly. Meanwhile Radius Apollinarievich's right foot was at play in Tamara's crotch, in which a special role was allotted to the sculptor's big toe.

The form is quite delightful, but as a piece of composition it leaves something to be desired, thought the sculptor. There's a certain touch of dilettantism about this arrangement.

He quickly regrouped the trio. Now Tamara became the center of the composition. Entering her from behind, he lay on his stomach over her back, which was curved like the bow of Artemis, and cupped her pendulous breasts from below with his palms. Klara, squealing with jealousy, fastened her lower parts to Tamara's face, while she inserted her index finger into Radius Apollinarievich's posterior orifice. From the movements of Tamara's head, the sculptor noted that the two girls were already united.

A tried and tested masterpiece, he thought, with a sideways glance into the mirror. Not exactly original, but beautiful! Ah, Hellas, mother of us all!

"OK, girls, this position is approved!" he shouted, and the shape set up a steady, rhythmic movement, charged with poetic but explosive force.

No doubt owing to a certain erotic satiety, Radius Apollinarievich worked hard but somewhat mechanically. More and more often he caught himself thinking that he now arranged these games à trois, which had undoubtedly started as a result of his debauched artistic nature, less for his own than for the girls' benefit.

By now all three of them were so well attuned to each other that the slightest movement, even somewhere out on the periphery, immediately sent an electric charge through the whole group, and the moment of truth always came to all three simultaneously, and then, even at the very start of the split-second spasm of pleasure, they already began to feel regret for the imminent breakup, the inevitable coming apart, and so for a long time the form continued to stir, pining with tenderness and gratitude, while all of them covered each other's still-warm parts with a delicate rain of fluttering kisses and whispered, "Radik, Radik, darling . . ." "Klara, my sweetest, Klara . . ." "Tamarochka, my little bunny rabbit . . ." "Oh, Radik, Radik, Klara, Tamara . . ."

Radius Apollinarievich stroked the two excited, panting heads nestling on his broad chest, and his feelings for them were almost paternal.

Funnily enough, it was just this "debauchery" that now maintained their inner calm and equilibrium: Klara, the little whore from Samarkand, had ceased her perpetual copulating with colored students in the dormitories of Moscow State University and was studying hard to get the best grades, while Tamara, gentle daughter of the Dnieper, had given up her shameful work in the foreign-currency bar, was drinking less alcohol, and was no longer lying down under wretched Swedish businessmen in order to extract their little secrets – trivial, but much needed by the KGB. Radius himself was more relaxed – loving these two little hookers chimed in favorably with his current attempt to reestablish himself.

Now he no longer needed to rummage in blind, feverish searches through all the garbage dumps of Moscow. At last the celebrated artist had found his sexual ideal. Sometimes he even thought that the two young whores were the incarnation of his romantic image of woman, in the search for which he had committed so many loathsome stupidities. The mere recollection of them was appalling; quite recently, for example, a squad of police had had to remove Khvastishchev from a drainpipe on the skyscraper that housed the Ministry of Transportation. What had brought him there? A sequence of sickening misadventures in search of the golden-haired Alisa Fokusova, who had flashed disturbingly across his field of vision one afternoon behind the wheel of her Volkswagen and illuminated the dim brain of Khvastishchev, stuck at the traffic lights at Insurrection Square, with the thought, There she is, my dream!

After that he had mooned about all day trying to get his bearings, wanting to sculpt, to immortalize in bronze the little pointed face and cascading hair, the childishly thin shoulder – the profile of the goddess Isis . . . Silence, night, a woman running past the pedestal of a monstrous thirty-story statue, a momentary turn of her head, flash of a face disappearing behind an oak door of the "great epoch". He had a fight with an Armenian-Italian-looking playboy, who had insulted Isis by hinting at sexual contact with her. He had spat in the ear of a doorman, who wouldn't let him into the club, where she, of course, was sitting and "breathing perfume and mistiness". He had been beaten up by three savage bloodhounds masquerading as waiters at the Labyrinth bar. And finally, night, silence, a monstrous stone monument to the Stalin era, lights burning on the tenth floor. She was there, of course, at a ball, in an atmosphere of subtle tension, and now he would appear at the window like some "mysterious figure in the night." The building turned out to be the Ministry of Transportation, and the creature lurking behind those windows turned out to be someone quite different – Beshchev, the Minister of Transportation, in fact.

Now all those former infatuations, including Alisa, wife of the prizewinning academician and mistress of every pig in Moscow, were in the past, behind him. Now he had both love and lust at home under his own roof, provided by these two dear creatures, little bitches, little kittens. He had stopped drinking; he was working and earning money. He was not a debauchee but the head of a family. He pondered calmly and wisely on art, as great artists should, and a couple of times a week he would actually go up to the marble flank of his favorite offspring, the dinosaur *Humility,* and hack at it with a chisel. At these moments the girls became as quiet as mice, because they understood: This was Art!

Their bed, or rather their communal couch, was situated in a little room right under the ceiling of the studio, and now, puffing at a cigarette and slapping his girlfriends' moist buttocks, he could see through a little window the simple peasantlike face of his dinosaur lit up by a neon light shining in from the street. It only needed a little work to round off the folds of the upper lip, and in this sort of lighting the creature would acquire a sardonic expression. This, of course, was quite unacceptable: Sardonic looks were quite out of place on such a simple-minded, herbivorous creature.

The telephone rang. Klara picked up the receiver. "Radius Apollinarievich? No, no, you're not disturbing us! Yes, he was working, but right now, unfortunately, he's not working." She tugged at her lord and master's male organ. "It's for you, Radik."

The voice in the receiver might have been familiar or unfamiliar, but at least it sounded like "one of us". From the first syllable Khvastishchev recognized it as being "one of our sort."

"Forgive me, Radius. You don't know me, but you and I have many friends in common. This is Pantelei Pantelei speaking, the writer."

"Are you sure we haven't met, Pantelei? I think you once came to my studio, old man."

"Possibly. I don't remember. Right now I've stopped drinking and I'm getting to know everybody all over again."

"I'm in a similar situation. Do you want to come over?"

"Thanks. I certainly will come. In fact, I've been meaning to come for a long time, but right now I'm calling you on another matter."

What a guy. I try to be chummy but he keeps his distance, thought Khvastishchev.

"Do you have a transistor radio. Tune in to the BBC; they're broadcasting something that's important to you. I'll call back later." Pantelei hung up.

In recent years Khvastishchev had stopped listening to foreign radio stations, seeing no need for it: Nobody from abroad was able to tell him anything new about his own country, and as for the Arab sheikhs and their oil, they could go fuck themselves! He didn't know where their radio set was, but even before he had put down the receiver he heard Klara turn on the radio and search boldly across the dial.

"What sharp ears you have, my little Tatar," he said, tickling Klara's navel.

"Professional training," said Tamara, laughing from the darkness.

Khvastishchev had not even had time to grasp this sly little dig when he had a feeling as if the marble foot of his dinosaur was treading on his stomach. What he heard took his breath away. Very close, right beside his ear, there rang out the voice of his friend Igor Serebro: "How shall I put it? Of course, it was always a source of secret torment. They degraded me. It finally became obvious that the whole of my life, both as an artist and as a private individual, depended on their goodwill."

"Does that mean, Igor Yevstigneyevich, that you were a secret KGB informer for twelve years?" The voice of the English interviewer sounded like the tones of a psychiatrist.

"The fact is they never actually called me a collaborator as such. On the contrary, they always insisted that I was a free artist, that they appreciated my talent and respected my patriotism, but . . . What the hell, it's time to call a spade a spade: yes, for twelve years I acted as a secret informer. A person only has to sign a piece of paper in a moment of cowardice and after that they never let you go. Twelve years! I couldn't bear it any longer!"

"Do you mean that your decision to stay in the West was motivated by that reason?"

"It's only one of the reasons, but probably the most important."

"What did your work as an informer consist of?"

"They wanted information about the moods, the attitudes of my friends and colleagues and about the creative intelligentsia as a whole."

"And did you give them that information?"

"I tried not to harm any decent people. Most of the time I was successful in this, but sometimes they made tape recordings of our conversations."

"Igor Yevstigneyevich, we have agreed that you don't have to answer all my questions if you don't want to."

"No, I'll answer them all. I want to get it all off my chest!"

"An admirable intention. Well now, let's see . . . Did you know your conversations were being taperecorded?"

"No . . . yes . . . sometimes I guessed they were."

"I see. Tell me, Mr. Serebro, why did you choose this particular occasion to request political asylum? After all, you've been to the West many times before, haven't you?"

"Life in our country has become more and more stifling since the political trials, since the occupation of Czechoslovakia and the rebirth of the spirit of Stalinism. My ideal of democratic socialism was totally destroyed. The whole of our movement of the sixties had perished; the 'new wave' had subsided into nothing more than a puddle."

"Do you consider yourself as belonging to that movement?"

"Mr. Eizenshtuk, you amaze me! I was one of the leaders of the Russian 'new wave!' "

"Pig! What a pig!" screamed Tamara.

"Radik, he was informing on you, too!" groaned Klara.

"Shut up, you little fools!" barked Khvastishchev.

Somewhere in the ether, and not very far away, the jamming signal began to gather strength. On a nearby frequency someone was pounding out Chuck Berry's "Johnny Be Good."

"And you were doing it, too, you cheap little Tatar whore!" Tamara suddenly yelled, and began to cry. "I know who you go to see when you go to the Kuznetsky Bridge!"

"Why, you bitch!" squealed Klara, clutching at Tamara's hair. "I've never said anything bad about Radik. On the contrary, I tell them he's a communist at heart! You, of course, prefer operating in the foreign-currency bar, *Lieutenant!*"

"I never did!" cried Tamara.

"I never did!" Klara sobbed hysterically.

The voice of the leader of the Russian "new wave" again came clearly through the jamming signal and the sound of Chuck Berry.

"Recently they became dissatisfied with me. I realized that I would never make it out to the West unless I dreamed up some dodge. They were interested in my friend Radius Khvastishchev, the famous surrealist sculptor. I went to see him, and took a bottle of whiskey with me in the absolute certainty that the outcome would be something totally absurd. Khvastishchev is completely apolitical. He's the impulsive, creative type, and his drunken speeches are nothing but delirious ravings. It didn't quite work out like that, but I wrote a purposely absurd report, in which I said that Khvastishchev was a religious obscurantist, that he maintained contact with the Vatican's Jesuit intelligence service and was recruiting people into this clerical spy network – people like the writer Pantelei, the mathematician Kunitser, Dr. Malkolmov, and even Sabler, a jazz musician. I specially picked them out at random from among the people I knew so that the combination would look utterly absurd. Khvastishchev, in fact, has never set eyes on any of them in his life."

"And did the authorities believe you?"

"I doubt it. But my efforts were rewarded – I was allowed to go to England. Now I'm free!"

"Wasn't that rather a high price for your freedom, Mr. Serebro? After all, your friend – what did you say his name was? Khvostov? – might find himself in trouble?"

"Oh, no! Not now that I've told all about it on the radio. Now I'm what's known as a 'traitor to the motherland' – my credibility is completely destroyed."

After a slight pause, the chilly voice of Abram Gavrilovich Eizenshtuk, the famous commentator, inquired with a hint of disgust, "Well, what are your plans, Mr. Serebro?"

"Chuck it all overboard!" exclaimed Igor, recovering his previous inspired tone. "I shall burn everything I brought with me! Even my name! I'll become a new man! All I need is stone and chisel! I shall carve pure abstract forms! No politics, no literature, no philosophy. I just want to join the club of the free artists of the West!"

"You'll find it difficult," grunted Abram Gavrilovich in farewell.

Then came a short news bulletin. Only then did the crazy jamming signal rise to its full power, blotting out the travels of Henry Kissinger, a statement by Reza Pahlevi, Shah of Iran, and the latest deals by Patolichev, the Soviet Minister of Foreign Trade – all things, in fact, that needn't have been jammed at all.

Khvastishchev crawled out of his vast bed, and first of all, for some reason, he pulled on his pants. His two beloved creatures were squealing and slapping each other at the other end of their communal couch.

"Stop it, girls," he said with a frown. "Why are you being so paranoid? So Klara too was recruited by the KGB. Big deal! Clearly the world situation is serious. If even Igor was a stool pigeon for twelve years, then for pretty hookers it's obviously inevitable. Humility, my little whores. Learn some humility from our dinosaur."

The girls calmed down and seated themselves crosslegged, gazing at their nabob. Their eyes glittered in the darkness. The jamming signal howled.

When were he and I last together at Tolstoy's estate, Yasnaya Polyana? "Look, Khvast," he had said. "There is the tomb of Leo Nikolayevich. To the left a white forest, to the right a black one, and the white and black branches are interlaced overhead. A natural church! All that's lacking, up there in that corner, is a little portrait of Johann Sebastian Bach in stained glass, like the one in the Church of St. Thomas in Leipzig. Do you like those great slabs of Tolstoyan prose that are extraneous to the plot? They're like the music of Bach. Tolstoy would have made a splendid sculptor, with his baggy shirt and his white beard, certainly no worse than Konenkov, for instance. He had a sculptor's powerful hands, and feel for wood and metal. Russia hasn't produced any great sculptors. If Tolstoy had been a sculptor, he would still have been Tolstoy. What a pity he never became a sculptor, Khvastishchev, my friend!"

When were he and I together at Yasnaya Polyana? It must have been thirteen years ago, before he started "passing information." Wait a minute. No, it was eleven years ago. By then he was already a stool pigeon.

When did he and I first visit Erik Neizvestny? It was then that he asked Erik about the "Man Shattered by an Explosion." What did it mean? Wasn't it a symbol? Wasn't it a symbol of our generation? No, it's not a symbol, Erik had replied, it's simply a man shattered by the explosion of an antitank mine. Your generation didn't know about such things. That had been fourteen years ago, before Serebro became a stool pigeon.

Oh, Igor! How many times he and I used to curse all informers and stool pigeons! Why, we even beat them up on more than one occasion!

"Radik," Tamara called out plaintively. "You must be getting hungry. It's time for supper. Shall I make you some scrambled eggs with tomatoes?" How like a kind old Ukrainian momma!

"Radik, I'll just run out for a loaf of bread!" said Klara, jumping up as though nothing had happened. What a sweet, bright little student she is!

"Comrade officers, attention!" said Khvastishchev, and switched on all the lights in the bedroom and the studio.

The light was very strong. They all looked white, like an overexposed photograph. A brothel. The ugly white bodies of beautiful whores.

"Hey, girls, do you remember, Serebro once brought us a bottle of Johnny Walker, didn't he? Where is it? We haven't drunk it yet, have we?"

Tamara at once ran off – naked, slim, white, so much the "brown-eyed, black-browed" beauty of Ukrainian tradition that he almost felt like fucking her again! – and came back with the very same bottle that Igor Serebro had just been describing to the whole of thinking humanity.

"That's right, Radik! Smash it against the wall! We don't want a trace of him left here!"

Khvastishchev took the bottle, read the label: "Blended Scotch Whisky . . . By Appointment to Her Majesty . . . ," unscrewed the cap with its striding optimist in tight white pants, looked inside for some reason, then shook it, and began to gulp it down.

Right after the first few mouthfuls he realized that the past was coming back, the mysterious evenings like youthful masturbation, the fascination with objects, a presentiment of love, and dusty, stifling mornings-after at the Men's Club.

The girls embraced and wept over him, keening over him as though he were dead.

SO LET'S REALLY DRINK SOME TEA

as the comrades suggested!

The thin, desiccated Verochka sat down beside Kunitser with a glass of weak tea. He noticed a diamond ring on her finger. A ring like that must have set someone back at least two thousand. Once he had himself been married and had given his wife presents like that.

"Tell me Aristarkh, where is Nathalie nowadays?"

"?"

"I mean your wife, we used to know each other at one time."

"The mother of my children is now far away from here, in the 'land of equal opportunity.' "

"In the States?"

"Yes . . . more or less . . . somewhere around there . . . in Brazil . . ."

"Did she emigrate via Israel? And what about you, Arik?"

Verochka's carefully laundered dress and her blouse from the Sintetica store smelled of Madame Rochas perfume. Verochka, a charming woman of around forty, warm in her own way and not at all sentimental, moved closer, put her elbow on the table, rested her chin on her hand, and looked non-committally into his eyes.

"The husband of the mother of my children is a talented Zionist, while I am a Russian, Verochka, although that may seem strange to you, and my name comes from the Russian word *kunitsa,* a marten. In the distant past I was slightly Jewish, but now I have a great future before me."

She gave a charming laugh. "You haven't changed, Kun! I remember once, when you were with us at Izmailovo –"

"With you at Izmailovo?"

"Don't you remember?" This time she laughed quite entrancingly and even slightly mysteriously. "And who fucked me in the bathroom?"

Something touched Kunitser's shoulder, quivering. He looked around – it was Nina.

"Perhaps we could go now, Aristarkh Apollinarievich? You did want to give me some more dictation."

The slender Verochka looked at her, smiling an intent little smile that caused all her charming little wrinkles to bunch together. "Can such very young women still be jealous of me?"

A fist crashing hard on the table interrupted this, to say the least, strange little scene. "This is disgusting!" said Argentov loudly and furiously. "Society gossip, flirting, jealous scenes! Are you people out of your minds?"

Kunitser felt slightly ashamed. In fact, Argent was right – it was odd, at the very least, to behave like this in a secret political meeting that has just been raided. Even so, they couldn't just go on sitting there in silence either. Why were they all so silent?

Everyone maintained a dumb, hopeless silence, not because they had been particularly frightened but from lack of experience. The new Russian Social Democrats did not yet know how to behave after a raid by the secret police.

Verochka moved away from Kunitser and turned to Argentov with a malicious smile. "All right, then, say something, Argent! Enough of sitting there like a statue! You must write the rest of this chapter of history."

"Vera, either shut up or get out of here!" Argentov said more calmly. "Well, my friends, let's put our heads together and try and think how this happened. They knew everything – where everything was hidden, who was present. They even knew that I had invited Kun today. Aha, now there, perhaps, is a clue!"

"Obviously there's a stool pigeon," boomed a male voice from a dark corner. "One of us is an informer."

"Now begins the melodrama *à la francaise! Franc-tireurs! Maquis!*" said Verochka, bursting into laughter. By now she was sitting on the windowledge, the very spot from which a few years ago a man toppled into the street. Beside her was a bottle. When she had stopped laughing, she poured herself a glassful of dark liquid – brandy, Kunitser decided from the smell – and drank it down in one gulp, "tossed it back" as the saying goes.

"Comrades, we won't find the stool pigeon now anyway," said the recent lecturer, Yakov Shalashnikov, in a muffled voice. "We'd better all go home."

Once again, Argentov thumped the table with his fist. "We can't just break it up like that!"

"He's upset because they didn't arrest him," Verochka explained kindly from the windowledge. "He's afraid they might not have suspected him."

Argentov stood up brusquely. Kunitser also jumped to his feet, intending to bar his friend's way to that dangerous window, but Argentov went in a different direction and switched on all the lights – a chandelier and three candelabra. Then he leaned his clenched fists on the table and announced, jerkily and with a vague smile on his lips, "Only four people knew that Kun was coming: myself, Vera, Nolan, and Maiboroda. The last is at the moment in Rostov. I propose that all four of us be placed under suspicion."

"My poor dear would-be martyr," said Vera, pouring herself another brandy. This time, Kunitser noticed the label on the bottle – Rémy Martin, no less!

"You see, comrades," she said in a lively voice, "by making this proposition, our wise Argentik has already halfway rehabilitated himself."

"And what would *you* propose, Madame Chief Conspirator?" Argentov swung around to face her, and Kunitser realized at this moment that they had loved each other for a long time and that the tension that was crackling between them was much more important to them than any struggle for social democracy or whatever.

"I propose we finish with all this," said Verochka, her voice suddenly hoarse. "Tomorrow let's all go out on Pushkin Square, announce our existence, and then let them arrest us all!"

"Agreed!" exclaimed Kunitser to his own surprise. "But why wait till tomorrow? We must go and do it now, immediately!"

"That, of course, is not a serious suggestion," said Shalashnikov morosely. "If there's to be self-immolation, then at least make it worthwhile. We would have to prepare ourselves, warn the appropriate people." He stood up, zipped up his worn leather jacket, and put on a black peaked cap with the letter *T* on its band. So he really was a taxi driver.

"You're too late to go to the Visa and Registration Office, Shalashnikov!"

A young man with a small fluffy beard and very, very hard little eyes emerged from a corner of the room. In his buttoned-up, high-collared Russian shirt and rumpled jacket he looked so much the perfect nineteenth-century revolutionary of the People's Will movement that it was too good to be true, as if he were playing the part in a movie.

"The Visa and Registration Office closed long ago," he persisted, staring at Shalashnikov.

Visibly embarrassed, Shalashnikov pretended to be looking for something in his pockets and tying the tapes of the portfolio containing his lecture notes.

"Visa Office, Visa Office . . ." he muttered to himself. "I have to go to work now . . . I work the night shift . . . Try feeding a family on the daytime rate of thirty-five rubles per shift . . . I'm not as young as I was . . . and my sight's getting weaker."

"What's the matter, Kershuni?" said Argentov reluctantly, through clenched teeth, as he turned toward the young man from the People's Will.

All the Social Democrats had by now left their corners and had clustered round the table, looking at Shalashnikov and Kershuni. Kunitser looked from one to the other. It was as if they were all foreseeing the outcome of this scene and were only waiting for the ace of spades and pistols for two.

Nina's soft lips touched Kunitser's ear. "Aristarkh, let's get out of here. I implore you."

He pushed her away rudely.

"What is there for me to say?" Kershuni said with a malicious smile. "Shalashnikov is the one who ought to be telling you how he exchanged a two-room apartment in Chertanovo for a three-room one in Tel Aviv."

Shalashnikov raised his arm to give the young man a slap in the face, but allowed his friends standing nearby to restrain him.

"So what, I've nothing to hide. I wasn't planning to desert, but I did submit an application . . . as a last resort. Revolutionary tactics justify it."

"There, what did I tell you?" said Kershuni in a blaze of triumph and turned around to all the others, clearly expecting a corresponding reaction.

The small group around the table remained silent.

"Well?" said Kershuni, perplexed.

"Argentik, why don't you say something?" Verochka shouted mockingly from the windowledge.

Kunitser glanced rapidly in her direction – the bottle was already two-thirds empty.

"I suppose I'm a complete idiot!" screamed Kershuni. He started to run away, came back, grabbed his cap, and tugged at the collar of his Russian shirt.

"Easy, easy, Moishe." Argentov made a move toward him. "After all, Shalashnikov –"

The door had already slammed behind Kershuni.

"Moishe, come back!" The cry was cut off by the clang of the elevator's steel door.

"A naïve Jewish idealist, and a Russian patriot," said Verochka, giggling. "He must be expelled from the Social Democratic party. Isn't that right, Argentum? We are all genuine materialists, sober politicians. Isn't that so, Nikodimchik? All of us have already made our independent arrangements for a retreat. We've thought it all out down to the last detail, haven't we? What make of car will you use to drive away abroad? I suggest a Jaguar. Will you give me a Jaguar, Argentik? Your memoirs, entitled *Underground,* will be selling well, so –"

"How disgusting!" Argentov shouted into her face, his features distorted with hatred, tense and trembling.

"To hell with these Soviet rags of yours!" In a split-second movement, Verochka tore her old and worn dress in half. "I want to be dressed by Dior! I want *la vie de luxe!* I want a man who knows what he's doing! Hey, Kun, come with me! Chuck that little hooker of yours. She can't do anything!"

The other, silent, thin woman grasped Verochka by the shoulders and pulled her into the next room. The silent woman's face expressed nothing; it seemed to have frozen in a look of pain, while Verochka, looking amazingly younger and defiant, was staring around her with unseeing eyes and calling for someone, rubbing her hip with one hand and with the other pushing her breasts up from underneath.

"Take me all the way!"

The door closed behind the two women. The men, staring at the floor, picked up their hats and one after another departed from Argentov's apartment. The master of the house, groaning with despair, was pacing from corner to corner.

"How disgusting, how disgusting. Believe me, Kun, we're not really like this at all."

Kunitser walked over to the window and poured the rest of the Rémy Martin into a glass. There was almost a glassful. He drank it down without stopping, then reached for the telephone.

"Who are you calling?" Argentov asked.

"My laboratory. They'll be looking for me, and I can't wait to find out how my calculations for a weapon of mass destruction are working out."

"I'VE NEVER EARNED A SINGLE RUBLE WITH MY VERSES"

said Pantelei to Mayakovsky, seated on the plinth of the poet's statue.

"As you see, you and I have something in common, Vladim Vladimych. But there is a difference, my old friend: You sang of your Soviet republic as the spring of mankind, whereas the great swarm of *my* republics, including even the Komi Autonomous Soviet Socialist Republic, is suffering from a prolonged drought. My love for you, however, has not diminished, my dear and famous friend, who splashed paint out of a glass, and in the distant past astounded young Von Steinbock with your arrogant looks, the features of a rebellious young European."

Pantelei gazed up from below at the massive creases in the huge, flared pants, weighted down, according to the idea of the sculptor, Kibalnikov, by enormous metal cuffs, and thought how this ponderous, granitelike figure of Mayakovsky had always struck him as unattainably elderly, played out and past its prime, and seemed so now, even though the inscription stated that he had died at the age of thirty-seven – in other words, at a younger age than Pantelei was himself who was sitting on the plinth of the statue, an aging youth, a perpetual friend of the handsome twenty-two-year-old Mayakovsky who had splashed paint out of the glass.

Twice already a group of vigilantes had walked past Pantelei, three stout hefty workmen in their best suits adorned with medals. Despite the fact that they were obviously well fed, they were talking about meat.

"Do you get a regular supply of meat there?"

"Yes, plenty. Pork, of course. There's never any beef."

"Some people turn up their noses at pork, but I think it's a tasty, juicy meat."

"The Tatars eat horseflesh."

"Horseflesh can be tender, too."

Although they were absorbed in their conversation, every time they passed Pantelei, they looked him over intently. A policeman, standing by the metro station, was also looking at him.

They're afraid I'm a foreigner, thought Pantelei, who may suddenly chain himself to the monument and demand freedom for Bukovsky. There have been incidents of that sort with foreigners in Moscow. Obviously it could never happen with Russians. Where would a Russian get chains from?

He remembered how ten years before, a crowd had gathered around this Statue and recited poetry, how the "smogists" had demonstrated here, and how Bukovsky himself, the hero of Russian youth, had also declaimed poetry, as yet undisturbed by thoughts of the Vladimir Central Prison. Today's young people would regard such demonstrations as impossible. Some of them imagined that such things had only happened before the Revolution.

"What's the time, please?" asked one of the vigilantes.

They had finally decided to find out whether he was a foreigner or one of ours. He would now show them that he was one hundred percent Soviet, in spite of his long hair and suede sneakers.

"You wouldn't happen to have a ruble to spare, would you, dad?" He answered their question with another question in a hoarse, desperate voice. "My soul's on fire. I've just been discharged from the hospital for infectious diseases. I don't want to go back to stealing. Just enough for a plate of soup."

The vigilantes gave a sigh of relief – he's one of ours all right!

"Shove off out of here while you're still in one piece," said one of them.

"We should arrest this comrade," said the second.

"Why push him back on the road to crime?" reasoned the third.

The first man immediately agreed and hauled out some small change from his pocket.

"Thanks, lads," said Pantelei, touched by such generosity. "I can see you're old frontline soldiers . . . does you credit . . . won't forget. I'll pay it back with interest . . . to the motherland. Would you like my passport as security?"

"OK, move on, pal," they said, giving him a dig in the belly for encouragement. "Sober up, go sleep it off, and keep off the slippery slope."

Pantelei at once set off toward nearby Sovremennik Theater. He counted the small change. Not bad – it added up to about eighty kopeks. He could make use of it if he got hungry. He felt really grateful to the vanguard of progressive humanity. It really was true that in the Soviet Union no one need starve. Either they beat you up and threw you in jail to eat prison slop, or they put their hands in their pockets and at least gave you enough for a bowl of soup. Joking aside, though, I love my generous motherland.

Like it or not, he must now go to the Sovremennik. He had been sitting by the monument, in fact, because he hadn't wanted to go into the theater: Alisa Fokusova, her husband, and their gang of hangers-on were in there. After the scandalous affair in the club, they had gone on to the late-night preview of a new play, which had, of course, already been banned by Kakarzhevsky, the *bête noire* of all Moscow progressives.

Pantelei hadn't gone with them for two reasons: firstly, because he didn't want to be counted as one of Alisa's hangers-on, all those big-deal sycophants who surrounded his beloved – yes, his beloved!!! – and secondly . . . well, secondly, because he hadn't gone with them!

Tonight he was going to shadow Alisa and the "blazer." He would tail them and put a stop to their sordid cold-blooded fucking session. That fuck was not going to take place if he could help it!

Where were they planning to go? To some fenced-off construction site? To the stinking hallway of some apartment house, where they would do it standing up? By the way, was the gear shift in a Mercedes on the floor or the steering column? And did that heap have fully reclining front seats?

As he considered different varieties of fucking, drawn, incidentally, from his own experience, Pantelei broke out in a hot sweat of hatred. These ladies of Moscow's "society" were really the most perverted whores, and as for the "blazer," well, he was nothing but a professional stud of the wham-bam variety without even a thank-you-ma'am. He had never caressed her hip in his dreams, never seen her in the guise of a Polish prisoner, had never wandered with her through a ruined castle, had never sailed around the earth with her in a rusty cable car.

Hell, I'm not drunk now. I'm sober and determined. In the past, when I was a drunkard, insolent, and inspired, I would have slept with her long ago by now, fucked her until I lost interest and then passed her on to others. Now I shall take her away from them all, including her husband the academician. He's been enjoying my beloved long enough!

Pantelei now needed Alisa as an essential element of his new, simple, and sober life. In the past she had been the very incarnation of a Moscow that was promiscuous, knowing, and corrupt, a false, ephemeral, "pseudo-Hemingwayesque," café-society sort of existence. Now he would create a new image for her, and she would wind her golden hair into a bun and sit with her feet up on some grubby old sofa, she would smoke and listen to music and gaze devotedly at the back of his neck as he toiled away with his pen. By day she would be silent, and at night they would make love . . . endless caresses . . . And above them would rustle the many-tiered trees, whose leaves so generously reflect the moonlight. Awakening, they would talk of the trees. In the end, perhaps they would themselves grow into trees and stand with their branches touching each other, and when their branches went numb from immobility, they would summon up the wind . . . But what shall we do when we rot and decay?

In the Sovremennik Theater, its artistic director, Oleg Tabakov, was sitting in his office. He was wearing a huge red wig, a revolting brocade minidress, black fishnet stockings, and stiletto-heeled shoes. Obviously he was playing the part of some shameless female in tonight's show, and now, between entrances, he was signing character references to assist in the candidacy of several of his colleagues for the title of Honored Artist of the RSFSR. Catching sight of Pantelei in the doorway, Tabakov stood up, opened his arms wide, and came forward to meet his visitor with his inimitable, depraved smile. "Pantelyata! I'm all yours!" Lifting up his padded breasts, he pressed himself against Pantelei, breathing with suffocating passion.

Pantelei loved Tabakov, in the way that one loves any perfect work of art. The man who was now director of this popular theater was a born actor. The stage wasn't enough for his acting talent. He acted everywhere – at home, in the family circle, in the Ministry of Culture, among bureaucrats, even when he was all alone. When there was no acting for him to do, he simply looked at other people with his "inimitable" look, which seemed to say, I know a great deal about you, as you no doubt know a great deal about me.

"Why are you so late, Pantelyata? Everyone in the theater has been trying to reach you by phone. It's scandalous! There are a hundred Americans in the auditorium and two hundred stool pigeons. All the big wheels, all the top bananas, all the beautiful women of Moscow, and there's no sign of our Pantelei. But we love you, Pantelyata, don't you know that? We're expecting a masterpiece from you. I hear you're working on an idea to do with a Heron, isn't that right, Pantelyata?"

"What?" Pantelei was thunderstruck. "How did you hear about the Heron, Oleg? I only thought of it today."

"From Vadim Serebryanikov. Our tame genius Pantelei, he says, has gotten an idea for a paraphrase of *The Seagull* by a certain Chekhonte, aka Chekhov."

"But only an hour ago he was smashed out of his mind!"

"*Yoo ar nie rait,* Pantelyata, *nie rait* at all! Vadim Serebryanikov was sitting in this very office, before the show, as sober as a judge, along with Tovstonogov, Yefremov, Kakarzhevsky, Donald Hughes, Academician Fokusov, and other big wheels. It was then that he told us about the Heron. He said he wanted to link it up with the events in Chile. And perhaps you'll give it to us, Pantelyata. Will you?"

"It's fantastic!" Pantelei scratched his unshaved chin. "This morning he was blind drunk, disgustingly drunk. In front of everyone he kissed the backs of a waitress's legs above her stocking tops. Do you realize–"

"We know how to pull ourselves together!" said Tabakov, beaming, admiring the invisible Serebryanikov. "It's our great strength! That's why our masters love us – because we never completely let ourselves go. We may throw up, we may scream our heads off, we may, as you claim, kiss the backs of someone's legs, but today we have to turn up at the Sovremennik, today we *must* appear there, today EVERYONE is there – so we turn up. Look . . ." Without taking off his makeup, he acted out the appearance of his friend Vadim, with eyes that were white and staring but full of expression, upright as a post, his lips twisted from the effort to remain vertical. "And so we enter, with Academician Fokusov" – he acted out the dignified look of an aging sportsman, the stiff movements of his patrician features – "and with Madame Alisa" – a quick tossing back of the hair, a wink flashed to the left-hand corner, and a bright smile straight at the right-hand corner of the room.

It was all done with great verisimilitude. Pantelei gripped Tabakov by his padded breasts. "What was that bastard doing with the Fokusovs?"

"Let me go, you rough boy, I'm not that sort of girl." Tabakov giggled, slipping back into his female role. He pulled himself free and instantly started playing the part of Academician Fokusov, speaking in a hoarse voice, slightly rolling his r's, just like the famous designer of tractors. "Excuse me, my friend, but over the last twenty years Serebryanikov and I have been through a lot together: Vietnam, Cambodia, the Battle of Smolensk . . . Oh, sorry, that's the wrong record. In other words, many of the hot spots of this planet of ours."

The voice of the assistant director came booming over the loudspeaker: "Oleg Pavlovich, you're on!"

"That's all! I must run. Pantelyata, sit down in this chair. And don't leave without me! Do we get the Heron?"

"But it's not even written yet," muttered Pantelei, flopping into the director's chair.

Tabakov rubbed his hands together, all his features twisted into his "inimitable" smile. "Now I'm going to show them Miss Soviet Union! It'll be a sensation, Pantelyata! Pity about this business with Serebro. Traitors to the country make things awkward for us, distinctly awkward. Sensation after sensation, and what's the result, Pantelyata? Nothing, that's what!"

"What sensation? Who's a traitor?" asked Pantelei in amazement.

His eyes glittering with diabolical amusement, Tabakov produced a Zenith Transoceanic radio set from under his desk, plunked it down in front of Pantelei, and whispered hotly to him in the voice that could give a whole audience gooseflesh, "Find the BBC, Pantelei!" Whereupon he became transformed and made his exit completely in character, wiggling his bottom and thrusting out his breasts.

Silence reigned in the office, disturbed only by the mumble of onstage dialogue coming from the loudspeaker. Pantelei decided to stay and sit it out. After the show, a crowd of celebrities would show up here to drink whiskey and congratulate Tabokov and Volchek, giving voice to "progressive public opinion" in front of the political bosses. Alisa would be among them, of course. Would the "blazer" come too? When were they going to meet today? Surely she couldn't be planning to slip away from her husband tonight?

So Vadim was here too, was he? That was news – Serebryanikov was a friend of Fokusov's. "The hot spots of this planet of ours?" It was true that they were often photographed together at all sorts of congresses and conferences. Was Vadim really planning to produce the Heron? If so, then all was still not lost. The Heron and the Vixen, the Fox and the Heron . . . When she was young she had been a heron of the Polish marshes, and now she had become sophisticated and smooth, a golden Moscow vixen. Was all really not yet lost?

Thinking about all this, Pantelei was twirling the knob on the Zenith until he finally hit the wavelength of the BBC. There was indeed a genuine, full-blown sensation: the sculptor Igor Serebro had defected to the West, Igor the famous, happy-go-lucky, irreverent, scandalous darling of Moscow. And not only had he defected, but he had also stripped before the eyes of the whole world and revealed . . . not the figure of a Greek god but the hairy thighs of an old stool pigeon, a longtime secret informer for the KGB.

The mores of the time have taught us not to be astonished by such news. Furthermore, Pantelei had never felt any great liking for Serebro, although the two of them were regarded as pals, comrades-in-arms, and fellow nonconformists. There was that other sculptor, Radik Khvastishchev, Pantelei remembered, a friend of that two-faced bastard; now there was a really worthwhile guy. What an idiotic life one led – drinking and hobnobbing with all sorts of riffraff, never managing to get on close terms with the real, decent people.

Pantelei found Khvastishchev's number in the phone book on Tabakov's desk and called him up. Maybe Khvast hadn't yet heard the news about his old buddy, his bosom pal.

Such, indeed, was the case. Having alerted Khvastishchev and hung up the receiver, it was only then that Pantelei remembered that he was supposed to be meeting Sabler that evening at a jazz concert. That was another lousy thing. I did, after all, write the script of *The Battle Between the Gods and the Giants* for those guys. I meant to go to the concert, meet them, and give them moral support, instead of which here I am chasing after some piece of ass. Alas, we are not free agents, we're not genuine personalities, not gods, and not giants. We just let Moscow churn us around at will in its meat grinder.

Now the show was over, and everyone poured into the office. From his corner, Pantelei caught sight of Serebryanikov, who was, indeed, sober and stern. While chatting to Popov, the deputy minister, he sternly rested his elbow on Tovstonogov's shoulder and sternly put his arm around Yefremov's waist. Pantelei also saw Academician Fokusov, who was talking to the two foreigners, Hughes and Morales, switching easily from English to Spanish, and glancing rapidly and furtively around him in search of his wife. Pantelei also saw Alisa, wearing a little black dress (when had she found time to change?), her intelligent face looking slightly puffy and hence somewhat childish, talking to Tanya Lavrova and Galya Volchek, pretending not to notice all the men who were looking at her. Pantelei also saw the "blazer." The latter turned up last, looking haggard and grubby, and with a black eye. He wasn't talking to anyone, but attached himself first to one group and then another, clearly trying to edge his way closer to Alisa.

"Bagrationsky, lend me five rubles!" Pantelei shouted to him.

The "blazer" willingly searched through his pockets and pulled out something small and miserable-looking, more wretched than a dead sparrow. "Sorry, old man, three rubles is all I can manage."

"Give me three, then. I need them for a taxi to chase after the woman of my dreams, the girl of the Golden West, understand?"

"And what am I going to ride in, old man? My bitch of a wife from Luxembourg has taken the rotor arm out of the Mercedes, and I have a date for a blow job tonight."

"Where are you going for your blow job? Maybe I can give you a lift," said Pantelei, feeling a thrill of childish excitement in the pit of his stomach. He suddenly noticed Alisa staring intently at both of them.

"To be honest, old man, I don't particularly want to keep this date after today's ghastly fiasco," Bagrationsky whined in his ear. "An hour ago, because my nerves were in shreds, I had a quickie with a paramedic in the Central Committee clinic. Why did I do it? What on earth for, I ask myself? What's happening to me?"

And what's the matter with me? thought Pantelei. When she looks at me, I ought to wink back at her, with a quick, cynical glance and a half-drunken grin, yet here I am getting butterflies in my belly like Tolya von Steinbock meeting Lyuda Guly.

Morales blocked the view of Alisa with his hefty shoulder, a pillar of the future Latin American revolution.

"I must go," moaned the "blazer." "I've made a date with the woman, so I have to go. Otherwise, my impeccable reputation will suffer."

Suddenly the evil genius of ideology, Kakarzhevsky himself, pushed his way into their corner. "And how did you like the show, Pantelei Apollinarievich, and you, Nikita Andreyevich?"

Pantelei and Bagrationsky exchanged momentary winks.

"Not very much," said the "blazer." "But my father liked it a lot. He couldn't stay – he had to go to the Finnish sauna . . . Well, you know the one I mean. He'd arranged a meeting there with . . . well, you know who . . ."

The evil genius was so fascinated that the skin of his face was positively flapping, and his desiccated head was craning upward out of his collar.

"Really, really . . ."

"And I didn't like it at all," said Pantelei. "The Sovremennik has started to shy away from problems and is taking refuge in musical comedy. Cozy conformism, an easy cop-out – that's what this show is!"

Kakarzhevsky beamed, with difficulty concealing his pleasure. "Oh, come, Pantelei Apollinarievich, surely you're being a bit too hard on it."

Tabakov, who had heard it all across three dozen talking heads, silently applauded Pantelei and Bagrationsky. Well done, boys, thank you very much! If two such unreliable types as Pantelei and Bagrationsky had praised his play, it would have only harmed the show.

Suddenly the Fokusovs started to go, inviting people to come to their place. The foreigners, of course, accepted at once, and a few girls also went. Serebryanikov embraced Fokusov and patted Alisa on the shoulder, as if to say, Excuse me, friends, but Oleg, Goga Tovstonogov and I still have some business to attend to, matters concerning the theater academy. Fokusov said casually to the "blazer," "Bagrationsky, would you like to hear *Jesus Christ Superstar*? I recently brought the album back with me from California."

The "blazer" was about to accept eagerly, but Pantelei held him back by the tail of his coat: "Don't forget your date!"

There was no invitation for Pantelei. Alisa looked questioningly at her husband, but he gave a negative twitch of his shoulder. From the doorway Alisa still managed to give the uninivited Pantelei a sidelong glance with laughing eyes, meaning that she hoped he realized what this was all about. Pantelei once more melted under her gaze, as though he were Tolya von Steinbock.

They all drove away, looking rather like the sort of company that figures in Fellini's films – captains of industry, a few good-looking whores, and a bunch of hangers-on from the fringes of bohemia. Meanwhile the professionals engaged in the arts – Tovstonogov, Kakarzhevsky, Yefremov, Madame Shaposhnikova from the Ministry of Culture, Serebryanikov, Tabakov, and Volchek – took their seats in a circle of armchairs.

At this point, Pantelei and the "blazer" slipped away.

Moscow at night, empty. An enormous multicolored advertising panel pulsating, meaninglessly but beautifully, above the Sophia Restaurant. This Japanese device had somehow escaped control by our improvers, and it displayed neither slogans nor advertisements, simply pulsated at night, beautifully but pointlessly. The group of cars carrying the Fokusov party was rolling away down the Sadovoye Ring toward an overpass. An empty taxi, its green light glowing, came out of the tunnel and headed for the Sovremennik Theater.

"Pantelei, I gave you all my money," said the "blazer." "Give me a lift to my date."

"Sure, jump in. Where's your woman?"

"Driver, follow those cars over there that are heading for the overpass," said Bagrationsky.

They rapidly caught up with the four cars in which the cheerful party was traveling – two Zhigulis, a Volkswagen, and a Volga.

"That's the Fokusovs," said Pantelei. "Look, Alisa's at the wheel."

"Yes, I see," said the "blazer," grinning. "Keep after them, driver. By the way, Pant, old man, in all the fuss you and I forgot to talk about the main thing. So do you agree?"

"?" asked Pantelei.

"*Crime and Punishment,* of course. Can I cable Paris?"

"You can. Cable away."

"Excellent!" the "blazer" exclaimed with a violence that seemed completely out of place. He rolled down the window and stuck his lacerated and badly battered face out into the stream of air. "Hell, it's a good life in spite of everything! Moscow! The night! Gasoline! You're going to see a woman who wants you! You're sitting beside a friend who understands you!"

"Don't you dare throw up in the back there," said the driver sternly. "If you feel you're going to throw up, tell me and we'll stop."

They turned and drove across Mayakovsky Square, past Tchaikovsky Hall, down Gorky Street, through Pushkin Square, into Art Theater Street – in other words, along the route marking the Russian people's love for their national art. Everyone remembers it, of course – a pistol, chocolate candies, another pistol . . .* Then the familiar Petrovka brought them to the familiar Kuznetsky Bridge. It was here, incidentally, that the creative agonies of our new society first began – the taxi drove past the monument to the Knight of the Revolution, Felix Dzerzhinsky, founder of the Soviet secret police. God, what an absurdly small head he has, and what a silly billy goat's beard! And as for that terrifying gap between the top of the plinth and the bottom of his long cavalry greatcoat, it's really too much!

Finally the massive building that housed Academician Fokusov's apartment appeared on the horizon. It soared upward, standing to the right of the famous Kotelnichesky skyscraper, to which it conceded nothing in dimensions or monumentality. Together these two enormous buildings completely blotted out the eastern slopes of the Moscow skyline. Both these memorials to the "great epoch" of Stalinism were so alike that even the cockroaches got confused and would often, in the course of their nocturnal affairs, run into the wrong building. In the gap between the two skyscrapers stretched a slogan made up of ever-burning electric light bulbs: "Communism equals Soviet power plus the electrification of the whole country!"

And that's all, Pantelei thought every time he passed by that slogan. In that case, what's missing? Surely we've long since electrified the whole country, haven't we? Are there really still remote corners where obstinate reactionaries still light tallow dips?

---

*A shorthand allusion to the methods whereby Mayakovsky, Gorky and Pushkin met their deaths.

So they drove into the vast courtyard, surrounded by the multistory walls of the building. High above, on the roofs and cornices, could be seen the huge, moonlit stone figures of workers, peasant women, and soldiers – The Ones Who Don't Drink.

"This is where you and I say goodbye, Pantelei!" The "blazer" briefly clasped his friend's hand and evaporated in an instant. Pantelei didn't even have time to notice into which of twelve doorways his future collaborator in the synthetic arts disappeared.

The cars that had brought the Fokusov party were standing outside entrance seven. Soon a long row of windows came alight on the eleventh floor, the Fokusovs' apartment. Up there, shadows were seen flitting back and forth.

Pantelei climbed the stone steps to the upper part of the courtyard, where there was a tennis court. Here he found a rickety box that had once contained Moroccan oranges, and sat down on it, leaning his back against the wire fencing around the tennis court.

No doubt they would try and slip away in the middle of the night to some girl friend's apartment, some shed where they would be out of sight. We know how it's done, we've sneaked away ourselves in our time. I'll sit here and won't let them get away.

Between the tennis court and the black, fireproof wall of the massive pile was a balustrade, ornamented with a row of wobbly, insecure stone knobs, in front of which slumbered a little lakelike expanse of asphalt, glittering with two or three patches of moonlight. He was seated in shadow, well concealed, as he observed the lighted windows, in which moved the shadows of various international observers, inveterate liars and scoundrels, freeloaders, sham-naïve foreigners, talented but weak-willed actors, and delightful women who throughout the ages have been the prey of such riff-raff.

My God, how stupid my life is! I'm forty and a bit, and here am I tailing my beloved like a seventeen-year-old. I've never done the really important things that I should have done. I abandon everything halfway even though when I was young I made a rule to finish whatever I had started. I've drunk so much and I've messed up my life so badly that now it's as gritty as sandpaper. Why on earth did I drink so much? Was it to hold on to the fleeting moment?

Once I was walking in Paris (or somewhere in France) along the Boulevard des Italiens (or some other boulevard). It was an urgent, blustery March day, with clouds scudding overhead and women flitting past in their ephemeral beauty. Suddenly I was overcome by a feeling of bitterness amid the transient paradise around me. In those days I knew of only one remedy for bitterness, and went into a bar. After three glasses of brandy, it seemed to me that I could now grasp that moment and make it stand still, all those gusts of wind, turning faces, all mixed up with those flying clouds, the changing light, and the creak of branches.

Then came a time when I ceased to perceive how this gorgeous life of ours was eternally slipping away. Everything in me became coarse and harsh, like sandpaper. But now the perception has returned again, and I am trying to catch Alisa and her fleeting, inconstant beauty.

She and I have never kissed, yet I am afraid for her beauty. I feel so bitterly sad that her beauty may fly away, like that March day in Paris.

When the gods and the giants fought each other in the days when the world was uninhabited, did they understand the true meaning of the battle? Zeus, no doubt, understood it; after all, if someone hadn't pushed a stone into Cronus' mouth instead of the baby Zeus, Olympus would have been uninhabited too. Yes, they were fighting in order to be perpetuated in marble. In the same way, we artists use every trick in the book in an attempt to make Cronus eat a stone instead of a living body. How much time can we buy in this way? A century, a thousand years? But he always gets it back, be it in marble, on canvas, in words, in any medium. In the end he devours it all.

On stormy nights, in their hut in the Third Medical Complex, Tolya von Steinbock used to listen to the cozy stories that the grown-ups told. One such story ran thus: Once in every hundred thousand years, a canary flies to the top of the Pyramid of Khufu and gives it a couple of taps with its beak. Even when the little bird has worn down the entire pyramid to its foundation, less than a moment of eternity will have passed. And yet, when I strike a match, a moment has passed; when I turn my head, a moment has passed. It is absurd to attack Cronus with upraised sword. There is only one warrior who is ready for victory – the unarmed, the timeless Jesus Christ.

A black Volga drove noiselessly around the corner of the building onto the expanse of asphalt and stopped near the wire mesh surrounding the tennis court no more than three paces away from Pantelei. Both of its front doors opened and two people got out of the car – Serebryanikov and his chauffeur.

Still sober, though giving off a faint whiff of something unpleasant, Vadim Nikolayevich walked over to the balustrade and looked at the deserted courtyard, surrounded by massive great walls, dark windows, and dim doorways. Only one bright strip shone out over the courtyard – the Fokusovs'' windows.

"OK, you can go, Talonov," said Serebryanikov in a low voice. "Lower the backs of the front seats and go for a walk. She'll be coming out at any moment."

"There is no end to my amazement at the female sex," said Talonov, busy inside the car.

"Off you go, philosopher," said Serebryanikov with a laugh. He lit a cigarette and leaned his elbows on the balustrade.

At that moment one of the entrance doors slammed, and the sound instantly reverberated around the stone shaft. Alisa ran out of entrance Number 7. Her platform heels clattered over the asphalt.

Pantelei saw her running straight toward the tennis court, toward the black Volga with its reclined seats, toward Serebryanikov. Now she was approaching, hair flying, mouth half-open, eyes glittering. Vadim Nikolayevich threw away his cigarette and carefully stubbed it out with his heel.

"You're crazy," said Alisa with a suppressed laugh. "Look where you've parked the car! Right in view of everybody!"

"It doesn't matter," muttered Serebryanikov as he took her by the shoulders and ran his hands all over her body, pulling up her already short dress. "The moon will go behind the tower in a moment and it'll be dark."

It was then that Pantelei emerged quietly from the shadows. Serebryanikov and Alisa turned and looked at him, their bodies pressed closely together, their faces distorted and white in the moonlight. A second later Vadim Nikolayevich's prophecy was fulfilled – the moon disappeared behind the castellated tower of the stone monster. The lovers' faces disappeared, leaving only the gleam of Alisa's eyes and the narrow little crescent of her teeth. Another second later a dark, threatening blob was thrust toward Pantelei – his friend's face.

"What are you doing here?"

"And what are *you* doing here?" Pantelei took another step forward. "She's my woman! Give her back to me!"

"Have you gone out of your mind, Pant?!" The voice of the dark face sounded conciliatory. "She and I have been meeting for three years. Only it's a great secret."

"I don't care if you've been meeting for thirty years," said Pantelei.

"To hell with you. You and I have never traveled together to the hot spots of this planet of ours. You're no friend of mine."

For a moment he was seized by the feeling that this wasn't he, Pantelei, who was fighting for his love so boldly and uncompromisingly but some other person.

"You'd do better not to disturb us, Pant." The grating sound of metal ball bearings could now be heard in the voice of the dark blob. "Go and have fun with your whores. Alisa is not for you. Come and see me tomorrow and sign a contract for the Heron. You and I will see that the Heron gets produced, Pant. Otherwise, I'll call Talonov, and he's got the car's crank."

"Don't threaten me with the crank." Pantelei took another step forward. "You'd do better to give me back my woman."

"Are you his woman?" Serebryanikov shook Alisa, who had so far kept silent. "Why don't you say something? Are you sleeping with Pantelei too? Bitch!"

The eclipse of the moon did not last long. The heavenly body was moving in its orbit a degree higher tonight than Serebryanikov had supposed. Light fell once again on the asphalt lake and on the three figures in the drama. Admittedly, a certain very significant novelty had now been added – the shadow of the wire mesh lay across their faces. Suddenly Alisa wrenched herself free. "It's true, I've had enough," she said in a hoarse, unpleasant croak. "I've had enough of you and me behaving in this disgusting way. I'd rather run off with Pantelei. He's my man. I've felt it for a long time."

"Talonov, come here!" shouted Vadim Nikolayevich.

He made an extremely clumsy lunge at Pantelei, missed him, lost his balance, and fell against the balustrade.

Alisa and Pantelei were already running down the steps. Headlong moments of life whistled around them, chased them, and beat against their chests, whirled around their arms like hurricanes, ruffled their hair, and turned their cheeks cold. All the moments of life carried them in a whirlwind to a taxistand at the deserted confluence of two minor Moscow rivers, amid semi-circles of reinforced concrete. Everything whistled and quivered in the vortex of moments. He clasped her around her waist, her face bobbed around his shoulders, her hot lips, like blind kittens, thrust at his neck, his chin, his hand, while her gentle voice roamed all over his skin.

"Well, where are we going, my dear Pantelei? Do you have somewhere to go? We don't need much, but do you at least have a somewhere?"

"A two-room apartment," he replied with a strange feeling of pride. "An ordinary two-room apartment. I'll give you a heap of sweaters, pants, and blankets to keep you warm. We'll hide there today, and tomorrow we'll run away. You ask where to? Wherever fate has destined us to go. We'll escape to the mountains! There's a house there on the edge of the forest, and right beside it the moon spends the night in the snow.

"You'll gather your hair into a bun and you'll always wear it like that, without showing your hair to anyone. Only I will loosen it when I make love to you. You'll sit on a little couch, smoking a cigarette and listening to music, classical or jazz, and you'll watch the back of my neck while I diligently cover a papyrus with written characters.

"Oh, yes, and another thing – at night, while we make love, above us the many-tiered trees will rustle their leaves, so generous with reflected moonlight. And, baby, if you get bored of being my wife and you want to recall the past, you can be my whore – I love whores, too, you see. And when we've well and truly made love, baby, we'll talk about the trees. After all, wouldn't it be good if we could just grow into trees, my dear! Just to stand there, our branches touching, and when our branches grow numb, we'll summon up the wind. And what shall we do when we rot and decay?"

"Shall we turn into two bits of rotten wood?" she suggested in the tenderest, gentlest, funniest whisper, for the sake of which alone life was worth living.

"Right, my love! We'll be two luminous pieces of rotten wood! By day we'll just be two ordinary rotting logs, but at night we'll be luminous. Glowing microorganisms will live on us in memory of this night, and we will quietly wait."

"For what?"

"Not for what, but for whom. The one that all people wait for."

"They're coming," Alisa suddenly said in a changed, sober voice. "They're running this way, can't you see? We'll never get away!"

Three men were running toward them from under the archway: the two friends – Fokusov and Serebryanikov – and Talonov the driver, grasping a hefty-looking monkey wrench in his right hand.

"Big deal!" said Pantelei, strangely boastful. "Now you'll see some cinema! Three against one? Big deal!"

"There he is – the traitor!" shouted Serebryanikov, running up on unsteady legs. "Pantelei's a traitor! Shame on you, Alisa!"

Without wasting words, Academician Fokusov was already raising his fist for a cruel punch on the jaw of the seducer, the traitor, the scoundrel Pantelei!

As he approached the field of battle, Talonov put the monkey wrench into his pocket. "Where are you going, comrades?" he inquired. "Maybe I can give you a ride."

Fokusov hit Pantelei hard, while the latter simultaneously swung a punch at Serebryanikov. The result was a most disgusting scene – all three of them fell onto the grass.

"Personally I'm opposed to violence in the sexual sphere," said Talonov. "If you love the man, then go off with him, provided the money's there."

Around the field of battle there were several newsstands and the canopy of a bus stop. As he picked himself up from the grass, Pantelei saw several of the ladies and gentlemen of Fokusov's party hovering behind the newsstands. Obviously this nocturnal scene was developing into a full-blown scandal. The phone calls that would be buzzing around Moscow tomorrow!

Fokusov and Serebryanikov were now holding Pantelei by his arms. The courageous faces of the two friends, wet with sweat, tendons bulging, were blazing with righteous fury.

"Talonov, call up General Fatakhov at Police Headquarters," croaked Serebryanikov. "Tell him to send a patrol. Say Vadim asked him to."

"Let the general come here himself," shouted Fokusov. "He can deal with it on the spot."

"Administrative exile at the very least! Send him to the swamps, to the herons!" yelled Serebryanikov. He seemed to be fighting drunk again. "You can fuck your heron, not Alisa!"

Pantelei struggled hard, and the three of them fell to the ground again. One of the Fokusovs' guests kicked Pantelei in the ribs.

"Let him go!" he heard Alisa shout. "I hate you all! Let Pantelei go! I love him!"

"Disgraceful! How disgraceful!" squealed a female voice from behind the newsstands. Suddenly a man burst upon the scene, shoved everyone aside, picked Pantelei up from the ground, and used his own sleeve to wipe Pantelei's face.

"How dare you treat a writer like this? What do you mean by kicking a writer? That's no way for civilized Europeans to behave, gentlemen!"

Pantelei found himself leaning on the "blazer's" shoulders. Facing them were no less than five hostile men, all quivering with excitement and indignation.

"He wanted to steal another man's wife!" said someone.

"Shut up, you creep!" Bagrationsky shouted at the "someone," and then turned to the others. "Pantelei is a poet and a dreamer. All Moscow knows that he's in love with Alisa. Shame on you, gentlemen!"

There came a pause, during which Pantelei was able to raise his head and look around to find the chief culprit of the melodrama. She was standing with her arms clasping a lamppost, her long hair hanging down and hiding her face.

"Yes, it is disgraceful," said someone else in the silence.

Carefully skirting the lamppost, Fokusov crossed the grass and began to walk quietly away, his heels hardly making a sound on the asphalt. Everyone stared after him in silence.

"Alisa!" Pantelei cried out in desperation.

She raised her head, but instead of looking at her beloved she looked at her husband's back as he approached the vault of the huge, gloomy archway. Poor Alisa – her face was swollen with tears. The great designer of tractors was departing in an air of silence and doom into a future of loneliness, into his huge Alisaless apartment.

At this point Pantelei should have uttered some sort of quavering, despairing cry and thus seized the initiative, but he suddenly felt sickened by the banality of the whole scene. He already knew how it would all end. Her heart would be unable to stand the struggle and she would run after her old husband, with whom she had passed so many "years and milestones," as the saying goes. Such was the inevitable dénouement of such a solid cast-iron plot and there could be none other, because we are in the land of socialist realism.

"What are you going to do?"

He yawned convulsively.

And so it all happened. Head bowed, without even looking at him, she walked past Pantelei and then broke into a run, desperate and dramatic, the sickening end to a little real-life Soviet drama.

Everyone left the field of battle feeling thoroughly satisfied. Talonov the chauffeur loaded Vadim Nikolayevich, who had reverted to his usual state of collapse, into his car. Only one guest lingered a little behind the others and stood facing Pantelei. He was both old and yet not old. Gray hair in a bristly crew cut, thick bony ridges above his eyebrows, two eyes like hot little beads, a boxer's broken nose, and a massive, mottled, goitrous double chin.

"I recognized you, you swine," Pantelei said to this guest. "And now I'm going to denounce you, warrior of the invisible front! You haven't forgotten the instructions issued by Marshal Yezhov, have you? You still know by heart all twenty-two methods of active interrogation, don't you?"

"Sorry, sir! I see you're out of your mind."

The guest turned around and walked away with the gait of a successful American of the fifties – shoulders back, legs thrusting forward.

"Bagrationsky, my legs won't hold me up. Chase after that bastard and give him a rabbit punch in the back of the neck," Pantelei begged.

"That's Hughes," said Bagrationsky, "Douglas Hughes, the progressive industrialist."

"Oh, all right then." Pantelei dismissed him with a gesture. "In that case, the Americans can take care of him. Let Patrick Percy Thunderjet punch him in the belly for me."

He staggered and sat down on the grass right under the display cases with the newspaper *Socialist Industry*. Bagrationsky sat down beside him. "Let her go, Pant!"

"No, I won't."

"She's a liar and a cheat."

"I don't believe it."

"But she's nothing but a whore! Everyone's had her."

"I don't believe it."

"I've had her myself."

"I don't believe that either."

"Well, almost. I could have if I'd wanted to."

"I don't believe you."

"Look what my woman gave me."

He pulled out of his hip pocket a flat flask of liquor with a picture of a black grouse on the label.

"She gave you a flask of vodka."

"It's Hunter's Vodka! Want a slug?"

"Why not? Hand it over!"

"Forget all this, Pant. Moscow's too provincial for us. Soon you and I will be going to Paris!"

"You may be going, but I'm not."

"Why not? We'll go together, and when we get there we'll paint the town red!"

"You can paint it red, but I won't. They won't give me an exit visa because I signed the same letters of protest as Radik Khvastishchev."

"That's a shame, Pant, a great shame. So you might as well spit on Paris, too!"

"No, I won't spit on Paris! I'll never spit on Paris! Whatever happens to me, or to Paris, I'll never, never spit on Paris!"

"Oh, come on, don't cry, Pant! I can't bear seeing brave people cry. I would never cry for her. She's not worth our tears."

"Who isn't?"

"Alisa."

"Yes, she is."

"She'll never leave that husband of hers because he has a salary of five thousand rubles a month, a permanent exit visa, the family jewels, twelve mink coats packed away in trunks, several chinchillas, the Little Koh-i-Noor . . . She's a whore . . . a whore."

"I don't believe it."

"She's a major in the KGB."

"Now that I do believe."

By now they were sobbing, and a copy of *Socialist Industry,* blown off the newsstand, fluttered over them like a consoling angel.

AT FIRST SAMSIK DIDN'T UNDERSTAND

what had happened. At the very start of the program, after the introduction and Makkar's vocal solo, he broke out of the general din and began to improvise on the theme of "The Streets of Nighttime Cities." He had a new electronic mute, which he put into his sax at moments when he wanted to say slightly more than he otherwise could say. He had affixed his mute, closed his eyes, and begun to play, when he suddenly realized that he couldn't hear his own sounds. He looked around and saw that Makkar was also opening his mouth soundlessly, while Tar Baby and the others were running around the stage as if they had gone crazy.

He then discovered that Silvester was not beside him. Silvester should have been right alongside him with his tenor sax, waiting to start playing immediately after Samsik. But Silvester wasn't there. Then he noticed that there were strangers on the stage.

They were a bunch of nimble young men neatly dressed in blue jackets and ties. They were moving purposefully about the stage, tugging at wires, disconnecting loudspeakers, and switching off microphones. A whole detachment of these youths was also standing in the wings.

"Curtain!" came a loud whisper from right across the hall.

A few seconds later the cream-colored curtain cut off Samsik from

the auditorium and from his beloved "people," who were sitting in
disconsolate silence. The boys from the band came running up, almost
in tears. "Sam, we've been raided by a squad of vigilantes! Don't you
see? They won't let us play."

(Hephaestus with a lantern over the stone-hard body. The resuscitation team's working well!)

"But what about the rest? What about our people?" stammered
Samsik.

"The rest is silence."

Pale, his beard quivering slightly, Silvester now appeared, and alongside him was none other than the leading Komsomol official Shura
Skop, who had supported them throughout the past decade in developing "jazz with a Russian accent."

"Look, you guys, I'm advising you for your own good, break it up
and go home," he whispered. "Someone sent in a report claiming that
you're planning to play religious music and that this supposedly isn't
a concert but a political demonstration." He glanced furtively around,
and then added in a much louder voice, "Go on, go on, collect all
their equipment! We won't stand for this sort of thing in our city!"

They were approached by one of Skop's subordinates, a solidly built
kid with a small mouth, hot little beady eyes, and a boxer's pug nose.
"You, Comrade Silvestrov, will inform the audience, politely, that the
concert is canceled for technical reasons. And you" – the youth turned
to Samsik – "you, Sabler, will bring your script and your music to the
Cultural Department. You will also be required to explain who invited
the correspondents of the imperialist press."

"Your name isn't Cheptsov, by any chance?" Samsik asked him.
"The son of the State Security man of that name?"

"My name happens to be Chechilyev," said the youth, furious but
restraining himself. "And what the hell is that to you? Pick up your
music!"

"And you, you young cunt, will be picking up your bones in a
minute!" said Samsik, and gave the innocent young Chechilyev a
violent blow on the head with his saxophone.

Shura Skop twisted the crazed Samsik's arm behind his back and
dragged him into the wings. "Are you out of your mind, Samsik?" he
whispered. "They'll take you apart for that!"

"It'll be your turn next, you cocksucker," said Samsik to his
protector.

At that moment Silvestrov announced to the audience: "Dear
comrades, we are obliged to disappoint you. For technical reasons our

concert will not take place . . . er, is postponed . . . will be announced
in due course. I'm sorry."

Samsik struggled, but he was held in a firm grip. Silvester disentangled himself from the cream-colored curtains and let his arms drop
helplessly to his sides, like an exhausted penguin.

"Bastard!" Samsik shouted at him. "Tell the people that we've been
gagged! Makkar, Tar Baby, are you men or mice?"

"Cut it out, Samsik!" Silvester stretched his arms out toward him.
"I'll go to the Cultural Department tomorrow and get it all officially
cleared!"

"But it's all been cleared already! Do you hear, Shura, you son of
a bitch? There's a member of the Central Committee of the French
Communist Party sitting out there! Where's Shura?"

"Shura's blown the joint."

"Why are you holding me? Let me go, you cunts! Makkar, you're
a karate expert. Chop one of them! Gods, giants, our mother Gaea,
rise up and strike them!"

Meanwhile onstage the members of the "rock generation," trying
to avoid looking at their leader, gathered their possessions. Samsik
alone continued to struggle hysterically, refusing to accept the collapse
of all his hopes.

Chechilyev Junior approached, wiping his forehead with a handkerchief, his lips twisted into that same look of disgust and class hatred that
Samsik knew so well, but which wasn't to be seen so often nowadays.

"There sure is some shit around here," he said, staring at Samsik.

"Easy, easy, Chechilyev. Don't lose your temper," muttered one of
the vigilantes.

"He cut my forehead open! Am I a man or not?"

Chechilyev must have weighed at least one hundred and ten kilograms, and all those kilograms, plus all his class hatred, smashed into
the face of the cursing, spitting musician, who was not, it must be
admitted, in the nicest of moods at that moment.

Samson Apollinarievich came to his senses in familiar surroundings –
in the boiler room of the institute. It was hot and dry. Dim light,
insulated pipes writhing along the warm, clean walls. It was comfortably crowded. Behind his back someone was gently strumming a guitar
and singing one of Vysotsky's songs, "The Ballad of the Sentimental
Boxer":

A punch, a punch, another punch,
A left and then a right
And now Butkeyev (Krasnodar)
Lets loose an uppercut . . .

It turned out to be Volodya Vysotsky himself who was singing.
Samsik was lying on the floor, and at his feet, wrapped in a rainbow-
colored shawl, sat Marina Vlady, her hair the color of wheat. On
Sabler's chest lay a woman's hand, no longer young but very dear,
bearing the mark where once there had been a wedding ring. Whose
hand was it. Surely not Alisa's, the Polish girl's? His glance followed
this hand as far as the shoulder. He saw the high cheekbone and nose
of Doctor Arina Belyakova, his first love in the days when he lived on
Barmaleyev Street. So I'm not going to die, he thought, with a little
shiver of pleasure. But where's my sax? Did I manage to save my
saxophone? His sax was lying alongside him, with a little drop of the
enemy's blood still stuck to its bell. Proud sax, golden weapon!

The musicians were sitting quietly all around him – Silvester,
Makkar, Tar Baby, Thomas Gorchiashvili, Frumkin, Levin, Karpovets
. . . the whole group and their chicks. What a place for a jam session!
Back in the boiler room! The refuge of the first Christians – the
catacombs of the Third Rome! Not a bad place, not bad, not bad at
all.

In the midst of this circle of exiles stood lined upon the floor a whole
battery of large black bottles full of the repulsive liquid known in the
Soviet Union as port wine. Samsik remembered that in his old, drinking
days these bottles were called ink bombs.

"The comrade is regaining consciousness," said the female doctor's
voice above his head.

Samsik stroked her long thigh. In the past, it seemed, her sport had
been the steeplechase. "And did you recognize the comrade?" he
asked happily.

Ah, what bliss!

Leaning over him, she removed a cigarette from her mouth with
fingers from which the nail polish was peeling.

"The comrade need be in no doubt. The comrade has been
recognized."

"And I recognized you, too," said Vlady.

"Even you, madam?" Samsik quivered all over with happiness, well-
being, and warmth. "Even you? And isn't the third woman here?"

"Don't get upset, Sam." The guilty features of Silvester appeared in his field of vision. "I acted a bit cowardly, I'm afraid, but what could I do? Those bastards at the regional committee raided us, behind the back of the city committee. Get it? Skop has already hinted – and I'll check it out – that we'll be allowed to perform at the Highway Technicum at a meeting that's being held in solidarity with the people of Zimbabwe, who are fighting for freedom. OK?"

"OK." Samsik stretched blissfully. "I've always sympathized with the people of Zimbabwe. They're a delightful oppressed people. Of course we'll play in their honor. And in honor of the city committee."

The boys laughed. "Bully for you, Sam! Witty as ever, daddy-o!"

Tar Baby was already looking glassy-eyed – he had obviously been drowning his sorrows. Alongside him Samsik noticed an ink bomb that was three-quarters empty.

"Who drank all that? Surely it wasn't you, my dear doctor?"

The boys laughed even louder.

"You drank it yourself, daddy Sam! We treated you with a generous dose of ink and you came back to life! Say, didn't you give up the booze? Didn't you sign the pledge and tie it up with pink string? Well, that string's shot to hell now! Let the Zimbabweans tie their own string if they want to!"

"Right," said Samsik. "They can tie it, and we'll untie it again, because we have legs like snakes, torsos of gods, and the heads of centaurs. The Zimbabweans can eat their pumpkin mush if they like, and we'll swallow ink as a sign of solidarity!"

Where did he get this sudden burst of energy? He jumped to his feet and ran into the middle of the boiler room. He raised a bottle over his head and cast his eyes around the familiar scene for the last time: his friends, the women with wheat-colored hair, and his intransigent little golden friend with traces of the enemy's bloodstains, curled up like the embryo of a god on the cement floor.

"Samsik, don't drink, you fool!"

He turned away and began gulping down the revolting chemical port wine. Now before his very eyes the mighty, hitherto sleeping, asbestos-skinned snake of Zimbabwe began to twitch.

A LITTER OF DIFFERENT COLORED KITTENS ON GREEN WET GRASS

In the 50th Precinct station (known as the Half-Ruble), which is in the very center of Moscow, they had long since grown accustomed to dealing with the most unexpected customers. Sometimes they even roughed up deputies of the Supreme Soviet if they disgraced the title of "servant of the people." Members of the nighttime duty squad were generally unimpressed by official ID cards, but simply slung all drunks into the cells if there was no room for them in the sobering-up station – we'll sort you out in the morning.

The five who were brought in that night were not kicking up a fuss but calmly filing down the corridor: someone was whistling, someone was humming a song, while others were making with the usual anti-Soviet talk.

There was, of course, no room for them in the precinct sobering-up station. The stations of the Proletarsky and Leningradsky Districts also refused to accept any more clients, so all five were crammed into a "solitary" cell meant for specially dangerous prisoners, although, we must repeat, there was nothing special about these five. Sergeant Chebotarev was ordered to take a look at them. Two or three times he opened the cell door and listened to the murmured talk.

The situation was absolutely normal: One of them was complaining that someone had squealed on them, another was cursing some woman, a third was being rude about an auxiliary vigilante squad, the fourth had apparently invented some terrible new weapon, while the fifth man had just resuscitated a sadistic, murderous State Security officer. In other words – normal.

In the morning all five were peacefully smoking and telling each other their dreams. It seemed that they had all had the same dream: a litter of different colored kittens on wet green grass. At first it was as if they were looking at them out of a window, then apparently from a bird's-eye view, then higher and higher, smaller and smaller, higher and higher, smaller and smaller . . .

Book Three
THE VICTIM'S LAST ADVENTURE

Or the dream in which, once whole,
I explode and fly apart,
Like mud, splattered by a tire,
Over alien spheres of existence.

— *Vladislav Khodasevich*

He enters (or do I?) the Supersam department store. The meaning of that name is not particularly clear to him, nor indeed to all the other citizens: Does it stand for Supersamson? Supersamovar? Supersamoyed?

The first thing that catches your eye is a row of huge stacks of soap. Household soap, toilet soap, laundry soap, pine-scented soap, palm-oil soap, pineapple soap . . . An amazing abundance! Yet there were times when people were put up against a wall and shot because of a piece of soap! Man has always loved cleanliness, and having acquired the legal right to a piece of soap, he was often likely to put anyone who illegally acquired his piece of soap in front of a firing squad.

Tragic childhood memories are connected with soap. When the dog catcher's prison van used to travel the streets, the dogs would push their dear little muzzles through the bars, trying to savor the aroma of their favorite garbage dumps before being turned into soap.

"The dogs are being taken away to be made into soap."

The number of dogs that must have been needed to put such mountains of soap into the stores! To hell with your hygiene if it requires the destruction of all those splendid, lively creatures with their wagging tails! Thoughts like these passed through the mind of more than one little boy in the days before the development of our mighty chemical industry. Even now, incidentally, we grown-ups still remember snowless winters when the city was littered with trash, foul inedible garbage in backyards, the smell of fish oil, a prickling under the collar, the pathetic howling from the dog catcher's barred van.

The way things work in supersamsons is as follows. You go in; it is desirable to produce an immediate good impression for the benefit of the closed-circuit television spy cameras, so you smile, you whistle a tune, you try and create the effect of being somewhat vague and absentminded, just to prove you're not a thief. You leave your shopping bag in a special section, and in exchange you are given a metal tag, in order later to distinguish your lawful possessions from anything you may steal. You pick up a wire basket and disappear into the labyrinth of American-type shelves and racks. As a diversionary move you throw into your basket a piece of Carmen brand soap, 1898 vintage (a contemporary of the Russian .30–caliber rifle), but in the children's toy section you pick up an enormous rubber fish, let the air out of it, then hide the plug in your mouth and the flattened fish under your sweater. Calmly, though slightly weighed down (the fish, after all, is resting on your stomach), you pass through the checkout, where you only pay for the soap and keep quiet about the fish. Risky, you may say? Sure, there is a risk, but not a very great one. Riding a motorbike, for instance, is a lot riskier.

The chase was fast and furious, as though he had stolen something edible instead of just a rubber fish. He had never imagined he had such talent as a sprinter. Psychologists ought to convince all sprinters that they have stolen a fish. Every sprinter ought to crouch at the starting blocks believing that he has just shoplifted a huge rubber fish from a super-samoyed.

So there I was, in absolute safety, on Tsvetnoi Boulevard. Idyllic surroundings. Old Moscow. In front of me was a street climbing up a slope toward Sretenka. A boy was coming down this street. He would certainly not refuse the offer of a fish.

"Hey kid, come here! Want a fish?"

Why the hell am I lisping? Oh yes, of course, I'm holding the plug in my mouth! The kid and I blow up the fish and push the plug into the hole under its tail. On your way, kid, and think of your kind shoplifting friend now and again.

Now the passersby have no reason to stare at me; it must annoy them that I arouse no suspicion, unlike the roof of that vegetable store that is projecting sideways into the street. The roof of that house, which in the interval between its vegetable periods was apparently occupied by something nonvegetable, is now giving cause for serious alarm. Outwardly no different from hundreds of other roofs (it even has a cat standing by its chimney), it nevertheless conceals within it a danger to our whole way of life.

Aha, it's swelling! The zinc plating of the roof has buckled into a hump and is now cracking at the seams. What difference does it make whether I look at it or not? It will still burst out of there, because it's growing, because as the years go by there is less and less room for it.

Even so, it's better not to look at it. Better read *Soviet Sport* instead. Aw, shit, they've lost again! Better think about dogs, about Turgenev's immortal *Mumu*. Why don't I write a story entitled "How I rewrote *Mumu*?" One could say a lot in that story. One could say something about Russia's great literary culture, which is, of course, inaccessible to those from other countries. Some peoples of this world suffer from cosmopolitanism, others from nationalism. We don't suffer from either. Or should I write about our health? However, they wouldn't publish the story unless it contained a good dose of Marxism, that age-old Russian ailment. But then why write a story if no one is going to read it? For the good of my soul. I'll crumple the story up into a ball of paper, stuff it down Lesyuchevsky's throat, and with any luck he'll choke. If he doesn't choke, he'll swallow it! There's no point in writing stories: editors like Lesyuchevsky and Polevoi just swallow them, like nice sharks devouring stools. Better just sit here and think about Turgenev. And not look over there.

I could of course walk across the boulevard and slip into that café. They don't only serve dairy products there. It's a place where one can recharge one's batteries. Through the window I can see a semicircular counter, a woman in a white smock standing behind it, and endless quantities of brandy on a shelf above her head. One gram of brandy costs 1.6 kopeks. So count up your cash.

With the end of his Parker pen he multiplied some numbers in the sand – he had enough money for 3,578.5 grams of brandy. The resultant amount gave him a pleasant surprise and greatly improved the whole situation. He stood up and walked into the café with an air of solid respectability.

He did not stop in the doorway, but all the same he cast a backward glance at the alarming intersection and the dangerous roof. No point in starting a panic. Nothing special was happening over there. The roof of the vegetable store had indeed burst, although not at the seams but in the form of a star-shaped hole. A pair of round marble ears were now sticking out above the roof, but there was nothing terrible about this apparition. If one stood there a little longer, no doubt one would soon see the eyes as well. Yes, there they were, the small, sleepy-looking eyes of some harmless creature.

Clouds were floating past. A flock of rooks was flying overhead. The asphalt had dried up. The passersby were enjoying the warm weather. A face, like the simple face of a Ryazan peasant, was rising out of the roof of that little old house. I went into the café and asked in a loud voice, "Have you ever seen a marble dinosaur?"

The answer was silence. The customers were eating: Some were eating borshch, some were eating hamburgers, and some were eating whipped cream with crushed nuts. I walked around the café, looking into people's faces, trying to discover whether anyone was interested in the phenomenon of a marble dinosaur bursting out of a vegetable store. Getting no reply to my question, I went over to the counter, leaned on it as though I were somewhere in Paris, and drew the barmaid's attention to a bottle of the most expensive brandy.

"Instead of calling up you-know-where, pour him a glass," said a voice from one of the tables.

"It's none of your business," said the barmaid to the voice from the table. "I'm paid to pour drinks. You get on with your food."

With the majestic air typical of Russian barmaids, she put my brandy in front of me.

"What a weirdo," I said to the barmaid. "He thinks I'm some kind of stool pigeon trying to create a scare. You're a local resident and of course you know that I'm referring to the marble dinosaur in that house where a sculptor once used to live. By the way, what became of the poor guy? Did he move out?"

As I sipped my brandy I gazed out of the large window at a pleasant, rather gray day with a slight breeze blowing, and at the lively movement of the passersby. Very long, very bright scarves flapped in the wind. A bright green bus drove past, on its side an advertisement for Dubonnet.

"Do you like it here, monsieur?" asked the barmaid. "It's nice here, isn't it?"

"Is it nice here? I don't deny that it's delightful. Salvation, however, is not to be sought here but deep in the heart of Russia, still untouched by corruption. I know, you'll talk of the Suez Canal, the oil embargo, the Concorde, and the TU-144. There is much that separates us, but all the same, I shall risk telling you my simple story.

"I had a mistress who came from a White Russian émigré family. Together we fought to save human lives in Africa. Yes, it does happen, madam – white turns pink, red bursts into flower. They long for revolution, we thirst for greatness. There can be no compromise however much blue you may add to those two colours in an attempt to make the tricolor. We met once every three years over a period of ten years. It now appears that Masha bore me children. And I've not come here for the peace movement, nor on business, but simply to see my children. *Vous comprenez?*"

"We're closing," said the barmaid, "for our lunch break."

"Right," I agreed. "The cook has to eat too."

"I'm glad you think so," said the barmaid. "Some people are not so understanding."

"Of course, of course!" I exclaimed. "Many people think Fima never comes out of the kitchen, and that casts aspersions on you as his legal spouse, Sophia Stepanovna."

The barmaid was so touched by such unexpected empathy that she invited me to spend the lunch break with them.

"But you will not infringe upon my personal freedom, will you, madam?"

"Of course not. Don't worry. If you wear out your nerve cells by worrying, you know, they're never replaced. Fima, give monsieur something to eat."

Fima appeared, cheerful, careful, and kind-hearted – delightful fellow! – and placed a dish of nerve cells in front of me.

It was a pleasure to behold this ex-butcher. Time had treated him well. He was what you'd call a handsome man, clean, brainwashed, dressed in safari-style garb. Cooking, for him, was only one of the means of existence, and perhaps simply a hobby. His main activity was the drama section of Radio Liberty, where he was in charge of a weekly review program on Soviet theaters.

"Eat your brain cells, sir. They can't be replaced, but we cook them in a Barbizon sauce."

Ah, the age-old culture of France! Roast Gascon chicken in a sharp Gallic sauce – the ocean to the left, the grim Germanic genius to the right. Remember La Rochelle? That was where it all began: "Beat our own people to frighten the others."

Fima and Sophia Stepanovna dove behind the counter for the lunch break. Sophia first sang and then moaned like a little girl, while the gallant Fima only wheezed a little; obviously he kept himself well supplied with fresh filet steaks through his old connections in the meat trade.

I finished eating the brains and went out onto the street. It was strange how the weather had changed while I had been cooling off in the café. From being a nice, slightly dull, routine day, it had become extremely Atlantic and disturbingly beautiful. Clouds big and small, shaped like little wheels, sheets of newspaper or ribbons, and the like were scudding across the sky. One had the feeling that somewhere over there, behind the houses, was the sea, painted by Marquet.

"We will fight for every letter of the Atlantic Charter!"

And the things to be seen there, on that street corner! An old man wearing a leather apron was selling oysters. The lumps of ice and strands of seaweed in his baskets added to their already remarkable air of freshness. In the nearby tobacco kiosk the ghosts of our youth were shining in all the colors of the spectrum: Marlboro County, the town of Salem, famous not only for its witches but also for its menthol. A woman selling flowers, looking like an old Bolshevik, was offering her wares: Parma violets, Senegalese perpetual gladioli, forced Belgian carnations. Pairs of suede pants hung placidly in a store window, a celluloid piglet grazing beneath them. Several vending machines pined with desire to regurgitate things of use to man – chewing gum, Pepsi-Cola, hot drinks.

Just as I reached the intersection, across it walked a sailor, two nuns, a traveling representative of Soyuzmashmekhimport with his wife and a friend, also the handsome mercenary bandit Jan Strudelmacher. Before I had time to take it all in, these people had passed by and disappeared, except for one long leg of Jan Strudelmacher's, but a moment later that too had vanished and the intersection had already filled up with other people – walking, running, hobbling: two female students, one with a beautiful bust, the other with a beautiful behind; a veteran with a bulldog; the philosopher Sartre, who stopped for a moment to sniff the oysters. There also appeared the new heroes of my moment – a couple of rockers in leather jackets, a Spanish beggar, an excursion party of Japanese schoolgirls, a Catholic priest, a whore, a tall, bony old man with three children, a large intelligent dog. But then these too disappeared, as did the next group of passersby, and it all became too much for me.

"We will fight for every letter of the Atlantic Charter!"

This was spoken by an elderly playboy, seated on a sturdy-looking chair with curved wrought-iron legs. In a nonchalant pose, he was greedily enjoying sitting there on the boulevard, taking an avid pleasure in his expensive, ultrafashionable suit tailored in Scottish flannel, the bright foulard at his neck, his bushy walrus moustache, his pipe, a glass of iced Campari, and every letter of the Atlantic Charter.

The old man was seated firmly, and around him other people were sitting equally firmly on chairs with curved wrought-iron legs. I moved toward them, because they were not disappearing like the others. Someone waved to me from the far edge of Paris. It must have been Hemingway.

I don't know whether the French appreciate Hemingway and whether they realize what charm this foreigner gave to their beloved Paris. There were times when Paris was only dear to me because

Hemingway was there. Right now young Americans of the twenties were sitting on this boulevard – the Kohns, the Gordons and the Fitzgeralds – and they too lent Paris additional, immeasurable, extra-Parisian charm.

I sat down beside Hemingway. "Hello!"

"Hello. Many Soviet people shun me. They think I'm not the real Hemingway, that I'm a Soviet agent disguised as Hemingway."

"I know that you're genuine."

"What will you have to drink?"

"I don't care. Anything, just to get drunk; otherwise, a sense of unreality sometimes arises."

He poured each of us a glass of wine, looked at me, and smiled into his beard. "How times change! It is a good thing that Soviet people are free to travel now, to spend a weekend in Hawaii. The day before yesterday I met Yevtushenko in Honolulu."

"The real one?"

"If he wasn't, it was a successful imitation."

"Excuse me, Ernest, but its customary for writers to compliment each other."

"Yes, yes, don't worry. I've been preparing a compliment to make to you. I recently read in the *Times Literary Supplement* your story called "How I rewrote *Mumu*.' Congratulations!"

"One compliment deserves another, Ernest! Your 'Cat in the Rain' changed my whole life. Thank you for that overkill."

Just then, at the far end of Paris, the life-loving old man articulated something with his lips. A minute later the words reached us: "We are ready to fight for every letter of the Atlantic Charter!"

I smiled, trying to show myself as a connoisseur of the Western spirit of freedom. "Ridiculous old man, isn't he?"

"Not at all." Hemingway rejected the gibe. "I agree with him. I'm ready to fight for all the letters of all alphabets. Except the Russian letter for 'shch' – щ "

"I beg your pardon?"

"I love Russian literature, but I have the impression that even your classical writers shun that strange letter."

"Really, Hem? Do you really think so? What about *borshch*? You can see that three-headed beast with its little tail in Turgenev's *A Sportsman's Sketches*. You should be nicer about it, old man! Maybe it's destined to be the first to break through the ideological iron curtain."

"The future will show us. I don't like arguing." With a motion of his chin, Hemingway drew my attention to another part of Paris. "Look, they're coming for you!"

Across the mirror-bright ashpalt of the sated West, across an alien world unwarmed by either Hemingway or Balzac, across a world glittering on various planes, twining themselves into knots, disappearing underground and flying up into the heavens, a familiar red shape came relentlessly toward me.

It was Masha Coulagot driving an open Ferrari. It was hard to recognize in this elegant lady the erstwhile perpetually drunk girl who used to start taking off her jeans the minute before the corresponding proposition was made to her. A charming severity, a sad little smile, were framed by the costly fur of wild beasts and the Moroccan leather of the costly automobile.

Finally, twisting and turning around all the spirals of supercivilization, she drove into our old Paris and pulled up beside our little cast-iron table. "Ernest, I'm going to kidnap your companion."

Simply and sincerely she presented me with her cheek to kiss. Unnoticed by everyone, indeed unnoticed by myself, my hand swiftly touched her breasts and belly. She led me to the life-loving old man, who was watching us, his whiskers fluttering in the breeze.

"Let me introduce you: This is my husband, Admiral Brudpeister."

"I warned you, Admiral, that he would turn up one day," she said to her husband.

"But of course," said the admiral, "you must invite the father of your children to lunch with us, madam. We shall see what his manners are like – whether he knows how to use lobster tongs, how he cuts fruit, whether he fumbles with his napkin. By the way, sir, all propaganda is forbidden at the table in our household. During the years of your absence, your children have been raised in the Atlantic spirit. We won't give up a single stone without a fight! Please accept my invitation."

The table was set beneath an immemorial oak tree in a glade in the county of Sussex. Now and again oak leaves fell into the soup as spontaneously as if the setting had been in the Russian province of Ryazan. The admiral watched covertly to see how the Russian would cope with this and whether he would keep his dignity.

The Russian picked the leaves out of his soup and carefully sucked them clean, because the oxtail soup was delicious. The children were thrilled by the behavior of their foreign father. Their father skillfully used the lobster tongs to scoop out the contents of an avocado, while he crushed the shell of the arthropod with blows of his fist. Apart from that, he disappeared under the table every few minutes, at which their mother shuddered slightly. The children glanced occasionally at their beloved grandfather, Coulagot of the White Guard.

"You, my friend, no doubt are of Jewish commissar stock?" the grandfather asked their father, raising his left eyebrow. "Didn't your father fight the Russian forces on the southwestern front?"

The father then surprised everyone, including the mother of his children. "On one side of my family, I am Baron von Steinbock; on the other side, my father was a proletarian, Comrade Bokov. How do you like that?"

"That's something new."

"It's something old, like the whole of our life."

The dessert was served. Port was wheeled in on a little cart. At the sight of the cart, the children's father became extremely excited. "Aha, red wine! I could do with a nice drop of red wine right now!" He accepted the cut-crystal decanter of glittering port from the servant's hands, quickly took a swig, burped violently into his hand, and said to the admiral, "What proof was that?"

"My friend, you have passed the test," said the admiral. "You are simple, natural, in a word, *comme il faut.* I'm not surprised that Masha fell in love with you."

Old Coulagot had not yet "accepted" the guest, was still grumbling at him for having usurped the Russian Revolution, was still showing off his republican sentiments to his "commissar," but even he, without any doubt, was melting: He liked this new pseudo-Russian, the father of his beloved grandchildrenskis.

Duchess Brudpeister was charming to everyone, smiling and condescending, a real lady, if one overlooked the fact that sometimes her fingers would lift the edge of the tablecloth and touch the pseudo-baron's cocking piece, or perhaps even if one included this fact. During one such moment she said gently to her father, "Tell me, Daddy, can you see him sitting beside you in the cockpit of the *Knight of Russia,* the world's first multiengine bomber?"

The profile of the humiliated but still defiant Republic of Russia shuddered, and through the old man's features, through his wrinkles, there could be seen the young Coulagot, trusting and brave. I stretched out my hand, put it on the table, and recited some lines from my favorite poet:

I walked along a street unknown
And heard a raven croaking from afar,
The sounds of lute and distant thunder's groan:
Toward me down the street there flew a streetcar.

The old man's hand rested on mine. "Damn me, Von Steinbock," he said in a youthful voice that broke through his senile coughing. "You may be a kike, Von Steinbock, but I do believe that you and I devised the method of towing a glider at Oranienbaum in 1915!"

My children all started shouting, "Sure! Fine! Lovely Daddy! Lovely Grandpa!" Masha burst into tears. Admiral Brudpeister produced a smokescreen from his Dunhill pipe in order to hide the sentimental expression that had overcome his features.

How marvelous it all was! Like the *Nautilus,* the county of Sussex was gently sinking into the pink Atlantic sunset. The tender green countryside, it seemed, was free of ecological problems. The round clumps of tall British trees unobtrusively enlivened the horizon. The gently glowing lamp, brought by a modestly smiling manservant, was still pale against the gold of the dusk. With their bright little faces and their happy, fun-filled eyes, the intelligent children provided a remarkable contrast to the slightly melancholy restraint of the adult faces, heavily scored by time yet not without their own attraction. The frosted cake, sliced fanwise by the admiral, stood in the midst of the tablecloth like a tropical island amid the ice of Antarctica. A delicate stream of coffee vapor quivered above the Wedgwood china which was decorated with an eighteenth-century hunting scene. Everything was marvelous if you disregarded a few minor details – if you overlooked the fact that the marble head of a dinosaur was gradually rising above the hill behind the house and grounds; if you overlooked the fact that the vile three-headed reptile щ with its little tail was gradually crawling, wriggling, and lurking toward our hands; if you didn't count the fact that a huge Nelson television screen was gleaming on the admiral's veranda and that from this screen our dinner party was being watched intently by the retired Lieutenant-Colonel Cheptsov, recently resuscitated by progressive Soviet medical science.

On the whole, it was like the kind of dream you have when you are getting over an illness – a gentle evening, slipping out of one's memory, a sense of fragile happiness, the hope of reliving it.

The Lament of Lady Brudpeister née Marianne Coulagot

Once there lived Princess Daydream . . . girlish games among
the birch
trees . . . Russia and the birch trees lived . . . in the Beryozka
stores now there's vodka and caviar . . .
I became an English lady . . . but my drunken husband said . . .
you should
have been a Moscow whore . . . plying your trade at the Kazan
Station . . . My
husband returned from campaigning . . . wounded by anguish . . .
It's all behind
us now – the years of drinking bouts . . . the flights of a drunken
hoopoe . . .
and a spoonful of honey in the barrel of pitch . . . the Arbat in the
moment
before dawn . . . Nature assures me that all will be well in the
future . . .
but art Thou living, oh God, over Moscow?

No use hiding the fact that at the same time, in the Timiryazev District
of Moscow, a wedding was in progress on Planetnaya Street. The
retired Lieutenant-Colonel Cheptsov was marrying off his daughter,
Nina, to Grisha Koltun, a major in the airborne troops.

At first the table was set, very properly, every bottle beyond
reproach – all imported stuff from the foreign-currency store! Then
suddenly the bridegroom's relatives showed up, laden with buckets:
five buckets of hot pies, five buckets of Russian salad, five buckets of
meat and fish in aspic. No matter, it was all good stuff. They fell on
the aspic with as much enthusiasm as they hit the bottles.

"A matzo for Abe! A matzo for Reuben! Some matzo for Nathan!
A piece of chicken in aspic for good old Vanya!"

Major Koltun, a tall, well-built young man with the straight back of
a good athlete, glanced sideways at his bride. She was as thin as a
rake, was Nina, nothing much to get hold of. Of course, it was a big
plus that her parents guaranteed her maidenly honor. Finding a virgin
nowadays was as great a stroke of luck as winning a Zhiguli in a lottery.
Another important factor, of course, was the apartment, located near
the Air Force Academy, where Koltun had just applied to take the
entrance exam.

At times the unfailing efficiency of his own body amazed even Koltun himself. After an evening of heavy boozing, all his comrades would be groaning, yet he would wake up with a steady pulse and a mood of cheerful optimism. The major was thirty-eight, yet according to the medical authorities, all his reflexes were those of a man of twenty-five. Reflexes plus experience – the result is splendid: but without experience one is apt to land in a ridiculous situation. Here's an example.

"In 1968, when we were helping fraternal Czechoslovakia out of a spot of trouble, I landed in a ridiculous situation, but later I was decorated with this Order of Military Glory. Does anyone want to listen? Then I'll tell it just the way it happened. Shut up, brother-in-law!

"OK, so we landed at night for camouflage purposes. The objective was clear – to isolate a group of hostile agents in the offices of a magazine called *I and You*. See here, Igor, old man, let's get this straight – either you sing songs or you listen to my military experiences. You're going to listen? OK, then shut up!

"So we rolled out of the Antonov in an amphibious armored personnel carrier and drove off. With us was a Czech patriot, a bookkeeper from their state security forces. The amphibian's a good vehicle, very roomy inside and stable in the water . . . only fu— excuse me, Nina, only not much use in medieval European cities."

"Are there a lot of Jews there, Grisha?"

"Questions afterward, please. Well, OK, OK, I'll answer now. Over there, comrades, are a lot of things that Soviet people can't understand: Jews and Europeans – they all merge into one faceless mass. So there we were, driving through the sleeping streets of this hostile city in the fraternal country. The boys were attracted by the contents of the store windows, in particular the knitwear, but the moral and political standards in our unit were tiptop and they all kept quiet. So we were driving along. The amphibian kept bumping against the corners of the streets, which were not well designed widthwise. What the fu— what the hell they gave us that amphibian for I don't know. After all, this wasn't the Suez Canal; an ordinary jeep would have been more suitable. However, we made do with what we were given.

"Suddenly our Czech started babbling – yak, yak, yak, stop the motor, *soudruzi* (that's Czech for 'comrades' – I'd learnt that much!). He jumped out and vanished into the night. So they were right when they said he was a rogue, who had fu— sorry, absconded with Dubček's official funds and had run away to us, the homeland of socialism.

"Where were we to go? Nobody knew. We saw a Jewish woman in pants walking along the street. We slowly followed her, but felt awkward about asking the way because of not knowing the language. It was starting to rain. Tough situation. Suddenly this Jewish woman – well, maybe she wasn't Jewish, I wouldn't like to swear an oath on it – Shut up, brother-in-law! – In short, this hooker stopped on the corner, pressed a button on this kind of stick she was carrying, and out of the stick, comrades, there flew . . . Sergeant Ravil Shalikoyev – great reflexes, that kid! – fired a round. It turned out the woman wasn't carrying a gun but a pushbutton umbrella. So there was one less blonde, unfortunately. Sergeant Shalikoyev's lack of experience showed him up, but his reflexes didn't let him down!"

"Is that the end of the story? Kiss the bride! Kiss the bride!"

Major Koltun turned to his bride. She was sitting there looking pale, staring straight ahead, exactly like the young bride in the classic painting *An Unequal Match,* although Major Koltun certainly wasn't an old serf-owner but a candidate for training as a cosmonaut, a lad whom all the girls in Golitsyno used to run after. Ah, if only there wasn't that apartment!

Doing his duty, the major put his lips to the cold lips of his bride, and suddenly he felt overcome by something, something he had never felt before, and he could not tear himself away from those cold lips. He pressed closer and closer, closer and closer, to those lips until something fell over with a crash at the parents' end of the table.

"Excuse me, I'll go on with my story about the value of experience in military operations. After the incident with the umbrella we drove into a little square, with a fountain and a neon sign. As the ranking officer I began to read the sign. What the fu— what the hell, I thought, it's all in double Dutch. The first letter was a Я but written backward, the second was a normal E, and then a sort of squiggle like a caterpillar. Admittedly this was followed by a good old familiar T, then a completely incomprehensible blob, then the backward Я again, after that an ordinary A, and then, comrades, just an N for 'number,' with the last letter the landing sign, the letter T which every airborne man knows so well. Have you guessed, comrades? Got it, brother-in-law? I'll tell you, I was so nervous and inexperienced that I forgot they use the Latin alphabet abroad. The sign said 'Restaurant,' and I had read it as something like ' Яе таияа т ,' minus the caterpillar and the number. So, I thought, this must be their way of spelling 'I and You' – in Russian, ' я и ты '."

" 'Halt! Weapons ready! Shalikoyev, Gusev, Yankyavichus, follow me!' We burst into the building, and we saw what looked like a tribe of monkeys, long-haired old men sitting around a table. Soviet Army!

Stand up! Hands up and face the wall! Good thing the Czechs understand Russian. It would be more complicated in other countries. We
frisked them all. No weapons were found, but we did find some pornographic postcards, evidence of bourgeois influence. I reported by radio
to brigade headquarters: Task force has occupied the premises of the
magazine *I and You*. Couldn't hear a fu— not a damn word from
headquarters. I wondered if they were all drunk, because all I could
hear was them laughing. Hell, Koltun, they said eventually, you
baboon, you've just attacked and seized a restaurant!

"Then I suddenly realized that all the letters were written backward,
and remembered German lessons in school when we had all read a
book called *Ich Liebe Mein Vaterland*. Well, I thought, my career is
well and truly fu— I mean finished! I asked, 'Should I release the
prisoners'? 'Do no such thing,' came the answer. 'We're sending you
a Special Duties squad.' And what happened? Why, good old Lady
Luck, it seems, was on my side! Those guys in the restaurant were all
from the staff of that magazine *I and You!* We'd stumbled right on
them! So I was recommended for a decoration."

Only a few people around the table had been listening to the bridegroom's long, drawn-out story: the host, Nina, myself, and my friend
the hockey champion Alik Neyarky, ex-forward, now the number one
defenseman of the national ice-hockey team. All the other guests were
digging into the aspic, twisting the legs off a Hungarian turkey, and
singing the traditional wedding song: "One day there'll be mountains
of gold, and rivers running with wine."

Seeing this, the major said confidentially to his bride, "That episode
did me some good, though, Nina. In view of the developing situation
and the relaxation of international tension, I took a crash course in
English." And he added in English, "Here you are, Nina!"

Having moistened a lock of his hair and pressed it to his brow with
his hand, he began to recite "The Ballad of Reading Jail" to his bride
in a Cambridge accent.

"I hope, Major, there was no violence?" old man Cheptsov growled
at him down the whole length of the table. He was sitting with his
elbows planted on some bits of food, his eyes burning his detested son-
in-law with a glance that out-dazzled the medallions on the bottles of
prizewinning Russian vodka.

"What was that, dad?" Koltun asked casually, without even turning
around. His heart thumping with happiness, he gazed at his bride's
lips, which were trembling very slightly.

What's happening to me? thought the future conqueror of the

asteroids. I always used to like my women well endowed, yet now I can't take my eyes off this bag of bones. Can it be the influence of the West?

Cheptsov pulled a slice of meatloaf from under his elbow and threw it at the bridegroom. "Hey, sonny boy, did you use violence on the people in that restaurant?"

"What a thing to say, dad!" Irritated, Koltun wiped the meatloaf from his cheeks as though it were a gadfly. "The Czech comrades knew the score: They were all members of the Czech Communist Party and the Komsomol, even though they looked a bit like hippies."

"Like me, for instance," said Neyarky with a laugh and shook his new blond hairdo à la Bobby Orr.

"We took them on the basis of reciprocal, reciprocal—" Major Koltun did not finish the sentence and stared at the trembling lips of his bride.

Alik was seized with the urge for a good-humored joke. He stood up, grabbed the bridegroom's hefty arm from behind, and twisted it backward with his own two hands, also far from weak. Hey, comrade, help me – he winked to me. So with the shaft of my halberd I pressed hard on the major's adam's apple. Sweating in our leather jerkins with their steel shoulder straps, together Alik and I dragged the major to the wall.

"You didn't take them like this, did you?" asked Alik. "You didn't drag the Prague Komsomols like this, did you?"

The major rolled his eyes in exasperation, meaning, No, we didn't treat them like this. With a firm grip on the shaft of my halberd, I looked into the calm, clean face of the airborne officer and saw that right now he didn't have a very clear memory of that Prague restaurant. Did he remember pressing his carbine against the windpipe of Ludek Travka, the modest walking encyclopedia from the foreign section of *I and You*? He could have forgotten. Of course he remembered perfectly all the orders he received and gave, and the names of the men in his task force squad, but did he remember that far-off night in every detail: the color of the tablecloths, the faint smell of urine coming from the nearby toilets, the shape of the glasses on the bartender's nose, the little picture on the wall calendar – maybe an Alpine landscape, maybe a seashore – the smoking cigarettes in the ashtrays, decorated with some inscription, the jackets hanging on the coat rack in the corner, the lighted dial of the radio set and the song that started playing at the start of the operation and went on until it was finished, namely three and a half minutes – was it "Strangers in the Night" or "Summertime?" I don't remember.

Did Major Koltun remember all the details of that night – the *whole* of that night – and if he didn't, if that night has perhaps largely ceased to exist for him, then was he to blame for it? Was he guilty? Did the Czech intellectuals who were arrested remember all the details of that night, and if not, were *they* guilty? Curiously enough, I don't have a very clear memory of the details of that night either, so therefore I am not guilty of staying in the back room with Helenka, of failing to go out and fight the occupying troops, and of not redeeming the shameful action of my mighty country by my death.

What are they worth, those blurred, faded nights, days, and evenings of ours? What indeed are our blurred, faded memories worth at all? What price our whole past life? And did it ever happen at all if we remember so little about it?

I was walking along Na Příkopé, past some trenches – no, not defensive trenches, there was no attempt at defense here – past some trenches being dug for sewage pipes: Prague had wanted to pump out the superfluous shit, but had not managed to do it. The motionless hulks of tanks loomed out of the predawn mist (or the revisionist smog). The slack, weary figures of the tank crews were sitting on the armored hulls. Many of them were reading a yellow-covered issue of the magazine *Youth,* in which there was a story by one Aksyonov entitled "A Surplus of Empty Barrels." The cannons and the antiaircraft machine guns mounted on the turrets looked utterly ridiculous in these everyday surroundings.

Even on that night, around the ever-open kiosks selling *spekačky* there were crowds of the ordinary nighttime folk of Prague: several whores shivering in the chilly air, a cosmopolitan bunch of drunken jazzmen, two or three taxi drivers, a priest who was clearly suffering from insomnia . . . The usual nervous laughter, unintelligible chatter, the gurgle of beer flowing down parched throats.

The priest – or maybe he wasn't a priest, just a man in a black sweater with a narrow strip of white shirt collar around his throat – was standing a little aside from all the rest, drinking Prazdroj beer straight from the bottle in short gulps and puffing a cigarette between gulps. The shadow of a lime tree hid his face from me, but his wiry, athletic figure was clearly outlined in the semidarkness.

I had already almost guessed who this was, standing in front of me, but at that moment an armored car of the occupying forces stopped beside the monument to St. Wenceslas and beamed a powerful searchlight at the sidewalk. Then I saw his face, with two deep vertical folds running down the cheeks from his eyes, looking at me with a grin of harsh derision.

"Hello," he said.

"Hi, Sanya," I said.

"When we met in Rome," he said, "why did you and I play games with each other? I recognized you right away."

"It was so that we could meet today," I said.

"Could be," he said.

"Sanya, what is on God's mind tonight?" I asked.

"Sadness, I expect," he replied. "Sadness and pity."

"Does he pity Dubček?"

"Yes, Dubček too."

"And Brezhnev?"

"And Brezhnev, of course, and you and me, and that girl over there who was forced to suck off five bastards today and nearly choked when the sperm got into her windpipe. He pities those five bastards too."

"The old man sure has a lot of pity in him. Has he no anger?"

"Neither anger nor contempt."

"So now he's just looking down on Prague feeling sad?"

"Why only on Prague? Right now he's looking down with equal sadness on Rio de Janeiro, where no doubt five men are beating up one lone wretch, or on Bombay, where an Untouchable is doubled up with hunger-induced nausea two steps away from a bakery. The scale of events means nothing to the Heavenly Father. It is the meaning of the events that saddens him. He leaves the scale for mankind to worry about."

"But Sanya, Sanya! At least move out of the searchlight beam, Sanya. What am I to do if I'm shaking with anger, contempt, and shame?"

"Keep shaking. You can't imitate God."

"Console me, Sanya, and at least tell me that He doesn't pity that gun, that bitch of a gun, that whore of a missile armed with a warhead?"

"Console yourself, Tolya; He doesn't pity them."

"Well, thanks for that, at least. You talk about God with such authority. Are you a doctor of theology by now?"

"What difference does it make which of us asks the questions and which of us answers them? You can pretend that I was asking you the questions if you like. I know no more about God than you do, although I actually am a doctor of theology, and you, Von Steinbock, are an ordinary drunkard."

A roar came from the direction of Na Příkopé – the column of tanks positioned there had started to warm up its engines.

"I must get moving," said Dr. Gurchenko. "I didn't sail across the Bering Strait in 1951 just so that the commies could grab me back again in Prague in 1968."

We moved quickly into a little side street, where for the last few months the poor Czechs had tried to make everything look "just like in Europe": There were advertisements for Cinzano, a sign reading "Bar and Grill" in English, and all sorts of other small, shining objects and lettering that turned this little street, with its huge old-fashioned houses, into a mysterious corner of some truly European capital. Cars of various makes and countries were parked along the sidewalk, among then Sanya's little Fiat.

"We can reach the frontier in a few hours," he said. "There's total confusion at all the checkpoints right now. A very lucky situation for you."

We got into the car. Sanya wrenched the wheel around to the left, in order to get out of the line of parked cars. From all around us, sometimes getting closer, sometimes fading away, came the roar of tank engines.

HOW HE CROSSED THE BERING STRAIT IN THE VERY HOT SUMMER OF 1951

Boy, did they fuck me up, Tolya, from the first to the last day of my interrogation! I'd rather not talk about it. You were saying that memories aren't worth a damn, but you're wrong. There are days when memories make you groan all over, and you can't make out whether it's the flesh that's groaning or the spirit. On bad days, fragments of that year move about and itch under my skin.

After that, with a twenty-five-year sentence under my belt, I was shipped off to the Chukchi Peninsula, to the First Directorate of Corrective Labor – you know, the uranium mines. In those mines the entire work force was made up of "twenty-fivers," all the most terrible enemies of the Soviet regime, but they even gave us an extra butter ration, and all the chow was better and more substantial than in the regular camps so that we wouldn't kick the bucket too soon, because the country needed the uranium to defend itself against imperialism. They even reduced our sentences there – one year counted as five. After five years they'll send you to Yalta to drink wine in a sanatorium, the guards used to tell us. Everyone knew, of course, that we wouldn't be leaving that place in five years but in six months, and we'd be going somewhere a lot farther away than Yalta. They put us into the mines without any kind of protective clothing, and the ulcers on their bodies that those miserable prisoners used to develop are another thing I'd rather not talk about.

Fortunately I arrived there in the summer. At roll call I could see the mountains lit up by the sun – at morning roll call the mountains to the west, in the evening those in the east. In winter, no doubt, I would have simply died, silently, in the perpetual darkness. Summer is a dangerous time for the uranium mines.

Do you think I was just going to let myself be turned into a draft horse? There in front of me were the eastern mountains, covered with great sheets of snow and blue pockets of shadow between them. Cross all those mountains one after another or die on one of them! Perhaps you'll see the ocean, too, with its floating ice floes. Cross that sea or die in it! Surely you haven't forgotten how to grab a rifle from a guard? Run off with a rifle or get a bullet in your back! A bullet, the rope, the fangs of a guard dog – every variant was better than the uranium mines.

It turned out that a few other guys in the camp were racked by the same questions. The organization of the guards there was chaotic. The bosses of Dalstroy considered, quite rightly, that the best form of security was the Chukchi Peninsula itself. Disarming the perpetually drunken guards was simply no problem for us, a dozen experienced veterans of the war in Europe.

We marched eastward for twenty-seven days. In that isolated part of the northeast, the Chukchi Peninsula really is one vast, secure prison. Gangrene, heat diarrhea, frostbite, scratches that never heal, snow, swamp – all of that together is, perhaps, only a little better than the uranium mines. And, my friend, we had to use violence: we attacked the natives, the Lourovetlans, and took away their miserable food, their reindeer skins, matches, and vodka. By all accounts the Lourovetlans are a peaceful folk, and I hope they won't keep on hating that bunch of half-crazy prisoners for too long. When I reached Alaska, I sent the Lourovetlans a prayer begging for forgiveness, sent it with the wind, with the sun, with the birds, by the only ways God provided, and I hope my prayer reached them.

When we reached the Bering Strait there were five of us left. Six had been left behind in the permafrost, but it wasn't the march that killed them: They had simply been in the uranium mines a few weeks longer than we had. Radiation . . . In those days we hadn't even heard the word.

From those black cliffs above the cold, rippling straits, we looked out over a vast and lifeless world, a world of inorganic nature. Rocks, water, and ice – nothing more. I can tell you, I was gripped with fear, and I doubted Christ. You see, if there's life around you – trees, children, dogs, even grass, even just lichen – you can always believe that Jesus lives! On Cape Dezhnev I saw a vision of the Other, the Ungod, powerful and mocking, with his pillarlike legs straddling the strait between America and Russia.

It seemed to us that we had reached the end, the borderline between two worlds that no one could cross, and that here we should turn into lumps of cold decay, when we suddenly saw a long kayak at the foot of the cliffs.

Yes, down there on the pebbles lay a boat, sewn out of skins stretched over a framework of walrus bones, with not a human soul to be seen, while on the horizon were some long dark streaks that maybe were just clouds but just might be Alaska!

We began to climb down to the seashore, and it was then that we were found by a frontier patrol. At first the three soldiers shouted at us, then opened fire. They had semiautomatic weapons, and we only had the lousy .30-caliber rifles issued to prison guards, but . . . But if those frontier troopers had known how much stronger and more desperate we were than they were and how badly we needed that kayak, no doubt they would have hesitated to join battle with us.

I think I have only fought with such passion on one other occasion, and that was in a detachment of the French *maquis,* when we captured a warehouse full of wine from the Germans in Châtillon. God forgive me!

It was all over in half an hour; all the others, on both sides, were killed, and I was left alone in the silence. I was only wounded in the arm. Even now I can clearly see the ash-blond head of one of the frontier guards, leaning against a rock. He seemed to be listening to something inside the rock, and the wind was ruffling his hair, like wheat in a year of bad harvest.

All my comrades were left there among the rocks of the Chukchi Peninsula – Dmitro and Oleg, and Gediminas and Borya. The only one to reach the kayak was Alexander Gurchenko, now a doctor of theology at the University of Rome. Suddenly a mist came in from the sea, thick as a smokescreen. I pushed the boat into the water, fell into it, and lost consciousness.

It's hard to say how long I bobbed about on the waves in that boat. There were times when I had the impression that I could see the sky, sometimes dark blue in the evening, sometimes gold. A strange smile settled on me at such moments of lucidity. With that smile on my lips I watched God and Nature fighting over me. Nature tormented me, sucked the blood out of me, hung over me in a green wall of water with a foaming crest – not with malice, of course, but only in obedience to her own laws. God sent me birds, to encourage me. Big and white, they flew across the empty heavens, reminding me of life. I felt neither fear nor bravery, but simply awaited the outcome with that strange smile.

One day a bird alighted on the stern of the kayak and looked at me with anticipation, just like a woman – that dumb, avid, expectant look of a woman naked and sexually aroused. Suddenly all my life's experiences with women passed before my eyes in a momentary but slow, expiring cycle. Joy, warmth, gratitude, and hope overwhelmed me. It's like that when you give yourself a shot of morphine. Next moment I had the strange feeling that I would never see a woman again. Then I sat up in the kayak and grabbed the paddle. Obviously, God and Nature had come to terms.

A month later I was discharged from the U.S. Navy hospital in Fairbanks, Alaska, and began broadcasting on the Voice of America. The cold war was at its height, and no holds were barred on the airwaves in those days. Did you ever hear my broadcasts?

No, I didn't hear his broadcasts. That summer, my freshman year, I was dancing to the "Domino" waltz. I had first picked up that hit tune on the wavelength of Radio Monte Carlo and was always singing,

> Domino, domino
> As you flit through the crowd of the dancers
> Domino, domino
> So you hold out a hope of love's chances. . . .

Yolkin the accordion player heard me. "What's that you're singing, kid? Let's see if I can pick up the tune and play it." He picked it up, and soon the whole band joined in. Every evening Monte Carlo would sing the song about the mysterious domino. Europe, having forgotten about the war, was furiously whirling to this insistent petty-bourgeois music. Domino fuddled the brains of the proletariat. We thought that

THE BURN

"today in the docks the French are not sleeping, the dockers are standing on guard for peace." Alas, they were indeed not asleep, but they had clean forgotten to stand guard for peace – they were dancing the "Domino" waltz instead.

"Why don't you play it, kid?" Yolkin said to me reproachfully. "Go on, take Erik's horn – he's gone out for a piss – play it until he comes back."

"I don't want to play. I want to dance. I've only just learned. Can you see Galya the gymnast over there? She has pink cheeks and white teeth, her back is as supple as a cat's, and she's as mysterious as 'Domino.' "

"Don't tangle with Galya, kid. They're always fighting over her. It's the law of the jungle!"

"Who cares! 'Domino, domino . . . ' "

I danced with her once too often, and was thrown out of a second-floor window onto a coal heap.

"So you had an interesting summer too."

"What about the woman, Sanya? The one sitting on the stern?"

"God sent her to me to save me from the waters. Since then I have never again experienced anything like it. Each year I wanted women less and less, and now it's years since I, you know . . ."

"Is that true, Sanya?"

"Yes, of course." He nodded casually, and then explained in one word: "Uranium."

We were getting closer. The Eternal City rose out of the mist. The Fiat was sailing over the hills of Lombardy, yet we could already see Rome. From the banks of the Arno we could see the banks of the Tiber. It was strange how farsighted we were. No stranger, though, than our clear, exact memories.

Oh, those clear memories of ours! We remembered driving toward the City of Seven Hills, and the city was already flowing past us: Via del Corso, Piazza Madama, Via Veneto, and St. Peter's Square, and there was the Pope, seen for a moment at a high window wearing a khaki tunic and a peaked cap à la Kirov – ah, those clear memories! As the city flowed past us with its countless cars, we went on rolling from hill to hill and recalling the Appian Way, Alexander Suvorov's crossing of the Alps, and there they were, marching past us, Suvorov's grenadiers in their comic shakos, come to liberate Europe from the yoke of forcibly imposed democracy.

"It'll be a hot day today. Let us pray for them. They're dying of thirst."

However, when we got out of the car in front of a roadside crucifix, there was no sign of heat; it was damp and cold, and the cry of a bird could be heard, just as in Lithuania. Not far away, a Soviet tank was positioned on top of a demolished house. The four tankmen, lying beside the tracks, were slicing a Hungarian sausage into small pieces.

"We're in trouble, guys. We're lost," moaned one of them upon catching sight of two fellow Russians. "We don't know where the fuck we're going. They don't like us here. Russian pigs, they say. We want a drink, but we haven't any Italian money. Pawn the tank? We'd be shot for it. Pawn the ammunition? They'd shoot us for that, too. You can't go far on one Hungarian sausage. We want to go home, boys! Would you show us the way home?"

I recalled my home, and the bottomless abyss of humiliation. All those sons of bitches, trembling lest they lose their special rations. And I remembered those rations. A special Kremlin ration emptied out onto the newly washed tabletop. Everything instantly reversed. A moment before, there was nothing; now suddenly we're swamped with goodies, truly Russian goodies – king crab, Borzhomi mineral water, brandy, delicious herrings, the likes of which are not to be found on the surface anywhere in Russia but are only caught in underground rivers. I suddenly remembered a litter of different-colored kittens on wet green grass, moving farther and farther away from me, higher and higher, lower and lower, getting smaller and smaller . . .

"What's that beating in the belly of your tank?" I asked the tank crew.

"The loud heart of Russia, still untouched by corruption."

I looked at Sanya and noticed that he had aged considerably since that night in Prague, since that memorable night of the invasion. I also saw that his nerves were not in the best of shape either: A chain of little tears was rolling across the huge Lombard plain of his face. It cost me no little effort to hide myself behind the tank.

"Sanya, I didn't sail across the Bering Strait. That summer I was dancing the 'Domino' waltz."

"God speed, boys," he said, and blessed us with the sign of the cross. "And may you not die of thirst on the way."

We drove off. Sitting alongside the driver, watching the road through the vision slit and the periscope, I gave the orders, "Drive onto the highway! Signal a right turn, let the Lancia pass! Move over into the left lane, let the Volvo and the Mercedes pass, turn on the left-turn

signal! Turn it off! Accelerate! Halt at the 'stop' line! Turn on the
signal again, but wait! Why? Because, you prick, we only move on the
green arrow, and the arrow isn't showing green yet. Now it's green!
Cross the intersection, but let that Leyland pass . . ."

The driver, a sweating Georgian, was groaning with pleasure and
gratitude. "Ah, *katso,* this is the way to drive! What would I do without
you? I'd have died of shame!"

The commander of the crew, Lieutenant Khryakov, was sitting on
the turret and shouting in Italian into the windows of tourist buses
driving alongside us (I had written out the words for him in Russian
letters): "Soviet tank, ladies and gentlemen! We've lost our way! We
are dying of thirst! Please give us a few bottles of Coca-Cola or some
money! Thank you with all my heart!"

The tourists gladly gave us water, and money, and sandwiches. The
boys cheered up – this was the way to travel! Although it had calmed
down, the tank still felt terrible, and it flew along the highway like an
accursed wanderer, like one of Hannibal's elephants that had fallen
out and been left behind by a Carthaginian column.

"Will we get back home one of these days?" the gunner–radio
operator Mukhamedzhanov asked cheerfully.

All around us the twilight of a super civilization burned with a dull
glow; through clouds of orange- and cherry-colored smoke could be
seen neon signs, the glass cubes of factories, the bowels and writhing
guts of oil refineries.

"Look, it's night already and we haven't seen a single statue of
Lenin," observed Makhnushkin.

"Do you remember your homeland, Makhnushkin?" I asked him
sternly. "It is a great country. Do you remember, Makhnushkin, how
you fell ill with diabetes and your country generously cured you in its
hospital near Klaipeda?"

"Yes, sir, I remember," said Makhnushkin, "In those days I was a
Seaman First Class in the missile cruiser *Strazha,* and I picked up
diabetes somewhere or other. I remember you treating me, comrade.
I remember your hypodermic very well, but I've forgotten your name."

"And do you remember, Makhnushkin, that litter of different-
colored kittens that used to play everyday on the grass of the stadium
alongside the hospital? You used to stroke them sometimes."

"Yes, sir, I remember them. And I strangled their mother on the
orders of the chief surgeon."

"How good that you have such an excellant memory, my dear
Makhnushkin."

"My memory rarely lets me down, comrade citizen of the Soviet Union. They were lovely kittens. Little she-cats."

"No, they were tomcats, Makhnushkin."

"No, sir, they were females."

"There, you see? Your memory *has* let you down. They were tomcats!"

"No, sir—"

Suddenly the highway came to an end, and we were crawling up a sloping valley, the hills around which were fringed with groves of oak trees. At the head of the valley stood a white house, within and around which glowed gentle welcoming lights. It all came rapidly and silently nearer, looking like a picture painted by some placid English landscape artist.

At last I saw myself in the circle of my new family: Lady Brudpeister, the childrenskis, old man Coulagot, and the admiral. As I drank my coffee and sipped chartreuse (made at La Grande Chartreuse monastery, and not at some Soviet distillery), I would glance occasionally at the house, standing there as calm and reassuring as early childhood, and saw through the second-floor windows the servants, with their kindly, humorous expressions, preparing the beds for the night: the big mahogany bed, as large as a frigate, for Masha and myself, a hammock for the admiral, bright modern bunk beds for the children, and a republican-Russian folding cot for old Coulagot.

All of us around the table smiled tenderly and cautiously at one another, afraid to spoil the enchanted moment. For the time being, all was calm. That little imp, the letter щ was peacefully burrowing inside the frosted cake. Stretching out its neck, the marble dinosaur was cautiously, as though for the first time, sniffing the sunset over the Atlantic. Lieutenant-Colonel Cheptsov, his eyes closed, was sitting motionless on the TV screen, looking like an Easter Island statue. We pretended not to notice these new arrivals, as though excluding them from the fragile charm of the moment. None of us noticed the tank's stupid great cannon thrusting itself through the bushes.

"Go into reverse, Rezo," I said to the driver. "We've taken the wrong road."

The people over there at the table did not even hear the roar of our tank as we raced backward. Preserving their enchanted moment, they rushed away from us, with their steaming coffee cups and their tablecloth of Versailles lace glowing in the twilight.

The tank drove backward into the kingdom of red calico, into the sea of glittering new buildings around Moscow the Beautiful.

"All for the people," "All in the name of the people," "Glory to the CPSU," "Party and people are one," "The ideas of Lenin are eternal," "Our aim is communism:" "Glory to the CPSU," the lower stories of the Moscow sky assured us, and in the middle of the sky hung a sputnik with its antennas spread out like five wide-open fingers, hung there, and sang the imperishable song "The Valiant Khaz-Bulat." Also audible was a dialogue between the two highest points, the two Ostankino television towers, one of which stood at home in Ostankino, and the other, swaying slightly, was wandering somewhere in the night haze of God knows where.

"The whole charging apparatus has been concentrated into one enlarged unit weighing one hundred and twenty tons," said one tower. "Reducing by slightly over three times the time needed to repair the assembly, the group has enabled the blast-furnace operatives to smelt an extra thousand tons of pig iron, which is hundreds of tons more than in the corresponding quarter last year."

"The amount of weeds and the susceptibility of the cotton plants to black rootrot are being reduced," said the other tower. "Before achieving the exclusive rotation of two crops – cotton and alfalfa – intermediate cultures play a truly invaluable role. All is ready for sowing in conformity with a decision of the Central Committee of the Communist Party of the Soviet Union."

"Well, we're home again, thank God," said Lieutenant Khryapov and crossed himself with a sweeping gesture.

"Is it seven o'clock yet?" said Makhnushkin. "Will we make it before the liquor stores close?"

"You, ugly mug, murderer of my kittens" mother, do you want some cold meat in aspic?" I asked him.

"Pork or beef?" he inquired with interest. "Veal? I don't believe it!"

The eternal Soviet soldier, starting from Khalkin-Gol, going through the Finnish War and World War II, ending with this last reconnaissance into Lombardy, eternally young as he moved from one arm of the service to another, Theodorus Makhnushkin, a rival to the poet Tvardovsky's soldier-hero Vassily Tyorkin, had little faith in the smile of fortune, never counted on the bitch-goddess smiling on him, and if he ever received the slightest windfall, he was as happy as a little kid. And suddenly here were five buckets of amber-colored calf's-foot jelly! It was enough to knock you down!

There was more than enough food and drink at the wedding party, and the guests, having grossly overeaten, had drifted away from the table and dispersed all over the apartment. Somewhere a male quartet was singing. Somewhere the cheeky Yurik was being taught to love his country by being flung from one corner of the room to another. Somewhere else Alik Neyarky was spinning the bridegroom around and around in a centrifuge used to simulate weightlessness in space, and the bridegroom was begging him, "More, more, give me another hundred turns, Alik. A bit more training never does me any harm." Somewhere they were dancing the shake to a protest song sung by Dean Reed. Cheptsov's colleague, General Lygher, his fellow fighter on the invisible front from the cloakroom of the foreign-currency bar, was shaking parts of his body, together with Paulina Arkadievna, his erstwhile legal spouse. She was doing pretty well for someone who had been paralyzed for twenty years! The master of the house, Cheptsov himself, was dancing a tango – to the rhythm of the shake – with the bride, pressing his daughter to his body and imagining that she was a little girl and he was giving her a ride on the crossbar of his bicycle.

"Stop it, Dad! It's supposed to be the shake! Let me go!" Nina threw back her head, trying to keep her mouth away from the old man's harsh lips and her nostrils from his garlic-laden breath.

"Sing, kid, sing your protest song," croaked Cheptsov.

The Protest Song of Soviet Youth Sung by Nina Lygher-Cheptsova,
Typist and Mime Artiste

To the corrupt rulers of Pretoria we raise our protest . . .
to the valiant Arab warriors we send greetings – all the best! . . .
My beloved you have left me . . . gone is the young moon . . .
I'm being forced to marry . . . the cosmonaut Koltun . . .
We tell Lon Nol in anger – Cambodia belongs to its prince by right!
    . . .
We despise Honolulu and all its queens of the night!
My beloved, the memory of you poisons my brain . . .
I wither, as grass withers, as the old man paws me again . . .
Shame on the arrogant Portuguese! Success to the spears of
    Frelimo!
We clench our fingers into a fist . . . Pantomino! Pantomimo!

Meanwhile her beloved was lying in a garbage can on the balcony and tearfully begging all and sundry, "One little glassful! Just a mouthful! Help, boys! I'm dying! I'm burning, I'm drowning, I'm tying myself into a knot!"

Suddenly he saw a gigantic fountain of fire above the rooftops.

Following the fountain, a glittering emerald nucleus rose into the sky and there burst into hundreds of stars, some white, some yellow, some lilac-colored. The quivering light lit up the mighty city, and in that light the Victim saw far away, beyond Khodynka Field, the clearly defined figure of a dinosaur as tall as the Ministry of Foreign Affairs, maybe even taller. The saluting rockets illuminated its little – but still no smaller than a tank! – head with the simple face of a Ryazan peasant, the serpentine neck widening as it went down and turned into an unthinkable vast asshole-belly with bulging lumps of muscle.

"Comrades, help! There's a dinosaur in the capital! Ring the bells! Sound the alarm!" shouted the Victim.

The guests crowded through the balcony doors, breathing the fresh air and admiring the fireworks.

"It really is a dinosaur, look at its size!"

"Oh, my God, it must be crushing people over there on Smolenskaya!"

"Don't worry. The government will take measures!"

"Think so?"

"And what do you think? That they won't?"

"Someone ought to drop a bomb on it. It's the Chinese – another one of their dirty tricks! Drop an atomic bomb on it!"

"What harm is it doing you?"

"But it's crushing people on Smolenskaya, it's making the buildings shake, and it's blocking traffic!"

"It doesn't worry me personally. How many salvos in the salute today?"

"The cab fare from here to Smolenskaya is only three rubles."

"Maybe we should call the authorities?"

"Forget it! The government will take steps, that's what the people have given them heads for."

"Call that a salute? That's just a shower of ashes, not a salute. Japanese pyrotechnics! Chemistry! Junk! Now, in the old days there were real salutes! Stalin was suspended in a dirigible, and the dirigible was camouflaged to look like a cloud, so that Stalin seemed to be hanging in the air by himself looking down on every citizen, and all around there were roses, fountains, and streams of fire."

"In those days everything was simpler, more natural, tastier."

"And prices went down *every year*! Whenever spring came around again you waited to see what else would get cheaper."

The fireworks ended, the city was sunk in darkness again, and the dinosaur vanished.

"There you are, no dinosaur! They were just shooting a film, comrades! Let's go eat, comrades!"

There was no hiding the fact that everyone was worried by the huge amount of leftover food and drink, and they all surged toward the table. The tank crew even helped the Victim to climb out of the container and join in the wedding celebrations.

The table looked like the evening of the last day of Pompeii. There was a certain strangeness in the air around the table, but people tried not to notice, in order not to disturb the eating and drinking. Even after a glass or two of vodka, however, the strangeness did not go away and finally it reached everyone – the strangeness was expressed in the absence of the host, retired Lieutenant-Colonel Cheptsov.

It was not true, however, that he wasn't there at all. His huge face stared at the guests from the TV screen. A most curious situation had been created: it seemed it wasn't a wedding party any longer but Amateur Hour!

"Repent!" said Cheptsov in a dull voice to the vast television audience. "I was recently in the other world and I now advise you to repent. Repent of violence, cruelty, cowardice, and lies! Repent, you cohorts of steel and you sportsmen, heroes of the Munich Olymp—"

For some reason he was unable to finish the sentence, and flew, arms and legs spreadeagled like a skydiver, into the depths of the television set.

What a burst of laughter there was! Noise, clatter, hiccups! Cheerful and lively, everyone talked at once, everyone settled more comfortably in their chairs, expecting more surprises from Central Television.

Only the Victim left the table and flung himself in horror toward the garbage can. Only there can I be saved! There's too much open space here! A vast smoking abyss and down below a field of battle, no one to stretch out an arm to, no one to shout to. Faces somewhere in the unthinkably far distance, like some insane flaw in nature. I'm just about to fall somewhere, but there's nowhere to fall to! How terrible to be afraid of falling when there's nowhere to fall!

He dove head first into the garbage can and swam. Through the waves of garbage a man was swimming, pushing aside old tin cans smeared with various glutinous liquids, used condoms, lumps of matted hair, eggshells, countless nail clippings, blobs of cotton, used tampons, congealed fat, rotten vegetables, used toilet paper – yes, he was swimming! He was getting short of breath, but kept on going deeper and deeper, resisting the efforts of the person who was tugging at his pants – come back!

"Don't be afraid, darling! It's me, Alisa!"

What a delicious enticement! This was just how the sirens once tried to corrupt Odysseus! What, Alisa? Do you really want to hand me over to my executioners, that rabble from Supersamson?

The gang of pursuers burst out of an underground Finnish sauna, where they had just gone for some underground Danish beer, and were now pursuing the Victim with fiendish whoops.

"Stop thief! He's stolen a fish! Grab the bastard! To the pillory with him! To the pillory of history!"

They ran naked, huge and pink, their pores wide open after the sauna, making much use of their elbows as they ran, shaking their large but by no means female breasts, these subterranean lovers of the workers" five-kopek subway fares.

He knew that he wouldn't get away, but male pride demanded that he keep running till the end, till the very last moment, and he ran on, past a torn and crumpled milk carton, like a slave running past the foundations of a pyramid, falling and panting for breath, and forced his way through a ripped nylon stocking. He gulped a mouthful from a puddle of curdled mayonnaise, hid behind a halfeaten cucumber, and ran on again until he tripped over a gnawed chicken's neck and collapsed on a bed of cotton stained with patches of menstrual blood. Here his male pride left him, and he lay there awaiting the blow, like a frog in the rain.

"Relax, darling! Don't be afraid, don't worry! It's me, Alisa! We're together now, don't be afraid, darling!"

And finally I saw reality. Before me stood the golden-haired Alisa, her face contorted with pity and disgust. How clearly I saw her whole being, her clothes: a light leather jacket, a high-necked sweater, and wide tweed pants.

Behind her head, behind Alisa's tousled hair, there shone such a dear, natural, beloved, and thrilling landscape: a Russian boulevard, Russian lime trees, Russian rooks on Russian nests, rapidly moving Russian clouds in a lilac sky, still unharmed by the Mongol cavalry.

I burst into tears. My love, my sweetness – Russia, Alisa, Moscow! I leaned my back against the garbage can. Everything around me was normal and simple. Occasional passersby flitted past to one side, paying no attention to us. Near us, silent and faithful like a dog trained from puppyhood, was Alisa's car. Music flowed from its window, a joyous yet quiet passage of music played by a dozen violins.

"It's Mozart, isn't it?" I asked through my tears.

"Yes, of course it's Mozart," said my beloved casually. "The Minuet in D Major."

"Alisa, my dear, I haven't really done anything very bad! I only stole a fish, a silly rubber fish. I can even pay back the cost of it."

"Oh, to hell with you and your fish!" said Alisa, pretending to be angry. Happiness had smoothed out the wrinkles on her face, which was beginning to glow with youth, love, and ocean. "I'm bored to death with your fish! Let's wash. I'm going to wash you in the bathtub, you wretched scoundrel!"

Apparently she had long been searching for me all over Moscow, and had even been to Leningrad and Riga, where I had also allegedly been during that time. She had, it seemed, done the rounds of all my hide aways and had despaired of finding me. Finally she had run across me quite by chance.

Three women in white coats had been running along the boulevard and shouting "Stop thief! Stop thief!" at a man ahead of them who was obviously trying to escape from them. This fugitive was myself. With the aid of a couple of ten-ruble bills Alisa had stopped the chase and the vengeance that would have caught up with me. How neat, I thought admiringly, to put an end to this nightmare with two pink Soviet treasury bills. You must be a sorceress, Alisa!

"And you're a scarecrow!"

I was wallowing blissfully in germicidal foam, while Alisa, wearing only a bra and a tiny pair of panties, was scrubbing my head, growling and snorting with enjoyment as she did so. Scraping clean the stinking head of the man she loved was obviously something that gave her great pleasure.

"Where are we?" I asked.

"In a safe place," she said. "It's an apartment that belongs to a girlfriend of mine. She's in Morocco, where she's been for over a year."

"No doubt you've entertained quite a few visitors here during that year?" I asked.

"There were some." She giggled.

"Bastards!" I exclaimed. "How I hate all those pigs, your lovers!"

"Oh, come now," she said, laughing softly. "Why are they *all* pigs?"

"Scum! Riffraff! How dare they touch you? If only you knew how jealous I am! Don't tell me you still see some of them?"

"I've given it up," she said gaily, covering my head with a terry-cloth towel and rubbing it very, very hard.

"And have you been seeing these . . . various men . . . for a long time, hm?"

I pulled the stopper out of the bathtub with my foot, and the foam began to subside. Alisa continued rubbing my head, saying nothing.

"And did you spend a long time with each of those shits?" I asked.

She still kept silent. I pulled away the towel and stood up in the tub.

"And how many shits did you have at a time? Two, three, five?"

She stepped back a pace from the bathtub. She was looking away, and her lips were trembling very slightly. "I must say, you ask some funny questions," she muttered in a hoarse, unfamiliar voice.

They were indeed funny questions, I thought. Somehow I was doing it all wrong. Here we were alone in the bathroom – she in a bra and panties, I stark naked – and I already felt as though we had a long life as lovers behind us. It was as if I had simply come back from some trip and was now acting jealous by right, and yet we didn't even know each other properly. Shame and tenderness overcame me. I took her hand and placed it on that part of my body with which she was as yet unacquainted. Like a blind woman she ran her fingers over it and grasped it. I looked at her face. Her eyes were closed, her lips muttering something inaudible. Very gently, hardly touching her, I ran my hands over her shoulders. What felt like little needles of electricity pricked my hands. I stepped over the edge of the bathtub, turned her around with her back to me, and gently pushed her forward.

She walked into the semidark room, then stopped halfway across it. At that moment I was completely overwhelmed with desire. It was a new kind of desire, so much stronger than normal lust that it couldn't be called lust. It was another, hitherto unknown urge. Even so, I told myself, it was the usual lust. I unhooked Alisa's bra and clasped her small breasts. Then I pushed her tiny panties down to the floor, and she stepped out of them.

This is a priestess of love, a lioness, I assured myself. Don't stand on ceremony, take her at once, like a lioness, you dissipated pig, take her without playing around. I told myself this, but my hands and skin were hearing something different. Again I gave her a slight push in the back, moving her toward the couch, and began to bend her over.

"What are you doing?" she mumbled. "Do you want it like this? Right away? Why?"

Now for the first time I felt a weak resistance, a faint hostility, but I pushed her harder, gripped her hips tighter, and then she obediently sank down on to her knees and elbows.

Overcoming the tender, defenseless, as it were, ever-virginal resistance, I entered her. She moved her legs wider apart, shook her head
a little, and threw her golden mane onto her back. With one hand I
gripped her hair, and with the other clasped both her breasts.

"Oh, God, what are you doing to me?" she whispered.

There was no knowing how much time passed. Then I turned her
over on her back, laid her body out along the whole length of the
couch, and lay down beside her. I touched her nipples, touched her
ribs and stomach, stroked her soft pubic hair, ran my hand over her
neck, and finding some wrinkles there, I kissed them, buried my nose
in her golden mane, where I found her little earlobe and held it in my
teeth, biting it ever so gently, then kissed her half-open mouth and
half-closed eyes, then lay on top of her, and pushed her legs apart
with my knee. She threw her arms behind her head so wearily, but
with such an air of willingness, with such inexpressible submission! I
pushed my face into the space between her arm and her cheek, and this
time she took me without the slightest resistance but with a welcoming
tenderness, which, although touched with weariness, breathed perma-
nence, as though for eternity. I went into her as though into an old,
familiar home, and asked her to open her eyes, but she whispered that
she never opened her eyes, and at this I got a little bit angry and
rrdered her to open her eyes, and she opened them, and in them was
a warm, vaporous mist, and she kept her eyes open, and then shut
them again all the same, because she was always used to doing it with
her eyes closed. She was forty-three years old, after all, and in that
time she had gotten used to lying under a man with her eyes shut, but
I knew then that I had to open them, open them at all costs and
without saying a word, without ordering her, and so I began to open
them, open them, open them, with even a certain fury, until she began
to groan, to wail, until she opened her eyes, and in them I suddenly
saw a joyful, astonished little girl and not a lioness at all.

A most peculiar awakening. The Victim woke up already sitting in a
car, already shaved, washed, and obviously having had breakfast.

"What about breakfast?" he sternly asked Alisa, who was driving.

"Ah, darling." The woman looked at him with humble tenderness.
The memory of last night was obviously still alive in her, whereas he
suddenly discovered he had no particular memory of it at all, only
remembering that he had slept with her but with no recollection of
any of the nuances.

The car was driving through the clutter of Moscow's traffic. To the right it was being crowded by the horrendous rusty sides of garbage trucks and trailers; to the left it was passed at high speed by something pistachio-colored with bobbing balloons, ribbons, and dolls – weddings, weddings, weddings one after another – followed by something massive and black, an official limousine like a battleship with cream-colored blinds, the proxy father of all those pistachio weddings.

"What did we have for breakfast?" the Victim repeated his question in more precise form.

Busy as she was with the gear shift and with watching the traffic lights, Alisa still managed to find moments to glance at her beloved. "We had what all normal people have for breakfast," she replied. "We drank coffee. Butter, toast, cheese, sausage, orange juice . . ."

"Aha!" The Victim cheered up a little. "So we drank gin and juice, did we? Gin fizz!"

He lowered the sun visor and looked into the little mirror, examining his puffy face with cheerful morning sympathy, as though it were a mischievous guttersnipe.

"We didn't drink any gin," retorted Alisa. "Your gin-drinking days are over!"

He suddenly shuddered from a powerful sensation like imminent nausea, a feeling of falsehood. He was surrounded by false leather, false metal, a dubious mistress. He was living and dying in one gigantic lie!

"Where are we going? To a hospital?" he asked gloomily and suspiciously.

There was no need for her to answer, he knew it anyway: to a hospital, under a steel net, into a bed covered with netting. Seryozha, switch on the headlights!

"What hospital?" She brushed the idea aside with affectionate irritation. "Which of us needs treatment? We're both healthy."

"What, am I perfectly healthy too?"

"You! Oho! I'll say you are!"

"Then where are we going?"

"Where you wanted to go. To that little town. Have you forgotten?"

"Oh, yes, I remember – to the town where it's insanely hot, where everything glows with the heat. The town that's like eggs frying in a skillet, that's where we're going. We'll live there until the heat drops, and when it does, we'll move on to another town, where it's wet. Ah, Alisa, it'll be so damp there that everything will squelch with dampness and our dwelling will be adorned with thick, hairy mold, and we'll lie in sheets so damp that we won't be able to tell whether it's our passion, our blood, our sweat, or our tears. You and I will live there through all the years of rain, and when it stops we'll go away to another town, where there's frost – to an icebound town, where a kerosene lamp is transformed instantly into a gleaming icicle. Why are you looking at me like that? Have I said something I shouldn't have?"

"Talk, my darling," said Alisa, laughing with the shortsighted happiness of the moment. "You talk like, like–" and she hesitated.

"Like what? Aha, I know: I talk in the way that a certain unfortunate writer used to write. By the way, what's become of him? How can he have disappeared so completely?"

"Oh, don't bring that up, darling!" A faint cloud passed over the sky of her shortsighted happiness, but it immediately evaporated. "Keep on talking, darling, I simply love it when you talk like that."

He continued his story about the town where they were going, but if she hadn't been so absorbed in her shortsighted happiness, she would have noticed that he was frowning with nausea and fidgeting. The conviction was growing in him that he was being taken to the hospital.

Alisa edged between some trucks in the right-hand lane, and then drove into a side street. They skirted a little square before taking a road that led uphill.

"Careful, Alisa," the Victim gently begged her. "Be more careful, but bolder. Caution does no harm, but without a little boldness, too, we'll never make it. You notice how incredibly he's grown lately. His dimensions are growing, but his movements are getting slower and slower. You'll see, in a few years' time he'll change from being a destroyer and will simply become a monument, one of the sights of our capital. I suggest that you drive slowly along the whole length of his tail, then under the archway formed by his sexual organ and the bend of his hip. When you're under the archway, shift into second gear, step on the gas, and you'll pass right under his belly without any trouble. In a moment he'll be at the halfway phase of his step, and we'll be out of danger."

"This time I don't know what on earth you're talking about," said Alisa. "I think you've overdone it a bit, darling. Couldn't you say it more clearly?"

"Keep going, keep going! If you're frightened, let me drive. That's it – hard a-starboard! Now – give her gas! Excellent! Dark? Don't be afraid! Do you see that gleam of light? That's the transverse spiritual artery, and light passes through it. In a moment we'll turn into the little street. It's odd that the marble monster is still so attached to this part of town, where it was born. It's odd, isn't it?"

"What *are* you talking about?" asked Alisa, terrified.

They were driving up a steep, humpbacked little side street. Sweet old Moscow ladies were gossiping outside a dairy. Wire baskets holding cartons of kefir were stacked on the sidewalk.

"I'm talking about this street," the Victim explained to his beloved. "A sculptor used to live here once. Maybe you remember him? You didn't by chance sleep with him, did you? Seems like he died or something of the sort."

"Don't talk like that, darling," Alisa whispered imploringly. "Please don't. Why upset yourself?"

They drove past the dairy, past a vegetable store, past a bakery, slowed down outside a delicatessen, but only in order to let a stream of cars go past, and then moved out onto a noisy highway, where everything concerned with simple human consumption merges into the endless, horrible shredder, and together with propaganda centers, secondhand clothing stores, Party district committees and offices, it roars past without the slightest hope – to the hospital!

"Let's first say goodbye," the Victim suggested, with proper male dignity, "I invite you to a restaurant."

"Oh, you fool!" She laughed with relief. "And I thought you'd really gone crazy. The restaurant's a great idea! I like it! Except we won't be saying goodbye but starting our honeymoon!"

"Do you remember any Polish?" he asked cautiously.

"Never knew a word of it."

"But you still remember your English."

"Spika leetle."

"Good." He smiled. "So we can start our jolly, illicit honeymoon." And thought, It's all over, she's taking me to the hospital.

"Yes, we're refugees, a boy and a girl!" She shook her mane. "You know, darling, right now I feel as though I never had anyone before you!"

Here we go! he thought grimly. You've had it all.

At that moment he suddenly had a very clear vision of himself under a tight nylon net and began to choke, clutching at his throat with his hands. Alisa did not notice this. She was too absorbed in maneuvering through the traffic, as she was trying to pull over to a filling station between taxis, official cars, and privately owned Zhigulis. Finally she hit the curb with her rear bumper and stopped. In front, two cars were waiting in line to fill up.

The Victim swallowed his choking feeling and climbed out of the Volkswagen. The bustle, swearing, and smell of gasoline bucked him up. The cold sky above the filling station and a massive nearby apartment house reminded him of the sky over the Baltic. There on the Baltic, in his young days, he had stood in the latrine of the crew's quarters of a warship and looked out at a sky exactly like this, wondering about his future. Now, in the midst of that future of his, he recalled his cold, windswept Baltic past, and that, too, bucked him up.

The filling station was packed with cars. Apart from sedans, there were several blue Zil dump-trucks, and, slightly apart from the rest, a minibus ambulance, open and empty. The Victim walked past the minibus and glanced, apparently casually, into the cab. The dashboard was completely covered with color pictures cut out of magazines – a bunch of unknown movie actresses and a reproduction of a landscape called *The Oak Grove*.

He looked around at the crowd and spotted the driver of the ambulance. This obvious rogue was drinking kefir out of a bottle and talking to a taxidriver. The Victim moved closer and listened. These two typical street-wise Moscow villains, grinning crookedly, were looking at Alisa's car.

"Say, Petya, see that little red VW, looks like a little polished shoe."

"Sure, and a nice-looking hooker sitting in it!"

"The guy who fucks her must be quite a big shot."

"Uh-uh, some top banana."

The Victim walked quickly over to his beloved to amuse her by recounting this conversation, but he couldn't get the open ambulance out of his mind and the landscape on the dashboard.

Meanwhile Alisa had been edging closer and closer to the pump. She handed him a ten-ruble bill through the window and asked, "Darling, pay for thirty liters."

Out of the car's window, flowing past Alisa's bony little shoulder, came the confident, strict-tempo sound of a jazz band playing "Take Five."

"Will there be any change?" the Victim asked dully. Anxiety was already burning his guts as he stood trembling with the ten-ruble bill in his hand, but Alisa didn't notice it, being busy with a complex maneuver.

"Alisa, do you remember, there used to be a great guy among us, a saxophonist?" he suddenly asked.

She shuddered and turned her face toward him, frowning with some painful thought.

"He played 'Take Five' damn well!" said the Victim loudly and challengingly.

The men standing around the filling station turned to look at him – the two drivers and a couple of traffic police officers with strong masculine faces, only slightly corrupted by an excess of power.

"Don't, darling!" Alisa begged imploringly. "Please don't move! Stay where you are! I'll come over to you in a minute."

"Where is he, that musician?" asked the Victim even more loudly. "Has he died, or what? Tell me honestly, has he kicked the bucket?"

"Stop it, darling!" Alisa opened the door of the Volkswagen and slowly put her leg out, as though afraid of frightening him away.

The Victim, however, was already running. In the moment that time stood still he raced through the cluster of figures, frozen in astonishment. He ran fast but without the slightest joy and only for the sake of the remnants of his male honor. A man, after all, must fight on to the end and fight for every last stone of his ruin; he had cultivated this view all his life, despite the "abyss of humiliations". He ran past the police patrol car, flew along a row of blue dump-trucks, stole from the last of these a nylon windbreaker and a pack of Rhodope cigarettes, leaped into the ambulance, started the engine, shifted into reverse, and pressed on the gas.

Its open doors flapping, the ambulance flew backward across a flower bed, turned wildly around in a puddle, and, furiously gathering speed, shot straight into the thick of the Moscow traffic. It took the traffic officers only a few seconds to come to their senses and hurl themselves in pursuit, but the ambulance, siren screaming, had already crossed the intersection and had plunged into the black throat of the tunnel.

Alisa's cry was still ringing in my ears, but it was growing fainter with every kilometer and changed into a distant and not wholly comprehensible sound – perhaps church bells, perhaps an alarm, perhaps the noise of a train, perhaps the sound of water on a water mill. Before my eyes was the landscape of the oak grove, the fresh grass dappled with sunlight, and that was where I was heading.

There she is, my Russia, minty motherland, fair meadow under the oaks, dappled like a humble little cow! Away, moldy, mothballed Jewish suitcases, preserving in their bellies a dark age-old treasure: Jewish misfortune! Farewell, crowded, mystic Middle East! Greetings, chilly north! Greetings, heart of Russia, still untouched by corruption!

The grass was so fresh that it seemed a shame to crush it with the wheels. I looked into the rearview mirror: a trail of tire tracks stretched out behind the ambulance, but the strong, fresh grass straightened up again and the trail disappeared. When the ambulance stopped, it stood amid uncrushed grass, as though it had been dropped from the sky.

I switched off the engine, and at once there was heard the sound of a choir of Russian birds, sweet, peaceful, and unobtrusive. Surely those vast propagandist choirs, with their elephantine roaring, couldn't exist in a country like this? There's the robin, pouring out its song in the bushes, there's the blackbird hard at work, there's the lark timidly essaying a trill, there's a wagtail quivering in embarrassed silence, while the chaffinch modestly repeats its "please come in, please come in, please come in."

Everything about me was asking for God's grace and every living creature gratefully accepted that grace: the spider hanging in the air, the squirrel on a branch, and my father Apollinary Bokov, who was standing quietly in the grass, leaning on his .30-caliber rifle and rubbing a little red-currant leaf in his rough fingers.

"Greetings, comrade!" I said to him. "I see you're here to ask for God's grace."

"Or rather, I'm admiring nature," replied my father with a smile. "Don't try and involve me in your fashionable idealism, my friend."

He was old, my father, but dressed in the Red Guards' dress of his boyhood: a peaked cap with a red star, pants made out of drapes from the landlord's mansion, and an ancient white, baggy "Tolstoy" shirt.

"Why do you need a gun?" I asked.

"This is dangerous country," he explained. "Very strong influence of the Social Revolutionaries in these parts."

"Why don't you join forces with the Social Revolutionaries?" I advised him bitterly. "After all, you fought side by side against the tsar all those years, you were shut up in the same prisons."

"Ah, my friend, they were intolerant," my father explained eagerly. "The Social Revolutionaries were always distinguished by their intolerance; they didn't want to admit their mistakes."

"And what about you?"

"*We* Bolsheviks brought the people scientific truths!"

"Do you recognize me?" I asked my father.

"You're my son." He smiled. "When I saw that minibus, I realized at once that my son was arriving, and I wasn't mistaken."

"I stole that vehicle," I said.

"Leave it here, and let's go," he said. "Let's walk to the village."

"And you leave that silly rifle of yours."

"Sure."

He threw the rusty old .30-caliber away, and the grass immediately swallowed it up.

"Tell me, father, did you kill many people?" I asked as we strode over the soil of our home country, over our brown mother earth toward the village, whose roofs could already be seen crouching behind a mound.

"Maybe not one," he said. "Out here we chiefly fought the Social Revolutionaries by swearing at them; after all, they were just ordinary peasants. During the Civil War I never saw the enemy at all, simply loosed off bullets from a trench. God knows where they went."

"God knows," I said with a nod.

"There you go with your mysticism again," he said, twitching with irritation. "They were shooting at me, too, you know." With much fuss he untied his rope belt, lowered his pants, and showed me a scar on the inside of his thigh. "See that? An inch or so higher, and you wouldn't have existed. Say, let's not imitate Solzhenitsyn by counting every bullet; we'd never manage to count them all anyway. Maybe one day somebody will."

"And you say you're not an idealist."

"That's enough!" He frowned. "At least let's not talk about that here. The people who live here are simple people; they till the soil, sow their seeds and feed their cattle. They live all their lives here; they don't wander off to the front lines or the prison camps, and they don't, by the way, steal cars. This is our home."

We have lived here for six hundred years beside a thin little creek called the Mostya, which winds so capriciously over the flat plain, as though its main objective was not simply to flow but to break down the clay banks.

Once we ran away from the sweating horses of a detachment of Mongol cavalry, or rather we didn't run away but dug holes in the local clay and buried ourselves in them at twilight and the horsemen galloped past. For a long time we waited in terror for them to return, but they didn't appear for a whole century, and by then we had built a village out of clay.

Today there gleams on the main street of our village the same puddle that shone there two hundred years ago, and only the television antennas distinguish the little houses from the houses of those days. Eternal pigs wallow in an eternal puddle. Eternal chickens scratch in the eternal dust. A skeletal bell tower stands over the village. A hideous, big-headed plaster statue of Lenin with a strange extraterrestrial smile looks down on the collective-farm yard, where a few men are sitting, with arms folded, on a log and waiting with sly peasant resignation for a miracle to happen – either for the broken-down harvesting combines to turn into fabulous pink horses or for some bottles of vodka to appear.

"As you can see, son, we've been through it all here. It has all come and gone – the Civil War, the New Economic Policy, collectivization, the war – and all that is left are the peasants' hands. Do you see them – the scars, the ingrained soil, the black hands of Russia? Touch that hand and feel it! Don't be afraid it, won't break."

And to show me by example, Apollinary Bokov put his old Party-member's hand on a peasant's hand that was resting peacefully on the man's knee, like a dead soldier on top of a mound. It was only a matter of minutes, of course, before a third, unknown hand appeared there and covered my father's hand: "A ruble apiece, and we can buy a bottle of vodka and split it three ways."

Suddenly I found myself on my knees in the biggest puddle in the village, the same puddle that had not submitted to feudalism, then had trickled away from capitalism to socialism, back to its former position. Fluff, small feathers, little lumps of horse shit, and the detritus of the twentieth century – cellophane and tinfoil – floated on its surface.

"Are you waiting for the Son of God, you Russian peasants, or have you forgotten about him?" I asked.

I heard not a sound in reply, but I saw the strangest scene: Through the suffering eyes of my father as they drew nearer, I saw the peasant mechanics, still sitting motionless on a log yet disappearing at incredible speed; I saw an empty pepper vodka bottle as high as the bell tower, a small plaster Kalmuk idol surrounded by huge birds, and the overturned sign of a teahouse leaning against the mangy flank of a dog, and three saucepans on a fence, and a motorbike, resting thoughtfully on its back wheel. Through a tiny private oasis of mignonettes and begonias, the whole of this little world, myself included, was being kept under observation by a television screen, on which were the incomprehensibly frowning features of Lieutenant-Colonel Cheptsov.

And are *you* waiting for him? I asked myself. Is your liver, are your blood vessels and lymph, waiting for him? Isn't your "liquid soul" flowing out of you through brawling in Yalta, through other people's beds, through sobering-up stations?

Suddenly something happened. The picture came to life again, the scale reverted to normal, and sound returned to the world again: a potato-sorting combine drove into the collective-farm yard. With the faint murmur typical of sophisticated modern machinery it set about its work, greedily swallowing potatoes, sorting them in an instant, cleaning them with brushes, and dumping them out – the big ones into nylon mesh bags, the little ones into a container for cattle feed.

"Good old West German efficiency!" said one of the men sitting on the log, not without pride.

A little piebald chestnut-gray horse pulled a cartload of potatoes alongside the combine, and the potatoes were flung into its maw with a bucket by a handsome old woman, her features distorted by the emotions of a wild and beautiful song:

> On Saturday, on Saturday,
> The wet and windy latter day
> No working in the fields, in the fields!

Absorbed with each other and paying no attention to anyone else, this trio made its way across the farmyard and disappeared in the fields beyond.

"What's that amateur theater show going on over there in the pond?" inquired a stern Komsomol voice from a window of the farm office.

"This comrade's interested in God," came the laughing reply from the log. "Seems like he's had a few drinks."

"By the way, Comrade Plyuzgin, this here old Bolshevik from out of town has given us five rubles."

"We're Bokovs! We come from these parts," exclaimed my father. "I'm the son of Ustin Bokov, and that's my son over there in the pond. He's not well."

"We know, we know, we were notified. You are Apollinary Ustinovich Bokov, a rehabilitated enemy of the people, and all of us here are your relatives: Edward Mishkin, Leopold Bodkin, Valery Rychkov, the two Pryakhin brothers, Marat and Spartak, and Vladlen Zhmukhin – all the most active members of the collective farm."

This was spoken by a young man of thoroughly urban appearance, who approached my father with the measured, authoritative gait of a cossack chieftain, looking as if he had come straight from a Komsomol congress – neat blue jacket adorned with badges for achievement in labor and sports, neatly parted hair, a neat little tie on an elastic band.

"And I am your distant nephew Igor Plyuzgin, junior inspector of the Office for the Prevention of the Theft of Socialist Property, so you may regard yourselves as my guests. Everything here is ours!"

"But *what* is there here that's yours?" I yelled from the pond. "There's nothing here! This part of Russia is an empty wilderness!"

"You're wrong, you're wrong! Our region is growing rich, and time has not passed us by! We don't lack what's needed to welcome veterans of the Revolution!"

It turned out that power in the village, and partly in the surrounding region too, had been seized by the large and widely spread Plyuzgin family; they were in the district committee of the Party, in the police, in the retail store network, and the related clans of the Mishkins, Bodkins, Rychkovs, Pryakhins and Zhmukhins also had their fingers in the pork barrel – in other words, they were the local elite.

Having locked themselves in the "teahouse", the table was set with almost Georgian lavishness. There was butter (Where from?); there were eggs (Where from? From Polish chickens!), there was salmon (From the seas of the Orient!), a dozen bottles of government vodka, and a large wooden pitcher of moonshine. Don't worry, we'll write it all off against the culture-for-the-masses account!

My father and I gazed in horror at this table; he, perhaps, was remembering his barefoot detachment of Bolsheviks fighting its way through the hostile country of abundance, camouflaging themselves behind pyramids of baked pies, forcing a passage through a plateful of suckling pig in aspic, wearily and hopelessly striving to find and suppress the last hotbed of Social Revolutionary influence. Can it be lurking in that ashtray full of butts of Bulgarian cigarettes?

"Dear Comrade Bokov, the village activists greet you! You see before you the fruits of progress between town and country! Nowadays the country worker wants to live as well as they do in the Bulgarian Peoples' Republic. Comrade Shmonin, a graduate by correspondence course of the Higher Party School, has the floor! 'When there will be mountains of gold!' Hey, you motherfucker, get your fingers out of that dish! I'm standing at the railroad station in a beautiful fur-lined jacket! Russia is alive, and our flag is in the Mediterranean Sea! Comrade Stalin's chief mistake was halting our troops on the Elbe River! Drink up, comrades, don't worry. If there's not enough, I'll bring more. The decision has been prepared to unveil a new statue of Lenin in the village of Fanino! To celebrate the forty-fifth anniversary of communal hay cultivation! We have plenty to be proud of; even the enemy admits that! Why are your glasses empty?"

I had long been quietly standing on the field of battle alongside a can of sardines, looking like the last Social Revolutionary preparing to capitulate with a white flag. Further resistance was pointless. I am showing tolerance and I hereby renounce unscientific ideas. It is stupid to fight, now that lumps of greasy Russian salad and the half-chewed guts of salt herring are falling on the snow-covered plain. Indeed, is this really Russia spread out before me? Isn't it America, rich and heartless? Isn't it Chicago in the twenties? It's enough to make you choke yourself on vodka!

They opened fire from the mountain of pies, as though from Sevastopol's Malakhov Hill. No doubt they hadn't seen my flag of surrender. Surely they can't think I'm carrying the flag of Russian democracy, that incurable venereal consumption?

Then I crawled along someone's private garden fence, woven out of willow branches, strengthened with planks, wire, and runway reinforcement strips stolen from some airfield. Through a crack I suddenly saw a tiny, neatly kept flourishing orchard of fruit trees, so flourishing and so neat, in fact, that one inevitably wondered whether some person wasn't concealed there as well.

Sure enough, there was! A clean-shaven old man dressed in pristine gray canvas garb, with a gentle but sly and secretive expression on his face, was sitting under an apple tree at a rickety little table and reading the Bible by candlelight. The warm night enveloped his sly solitude in a cloak of concealment.

Empty and full vodka bottles towered above the hills on the horizon. The bullets of the punitive detachment banged into some nearby cans of food. Heavy television music spread itself over the plain like a fog, but here in this secret orchard, it was quiet, and not a single sound penetrated into it from the surroundings.

The old man turned his face toward me, a face scrubbed clean to the last wrinkle. How deeply his eyes were set among those wrinkles and how they sparkled with sly, concealed goodness! How blue they were! Laying his huge yellow finger on the Bible, he said to me, as though to a good friend, "Know, thou suffering brother, what is written here: '. . . as the lightning cometh out of the East and is seen even unto the West, such will be the coming of the Son of Man.' "

Having thus spoken, he stood up with candle and book, walked past the apple tree, adjusting its branches, and began quietly to descend into a small rectangular opening in the ground.

"Who are you and why are you going down into the ground?" I asked.

"I am an underground inhabitant of Holy Russia, and my length of service is not yet sufficient for life above ground." He had already disappeared into the ground to waist level, but paused to continue his explanations. "My time of probation ended in the 1930s, when Russia was being mobilized for communism. It was then, nephew, that I went underground. Here is my abode, under my native earth. Here I think about the Lord and about the roots of the apple trees, while up above lives my old woman, having completed her probation, and it is she who keeps me supplied with food."

He took another pace downward and descended to the level of his chest.

How quiet it was here, behind these overgrown fences on this patch of beneficent earth, so secluded amid the vomit-spattered tablecloth of this grossly opulent feast.

"But if you are so firmly established among your roots, why don't you bring culture and the word of God out onto the earth's surface?" I asked the old man. "Everywhere, you know, people eat absolutely anything with their rotten teeth and belch it up from their sick stomachs. Here people are ashamed of asking anyone about God, because they bow down to idols of plaster and plywood."

The sly benevolence in the old man's eyes now changed to pinpoint sparks of suffering.

Suddenly the ancient fence shook along its whole length as though a mad dog were running alongside and bumping against it with its flanks. The old man shuddered and crossed himself. "I am a weak gardener, not a shepherd of souls."

Again the mad dog raced along the fence.

"You see, they're firing from a machine gun again; it's 1918 all over again. Come with me, suffering nephew. We will wait together and read the book and tend the roots of the earth."

I suddenly remembered the white flag in my hand. Perhaps my vocation was capitulation? "Perhaps if we meekly accept those machine-gun ideas, we could stop any future bloodshed, shut off the artery?"

"See here, nephew, they'll skin you alive for surrendering," said the old man. "What effrontery – to surrender! Go on, look, see for yourself, and don't be angry at me for living in retreat."

I wanted so much to take his candle from him, to sit down under the tree with the ancient book, and to be transported once more two thousand years back in time to that hot country, thrilled by the appearance of the strange Messenger, but . . . but my mission at present consisted of surrender.

"Farewell, uncle, and let's kiss goodbye!"

I opened the gate and ran out into the snowy expanse. Was it snow or was it starch? My flag blended into the color of the plain; the

punitive detachment couldn't see it, and took me for a militant Social
Revolutionary. I flung myself for safety into the debris of a heap of
chewed chicken bones. But they can easily see me among the bones and
half-eaten giblets. Like a Paris communard on a shattered barricade, I
waved my white flag, but even so, bullets kept on whistling around
me. Surrendering seems to be a pretty risky business. Flinging the
bones aside, I again ran out into the hazardous open ground and
unexpectedly found myself rolling down a warm spring slope, through
ferns and buttercups, through the sticky black earth of my childhood
to the bottom of a gully.

There, like a lake, lay a solid dish of aspic with patterned earthenware shores and my father standing in it up to his knees.

I was now looking down on him slightly from above. The sun, shining
above the gully, cast a steady light over the pseudomarble surface of
the aspic, through which could be seen rings of onion and halved hard-
boiled eggs. My father was standing deep in thought, holding in one
hand a red velvet flag and in the other a little idol with a head like the
carved knob of a walking stick, a look of cunning on its face.

There was my poor dear father, who grew up in the Revolution, a
pilgrim of the Soviet decades, my dear old dad up to his knees in aspic!
Could he and I do anything for each other? No, salvation was out of
the question. There was no saving us! The only possibility was mutual
assistance, which called for courage.

I waded through the aspic to my father and planted my white flag
beside him, and he carefully put his red flag next to it.

"Let's at least keep this little fellow," my father said with an embarrassed smile, nodding at the little plaster creature resting in the crook
of his arm. "He never meant anyone any harm."

"We'll put him in the very center of the village of Fanino, if you
like," I said. "Who knows what he was thinking when he was deprived
of speech. It will be a little memorial to a man who was deprived of
the gift of speech not long before his death."

We clasped each other around the shoulders and set off. A considerable quantity of heavy, indigestible food covered all our land. Above
us, like Olympian thunder, the feast of the village activists rumbled
on.

"I know, you bastard, that you're collecting evidence against me! Is
it my job you want?"

"Yakov Mikhailovich Sverdlov, Lenin's right-hand man, taught us
to be modest and frugal! He wore nothing but the same leather jacket
all his life."

"You are my melody, I am your faithful Morpheus."

"We'd better try and come to a sensible agreement, you mother-fucker! Tomorrow I'm going to regional headquarters, and Guskov has invited me to his Finnish sauna!"

"Let's drink to the cause of our fathers, to our hard-working tribe of collective farmers, to the great Stalin – we're all on the same side here!"

The sad autumnal plain stretched before us. In five hundred years our village had not managed to move itself up to the dry ground on Mamin Hill, or to pave its streets with good stone from the Pichugin Quarry, or, as the lousy Germans did, to put streetlamps in the village square, or to surround the square with neat little restaurants, a pharmacy, and a brothel, or to embellish it with a little fountain so that the place would be pleasant even in bad weather, as the lousy Germans did, so that it would be a shame to knock it all down. Alas, no, they never managed to do that; instead, the village only succeeded in sprawling several versts along the damp gulleys, and now it lay scattered amid the banqueting table like useless garbage.

The village activists were really letting it rip. An old Volga M-21, a battered jeep, and a couple of motorbikes were getting soaked in the rain alongside the "teahouse," from whence came climactic shouts, hoarse, half-smothered cries, a ragged chorus singing "Tenderness," the sound of crockery being smashed, and the noise of chairs breaking as they were flung around the room.

Suddenly, in the deepening twilight, the brothers Pryakhin, Marat and Spartak, were flung out, no doubt for being unsuitable due to their slightly advanced age. Coughing up their shattered bronchi, staggering bowlegged toward one of the motorbikes, they started it as though it were an ancient kerosene burner and drove off over potholes and ruts to the village store, where the entire surviving population of the village was already standing in line waiting for a delivery of goods.

"Son, my friend, do me a favor. Crawl out of the maelstrom of alcoholic nihilism and just find a few pebbles on the surface that we two can catch hold of. Let's go to the village store, and there you'll see your people."

"Very well, father, my friend, let's try. Let us pass through the temple of the past into the temple of the future, into the village store, where our people await new supplies with peaceful goodwill."

The ruins of a cemetery were all around us, broken glass was crunching underfoot, while beyond the cemetery a number of objects were to be seen: a dark wooden outhouse with open door and a heap of feces above the hole, three proud trees, wet and black with dampness, a huge vase of green blown glass containing some broken cookies and a dozen or so candies, a transformer whose wires stretched out to the television flickering through a clump of oaks, with its horned antenna, and the stripped, desecrated Church of the Transfiguration-on-the-Sands.

The desecration inside the church was so recent that it seemed as if only yesterday a Mongolian detachment had bivouacked here or Red cavalrymen had vandalized the place. The frescoes had not faded over the centuries, but there was not a single spot on them left alive: faces, haloes, the folds of garments, the tails of dragons, rays of light, and clouds – everything was spattered with audacious, freedom-loving graffiti. Here too broken glass crunched under our feet, and on the cornice under the shattered dome perched pigeons, hunched up against the cold like tired pilgrims. A most curious detail – in one of the side chapels stood a monument to "war communism," a genuine *bourzhuika* pot-bellied stove with its many-elbowed pipe.

"Well, as you see," – my father cleared his throat in embarrassment – "well, as you see, the crisis of religion—"

"Dad, was this a beautiful church?"

"Oh, it was!" he exclaimed despairingly, and, it seemed to me, almost dropped to his knees together with his little gray idol.

"Dad, tell me how beautiful this church was when you were a boy. After all, what is there left of your childhood if not this church, which shone with its azure-blue dome, its gilded crosses and stars, when they brought you here as a little boy under the fresh young greenery to celebrate Pentecost? Tell me about the little shirt you wore, embroidered with roosters, and about the smell of your hair that your mother, Avdotya, had anointed with sunflower-seed oil. Tell me how all you Bokovs went decorously to church and how proud you were of your clean, respectable parents that day, and what it smelt like in church on that dry, clear day of early summer, and how the altar glittered, and how the deacon's voice rolled out, spreading until it filled the whole space of the church as he formed the responses into a shape that was almost like an air-filled Easter cake: "We pr-a-a-ay unto the-e-e o Lo-o-o-o-rd . . ."

"That's how it all was, that's how it always has been, that *is* my childhood!" My father turned sharply away from me and walked past a pillar. A minute later his voice came from behind it: "Come here!"

In another side chapel we saw a live crucifixion – Igor Plyuzgin, the young inspector of the Office for the Prevention of the Theft of Socialist

Property, was executing the cross on gymnastics rings. His muscles stood out in bold relief, and his lips were set in a prolonged smile.

"The decision has been taken to hand over historic monuments to the care of the Sputnik youth travel agency," he informed us with his navel, that was pulsating like a lily. "Soon the protest songs of international youth will sound beneath these vaults. If you will leave your statue here, it will be labeled as the gift of a veteran, the baton that he hands on to future generations. Downstairs we'll have our own Finnish sauna, where we can raise as much hell as we like."

"You're wrong, Igor," I replied on behalf of my father, who was standing there in despondent silence. "The statuette of the man who lost the power of speech will be set up in the modern equivalent of the church – the village store. The stern look of this dumbstruck gentleman will restrain the workers in the retail trade from any impulses to embezzle socialist property."

"And what am I supposed to do? Keep hanging here?" Igor asked tearfully. "So you mean young people from all over the world will come and admire my muscles but I never get to eat or drink?"

The plaintive voice of the Soviet gymnast was still ringing in our ears when we came to a barely visible little door, wreathed in Palestinian ivy. The door opened soundlessly, and we at once found ourselves in the new building of the village store, enclosed by glass walls and with glass counters beneath a freshly painted slogan that proclaimed something about "ever-increasing demands" – and there stood our people.

Our people largely consisted of the female sex, if one didn't count the Pryakhin brothers, who were noisily demanding red wine as they fooled around in a corner, incapable of approaching the counter, wrestling with each other, and punching each other in the face for lack of anyone else to talk to. Our female population, wearing the usual little short velvet jackets, was chewing sunflower seeds as it waited for the van, which, according to rumor, was supposed to be delivering meat and meat by-products, including kidneys and hearts, from the district slaughterhouse. The leader of our people, the sales clerk Zina Plyuzgina, was keeping a stern eye on the situation. An ancient, righteous-looking old man with empty, Homeric eyes, was sitting on a box beside a radiator, against which he was wiping the five-hundred-year-old mud from his feet.

On catching sight of the old man, I rejoiced: There he is, the righteous man of Old Russia, and sitting up here on the surface, not underground! Even if it was only the village store, even if he was sitting beside a cold radiator with no heating system to which to connect it, as long as a righteous man is to be found on the porch, Old Russia is not dead!

All around I saw our great achievements: cakes and pastries, macaroni, buckwheat, and a certain quantity of knitwear. I saw our good women, who get so little of a woman's due from their awful men that by thirty they have forgotten about the joys of nocturnal life and turn into sexless, dimwitted, kind-hearted young-old women. I saw Spartak and Marat, as they carried on their revolutionary struggle in the corner, falling over each other and picking themselves up only to fall down again. I also saw, however, the righteous old man with the Homeric eyes, who was muttering something inaudible with his slack mouth, and I went over to him – was not he the guardian of some secret?

"He is a righteous man," I said to my father. "He is the keeper of a secret."

"Wait." My father stopped me. "You'd do better to take a look at the abundance of consumer goods."

"I don't need consumer goods, father! I need to know the secret of our Russian nature, the secret of why it is so inert, the metaphysical significance of unanimous approval."

"Wait," said my father, strangely upset. "Let's talk instead to these women about something simple – about the prospects for the harvest."

I had the impression that for some reason my father was purposely trying to get me away from the old man, as though he didn't want the latter to see him with his unseeing eyes.

Nevertheless, I went over and sat down beside the old man on the empty soap box. He nodded to me and raised his ancient hand to his mouth. I saw that he was munching a little piece of strawberry cookie with his lips and toothless gums.

"Greetings to you, grandad!" I said into his ear. "Greetings, Russian Homer! What horsemen are flying across the plains of your memory? What ships are burning on your shores? Does Troy still stand? Is Ryazan flourishing?"

"Greetings," said the old man in a firm voice. "We have had big successes on the root-crop front. Tell the St. Petersburg proletariat to hold on, and we won't let them die of hunger. Death to the enemies of the Revolution! The Party unmasked Khrushchev as a landowner and a rich man; at Bakhmach Station he handed me over to a constable who subjected me to feudal torture. There have been a lot of cattle abortions in the past five-year plan, a direct result of the consequences of arrant Trotskyism. Many immature citizens have been poisoning the wells in places where the Red cavalry is to pass. Why doesn't district headquarters pay attention to the signals from the localities? Sometimes a lad's walking around, and when you take his pants off, it's a woman. The other day I personally dug up ten tons of potatoes for the St. Petersburg workers. I got a personal letter from Comrade Shvernik. He explained the situation about strengthening the collective-farm system, and I was given a personal pension, seventeen rubles, for collecting surplus nonferrous metal from a kulak's wife. 'Ow,' she says, 'you're hurting me, boo-hoo,' and I say to her, 'No good saying boo-hoo; get your stuff together and hand it over or we'll drag you all out onto the village threshing floor, where our enemies are lying already like so many sheep with their throats cut.' Comrade Shvernik decreed that I should personally be paid seventeen rubles a month for unmasking the cult of the personality, and no matter how hard the enemy attacks, we won't retreat a single step from the commanding heights!"

I put my hands over my eyes to close them. The old villain burbled on like an unstoppable trickle of prussic acid, yet it grew quieter, as though his words were not reaching my mind through my ears but through my eyes.

"Leave him," said my father. "He's a very cruel man. He was once in our detachment, but we all went away to the front while he stayed here in the Political Police and tyrannized the population. There's not a house in our village in which he didn't commit some atrocity. Come on, son, forget him. He's senile."

Darkness covered my soul and I was permeated with murk, like an old-fashioned hot-air balloon filling with wood smoke, and the only reason why I didn't fly away was that the old sage-turned-butcher seized me by the knee and held me in an anchorlike grip of iron.

" 'Boo-hoo,' she said, 'boo-hoo.' 'Shut up, you bitch! Where are you hiding your samovar, you kulak? The hydras are persecuting our class and you're eating buckwheat pancakes. Potatoes, carrots, cucumbers, cabbages, geese – we'll send it all as per instructions . . . to the St. Petersburg workers.' "

When I opened my eyes, there was movement in the village store. The housewives were leaving the counter with their purchases, and each one threw something into the old man's sack as he sat there mumbling – a cracker, a candy, a piece of butter wrapped in newspaper.

"You'd do better to look at the women – look, look, they are the ones with the secret," whispered my father.

They were filing past us in their little short jackets, quilted coats, and rubber boots, these dumpy, overweight, dimwitted, but kind-hearted, ageless women, and I saw as they passed by that they were all *my* women, all my erstwhile tender, juicy girlfriends: Masha Coulagot, Nina the little mime artiste, Tamara and Klara, Natalya the Wasp-Waisted, Arina Belyakova. Poor things, what has become of you?

Suddenly one of them rushed toward me from the counter, meat by-products and butter spilling all over the tiled floor. She was naked under her quilted jacket, with grubby, protruding collarbones and thrusting breasts, naked with her wizened yet youthful features, her huge blue eyes like warning lights, Alisa my little girl prisoner from Kolyma.

"Run, Von Steinbock, or they'll hit you with a prison sentence! Don't you see the minibus coming? Run, or our activists will beat you up."

I looked out through the glass wall. Across the land of nightingales, over the lilac-colored hills, my stolen ambulance was crawling toward the village store without a driver, its doors swinging open, its headlights blazing, grinning stupidly, apparently looking for something or someone. Me! Its abductor!

By now everyone was watching the approaching vehicle. The doors of the "teahouse" were flung open, and there on the threshold stood all the activists. The brothers Pryakhin were quietly sneaking up on me from behind. Sitting on its pedestal with legs crossed, the little plaster idol was smoking, awaiting the denouement with patronizing expectancy. Igor Plyuzgin jumped down from the gymnastics rings and was now flying toward the center of events in a slow-motion somersault. The moment stretched itself out interminably.

"There's a dead man inside it!" came a voice from the pedestal with a heavy pseudo-Georgian accent.

Igor finally landed, neatly and without any faults, gaining the maximum number of points. Having hastily combed his hair, he strode over to the ambulance and made a sign to the Pryakhin brothers. "Bring the prisoner over here!"

The ambulance turned around in a puddle, presenting its rear end. Holding me by the elbows in a bear's grip, the brothers led me to it. Everyone, people and activists, gathered around in a circle.

Inside the ambulance there really was a dead man sitting on a stretcher – it was Cheptsov, looking as hard and waxy as a candle. Gazing at the Russian people with a look of glum indifference, he was smoking something, slowly, but without any smoke.

"Shmonin, take down a statement!" Igor ordered boldly, turning to me with a polite frown. "Where did you get this dead man from, citizen?"

"Comrades, that's no dead man!" my father interjected nervously. "Look, the comrade was given first aid in time and he's been resuscitated! I swear he looks considerably better now than he did in 1949, when he was in the prison-camp administration, in the strict-regime hut, and he used active correctional methods on us, prisoners."

"I have no complaints," said Cheptsov gloomily, regaining consciousness. "It was all done according to regulations. I was destroyed by being resuscitated through the introduction of someone else's Lymph-D into my body."

Slowly but confidently he clambered out of the ambulance, knelt down in the puddle, and, in a vast, ever-rising, endless roar like the thunder of a space rocket, shouted, "Confess, people!"

At this point, our righteous old man with the white eyes leaped forward like a sprightly little mutt. "Put them up against a wall! Shoot the lot of them!" he shrieked. "And this," he untied his sack and shook its contents of crackers, cookies, gingerbread, scraps of salami, kidneys, hearts, slices of bacon, candies into the puddle, "and give all this to the children! Send it to a kindergarten! For the children starving in the blockade! They can eat it! I don't need it!"

"Run, before it's too late! Run away to the south!" my father hissed to me in a loud whisper. "Run and don't look back!"

The engine roared, the broken muffler spluttered furiously. Tugging at the shift and accelerating wildly, I tried to drive out of the puddle. I knew that I could never get out, that I was just one minute too late, that any minute now I would be hauled in front of a kangaroo court set up by the activists, and the trial would be short and unjust.

Just or unjust, who knows? Perhaps they, all the swindlers, hypocrites, and bullies, were in the right? After all, their arguments were there for all to see – the crackers, the cookies, the butter in the village store – and even though these arguments were so much deceptive junk, they were better than nothing. And where, pray, is *our* truth, *our* justice, my dear half-Jew?

Suddenly all was calm. The engine was humming steadily, it was night, and we were barreling along a smooth highway with a bright, white, central dividing line. The gentle, affectionate landscape of Russia was flying past on either side, beautifully lit by the moon. A warm, exciting wind was blowing into the cab through the ventilators. As our speed increased, my breathing steadied and the two halves of me, Jewish and Russian, merged into one. I was flying somewhere, I was saved, I was racing away, probably to the south, to my youth, into the far, life-giving distance!

Ahead several lights were shining, a strip of reflecting glass, road signs flashed by, marked in luminous paint: reduce speed to 80, to 60, to 40 kilometers . . . a traffic police post.

Over the highway, placed on a semicircular concrete arch, was an internally lit aquarium, and in it two officers were calmly drinking tea and eating buns. A blue and yellow police Volga and a motorbike were parked underneath. A traffic light was winking over the intersection at regular intervals. Four roads, silvered by the moonlight, stretched out crosswise. Slowly, as instructed, I drove up to the intersection, looking up at the bundle of colored arrows at the end of the tall, curved stalk. The officers in the aquarium glanced down at my car and turned their concentration to their tea.

Suddenly a huge, long, flexible neck popped up above a nearby wood with amazing swiftness, and in an instant the cruel jaws of a dinosaur had devoured the moon. A siren howled in the sudden darkness. From all sides came the desperate squealing of brakes of all sizes, and dazzling headlights began to converge on me. A blinding flash from the rearview mirror burned my left eye, while my right eye was closed by a blob of hot diesel oil. I felt a violent bump under the wheels, and there was a crunching sound. Realizing that something irreparable had happened, I pressed on the brake pedal and switched off the engine. Powerful hands dragged me out of the cab and pushed my face under the chassis into a yellow circle cast by a flashlight.

"Look at that, you cocksucker. Look at what you've done!"

Under the wheels lay Lieutenant-Colonel Cheptsov, sliced into two halves. His lower half was in its death agony, looking like a huge spider as its legs twitched and jerked, while the upper half lay there quite peacefully, the right hand under the head, while with the left hand it was extracting something from a tunic pocket and calmly eating it.

In a deep but expressionless voice the halved man announced, "I have no complaints. I was run over strictly according to regulations."

I broke down and sobbed bitterly, knowing that nothing could help me now. And immediately a tow truck that had driven up to the scene of the accident began to cover me from head to foot in blobs of hot diesel oil, while several efficient young men – all excellent athletes of course! – busied themselves with lowering a large hook on a frayed steel cable.

"Let him go, let him go!" came the sound of a piercing female voice, like a St. Petersburg flute. "Let him go, I won't let you have him! Give him to me!"

"Why do you want him? A shit like him? What good is he to anyone?" The tow truck's crew, tough Moscow ice-hockey players, were encircling my body with the frayed cable.

The cable cut into my swollen body. I was dying, and could only beg for vodka. Nothing but vodka could mitigate the horror of death by a tow truck!

"Darling! What have you done to yourself?" wailed the female voice. "Look at the state of your liver, my dear! Your liver is all black and swollen with venous blood!"

"Out of the way, doll!" the boys said to the woman. They were my friends from the Men's Club, who were now killing me. "Why the fuck did he go for you anyway, with a liver like that? Not a sign of life in him now. Out of the way!"

They finished wrapping me up, secured one end of the cable with a block, and began hauling on the other end with the crane. OK, haul away! Haul away! Can such monstrous force be necessary just to crush one man? I was dying, and was only just able to beg faintly for vodka. Then I forgot about the vodka.

"Darling, darling, what horrible blood vessels you have! Such hemorrhages in your mucous membranes. You're so revolting, so swollen, so stagnant, so decayed! Oh, can it be, can it really be?"

Where was this crying coming from? Around me was nothing; there was nothing but this steel tourniquet, crushing my head, my neck, chest, stomach, crotch, arms, and legs. Surely she can't be shouting like that from *inside me*? Can it be that they're crushing her to death too?

And only because of her, for the sake of that dear beloved part of myself, I bit off the neck of a bottle of cologne that had appeared from nowhere.

She was now standing over him on all fours in the dear, cozy fuzziness of real life. With particular clarity he noticed around him the objects in this unknown but pleasant little den, the lair of some nice, likable intellectual where they had found refuge.

Shelves full of miscellaneous books, many paperbacks with colored edges to the pages. A picture by Oleg Tselkov from his red period, fifty by fifty centimeters. Three antique samovars, one in the form of a small barrel with a little horse on the lid. A reproduction of the famous *Uncreated* icon of the face of Christ. A Mexican sombrero. A poncho. A pair of peasant shoes made of plaited lime bark. An artificial fireplace gleaming in a corner. A shaggy Bulgarian carpet. A pair of White Star downhill skis.

The Victim was lying on his back and feeling calm, peaceful, and safe. Alisa was squatting on her haunches over his legs. Letting her hair hang down to his stomach, she was looking straight into his face with happy, loving eyes.

"You thief," she said. "First you steal a rubber fish, then a car."

She lifted up the Victim's sweater and kissed him on the stomach. On the navel. She gave a funny little sneeze. She stuck a finger in his navel and with sweet mock horror dug out of it a lump of matted fluff. Then she kissed him again below the navel, put her hand there, and found what she was looking for. She gently pulled down the zipper on his jeans, unfastened the button, kissed him again, flashed her quick gamine smile, and then sighed with relief and liberation, with such fullness of female happiness, like a soldier's wife meeting her long-awaited husband.

"Poor thief," she purred, like a cat. "My poor-r-r old thief."

In the middle of the night they drank tea and talked. Around their bed all the charming objects were picturesquely disposed, creating somehow more than a Flemish still-life, a cosmopolitan riot of pop art: a Philips record player and several records with faces of the stars of jazz and progressive rock, an Ocean radio set from Byelorussia, a big jar of Brazilian Nescafé, packs of different cigarettes – Marlboro, blue Gitanes, yellow Dukats – that recalled my student days, a red Czech telephone, Arab slippers with pointed turned-up toes, a Chinese thermos, a Soviet immersion heater and enameled saucepan, imitation Meissen cups, cellophane packets of nuts, Moroccan oranges, long crusty French loaves, half a block of Swiss cheese, a salami, several cans of Carlsberg beer, Schweppes tonic water, kefir, milk, a bulbous bottle of Johnnie Walker, loose tablets of painkillers and anticonvulsants, lemons, several books, among them an anthology of Russian poetry from Sumarokov to Akhmadulina. Without getting out of bed they could remain in constant bodily contact and at the same time drink tea, smoke, eat, and make phone calls. The Victim was able, for instance, to stretch out his hand, take a book and open it, as though to order, at Annensky's poem "September:"

> The heart perceives alone the beauty of the fall,
> And feels alone the rapture in its magic power;
> All those whose lips have tasted of the lotus flower
> Are by the autumnal, subtle incense held in thrall.

The Victim's skin twitched with a shiver of excitement, and that was
a good sign – his feelings were coming to life. He was about to read
the rest of the little collection of Annensky's poetry in this anthology,
but just then he felt her knee trembling very slightly, and he turned
toward her in full readiness.

"Why did you tremble then?"

She gave a gentle laugh. "It was just my knee trembling a bit . . .
with tiredness."

"May I? May I . . . a little more?"

"Why do you ask? Of course you may. As much as you like."

"You're tired, poor little thing."

"Yes, the poor little thing's tired."

"Well, I'll do it just a little and very gently."

"Please do, as much as you like."

"You're frowning slightly. What's wrong? Does it hurt?"

"Yes, it does hurt a bit, but it doesn't matter."

"I hurt a little too. I'm slightly sore on one side."

"My poor little soldier boy! Why does he try so hard?"

"He's not trying. That's the way it goes."

"And you're not bored?"

"No, I'm not bored. No doubt tonight is somehow special. When
morning comes, I'll chuck you in the garbage heap."

"The garbage heap? I shall cry there."

"Go ahead and cry on the garbage heap."

"Oh, my God! There won't be anything for you to throw out! Look
how thin I've become because of you. I'd better stick to you. Don't
throw me into the trashcan."

"OK, I'll wear you under my sweater."

How blissful, how magical was that reality and those real, very
tender, very strong sensations! From whence had he floated up into
this world? How long had he been swimming that night through those
terrible but by no means forgotten depths?

I shall never leave this world, the Victim insisted to himself, caressing
his beloved, smoking a cigarette, munching nuts, sipping tonic water,
and not turning his head toward the window, without even thinking
about that window, turning away without the slightest effort from that
window, to which was glued an eye. He knew, of course, that the
window was covered on the outside by the huge eye of a portrait
placard used in holiday processions, but he had enough strength not
to turn around and, instead, to imagine that outside the window was

a starry night, branches of trees, the pulsation of some kind of distant living mass, in a word – life.

How splendid it was all around – ah, there's the phone ringing! A construct of human hands, product of Czechoslovak industry, a red plastic shell, within it a blob of human genius that began with Edison! All those vibrating membranes, little bundles of wires, ebonite plugs – what could be better? The transmission of sounds, and therefore of thought, over distance! You're lying on a couch surrounded by unimaginable reality, and at the same time you are linked with the whole world! In fact you can become a unique kind of center of the world, from Yakutia to Tasmania! Use the dial, call up cities – Paris, Brussels, Los Angeles – and if you keep trying long enough, you can become the center of the world! And all thanks to this simple, red beetle, like a Volkswagen, this laconic plastic shape! No, all this talk about the alienation of contemporary man is pure snobbery!

My beloved was talking to someone. Someone was chirping to her about something. Women's talk. Nonsense. And what if, while she's talking, I were to begin my next – excuse me, my love – my next tender assault?

"No, no, I won't disturb you. Keep talking, just turn a little bit this way, just a little bit that way. Keep talking."

As he was enjoying the sensations of real life, she continued to talk on the phone and frowned. Why was she frowning?

"No, that's impossible," she said. "Both? In one day?!"

"But it's unthinkable!" she said. "Both? In one day?!"

"How awful!" she said. "I can't believe it."

At this point her womb and the walls of her vagina began to contract, she groaned softly, and dropped the receiver.

And all this time, while her tumescent organs were contracting, while her secretions were flowing, the red receiver with its ebonite earpiece was twittering away in a squeaky, childish voice: "Yes, yes . . . just imagine . . . both in one day . . . both in one day . . . ."

Suddenly he guessed it. He was being deceived! More lies! Another web of lies! He pulled himself out, without savoring the last, few, sweetest seconds, and began pacing about the room, barefoot over the soft carpet, until finally he turned sharply toward the window, toward that weird eye!

"Who are these two? What's happened to them?"

The eye was just an eye: the white, the pupil, the network of blood vessels, the total absence of thought, emotion, ideas, soul – in other words, a normal eye.

"Why don't you answer? What's happened to those two?"

She raised herself on one elbow. Her little breasts, so fiercely mauled by him, hung down to one side like two little animals. She was all wet and very young, despite her age.

"Who are you talking about, darling? I don't understand. What two?"

He noticed that her finger was depressing the phone cradle, and now a kindly but tedious little Czechoslovak mosquito was buzzing monotonously in the handset. The lie trap had snapped shut!

"You're hiding the truth from me again! Tell me straight – what has happened to those two, those two scientists? Are they dead? Have they turned up their toes? Don't treat me like a fool?"

"Don't!" she shrieked in despair. "Stop it! Don't talk about it like that! It's nothing, it's all nonsense! Love me, love me, love me!"

"You can cut out the hysterics," he said calmly. "Lies never saved anyone and never did any good. The truth – that is our only weapon!"

He had long been hatching a plan, but only now, as he turned away sobbing, could he put it into effect. He thrust the precious object, the little red telephone, behind his shirtfront, quickly snipped the cord with a pair of scissors, took a long run, pushed off with both feet, and dove, as though into water, head first into the eye.

Passing easily through the eye, he found himself in a space that was airless but entirely suitable for turning somersaults. He was expecting to see an abyss, but no sense of an abyss came to him, although no end or edge to that space was visible, and the whole space was made up of an innumerable multitude of invisible black particles. But if any single particle were to separate itself from that invisible multitude, it could mean only one thing – that particle is like you, and the two of you are approaching. Yes, he and Patrick Thunderjet were approaching each other.

Good old Pat. Long time no see! When was the last time? When? Who are you anyway?

He too was wearing no pants, and his whole self was leaning slightly to the side, for in that space, of course, weightlessness prevailed.

Faint smiles appeared on our faces as we approached. The feeble simulacrum of recollections came to us both. All that would come to mind were vile things, certain revolting details that people usually don't remember about each other: a toilet, a drunken table covered with sodden cigarette butts, some shameful chase – maybe an escape, maybe a pursuit – ugly, piglike faces flashing momentarily past in the dark, a horrible feeling in the chest, either fear, or, on the contrary, an awareness of one's own crass, irrepressible loutish strength . . . when suddenly . . .

When suddenly there came the memory of something true, something alarming and familiar: night, the main doorway of the old Hotel National, a ground wind blowing on a broad front across Manège Square.

"But we're flying to the moon! Don't you realize?!"

Then we saw the huge silvery plate and everything fell into place. We once more acquired a sense of which way was up and which was down, the plate filled half our space, we entered the field of the moon's gravitational pull, and began to fall toward a glade between low pointed lunar hills.

Having landed on the moon's surface we saw in front of us, amid the brown and faintly luminous dust, a lifeless concrete block of indeterminate function. Looking around, we saw a similiar block. There was no getting away from it – it surrounded us on all sides. Two stories of long balconies stretched along the front of the block, with a long red strip carrying a slogan attached between them. Here and there, in the black cosmic sky above the top of the block, rose the peaks of lunar mountains, looking like the roots of teeth, and in one place could be seen a damp wine-red slope – as I guessed, it was my own liver.

Since we had last parted, Patrick, it seems, had learned sign language. With a funny little grin on his face, he sketched something by twiddling his fingers, as though explaining to me everything about our surroundings and what awaited us, as though he were completely in the picture. He seemed to be warning me about some danger.

"Nonsense!" I said to him into the stolen telephone, which was now suspended weightlessly in front of me. "Stop playing the fool, old pal! Who is there to be afraid of here? It's obvious that this fort was built thousands of years ago by Chinese Marxists. It's equally obvious that they're all dead by now. There's no one here."

At that moment we heard a booming voice: "Hi, there! Sit down and tell us what's new."

Lieutenant-Colonel Cheptsov, retired, killed by resuscitation, moved slowly along the second floor of the lunar block, looking exactly like the leader of some totalitarian state. He was clearly trying to create an AUTHORITATIVE impression. Maybe this manner still has some effect on Englishmen, but we middle-aged Russians have had to swallow so much of that stuff that our reaction to that sort of bigwig is to want to give them a "penalty kick up the ass," as my beer-drinking pals in the Men's Club used to say.

"Ha, ha," my foreign friend said to me, cracking his finger joints, flicking his throat, making his eyes pop, and sticking out his tongue. "You Russians are an inert, thickheaded people, completely under the spell of the herd instinct. We free Celto-Norman-Anglo-Saxon-Americans would have long since pissed on the kind of government you have."

Suddenly Cheptsov acted in the most unexpected way. Drawing level with us, he threw off the persona of a grim Party boss and leaned over the balcony, for all the world like a cheerful, friendly old janitor, all his wrinkles creasing into a smile of pleasure at this encounter with two fellow earthlings. "A fine job they found for me in my old age," he said with a giggle, with both arms gesturing toward the hideous, lifeless building. "Janitor in a Chinese museum. Don't be embarrassed, boys. I don't know you, you don't know me. That's it, no reminiscences! Everything and everyone have been forgotten. A simple meeting on the dusty paths of distant planets. Don't think I'm the man I was. I'm not a Russian and not an American, and my past life has long since come to an end. I've forgotten the insults, the humiliations, the hints at mental inadequacy – in other words, everything that made our biogroup take up arms. By the way, I'm now not even a man at all. I'm a philosophical construct. Here I sit and think in silence about religion. There's a totem pole, there's a cross, there's Buddha, Osiris, Shinto, Zen, the hammer and sickle." He pointed affably at various points on the block, at which the religious symbols were each illuminated for a few moments.

"It's not an easy job." The construct, previously known as Lieutenant-Colonel Cheptsov, cleared his throat deferentially. "I'll say more – it's a job that calls for finesse. I think long and hard, and I make no concessions to myself or to them. We make out, of course, but there have been some tricky moments."

A fierce spasm of premortal banality shook us all.

"Oh, God, why did you punish us by flinging us out to this distant surface?"

"And does God's power exist here too?"

At this point everything went quiet for one single moment, a moment full of piercing hope, after which a melancholy utterance came to our ears from somewhere behind the lunar mountains: "God does not punish and his strength lies not in power. God is only good and only love and never evil. Know that whenever you feel goodness and love, or delight, or pity, or something even more sublime, you are coming nearer to God. Know that when you feel malice or something even baser, you are rejecting God. In times of misfortune, God gives you hope. When you suffer despair, you push God away. God is always joy, greatness, beauty. Joylessness, baseness, ugliness, are not of God. You have been given the gift of will, enabling you to be near to God or to go away from Him, because you are human. At this moment, you have fallen away from God and are surrounded by the terrible symbols of your own unhappiness, but God sends you thoughts of Himself, and that is hope. Await, like all who await His Son, and await the mom—"

Here the utterance was suddenly broken off, and everything vanished. Everything that still linked us to God and to our former life dissolved in blackness, and there approached us only objects of horror, almost none of which could we either recognize or give a name to, and those things that we could name were, perhaps, more terrible than the unnamed.

Over the dust around us passed a stream of urine, powerful, concentrated, and taut as a steel cable. Swaying, a curtain of dust moved toward us, toward me, toward him, toward them, toward the one who was still thrashing furiously about like a half-crushed spider. The black window of the cosmos lit up in a vast, mocking smile. The dust settled, and soon the whole expanse of the cosmos shone with a gigantic, mocking smile.

. . . And amid invisible space there rose up a perfect, iridescent teardrop: the earth.

There is a strange crossroads in Moscow. It is where the Sadovoye Ring curves towards the Kursk Station, Novo-Basmannaya Street runs off toward Razgulyai, while another stream flows into that positive inferno, Three Stations' Square. Every hour, fifteen thousand vehicles cross that intersection.

Well, what's strange about it? The reader will ask, exhausted as he already is by the oddities of this book. What we see here is a very ordinary Moscow crossroads, he will say, and he will be profoundly wrong.

Firstly, there are no unstrange crossroads in Moscow – each one is strange with its own special strangeness. Secondly, just look, and you'll see why!

Here, like some crazy Constructivist promontory or one of Mussolini's old dreadnoughts, there rises the building of the Ministry of Transportation, while opposite it is the ministry's newer building, a

Stalinist skyscraper wearing cream-colored curlicues on its mighty shoulders. Between them, like a marble, alien youth, stands an officer of the Guards' cavalry, a Russian Scotsman, victim of his accursed mother country. Behind his back the gilded crosses of one of Moscow's few surviving churches gleam modestly. On a diagonal from the youth, across the huge asphalt mound, can be seen a most extraordinary shell with a dark, bottomless maw, the entrance to the Red Gates metro station.

Here, if you stand under the central overhead traffic light on the top of the asphalt mound, and look down toward the Sukharevka, you have the feeling that you are witnessing the Great Migration of Peoples, so endless is the stream of cars and trucks pouring up and down.

Power-brake systems hissing, the giant Kraz and Urals trucks and the medium-sized workhorses, the Mazes and the Zils, roll day and night; the new horses of Russia, the Fiats, dart and buzz; pistachio-colored Volga taxis and black official sedans stream past, mixed with Java and Izh-Planeta motorbikes, wedding Chaikas, funeral Gazes, cautious, worn-out old Moskviches, and snooty foreign diplomats – and all of this flows, like a school of salmon swimming to their unknown spawning ground, and it was amid all this that the Victim was borne upon, as they say, his last journey.

And it was amid all this, at this particular intersection, that the Victim was struck by a moment of alarm, the moment when all Moscow came to a halt.

Nobody realized what it was, but all at once everything stopped, and all of Moscow's millions froze in deadly-keen foreboding, in a deadly-joyful hope, in expectation of something mortally imminent. For a few seconds the police and security forces bustled about on the median strips and in the reserved lanes of the highways, still thinking, by inertia, that this feeling of the Imminence of Something was simply a secret order to allow free passage for some convoy of bigwigs; then they too froze into stillness.

"What is it?" the Victim asked in a low voice. "Alisa, what's happening? Can it be?"

She laid her warming hand on his forehead. She could say nothing. Her soul was trembling.

Everyone was looking in different directions, at different angles of the earth and sky, from whence, they felt, the Thing that they were expecting should appear: in the clouds, perhaps, from over the roof-tops, or maybe in that strange shell of the metro station . . . A momentary and deafening silence settled over Moscow, and in that silence millions of souls were trembling – not with fear, but with the Imminence of an encounter, with a nameless emotion.

How long it lasted, we knew not. Then everything started moving again.

1969–1975

About the Author

VASSILY PAVLOVICH AKSYONOV, who is generally acknowledged as the leading Soviet writer of his generation, was born in Kazan in 1932. His father was a Communist Party official. His mother, Eugenia Ginzburg, a historian, won international fame as the author of the memoirs *Journey into the Whirlwind* and *Within the Whirlwind,* in which she recounted her experiences of nearly two decades in Stalin's camps.

Aksyonov spent part of his childhood with his mother in exile in Magadan, Siberia, "farther from Moscow than from California," as he puts it, and his own re-creation of that experience can be found in the pages of *The Burn*. He was later educated as a doctor, graduating from the First Medical Institute of Leningrad in 1956. His first novel, *The Colleagues,* published in 1960, was followed in 1961 by *Half-way to the Moon,* which attracted the attention of the world press and established his reputation as the representative of a new, Western-oriented, questioning generation of Soviet youth.

Aksyonov's prodigious activity as a novelist, short-story writer, dramatist, and screenwriter soon earned him a place at the forefront of Soviet cultural life. Although frequent clashes with government authorities made it increasingly difficult for him to publish at home, he was one of a few writers permitted to travel abroad. In 1975 he was a visiting lecturer at the University of California at Los Angeles.

In 1979 he spearheaded the effort to create a literary anthology free of censorship, *Metropol,* and resigned from the Writers' Union after two of his fellow editors were expelled. Forced to emigrate from the Soviet Union in 1980 when *The Burn* was published in Italy, he now lives in Washington, D.C., with his wife, Maya. He has been a Fellow of the Kennan Institute for Advanced Russian Studies there and is currently teaching at Goucher College and at Johns Hopkins University in Maryland.

Aksyonov's work is now published throughout the Western world. A collection of short stories, *The Steel Bird and Other Stories,* appeared in translation in 1979. His satiric fantasy, *The Island of Crimea,* was published in America to wide acclaim in 1983. Two new works—a nonfiction book about the United States and a new novel, *Say Cheese*—are forthcoming.